The Priest

Other books by Ralph McInerny

JOLLY ROGERSON
A NARROW TIME

The Priest

Ralph McInerny

HARPER & ROW, PUBLISHERS
New York · Evanston
San Francisco · London

FIRST EDITION

STANDARD BOOK NUMBER: 06-012912-3

LIBRARY OF CONGRESS CATALOG CARD NUMBER: 72-9173

Designed by C. Linda Dingler

For Connie

And I have asked to be
Where no storms come,
Where the green swell is in the havens dumb,
And out of the swing of the sea.

Gerard Manley Hopkins

Part One

1 Arthur Rupp jogged with the joyless determination of a man working off the temporal punishment due to sin and thus was not disposed to feel indulgent one May morning when a yapping terrier began to pursue him with the tenacity of the Hound of Heaven. Arthur flung a dissuading heel at his tormentor but succeeded only in shaking the dust from memories of long since subsided conga lines. Knees churning, dog at his heels, he seemed a half-heroic, half-ludicrous figure on the residential streets, doing the public penance which would save his body if not his soul.

When he reached his own driveway, Arthur turned on the dog, shouting and throwing out his arms in a shooing gesture. The dog retreated into the next yard, where he lifted a leg and left his moist signature on the mottled bark of a sycamore. Arthur continued on numb legs to his front door.

Red of eye, face flushed, his sweat suit limp as a bath towel, Arthur was in no mood for the morning's news which Clara brought immediately to his attention, her smile the thin-lipped one that told Arthur the universe had done it again. He could not agree more. While he read the story he rubbed with sweaty palm what hair his fifty years had left him. He began to groan. He rocked back and forth on sneakered feet and exchanged enraged looks with Clara.

"Well?" she said.

Arthur slumped into his chair at the dining room table. He still held the paper, rolled now into a baton. He might have been a defeated relay runner. His breath came in gasps, an effect of the jogging, of course, though the newspaper aggravated the aftermath of his efforts to bring his weight down to 190.

"Why do they print such garbage?" He picked up his orange juice and drank it to the dregs.

"It's scarcely the paper's fault, Arthur."

Clara, dear Clara. Had she any idea what might be printed if editors

3

opened the floodgates? It was the paper as much as anything at which his wrath was aimed. They had sought the man out, interviewed him at length, taken all these pictures. Arthur got to his feet.

"I'm going to call them."

"Shower first. You'll catch cold."

Arthur paused in the doorway, then shook his head. What priority could his health claim at a time like this? Continuing to the den, he was assailed by remembered scenes from *Yellow Jack*, a movie he had seen a dozen times. When he put the phone to his ear, its buzz was the whine of the tsetse fly. Or had it been mosquitoes?

"So I told him where to shove it," a female voice said into Arthur's ear.

"I beg your pardon."

"Who's this?"

"Are you Mary Muscatelli?"

"That's right."

"Arthur Rupp here. I'm calling about the appalling story on Father Bullard in this morning's paper."

"No, not in the ear!" Miss Muscatelli cried. She seemed not to be speaking into the phone. Her voice came to Arthur against a frieze of other voices, conversations, giggles, the clatter of typewriters. "What about the story?" she said into Arthur's ear.

"I think it's dreadful."

"Who'd you say this is?"

"Arthur Rupp." He straightened in his chair, as if to take more complete occupancy of his commodious sweat suit. "I am the chairman of Te Deum."

"Tedium?"

"Te *Deum*."

"Tum ta dum."

"Now see here, miss." To Arthur's consternation, Clara had come into the room and now stood watching him.

"You don't like the story," Miss Muscatelli said.

"I most certainly do not."

"What is this tedium outfit anyway?"

Arthur closed his eyes, pressed their lids with his fingertips, saw a riot of black and red. "Te *Deum*. Young lady, if you were alert to the real religious news of this community—"

"You're religious?"

"Te Deum is an organization of Catholic lay people. Intellectuals. We meet to discuss foreign policy, the liberal menace, the lost tradition. Surely you've heard of us."

4

"Ooooh. That right wing thing."

Arthur exploded. "If that isn't a typically stupid knee-jerk liberal—"

The phone went dead. Clara had depressed the cradle. She took the phone gently from him, shaking her head.

"Don't, Arthur. Don't get upset."

Arthur allowed himself to be mollified. Clara could be so soothing at times like this. Honest to God, sometimes he could believe that the whole country, and the Church with it, was going to hell in a handbasket. Imagine running a story that length on a beatnik like Bullard. Arthur could recall halcyon days when clergymen in trouble were kept out of the public print as a matter of policy, and a damned decent policy it had been. Now scarcely a day went by that one wasn't reading of clerical embezzlers, supposedly celibate bigamists and, just last week, a Southern Baptist preacher who supplemented his income by writing pornographic paperbacks under a pseudonym. What of good priests? How long had it been since there was adequate coverage of a Te Deum lecture or an interview with Monsignor Eisenbarth, its founder?

"Eisenbarth," Arthur breathed against Clara's bosom. "I should have called him in the first place."

"Take a shower now, Arthur. You can call him later."

From outside came the sound of barking. Arthur went to the window. The terrier was out there, refusing the mailman entry to the Rupp driveway.

"That goddam dog," Arthur raged.

Clara took his elbow and led him to the stairs.

"I'll get rid of him, Arthur. You go up and take your shower."

Civility without conversation was the unwritten rule of the seminary faculty breakfast room. Whether it was based on the pious desire to husband the spiritual glow left from saying Mass, or on the far more human disinclination to find one's fellows tolerable before nine, this rule had had the effect, over the years, of getting the faculty started on a new day in a merely private gloom. Internecine sniping was postponed until the noon meal, when they dined at the head table in the refectory upstairs.

Monsignor Randolph Eisenbarth, the rector, came in from saying the community Mass, his walk an odd bias, as if from defying prevailing winds. His chin was tucked in so that his head seemed to regard the world from the shelf of his chest. He put bread in the toaster, poured himself a cup of coffee and sat at the table. Its only other occupants were

Fathers Sweeney and Ewing. Father Sweeney, ancient, learned, gentle, bobbed his head and said shyly, "Buon giorno."

"Good morning, Father." The rector added a belated *s*, wanting the one greeting to suffice for both men. But Father Ewing, muttering over the morning paper, seemed unaware of his arrival. The toast popped and the rector got it, returned to his chair and began to spread the tan porous surfaces with butter. Father Ewing appeared to be in pain.

"Is something wrong, Father?"

"My God," Ewing murmured, continuing to read. He had raised his hand as if to hold the rector's attention. Please don't let him read aloud, Monsignor Eisenbarth prayed. His father had read aloud to his children as if he were rearing a pack of illiterates. No, that wasn't fair. The old man had been inordinately proud of his command of this new language, a command less complete than he had realized. Those occasions had left their mark and even now the rector would have half expected Father Ewing to come forth with broken English if he should, which God forbid, begin to read the paper aloud.

"Remember Bullard?" Ewing demanded suddenly.

"Has something happened to him?"

Ewing handed the rector the paper. He might have been notifying the next of kin.

The story was on the first page of the second section, more photographs than text, and in each of the photographs young Bullard, clad in the very antithesis of clerical clothing, figured prominently. He seemed to be playing a guitar, he seemed to be crooning, he was most certainly quaffing a foaming schooner of beer. The rector sought some alleviation of his shock in the legends beneath the pictures. They did not help. His slice of toast cooled in his hand.

"He has lost his mind," Monsignor Eisenbarth said.

"Oh, no, Randolph. Read the story. We're crazy, not Bullard."

Bullard. Bullard. He had been ordained but a few years before. The rector had no distinct memories of the man as a seminarian but the photographed face before him was familiar enough. Puffy bunny cheeks, thin blond hair, the comic separation of his rather prominent front teeth. In every photograph Bullard smiled with relentless lack of humor.

" 'On skid row,' " the rector read.

" 'Where the action is,' " Ewing quoted, wincing.

"But this is incredible." The rector looked at his two colleagues, his expression one of acute pain. "Incredible."

"He feels unfulfilled," Ewing said. "His priesthood has become hollow. It's all there."

6

And indeed it was. Bullard had appointed himself missionary to the degenerates on skid row, at least for an evening, and had taken along a group of young people from the university. This is where Christ would be if he were on earth today, Bullard had assured the writer, whose lavish eulogistic prose recounted the spiritual saga of Philip Bullard, one of the new breed of Roman Catholic priests who were seeking to break out of the clerical ghetto and lead more relevant lives. Bullard's vitriolic comments on his fellow priests, if he had been accurately quoted, were slanderous.

"We are the agents of the middle class," Ewing said with mournful glee. He was quoting Bullard. "We are fat and comfortable and an insult to the Christianity of the New Testament. Worst of all, we are irrelevant." Ewing half sang *irrelevant*, giving it two accents instead of one, according it an iambic lilt.

Eisenbarth looked at Father Ewing. The professor of moral theology was sixty and looked seventy. His ears were luxuriant with hair, his nostrils needed barbering, but his pate was as smooth as a penitent's knee.

Ewing said, "He thinks bums are good because they're not bad in the same way laborers and bankers and surgeons are. He thinks they're saints."

"Oh, he doesn't go that far."

"Indeed he does."

"They do have souls," Father Sweeney said softly.

"Sure they have souls," Ewing agreed. "Souls in bad shape. That's what Bullard misses. Where Christ would be! If he were he wouldn't be telling reporters those bums are paragons."

"Perhaps he means they're not hypocrites," Father Sweeney said.

"I hope he's right. But there are people who take a morbid pleasure from failure. It can look like humility."

Father Sweeney wanted to object. He held up his spoon as if to be recognized but he said nothing. Years in the confessional had made him familiar with the type Father Ewing might have in mind: whining women whispering with relish their catalog of faults, gruff male voices, bodiless in the dark, laying claim to fierce and uncontrollable passions and daring the priest to say temptations could be conquered. The previous Saturday a woman had kept repeating in mournful Mediterranean tones that she had the "fleshly desires," the phrase her warrant for a lechery Father Sweeney had begun to suspect was largely imaginary.

"Well," Father Ewing said, getting to his feet. "That young pup isn't going to ruin my day. Let George worry about him." Crumpling his napkin, he smiled. "This is the day young Ascue comes home."

7

"Is that so," Father Sweeney said.

"Today's the day."

"Well, well. I'll come along with you, Father."

Left alone, the rector read the newspaper story again. How ill bred the new breed seemed. Quite odd in Bullard's case. He came from a rather wealthy family downstate. Socially speaking, the priesthood had been a step downward for young Bullard. The rector's gaze lifted, went to the window, saw nothing. His own vocation had been greeted by his parents with awe and gratitude. A son a priest. What more could a family ask? But hadn't his parents seen it as a step up in the world rather than a turning aside from secular pursuits? Young Bullard's accusations made Monsignor Eisenbarth vaguely uneasy. His own ministry, outside the seminary, brought him among the well-to-do. But they could not be called complacent people. They were anxious about the fate of their country and their church. How edifying their alertness to the dangers of liberalism, their sadness at the loss of religious values. No, they were not complacent. They had been frugal and industrious and it was wrong of Father Bullard to compare them unfavorably with drunks and fallen women.

Monsignor Eisenbarth rose from the table, slipped his napkin into its ring and left the breakfast room. He shot an immaculate cuff and slid it back to reveal his watch. On schedule. He prided himself that his day was measured with an exactness which bespoke discipline and dependability, virtues that must be inculcated in young men aspiring to the priesthood.

In the hallway outside his office the rector came upon a janitor brooming clumps of sweeping compound over the tiled floor. The man took on symbolic force: here was a typical representative of the simple faithful.

"Good morning," Monsignor Eisenbarth said cheerily, drawing to a halt. What *was* this fellow's name? Janitors came and went so rapidly nowadays it was difficult to keep track.

The man shot a foot-wide swath of detritus to within inches of the rector's polished toe.

"Good morning, Reverend."

Reverend? Wasn't the fellow Catholic? The janitor had floored his broom with one foot and was twisting its handle in order to tighten it, an operation accompanied by an irksome squeak. He looked angrily at the broom.

"Could use some new equipment around here."

Monsignor Eisenbarth managed a smile. One of the little ones, this man must be reached. He felt as if young Bullard were a witness of this chance encounter.

"A new broom? I think we can handle that."

The man tugged at his ear lobe with leathery fingers and squinted down the hall as if its waiting length depressed him.

"The handle's all right. But look at these bristles."

He raised the broom and thrust it at the rector. Eisenbarth backed off, staring at the flattened brush festooned with bolls of dust. Was this man unbalanced? The broom was scarcely a foot from the rector's face.

"Worn out. See?"

"I see." Monsignor Eisenbarth moved farther back, as if getting perspective on the offending broom. Circling the man—mad, anticlerical or both—he continued to his office. When he had a hand on the doorknob, he called over his shoulder, "Keep up the good work."

But faith seemed more necessary than good works when he stood with the door closed behind him, sighing with undeniable relief. Where in the world was help being gotten nowadays? That janitor would be more at home in one of the bars Bullard had visited than in the peaceful otherworldliness of the seminary.

His phone rang and Monsignor Eisenbarth was happy to be distracted from thoughts of Bullard and of his own less than magnificent encounter with the janitor.

"Arthur," he cried. "Good morning. What's on your mind so bright and early?"

Phone to his ear, still standing, he listened with returning gloom to what was on Arthur Rupp's mind so bright and early. From his window he saw Father Ewing on the walk, heading across campus to his first class of the day. How insouciant the professor of moral theology looked. Ah, yes, the return of Father Ascue from Rome. Monsignor Eisenbarth watched his colleague with a sad smile while in his ear Arthur's irate voice went on. Let George worry about Bullard, Father Ewing had said. Let George do it. Poor Father Ewing, elated that Francis Ascue was returning. Eventually he would learn that George—the bishop—had indeed done it.

Birdsong, with here and there a chesty robin on the shimmering grass, head cocked, waiting. Earthworms through earth and vice versa move. And both through birds, eventually. Father Ewing sidestepped a chalky fried-egg-like besmirchment that formed on the walk before him and lifted a wary eye to a burgeoning but fortunately now birdless branch above him. A passing covey of seminarians tipped their birettas and the priest returned the courtesy. There was a forsythia bush near the entrance of the classroom building and Father Ewing paused on the steps to enjoy its splendor and then looked back the way he had come.

Smiling, he breathed deeply. The season meant the end of the semester, the end of the school year, the end, *deo volente,* of his final year as professor of moral theology. The egg blue of the sky promised not only a fair day but the arrival home of Father Ascue. Clutching the manila folder which held his yellowing lecture notes, Father Ewing plunged into the classroom building.

Within there was a single season, the winter of his discontent. No boy had gone less willingly to school than he, and yet, for over thirty years, he had been entering this building, ascending to the *aula maxima* on the second floor and reading to class after class the contents of his notes. At first, long ago, there had been some satisfaction in the task. In those days he had been writing his lectures. If preaching palls, teaching is worse. He had his syllabus. He had his doctrine. He had long since stopped pretending to "keep up with the field." He had not been to a theological convention since 1955. It wasn't that he objected to heavy drinking: hotels depressed him and there was always some ass who wanted to discuss the papers that had been read. The content of those papers had begun to change almost imperceptibly; Father Ewing had now reached the point where he read theological journals as a lenten penance and, on Holy Saturday, celebrated by reading a sober page or two of Alphonse Liguori. It was hard to date the beginning of his desire to be freed from his post on the seminary faculty—it sometimes seemed to him now that he had never liked it here, that he had always longed for release and real priestly work and, of course, to be his own boss— but, if he had to choose a year, roughly 1955 would serve.

Outside the aula door, Father Ewing lit a cigarette and leaned against the railing. He was concealed from the students waiting for him inside, but their sibilant preclass chatter oozed from the open double doors. The truth was that he dreaded facing the young now. It had all changed —the seminary, the Church, everything—and not for the better. No one would ever convince him that all this whiz-bang, guitar-plucking racket at Mass, and all the rest of it, was an improvement. He glared at the discolored filter of his cigarette. Damned tasteless things. Since he had switched to filters, he smoked twice as much as he had before and just the other day Eisenbarth had read an article to him which claimed that filters were more rather than less hazardous to health. He could believe it, he could believe it. The promised improvement was always a turn for the worse. He dragged hungrily on his cigarette.

A seminarian came out of the aula, saw Father Ewing, smiled sickly and went back inside. The lookout. Ten minutes late and they could assume the class was canceled and flee to their rooms. His watch told him that he had five minutes more of grace. He would finish his unsatisfying cigarette and then go in and talk for forty-five minutes on natural law, allow no questions, just let them have sound doctrine right between the eyes. That way, *his* obligation at any rate would be met.

Not that he thought they would swallow it. The faculty wasted hours at their monthly meetings trying to figure out what had happened to the spirit of the place. Knacker, who lived in dread that the Code of Canon Law (which he had committed to memory in his youth and had put generations of students to sleep with) was going to be completely rewritten, would shake his head and quote from the Apocalypse, thereby bringing down on his head the exegetical inconsequences of Baldie Barfield, whose beagle, Maccabee, had gone blind and now accompanied him to class and, inevitably, to faculty meetings as well. It was disconcerting when the hound crawled into Barfield's lap and stared across the table with his milky sightless eyes. Maccabee was as equipped as any of them to be a leader here. Of course a few like Tremplin thought everything was fine. Students were leaving like rats from a sinking ship, but everything was fine. Tremplin had raised a fuss about taking the oath against Modernism when he joined the faculty, but then what could you expect from a seminary professor who had earned his degree at Yale!

Father Ewing put out his cigarette and inhaled some smokeless air. His lungs wheezed with the effort. He missed the sense of peace he had had briefly on his way across campus. There was a far-off sound of a plane and Father Ewing smiled. That was it. Concentrate on that. Frank Ascue was returning from Rome today.

Charlotte Nygaard opened a kitchen cupboard. Taped to the inside of the door was a large sheet of paper bearing the crayoned message: LOVE GOD AND DO WHAT YOU WILL. There were no clean cups.

"They're all in the washer," her daughter Beverly said. "Unwashed. I rinsed this one out."

"Unwashed!"

"You forgot to turn it on last night."

"But that's your job."

Charlotte's claim could be verified by consulting the bulletin board which hung beside the kitchen door. She liked to think of her family as a well-organized team, each with his allotted chore, moving through the day in an allegro of camaraderie. The patristic and liturgical graffiti which greeted one on opening closet or cupboard were part of that.

"Howard!" she called. "It's going on nine."

"Want me to rinse out more cups?" Beverly did not rise from the breakfast nook. There was a notebook open beside her, which she had been listlessly reading when Charlotte came back from sending Beth and David up the street to the parish school.

"I'll do it. I wish your father would hurry."

"Say," Beverly said. "Doesn't Uncle Frank get in today?"

After the slightest pause, Charlotte said, "His plane is due at three."

"What airline?"

From the street came the insistent sound of a horn. Beverly scrambled to her feet. "Gotta run. See you, Mom."

Charlotte put out her cheek and got a hurried kiss. "Have you eaten anything at all?"

"I spend half my day at the Center. I won't starve."

"Did you have juice?" The car horn sounded again.

"You forgot to defrost it. I may see you at the airport."

Notebook in hand, Beverly ran to the front door. She scooped up her coat on her way through the living room.

"What did she mean, airport?" Howard stood on the stairs, looking at Charlotte, who had pursued Beverly from the kitchen and come to a confused halt by the front door.

"Frank's plane is due at three."

"Today?" Howard's hand gripped the newel post.

"Did you forget?" Charlotte returned to the kitchen, where she took a can of frozen juice from the refrigerator. She put it in the sink and let hot water run on it.

"Charlotte, I can't possibly get away this afternoon. I had no idea today was the day." He rubbed his forehead with his fingertips. "Could he possibly take a cab?"

"A cab!" Charlotte seemed to shrink with her kimono. "After three years in Rome, you want him to come home with no one to meet him and have to take a taxi?"

"Of course I don't *want* it." Howard opened the refrigerator. "Where's the juice?"

"It'll be ready in a minute."

"I'll just have coffee."

Charlotte held a cup under the running water. The stream swirled in it, then shot out, splashing her kimono. She darted back from the sink, emitting a little cry. Oh God, it was going to be one of those days. Howard took the cup from her and dried it.

"Better change, Char."

"I'm okay." She poured his coffee. He tasted it and put it down.

"Who made the coffee?"

"Howard, what are we going to do about Frank?"

"Why don't you drive me to the office and keep the car? At least you can meet him."

"Perfect! I'll run up and dress."

"There isn't time. You can go like that. You won't have to get out of the car."

"But what if something happened?" Charlotte had every woman's dread of being wheeled into Emergency in unpresentable attire.

"Nothing is going to happen."

"You haven't had breakfast. Beverly had no breakfast. Would you like some cereal?" Cereal made Beth and David's breakfast a snap.

"Good God, no. Come on, we'd better get going."

Charlotte drove. Howard, happy for the chance to ignore the morning traffic, read the newspaper. Charlotte talked incessantly. They were just going to have to be better organized in the morning. She would prepare breakfast before going to bed if she had to. They would all come down with rickets or beriberi if they went on like this. She applied her slipper to the brake. They were downtown now, only blocks from Howard's office. The walks were filled with sleepy people hurrying to work. For a moment Charlotte envied them their purposeful day. She was jarred from incipient reverie by the blast of a horn behind her.

"The light's green," Howard said.

"Thanks," Charlotte snapped, and the car lurched forward.

"Do you know a priest named Bullard?"

"Philip Bullard?"

"Yes."

"He was a classmate of Frank's. Why?"

But they had arrived at his building. Howard was jamming the newspaper into his briefcase so that their stay in the No Parking zone would be brief. He leaned over and kissed her and was gone. Charlotte watched him go, feeling slightly abandoned. Then, to the accompaniment of screeching brakes and furious horns, she got the car back into traffic.

Auxiliary Bishop Sean Brophy, vigorous and forty-four, had, like the vice-president of the United States, some pomp but little power. As much as the other priests of the diocese, he was at the beck and call of Bishop George Caldron, whose see Fort Elbow was. Indeed Brophy's case, though one would never have guessed it from the taut line of his jaw, his glistening smile, short-cropped hair and firm handclasp (given quickly lest those he met lapse into a medieval swoon, genuflecting to kiss the episcopal ring), was perhaps worse than that of the simple priest. Others had for the most part a saving daily distance from George, while Brophy was resident in the cathedral rectory and all too easily summoned into the senior episcopal presence at the palace two blocks away.

This morning, taking the stairs two at a time as he went up to his suite on the second floor of the rectory, he could look forward to a Chamber of Commerce luncheon and, later, a meeting with Rabbi Rapoport and Reverend Martin Tetzel, his opposite numbers on the Conference of Christians and Jews. His luncheon speech would be a much used one on the separation of church and state. With Rapoport and Tetzel there would be long-range planning for a civic fusion of the celebrations of Hanukkah and Christmas, a project running into opposition from some outspoken and likely dubious Sufis in the radiation laboratory at the university.

When he reached his room, he was greeted by the roar of a vacuum cleaner. Mrs. Ryan had not yet finished her housework. She smiled apologetically, plying her ancient Hoover like a bagpipe on wheels.

"Through in a minute, Bishop."

"Take your time, take your time."

She turned off the machine. "What?"

"I said to take your time." He went to his desk and consulted his calendar. The roar of the vacuum did not resume.

"I suppose you read this morning's paper, Bishop."

He nodded without turning. He would not get into a discussion of the Six Counties or of how Paisley got into print.

"I say it's a crying shame, carrying on like that."

"Ah, well," Bishop Brophy said, trying to invest those ambiguous syllables with the full freight of a Boethian consolation.

"The sad thing is, he's taking advantage of those wretches."

What on earth was she talking about? The bishop glanced significantly at the deflated bag of the vacuum.

"Ah, yurr lordship, good morning to you." Monsignor Yorick, the chancellor of the diocese, stood in the doorway, smiling ironically. In one hand he palmed his breviary like a bootlegging quarterback. "And good morning to yourself, Mrs. Ryan."

"Good morning, Monsignor. We was just speaking of that business in the paper."

"And what business would that be?" Yorick affected a stage brogue

14

with Mrs. Ryan. Brophy did not know if Yorick had ever seen the Emerald Isle, but four generations separated Mrs. Ryan's family from the sod and on her husband's side at that. Her maiden name had been Bauer but marriage, two world wars against the Hun and a succession of rectory jobs had turned her into an aging colleen.

"That Father Bullard," Mrs. Ryan hissed.

Bishop Brophy's brows shot up in a practiced way. "Is that what you were referring to, Greta?"

Mrs. Ryan disliked being addressed by her Christian name. She ignored the bishop, speaking to Monsignor Yorick. "What's got into the young priests anyway?"

Yorick looked as if he might say, Faith and begorra, Mrs. Ryan, I wish I knew. Brophy headed him off. "You mustn't be upset, Mrs. Ryan. Remember that people murmured about the company Our Lord kept."

"Aw, come on, Sean."

Yorick's indignation invited a further dig, but Bishop Brophy was not one to waste time in idle argument. Besides, anything he said to the chancellor would eventually arrive distorted to Caldron's ear. Brophy had learned during the past two years that George Caldron did not consider his auxiliary a peer with a right to an independent opinion. Particularly about his, George's, clergy. Caldron would tick off the number of priests in the diocese like a prince in Tolstoy counting serfs. George had never actually said it, but his actions made it clear that the sooner Brophy got his own diocese, the happier they both would be. Had George learned of his rejection of the Wyoming see? God knows, even that had been tempting after playing second fiddle to Caldron, but Bishop Brophy's mentors in the East had counseled patience. Far better things than the wastelands of Wyoming were in store for a man of Brophy's caliber.

"Try sinning on the side of charity, Monsignor."

Mrs. Ryan snorted and flicked on the vacuum. Yorick winced at the racket and beckoned Bishop Brophy into the hall.

"George *will* hit the ceiling on Bullard."

Brophy nodded, saying nothing, his expression readable as Yorick wished.

"She's right, you know." Yorick nodded toward the noise. "The junior clergy are losing their minds. Did I ever tell you of the talk I had with Father Tremplin?"

Yorick had told him, ad nauseam. Brophy looked at his watch, though his smile never wavered. Caught in its beam, Yorick could only have felt encouraged to go on.

15

"Tremplin should have been sent to Rome to study." Suddenly Yorick brightened. "Like Ascue. He's due back, you know."

"Ascue? Do I know him?"

"Frank Ascue. No, you wouldn't know him. He's been in Rome for three years. Studying."

Mrs. Ryan, through with the bishop's rooms, came into the hall, sighing a righteous sigh, that small part of her endless drudgery behind her. Her manner galvanized Yorick.

"Got to get to the office. Is it today you have confirmations in Stillville?"

"Thursday."

The thought seemed to please Yorick and he bounced away. Stillville was a dull fifty-mile drive into the southwest corner of the diocese. But that was the point of having an auxiliary: let him do the confirming and distant visitations. Brophy went into his room.

The reminder of Stillville filled him with momentary despondency. Father Garish, the young master of ceremonies they had wished on him, would drive, all the while uttering pious platitudes. On their first trip, Garish had suggested they recite the rosary to pass the time but Brophy had squelched that. Sighing, he crossed the room.

The view from his window was cluttered with buildings but for a moment Bishop Brophy might have been regarding the liberating expanse of Wyoming. Down the hall Mrs. Ryan's machine started up again. Abhorring, like nature, a vacuum, Bishop Brophy gathered up his keys and fountain pen and fled.

Arthur Rupp was a first drip followed by many more until the flood was full and Miss Mary Muscatelli, phone to her ear, a smile on her pale pink lips, sat ecstatic at her desk among the clattering typewriters and ringing telephones.

Her current caller, like most of the others, was angry. In a husky voice the woman droned on about the national moral fiber while Mary answered monosyllabically and entertained visions of a Pulitzer. Dominic Serge, a reporter's reporter, had saluted her with a copy of the morning edition, folded to her story, then stooped over the water fountain to let the icy stream play on his face, seeking in that chill ablution the memory of sobriety. Ralph the copyboy had looked her in the eye instead of the chest when he said good morning. Her sense of euphoria was a pleasant counterpoint to the vituperation that had been coming to her over the phone for more than an hour. The purpose of a good reporter is to enrage his readers. Fame, acclaim, perhaps a raise. Absentmindedly, with a pencil, she separated the spiky bangs on her broad forehead.

Suddenly the connection was broken and the switchboard girl said, "Go ahead, Mrs. Crawley."

"Muscatelli?" This voice was level and authoritative, that of the secretary of Quill.

"Yes." Mary's eyes lifted. At the far end of the room she could see Mrs. Crawley in her glassed-in office and, beyond her, faintly, behind another layer of glass, Quill himself.

"Your story in the morning edition. Quill wants a follow-up."

"All right."

"There's been quite a reaction."

"I know! I've had a hundred—"

"Check with the priest, see what flak he's been getting. You've been getting calls?"

"All morning."

"Check them out. Are they angry?"

"Splenetic. One woman told me—"

"They're the best. Go interview them."

"Most of the calls are anonymous."

"Check those that aren't. Can you handle this?"

Mary's eyes met Mrs. Crawley's: the fifty yards between them were busy with distractions, but Mary's sudden pique erased it all. "Of course. Do I get a photographer?"

"Just interviews for now."

Click. That was it. Serge had described a call from Mrs. Crawley as *conversatio interrupta*, his brows dancing suggestively as he mouthed the words like an instructor of freshman Latin. Mary became aware of a flaming match inches in front of her face. It was held in the trembling fingers of Serge, who stood beside her desk. She dipped forward, inhaled, brought the filtered smoke into her lungs, smiled a thank you.

"Someone's been taking notes on your forehead."

"What?"

Serge leaned toward her, squinting his red eyes, and parted her bangs. "A shorthand I can't read. Definitely pencil."

"I'll wash." Mary stood, startling Serge. "I have to go anyway. My story."

"Ah," he said, nodding. On his brow a less eradicable stenography was all too legible. Mary squeezed his tweedy arm, crushed her cigarette in the ashtray, swept her purse onto her arm. She felt an impulse to phone Diane but checked it. Her roommate would have reason to gloat over this. Bullard had been Diane's suggestion and, despite herself, it was

Diane's attitude toward the priest that Mary had forced into her prose when she wrote the story.

Going down in the elevator, she thought with vague distaste that her own feeling of triumph was parasitic. She had made a hero out of Bullard—*saint* was the word she had edged close to then thought better of—and at the same time, she hoped, a heroine of herself. Somehow it seemed too high a price to pay. She had not liked Bullard.

In her Volkswagen, revving the fluttery undependable motor, preparing to leave the parking lot, Mary decided that she had not liked Bullard at all. While she drove through the busy morning streets to the local campus of the state university and to the Catholic Student Center there where Bullard dwelt, she thought of the weird hours interviewing him.

Love me. Those were the words that might have been scrawled across Bullard's forehead in pencil or crayon or simply in the natural lines that rippled on Dom Serge's. No, not lines. Bullard had that pink smooth complexion so out of place on a man. Mary's gloved hand stroked her own cheek. Did he even shave? She could believe that he did not have to. There was something childlike, even infantile, in his smile: shy, head ducked, eyes searching, for what? He had told her he wanted to be a friend first, a priest later, if ever, to people. His thin yellow hair was brushed forward over the coconut-shaped head, the style now, of course, but Mary suspected that in Bullard's case it had more to do with concealing his baldness.

"He'd make a perfect story," Diane had said. She had met him at a party, a short, shy man in a black Nehru jacket and white turtleneck, an outfit she had thought a parody of clerical dress and imagine her surprise when Phil confessed that he was indeed a priest. "He was just like anyone else," Diane said. "And he does all these fabulous things."

Fabulous indeed, as Mary had learned. When she interviewed him, Bullard seemed almost eager to tick off the idiosyncratic things he had done.

"Once I sat for an hour and a half on the top of a condemned building watching the artistry of prethunderstorm lightning."

"Why?" Mary asked.

Those green eyes with their yellow flecks lifted quickly, alert, on guard. He seemed to consider the statement and the episode to be self-justifying. "Why," he repeated. "Well, for one thing, I like to break out of here." A limp hand indicated the chaos of his office. "Into the streets. There are so many lonely people." His hand, returning from its gesture, lay on the desk and he contemplated it as if it were a homeless creature. "I go to be a friend. To be of service." He added quickly, "And

18

to learn. Showing interest in a person helps him to increase the value of his own worth. It shows that somebody gives a damn about him regardless of how he dresses or wears his hair or what color his skin is."

Mary imagined a headline. The Priest Who Gives a Damn. He kept her writing for hours. Once he had said Mass in a restaurant while on a skiing trip with a group of students. "It was the only place open," he explained with a smile.

"Oh, it's marvy, it really is," Diane had said at two this morning when she read the story. "You've caught him, Mary."

"The photographs help."

The editor had made a good selection from the dozens Earl had taken. Trust old Earl to have coeds in most of them, young nubile girls looking wistfully at Bullard in a knit Arnold Palmer T-shirt. Bullard in vestments presiding at the wedding of two agnostics in the chapel of the Student Center. "Who knows who's in God's Who's Who?" he had asked with an owllike expression. "I don't. They wanted to be married in this chapel. They're friends of mine." His hands opened in a palmy *ergo*.

"What do your superiors think of that sort of thing?"

An index finger went to his lips, as if to hide the gap between his teeth. Winking, he said, "Are you going to tell on me?"

"Should I keep that out of the story?"

Bullard ignored the question. "I want people to come to know me as me. Phil Bullard. Not as a priest or minister, someone on a pedestal. If they see I have the same kind of feelings, temptations, strengths and weaknesses, as well as the element of faith, well, they're less likely to find faith alien."

"Finally you want to convert them, don't you?"

Bullard laughed. "No. I told you. I want to serve. And to learn. I burned my draft card, you know."

"Are priests draftable?"

Mary had known of the draft card burning. The paper had covered it but Bullard had been only one of a dozen clergymen surrounded by fifty young men.

"There, you see." Bullard sat forward, triumphant. "You think of a priest as of another species, don't you? Why should I be considered different from other men?"

"*I* don't know. But why be a priest at all if it isn't something different? I mean, you are different, aren't you?"

"I would say that priests have to become different. Different from what they've been. That's what's going on in the church now. If you don't change, you're static. You have to adjust to survive, like the dinosaur."

Mary blinked. Had dinosaurs survived? She asked about his post. He had been in a parish but was happy to have escaped to the Catholic Student Center. People in the parish had thought he was unhappy to be a priest because he did not wear a Roman collar. On campus the kids understood him.

They certainly seemed to. "He's a real buddy," a girl with red hair and blue eyeliner told Mary, staring steadily at her. The girl seemed never to blink. "I'm not a Catholic myself but this is the only place on campus where I feel at home. Do you know, I attended half a dozen Masses before I realized what was going on? Somehow it's not like religion here, know what I mean?"

"Phil? Great guy." The boy who told her this held his nose as if it were a cigarette. "Say we're sitting around at night, bored, you know, and someone says, Let's go. Phil comes along. Out to a bar, anywhere, he'll come. And none of this crappy attitude that he's slumming or something."

Mary wrote it all down. "It's where Jesus spent his time," Bullard explained when she asked about stories that he went to bars. He had already offered to bring Earl along on one of his excursions. Mary begged off.

"You should have gone," Diane protested.

"No, thanks."

"It's where Jesus spent his time." Diane giggled.

"Maybe. But I'm no Mary Magdalene."

No, she thought, pulling into the parking lot of the Student Center, I don't like Bullard. She felt as if, almost unwittingly, he was using her, that the story was merely a broader cast of the plea she had imagined inscribed on his ingenuous smiling face. Love me.

His passage through the lounge was accompanied by cheers and triumphant flourishes of the morning paper, a tribute almost surprising since, though this was home ground, the kids here this early in the day were the buttoned-down type who never missed class. They used the Center as a place to study and to eat the lunches they brought in bags from home. Not really his people at all. Moved, moving at a good clip, head ducked to avoid confetti or receive the laurel, Philip Bullard was on his way to his office, where Janice had said Mary Muscatelli awaited him. He was not really annoyed when his way was blocked by a trio of girls who sprang from chairs to confront him.

"Have a minute, Father?"

"Sure." He smiled. Being available, that was his job, his creed. Others began to cluster around and Bullard could feel that these kids considered him one of themselves. His pale brows rose receptively, but he warned, "I've got someone waiting in the office."

"Do you say Mass in homes?" The questioner was a fat girl. Her unwashed hair lay over her ridged forehead. "I mean, you know, where people live."

"Why do you ask?" But he directed the question at the shy pretty girl beside the first.

The fat girl said, "We wondered if you'd come say Mass in the house where I room. Everyone would be welcome." She turned a pathetic smile at those who had drawn near.

"Hey, Father," a boy called. "You going to get into trouble about that story in the paper?"

Glad for the distraction, Bullard turned, paused a moment, then winked. "We'll see." He turned to the fat girl and repeated, "We'll see."

Appreciative murmurs behind him, he was happy to have avoided a commitment to the fat girl and her friends. The home liturgy worked better when you knew the people and the fat girl had been a stranger. And why didn't she keep her hair clean?

Out of the lounge and into the hall that led to his office, he slowed his pace. He had been reading the paper when Janice rang his room to tell him Miss Muscatelli was waiting downstairs. The story was a good one, no doubt about that, better than he had expected from her. He had detected skepticism in her during the interviewing and when she declined to come along to the bars he had felt her cool appraising eye upon him. It was the old story, the distance between the priest and others. But perhaps he had misjudged her. He could hardly complain of what she had written.

Only Janice looked up when he came into the office. Miss Muscatelli, facing Janice, might have been quizzing her. Janice looked relieved to see him. "Here's Father now," she cried.

Miss Muscatelli turned and her smile seemed genuine enough. "Good morning, Father Bullard. Have you read the story?"

He hesitated, then wished he had not. "Yes. Of course."

"You're not the only one. Have you had many calls?"

"Have you?"

"Nothing but, all morning. My editor wants a follow-up."

"What kind of calls?"

She tipped her head and her lower lip puffed out. "Let's just say they weren't fans of yours."

"I was afraid of that. Sit down, won't you? Janice, see if you can scare us up some coffee."

"Are you really surprised? Surely you didn't expect people to find you an ordinary priest."

He might have taken her remark as flattery if her tone had not been taunting. Janice, on the way out of the office, looked back and frowned at Miss Muscatelli.

"I couldn't know what the story would be like, could I?"

"Oh, come on. It's little more than direct quotes. Do you know anything of the Te Deum group?"

"Aha. I would expect them to be upset. Did Monsignor Eisenbarth call?"

"No. A man named Rupp."

"I don't know him."

"I had hoped you'd have had calls too. How about your bishop?"

"My bishop?" He looked at her warily, but the question did not seem pointed. "I hardly expect him to call."

At which moment the phone rang. They both jumped. He laughed and so did she. "We'll let someone else take that."

"Could people have phoned and you not know?"

"You'd have to ask Janice."

"I did. She told me to ask you. Frankly, my editor hopes for a little commotion. The calls we're getting seem to promise that."

He picked up a glass cube from his desk. A paperweight, its facets were smudged with fingerprints. "Mary, I'm not interested in causing a commotion. I am interested in doing what I think I ought to do. It's that simple. I just can't settle into a sleek comfortable clerical life. I tried that for a couple of years. When I was assigned here, it became clear to me that there are all sorts of ways to be a priest, more relevant ways. . . ."

She took notes while he talked, and, for the first time, he had real misgivings about this kind of publicity. Oh, admit it, he took pleasure in the notoriety the story promised. His assignment to the Center had opened vistas, he liked this job, had been happy to get out of the parish that was his first assignment. That had been too much like the seminary.

He had not liked the seminary. His forte had been athletics and when he had tried to associate with the seminary brains they had never taken him seriously. He had been classified as a jock. A sudden memory took shape in his mind: Frank Ascue before a metaphysics exam conveying to his slower classmates the burden of the course. Phil Bullard had kept to the outer fringe of those surrounding Ascue, needing the help, not wanting to admit it. Ascue. He must be nearly finished with his studies in Rome. Bullard brushed the memory away. Everyone admitted now that the seminary curriculum was hopelessly irrelevant. Nowadays a student could not be at a disadvantage just because his Latin was poor. Ordination had promised freedom, but his parish assignment was only a different kind of incarceration. Before a year was up he was pestering Yorick for an appointment with the bishop. Ignoring the counsels of prudence, he was determined to ask outright for a change. He would have liked to be sent on for further study, in sociology or psychology, earn a degree and get sprung permanently from parish work. No doubt the bishop had thought assigning him to the Center was a good joke. This branch of the university offered no graduate courses. It hadn't mattered. He had taken over a joke and turned it into a real haven for kids. The joke was on the bishop, finally. Father Bullard wondered what the bishop would make of the story in the morning paper.

Janice came in with two mugs of coffee. Miss Muscatelli put hers on the table beside her chair. Father Bullard said, "Have we had many calls this morning, Janice?"

"You're kidding."

"Who?"

"Well, among others, Bishop Brophy. He said not to disturb you but to tell you, 'Excelsior.' "

Bullard beamed. Brophy was all right.

"And the chancery."

"The chancery?" Miss Muscatelli sat forward, pencil poised.

"Who made the call?" Father Bullard was glad his voice betrayed no excitement.

"Monsignor Yorick. You have an appointment for Thursday."

"A summons?" Miss Muscatelli asked.

Bullard allowed an enigmatic smile to suffice for an answer. Miss Muscatelli clearly felt rewarded for her visit. Well, let her make of it what she liked.

After he showed Miss Muscatelli out he went upstairs to his room. He was glad Janice was not bothering him with phone calls. He did not want to talk to Diane now. Things suddenly looked very different. What he had said to Mary Muscatelli was more than words. He did have a role, an evolving one. Who knew what might come of all this? The appointment with the bishop he had been requesting for weeks no longer seemed desirable. How ironic that, after so much delay, he should hear from the bishop now.

He picked up the paper and glanced again at the story. He thought of others reading it, the bishop, his intellectual classmates. He would love to see *their* reaction. Had any of them made this kind of splash? It was too bad that Frank Ascue was not in town to read it.

2 The flight from Rome was never smooth but when the plane neared North America real turbulence began. Beneath two belts, his own and that which strapped him to his seat, Francis Ascue's stomach developed a few analogical air pockets of its own. There was a light pressure on his sleeve, Miss Simpson's hand, and a preparatory clearing of her throat.

"My, my, Father, isn't this unusual?"

She sat in the aisle seat in a bank of three. Father Ascue was in the middle. On his right a Mr. Kieffer slept, his head resting against the window. Father Ascue conveyed to Miss Simpson a reassurance he did not feel and plucked from the pouch at his knees a plastic card which he began to read. Miss Simpson's ancient hand rejoined its mate, clutching her purse.

The seasoned traveler, Father Ascue read, indeed the captain himself, always keeps his seat belt buckled except when moving about in the aircraft. He felt no camaraderie with seasoned travelers. Three years before he had gone by boat to Europe, a wretched retching week he had had no desire to repeat, but ever since they had taken off from Fiumicino he had been regretting his decision to fly. In a way he was a seasoned traveler.

During two summers he had wandered around Europe by train and bus and rented car with other student priests. When he wrote Charlotte from Paris or Brussels or Barcelona, he wondered if she thought of him as a knowledgeable cosmopolitan, moving with polyglot ease through legendary places. No doubt she did, since his letters veered toward fiction, seeking the awaiting genre of the touring intellectual's notes on foreign places. For himself the fanciful image dissolved into his shy presence in various third-rate hotels, the sense of imposture he sometimes felt when he came into a strange sacristy and asked permission to say Mass, treks with other tourists through galleries and churches, an indistinguishable member of the great American diaspora. The gap between the real and the ideal was lessened, almost closed, when he traveled with Tony Grosvenor, an English priest, a convert from Anglicanism, who had a British condescension toward the continental and did not hesitate to babble imperiously in languages he imperfectly understood. There had been some memorable trips with Tony, not least a mad three-week invasion of Germany by motorcycle, the two of them on one machine, Tony in control, the wind a roaring vortex amplified by their safety helmets as they raced along the *autobahnen.* Tony was particularly severe with Teutons and they left in their wake a series of insulted and outhaggled innkeepers. Unfortunately he did not see Tony often in Rome. His English friend was at the Greg, the Jesuit college, and intent on finishing and getting home. He found Latins annoyingly childish and emotional, his chill northern faith threatened by all that sun and garlic and impossible noise.

"And then there's the pope, Frank. He makes me nervous. You do understand?"

"I understand," Frank lied.

Frank returned the plastic card to its pouch and blotted from his mind its instructions on what to do when the plane crashed. When, not if. The card was subjunctive about it but Frank had found a prediction there. Miss Simpson's hand again, the clearing of her throat.

"I'm glad you're beside me, Father," she whispered. The tips of her teeth appeared beneath a colorless upper lip. "In case something happens," she added, leaving nothing to surmise.

"Nothing is going to happen." Fortunately his words did not sound like the semiprayer they were.

Miss Simpson sighed. She had been to Lourdes and Fatima as well as Rome, bargaining with God and his Holy Mother. What does she pray for? he wondered. More life? Well, who doesn't? That was precisely what he asked for himself. Still it annoyed him to have his priestly function reduced to that of celestial laundryman: the wave of his hand in absolution before the final dark descended.

A burst of static and then as from a cloud the captain's voice. Kieffer came awake, or stopped pretending to sleep.

"What did he say? Did you hear?"

"He says we've encountered turbulence."

"No shit." Followed by an apologetic smile.

The plane suddenly seemed to become lighter, to drop vertiginously. With a lurch, it asserted its weight once more and seemed to resume an onward movement. Clutching the backs of seats, a stewardess came down the aisle, her functional smile intact. Kieffer called to her.

"Bring me a bourbon, okay?" He turned to Frank. "Care for a drink?"

"No, thanks."

Kieffer leaned forward to look at Miss Simpson, seemed about to ask if she would join him, then decided against it, doubtless put off by her disapproving profile. Imagine, inviting a priest to have a public drink!

The stewardess went away, Kieffer consulted the window, Father Ascue's eyes dropped to the pouch in front of him. His stomach felt ominously convulsive. There was a sky blue paper bag in the pouch. He pressed his eyes shut, breathed deeply and tried to steel himself by recalling Paul's accounts of his journeys. But the apostolic vicissitudes with their vivid evocations of *mal de mer* caused him to open his eyes. He had the distinct feeling that the plane was being borne against its bent on swirling gusts of wind.

"Bourbon," the returned stewardess announced cheerily. Kieffer pressed a button and a tray unfolded over his knees. He reached across Frank to take his drink.

"Sure you don't want anything, Father?"

"Positive."

"Are you feeling queasy?" the stewardess asked.

Father Ascue shook his head. The girl hesitated but finally went away. He *was* going to be sick.

"Three years in Rome," Kieffer said, smacking his lips. "I envy you."

Miss Simpson stiffened at Kieffer's tone. "Father was very fortunate to spend so much time in the *Holy* City."

Father Ascue felt caught between them. He seemed to be swallowing involuntarily. Oh, God, here it comes. He snatched the paper sack from the pouch and brought it to his face. It inflated and collapsed with his breathing but nothing happened. Kieffer had moved back against the window, eyes wide. With the bag still pressed to his face, Father Ascue tried to convey with his eyes that all was under control, but he only felt more foolish. He was not going to be sick after all. He blew into the bag, closed its throat with thumb and finger and brought it smashing into his palm. It did not bang. The air escaped obscenely. Kieffer followed all this with dreadful fascination.

"Okay?" he asked dubiously.

"False alarm."

Miss Simpson said, "Would you like to sit on the aisle, Father?"

He hesitated, but only for a moment. Kieffer awake was something else than Kieffer asleep. Before the man had dropped off, he had quizzed Father Ascue about his years in Rome and could not be made to talk of himself. All Frank had learned was that Kieffer was in heavy machinery. What other kind is there? He sensed that Kieffer did not understand him, could not grasp why any man would want to be a priest. Celibacy, of course, though Kieffer's manner indicated that he was skeptical that it was really observed. The received view was once more that of Chaucer, Boccaccio, Balzac. Small wonder, with priestly defections making the news almost every day. It would have been pointless to try to explain what it meant to be a priest, what it meant to him.

"Thank you," he said to Miss Simpson, unfastening his seat belt. When the transfer had been made he did feel better. Not good, but better. The windows streamed with rain. He did not avail himself of the seat belt.

"The stewardess could bring you some Dramamine," Miss Simpson said.

"I think I'll be all right now."

"It doesn't hurt to be safe."

"If I feel sick again I'll call her."

"It must have been sad for you to leave Rome."

Father Ascue looked at her. "It's nice to be going home, Miss Simpson."

"Oh, I'm sure it is. Will you be doing parish work?"

He shrugged and smiled. "Perhaps. Perhaps teach. That's up to the bishop."

But of course the three years in Rome and the S.T.D. were meant to prepare him for the seminary faculty. Somewhat to his own surprise he had not liked Rome, the Collegio where he had lived, any of it. Oh, for several months he had been awed, like any tourist, but it is impossible to remain a tourist for three whole years. He had arrived in Rome after the Council was over and the Vatican did not seem the center of post-conciliar activity. The exciting news bore any dateline but that of Rome and he had found himself anxious to get away. Partly what he had felt was the expatriate's usual chauvinism and he developed a nostalgic longing for his native land.

It had started off nicely enough. The tile roof and pink walls of the Collegio had seemed the realization of a scarcely permitted dream when he first saw the place, only three months a priest at the time, new and eager for study. His cell-like room, never really warm and bitterly chill in the morning, was redeemed by the view from its window. A roof across the way was alive with lichen and, through an interstice of buildings, he could see a fountain. His mood wavered from medieval to Renaissance and, if it had not been for the constant whine of traffic, he might have been in another age.

But how long can a picture postcard enthrall? There were the droning Latin lectures, the scruffy professors, the obsequious students. The very prevalence of clergy seemed to devalue his calling. The Council might never have taken place. There were only two other Americans living in the Collegio. Few bishops were so uninformed as to send a man to live there rather than at the North American College. Father Ascue's bishop had been conned into favoring the place by its rector, Archbishop Cacciatore. Cacciatore no doubt gave Bishop Caldron, far off in rural Ohio, the reassuring illusion of having an advocate in Rome. The truth was that the rector was held in catholic contempt in the Eternal City. His younger brother, Giulio, was a papal count whose orgies were notorious and, well, Roman. The one thing that sustained Father Ascue as time passed was the thought that, his exile done and his degree obtained, he would be assigned to the faculty of the major seminary at home.

His ambition to teach, never openly acknowledged except to old and close friends like Bob Wintheiser and Gerry Doyle, had first gripped him fifteen years before as a freshman in the minor seminary on Lake Glister. That school, sold after years of dwindling enrollments lent unavoidable force to the negative view of taking boys from their families at thirteen or fourteen, loomed very large in Frank Ascue's private mythology. There he had been taught the classics and been introduced to the life of the mind; there he had read such Catholic heroes as Belloc, Chesterton, Newman, Hopkins and Brownson. It was odd that so many were converts or English or both. The school comprised six years, so that at thirteen Frank had been able to choose his local heroes from among the college men and the ones he chose and patterned himself upon were the editors of the school magazine, the president of the Literary and Dramatic Society, the officers of the Classics Club. Throughout high school, sleeping in dorms, he had dreamed of the time when he would have a room on the college corridor and, once there, his daydreams centered on a faculty suite. It had been a bitter day when, as a major seminarian, in his second year of theology, he had learned that the school on Lake Glister was to be closed. He had never been a good one to ask about the value of minor seminaries. He had loved the school on Lake Glister so much it was impossible for him to be objective on the subject. Of course only he and Wintheiser and Doyle had stayed the twelve-year course to ordination. Frank had not felt snatched from the bosom of his family in tender years. His parents were dead and while he loved his aunt and uncle, retired now in Arizona, they were not after all his parents. A decade separated him from his older sister Charlotte and, besides, she had been almost as excited about his going to the minor seminary as he was. With the closing of the school, his ambition to teach had been transferred to the major seminary and in this he had been encouraged by Father Ewing.

28

"Rome!" Father Ewing had cried the morning of Frank's ordination. They were in the cathedral sacristy, which was filled with newly ordained priests, still vested, tearing open the envelopes which contained their first assignments. Father Ewing stared in disbelief at Frank's letter. "I begged him to send you to Louvain. I was sure I had convinced him."

"But Rome is . . ." Father Ascue, trying to conceal his elation, sought the appropriate word. "Rome," he said finally, grinning despite himself.

"Rome is Rome," Father Ewing repeated. "How terribly true that is. It requires the strongest faith to survive study in Rome." He handed the letter to Frank and began pulling his surplice over his head.

Relatives of the newly ordained were waiting outside for a first blessing. Father Ewing dropped to his knees and Frank blessed him; it was an odd sensation to bring his palms down on his old professor's bald head. When Frank helped him to his feet Father Ewing wore a sunny expression.

"One thing, Frank. It won't take long. A Roman degree is the easiest in the world."

"I'll work hard, Father."

Frank had intended this as added consolation but Father Ewing looked at him as if he could no longer fathom such resolution.

"Just work fast," he said.

Either the flight had become smoother or his stomach was becoming used to turbulence. The bland music which emanated from God knew where was once more audible. Hardly celestial strains. There was a tinkle of ice as Kieffer returned his glass to the tray. Miss Simpson seemed to be humming along with the Muzak. Father Ascue's own heart felt light. In hours he would be home. He would see Charlotte and her family and, best of all, he would at long last begin his real life as a priest.

The airport parking lot, though not full, was too far from the terminal, so Charlotte Nygaard slid into a space reserved for cabs. Two forty-five. She got out of the car, slammed the door and looked up at the sky as if Frank's plane might put in an appearance on command of her expectant eye. But only a blank blue expanse looked back at her.

A cab pulled alongside her parked car and the driver glared at it. His mouth moved eloquently with inaudible oaths. Charlotte turned and fled into the terminal.

How incredibly crowded the place was. Weaving through the crowd, heading for the waiting room, Charlotte prayed that her path would cross her daughter's. If she was here. It had been such a hectic day. She had tried a dozen times to reach Bev at the Center but all she could get was the busy signal. Kids. And then that Bullard story. The noon news on the radio had alerted Charlotte and sent her in search of a morning paper when she remembered that Howard had taken theirs to work. She could hardly wait to discuss Bullard with Frank. What a hero the man had suddenly become.

Neither she nor Frank was much of a correspondent. While he was in Rome they had exchanged perhaps half a dozen letters, not counting Christmas cards, and his were largely accounts of trips he had taken, hers reports on her family. Those impersonal letters were just a point of surface contact, however; Frank was with her always, subconsciously. She never thought of him as far away. They were attuned. Frank knew without her telling him that she was trying to create for Howard and the kids the kind of home they had never had, she and Frank. Oh, Aunt Mildred and Uncle Harry had been wonderful, it had been immensely generous of them to assume responsibility for their orphaned niece and nephew, but throughout her childhood Charlotte had been conscious that she and Frank were deprived of what other kids had.

She had reached the waiting area. Here there were beige leatherette couches and ebony plastic tables. Close to the huge windows were backless benches, maroon leather cushions on stainless steel frames. Charlotte claimed the end of a bench near the window, lit a cigarette and, like everyone else, stared out the window as if in a trance. A chain link fence separated the ramp from the outside waiting area. A plane stood out there, surrounded by maintenance men. A tractor pulling baggage carts snaked toward it. Several people were clustered near a gate. Passengers. Well-wishers. Sad. Partings always sad. Yet when Frank left for Rome it had been only a matter of putting him on a train to New York. It had been difficult to think of someone boarding a train as bound for Rome. Which had made it easier. She had not let herself think that she would not see him for years. Her brother. Her flesh and blood. The only real family she had. Of course he would become a priest.

The gate in the chain link fence opened. Passengers were admitted to the ramp by a gangly man in uniform who made an announcement over the PA system before opening the gate. The people started toward the plane, their leader moving tentatively as if he had not wished to be a guide in this adventure. He kept looking over his shoulder, which gave the impression that he was being pursued rather than followed. Framed in the door of the aircraft, a stewardess awaited her wards.

The ash from her cigarette dropped and Charlotte, anxious to avoid catching it in her lap, swung her knees to the side.

"Excuse me," she said to the startled man beside her and then, noticing his collar, added, "Father."

"Not at all." His hand went to his hat but stopped en route.

"I'm Charlotte Nygaard. The sister of Francis Ascue. Father Ascue. Do you know him?"

The hat came off. How bald he was. "Father Ewing. Indeed I know him. I'm here to meet his plane."

"How nice." Who was he? There was something vaguely familiar in the name. Ewing? Ewing?

"I imagine you're here for the same purpose."

"Oh, yes."

"That's reassuring. I had begun to think I'd made a mistake."

Charlotte pushed back her sleeve. Five after three.

"It's today all right. His plane is late, though. He changes planes in Cleveland."

Charlotte dropped her cigarette to the floor and covered it with her shoe, making a grinding motion. Father Ewing looked away, as if discreetly.

"I'm expecting my daughter to be here too. Father Frank is the only real uncle she has and it's been such a long time."

Charlotte stood and looked over the crowd for some sign of Beverly and suddenly remembered who Ewing was. "You teach at the seminary," she cried.

His head jerked up as if he had been accused. Charlotte sat.

"Frank will be assigned there, won't he? To the seminary?"

For the first time Father Ewing's face looked pleasant. "I devoutly hope so."

The plane that had been loading taxied away and, on cue, everyone stood to watch it go. It lumbered across the field to the end of a runway. Moments went by and then it began to roll; it lifted gracefully and rose in a lazy arc and disappeared into the east. They were still standing when Beverly arrived.

"Are we in time?" she asked breathlessly. "I was sure we'd be late and miss you."

The two girls with Bev nodded a greeting, their faces flushed. Charlotte wondered if she should introduce the girls to Father Ewing but decided to spare him. Suddenly he was on his feet again and Charlotte followed his gaze. A plane was coming in.

The next half hour was pandemonium. The crush to the door, milling about by the chain link fence, waiting, waiting, and then Frank emerged from the plane, hesitated, looking in the wrong direction with an expectant smile. He bounced down the steps and came across the apron, looking young and happy and thin. It was Father Ewing he had spied, the clerical garb making him an easy target, but finally he saw Charlotte and was through the gate and she was hugging him and, for God's sake, crying, blubbering like a big baby at seeing her little brother again. She was conscious of the stares of onlookers, the mild shock until they decided that the clinging woman must be his sister or something; after all, the man was a priest. She broke away and brought Bev forward, Bev suddenly shy and awkward and Frank saving it, he was so suave when he had to be. When they turned to go into the terminal she sensed that Frank felt pulled between her and Father Ewing, that he wanted to talk to her but could not ignore the older priest. The shoving crowd made the choice for him, pushing him with Father Ewing. She called to Frank, asking for his baggage stubs.

His hand reached through to her, giving her the stubs. Father Ewing was now flourishing a newspaper and speaking with great intensity. Charlotte broke through the crowd and joined the two priests. Bullard's name was mentioned.

"What do you think of him, Frank?" she asked. "Wasn't he in your class?"

"Yes."

"Not very bright," Ewing growled.

Charlotte gripped Frank's arm. To hell with Bullard. How thin Frank was. But he was well and happy and home again and that was good.

Father Ewing excused himself. He shook Frank's hand, held it for a moment. "I can't tell you how I've waited for this day. Welcome home. But for now I'll leave you with your family."

"I'll phone, Father. Soon."

"Good. But get some rest now."

Bev and the girls joined them now and Charlotte said, "Come on, Frank. Let's get your bags."

The chancery office was a squat granite building, an afterthought on a narrow lot, wedged between the cathedral and the rectory. It was a place of legend rather than of experience for Father Ascue and he mounted the steps two days after his arrival home with appropriate trepidation. Inside was a small empty vestibule and, beyond, a long corridor lined with doors. At the far end, on a pedestal and bathed in the weak light of a ceiling spot, was a statue of Saint Rose of Lima. Father Ascue went from the vestibule into the corridor and stopped.

"Yes?" A woman's voice; it had emanated from an open door to his left. There was no one visible. Father Ascue went to the door and looked inside.

"Yes?" The woman sat in profile. She had not turned. She was behind a desk on which stood a wedge of varnished wood bearing the legend *Receptionist.* Her arms, v'd at the elbow, were held out from her body, clawlike fingers poised over the keyboard of her typewriter, but her closed eyes and expectant air made her seem a figure at a séance.

"Father Ascue," Father Ascue said.

"Do you have an appointment?"

"Yes, I do."

"With whom?" She turned abruptly, the movement causing her eyes to snap open. She might have been catching him in a lie.

"Monsignor Yorick asked me to come in today. I phoned yesterday. To see the bishop." He blurted this out, then held his tongue. This crone put him on the defensive, made him feel an impostor.

"What time was your appointment?"

"It *is* at ten o'clock. Would you tell Monsignor Yorick I'm here?"

"What was the name?" Her nose wrinkled, her brows knit.

"Father Francis Ascue."

He marched to the wall and studied the photograph of Bishop Caldron hanging there. The woman rose, fidgeted, did not move. Father Ascue realized that he was glaring at his bishop's visage. He was involved in some childish contest with this woman and it would be fatal to so much as shift his weight. Footsteps. She came around the desk, went past him to the door, stood there a moment and then continued down the hall.

Father Ascue exhaled in triumph. He turned and noticed an intercom on the desk. Why in the world hadn't she used it? The chancery was as bad as everyone said, Byzantine. Rome itself might envy this bureaucratic insolence. He heard voices approaching, the woman's and, unmistakably, Monsignor Yorick's.

The chancellor, in monsignorial garb, the red piping of his cassock almost luminescent, swept into the room, his broad face aglow. His right hand was extended. With his left he brushed back the sparse hair worn in what Father Ascue's Aunt Mildred would have called a pompadour.

"Father," Yorick said in a reedy voice. He gripped Ascue's hand. "Welcome home. Welcome home." He turned to the harridan, who had skulked to her desk, where she seemed to shrivel within herself.

"Agnes, this is Father Ascue. He's been in Rome for years and years." He beamed at Father Ascue. "When did you get in?"

"Tuesday." He had told Yorick this yesterday on the phone.

"And can't wait to go to work? Good. What do you think of that, Agnes?"

Something happened to the embalmed line of Agnes's mouth, as if she were trying to pop the stitches and scream that she was still alive. Father Ascue decided it was intended for a smile. Embarrassed by her levity, Agnes began to shuffle things about on her desk.

"Can't wait to get to work," Yorick repeated with a chuckle. He took Ascue's elbow and steered him into the hall.

Father Ascue made a neutral noise, looking at the illumined statue at the end of the corridor. Yorick's eyes were on him but when he turned the chancellor's expression was unrevealing. Yorick twisted his neck and began to move more rapidly. His head made an odd to-and-fro movement as he walked. The Chanticleer, Father Ewing called Yorick, and Ascue saw that it was not merely a poor pun.

"Here we are." This office was cheerful after the receptionist's lair. Sunlight entered through high windows, the tilted blades of the blinds laid bright bars of sun on desk, on leather chairs, on bookcases and on a startling array of trophies enshrined on a table against a wall. Yorick seemed to have been waiting for Father Ascue to notice the display.

"Do you bowl, Father?"

"No. But I used to."

Monsignor Yorick thumped his pouter pigeon chest. "Best sport in the world. Far better than golf. It's a game for all seasons."

"There aren't many alleys in Rome."

"I don't suppose."

"Not that I had much time for bowling."

Yorick, seated behind his desk now, frowned. His eyes dropped to the newspaper spread open on his desk and the frown deepened.

"Weren't you and Bullard classmates?"

"Yes."

"Have you heard of his shenanigans?"

"Only what I've seen in the papers."

"Only!" Yorick hunched forward. "Tell me, Father. What gets into these young guys?"

Father Ascue assumed a thoughtful expression, searched for a prudent remark. "I'm hardly the one to say. After all, three years away . . ."

"All the better. You have perspective. They must be discussing these things in Rome. If only they'd *do* something."

Did he really think Rome was the buzzing center of it all, a place where clear-sighted cardinals wisely appraise the problems of the world? The somnolence and inefficiency of the Vatican were light-years distant from the Rome Monsignor Yorick invoked with his angry sigh. Like Monaco and San Marino, its major industry was postage stamps.

"Agnes is a pretty disconcerting person to meet this early in the day," he said, making a ninety-degree turn from these stormy waters. To Father Ascue's surprise Yorick brought a finger to his lips.

"The bishop's cousin," he said in a stage whisper.

"I didn't know," Father Ascue said feebly.

"She's not a bad old thing. And she keeps out the cranks."

Cranks? Did Yorick mean the clergy of the diocese? The chancellor rocked in his chair, studying Father Ascue in a not unkind way. He picked up a half-smoked cigar from a tray on the desk and applied a match to it. Wreathed in bluish smoke, he said, "Have you seen Ewing yet?"

"He met my plane."

"Did he? He and I are shirttail relatives, you know."

Father Ascue knew. From the asperity with which Father Ewing spoke of Yorick ("my half-ass cousin"), Ascue had surmised the rivalry between the two men. Yorick's eminence in the diocese, as chancellor, had eclipsed the accomplishments of the older man, who was shown only the amused and wary deference accorded seminary professors. A series of lost battles had culminated in Yorick's being selected by the bishop to act as his *peritus* during the recent Council in Rome.

"The idiot knows nothing beyond Tanquerey," Ewing had exploded. "And his knowledge of Latin is piggish." With masochistic relish Ewing had intoned Yorick's rendition of "Happy Birthday" at a clerical cele-bration. *"Beata natalitia tibi, beata natalitia tibi . . ."* As a seminarian, Ascue had been regaled by Ewing's reading Yorick's letters from the Council. The other *periti*—the *other!*—were heretics. There was that nitwit Rahner, that idiot Küng. That Ewing shared these assessments did not diminish his mordant mirth.

Father Ascue glanced at his watch, but Yorick, puffing on his cigar, continued to act as if this appointment had been to see him.

"You get your degree, Father?"

"Yes, I did."

"What did your professors make of this new theology?"

"I don't think many of them had heard of it."

"Good. Good!" Yorick produced a billow of smoke through which his satisfied expression made its way. "That's encouraging."

"In many ways their indifference is surprising."

35

"Oh?"

"This is a time of change, after all. Of renewal." Father Ascue inhaled. "Of *aggiornamento.*"

"Sure it is. But change, not revolution." Yorick's hand came down with a bang on the newpaper before him.

"A lot of the new stuff is good, Monsignor."

Yorick waved away smoke and with it that topic of conversation. "You'll learn," he said enigmatically. "Once you get into the pea patch and are doing a priest's work you'll be all right."

Father Ascue found himself smiling in bewilderment at the sunny Venetian blinds.

Yorick said, "Ewing's a pretty good teacher, isn't he?"

"Yes, he is."

"Then why does he want to play Hamlet?"

"Hamlet?"

"He's been trying to get out of teaching for years."

"Is that right?"

"He wants a parish so bad he can taste it." The chancellor chuckled. "Who would replace him? He's the only man in the diocese who can teach moral."

Father Ascue's recent degree was in moral theology. Did Yorick realize that Ewing regarded him as his replacement? Father Ascue began to hope that the chancellor did not suspect, though this involved the unsettling realization that Ewing's assurances about his being destined for the seminary were not based on any understanding here at the chancery.

"I suppose it's only natural to want to do parish work."

Monsignor Yorick put his elbows on the desk and nodded. "The true work of the priest. You're right, Father. It's the most natural thing in the world."

"All those years a priest and nothing but teaching," Father Ascue mused. It occurred to him that the chancellor had never been a parish priest either and he added, "I don't mean that teaching isn't important. There are many things a priest does . . ."

What a ridiculous conversation this was. Why didn't Yorick mention the bishop?

"All his classmates are pastors," Yorick said. "Have been for years. Every one of them. Good parishes too."

Silence fell and Father Ascue eased back his cuff and looked at his watch. It was well after ten-thirty. His eyes met Yorick's when he looked up.

"The boss will buzz when he's ready for you."

Father Ascue laughed nervously. "I'm in no hurry."

"Where are you staying?"

"At my sister's."

"What parish she in?"

"Saint Barnabas."

"Oder."

The pastor. "Yes."

"Know him?"

"Not really."

"What's your sister think of him?"

"They like him."

Yorick ground his cigar in the ashtray. He glanced at the intercom as if he too wished the bishop would buzz for Father Ascue. "Were you at the Angelicum, Father?"

"No," Father Ascue said, crestfallen. Didn't they even know where he had been the past three years? "I lived at the Collegio. . . ."

"That's right. Cacciatore."

"He always spoke highly of Bishop Caldron."

"Is that a fact? Good. Good." A friend in Rome. The lingering smoke from the chancellor's cigar made Frank feel vaguely ill. "The thing is, Father, and I'll be frank, we need men like you very much just now. You're young and that helps; most important, you've had good solid training. You can be a yeast."

Frank remembered the little foil-wrapped cubes, Fleischmann's, that Charlotte had eaten for her pimples. "I want to do whatever I can." He felt like a nitwit occupying the Eagle Scout role Yorick had cast him for.

"The young men ordained nowadays . . ." The chancellor brushed a hand back over his hair, causing his eyes to lift to the ceiling. "I don't know what it is, Father. No docility. No sense of what it is to be a priest."

Maybe not, Frank thought. But Yorick was not his idea of a priest either, sitting here in an office among his trophies, puffing on cigars, thankful that Agnes kept out the cranks. If it weren't for the cassock, Yorick might have been a harried businessman. What right did he have to complain about priests in parish work and to speak condescendingly of Father Ewing? Frank wanted to escape but at the same time he was cheered by the direction of the conversation. Yorick's remarks brought to mind visions of malleable seminarians: young idealistic men, eager to be shown what the priesthood is. Frank's previous doubts went and with them his annoyance with the chancellor. He wanted to assure Yorick that he would very much like to take part in the formation of young priests. Things were indeed getting out of hand.

The intercom on Yorick's desk made an indecisive noise. The chancellor swooped toward it and depressed a button.

"Is he there, Monsignor?"

"I'll send him in, Bishop."

Father Ascue stood and waited for Yorick to come around the desk and precede him to the bishop's office. His eye fell to the newspaper and Phil Bullard's name, upside down, leaped for his seeing. Frank felt no sympathy at all with his wayward classmate, not now, not here, with the chancellor of the diocese about to usher him in to see his bishop.

Thus it was that, expectant, disponible, feeling slightly smug, Father Ascue came out of Yorick's office and encountered Phil Bullard in the hallway.

"Hello, Frank." Phil Bullard pulled the door of the bishop's office closed behind him. Too late, he realized that this impeded Ascue and Yorick. He felt a blush suffuse his face. This was like emerging from an extended stay in the confessional to face the next penitent.

"Hi, Phil."

"When did you get in?"

"Just a few days ago." Ascue's expression suggested that he had been reading the papers.

Bullard, smiling half defiantly at the chancellor, said, "Well, things are changing. Isn't that right, Monsignor?"

Yorick grunted and pointed Ascue at the bishop's door. "Just knock and go in, Father. He's expecting you."

"Good luck," Bullard said.

"Thanks, Phil. I hope I don't need it."

"We all do."

Ascue knocked and entered and the door closed behind him. Bullard was left in the corridor with Yorick. The chancellor started to walk away, then stopped. "You can find your way out, can't you?" After a millisecond, he added, "Father?"

"Yes, Monsignor. I know my way out."

"Good."

"I meant out of the building."

"That's what I thought you meant."

"Just wanted to make sure."

Yorick now waited for Bullard to go ahead of him and, doing so, Phil felt he was getting the bum's rush. He slowed his pace but too late. Yorick was already at his own door. He disappeared into his office without another word. Angry, Bullard hurried out of the building and began to walk downtown where he had left his car.

Yorick would know of his request, of course; the appointment with the bishop this morning had resulted from it. The chancellor's attitude was not surprising. Just so, in the seminary, a class achieved a sudden and evanescent esprit de corps when one of its members left. No, not left. Quit. Men who left the seminary were quitters, the word suggesting that they hadn't what it takes, that they had weakened. In the wake of their going, the survivors were seized by a mood of unspoken self-congratulation. They were still there. They would make it. For a week they would gossip about the quitter, recall portents and signs of his going, the anecdotes summing up a man and finding him wanting. How many had been influenced by memories of such camaraderie when they had doubted that they belonged in the seminary? It was easy to think that the priesthood was not a lonely decision but a group affair, something they were all doing together, so that the individual's doubts could be swallowed up in the collective confidence.

Bullard knew that he himself had been intimidated by the thought that none of his classmates doubted the rightness of their being in the seminary and destined for the priethood. Alone in his room at night, especially in fall and spring when the sounds of the city drifted through his open window, the sounds of that other life which to an apprentice celibate took on a mystery and fascination those engaged in it would never have believed, Phil Bullard had sometimes thought of the future with sinking melancholy rather than dread. The future seemed so joyless and he knew that he must endure it alone. Perhaps he did not have a vocation.

Of course when he mentioned his doubts in the confessional or to his spiritual director (old Nolan, dead now, tall, bald, birdlike, ordained early in the century, incapable of understanding anything Phil tried to tell him), the answer was predictable. A vocation is not magic or a miracle. A steady response to the grace of the moment. Pray, son. Pray incessantly. Doubt was temptation. "This is a seminary. You're here. Why? It's not an accident that you're here." Nolan seemed to be saying that the only way out of the seminary was via ordination.

Bullard went downhill from the chancery, scampered across Keasy Street. There was a bench there and he sat, watching the cars come down the hill and turn sharply to take Keasy into the business district. The drivers were male and female, people, plain people. Bullard stared at them as if he were surprised to find that he did not envy them. How he had romanticized their ordinary lives. A wife, love, ecstasy, someone who knew and accepted him, who welcomed him home and sat in rapt attention while he spoke. He knew marriages were not like that. Wives got bored and nagged and husbands directed at almost any woman not their wife the kind of vague inflated hopes that had surfaced in themselves. It was childish, he knew that, he felt he really knew that now. Even the bishop had been surprised.

Though it was warm, Bullard wore a topcoat, its collar turned up. Hatless, the coat navy blue, black trousers, but loafers adding a deceptive dash since his Roman collar, worn out of deference to the bishop, was concealed. No one would take him for a priest—unless they recognized him from his picture in the paper.

A woman approached. She carried a white shopping bag bearing the phony coat of arms of a department store. She glanced at him, looked immediately away, annoyed by his curious look. A negative reaction but generic, female to male. The woman went up the hill, her legs muscular with the effort of her ascent.

Cars, people, infrequent pedestrians, the people of God. The thought was not ironic. Philip Bullard felt his heart go out to them all, seen and unseen. It was them he wanted to serve. The publicity of the past week had thrown him into a confusion that had not gotten into the newspaper stories. All that had been a last desperate effort, truly desperate; hope had gone, or so he had thought, but his swan song had stirred the dead coal of zeal. The bishop had been wary but receptive. He thought of Ascue, in with the bishop now. How different their interviews would be. Frank had come to that office along a well-marked route. Everyone assumed he would be assigned to the seminary. That had seemed his manifest destiny ten years ago.

Bullard got to his feet and began to walk, his hands deep in the pockets of his topcoat, his spare hair lifting with his gait. He did not envy Ascue. Ascue least of all. What had happened to all the seminary luminaries? They had sunk into their assignments and become indistinguishable from everyone else. Not one of them seemed to grasp what was going on in the Church and in the world. They did not see that the old comfortable way was doomed. He would bet that Ascue was as Neanderthal as the rest. The real joke was that most of the so-called brains were now as conservative as hell.

"What make is it, fella?" The attendant in the parking lot took his ticket, made change, asked the question with easy man-to-man insolence.

"Mustang. Red. I see it."

"Right."

Fella, not Father. The way it ought to be. To hell with this phony aristocratic stuff. Why should a priest get more deference than a banker, say? Not that he thought the attendant would address a banker as fella, but the point seemed clear.

Into his car and buckled up, he eased it from the lot and felt an impulse to drive out of town, to hit a country road and just follow the hood where it took him. He did not want to go back to the Center, to his room, to the inevitable call from Diane. Oh, God, he groaned, slipping into traffic and with leaden reluctance turning in the direction of the Center. It was his fault, of course. He could not blame Diane. Last night he had not been very clear to her about his coming visit to the bishop, though he had meant to be, he really had, but no natural way of telling her had presented itself. She had assumed she knew what it was all about and it would have been cruel to disenchant her abruptly.

It was all different now, all changed. Certainly she would be able to see that. What a nuisance, what a pest. It was unfair to think of her like that, but it wasn't only a matter of the two of them. If he could have his personal way . . .

He drove on, rehearsing, anxious to have it over.

The bishop's office, like Monsignor Yorick's, was bright and cheerful after the gloom of the corridor. The Most Reverend George Timothy Caldron, in street clothes, his suit coat open to display the pectoral cross anchored in a buttonhole of his vest, had stood, though his diminutive height might have misled the unprepared to think he was still seated. Father Ascue felt like a schoolboy come to the principal's office. He advanced toward his spiritual superior, the man who had ordained him priest three years before. The bishop extended his right hand with its huge episcopal ring. Father Ascue took it, bobbed and brought his lips to the ring in the now outmoded gesture of fealty.

"No need for that," the bishop said.

Stupidly Father Ascue said, "I'm sorry."

"Whatever for? Please be seated, Father."

Seated himself, the bishop reached out and corrected the angle of a clock. "After eleven. *Tempus fugit*, Father. *Tempus fugit.*"

Father Ascue looked at his own watch and nodded.

The bishop was studying him over the bifocal inserts in his glasses. Chin drawn back so that his Roman collar was lost in flesh, Bishop Caldron bore a faint resemblance to the late pope. A meaty nose, wide full-lipped mouth, close-clipped white hair. The bishop's eyes twinkled in an effort to put Father Ascue at ease. Quite consciously, Father Ascue was ridding his mind of remembered phrases of Father Ewing's, tart descriptions and bitter excoriations of the bishop. The prelate's physical solidity seemed almost an argument for the permanence of the Church, even in this small Ohio diocese. Father Ascue thought of a mystical line extending back through time, connecting the chubby little man with the Apostles. Bishop Caldron was the visible continuation of the church Christ had founded. It was a damned shame the man was such a reactionary.

"How's your Latin, Father?"

"Quite good."

"Reading alone or speaking too?"

"We wrote our exams in Latin, of course."

"Is that so?"

"That's hardly an accomplishment."

The bishop's brows lifted. "I wouldn't say that, Father. Indeed I wouldn't. You can't imagine how difficult it is to find a man who can write Latin. For official correspondence."

Good God, did the bishop intend to make him a chancery flunky with the task of composing the letters and documents going to Rome? He should have downgraded his knowledge of Latin. He might have known the bishop would be impressed. The Council session had taught American bishops what a disadvantage it could be not to be fluent in the language of the Church. Ascue had heard how Bishop Caldron, with only Yorick to aid him, had sat through those first sessions in sullen frustration. His inability did not affect the bishop's views on the use of the vernacular at Mass, however. He had been foursquare for retaining Latin, the language of culture and scholarship, the traditional language of the divine services. He had written a series of letters in the diocesan paper devoted to the beauties of the Latin liturgy, a series rumored to have been penned by Yorick. "Who used a pony for every author after Caesar," Ewing had commented.

"You'd be surprised," the bishop said.

"I'm sure most priests in the diocese know Latin as well as I do."

"Then you must have had a difficult time in Rome. So you don't consider yourself an accomplished Latinist?"

Father Ascue felt intensely uncomfortable. Bishop Caldron had a reputation for thwarting anything he construed as ambition and it was the sad priest who made a direct request of him, since this almost guaranteed getting the opposite. Nor could the obvious ploy be worked, asking for what one did not want; the bishop was said to have an uncanny ability to discern the true direction of ambition. Ewing's illustration of this had been a priest who, wanting to enter the chaplain corps, told the bishop he had a contemplative vocation and would like to enter the Trappists. Within forty-eight hours he was installed as chaplain in a home for wayward girls with the added duty of being confessor to a convent of contemplative nuns. The bishop, in his letter of appointment (which the victim had framed and hung over his toilet), suggested that these new tasks would enable the priest to test the authenticity of his contemplative calling.

"Archbishop Cacciatore sent his regards," Father Ascue said.

"An excellent man."

"He has quite a reputation in Rome."

The bishop steepled his stubby fingers. "These are dark days, Father. Dark days. And the worst may not yet be upon us."

"A time of change," Ascue said, as if echoing these thoughts.

Uneasy as he felt, he was less impressed by Bishop Caldron than he would have liked to be. One of the great thrusts of the Council had been to decentralize the power of the Church and return to bishops fuller control over their dioceses. It was difficult to think that Bishop Caldron was the sort of ordinary the theologians who had been partisans of collegiality had in mind. Their arguments invoked wise, gentle pastors, guiding their flock with unfailing enlightenment once loosed from the bureaucratic fetters of the Vatican. Sitting across from Bishop Caldron, remembering his history of whimsy and caprice, it was difficult to believe the future would be much different from the past. It might even be worse, Father Ascue thought gloomily.

"Young men dream strange dreams, Father. Priests your age. You'll be hearing all about it soon. Older men demand that I do something. Well, it isn't as simple as it used to be. How can you discipline a man who has no conception of obedience?"

Was the bishop speaking of Phil Bullard? It was difficult not to think so and, thinking so, to say anything. Surely the bishop must realize that he and Phil had passed in the hallway outside. Frank wondered if his loyalty was being tested, but loyalty to whom? Caldron's expression was sibylline. How little the bishop had changed over the years. Frank had not seen him often in person but his photograph had hung in the hallway of the parish school, had been prominently on display in both minor and major seminaries and had looked out at readers of the *Fort Elbow Catholic* for over twenty years. This was the prelate who had confirmed Frank and whom he had seen come down the aisle of the seminary chapel to the strains of the *Ecce sacerdos magnus.* In many ways his life had orbited about this little man and, though Frank had aged and altered, the bishop had not. Such changelessness might have been reassuring if Caldron were less obscure. More than anything else, the boy beneath the priest he had become was called forth by this familiar if remote figure and Frank found it almost odd that the bishop should take time to chat with him—if chat was the word for what they were having. Yet the bishop did not make him uneasy in the way that Yorick did. Melancholy as his remark might sound, there was a little bow of a smile on Caldron's lips and it occurred to Frank that the bishop's capriciousness might stem from some extraordinary vantage point. Did he regard even the antics of his clergy *sub specie aeternitatis?*

"It all goes back to seminary training, of course."

Frank nodded, hoping that the bishop meant that there was a need for new directions. A good many suggestions had been made recently, suggestions for change and a new orientation. After all, the bishop had closed Lake Glister and that had been a dramatic step, however reluctantly taken. Frank's own pain at that came back to him and with it the realization that the windows the Council had opened must have introduced chilling winds for men who like the bishop had lived for many years under a seemingly unalterable regime.

"That is the key."

"Indeed it is." The bishop began to rock in his chair. "Now what sort of work would you like to do, Father?"

"Anything you wish, Bishop." They looked at one another across the desk. Obedience. Malleability. Frank knew that those were the sentiments he should feel. And he did feel them. Wherever the bishop sent him he would willingly go. Of course it helped that they had just arrived at an unstated agreement.

"No predilections at all?"

"I'll be happy with any assignment."

"Oh, I have no doubt of that. Your record is an excellent one."

The bishop turned in his chair, pulled his typewriter toward him and fed a heavy crinkling piece of diocesan stationery into it. He paused for a moment, then began to peck away, the tip of his tongue appearing as he typed. Frank felt that he had just passed an exam and it was odd to think that the staccato rhythm of the bishop's typewriter was tapping out his fate. He felt no apprehension now. An excellent record. Perhaps, on paper, but he had, he felt, few illusions about himself. And anyway it was not the bishop's praise he was after; bishops were often wrong, not least in their favorable opinions.

When he had finished typing, Bishop Caldron pulled the sheet from the machine and laid it on his desk. He read it through with obvious satisfaction, signed it and sealed it with the diocesan seal. When he had folded it and put it into an envelope, he rose.

"There you are, Father. I will telephone Monsignor and let him know you're coming. God bless you. It's good to have you back."

The bishop came with him to the door and showed him into the hallway. When the door had closed behind him, Frank started down the hall with a light step. Monsignor! The bishop had said he would phone Monsignor. When Frank passed Yorick's door he was stopped by a *Pssst* and the chancellor peeked out at him.

"Get it?"

"Got it." Frank flourished the envelope.

Yorick opened his door wide. "Where to?"

"Don't you know?"

Yorick glanced at the bishop's door. "It's never sure until he does it." His eyes dropped to the envelope. It was clear that he wanted Father Ascue to open it and tell him what assignment he had received. That seemed reasonable. The chancellor of the diocese ought to know such things. The intercom on Yorick's desk began to crackle insistently and the chancellor jumped. He looked over his shoulder and then at the closed door of the bishop's office. He looked at the envelope in Father Ascue's hand. Finally, he threw up his hands and retreated into his office. Frank escaped down the corridor. Yorick could get the news from the bishop.

He skipped down the chancery steps in the spring sunlight, holding in both hands the letter which contained his fate. He realized that he was whistling. He did not open the envelope until he was settled behind the wheel of Charlotte's car. "Dear Father Askew," the letter began. Frank's eyes moved rapidly down the page. Involuntarily, he cried out. He read the letter again, slowly, then stared straight ahead. The sun, high in the sky now, was bright on the car's hood. It reflected painfully, hurting Father Ascue's eyes and causing them to water.

Father Ewing, breviary in hand, but in no mood to read his office, paced the blacktop road which would bring young Ascue out of the city traffic onto the seminary grounds with the news of his interview with the bishop. It was wrong to be so eager, but he had found it impossible to remain in his rooms. The twitter of birds, the sound of a ball game brought to him on gusts of spring breeze, the vernal scented air, all seemed a composite symbol of hope and he could not wait to learn that Ascue had indeed been assigned to the seminary faculty. Once that was assured, his own request for a transfer would be in order. They could not deny him, not now.

Short of the entrance to the seminary grounds, Father Ewing wheeled and walked back toward the cluster of buildings. Behind the convent a covey of nuns were screeching through a game of badminton. With the idiotic new habits, it was a scene worthy of Boccaccio. The heavy woolen skirts stopped between knee and ankle, the headdress had given way to a diaphanous veil pinned halfway back on the head and this revealed a startling variety of hair: mouse gray, blond, auburn, white. Most older nuns, with the wisdom of vanity or tugged by tradition, had retained the old habit. Father Ewing flipped open his breviary. He glanced at it, the *sortes Vergilianae.* It had opened at complin. The Nunc Dimittis! He smiled, wanting to chant the words. "Now dost thou dismiss thy servant, O Lord, according to thy word in peace." It had to be an omen.

"Hi, Father. Great day."

Young Tremplin, clad in khaki pants, sneakers and a maroon sweat shirt, looking not much older than the seminarian with him, waved to Father Ewing, then stopped on the road, awaiting his approach.

"Good afternoon, Father." Ewing looked at the seminarian. "Cole?"

"That's right, Father."

Cole had been the prime mover behind the student protest over the refectory food some weeks ago. Probably put up to it by Tremplin. Father Ewing had considered the protest an excessive reaction to two mild cases of ptomaine. It had been traced to the German potato salad, of course, eaten by two unwarned first year men. They should have been told that no one ate German potato salad on its second and subsequent appearances at table. But the protest, fifty signatures, had smacked of rebellion and Father Ewing had not liked that at all.

Tremplin said, "What have you heard from Frank Ascue?"

"Ascue?" Ewing said. "The man who's been studying in Rome?"

Father Tremplin looked surprised. "Is there more than one Ascue?"

"I know we have a man of that name in Rome."

"There's only one Father Ascue in this diocese."

"Is that so?"

"I understand he's back." Tremplin's smile was the uneasy one he wore when he feared that his leg was being pulled.

"Is he?"

"I thought you'd know."

"I'm sure I would."

Tremplin gave up and Ewing was almost sorry. A moral theologian has several dozen ways of being less than candid; it would have been a minor challenge to withhold information from someone as normally insistent as Tremplin.

46

"Mr. Cole and I were speaking of *l'affaire* Bullard. The students wonder if there isn't some way they can show solidarity with him."

"With whom?"

"Philip Bullard."

"My God, you're not serious. What do you mean, solidarity?" Father Ewing directed this question at Cole.

"He seems to be a victim of the establishment. Why did the bishop summon him? We were thinking of a fast."

"A fast!"

"To show our sympathy with him."

"You'd be better advised to pray for him."

"Well, that's more or less the idea," Tremplin said. "A fast is dramatic, it will draw attention—"

"Whose attention?"

Tremplin, wary, shrugged.

"Father, I hope you're not encouraging the seminarians to pull some stupid publicity stunt. A fast! No doubt the same group that has been complaining about the food."

"I wouldn't call it a stunt," Tremplin said with quavering voice.

A car came in the road and Father Ewing looked up expectantly. But this huge expensive automobile could not be bringing Ascue. The three of them stepped to the side of the road and the car came to a halt. Monsignor Eisenbarth smiled from its window; behind the wheel was a layman.

"You know Mr. Rupp, don't you, Father Ewing?"

"We've met, Monsignor. We've met."

"Park here if you like, Arthur. This is fine."

Rupp pulled the car slightly closer to the side of the road and shut off the motor. He and Eisenbarth joined Ewing, Tremplin and Cole. Rupp seemed surprised to learn that Tremplin was a priest.

"What do *you* teach, Father?" he asked Cole.

Cole, flustered, told Rupp that he was not a priest.

"Not yet," Monsignor Eisenbarth amended. "Not yet."

They were still standing there a minute later when Father Ascue drove up. He parked behind Rupp's car and walked toward them. This was not the way Father Ewing had imagined receiving the news and he considered the possibility of whisking Ascue away before the others could object. But Eisenbarth had moved forward, pompously, as if through water, to offer his hand to Ascue.

"Welcome back, Father." His voice seemed to force its way through the bridge of his nose. "Welcome home from Rome." This last was clearly for Rupp's benefit. Eisenbarth's head had swung toward the layman though his eyes remained on Ascue.

Tremplin said, "Hello, Frank." The two young priests shook hands. Ascue was introduced to Rupp then and, perhaps inevitably, when they had formed a circle on the road, Eisenbarth asked, "And where will you be stationed, Father?"

Father Ascue glanced at Father Ewing. His eyes were wide and dull and a rather silly grin fixed itself to his mouth.

"I've just come from the chancery office."

Father Ewing heard his own voice ask, involuntarily, "What is your assignment?"

Did the birds stop twittering then, was some devilish deodorant employed to snuff from air the perfumes that had assailed him only moments before, did some pall fall upon the world? It seemed to Father Ewing that he heard Ascue's answer in some seasonless vacuum, a hygienic purgatorial place from which joy was wholly absent.

"I've been assigned to Saint Waldo's," Father Ascue said.

"Entweder," Eisenbarth said. "Ambrose Entweder."

"Congratulations, Father."

Ewing spun to see that Rupp was serious. He had a seignorial smile now and his hands were inserted to knuckle depth in the pockets of his vest.

"Congratulations, Father. Saint Waldo's is my parish."

Part Two

1 Fort Elbow is situated in northwestern Ohio, midway between Toledo as armpit and the Indiana border as wrist, the name derived, perhaps, from the bend in the Prune River on whose east bank the fort was located. The modern city is distributed along both banks of the Prune with business and industrial concerns favoring the east bank while crossriver the newer neighborhoods and eventually suburbs spread west, munching into orchards as they go, encircling Cobb County airport and then moving north, so that in the fullness of time the area will be subsumed into the threatened megalopolis which will extend from Buffalo to Milwaukee.

The terrain is hilly, especially in the older town, and the Catholic cathedral is clearly visible from the western suburbs, its massive dome prominent in the uptown silhouette at sundown and sparkling like a golden onion in the morning. This pride of place might be justified by the fact that French missionaries early passed this way (indeed a recurrent debate in the Cobb County Historical Society turns on the pros and cons of the town's name being a corruption of the French Fort Le Bois), but in the post-Revolutionary War period the influx into the Northwest Territory began. That portion of the Territory which, in 1803, became the state of Ohio began a laminating process which has left Fort Elbow in such a condition that it can fairly be described as the nation writ small. The ultimate origins of its citizens reflect, almost to the decimal point, the national figures and it is the far-out religious denomination indeed which is not represented by tent or tabernacle, temple or cathedral, meeting house or reading room.

To the Roman Catholic eye, taking as its vantage point the greening statue of Saint Jude atop the gold-leaf dome of the cathedral, the see city of the Fort Elbow diocese has its off-center nucleus on the east bank of the Prune: the Italian parish down the hill near Keasy Street, the Irish church due east from the chancery entrance, the Polish and Slovak churches glaring at one another across Kosciusko Avenue as if about to joust with their steeples (that of Saint Thaddeus several centimeters nearer the sky, thanks to the higher level of the north side of the avenue), and, of course, Saint Waldo's near the river, where the bank dips down from the promontory on which the old fort stood, Saint Waldo's whose pastor for thirty-odd years has been Ambrose Entweder.

If we imagine Francis Ascue taking once more his bearings on his native city from atop the cathedral, his pained eyes would lift quickly from Saint Waldo's and seek a kinder scene westward. His gaze would doubtless dwell on the puff of trees downriver which conceal from quasi-celestial viewers the buildings of the Fort Elbow Major Seminary. Then, albeit reluctantly, his eyes would lift and go down the pale vein of the freeway toward the airport, the freeway from whose exits each of the newer parishes can be reached, including the most notable of them, west-northwest, Saint Barnabas, the Nygaards' parish or, as a cleric would be more apt to regard it, the parish of the Reverend Donald Oder.

A more secular eye, from the same vantage point, would notice the swirl of banks and businesses downhill from the cathedral, the factories along the river and south of the old city and, in looking southward over the Prune see, not the seminary, but beyond it the Fort Elbow campus of the state university. In peering toward the airport, such an eye would consider the new industrial park with its squat steel and glass buildings southwest of the field. Banker, merchant, salesman, realtor, and the cleric too perhaps, would see a prosperous city of eighty thousand, a city busy and confused and thus no different from the nation itself as it blundered through the last years of the sixties.

The instructions in the bishop's letter had left Frank Ascue little time for such lofty contemplation of the scene of his future priestly activities, even if, in the stunned aftermath of its message, he had been so inclined. His transition from putative moral theology professor designate to junior assistant at Saint Waldo's was to be accomplished overnight. "Dear Father Askew," the bishop had typed, and it had been an added bitterness that he had misspelled the name, a bitterness increased by the suspicion that it had been deliberate. "Dear Father Askew, You will report to Monsignor Ambrose Entweder, pastor of St. Waldo's parish, on Friday, May 20 (tomorrow), before the noonday meal and present yourself as his new assistant. My prayers go with you in your new assignment asking that such talents and zeal as you possess will redound ad majorem gloriam dei. In Christo, + Georgius, episcopus castrelboiensis."

"Saint Waldo's?" Charlotte cried, her voice rising in a curl as if to describe in air a question mark.

"Old Saint Waldo's," Frank had said with husky bravado. "Monsignor Entweder."

"Is it a *permanent* assignment?"

He gave the letter to his sister. Howard turned from mixing drinks and handed his brother-in-law a glass. Frank took it and sipped as if from need. Careful, he warned himself. Howard mixed a deadly martini. During the evenings he had spent with Charlotte and her family since getting off the plane, Howard had managed to get the three of them half smashed before they sat down to the table. It had been a trifle difficult to play the role of Uncle Father Frank with a thick tongue and eyes that had a tendency to focus several inches before the chosen object of vision.

"What's this Latin at the end?"

"A Jesuit motto. Caldron is a graduate of Fordham. And that's the Church rendition of Fort Elbow."

"It doesn't say for how long. Do you think it could be just for the summer, Frank?"

"No."

He had to stop such speculation right now, in Charlotte, in Ewing, in himself. When Ewing had caught his breath after the blow, hope began to rise in him, like a barometer under pressure. He too had called it a summer assignment. They both knew it was nothing of the sort. If the bishop had wanted Father Ascue to teach at the seminary in the fall, he would have said so during the interview. Not even Caldron would send a man to a teaching post on a twenty-four-hour notice next September. No, this was it and there was no point in thinking otherwise.

"To Saint Waldo's," he said, lifting his glass. Howard and Charlotte, wondering whether he was mocking or serious, hesitated, but then the three glasses clinked and they were drinking to his new assignment.

He set off the next morning, by cab, having said Mass at Saint Barnabas. Oder was on vacation, stashed away in his retreat on Higgins Lake in Michigan. Frank felt under no obligation to explain to the assistant, Father Swivel, the fate that had befallen him. Let Swivel read of it in the *Fort Elbow Catholic,* the diocesan paper. He declined his invitation to breakfast and went back to the house, wanting to spend an hour or two with Charlotte before leaving.

"I'll drive you there, Frank. Howard left me the car."

She had made an elaborate breakfast and it seemed part of her apology for not attending his Mass. She sat across from him, holding her coffee cup in both hands, her eyes on its contents, her expression the serious one she reserved for farewells. How familiar that expression was: eyes downcast, corners of the mouth drooping, a general promise of tears. Thus she had seen him off after vacations though his destination had been merely crosstown, thus she had put him on the train to New York and the boat three years ago.

"No. I'll take a cab."

"You will not. I'm not going to have my only brother show up at his first job in a taxi."

He laughed. She made hired transportation seem a symbol of disgrace. Of failure. He pushed the thought away. It was not the cab that bothered him. Good God, how crazy he had been to plan on an assignment with no other assurance than Ewing's. Ewing had no clout at the chancery. Far from it. But there had been more to go on. Being sent away to study, to obtain a degree in moral theology, was presumptive evidence that this was meant to equip him for some intended work. But he did not want to be bitter. The bishop did not owe him a teaching assignment. The surprising truth was, and he had first realized this in the sacristy at Saint Barnabas less than an hour before, the truth was that he was excited by the prospect of parish work.

Yesterday, after he had left Ewing's rooms, he had found Tremplin waiting for him at the foot of the stairs. Tremplin glanced up into the gloom of the landing and hunched a shoulder for good measure. "You know he thought you were going to replace him here?"

"I know."

"I wish you were, Frank. I won't kid you about that. Believe me, the faculty could use some new blood. You've no idea the resistance I meet."

Tremplin took his arm and they walked out of the building and on toward Charlotte's car. The campus, its buildings and trees and walks, an old acquaintance like Tremplin beside him, brought a rush of memories. Still fresh from an orgy of lamentation with Ewing, Frank felt his throat tighten with nostalgia. This place had been the target of his hopes and now, in one whimsical move, the bishop had snatched it from him. It seemed cruel and childish. He could half expect to meet his younger self on these walks. He became aware of Tremplin speaking with great excitement, though in a hushed voice. They might have been whispering in a Sunday Vespers procession years ago. Naughty, naughty.

"The liturgy, Frank! They won't accept it. Our only English Mass is the community one. The rest of them still say private Masses, mumbling Latin at all those side altars as if it were a private devotion. The young men have to be given a proper understanding of the Eucharistic Celebration, learn that the Church is the *ecclesia*, the assembly of the People of God. Who can get together anywhere."

Tremplin spoke the last sentence with intensity, his lips moving with the words like a bad ventriloquist's. He had gripped Frank's arm and now turned to him.

"In February I said Mass in the trunk room." Tremplin's eyes glistened. "At eleven o'clock in the evening. I gathered together maybe a dozen seminarians and we went down into the trunk room. Only candlelight! I let them select the Scriptures to be read and then we just talked. Talked! There was such a sense of community. It might have been the catacombs, Frank." Tremplin waited for the image to establish itself, then squared his bony shoulders. "Then I consecrated crackers and grape juice. It was beautiful."

"Crackers and grape juice?"

"Does it matter, Frank? You know it doesn't. If you could have seen the rapport. There has never been anything to approach it in chapel. We dispersed in silence."

Tremplin seemed overcome by the memory. Frank was appalled. Mass in the trunk room? The catacombs! He wondered if Tremplin had ever seen a real catacomb. And who were the persecutors supposed to be?

"I thought they'd crucify me, Frank."

"Who?"

"You're kidding. Word got out." He sighed. "Some Judas among us. Eisenbarth confronted me with it as a lying rumor he wished me to deny. Of course I would not deny it. He made some guarded remarks about delating me to the bishop."

Tremplin was gripping his arm again and Frank found himself wanting to avoid the intensity of the other priest's gaze.

"Frank, I would have welcomed that. There must be martyrs. Witnesses to the spirit of the Council. Look at Bullard! Who would have thought that he would show the way? But Eisenbarth would not give me the satisfaction. Not that he cared what might happen to me. I am sure his concern was that it might reflect adversely on himself. I used the occasion to tell him what I think of the liturgy here. What the students think too, never fear. They are not the docile cattle we were, Frank. They *demand* relevance, as well they might."

"Where is everybody anyway?"

Tremplin looked puzzled.

"The seminarians. The place looks deserted."

"Oh, the enrollment is way down. What would you expect?"

"Down to what?"

"Sixty-eight. No, sixty-seven. One left this morning."

"Are you serious?"

Tremplin was amused. "Ah, you're remembering how it was in our time here."

"Our time? That was only three years ago for me. There were nearly three hundred seminarians then."

"I know, I know."

"What in the name of God happened?"

"Frank, what have I been telling you? This place never caught up with Vatican I. As far as most of my esteemed colleagues are concerned, the Second Vatican Council is a vicious rumor launched by *Newsweek* and the *National Catholic Reporter.*"

"Sixty-seven seminarians," Frank said. If they were evenly distributed, that would mean an average of eleven members per class.

"And the number will go down rather than up unless something is done."

Like Masses in the trunk room? Why hadn't Ewing mentioned this? Frank looked around him. The row of brick residence halls might have been a squadron of sinking ships.

"I envy you, Frank. Parish work. Out with people. There you can do what has to be done." He threw his hands into the air and his eyes lifted too, as if he had released an invisible object, lighter than air. Whatever it was—his zealous hopes, visions of experimental liturgies, an exact replica of a catacomb in an underground parking lot downtown—it drifted over the trees and was gone.

They had arrived at the car and Frank got in. Tremplin closed the door and stood there, gripping it as if it were the rail of the *Titanic.* Frank started the motor, thanked Tremplin and put the car in gear. The hands released the door and Tremplin stood in the middle of the road staring after the car. Frank watched him diminish in the rear-view mirror.

The strange conversation had softened what, with Ewing, had seemed only a crushing blow. Sixty-seven seminarians! He kept repeating that to himself as he drove to Charlotte's with his news. The freeway had changed the city, making it seem bigger and busier than he remembered it. His native city, like his visit to the bishop, intimidated him a bit, as if where he had been a child questioned his returning in an adult role.

"Everyone gone?" he asked Charlotte, covering his cup with his hand to prevent her refilling it.

"Howard and the little kids, yes. Bev doesn't have class until afternoon."

"How does she like the Fort Elbow campus?"

"Loves it."

56

"Does she see much of Phil Bullard?"

"Of course. Frank, what will happen to him?"

"I haven't any idea. Probably nothing." He did not tell her that he had run into Phil at the chancery yesterday.

"He's great with kids, Frank. He really is."

"I'm not surprised. He was quite an athlete."

"He was?"

"One of the best."

"He's so full of ideas."

Frank was sure that all Phil's ideas would turn out to be someone else's but he was not going to knock him with Charlotte. Phil should concentrate on some sort of athletic program at the Center, do something he was good at.

"Well, I'd best be going."

"Frank, let me drive you."

"No, Char. I mean it."

The expression again. He phoned for a cab and when it came she walked outside with him. He had only the bag he had carried on the plane. His books and other things were coming by ship. Frank put his arm around Char and she pressed her face against his chest and began to cry. His own throat tightened at the sound of her sobs. Good old Charlotte.

Good old Charlotte watched with blurred eyes as her brother walked out to the cab. One bag and the suit he wore; it seemed so sad. Before getting in, he turned and gave her a jaunty wave. She remained in the doorway until the cab went out of sight around the corner and then returned to the kitchen and her cold coffee and let the tears come.

Her little brother assigned to Saint Waldo's. She really did not know how she felt about that, mainly because she could not figure out what Frank's true feelings were. Was he disappointed or not? If he was he certainly wasn't showing it. But Saint Waldo's! Good grief, what kind of parish was that?"

The parish, and she wasn't alone in thinking so, nor was it simply the loyalty of the charter parishioner, was Saint Barnabas. Oder was the kind of pastor she could imagine Frank working with. She was not sure she had ever seen the pastor of Saint Waldo's; he certainly was seldom mentioned in the pages of the *Fort Elbow Catholic.* Hardly an issue went by without a story on events at Saint Barnabas and then there was Father Oder's column, a weekly feature. Nor was it only the Catholic press that kept an eye on Oder and Saint Barnabas. It was to Oder that the city paper had turned to get a Fort Elbow interpretation of the various sessions of the Vatican Council. Charlotte, who had heard her pastor's unguarded remarks about Bishop Caldron, had discerned in his pieces the faint edge of sarcasm.

There was the sound of water running upstairs. Beverly. Charlotte wiped her eyes and got up to turn the heat on under the coffee. She should get Bev's breakfast but she had expended all the energy she could summon in preparing Frank's. A nineteen-year-old girl could just feed herself, particularly when she lay abed until ten-thirty.

"Uncle Frank back from church yet?" Bev asked when she came into the kitchen. She was fully dressed, looked bright and rather pretty.

"Back! He's had his breakfast and gone."

"Darn. I wanted to talk to him."

"Well, he hasn't left the country." Charlotte lit a cigarette and blew smoke at the ceiling. "Talk to him about what?"

"Just talk. You know."

"You had three days to talk with him."

"Ha. Mother, you monopolize him, do you realize that? You treat him like a little boy when you aren't deferring to him as some kind of guru."

"Little boy indeed. Frank is a priest with a doctorate in theology."

Beverly spooned jam onto her toast. "He acts so young."

"What do you mean?"

Bev's mouth was full. She gestured to indicate an explanation was on its way. "Did he ever go out with girls?"

"What a ridiculous question."

"Did he?"

"Bev, he wanted to be a priest as long ago as I can remember. Of course he didn't go out with girls."

"I didn't think so."

"What exactly does that mean?" Her annoyance surprised Charlotte. It was as if Beverly had put into words her own awareness of Frank's, well, innocence. His indifference to girls, as far as she had been able to tell, indifference to them as girls, had seemed one of his strengths as a seminarian. Girls always seemed to be at the bottom of it when one of his classmates left.

Bev said, "I don't know, exactly. With some priests, celibacy seems a real sacrifice. And some of them are so darned good-looking."

"But your uncle's ugly?"

"You know he isn't. But he doesn't seem to have any curiosity about what it would be like not to be a priest. He really seems happy."

"Is that a crime? I think most priests are happy."

"Most? Maybe. But that leaves some, doesn't it?"

58

"It always has."

"But did they gripe about it before the way they do now? You should hear Phil Bullard on the subject of celibacy."

"When has he mentioned celibacy?"

Bev laughed. "When doesn't he, would be a better question. He votes no, I can tell you that." She sipped her coffee. "I have to get going."

"I thought you didn't have class till this afternoon."

"I don't."

What a pity that Father Oder had been out of town while Frank was staying with them. It was a recurrent dream of Charlotte's to have her pastor and her brother become friends now that they could meet on terms of equality, more or less. But how much better it would have been if Frank were a professor at the seminary. Father Oder had been impressed when Frank was sent to Rome but now that advantage seemed to have dissolved with his assignment to Saint Waldo's.

Oh, she mustn't brood about it. If Frank could accept it without bitterness, so could she. Charlotte glanced at the kitchen clock. He must be there by now.

The Saint Waldo parish plant, set in asphalt, occupied a city block. The four buildings were constructed of buff brick, had Spanish tile roofs and no shade at all. On hot days, mirages of water formed on the sizzling asphalt as if nature were trying to win back an imagined victory over the conquering art of building and blacktop. The church stood on the southwest corner, its entrance flush with the sidewalk; a driveway gave entrance to a portico at the south entrance and it was there that undertakers unloaded the casket for funerals. Weddings used the front door, of course. The steps and walks were littered with rice during the first days of every week, mementos of the Saturday nuptial Masses.

The rectory was behind the church, joined to it by a roofed loggia. To the right of the church was the parish school, ringed by basketball courts and bicycle racks with capacity for several hundred bikes. The convent, to the right of the school, at the far corner from the church, had greenery in its window boxes, artificial plants. On Sundays, at all the Masses but the earliest, the huge expanse of asphalt was covered with automobiles. Two off-duty policemen, members of the parish, directed traffic, hustling cars on their way to make room for the next mob of motorized Mass goers.

"You wanna get off at the church?" the cabby asked.

Father Ascue sat forward; they had passed the convent and school and were now approaching the church.

"I want the parish house."

The cabby slowed but now he eased across the intersection. He was not looking for the parish house. Annoyed at the lack of cooperation, Father Ascue nearly missed it himself.

"There it is. Behind the church."

"I'll have to go around the block."

"This is fine. I'll get out here."

Shaking his head, the man pointed the cab at the curb and drew to a halt. He flipped the flag on his meter. "Two and a quarter."

Father Ascue paid him and let himself out. He looked up at the huge old house before which he had alighted and saw that it was flanked by others of equal size and vintage, frame houses, with huge reflective windows making for a sad expression. Pink, a nauseous green, the one before him a dignified white. It was an old neighborhood but well preserved though many of the current dwellers seemed to have antic notions of decoration. Father Ascue had put his bag on the walk while he pocketed his change. Picking it up, he felt like a mendicant. At the corner he stood for a moment, looking to his left. Yes, that must be the rectory. He took a deep breath, felt his shoulders move back, and marched toward the house.

A moment after he rang the bell, having entered the deep tunnellike porch whose walls were a lattice of brickwork, a buzzer sounded. It stopped before he could get the screen door open and his hand on the doorknob. He rang the bell again, his hand gripping the knob, but the buzzer did not sound. He became aware of a pair of eyes, inches from his own, studying him through a small pane of glass in the door. Male or female, he could not tell; he seemed involved in a speakeasy scene from the old movie he had watched with Charlotte and Howard two nights before. He managed a smile and something happened to the watching eyes and the door opened.

"I thought it was Father Charles forgot his key; he always does."

The woman was massively fat and yet the sky blue wash dress she wore hung loosely on her. Her arms were at her sides, more or less; they hung slightly away from her body, like a gunslinger's.

"I'm Father Ascue."

"Of course, Father. Come in. Here, I'll take that." She whipped the bag from his hand. "Monsignor Entweder's home. Why don't you wait in the office there? I'll go get him."

"Thank you."

"I'm Hilda. Just sit down there, Father, and make yourself to home. He'll be here in no time at all. Is this all your luggage?" She lifted his bag, suspended from two pudgy fingers.

"For now."

"I should think. You're here to stay, after all."

The sound of her tread seemed the echo of her words. The office was a bleak impersonal room. A desk, several straight chairs, an easy chair in the corner, leather, unused looking, an ashtray standing beside it. Behind the desk, in a recessed bookshelf, half a dozen volumes stood. On the desk was a blotter, a pen angling from its holder, a crucifix. The only ornament was a lithograph of Christ, one of those vague simpering Jesuses more often seen on calendars than in frames.

Father Ascue lit a cigarette and stood at the window, looking at the back of the church. Exhaled smoke drifted to the window, flattened on the pane, lifted, dispersed. Here to stay. Why not? He turned to look at the room again. No doubt there were half a dozen like it, places to interview callers: couples intending to marry, prospective converts (probably not too much of that, at the moment), distraught wives with errant children or husbands who drank. The room as potential setting for those sad scenes brightened Father Ascue's mood. That was priestly work, that and celebrating Mass, bringing God to his people. It was stupid to regard this as less important than teaching in the seminary. When he thought of it, a teacher's life was pretty much like a seminarian's. Institutional life. Classes and meals and a room in a corridor, a solitary life and, it suddenly seemed, a rather too comfortable and remote one.

There was the sound of Hilda's returning tread and then she filled the doorway.

"Monsignor's on his way. Sit, Father. Sit. Would you like some coffee?"

"No, thanks."

She peered at her watch, hidden in a fold of flesh. "Nearly lunchtime anyway. I have to get back to the kitchen."

She went away. Father Ascue became aware of the aroma of cooking. He took a Bible from the shelf behind the desk and it flopped open at the Book of Psalms. "Behold how good it is, and how pleasant, where brethren dwell at one." There was a sound behind him, someone clearing his throat. Father Ascue turned to face Monsignor Ambrose Entweder.

Entweder wore a shiny, half-buttoned cassock, his head was sunk into his shoulders and he regarded Father Ascue over the rims of his glasses. A pink face, very white hair, finger-combed at most. His fingers now moved on the half-dozen pens and pencils clipped between two cassock buttons. He might have been limbering up a trumpet.

"I'm Francis Ascue, Monsignor." He took the bishop's letter from his pocket and handed it to Entweder.

Entweder accepted it, reluctantly it seemed, and walked slowly to the desk, where he sat. He unfolded the letter and lay it on the desk before him, smoothing it carefully, examining Father Ascue for half a minute before he began to read. His lips moved with the words, his head followed the lines like a typewriter carriage. He reached the end and read it through once more.

"When were you ordained, Father?"

"Three years ago."

"Three years," Monsignor Entweder mused. He took off his glasses and his eyes drifted to the window. "Three years. I suppose that seems a long time to you. Well, perhaps not a long time. I myself was ordained in 1925 and that was before you were born, wasn't it? Ordained by Bishop Floyd, who is long since dead. For that matter, over half of my classmates are dead, but God has let me linger on. For my sins, no doubt, for my sins. Is this your first assignment?"

"I've been in Rome, Monsignor."

"In Rome!" Glasses replaced, Entweder got his arms on the desk and looked at Father Ascue with new interest. "In Rome. Imagine that. I went to Rome for the Holy Year, just that one time. Nineteen-fifty. You were born then, I suppose. Such a wonderful city, truly eternal. What were you doing there, Father?"

"Studying."

"Ah. And were you ordained there?"

"Oh, no. I was sent there after ordination. Bishop Caldron ordained me, here in the cathedral."

"Studying, were you? Well, well. And now you're going to be a parish priest. What do you think of that?"

"What do you mean, Monsignor?"

"What do I mean?" The glasses came off, the pale blue eyes returned to the window. "Saint Waldo's was my first assignment too, Father." He smiled dreamily. "Little did I suspect when I came to the rectory door —not this house, of course, this house did not exist then—little did I suspect that forty years later I would still be here. How the Church has changed, Father."

Did he mean the parish or the whole Church? Probably the latter. Monsignor Entweder's face had become a mask of sadness.

"No discipline, Father. No dignity. Have you read of this young man who runs around to saloons and makes such a scandal?"

"Father Bullard?"

"That's the man. So you have heard of him. And the advice people are receiving, Father. In sermons, in the confessional. They want to invent a new religion of their own and still call it the Catholic Church. I'm fearful, Father. Surely this can't go on."

A bell tinkled. Monsignor Entweder rose from behind the desk. "Time for lunch, Father. Come along. I'll have Father Charles show you your room afterward. Charles McTear, my first assistant."

McTear. Father Ascue could not remember having heard of a priest named McTear. Certainly there had been no one in the seminary of that name. When he followed Entweder into the dining room and saw a tall bony priest with a red crew cut who could only be McTear, it was obvious that they could not have been contemporaries in the seminary. McTear was over forty, a surprise in itself; most men that age were pastors. Entweder introduced Ascue and McTear wrung his hand, then sat down, nodding to Hilda as he did so. Entweder sat too, waited for Father Ascue, bowed his head. He cleared his throat and eventually grace emerged, in Latin, riding his wheezing voice in a strong American accent.

"I raised Rio last night," McTear said when Entweder was done. Hilda lumbered in with a casserole which she placed before the pastor.

"Indeed," Entweder said.

"Clear as a bell."

"Father Ascue has just returned from Rome."

"I talk to people there all the time," McTear said. He grinned, exhibiting massive yellow teeth.

"You do?" Father Ascue said, puzzled.

"What were you doing there?"

Father Ascue told him, accepting the casserole from Entweder.

"Why'd Caldron assign you here?"

"Why not?"

"Oh, this is a great place. Don't get me wrong. Ambrose can't get rid of me. Isn't that right, Monsignor?"

Entweder winked at Ascue. "Father McTear has designs on my job. He's waiting for me to turn up my toes so he can take over."

"Aw, come on, Monsignor." McTear looked genuinely distraught. "You're going to live forever and you know it."

"I pray to God I do," Entweder said solemnly. "In the important sense."

"No worry there," McTear said. "And you know darn well the bishop would never make me pastor here."

"I'd hate to think of you moving all that equipment."

To Ascue, McTear said, "I've turned down three parishes. Caldron thinks I'm nuts. But the reception is perfect here."

"I wish you'd show Father Ascue around this afternoon. Help him settle in. Our routine is simple, Father Ascue. Office hours, sick calls when required, and the census. That is something we do not shirk at Saint Waldo's, the census. It's the best way to keep in touch, to flush out trouble, be of help. Our records are the equal of any parish in the diocese, I'm sure of that. A month ago Bishop Brophy was here and he simply could not believe how up to snuff our census is, praised it to the skies. And I was able to tell him that it had been like that when I came to Saint Waldo's and has continued so ever since. Census, Father Ascue, census. It seems a small thing, but believe me it is the key to a well-run parish. The societies, the school—they are nothing next to it. People have to be seen in their homes to be seen as they really are."

Father Ascue nodded. It seemed wise to him; he liked the thought of going out into the parish to visit parishioners. Any disappointment still remaining in his heart had gone. McTear was inscrutable—what did he mean, he talked to people in Rome?—and the pastor was old and wheezy and probably not too sharp anymore, but this seemed to be a place where a priest could work.

"Masses now, Father. I say the six and I'm afraid I'm rather selfish about it. You and Father McTear will alternate the seven and eight. The seven is in the convent chapel, the eight in the church. Work out office hours between you. For the afternoon. I am in the house every morning. Except Wednesday. My day off. An old man's indulgence."

"We'll work it out, Monsignor," McTear said. "Bascomb's room?"

"I think so, Father."

There was silence. Ascue looked at the two priests but they did not meet his eye. Entweder stirred his coffee, McTear polished his napkin ring on the tablecloth. They might have been commemorating the dead.

The moment passed when Entweder picked up a little bell and shook it. Hilda called from the kitchen, "Coming. Everyone want apple pie?"

Everyone wanted apple pie. The meal ended with grace. In the hallway, outside the dining room, McTear said, "Okay, Father. Ready for the grand tour?"

"What kind of priest is he?" Clara Rupp asked.

Arthur turned, the cocktail shaker in his hand sloshing toward silence. "What *kind* of priest?"

"You know—liberal, conservative, what?"

"Oh, Ascue's all right. I'm sure of it. Eisenbarth would have said something otherwise." Arthur resumed shaking, then once more stopped. "He spent three years in *Rome.*"

"Aha."

"Precisely."

Arthur poured and brought Clara her drink. They sat together on the couch, pensively sipping.

"What's going to be done about that other one? Bullard?"

"I don't know. Even Eisenbarth seemed discouraged. His first reaction was that there was scarcely any point in going to the bishop about it."

"He said that!"

"Not in so many words. You know Eisenbarth. But I had the distinct feeling that I would have to persuade him to go to Caldron."

"Surely he doesn't think that the bishop approves of that young man?"

"Oh, no. Certainly not. The question is how to stop that sort of thing. Stopping the man the wrong way could stir up others."

"Bishop Brophy was true to form."

"Why don't they give that man a diocese of his own? Say Fairbanks or Nome."

Arthur sipped in silence, glowering into the darkening room. He might have been a Roman watching the lights go out over the Empire as the barbarians swept down from the north.

"Sheila called today," Clara said softly.

Arthur stiffened but did not speak.

"I asked her to dinner when she returns from London."

"Can she spare the time?"

"Now, Arthur."

"Can she?"

"She'd love to come."

"Does that mean she will?"

Clara put her hand on Arthur's.

"We could invite Father Ascue as well. We could ask others too. Have a little dinner party."

"We might just as well. Sheila is bored to death with just the two of us. Or is it only with me?"

"Arthur, you know that isn't so. You've grown so sensitive about her."

"Why the hell doesn't she live at home where she belongs?"

Clara sighed. "When a girl is over twenty-one and has a career—"

"A career! You call that a career? Baby-sitting passengers on transatlantic flights. Flitting around strange cities. Fort Elbow is just another town to her now. Living in an apartment, as if she were a stranger."

"It's practical."

"It is not practical. She's seldom there. Why pay the rent? It's damned foolishness and you know it."

"They share the rent, Arthur. Sheila and the other girls. There's always one or more of them there. The fact is the place would be too small if they were all there together."

"She *is* coming to dinner?"

"Yes. Arthur, shall we make it a party? Father Ascue, Sheila, who else? The Hanrahans?"

"Good God, no. Oh, I like the idea of a party, a festive night. Yes. For Sheila, for us, but more than that, we can find out the sort of fellow Ascue is. Ask the Meyers."

"And the Bentlys!"

"The Bentlys. We'll surround him with the right type and see how he reacts. Yes." Arthur finished his drink and nodded as if the idea had been his. "Care for another drink?"

"Do you think you should? What's the point of that infernal jogging if you're going to have two drinks?"

"If I have two drinks I'll keep on jogging. At my age it's a victory to keep my weight steady. Turn on the news, it's time."

Clara peered at the clock on the mantel. "We have half an hour."

"I want to hear the local news too."

Clara turned on the television while Arthur refilled their glasses. They had settled back once more, almost content, when their fragile peace was shattered by the news. Another eruption, and in Eisenbarth's bailiwick. A hunger strike was in progress at the seminary, staged in sympathy with Father Philip Bullard.

"Expel them," Ewing snapped. "Throw them out."

"But Father Tremplin is out there with them."

"Leave him to the bishop. Expel the students."

Monsignor Eisenbarth drew a handkerchief from the sleeve of his cassock and looked at it as if he had surprised himself with a conjuror's trick. "You want me to summarily dismiss thirty seminarians? At the moment, that is nearly half the student body."

The two priests were in the rector's office, staring at the television set that Monsignor Eisenbarth had wheeled in from his bedroom. Seminarians in cassocks, carrying placards, moved across the screen. They were out on the public sidewalk picketing and raising havoc with the late afternoon traffic. The press had arrived as soon as the demonstration began, suggesting collusion, an advance warning. Father Ewing was calling off the names of the students on the screen.

"That's not necessary, Father. We can simply take note of those absent from the refectory."

"A hunger strike! That's the same bunch that was complaining about the food a few weeks ago. I wish they'd make up their minds."

Monsignor Eisenbarth felt more helpless now than he had when Arthur Rupp had badgered him about Bullard, wanting him to raise a fuss with the bishop. Did the man think that Caldron was unaware of Bullard? The man seemed to be followed by reporters wherever he went. The story that Father Bullard had been summoned by the bishop remained a mystery. When Monsignor Eisenbarth had told the bishop that Arthur Rupp and others in Te Deum were upset, Caldron had only said that if he were free to speak the situation would seem more bizarre than it already did.

Now, at Father Ewing's urging, Monsignor Eisenbarth tried to reach Bishop Caldron and was told he was not in. Nor did Yorick answer his phone. That left Sean Brophy, the vicar general, and Eisenbarth had no desire to speak to Caldron's auxiliary. How bitter it was that such a man had been raised to the episcopacy. *There* was a matter for lamentation if one wished to read the signs of the times.

Sean Brophy a bishop; it was preposterous. If his name were Smith it would be possible to believe that there had been confusion in Rome and the wrong man appointed, but how many Sean Brophys could there possibly be? There were no others in the *Catholic Directory;* Eisenbarth had looked. Of course Brophy had friends, powerful friends, and he was not the first Trojan horse among the hierarchy. They would bring in others of their ilk, just as the Irish had for so long ensured that the American hierarchy was dominated by Kelleys and Murrays and O'Brians and a hundred assorted Micks, Macks, Fitzes and O's. That old conspiracy did not explain Brophy. The Irish were generally sane and conservative, you had to give them that; they would not have been blinded by Brophy's blood. They knew the sort of rascal he was. But friends he had nonetheless. Eisenbarth was oppressed by sadness. He had had friends too, or so he had thought. Now he had passed the age when friends might be of help; indeed most of his friends had passed on.

"Randy, look."

On the screen, Tremplin was being interviewed by reporters. His petulant face now filled the screen as if he were directly addressing his two colleagues.

67

"An anachronism," Tremplin cried. "A bastion of indifference."

"He means the seminary, Randy."

"These young men," Tremplin went on, turning—and there was a shot of the seminarians wandering about on the sidewalk carrying their hand-lettered signs—"these young men are going to be priests. Out there. In this city. Yet this is the first time they have broken free of the shackles of the seminary to express their solidarity with future colleagues. Priests out there know that the work they do has no relation whatsoever to the training they received here as seminarians. This institution seems bent on making men *un*prepared for the priesthood. Well, today something has happened. This may be the first crack in the wall of indifference. The world is invading the seminary through the consciences of these young men. Who, let me remind you, are taking their future in their hands by what they do today."

Tremplin seemed on the verge of tears.

"He's through," Ewing said emphatically.

"That's up to George."

"Damn it, Randy, those students out there are your responsibility. You better do something."

"But what?"

"Listen, if you can't control a seminary with only sixty students in it . . ." Ewing stopped, calming himself, but Eisenbarth knew where the sentence would have gone. What would he do with a diocese of his own?

"Do you expect me to go out there and debate on the public streets with all those journalists about?"

"I'd go out and give them one minute to get the hell back to their rooms or consider themselves expelled."

"And if they didn't?"

"Then we're down to thirty seminarians."

"But do you think the boys out there would just go away? They would not. They would stay out there until doomsday, demanding reinstatement. In the present climate, all the sympathy would be with them. Tremplin isn't just an oddity. You know that. How many priests would agree with him?"

Silence followed and then the phone began to ring.

"That'll be the bishop," Ewing said with satisfaction.

Eisenbarth stood for a moment beside the desk, gathering his dignity. His eyes were lidded and serene when he picked up the phone and said hello. A moment later the flesh of his face sagged.

"Yes, Bishop Brophy," he said. "This is Monsignor Eisenbarth."

Bishop Brophy heard the catch of disappointment in Monsignor Eisenbarth's voice when the rector answered the phone. He had not really expected to reach Eisenbarth in his office. My God, imagine him holed up there while the seminary was going up in smoke. Brophy had his TV on, sound down, and he saw Tremplin in the center of the screen.

"What do you plan to do, Randy? Are you simply going to let the demonstration run its course?"

"I can scarcely use force, if that's what you mean."

Bishop Brophy laughed softly. "Force? Now I would hardly recommend that, Monsignor."

"What then?"

"Get on top of it. Haven't the reporters asked to see you?"

"I'm seeing no one."

"I was afraid of that."

"I have been trying to contact Bishop Caldron."

"That's impossible, Monsignor. This is his day of recollection. No one knows where he goes for it. He quite simply cannot be reached. My advice," Bishop Brophy said, then paused. He did not like to remind Eisenbarth that this was the vicar general calling. "My advice is to get out ahead on this thing, take the initiative away from Father Tremplin and those boys."

"How?"

"Call in the reporters. Be interviewed on television, anything and everything. Express your fundamental sympathy with the desire for renewal and updating of the work of the Church—"

"Are you suggesting that I endorse a revolt by my own seminarians?"

"*Your* seminarians, Randy? Now, now. And endorse is hardly the word. I am suggesting that you embrace the underlying principle. Once you've done that, you can chide the overenthusiasm of the young, question the wisdom of the particular means they have chosen. But grab their standard, Randy, and make it yours. Show that you are indeed the leader of those young men."

"Bishop Brophy, I have no intention of being interviewed on television. I have even less intention of subscribing to the sort of idiotic nonsense that has gripped Fathers Tremplin and Bullard. You do realize that this protest is an expression of sympathy with Philip Bullard? Do you sympathize with Father Bullard? I do not. He is a disgrace."

"A disgrace, Monsignor? Imprudent, perhaps overly dramatic . . ."

"He has insulted his fellow priests. In effect, he questions the authority of the bishop. That is not something I could endorse with however many distinctions and mental reservations."

Bishop Brophy imperfectly controlled his anger. "The main thing, Monsignor, the important thing, is to get those seminarians in off the street. I pointed out an astute way in which you might accomplish this. Since you find it distasteful, I suggest that you come up with an alternative. But, as vicar general, I am telling you to get those boys off the street!"

Bishop Brophy slammed down the phone. It was what he might have expected from an ass like Eisenbarth. Incommunicado in his office while his picketing seminarians were all over the television screen! The man was beyond belief. And so was his Te Deum group. Eisenbarth was full of wind about how the country should conduct its foreign policy, but given an opportunity for action all he could think to do was sit on his duff and await orders.

Bishop Brophy turned off the TV. His advice to Eisenbarth had been inspired, he was sure of it. He picked up his ringing phone. It was Quill, the editor of the *Fort Elbow Tribune*. Bishop Brophy settled into his chair.

"Yes. Mr. Quill, I know. I know."

Who could blame the man for being baffled by the rector's unwillingness to meet the press? Certainly not Bishop Brophy, something he managed to convey to Quill without in any way calling Eisenbarth's conduct into question. A solid front. Yes, that was right, Bishop Brophy was the vicar general of the diocese. Did *he* have a statement? He could have, and in short order. As a matter of fact, he would be holding a press conference within the hour.

In the improvised newsroom on the first floor of the cathedral rectory Bishop Brophy stood behind a table and smiled into the glare of the lamps. A cameraman asked him to be seated behind the desk while final focusing was done.

"Very well," Brophy said. He held up a single sheet of paper. "Shall we begin?"

"You're on," the cameraman called.

"Gentlemen," Bishop Brophy began, his eyes sweeping the room as if it were an auditorium. His eyes passed Mary Muscatelli, came back. "Ladies and gentlemen. I want to read a statement, after which I shall be happy to answer any questions you may have." He waited as if for permission, then began to read.

"In recent days there have been a number of incidents involving priests of this diocese and only this afternoon there was a demonstration at the diocesan seminary which was—as it should have been, let me add

70

—thoroughly covered by the various news media. Because of the public character of these manifestations, particularly that which took place, which may still be taking place, at our major seminary, I feel that some official comment is required. In the absence of the ordinary of the diocese, the Most Reverend George Caldron, that task falls to me as vicar general. I should like to address myself first of all to the members of my own faith, to the clergy but especially to the laity, for it is among the latter that many will be found who simply do not understand what is going on and who are shocked to find priests and junior clerics items in the daily news. Surprise if not shock is certainly understandable. We clergy have not been noted for rocking many boats, least of all the bark of Peter. It may be that, after so long an even ride, some now act in ways which are intemperate and ill-advised. In such times as the present I believe that forbearance is called for, particularly from those in authority. More important still, I think we should go beyond particular manifestations of unease to the underlying causes which are, or should be, the concern of all. We are living, as you know, in the immediate wake of the Second Vatican Council, which was convened by His Holiness Pope John XXIII, a man whose death left not only the Church in the narrower sense but the great globe itself a poorer place. This saintly man wished to call Catholics, and indeed all believers, from lives of comfort and complacency; he wished us to spend less time dwelling on the differences between the various Christian denominations, and between Christianity and Judaism, and to ask ourselves what we had done, what we are doing, what we intend to do to give our belief a greater impact on the sick world in which we live. He called for a time of renewal. In our groping, in our quest, which is an obligation on us all, many mistakes will be made, many things will be said, many deeds done, which will seem unwise to many. It may well be that such mistakes have been made in recent days. Sobeit. I wish to make but one point, lest others fall into the self-congratulating posture of negative criticism. Let each of us ask himself, when tempted to condemn the efforts of others, wise or unwise: what of a positive nature have I done on behalf of my faith? To paraphrase another noble departed John, ask not what your church can do for you, ask what you can do for your church."

For a moment, after he had finished reading, Bishop Brophy thought that there might be applause. But what broke the spell was an insistent female voice.

"Are you giving official approval to the picketing going on at the seminary?"

The bishop's smile might have been a plenary indulgence. "Miss Muscatelli, isn't it?"

"That's right."

"Then I know that you listened carefully to my statement. I am suggesting that we not get hung up on particular events but attend to the principles which underlie them."

"And which could justify them?"

"It may be. It may be."

"Bishop Brophy." Donovan, editor of the *Fort Elbow Catholic*, had been looking at Miss Muscatelli with annoyance and now lobbed one over. "Do you intend to make your views known to the rector of the seminary?"

"I have already spoken with Monsignor Eisenbarth on the phone. Of course he is in complete command of the situation."

"He wouldn't see us," someone complained.

"Perhaps he was on the phone talking with me. In any case, gentlemen, ladies and gentlemen, you must appreciate that we clerics are not accustomed to meeting with the press. . . ."

"Will we be given copies of your statement?" Mary Muscatelli again.

Brophy looked surprised, then contrite. "I'm afraid that I just tapped out these remarks without a thought to having copies made. How can we repair that oversight?"

Donovan offered to Xerox copies at the *Fort Elbow Catholic*, a few blocks away. Bishop Brophy decided not to linger. Waving good-bye in a gesture that permitted him a peek at his watch as well, Brophy excused himself and hurried up the stairs. Busy, busy. They must be made to see that the Church gave its leaders little time for rest.

On the second floor, at the back of the house, was a large room with deep comfortable chairs, a small refrigerator and a massive color TV. It was here in the evenings that Entweder nodded through dramas, cackled at the situation comedies and nursed a single beer while waiting for ten o'clock and the news. After that he would go to his room, finish his office and retire. The pastor rose at five. Father Ascue's last waking sound was the slow tread of McTear coming up from the basement, apparently trying to do so noiselessly and thus, inevitably, bringing Father Ascue out of his shallow sleep. This would be at two in the morning. At five Frank was wakened again, this time by the pastor's alarm clock, which was followed by coughing, running water, and odd groans and mumblings before Entweder banged down the stairs. The slam of the outside door and Entweder shuffling toward the church. Then Frank could roll over for another hour of sleep.

Tonight he had been more than willing to sit down with the pastor in front of the TV.

"Have a beer, Father. It's good for you."

"I think I'll have a soft drink."

"You don't drink?"

"I just don't seem to like it." The trouble was that he feared he could come to like it too much. Those cocktails with Charlotte and Howard had decided him on a nonalcoholic life.

"You're not a temperance fanatic, I hope."

"After all those years in Italy?"

Entweder had uncapped a beer and was pouring it into a glass, his eyes on the rising line of foam. His brows lifted at the mention of Italy, but that was all. Frank bit his lip. He had to stop making allusions to his years of study abroad. Entweder had never encouraged him to talk of his time in Rome and on those occasions when Frank did reminisce the pastor listened without great curiosity.

Ascue smoked and watched the antics on the screen, fascinated and repelled. He doubted that television could become a habit with him. Watching it was simply a matter of keeping the pastor company. In a little while he would slip away to his room.

He was still there at ten o'clock when the news came on and with it Bishop Brophy. At the sight of the auxiliary, Entweder rose and turned up the volume. The noise was deafening. Father Ascue was certain the set must be audible two blocks away. But for once he was grateful for the pastor's defective hearing. Both he and Entweder listened with rapt attention. The clip of the bishop ended rather abruptly when the statement had been read.

"He is a smoothie, Father," Entweder purred.

"It was a very careful statement."

"Yes. Very careful."

"Is Bishop Caldron away?"

"Bishop Caldron disappears one day a month. To make a small retreat. He is a holy man, Father Ascue. A holy man. You can imagine what an accomplishment that is for a bishop. I wonder how he will react to this."

"Certainly he can't object to anything Bishop Brophy said."

"Bishop Brophy put his seal of approval on a revolution. George Caldron is not going to like that. No, sir, he isn't."

Entweder turned the volume down a decibel or two and sat, wagging his head and sucking his lips. Scandal, scandal. Frank had no intention of arguing with him; he was certain that Entweder was mistaken about Bishop Caldron. Thank God, Brophy had spoken out in a temperate and positive vein. Look at us, he thought. Here we sit in isolated comfort, wasting an evening in front of a television set few lay people in the parish could afford. Those seminarians were willing to risk everything, to go hungry, to walk for hours. . . .

But then he thought of Bullard and Tremplin and relaxed. His righteous anger drained away. It was difficult to think of those two as heroes. But wasn't that the true genius of Bishop Brophy's statement? He mollified potentially dangerous rebels while at the same time trying to galvanize the rest of us into constructive action. Yes, it had been a smooth statement, a nuanced statement, but a forceful statement too.

Entweder turned off the set and in the sudden silence Father Ascue set off for his room. Bascomb's room. They still called it Bascomb's room. Poor Bascomb. Ordained a year ago, he had gone over the hill in March, fleeing to Las Vegas with some mad idea of turning a few hundred dollars into a fortune. He was now said to be working on the assembly line in a California factory. Father Ascue paused at the door of his room. From the basement came the muffled voice of McTear, repeating his call letters over and over, trying to raise other ham operators.

His trunks and boxes of books had arrived but even with the shelves and dresser and closet filled with familiar possessions, Frank found his room strange. Not that it was haunted by Bascomb, although when the room was still bare he sometimes lay awake at night and wondered what his unhappy predecessor had been like. The strangeness of the room arose from his occupancy of it. This is it, he told himself. Perhaps, like Entweder, he would still be here forty years from now. The thought had a dizzying effect, as if he were to be given a long life to be lived only in the present, without a future dimension, day after day to be spent doing essentially the same things. Up to now his life had been one of preparation, of looking ahead. At Lake Glister he had spent his high school years looking forward to being a college man and then he had looked ahead to the major seminary where it was the priesthood itself which lay at the term of six more years of study. In Rome it had been the degree and his return home, presumably to teach. The vertigo that gripped him now had nothing to do with his assignment; he would have felt the same way at the seminary. There too it would have occurred to him that finally, after so many years, he had come to a place where he would remain indefinitely. If married people felt this way it could not be to the same degree. Their children pulled them into an altering future, shaped their hopes, continued their expectations. For the first time Frank became aware of the frightening isolation and loneliness of the priesthood and, lying in the dark, he found it impossible to dismiss the realization. It was better to accept it, to dwell on it, to adjust to the reality of the life he had chosen. The recognition of his exceptional status was not an invitation to brood. Celibacy was meant to leave him free for others, a servant, an instrument.

As a seminarian he had read of the Curé d'Ars, he had also read Bernanos's novels about priests, and it had been easy to feel an almost sensual desire for an austere clerical life, to be a conduit of grace to others, their joys the only ones he asked for himself. Of course that had been a romantic aspiration. The truth was that the Curé d'Ars frightened him as only saints can frighten since by exhibiting the possibilities of holiness they make us conscious of our defects and end by repelling because they threaten what we are. Yet holiness was the ideal he had set before himself when he accepted ordination to the priesthood. What he dreaded, what they all dreaded, was letting it become a job, a career, merely the thing one did for a living. To love God in other people, to see men as called to an eternal happiness and to help them reach it. Who knew what that might demand of him? He didn't, he hadn't a clue. But he had to live each day finding it out or sure as sin the loneliness and isolation would do him in. In Bascomb's room. Poor devil. He would have to remember to pray for Bascomb. Maybe it was that damned mumbling rising from the basement half the night and Entweder's coughing that had sent young Bascomb barreling westward with his nest egg.

2   By the grand tour McTear had meant the parish plant
    but of course the buff brick buildings standing unshaded
    on asphalt could not be identified with the parish of Saint
Waldo's in any important sense of the term.

The real parish was a shifting concatenation of activities which
reached out from the church and school and parish house to involve in
various and changing ways the several thousand Catholics who lived
within the geographic boundaries of Saint Waldo's. Those boundaries
were odd ones. Father Ascue's first impression of the neighborhood had
been of older homes, well preserved, but he was to learn that from the
immediate environs as middle ground the parish moved uphill into an
area of real slums and downhill toward affluence, toward the park and
the wide tree-lined avenues where the houses, large and distinguished,
were inhabited by heavy contributors. The economic spectrum of the
parish overlay another, the spiritual one, and that respected geography
not at all.

On the wall of his study Monsignor Entweder had a huge map of the
parish which was covered with illegible or coded notations. The map
hung over a table which held a bank of filing boxes containing the
three-by-five-inch cards used in taking the census. For it was census
rather than office hours that the pastor had decided was the best initia-
tion to parish life. He stood before the map, regarding it with the
admiration others might reserve for old masters.

"There we are, Father. In a manner of speaking."

Entweder traced with trembling finger the firm line of Cavil Boulevard, which ran like a spine through the gridded map, leaving downtown and entering the upper poorer portion of the parish and, gathering speed, passed two blocks east of the rectory to graze, before it left
the map, the plush section bracketed by the park and river road.

"What was your home parish, Father?"

"Before I entered the seminary, my sister and I lived in Blessed

Sacrament." Frank put his finger on the map and ran it off the border in the direction of Blessed Sacrament. "My sister and her family live in Saint Barnabas now."

"Ah, well. We are not Saint Barnabas, Father."

"No." There was scarcely a building within the confines of Saint Barnabas parish that had been standing prior to 1950. The area had an aura of newness, of evanescence, as if all those rows of houses could be packed up and hauled away as swiftly as they had appeared upon the meadows and marshes of yesteryear. The ages of man had been reduced to two at Saint Barnabas: youth and early middle age. It was a funny thought that Charlotte and Howard were typical of the parish, happy among the brick veneer and plasterboard, romping among transplanted shrubs on instant lawns. The thought seemed disloyal, but Frank was glad to be at Saint Waldo's, where some faces other than white ones were seen, where age was not a rumor, either in houses or in people.

Entweder opened a drawer and took out a stack of census cards an inch thick. He handed them to Frank and made a notation on the map.

"Start with those, Father. You can see where you'll be." He pointed to where he had made the notation. "After you've finished with those, we'll send you into another neighborhood. It would take one man at least three years to cover the entire parish. Together we manage to get to everyone in the course of a year."

The cards Frank had been given took him into the lower, more affluent part of the parish and he wondered if this was the luck of the draw or if Entweder had wished to impress him. On his first day out he came to a large vine-covered house and stood before it puzzling over the card. Simpson? Simpson? He did not know why the name seemed familiar. A maid answered the door and Father Ascue thought that she might be Miss Simpson.

"Oh, no. Who shall I say is calling?"

"Father Ascue. From Saint Waldo's."

He was led into a dark living room with an Oriental rug and heavy furniture. The drapes were drawn but instead of opening them the maid turned on a lamp. Left alone, Father Ascue took out his pen, shuffled his cards and waited. He felt as he supposed salesmen must feel.

"Good morning, Father."

He rose to face the woman who had sat beside him on the flight from Rome. Recognition shone in her eyes too and she came toward him with a smile.

"Why, Father, what brings you here? Alice said it was one of the priests from Saint Waldo's."

"That's right. I've been assigned there."

"For heaven's sake. Sit down, Father. Do. Would you care for coffee?"

"No, thank you." McTear had warned him about accepting offers of coffee, topping the warning with the story of his own antic search for a men's room after having swilled a dozen cups on his rounds.

"But I thought you were to be a teacher after all that study in Rome."

"Apparently not, Miss Simpson. The bishop decided to send me to Saint Waldo's."

"Well, aren't you lucky? And aren't we lucky too."

"I like it."

"I meant that you're free of all that picketing and so on. Wasn't that disgraceful? Honestly, I don't know what things are coming to."

Father Ascue steered her away from that topic but made the mistake of mentioning her European trip to accomplish this. Miss Simpson settled back and commenced a nostalgic bout of reminiscing, saving her real enthusiasm for Lourdes.

"It may seem vain to say so, Father, but I think it did me a world of good. I can't tell you how much better I've felt since I went there. I brought back some Lourdes water and I dab on a little every day, as if it were perfume, and I know that sounds silly, as if I believed in magic or something, but I do believe in miracles and the fact is I feel better than I have in years."

Lest she begin a catalog of her ailments, Father Ascue referred to the census card, directing the conversation along the waiting lines of the printed questions. Miss Simpson had made her Easter duty, did not miss Mass, practiced her religion faithfully. Her answers were hardly surprising. She seemed happy to get *that* out of the way so they could continue their interesting conversation. Father Ascue stayed another ten minutes, declined her offer of several ounces of Lourdes water—she seemed to think that he would have a supply and was shocked when he told her he had none—and rose to go. He had many calls to make. Alarmed that she might have been impeding his priestly work, Miss Simpson took him to the door.

"Pray for me, Father," she called after him when he was going out the walk.

He turned and lifted his hand in farewell. In the doorway, Miss Simpson hurriedly crossed herself. He did bless her then, mumbling the words, then went quickly up the street.

The first week he drew the seven o'clock Mass in the convent chapel. McTear crowed in triumph when he did; it meant an extra hour of sleep for the first assistant after a hard night with his radio. The convent chapel was small and bright and smelled of furniture polish and paraffin. The nuns were on their prie-dieus reciting the Little Office when he came in. There was no sacristy, simply a vesting table to the left of the altar. Standing beside it was a gangly boy in cassock and surplice. The cassock stopped several inches below his knees and plaid-shirted arms extended from its sleeves. The boy looked acutely uncomfortable and the arrival of Father Ascue did not seem to help. He picked up a book of matches and moved to the altar to light the candles, stumbling on the raised platform. There was a caesura in the recitation of the office but the wavering voices went on when it was clear that disaster had been avoided. At the altar, the boy was having trouble with the matches, which flashed into flame and immediately died. Father Ascue, vesting, watched him. Finally the boy hitched up his cassock, took a Zippo from his trouser pocket and with a practiced flick of his thumb produced a roaring flame. He applied this to the candle wicks and turned with a triumphant blush. Father Ascue winked and made a friend.

His name was Basil, call me Buzz, and he was in the eighth grade of the parish school. When they emerged from the chapel after Mass, Father Ascue asked him where he would have breakfast.

"We feed the server," a voice trilled behind him.

Father Ascue turned to face a very pretty nun, who, unlike the others, had left her eyes wide open when she put out her tongue to receive the host at Communion time.

"That's the only way we can talk boys like Buzz into getting out of bed so early. Right?" She dug the boy in the ribs and he danced away, blushing but delighted. "I'm Sister Eloise," she said to Father Ascue.

"I'm Father Ascue."

"I know. Is it true you're just back from Rome?"

"Well, not just. It's been over a week."

"What was it like?" She wrinkled her nose and knitted her brows, prepared for the worst.

"Oh, it wasn't bad." He did not mind criticism of Rome if he began it but he rather resented this downgrading of his years abroad.

"I'd welcome you to Saint Waldo's but I'm basically an honest person."

"How do you find it here?"

She crossed her eyes, dropped her head to one shoulder and let her tongue loll like a hanged man's. "Dead," she whispered. "The Dark Ages."

Sister Eloise wore a dark skirt, white blouse, navy blue sweater, and had a veil pinned halfway back on her brown hair. The younger nuns in chapel had been dressed like Sister Eloise, but there were others trussed up in wimples and starched headdresses and the voluminous skirts of the traditional habit, their movements setting off a muted clacking of the long rosaries which hung from their cinctures.

"I'd ask you to breakfast too, Father, but we can't compete with Hilda."

Thanking her, he wondered if he was indeed refusing an invitation. He left the convent and set out across the blacktop toward the parish house. The area behind the school was already noisy with the first arrivals: several dozen bicycles stood in the racks and basketballs were arcing toward hoops. Piping voices called, "Good morning, Father," and Frank waved, deciding not to stop. What do you say to kids that age? Not that he felt inadequate. He was reveling in parish life and had not a bit of regret left. There was no need to force himself to thank God that the bishop had assigned him to Saint Waldo's.

Bishop Brophy, still in pajamas, was reading the morning paper when Caldron's secretary called to say that the bishop would like to have his auxiliary join him for breakfast.

"I'll say Mass in the chapel there, if I may."

Father Foster said that would be fine and, having hung up, Bishop Brophy returned to the paper. The coverage of his news conference was good, very good. He was not surprised that Caldron should wish to see him. Who knew? Maybe the old man would take his cue from this adroit handling of a very sticky situation. Humming, Bishop Brophy went into his bathroom.

The night before he had watched himself on the ten o'clock news and had been relieved to see that they had cut the questions and answers which had followed his reading of the statement. The statement was the important thing. And yet, later, in bed, he had begun to doubt. He had given the only copy of his remarks to the newsmen and he found himself unable to reconstruct what he had said. Had the statement been as carefully crafted as he thought? Tossing and turning, his mind a jumble of disconnected phrases which may or may not have been part of his statement, Bishop Brophy spent a restless night. Now, with the reassurance of the newspaper account and Caldron's invitation to breakfast, his confidence was restored.

The chapel in the episcopal palace was baroque, an object of gentle derision from Brophy when he was chatting with the clergy. One entered at the side of the chapel through double doors to see on the opposite wall three small stained-glass windows which created the saccharine effect of the witch's house in "Hansel and Gretel." Four pews of rich mahogany under an arched ceiling Brophy could almost touch on tiptoe; a riot of colors, painted angels and snippets from the Vulgate adorned the ceiling. The altar of marble and gold and gleaming linen supported enough candles to give a fire inspector nightmares. When Bishop Brophy arrived, Bishop Caldron had already finished offering his Mass and now knelt in a front pew making his thanksgiving. Caldron nodded in response to Brophy's mouthed good morning. His expression told Brophy nothing. Well, he had hardly expected a cheer. Nonetheless he began to vest for Mass with a light heart. It seemed to him now that his impulse to speak out last night had been not only shrewd but inspired, in the deeper sense. Had he not been, in the manner of a bishop, a mouthpiece of the Holy Spirit? It was a solemn, agreeable thought. Vested, he waited for a moment while the cadaverous Father Foster checked the cruets and then took up his stance behind Brophy. Over his shoulder the auxiliary bishop whispered, "Is the English missal out?"

"Yes, Bishop." Father Foster's mouth smacked in the morning, his tongue clacking off dry dentures.

Caldron cleared his throat. Brophy turned, the chasuble heavy on his arms as he brought his palms together, and followed Father Foster as if in procession the four baby steps it took to arrive at the foot of the altar.

After the consecration, Brophy heard Caldron rise and shuffle out. Brophy hurried reverently through his Mass, not wanting to keep Caldron waiting in the dining room.

Surprisingly, Yorick was at table with Bishop Caldron when Brophy swept into the dining room. Unfazed, Brophy called out a hearty good morning, crossed the room and stuck his face into the kitchen. Leon, the cook, pored over the sports page at the kitchen table.

"How about a poached egg, Leon?"

"Coming up, Bishop. Coming up."

When he sat at table Brophy noticed that Yorick had a copy of the morning paper folded and pinned under his elbow. The chancellor stirred his coffee noisily and studied the chandelier as if it had been recently installed. Brophy decided that he would leave the opening gambit to Caldron. The coffee was lukewarm and he downed half a cup without pain. Caldron had been trimming a cigar and now put it between his teeth. Yorick produced a match from his cassock pocket, ignited it with a flick of his thumbnail, and held it to the bishop's cigar. Caldron's beatific expression as he drew on his matutinal cigar reminded Brophy of one of those pinkish angels on the chapel ceiling.

"Smells like a Havana," Brophy said despite himself. He hated silence at meals, even breakfast.

"I believe it was made in Miami, Bishop Brophy."

"Where else?" *Bishop* Brophy? My, aren't we formal this morning. It occurred to Brophy that Yorick had been looking alternately sullen and smug. At the moment he was looking smug. What a lackey the man was.

"Any news from the seminary this morning?" Brophy asked. If they didn't have the grace to tell him well done, the incident itself should be discussed. He was gratified to see Yorick's expression drift toward sullenness again.

"The seminary, Bishop Brophy? Were you expecting a message?" Caldron was wreathed, in cigar smoke and in smiles.

"There was quite a bit of commotion over there yesterday."

"So the newspaper says. I must give Monsignor Eisenbarth a ring and ask what went on."

Randy would like the bishop's ring all right. But what was going on here? Brophy had the distinct feeling that he was the rodent in a cat and mouse game. Had Caldron somehow got a garbled version of what had taken place?

"I called Eisenbarth yesterday. Seminarians, as you must have read, were picketing on the street outside the seminary grounds. The press was there. My first knowledge of the situation came via television. Eisenbarth seemed to be barricaded in his office, refusing to talk to the press—"

"Is that why you praised him in your statement?" Yorick demanded.

"Monsignor, Monsignor," Caldron chided, putting a soothing hand on the chancellor's arm. "Why *did* you issue a statement, Sean?"

"The situation called for immediate action. As vicar general, I felt it should be put into perspective." He paused, sipped his coffee. Dear God in heaven! Caldron wanted him to *justify* what he had done. "I was contacted by the press and, in your absence, agreed to make a statement."

"You knew we'd be back in a matter of hours. What was the big rush?"

"Monsignor Yorick, please! I want you to leave Bishop Brophy and me alone to discuss this matter."

Yorick leaped to his feet, as if delighted to have a chance to get out of the auxiliary bishop's presence.

Leon entered with Bishop Brophy's poached egg and watched Yorick storm out of the room.

"Something wrong?"

"With the food, Leon?" Caldron asked. Leon had an insatiable curiosity about the clergy and confided to anyone who would listen that he himself would have made one hell of a priest. It was difficult to disagree. Rebuffed, Leon went sulkily back to his kitchen and the sports page.

"Now, Sean. I wish you had not brought up that matter while Monsignor Yorick was here. He was an unexpected visitor. Tell me now, what went on yesterday?"

Feeling better, Bishop Brophy summed up the events of the previous day as he ate his egg. He had intended to tell Leon to bring in some hot coffee but that would be a distraction now so he drank the tepid brew available and concentrated on his narrative.

"But what did Eisenbarth say when you phoned him?"

"He didn't know what to do. He wanted to talk to you, of course. He was holed up in his office, just waiting until he could reach you. Meanwhile, half his students were parading around on the sidewalk, covered by TV cameras, being interviewed—"

"The boys were interviewed?"

"No, not the boys. Father Tremplin."

"Ah. And precisely what were they demonstrating about?"

"It's in the paper. The essence of it."

Caldron opened the paper Yorick had left, did not read. "A hunger strike?"

"Yes."

"In support of Father Bullard? Protesting, I gather, my high-handed treatment of him."

"Of course they couldn't know all the facts of the case."

"No, *they* couldn't. But you do know, Sean. How then could you give the appearance of supporting them?"

"No, George. Not supporting them. I tried to be quite clear and explicit about that. It was important to avert a scandal. But there is a principle here and I pointed precisely to that. Misguided or not, those boys have a zeal the Church needs. I think it is important that their zeal be directed, not squelched."

"But what was the hurry?"

Bishop Brophy fought an impulse to anger. If Caldron had to have it spelled out for him, okay. "By agreeing to meet the press when they asked me I ensured that my statement would be part of the same day's events and thus cast what had gone on into perspective."

"That couldn't wait for my return?"

"These things exist in the media, on television, in the newspapers. They're here today and gone tomorrow. If I had not spoken, think of the impression that would have been created."

"You mean we might have looked foolish?"

"Of course we would."

"Is that so terribly important?"

Brophy inhaled. "Bishop, what do you think of my statement?"

Bishop Caldron turned over a spoon, a fork, the newspaper. "I find it odd that you can describe Philip Bullard in terms of zeal. You know all about that case. Since the commotion at the seminary was in support of Father Bullard, your statement can only be construed as blinking the facts of the case."

"I don't agree."

"I see."

"But *do* you? We can't afford to lose any more seminarians. You know that."

"Sean, I can afford even less to encourage the future clergy to question the authority and good sense of their bishop. To speak of me as suppressing Father Bullard is worse than fanciful. These young men are deluded and I am afraid that your statement can only encourage their delusion and confuse a great many others."

Bishop Brophy wiped egg from his lips. He found that he was not really surprised by Bishop Caldron's reaction. It had been ridiculous to expect that he would be praised for what he had done. But now was the moment to make the larger point he thought his statement had already made. He lit a cigarette and sat forward.

"Bishop, this goes beyond Bullard and Tremplin and those kids. The diocese is drifting. Oh, not just this one; most dioceses are. What is needed is for the chancery to take the initiative, to lead the way, to interpret the times in the light of the Council. We seem to be just sitting around waiting for an eruption and when it comes, we react. Reaction, not action. We're not renewing and that is the name of the game now. The seminary is moribund, the younger clergy is alienated, the older men are closed in on themselves, and the people are just turned off by it all."

"Our public relations are bad?"

"That isn't fair."

"Perhaps not. But I am dubious of this zeal which wants us to appear wise in the eyes of the world, to adjust, adapt. Sean, what is this impulse to march about, to make statements, to appear in print and on television? Are we selling soap? Are we in politics? I would find all this criticism of the Church more tolerable if it went hand in hand with a criticism of the world. Isn't that our task?"

"The communications media enable us to perform that task."

"Perhaps. But we are drifting from the point. The point is Father

Bullard. You known that he is a womanizer, that he applied for laicization and that I was perfectly willing to grant it, subject to the usual procedures. Suddenly, for reasons that are not perhaps difficult to find, he reversed himself and withdrew his application. He had become a celebrity and he liked it. Perhaps I should have sacked him. If I did not, it's because I pray that more will be at work in his life than his own poor efforts. Grace, Sean. Grace. What I must say is this. I am vastly displeased by what you did yesterday."

"I'm sorry to hear that."

"You'll be sorrier to hear the rest. I am sending you on an extended tour of the diocese. It will keep you out of the city for several weeks. During that time, no interviews. No public allusions to what has happened."

"But I have engagements, speeches. . . . Do you mean that I should cancel them?"

"Yes."

This could not be happening. This was a bad dream. Caldron was sending him into temporary exile for bailing out Eisenbarth and sparing the diocese a black eye. Caldron rose from his chair.

"You think I am being unjust. Perhaps I am. I don't think so. But if I am, you will not be the first to have suffered the stupidity of his ecclesiastical superiors."

Caldron left the room. Brophy stared at the door as if Caldron must soon reappear and cry, "April fool." His hand went out for his cup and he brought it to his lips. Sputtering, he exploded.

"Leon! Bring me some hot coffee."

She sounded all business on the phone.

"Father Bullard? This is Mary Muscatelli."

"Well, how are you? It's good to hear from you."

And it was. Her voice recalled all the excitement which, for a week now, had been little more than a memory. The attention which she had briefly directed on him had drifted elsewhere and while he told himself it was silly to regret this, the truth was that he missed being at the center of the stage. The protest at the seminary which had promised so much—for a moment it had been possible to believe that the diocese would rouse itself from decades of slumber and enter the twentieth century—had been turned into something else by Brophy's ambiguous statement. Now the auxiliary seemed to have gone into hiding and there was much speculation on his whereabouts. The paper said that calls to the chancery and cathedral rectory drew only the response that

Bishop Brophy was out of town. At the seminary all seemed returned to its previous quiescent state. Mary's call stirred up the hope that she might help him prevent the diocese from returning to somnolence.

"I'd like to talk with you," she said.

"Anytime."

"Not there."

"Wherever you say."

The restaurant she mentioned was unfamiliar to him but he told her it would be fine, he would meet her there.

She was in a booth in the bar when he arrived, a drink before her. Before sitting down, he flagged a waitress and ordered a Manhattan, up.

"Want another, Mary?"

"I'm fine."

"You're wearing your collar," she said when he was settled across from her.

He smiled. "I'm traveling incognito."

"Have you stopped being a rebel?"

"I'm not a rebel, just a revolutionary."

His drink came and he lifted it. She did not follow suit. He sipped. Too much bitters. "So what's on your mind?"

"Let's cut the crap, should we?"

If she had wanted to startle him, she succeeded. He was taking another sip of his drink when she spoke and he began to choke. She watched him try to regain control, watched him coolly, clinically, without any sympathy at all. When finally he caught his breath, he looked at her with tear-filled eyes. Several men at the bar had turned at the sound of his choking and were now huddling. Get a load of the priest with the broad.

Mary said, "I want to talk about Diane."

My God! He was seized by real panic. How had she found out about Diane? Mary's half-skeptical attitude when she had interviewed him was now an open animosity and the fact that she was a reporter, that she must regard his relations with Diane as news, seemed the potential of disaster. He had assured Caldron that his lapse had not been public or a matter of scandal and it had been clear that without that assurance the bishop would not have agreed to let him withdraw his application for laicization.

"Diane?"

She made a face. "Please don't say you don't remember."

"That's all over."

"Is it?"

"You can't publish something like that!"

He had succeeded in surprising her. She sat back and studied him through narrowed eyes. "Is that your only concern?"

"It's not news, Mary. You can't put it in the paper."

"Don't tell me what I can put in the paper."

He laid his hands flat on the table. He had to stop this pleading: it was only making things worse.

"Diane says that you want to dump her. Is that true?"

"When did you talk to her?"

"She's my roommate."

He was beyond surprise now. Roommate. How oddly proud she seemed to be of that. He had known Diane had a roommate, that was why he had never been able to go to her place, but he had never asked about the girl or what she did. Suddenly he understood why Mary had come to interview him. Diane, of course. Had she thought the publicity would speed things along for them?

"How much did she tell you?"

"Enough."

"Give me some idea."

"All right." Mary's expression hardened. "She shacked up with you on the assumption that you were through as a priest. You were going to marry her but first you had to get permission to leave so everything would be aboveboard. Permission was refused. So kaput with the marriage plans and bye-bye Diane."

"What more can I say?"

"Why is that permission important to you? You call yourself a revolutionary and then need some damned piece of paper to marry a girl you say you love!"

He traced the edge of his collar with his finger. "Aren't you a Catholic, Mary?"

"Oh, boy. Yes, I'm a Catholic. More or less."

"Then you should understand," he said softly.

"Understand what?"

He leaned toward her. "I am a priest. I have made promises, solemn promises. Unless I am relieved of them, officially, any attempt to marry would be a grievous sin. I can't do anything without that permission. Do you want me to condemn myself to hell?"

This appeal to the raging flames she must have imagined since childhood did not move her.

"Did you have permission to go to bed with her?"

He waited a moment before saying, "If you are a friend of Diane's, you wouldn't speak of it like that. As if it were dirty."

"Did you ever really intend to marry her?"

The noise in the bar, happy, bibulous, seemed symbolic of a carefree life that he was forever denied, that was always beyond his grasp. He felt trapped by Mary and her questions which led on to further questions, and where they might end frightened him. Surely it was only a white lie to let her believe that his request for laicization had been denied. He had not said that in so many words to Diane. How bitter it was to remember that he had thought Mary's telephone call was to the crusading priest who bore the banner of change and renewal. He swirled his drink, watching the liquid revolve in the hollow of the glass as if it, like himself, were seeking a horizon and equilibrium. He drew his lower lip between his teeth and bit hard to stop the trembling of his mouth. His eyes, still wet from choking, primed the tears and he could not look at Mary Muscatelli. Wouldn't it be easier to do what Mary suggested? Pitch everything and run off with Diane. He said in a small voice, "I never felt about anyone the way I felt about Diane."

"Bullshit."

He stared at her with shocked glistening eyes.

"Listen to me, Bullard. You're not going to drop her like a load of garbage. Understand? Maybe you fool Diane with this pizzle about permission, but I know you and I know you'd do anything you really want to do. And you'd better really want to think it over about Diane."

"Or what?"

"Or we'll see."

"I don't understand you. If she's your friend and I'm the monster you think, why don't you just leave it alone?"

"Have you any idea what that girl is going through?"

"Of course I do." Dear God, how could he tell someone as unsympathetic as her what joy he had known with Diane, the sense he had had that with her his life could begin all over again and begin on a note of happiness? He had turned away from that, had resumed his obligations with the determination to be a good priest.

"I think you just took her for a ride. She thinks you've done the noble spiritual thing. Bullard, I want Diane to know you for the bastard you really are."

He had never in his life, before or after ordination, been spoken to like that and he did not like it at all. This woman was unbelievable and what she was asking made no sense. He no longer thought that she would use this against him publicly. Her only concern was with Diane. She really hates me, he thought, and indeed her hatred was almost palpable, a third presence there in the booth. Or a fourth. Diane was with them too.

"How is she, Mary?"

"How do you think she is?"

In her widened eyes he could see contained the grieving Diane. Diane's grief had become Mary's, it inhabited her, and that explained this meeting and these bitter words which now began to make a kind of sense. Father Bullard stopped thinking of Mary as a threat.

"She's fortunate to have you as a friend. I don't blame you for what you think of me. I wish I could undo what I've done but I can't. But for me to see Diane wouldn't help, Mary. It certainly would not help her. If you can make it easier for her by convincing her I'm what you said, a bastard, well, go ahead. Tell her anything that will help her. Please."

"Oh, that's very big of you."

He ignored that; in any case, her sarcasm was muted. "You can help her, Mary. You know you can. I can't."

"No," she agreed. "You can't. Maybe nobody can. She just doesn't seem to care about anything or anyone now. It's frightening. . . ."

Her voice had become gentle, she might have been speaking to herself. Mary's head had dropped and she ran her finger up and down the stem of her glass, subdued, her anger spent. He put his hand on hers but she snatched it away. She did look at him, though, with tears in her eyes.

"Let's have lunch, Mary. We can talk more later."

She nodded, squeezing her eyes in an effort to dry them. This time she did not remove her hand when he covered it with his own.

"Father Oder can't come tonight," Charlotte said at breakfast.

"No meeting then?"

"Oh, we'll have the meeting. It just won't be the same."

"Then why have it? Cancel it, for crying out loud. We'll survive."

"Howard, I'd be the first to say that, *if* we weren't hosts tonight. But it would look funny if I said, Gee, no chaplain, no meeting. Now, if someone else suggests it . . ."

"Talk to people; give them a chance to suggest it."

She looked at him strangely. "Boy, you really want out of it, don't you?"

"It isn't that."

"Isn't it?"

"Okay. The thought of meeting with that bunch tonight does not excite me."

"It never does."

He looked at her warily. One admission could too easily be another. "Sometimes they're interesting."

When she phoned him at the office that afternoon he had forgotten the meeting altogether.

"No luck, Howard. It's on."

"Oh. The group." He had had to think.

"Oder is sending a substitute. Father Swivel."

With hope of reprieve gone, Howard had not complained. There would have been no point. He could wish now that he had not been so explicit about disliking those goddam meetings when Charlotte had brought it up that morning. But the prospect put lead in the afternoon and gloom in his heart. Before going home, he stopped in a bar up the street from his office and had two double bourbons. At home, he put a couple more on top of those and began to feel sufficiently anesthetized for the evening.

Swivel, confused about the time, arrived half an hour early. He accepted the offer of a drink. "Fill me in, Mr. Nygaard. I've never been to a CFM meeting before."

"Lucky you." It just slipped out. His eyes darted to the priest, but Swivel was delighted. For that matter, Howard was delighted to meet a priest who had never attended a Christian Family Movement meeting.

"That bad?"

"What's that thing monks used to have, a kind of sensitivity session?" Swivel looked alarmed. "A chapter of faults?"

"More the reverse of that. Public self-congratulation. Why we have a perfect marriage. Why aren't other couples as sweet as we?"

"Oh, boy." Swivel held out his glass. "May I?"

He might. Howard had another himself, knowing he should not. The others arrived before he finished it, but to hell with them, he polished it off and took the glass to the kitchen. Drinks were never served at the meetings. Charlotte was in charge now, getting people settled, introducing Swivel to those who did not know him. Howard took a dining room chair and sat under the arch between the two rooms, with the group but not of it, and prayed that time would pass swiftly.

Daydreaming, not really listening, his head hummed with a composite meeting. The speakers were usually the wives, although several of the husbands, notably the pasty-faced Hanker, managed to get the floor from time to time. The marriage relationship, a great mystery, sex made sublime and the depth of a union sacramental, on and on. What killed Howard, really killed him, was listening to Charlotte. She became a poet of the nuptial bed in public. Hearing her rave on about the role of sex in marriage, Howard wondered if others imagined her to be a real alley cat in bed. There was something quaintly defiant in all this talk of sex. "Now once the pope gets off the pot and speaks out on the pill, I'm sure we're going to have a golden age of Catholic marriage. The whole notion of periodic continence, rhythm, whatnot, may be all very well on paper, or when a dozen juiceless old cardinals are sitting around talking about it, but in the concrete, in the life married people lead, you just can't reduce sex to a schedule. Maybe we shouldn't get hung up on this. It's as sure as can be that the pope will say only what so many theologians have said. Don't you agree, Father Swivel?"

Howard opened one eye and looked at the priest. Swivel said, "I'm sure Father Oder would agree that it's a matter of personal conscience. I don't know how one can have a law which applies to every couple no matter what . . ."

Howard closed his eye. Swivel could be sure that Oder would agree. Charlotte was on the pill. Big deal. For several months it had changed things. She had loosened up, relaxed. They had made love several times a week. Whoopee. They had lost interest at the same time, as if to show how attuned to one another they had become. Too tired, too listless, it was a relief to be able simply to kiss good night and drift into simple sexless sleep. "Howard, we're getting old," Charlotte said whenever it had been established that neither of them wanted to, that sleep was pleasure enough. "Speak for yourself," he answered and tried to give her a purple heart. She twisted away, laughing, and that was the end of the great sexual revolution in the Nygaard bedroom.

Speak for yourself. Howard sat up, slipping into a more erect position, easing his eyes open as he did so. What a hypocrite he was, sitting here with these people. It was easy to think of them as silly and naïve, but in his heart Howard considered them good, really good. They were faithful, loving, loyal, good parents and good spouses.

Half drunk, remorseful, Howard wanted to stand up and confess it aloud to them all. To Swivel too, a chapter of faults, pleading for absolution. It was a mad impulse, but an appropriate one for a divided man. He looked from one male face to the next, going around the room, studying each in turn for some surface indication that there were darker depths, but he was sure that not one of these men had been unfaithful to his wife. Not a single one. If what he had was leprosy, he would have been issued a bell; he would have had to ring it before entering a room like this, a room filled to overflowing with the clean and the good.

Hilda rang his room to say that someone wanted to see him downstairs and when Frank came into the office, the same one in which he had awaited Entweder his first day here, Phil Bullard was sitting in the leather chair.

"Hi, Frank." Phil got to his feet. "Are you busy?"

"You're my first customer today. How've you been?"

The two priests shook hands. Phil was wearing a turtleneck sweater with his black suit. No, it wasn't a suit. Dark slacks and a navy blue jacket with metal buttons. Hilda must not have suspected that Phil was a priest.

"All right. You know."

"You're quite a celebrity."

Phil ducked his head and smiled bashfully.

"Why don't we go upstairs, Phil?"

"No. This is fine. Can we close the door?"

Frank closed the door. Phil was as nervous as a layman on his first visit to a rectory. Was it the atmosphere of the room? Frank had felt it himself that first day: it was a setting for the enactment of sad scenes. Trouble in the family, money, infidelity, liquor, ungrateful children. Phil sat, taking a straight chair nearer the desk. Frank hesitated and then went around the desk.

"So what brings you to Saint Waldo's?"

"I might ask you the same thing. It was a bit of a surprise, wasn't it, being assigned here?"

"Oh, I don't know. Anyway I like it."

"You're lucky. The place I was in—ugh."

"Things going well at the Center?"

"Oh, sure. The kids are in a panic right now though, with the semester coming to an end. Term papers, exams."

"I know what that's like."

Frank's eyes had gone to the window: this stilted conversation made him uneasy. When he looked back at Phil he was startled to see the abject expression on his classmate's face. Arms at his sides, palms pressed flat against the seat of the chair, Phil might have been about to lift himself off it. Tears stood in his eyes and his grief was shameless, almost defiant.

"Good Lord, Phil, what is it?"

"I'm in trouble."

"Trouble?" Those newspaper stories. Good God, had Caldron suspended Phil? "What kind of trouble?"

"I want to go to confession, Frank."

Seconds went past while the two priests, frozen, stared at one another. Frank felt for and found the drawer of the desk, opened it and groped for the stole kept there. How stupid to hesitate like that. It unnerved him to have lay people ask to confess in a parish office. For that matter, he was not yet used to hearing in his confessional in the church. That was a part of the priesthood that had been postponed during his student days in Rome. He unrolled the stole and slipped it around his neck. It was white side up and he turned it over to penitential purple. Phil insisted on kneeling beside him and Frank, acutely uncomfortable, listened to his classmate confess his sins.

"A *year* since your last confession?"

Phil, his eyes lowered, nodded. My God, a priest should confess once a week. A year! But then the flow of words began and Frank, numb, stared at the window where a lilac bush swayed in a light May breeze. He tried not to despise Phil, tried not to think that this was the worst set of sins he had yet heard as a confessor. What in God's name would he say to Phil when he had finished?

"Is the girl married?"

"No."

"Where did you meet her?"

"At a party. We started to talk. It just . . . happened."

"You don't intend to see her again?"

"I don't want to." Phil had hesitated.

"What's the problem? Do you have to see her?"

"Not the way you mean."

"Get up, Phil. Please. Sit down."

"Give me absolution, Frank."

"Sit down. We have to talk about this. You know there's no point in my giving you absolution if this is going to continue."

"I know." Phil got back on the chair. "And I know how incredible this must seem to you."

"Incredible?"

"All right, disgusting. I can't explain it."

"Not going to confession regularly is asking for trouble, Phil. You know that. Of course this isn't incredible. It's not disgusting either. *Are* you through with her?"

"I want to be."

"Does she? What about her?"

Phil rubbed his upper lip as if he were surprised not to find a mustache there. "She thought we were going to get married and go away together. I told her we would. And of course practically every day she reads in the paper of another priest leaving. She wants me to apply for laicization."

Frank tugged at the ends of the stole. "You could, Phil. Maybe you should."

"But I want to be a priest, Frank. Maybe that sounds strange after what I've told you, but it's true. I'm sorry for my sins. I want to start all over again."

Frank realized that he was trying to imagine the girl. There was another human being at issue here and it did not seem right that she should be regarded simply as someone Phil might accept or reject. And whoever she was she was right. Phil could leave. That would be a major step, of course, and certainly not an easy one to take. But it could not have been easy to get involved with the girl either and by doing that Phil had started to take that other step. But how could he urge Phil or anyone to abandon the priesthood?

"You can't ever see her again, Phil."

"I haven't seen her for nearly two weeks."

"Good."

"I wish I could believe that. She's taking it badly, Frank. I'm afraid she might do something."

"Do you mean harm herself?"

"It's not impossible. Her roommate came to see me." Phil rubbed his face.

"Would you talk to her, Frank? Would you go see her?"

"What good would that do?"

"It would do me a lot of good. I have to know that she's all right and if I go to see her . . ."

"All right." Phil had to stay away from the girl. "If it will make it easier for you, I'll talk to her."

Phil sighed with relief and relaxed in his chair. "Okay. Now I can promise that it's definitely over."

With dread Frank thought of something. "Have you been saying Mass?"

"I have to, Frank. Every day at the Center."

So there was sacrilege added to everything else. Every Mass Phil had said had been a mortal sin, an abomination, an offense far worse than the affair with the girl. It was not the multiplication of the event that was shocking—spiritually, too, you can only die once—but its character. Calling down God's mercy on sins of the flesh was easy, but the thought of a priest saying Mass in a sinful state was like trying to maintain a self-contradiction.

"I'll give you absolution now, Phil."

Phil Bullard sank to his knees and bowed his head and Frank, reciting the formula of absolution, felt that a burden was being lifted from them both. A nunnish fantasy of smiling angels hovering over the scene came to him and he found no urge to dismiss it or demythologize it. Phil got to his feet.

"Have you got a piece of paper, Frank? I'll write down her name and number." A moment later he looked up from his writing. "This phone number is where she works."

They went to the door together. Before Frank could open it, Phil put a hand on his shoulder. "The stole, Frank. You're still wearing the stole."

Frank took it off, rolled it up and put it back in the desk drawer. When they had come out of the office, he asked Phil where he was parked.

"Over in front of the school. I came across the playground."

"I'll walk you to your car."

He stopped at the kitchen to tell Hilda he would be right back and went outside to find Phil on the loggia connecting house and church. The playground was filled with kids now, enjoying the afternoon recess on a bright warm day.

"We can cut through the church, Phil."

"Oh, I can make it through the kids."

"Let's go."

"You don't have to come." Phil put out his hand. "I'm grateful, Frank."

"Forget it. I'll come along. It's good to get out of the house."

They started across the playground through careening, screaming kids. A hundred games seemed in progress: balls were being bounced, hit, banked off backboards.

"Father Ascue! Hello."

It was Sister Eloise, skipping rope. The two girls turning it were doing hot pepper and the nun bounced up and down, her veil and hair flying, her face aglow. She skipped free of the rope and came toward them, laughing, breathing heavily.

"Oh, that's fun," she cried, a picture of glowing youth.

"You were doing pretty well," Phil said.

"Pretty well!" The nun looked at Phil saucily and then, remembering, dropped her eyes.

"This is Father Phil Bullard, Sister."

Her eyes popped open and her smile returned. "Father Bullard! Of course. I *thought* you looked familiar." Her hand shot out and she grasped Phil's hand and began to pump it. "Keep up the good work, Father. I mean that. You've been great."

Phil looked sheepishly at Frank but he could not repress a pleased grin. The nun pointed at his sweater.

"I like that."

"It's comfortable."

"Those newspaper stories raised the roof in the convent, I can tell you. At the chapter meeting Mother Superior roasted you for fifteen minutes. If you think priests are backward, you should sit in on one of our chapter meetings. Not that they'd let you."

"Pretty terrible?"

"Sometimes I wonder if we'll wake up in time. There are days when I doubt it."

"Keep the faith, Sister," Frank advised.

"Right," Phil said. "Things are getting better."

"Let's hope so. I'm delighted to meet you, Father." She squeezed Phil's hand. "Well, back to work." She returned to her kids, the rope went into action again and Sister Eloise, bouncing like a ball, waved good-bye.

"Wow," Phil said when they had got off the playground. "Did she ever make me feel like a hypocrite."

"Forget that. It's what you do from now on that counts."

"Thanks again, Frank. You got that number?"

"I've got it."

Phil's red car took off with a roar. Frank watched it go and then, turning, went toward the church. Inside it was cool, empty and echoing in the afternoon. Outside the voices of the kids subsided and all was still. Frank sat in a pew and looked toward the altar and the tabernacle on it. Christ sacramentally present there whose grace had just wiped away Phil Bullard's sins. That mercy, the willingness to make the past as if it had never been, was impossible to understand. Sin, grace, life and death, the whole story of salvation working itself out imperceptibly in time—he believed that, he did not understand it. The impulse to despise Phil was still with him but it was easy to suppress here in the church. If God forgave Phil, how could he do less? What Phil had done was no favor to his fellow priests but the whole point of the Church was that sins could be forgiven, that the gap men opened between themselves and God could be closed. He should pray for Phil. He did. He prayed for the girl too, the girl he had agreed to see and, while he did, he realized what it was that frightened him about Phil. It could happen to me, Frank thought. It could happen to me. It seemed both plausible and wildly implausible, but however he regarded it, it was a useful thought, lending the weight of genuineness to his sympathy with Phil Bullard.

Beverly Nygaard divided the boys she knew into two groups. First there were the clowns who lay about the Center all day, missing classes, bumming coffee and having endless conversations about politics, the state of society and their intention not to sell out. Then there were the dull serious ones, aimed at a degree like arrows at a target, their real lives awaiting them maybe three or four years in the future. Dates with the first type were as dull as dates with the second. In either case she was expected to exhibit bottomless interest, since what *he* thought or felt or intended to do was always the topic of conversation. Her role was to listen and then pay for the privilege by subjecting herself to the last-minute fondling which was either desperately amateurish or frighteningly expert. Boys who professed to be concerned with their estrangement and loss of identity had a small edge over those destined to become like her father, a very small edge, on being the more intolerable. How anyone who spent twenty-four hours a day contemplating his navel could complain of a loss of identity was beyond Beverly.

"Who am I? I mean, who the hell am I, Bev?"

Thus, for example, Alfred Patch, while they sat in the converted hearse he drove, parked by the river, feasting on cheap hamburgers and sharing the warm beer.

"Alfred Patch." Bev freed a pickle slice that had been embedded like a fossil in the hamburger bun.

"Funny. But who is Alfred Patch?"

"The Dauphin?"

"What?"

"Nothing. A joke." Poor Alfred. Like most of his type, he claimed to be an English major. (And I'm an American general, Bev would say, drawing a grimace.) Apparently Alfred had not read *Huckleberry Finn*. It went without saying that he was ignorant of European history.

He brooded in silence for a time, swilling beer, glowering in the direction of the river, but no matter where he looked he saw the infinitely interesting landscape of himself. When he spoke again, he was more careful about framing rhetorical questions. Alfred Patch, said Alfred Patch, could not be reduced to external relations, his citizenship, his parents, his enrollment at the university. ("You're kidding," Bev interrupted. "Are you a student? What courses are you taking?" She knew that Alfred had indeed signed up for courses but stopped attending them after a week. Ever since, he had been in quest of himself, cruising around town in his hearse, lolling about in the Center lounge, talking about going to New Hampshire, then Wisconsin, then Indiana, for the primaries, but just talking about it. He never went.)

"What's your draft status, Alfie?"

"I'm a CO."

"What do they call it on your card?"

"Oh, that still reads 2-S. I'm going to have it changed."

"Let's go, shall we?"

"We just got here. Want some more beer?"

"No, thanks."

Warm beer from a bottle he'd been slobbering over—what a creep. What was she doing here, sitting in a hearse at riverside with Alfred Patch? For crying out loud.

"Who am I?" she asked.

"I hate a cynic," Alfred said. "The whole goddam world is falling apart and all you do is joke."

"I know. Let's go."

"Aw, come on. Where's to go?" His arm slithered along the back of the seat and his hand dropped clawlike to her shoulder. She sat up.

"I'll scream."

He laughed. His hand moved. She screamed.

"Jesus," he said. "Cut it out. You want to bring a cop or something?"

"Or something."

He looked at her, confused, hurt. He had bared his soul to her, such as it was, and now they were to cuddle and coo. She felt like throwing up. She told him that she really and truly wanted to go home, so start the damned motor and back out of here, would he, please? After a moment he did, in sullen silence. At her house, he pulled to the curb and waited, staring straight ahead.

"Good night, Alfred." She opened the door and hopped out.

"Good-bye!"

He roared away, his cracked muffler violating the suburban quiet. Good-bye, Alfie, she thought, waving after him. What an ass.

But it was catching, what Alfie had, and in bed she lay awake, wondering who on earth she was to attract creeps like Alfie. Who am I? What do I want? Where am I going? All those big questions were so easy to kid about when jerks like Alfred Patch asked them, but after all they were the only questions. Did she want to end up in a few years in her mother's situation: a house, a husband, children of her own? Why not? Why not? All she wanted was some boy who did not whine, who did not take himself so seriously, someone with a sense of humor. And she would like to have children, to hold, to love. She hugged her pillow and drifted into sleep where, vague, indistinct of face, but vastly different from any boy she knew, *he* awaited her. No doubt it was only because our dreams are shaped from the rag and bone shop of memory that his face, when it did take on contours, was very much like Uncle Frank's.

The girl, Diane, had been surprised when Father Ascue telephoned, then wary and evasive, but grudgingly she agreed to meet him. Where? His suggestion that he come to where she worked was okay with her. She would be waiting for him in the reception room at ten o'clock, the time of her coffee break.

Frank came out of the elevator into a maze of glass-partitioned offices. The acoustic ceiling sailed away, bearing with it dozens of fluorescent light fixtures. The whole place was filled with a muted clack and hum. How could he possibly speak with the girl here?

The receptionist looked up, saw the collar and tried to conceal her surprise with a functional smile. Almost immediately the sound of tapping heels approached and a girl said, "Father Ascue?"

"That's right."

She was not what he had expected. This was no *femme fatale*. She was not even especially pretty. Regular features, a scrubbed face, gray eyes and brown hair that was pulled back almost severely. She wore a light blue suit. She did not look like a girl who would get involved in an affair, let alone with a priest.

"We can talk down here." She led him among partitions until they came to a lounge in a corner of the floor. There was a coffee urn and he said, yes, he would like a cup. He waited for her to draw another for herself and then they sat. The others in the lounge tried not to stare. Diane sipped her coffee gingerly and Frank followed suit. It was very hot, hot and tasteless.

"You want to talk about Phil," she said.

"Yes." The lounge made him feel uncomfortable though the girl was at ease. He found the role of avuncular cleric difficult enough but in this bright echoing place, so brisk and busy and impersonal, he felt at a special disadvantage.

"Did the bishop send you?"

"Why would you think that?"

She shrugged. He was struck by her resignation, by her indifference to the curiosity of her fellow workers. "Phil told me they had turned him down. I thought perhaps you were sent to make it official."

"Turned him down?"

"His request. To be permitted to leave."

Was she being disingenuous or not? He could not decide. She looked simple as a dove. What had Phil told her? "Had he put in such a request?"

She stared at him for a moment, then her eyes drifted away, thoughtful. "He said he had. I wonder if it was the truth."

Father Ascue gritted his teeth. Had Phil lied to them both?

"It's all over, Diane. You know that, don't you?" He felt warm and uncomfortable. The coffee, perhaps, or the sun streaming through the windows, though the glass seemed to rob it of any salubrious effect.

"Yes, I know."

"What are your plans?" The question was prompted by her forlorn expression. She seemed drained of energy, of interest, of everything. Frank studied the paper cup he held, as if its design were a marvel. "Is this your home town?"

"No." Slowly, as if it were a recording, she told him of coming to Fort Elbow, of getting this job: it had all been something that might so easily not have happened. So many things would not have happened to her if she had not come to Fort Elbow. In her account, none of the things that had happened to her sounded very attractive. Frank became attuned to her mood; he thought of the surface of the globe, crisscrossed with the paths men make: a point of origin, travels to and fro making lines upon the earth which intersected other lines, and the intersections like the lines themselves might so very easily not have been. Eventually the paths stop, grow faint, disappear. There had to be a vantage point on the lives of men which lifted them above such finite tracings of absurdity.

"Why stay here?"

"Is that what they want?" she said quietly. "Is that what Phil wants?" Her voice had dropped until it was scarcely audible.

"It's not what *anyone* wants. I just thought you might find it easier if there were no chance of seeing him again. New friends, new surroundings . . ."

"Are you afraid I'll make trouble?"

"Of course not." The thought had crossed his mind on the way here but from the moment he met her he knew that could not have been the reason for Phil's concern.

"I would have thought they'd want to send him away."

"Diane, nobody wants anybody sent away. I'm here as a friend of Phil's. I'm sorry I mentioned leaving town. Where's your home?"

"In Illinois. I don't want to go back there."

Frank crushed his coffee cup. They both looked at its crumpled remains lying in the palm of his hand.

"Did you know your roommate went to see Phil?"

"She what!" Diane's voice rose, embarrassing them both. For a moment they sat in silence, as if to deny that she had almost shouted.

100

"She's worried about you. And of course when she told Phil he became worried as well. He asked me to come see you, see that you are all right."

"What did Mary tell him?"

"Is that her name?"

"Yes. Mary Muscatelli."

It seemed to Frank that he had already heard that name though he was not sure Phil had not mentioned it. "You know how painful it was to Phil to hear that you're despondent." He swallowed; it was strange to speak of him as Phil with this girl. "He loves you." His voice came forth oddly. "It is not going to be easy for either of you for a very long time."

"I'll go away. You're right. Mary shouldn't have talked to him. I'll go away."

"Do what you think is best, Diane. I'm sure that whatever you decide will be the right thing."

"With my record?"

"We've all made mistakes."

"I'm not a Catholic."

"I know."

"I never saw him in one of those." She meant the collar. "I didn't even know he was a priest at first. Maybe it would have been different if I had known."

"He should have told you."

"Don't blame him. I suppose it all sounds dirty to you. . . ."

"No, not dirty. But wrong. It would have been wrong even if he weren't a priest. The fact that he is a priest, for him, made it terribly wrong. Wrong, not dirty. What is your religion?"

"I haven't any. Not really."

"Do you believe in God?"

The question surprised her. "I think so. Yes, I do."

"Good." And it was good. That image of men crawling pointlessly over the face of the earth seemed to be erased, at least for her.

"Father, would it shock you to know that I don't think it was wrong? Phil and me? I believe in God, yes, but I don't think it was wrong. That we were wrong. We didn't hurt anyone, I mean anyone else."

"I hope you're right. But I wonder. We're all bound together, Diane. Parts of a body. Parts of a play with only minimal stage directions." He stopped. He sounded as if he were in the pulpit, reaching for a metaphor that was pretty obscure in any case. "What you did was wrong and it may have affected others in ways you'll never know. Surely if everyone broke his promises, as Phil did, life would be a mess. When we do things like that we count on others not doing them; we need others in order to be an exception ourselves. I'm not making sense. What we do counts."

"I'm only sorry that it ended. I thought we were going to be married. We both thought so. Maybe for a time it wasn't what it should have been, but we were going to make it right eventually. That's what we meant to do. And then they wouldn't let him. It really broke him up. He cried. A man. He cried and I cried and, oh God, it was awful, but that's all I'm sorry about, that it ended. The God I believe in is in favor of love because there's so darned little of it and when it comes and you have it, it's terrible to have it snuffed out by some stupid rule or promise a man made before he knew what life is all about."

"I'm sorry too, Diane."

"Sorry I'm not sorry?"

He smiled. "Something like that."

She looked at him with a little squinty smile. "You *are* a priest. Through and through. I think anyone would know that, talking with you, no matter what you were wearing."

"Nuns used to tell us that in school. That you could always tell a priest. It's a myth."

"Phil isn't like you."

"Of course he is. As a priest. We were classmates in the seminary. I've known him for years."

"I don't want to know those things about him. For me he isn't a priest. No offense."

"He's a priest, Diane. He always will be. He was tested and I never have been. I pray I never will be."

"I don't think you will be. He was ready for something to happen, I think, almost waiting for it. Oh, we were both ripe for one another when we met. But it wasn't dirty or sneaky or sordid. Nothing like that. We both meant it to be something wonderful."

The very brightness of the hope made the statement sad. They fell silent. The lounge was emptying. Diane sighed and threw back her shoulders. She had to get back to work.

"If you should decide to go, Diane, could you afford it?"

"On my savings I wouldn't get very far."

"If you'd like, I could raise the fare at least. To California, New York . . ."

"Good Lord, do you think I'm pregnant?"

"No. You're not, are you?"

She laughed. "In this day and age?"

"Thank God you're not."

102

"I do. But then I gave him an assist."

They retraced their steps to the elevator—more lines on the globe—where she waited with him until the car arrived. She stood looking at him while the doors cut her from view, a painless guillotine, and his descent to earth began. The poor girl. Something ought to be done for her. Phil had an obligation to her. If Diane decided to go he would collect some money from Phil and pass it on to her. It was the least Phil could do. He could not involve himself in another's life and then simply withdraw. And yet Phil did have to withdraw. The break had to be clean. There was no way out of the pain Diane and Phil had caused themselves. It did not seem fair that Diane was getting a disproportionate share of it.

Garish was on the front porch with the pastor's mother, having lemonade and cookies. Bishop Brophy sat in the rectory office with Jim Grimes, the pastor, wondering if he would have to suggest that they have a drink. Grimes was not one of the wet ones, Brophy was sure of that; such news traveled swiftly. When a priest did go under, it was either Punch or Judy, and if Grimes should slip, which seemed highly unlikely, Bishop Brophy was sure it would be booze. That mother of his might save him—or be his main motive. Mrs. Grimes was a *mulier fortis*, no doubt of that. Poor Grimes. This godforsaken parish in this godforsaken town.

From the front porch there was a perfect view of desolation. The parish house was on the edge of town, and edge in a permanent sense: hills rose perpendicularly, covered with scrub and anemic trees. The street on which the church and rectory stood was unpaved and descended like a draining ditch to the main street. Most foreign missionaries had it better than Grimes.

"Do you ever see Father Sweeney?" Grimes asked. He half sat on a straight-back chair, wringing his hands, smiling wistfully. He might have been asking news of the far side of the world.

"Larry Sweeney?"

Grimes nodded vigorously.

"Once in a while. I don't get over to the seminary much."

"Ah, the seminary," Grimes said.

Brophy was accustomed to the penchant of far-flung pastors for nostalgia. If he let them, they would go down the roster of the diocesan clergy, asking news, recalling anecdotes. In Grimes's case, it would have been cruel to cut him off immediately. Brophy wondered if the man subscribed to the Fort Elbow newspaper. Was there a television in the house? He looked at Grimes more closely. Sometimes priests, cut off like this and thrown on their own resources, engaged in bouts of asceticism which were too often a prelude to its opposite. The next thing you knew they were on the bottle or over the hill. The bishop's eyes went to the window. For Grimes, over the hill would be all too literal a description of his defecting.

"Cigarette, Father?" The bishop shook a package under Grimes's nose.

"No, thank you."

"You don't smoke?"

"Not anymore."

"Worried about your health?"

"Oh, no. It wasn't that." Grimes's eyes dropped and his smile became more shy.

Bishop Brophy smacked his lips. "A long drive dries me out."

"There's loads of lemonade. Would you like a glass?"

Grimes had leaped to his feet and Brophy did not have the heart to stop him. He could not remember when he had last had a glass of lemonade. He did not care to remember when he had last had a glass of lemonade. When Grimes was gone, the bishop turned sighing to the ledger on the desk.

The pity he felt for Grimes was, at least in part, refracted self-pity. He was in the second week of his exile from Fort Elbow, his days filled with driving or conversations like this. One or two confirmations, but mainly visitations. A look at the books, a tour of the plant. How many furnaces had he inspected, nodding through the incomprehensible praise or lamentation? The truth was that he understood very little of the lives of these men. He had never been in a parish, had never known its routine or problems or *modus operandi*, and his ignorance encompassed the financial as well as the physical side. Not that he considered this a deficiency in himself. Specialists were a dime a dozen; he had always preferred the big picture. He did not stay overnight in rectories often; that would have been too much. It did not lessen his depression to realize that the room they gave him and the bed he slept in were very likely the best they had to offer. He preferred motels and a professional boniface. Garish was shocked by the preference, of course. He liked to be near a church. The boy was given to making holy hours in front of the Blessed Sacrament. If he kept it up, he would surely crack. Too intense, too knotted up. Since when did religion have to turn you into a spook who could not carry on a decent conversation? Brophy had taken to riding in the back seat of the car now. The democratic impulse that had prompted him at first to sit up front with Garish had been

104

easily stifled. Now, when Garish spoke, Brophy would grunt and riffle papers and pretend to be busy as the devil back there.

"Here you are, Bishop." Grimes put a sweating glass of lemonade on the desk blotter.

"Everything looks in good shape here, Father." Brophy closed the ledger. Figures bored him and explanations of them bored him more, particularly at this penny-ante level. One had to presume that a pastor knew how to take care of his own shop.

"I hope to start paying off the principal of that loan fairly soon."

Brophy nodded. Loan? But he did not want to reopen the ledger. He picked up the glass of lemonade and applied its cool edge to his lips. "Mmmm," he said, putting it down.

"I've heard that things are pretty bad at the seminary."

"Bad? In what way?"

"Isn't the enrollment way down?"

"Temporarily, yes. Things are rather confusing just now and I suppose many young men who intend to enter the priesthood are holding back until things shake down a bit."

"I wonder. There isn't a single prospect of a vocation, male or female, in this parish. Not one."

"Well, there are many parishes." Brophy had difficulty imagining a future priest emerging from this place, but of course one never knew. Can any good come out of Nazareth?

"Not that I've been instrumental in many vocations anywhere else. In fact, the only vocation I've had a hand in at all is a boy, a young man, now at the seminary. I pray for him every day, Bishop. It upsets me when I hear stories about what's going on there. These liturgical experiments . . ." Grimes shook his head.

"How's the liturgy here, Father?"

"We're following all the diocesan directives. That is, we intend to. Change is slow in a place like this."

"Your altar faces the people, does it?"

"Nooo. It would cost quite a bit of money to turn it around. I'm told that it supports the wall and . . ."

"Most places leave the old altar where it is and put in a temporary one which faces the people."

"You must see our sanctuary. There isn't room for more than one server, even at High Mass. The sanctuary is smaller than this room."

"Well . . ." He had not meant to question Grimes. But these fellows alternated between nostalgia for the city and whining criticism. Brophy had not wanted to encourage Grimes in any jeremiad on the condition of the seminary; that might have led to talk of the hunger strike and the

105

wounds were too fresh. In any case, Grimes had his work cut out for him right here.

"All done?" Mrs. Grimes stood in the doorway, hands under her apron. She might have been Ma Barker concealing a weapon.

"All done, Mrs. Grimes. Where is that young master of ceremonies of mine?"

"He went over to the church. Such a nice young priest."

Brophy frowned at his watch. "We are going to have to press on, he and I."

"Now, Bishop, you must stay for lunch."

"I'd love to, Mrs. Grimes. I'd love to. But my time is not my own."

In his mother's presence, Grimes stood grinning like a little boy. It was clear as day who was running the show here. Probably just as well.

"Let's go find Father Garish," the bishop said to Grimes.

"You can take a look at that sanctuary, Bishop."

"Yes."

On the way to the church, Brophy's eyes were dragged toward the hills. He hadn't been here two hours and already he felt an impulse to take off up the nearest slope as fast as his legs would carry him and put this place forever behind him. He waited for Grimes to fall in beside him and put his arm over the priest's shoulders.

"Quite a parish you have here, Father. Quite a parish."

Both Bob Wintheiser and Gerry Doyle phoned when his appointment to Saint Waldo's appeared in the *Fort Elbow Catholic* and while neither came right out with it, Frank could sense their surprise that he had been assigned to a parish rather than the seminary.

"Have you seen Ewing?" Bob asked.

"Do you know he actually met my plane?"

"Aha. And how is he?"

"The same. You know."

"Good old Ewing."

After a pause into which Frank inserted no further information, Bob suggested that they get together with Gerry for dinner soon. Gerry made the same suggestion and for several weeks they called one another about it but it turned out to be difficult to find an evening when they were all free. Gerry's pastor was ailing and the full burden of the parish had fallen on his assistant. Finally, tiring of postponements, Bob suggested that they go ahead without Gerry. "This kind of fanfare would make the Last Supper a disappointment, Frank. Gerry will understand."

What Bob called two-thirds of the old triumvirate met at a restaurant several miles out of town and Frank was relieved to find Bob more intent on bringing him up to date on local news than on quizzing him about Rome. Not that Bob's range was wide: mainly he wanted to talk about his pastor, a fairly young man named Gilligan who, though he worked Bob hard, worked equally hard himself.

"My chief comfort is that Gilly is sane. This is rare, Frank, very rare. Even in men his age. Believe me, it was a dark day when I confided to him that Bullard and I were classmates." Bob sipped his second drink and crossed his eyes. "Bullard as intellectual, Frank. Bullard in the vanguard. Are these the last days or are they not?"

"Do you ever see him?"

"I'll forget you asked that. My spiritual director won't permit it. That's me. What would we talk about? What the age demands? My God! Get thee to a locker room. Jock in the pulpit. The last days, Frank. Incidentally, Gilly has a beautiful spiel based on the revelations of Malachi. You have to meet him."

Bob babbled on, his petulant mouth moist with drink. He plucked the cherry from his glass and ate it with relish. Bob had put on weight, his face seemed pasty, his hair had noticeably thinned. Frank was finding it difficult to rediscover the old camaraderie and it did not help when he vetoed the suggestion of a third drink. Bob seemed piqued and, after they had ordered, they sat in silence, suddenly aware of the distance three years can put between old friends.

The food, as Bob had promised, was excellent and when after-dinner drinks, courtesy of the house, a lure to the clerical trade, arrived, Bob settled back with a cigarette.

"Do you have many confessions at Saint Waldo's?"

"Enough. I've no basis of comparison, of course, but the three of us are kept busy every Saturday."

Bob's brows rose. "Oh?"

"What's wrong?"

"Ours have fallen off drastically. Contraception, needless to say. Gilly and I are Catholics and that makes us difficult. The simple faithful have learned that all they have to do is shop around to get the advice they want. I trust you people are holding the line."

"I suppose the question is, will the line hold?"

Bob sat forward, shocked. "Are you serious?"

"It's not impossible that there'll be a change, Bob. The pill, some kind of pill, could make it a whole new ball game."

Bob shook his head. "Wow. What kind of advice do you give in the confessional?"

Frank smiled. "The Church's position. What else? I can wait for the pope to give his verdict."

"Frank, if you expect any change, don't hold your breath. There isn't going to be any change. There can't be."

"Is that in Malachi too?"

"I'm serious. I'll bet you a *dinner* that the pope will simply restate the traditional doctrine."

"Why don't we just wait and see?"

"Don't hold your breath."

Frank agreed not to hold his breath. It was harder to hold his tongue. His vanity, he realized, had been stung by Bob's magisterial manner. You would have thought it was Bob who had the doctorate in moral theology. Ah, well. In other circumstances he might have been willing to discuss the matter with him, but not here, not after all those drinks. His head felt light and the real point was Bob's smug assumption that nothing would ever change, that the Church is what it is and will always be the same. What did that mean anyway? Clerical life as they had looked forward to it, dinners out with drinks on the house, laying down the law to the faithful, holding the line? No wonder people became angry with conservatives. Bibulous, speaking too loudly in the restaurant, Bob had revealed a Torquemada streak. Frank wished they had waited until Gerry was free. The evening had not turned out enjoyably at all.

"Where are you parked?" Bob asked when they came out of the restaurant into a night still uncomfortably warm.

"Can I bum a ride? I don't have a car."

Bob stared at him. "How did you get here?"

"Cab."

"Cab! Oh, that won't do. You have to have a car. You'll go broke riding cabs."

The car they went to seemed massive to Frank and Bob drove it with abandon, whisking along the road to town.

"How much did this car cost?"

Bob made a little croaking noise. "Too much. My one indulgence. Of course I got a deal. Hirsch gives a clerical discount, as well he might, selling indulgences. I'd advise you to trade there."

"I'd like to get along without a car if I can."

"You can't."

"We'll see."

Bob shrugged. Frank half expected to be told again not to hold his breath. When they drew up in front of the parish house, Bob turned off the motor.

108

"This is quite a place, Frank. Entweder was one of the builders, you have to give him that. The house air-conditioned?"

"We have air-conditioners."

"No central system?"

"No."

"A mistake. Much cheaper in the long run."

"Would you like to come in?"

"Better not. I have an early Mass." But there was more of overture than farewell in the sound of Bob's inhaling. "About Phil Bullard. Rumor has it that he's leaving."

"Really?" He tried to keep his tone neutral, tried not to feel a secret satisfaction that he knew the truth about Phil, not merely rumors. Of course he could give no indication of that.

"Not much of a surprise really. Everything points that way. Or do you think celibacy will be dropped when the pill is okayed?"

"I'm not making any predictions, Bob."

"Who knows? Maybe polygamy will make it too, if we wait long enough. And cannibalism. Good idea, that. A modest proposal. Solve everything. How would the encyclical be entitled? *De modesto proposito?*"

"Or *Maxima cum celeritate.*"

"The race is not to the Swift." They laughed and briefly it was like old times. Bob turned sideways in his seat. "What I can't take is all the whining. *They* won't let me marry. *They* have robbed me of my rights. They. Who the hell is they? We all knew what we were getting into. God knows we were reminded often enough."

"That's true. But some seem to find celibacy harder than others."

"Of course it's hard," Bob said vehemently. "That's the point of it. It's supposed to be a sacrifice. Whatever happened to the concept of sacrifice?"

"Good question."

"You're darn right."

At the corner a street lamp spilled an eerie light on curb and pavement. The rectory was dark except for a basement window. Frank yawned and Bob reached forward and twisted the ignition key. They agreed to get together again soon, this time with Gerry. Bob did not sound any more eager than he did.

When he got to his room, Frank went immediately to his air-conditioner, hesitated, decided not to turn it on. A little self-denial to balance an evening out. Later, lying in pajamas, no covers, trying to ignore the heat, he thought of the Reverend Robert Wintheiser, classmate, old friend, fellow priest. He almost dreaded seeing Gerry now. What would he be like? Unfair as it no doubt was, he had found Bob dull and repellent. Bob talked of working hard and he probably did but he looked fat and comfortable and had an inflexible answer for everything. Perhaps he was right about the pill, but, damn it, there are wrong ways of being right. Bob acted as if he would take it as a personal vindication, a cause for rejoicing, if the pope did indeed reaffirm the traditional teaching on contraception. Surely he must see that there are difficulties with it. For one thing, it seemed to demand heroic virtue of everyone and that was not like the Church, for whom there was usually a common measure first, the minimum requirement, and then, beyond that, the call to perfection, but as counsel not precept.

Good Lord, it was hot. Frank went to the window and flicked on the air-conditioner, letting the frigid blast ripple his pajamas. So much for mortification. When he returned to his bed, he knelt beside it and tried to pray, as if to justify his technological comfort by lifting his mind to God.

God. He tried to think of God but his mind was invaded by the image of an old bearded man thirty thousand feet above him in the sky. Think of Christ, he advised himself, but that image too was blurred, too much like the simpering picture in the office downstairs where he had first met Entweder. He shook his head. This was terrible. As a priest he was supposed to be another Christ and he could not even summon a convincing image of his model. Christ crucified. The ultimate sacrifice, greater love hath no man . . . But it was Bob he saw, plucking a cherry from his glass.

Frank got to his feet, sat on the edge of the bed and stared across the room where, above his purring air-conditioner, the slats of the blind admitted a pale light and threw a paler ladder on the floor. His hand went to his throat. No Roman collar there now, of course, only mortal flesh, the throat of a man, of a priest. A priest. What did that mean? He had the sudden prescient certainty that in a few years priests would stop wearing distinctive dress, that parish plants like Saint Waldo's would sink hopelessly into debt, be sold off one by one, causing a diaspora of priests and people that would take with it clerical discounts, courtesy after-dinner drinks, fat and complacent *fonctionnaires* like . . .

He stopped the thought, then let it complete itself. Why not? He felt that he was keeping an overdue rendezvous with his own soul. Like Bob Wintheiser. Like Oder. Like himself? He did not wish to exempt himself from the apocalyptic roll. McTear, Eisenbarth, Ewing too, in a way. Yorick. Phil Bullard, Tremplin. Why did the priesthood seem like a jest God was playing on the Church and on mankind? To go down the roster of priests he knew turned up too many he had no desire to emulate.

110

There were others, of course. Entweder, for example, and old Father Sweeney. But they were hardly models for him. Christ was his model, that innocent twisted body on the cross, nailed cruelly, lifted up above the earth on which men pursue a billion conflicting hopes which disguise their single need: eternal happiness with the risen God-Man.

Frank's fundamental vision of Christianity was derived from Chesterton. The cross was a commentary on the world, a mockery of its values, the assertion that the upside-down of failure was true success. That had been grafted onto a realization that he had had one winter afternoon in the sixth grade of Blessed Sacrament school: I shall never cease to be. That truth, conveyed in the flat indicative mood of a catechism answer, became a truth for him. Every man begins but he will exist forever; death, no matter how horrible, is no definite end. Forever and ever and ever, the perpetual motion clock of eternity a measure reducing the ambitions and fears of this testing mortal time to less than the lurch of its second hand. That, then Chesterton, and—surprise, surprise—Feuerbach, an enemy with a clear view of the opposition. The little arc from birth to death was at once comically unimportant and eternally important. Out of the drift of choices, daydreams, aspirations and deeds, a self is constituted which at death clears the last hurdle of alterability. Stale lectures and lively bull sessions in the rec room came back to him. Freedom, determinism, how could God create a soul he knew would be damned? In that dread possibility resides the seriousness of the stakes of life; eternal happiness implied a dark opposite without which freedom was nonsense. So much was clear, beyond one did not go, nor did the Church. The individual soul works out its destiny beyond the reach of finite witnesses. Over those billions of private struggles, which trace a mad geometry upon the earth which only God can read, the cross is raised. The Church is a communion of losers, in the world's eyes, the cross is a message of scandal and folly but, to him with eyes to read, the unique hope. As vehicle of that hope, the Church is a sign of contradiction, its priesthood a conduit of the grace won on Calvary, each priest a servant of the servants of God.

The shock of Bob Wintheiser, as earlier of Phil Bullard, brought Frank to the grim recognition that the ideal which had led him from Blessed Sacrament school to Lake Glister and on to the major seminary, though it had been progressively clarified along the way, had become tarnished too. Hadn't he hoped to make a good thing out of what, in the jargon of his trade, was called a sacrifice? The priesthood on his own terms. A teaching post, a soft satisfying life, the importation of the supposedly rejected standards of measurable success. But this was a night battle they were engaged in where triumph and failure could not be read off events, where even the easy interpretation of failure as success and triumph as defeat could lead to the smug conviction that one was not like the rest of men. Ever since he had come home, Frank had been hearing jeremiads, a description of the days as dark. Perhaps they are, but one man's dark was another's light and it was the human estimate they were supposed to transcend. Criticism could be the mask of pride or the coded concealment of lust. In whatever direction he turned he heard Cassandras complaining that the Church was not making it in the present age and, whether the complaint envisaged a threat to an efficient corporate structure or lamented the lack of attunement with more revolutionary trends, Frank found it hard to see where a human estimate of the role of the Church was distinguished from the unreadable divine direction of it. Seated on the edge of his bed, staring at the ladder of borrowed light which lay upon his floor, its upper rungs leading into darkness, he felt in his bones that the priesthood he had received three years before was going to carry him past all recognizable points of reference into a future known to God alone. The conviction was accompanied by a sensation not unlike that he had felt when his plane took off from Fiumicino and, feet flat on the floor, he realized that beneath the proximate support was only air, that the press of the seat against his back was a parody of security. Man rose above his earthly condition only by defying the laws of nature.

He was sitting there when he heard McTear come up. The switch in the hallway clicked and the thread of light beneath his door stopped competing with the chiaroscuro ladder on his rug. The footsteps of the first assistant might have been emissaries from the matter of fact, dispelling dead-of-night thoughts. But his vigil was not yet over. When Frank lay down and closed his eyes, coaxing sleep, he thought for the first time in years of Margaret.

Margaret! Margaret and Toohy. Eyes opened again, a smile on his lips, Frank stared at the ceiling and wondered what had reminded him of that. It had been thirteen years ago.

There had been a huge advertising backdrop on the stage of the parish school and before a recital or play the audience sat looking at it until eventually it was cranked up and the entertainment began. Local businesses rented space on the screen and, smack in the center, twice as large as any of the others, was the box proclaiming the location of Toohy's Pharmacy. This was only as it should be since Toohy's was the secular center of the parish. It was there that Frank would go during the first empty days of vacation from the preparatory seminary on Lake Glister.

Toohy was in his late forties but his pudgy shape seemed that of a teen-ager, as if no manly physique had intervened between boyish fat and middle-aged spread. His sandy hair was thin, his features merely emergent and his eyes, bright and usually red, the flush of his cheeks and the pocked raw round of his nose, told of his adult vice. Toohy was a drinker and the kind who rises with true contrition to take the pledge whenever the opportunity affords itself. He was a great parish man, too, a perennial officer of one club or another and on Sunday he ushered at two Masses.

While Frank was in grade school Toohy treated him with a generic kindness, but after he had become a seminarian his return to the drugstore was a festive occasion. Toohy would bustle out from the back room where he made up prescriptions and take over from the girl at the soda fountain. She would be sent on a delivery or to the front of the store to shoo kids away from the comic books and Toohy, wearing a funny frowning smile, would make up Frank's sundae with a prodigal disregard for the proper proportions of that delicacy.

"Well, Frank. Not much longer and you'll be going back."

Toohy said this even in early June, when the three months of summer stretched before Frank like an eternity.

"Tell me about it," Toohy would say, and he really meant it. He wanted to hear all about the seminary, when they got up in the morning, the refectory, the dorms, everything. Frank obliged, speaking like a returned sailor to some poor homebody begging to hear of the great world beyond.

"I nearly went myself when I was your age," Toohy said one day.

"You wanted to be a priest?"

"I thought of little else." Toohy smiled wistfully and his fat fingers counted the pens and pencils thrust into the breast pocket of his pharmacist's jacket. "I never really forgot."

"Why didn't you go?"

Toohy hummed and shook his head. He had taken a paper napkin from the chrome dispenser on the counter and folded it over and over until it was a wadded triangle which resisted reduction to smaller versions of its essential shape.

"A good question, Frank. A good question." Toohy put his hand on Frank's arm. "You stay with it, Frank. I mean it. When you're my age, you'll know it's the only life. Other things . . ." His hand went out in an impatient arc, dismissing the store, the street outside, the world itself. "Glitter. Don't let it fool you. It's all nothing. Everything."

Toohy's mention of his thwarted hopes embarrassed Frank, though he found he was not surprised. The druggist's deference eventually became annoying, however, and Frank began to suspect that one of

Toohy's motives in rushing out to the soda fountain was to prevent his talking with the counter girl, Margaret. Sometimes Frank did not even get to the fountain, having been waylaid by Toohy when he came into the store.

In her starched white uniform, a cap atop her deep black hair, Margaret reigned at the fountain, parrying with practiced authority the advances of the boys who came in droves to see her. Because of Toohy, because of his vocation to the priesthood, Frank was excluded from the worshipful throng and he wasn't sure he liked it.

"It's no picnic at the seminary," Frank said once, stopping Toohy's lyrical effusions. Margaret stood a few feet from them, leaning against a counter, indolently twisting a lock of hair as she read the instructions on the back of a home permanent kit. She became aware of Frank's eyes and looked up.

"Of course it isn't," Toohy said. "Whoever thought it was? It is a difficult life. But not too difficult, is it? You make up your mind and the Good Lord does the rest."

Frank got to know Margaret only because, quite by accident, he ran into her at the beach. He had spread his blanket on the sand and gone down to the water. The day was hot but the lake was cold and he stooped to rub water gingerly on his legs and arms. When he straightened, a girl in a white suit emerged a few feet out from where he stood. She tugged at the fastener of her cap and when she pulled it off the dry surprise of her hair contrasted with the wet suit clinging to her body, revealing small breasts.

"Hi," she said.

"Hello, Margaret."

They stood talking in the shallow water, she decided to go back in, afterward they sat together on his blanket. It was late afternoon when they left the beach. It was that easy and it was wonderful. He assumed that she did not know where he went to school but, in the car, going back to town, she said, "Tell me about it."

"What?"

"The seminary."

"You're as bad as Toohy. That's all he ever wants to talk about." Didn't she realize that he wasn't supposed to go out with girls? Not that meeting her at the beach was a date.

"I just want to know what it's like."

"Some other time, okay?"

At her house, she scrambled from the car, thanked him and ran to her door.

The next day he entered the drugstore and went directly to the

114

fountain, where he ordered a Coke before Toohy had a chance to put in an appearance. For several days his luck held and he managed to spend hours with Margaret. She would come around the counter and take a stool next to his and their reflection in the mirror was needed proof that this was really happening. Toohy, busy with prescriptions, looked on in dismay from the back of the store. And finally the pharmacist intercepted him on the walk outside.

"Frank," he began, and then seemed to forget a speech he had prepared.

"I'm not going back, Mr. Toohy." Frank startled himself with this flat announcement and he could not meet Toohy's weak red eyes.

"Don't say that, Frank."

"It's true. I've made up my mind."

"You're just having a spell, Frank. A moment of weakness."

"No. I don't have a vocation."

"How do you know? What do you expect, a visit from an angel? It's not like that, as you know perfectly well. You simply make up your mind."

"I have." Why did it seem cruel to insist upon it? "I'm not going back." Once said, the surprising sentence was easy to repeat.

"It's the girls, isn't it? Well, they're fine creatures and that's the truth. But they change, Frank, and you'll change too and what then? Do you want to end up like me, selling comic books and cigarettes and Kleenex and aspirin? Frank, you don't want that." Toohy looked at his store as if the sight of it made him sick.

"I don't know what I'll do, Mr. Toohy. Maybe I'll be a doctor. I don't know."

"That's not for you," Toohy said with finality. He grew agitated and gripped Frank's arm. "Look, I'll pray for you. All summer. I'll go to Mass every day. I won't drink." He received Frank's wondrous look with weary dignity. "I drink, Frank. Yes. I supposed you knew. God knows I've tried to stop. You can't understand that any more than I could at your age. But I'll stop now. For you. As a penance."

"Please, Mr. Toohy . . ."

"I want to, Frank. It's a special grace. For both of us. You'll see."

After Toohy's promise, or threat, Frank broke away and started home. When he looked back, Toohy still stood in front of his store, smiling with unsettling determination. The druggist waved in a benevolent, menacing way.

That night, after supper, Frank went out to the backyard, where his uncle was chipping with a nine iron.

"Uncle Harry, do you know Mr. Toohy at the drugstore?"

Uncle Harry lofted a ball with a meek metallic splut; it went its errant way and clattered against the garbage can. "What about Toohy?"

"Maybe I won't go back to the seminary." How easy it was to say that now, at least to Uncle Harry. He could not imagine telling Charlotte or Aunt Mildred.

His uncle continued to swing his club. "What's that got to do with Toohy?"

Frank told him. His uncle took the story as calmly as he had Frank's statement that he was not going back to the seminary. It was odd that Mr. Toohy took it so much more seriously.

"Toohy's a funny bastard," Uncle Harry said, inspecting the grip he had on his club. "But he's a good pharmacist. I don't know how many doctors have told me he's the best in the business. That's surprising, I guess. Or maybe not. I've never believed the stories that he drinks on the job."

"Does he really drink? Get drunk?"

"It's a sickness with him, Frank. In the end it will kill him. He knows that as well as anyone."

"He says he's going to quit now. I'm sure he meant it."

"I wouldn't worry about it."

"Don't you think he meant it?"

"I'm sure he means it every time he quits." Uncle Harry brought his club down and sent a massive divot flying. "I didn't know that Toohy was a spoiled priest." He retrieved the divot and tamped it back into place with the toe of his shoe. "You never know about people."

"I don't want to be his motive."

"I said not to worry about it. You just do what you want to do."

For several days Frank stayed away from the drugstore and from Margaret. In the morning he went to Mass and Toohy was always there. The sight of him, erect in a front pew, filled Frank with annoyance and dread. One night when Jim Mullen phoned and asked him over, Frank went by Scott's Bar, where Toohy had always hung out.

Jim said, "Say, old Toohy quit drinking."

"How do you know?"

"My brother Ed. Toohy hasn't been to Scott's all week. The regulars can't believe it."

"Maybe he's sick."

"That's what Scott thought. But he phoned and Toohy's fine."

"Did he say why he quit?"

"It's not the first time, you know. Toohy's a pretty religious guy. Probably took the pledge again."

They shot baskets behind the Mullen garage, using up the waning light, and when it got too dark for that, they went inside the garage, where Jim tinkered importantly with the engine of his car. This got boring for Frank and, after half an hour, when Jim had the entrails of the car spread around the garage, Frank went home.

At the corner, waiting to cross, he was aware of Scott's Bar behind him. A sharp smell of beer and liquor, a genial cacophony, drifted from the place. That was where Toohy should be and wasn't. His absence was a sign and portent, a judgment on Frank's attraction to Margaret and his desire to leave the seminary. Without really making it explicit, he had been praying that Toohy would get roaring drunk and set him free and the prayer was as much a bargain as Toohy's abstinence. But what if Toohy was right? Margaret, this summer, could be merely a passing weakness, a moment when he was being tested. What if he was turning away from the one life he was meant for? He remembered his uncle's words. In the end it will kill him. Was that what he had been praying for? Toohy's life seemed a high price to exact for his freedom. An amorphous, hedonist future with Margaret, with someone like Margaret anyway, the object of his recent dreams, seemed silly and self-indulgent.

Frank turned to look back at the bar and saw Toohy. He was crossing the room unsteadily, carrying a glass with tender concentration. For a full minute after he had disappeared from view Frank did not move, and then he rushed into Scott's, where he found Toohy sitting in a booth.

Toohy's eyes were pinched shut. His fat hands held the glass and in his abjectness he looked angelic. His eyes opened and he saw Frank and with the shock age took possession of his face. Frank felt a hand on his arm and then a bartender was propelling him to the door. "Frank," Toohy called after him. "Frank, wait." At the door the man let go of his arm and Frank went unaided into the night with Toohy at his heels. They faced one another on the sidewalk and tears stood in Toohy's eyes.

"I tried," he pleaded. His features jumped in the flickering light of the neon sign above them and he seemed to be having difficulty making out Frank's face. "I tried, but I failed you."

"That's not true, Mr. Toohy. It was my fault."

"Your fault?"

"In the store, with Margaret . . ." He could not say it. "I'm sorry, Mr. Toohy."

Toohy blinked and shook his head. "No, no. You're not responsible for me. Good God, I've been a failure for years and years."

"You're not a failure. You're a good man. Everybody knows that."

"I'm a wretch. A drunken wretch."

117

"It's a sickness. My uncle said so. And he told me you're the best druggist in town."

"He said that?"

"Yes, he did."

"He's a kind man."

Frank clenched his fists and stared at a spot above Toohy's head. "I'll go back to the seminary if you stop drinking." Margaret slid past his mind, moving down a slope of time. Her hand reached out, seeking his, but his arms were too leaden to move. All that was drifting away from him. He would never know it.

"Good God." Toohy was aghast.

"I'll go back, Mr. Toohy. But you have to stop drinking."

"You'll sacrifice yourself for me, is that it?"

"You have to promise."

Toohy tried to smile. He moved his head slowly from side to side. Frank felt deflated. "We're birds of a feather, Frank. Look, I'll tell you what. Let's agree to let one another alone. You do what you want to do, Frank. I won't bother you again."

Toohy was releasing him. Margaret was being summoned back, like Lazarus from the grave. Frank found he did not welcome her resurrection.

"It will kill you, Mr. Toohy."

"I know, Frank. That or something else. Don't worry about me."

After a moment, Frank dashed across the street. He ran for two blocks before he stopped to look back at the square of light that was Scott's. Had Toohy gone back inside? It no longer seemed Frank's business.

It was not the drink that killed Toohy but lung cancer. A nonsmoker, he was fifty-two. At the time, Frank was in the first year of the major seminary. For some months he remembered Toohy in his prayers but then he had been forgotten, forgotten like Margaret. What had happened to her? Certainly she would not remember him. There had been nothing between them, not really, and anyway he had been only one of many who had fallen half in love with her that summer. Whatever had brought the memory back now brought with it the shame he had felt at how easily he had considered leaving the seminary. Thank God he had never been tempted again. Perhaps his immunity was a result of that strange set of bargains he and Mr. Toohy had tried to strike with one another that summer ten years ago.

From a window in Sister Eloise's classroom on the second floor of the parish school, Frank looked down at the playground, where many kids

118

still lingered though school had been out for half an hour. They seemed reluctant to leave. Dribbled basketballs, a dozen unrelated metronomes, measured the going of the afternoon; aspiring pitchers, warming up for imaginary games, were encouraged by the mimicked chatter of their catchers; girls played hopscotch, skipping one-legged like laughing casualties from square to square. An unseasonal football carried its imprisoned air in a long arc to a racing receiver whose hands could not quite gather in the ball and glory.

"How long do they stay?" Frank asked Sister Eloise.

"As long as we'll let them. It's this way every day. Haven't you noticed?"

But of course Frank's day was not divided by the ringing of the school bells. When he did hear them, they did not signal for him as they would for Sister Eloise the beginning of recess or the end of the school day. Now that he thought of it, there seemed always to be the sound of kids on the playground, from early morning until almost suppertime.

"What bothers me, Father, is that in a week or so school'll be over and most of these kids have absolutely nowhere to go and nothing to do during the vacation. There are a hundred ways for them to get into trouble, of course, and we have no contact with them for three months."

Sister Eloise put her elbows on the windowsill and looked sadly down at the playing kids.

"Especially the eighth-graders, Father. This summer they're neither fish nor fowl. They won't be coming back here and they're not yet in high school really."

"Do they play here during the summer?"

"Nope."

"Where? Down in the park?"

"Not these kids. Most of those out there now are from the upper end of the parish. You know what that's like."

Frank knew; he had taken census there. The buildings were pressed against one another, a continuous erratic mass on either side of the narrow streets; on street level there were stores, many empty, their dusty windows sad with fingered graffiti, others bars, groceries, wholesale outlets, unsavory bookshops. Traffic clogged the streets. Climbing the narrow stairways of those buildings, Frank had held his breath against the odor of mildew and worse.

"Why *don't* they come down here?"

Sister Eloise turned toward him. "Because they couldn't get in. The

119

gym is locked, the school is locked, the gates of the playground are locked."

"But why?"

"It has something to do with insurance. And of course there would have to be someone here to supervise."

Frank looked at the vast expanse of the playground, anger leaping in him. What a waste for that to go unused all summer, particularly when you considered the alternative awaiting those kids. He could see the far gate and he imagined it closed, locked, and these kids outside for months. And just because of a little money for insurance!

"That's crazy, Sister. This place ought to be available to them. It's their parish."

"Of course it should be. But how?"

Insurance. And supervisors too. The nuns did not stay here during the summer but went to their mother house on the other side of the river.

"I don't know. But I'm going to find out. We ought to have a parish summer program. I can't believe that the insurance would be so high that the money for it couldn't be raised. And there must be parishioners, older kids, kids home from college, who would run it."

"Oh, Father, will you do it?" She took his arm and looked at him as if she feared he did not mean what he said.

"Of course I will."

They sat on desktops and talked of what a summer program could be. All the parish facilities would be used; there could be a recreation program during the day, and, several nights a week, dances in the gym. There would be picnics, trips to the museum and the zoo. As they talked, Frank imagined the parish plant blooming with a vitality it had never had before.

He said, "The most important thing would be to get someone really good to run the whole program."

"I'll do it!"

"You? How could you? Don't you have to—"

"No! I'll get special permission. I know I could. This is terribly important and I just know that Mother Superior would see that."

It became the topic of conversation whenever they met during the next two days. The nun's animated expression when she spoke of the program seemed the reflection of his own excitement. The idea might so easily not have come and it had been an inspiration, one they had to follow through on, for the sake of those kids, for the sake of Saint Waldo's.

The second day, Sister Eloise made Frank sit in the front row of her classroom, scooted around her desk and pulled open a drawer. She brought out a large card, which she placed in the chalk tray and leaned against the blackboard. The card was a psychedelic burst of colors from which, like numbers in a test for color blindness, a legend emerged. ST. WALDO'S YOUTH CLUB.

"What do you think?"

"Did you do it yourself?"

"So I'm not an artist."

"No, I like it. Sister, are you sure you'll be able to be here this summer?"

She made a face. "Are you sure you can convince the pastor?"

"Convince him? What I have to do is see about money for the insurance policy. Then I'll talk to him."

"That's the way to do it. They only understand *faits accomplis.*"

She made the phrase sound like "fat accomplices." Frank pulled in his stomach. Hilda was a sensational cook who seemed bent on making those she fed as ample as herself. He did not know how McTear remained so spare and the pastor almost gaunt.

"I could get some other sisters to help. Young ones, who wouldn't spook the kids. Phil Bullard said that some of the college kids who come to his Center would be glad to help."

"You talked with Father Bullard about this?"

"He'll keep it quiet. I told him it was still very hush-hush. He was so helpful and enthusiastic."

Frank tried not to feel resentment that she had talked with Phil. When? Where? He said, "He's had a lot of experience with this sort of thing."

"He liked the way we're going about it. Do what has to be done and nuts with superiors. Well, maybe not nuts. The thing is, if you hit them with a well-planned project, they have to come along with you."

"A *fait accompli?*"

"Right."

Was she thinking of her mother provincial or of Sister Gretchen, who was principal of the school as well as superior of the parish convent? Unlike Sister Eloise, the principal continued to wear the traditional habit of the order; her one concession to change had been to reassume her baptismal name, a choice that could not have been difficult. Her religious name had been Sister Henry. Sister Eloise was certainly capable of making the summer program work. If the kids needed the program, maybe she did too. Frank found her puzzling; so much of the time her wit was aimed against the life she had chosen. But then he was puzzled by the whole concept of nuns, at least those who taught school, maybe even those who were nurses in hospitals. Contemplative nuns, buried away in their convents, walled off from the world—that he could understand, even envy as he sometimes envied the Trappists. But other nuns seemed to be like the eighth-grade graduates Sister Eloise had mentioned, neither fish nor fowl. They were neither in the world nor out of it and, unlike priests, had no distinctive role to play. Now, with the disappearance of the habit, the one thing that had set them apart, their status was more ambiguous than ever. Frank felt that there was some deficiency in his view, some radical flaw, but he did not know what it was. Sister Eloise obviously saw the job of directing the summer program as just the sort of thing a nun should do. Well, it was certainly something that should be done.

"Have you found out yet what sort of insurance policy is needed, Father? How much money will you have to raise?"

"I'm going to talk with someone about that tonight." Frank had been invited to the Rupps' for dinner and Arthur Rupp had an insurance agency. "I'll let you know."

Sheila Rupp was a beautiful girl. By the alchemy of genetics her pudgy father and angular mother had produced a willowy girl who seemed taller than she was and whose eyes, when they moved about the room, seemed full of both wisdom and innocence. She stood six feet from Frank in the Rupp living room, which was filled with conversation and smoke. Whenever their eyes met she seemed to be wondering what Frank made of this. Next to her was a man who spoke out of the corner of his mouth, his eyes narrowed, and Sheila listened to him with the professional politeness Frank associated with airline stewardesses. Her judgment remained confined to her eyes. She looked at Frank again and this time her brows lifted.

"Do you ever fly to Rome?" Frank had almost shouted, and even at that she cupped a hand to her ear.

"Rome," he repeated, as if to a lip reader. She understood. She nodded. She began to move toward him but was detained by the man with the narrow eyes.

Frank subsided into silence. They had put him in a thronelike chair near the fireplace after a crazy passage through the room and a haze of introductions. Arthur Rupp was sitting on the piano bench, his feet just reaching the floor. Though he was nearly bald, his being perched there like that gave him a little-boy look. Frank could imagine what his host had looked like forty years ago. Clara Rupp, in a velvet hostess suit with bell-bottom slacks, was trying unsuccessfully to unify the group,

122

which was fragmented into half a dozen different conversations. She threw a despairing glance at Father Ascue.

The others had apparently come very early for cocktails and had had several before he arrived. Speech was slurred, eyes were too bright, the laughter tending toward the uncontrolled. Father Ascue decided to see what names he could remember. Maud and Dick Bently were together on the couch. Small and thin-legged, her wound-up hair piled like a dunce cap on her head, Maud was leaning forward, the stem of her glass pinched in a trinity of thumb and fingers, tapping with her free hand the knee of the man to whom she was speaking. He was Henry Meyer of Meyer's Condiments (Jams, Jellies, Cider and Apple Butter), whose wife, Peg, was in the twin of Father Ascue's throne on the other side of the fireplace. Mrs. Meyer had been flipping through copies of *National Review, Triumph* and *Twin Circle* pulled from the overflowing rack beside her. Next to her was a Mrs. Fish, who spoke rapidly and with darting eyes, as if she would like to disclaim ownership of her mouth. The man with Sheila Rupp was not Mr. Fish. His name was Fred and he was at least a decade younger than Mrs. Fish.

"Care for another, Father?" It was Sheila Rupp. Frank got to his feet.

"No, I'm fine."

"Few are." She glanced around the room. "You were wise to come late. They seem determined to numb their taste buds before we sit down to eat. Why did you ask about Rome?"

"Mainly to say something." His throat felt raw. The room was filled with smoke. "I spent some years there."

"Did you like it?"

"More or less."

"I see all kinds of cities, but of course I never stay long enough to visit more than the obvious places. After a while they blend into one indistinguishable glob. Except Fort Elbow, of course."

"This is a nice house."

She looked at him. "You're making conversation again."

"I know. But it is a nice house."

"I don't live here."

They were distracted by Maud Bently, who had succeeded where Clara Rupp had failed. She had everyone's attention now and she had a darling story. It concerned a bat in their upstairs. "And I don't mean yours truly," she said, rolling her eyes. She spoke very loudly and with exaggerated slowness, as if each word were a separate task. "I screamed, needless to say, and called Dick and told him to get that goddam bat out of there." Her mouth rounded in mock shame and she covered it with a many-ringed hand, winking at Father Ascue. Her husband did not oblige, being as much afraid of bats as she. Well, *she* went after it then, with a towel, and managed to knock it down and clamp a wastebasket over it. Then she called the Humane Society and they told her to call the police. When the police arrived, Maud met them at the door. "I said to this great big doll of a cop, 'He's upstairs, in the bedroom. He must have come in a window. I knocked him down and I think he's dead.' So he pulled out this great big gun, dears, and went loping up the stairs. He came upon Dick, who had been cowering in the bathroom during all my heroics, slammed him against the wall and began to frisk him." She looked at her husband, who stuck out his tongue.

"But why would they pick on Dick?"

"I thought you'd never ask. What a comedy of errors. The police had not been told it was a bat. And Dickie boy was so startled he could not utter one word and, honest to God, if I hadn't intervened, they would have driven away with him."

"But, Maud, don't you see? He was escaping!"

Dick assumed a silly smile and nodded vigorously.

"Dick?" Maud snorted. "Fat chance."

"Maud is sloshed," Sheila said.

"You may be right."

"I am and we'll all regret it. She is a very silly drunk."

Some minutes later, Father Ascue was joined by Arthur Rupp. It was necessary to refuse once more another drink. Frank began to suspect that dinner was still a long way off.

"Are many of these people in Te Deum?"

"Most of them are charter members."

"Is that so?"

"You should come to our meetings. I'm chairman, you know."

"Congratulations."

"It's a lot of work, a lot of grief. But if we're not ready to sacrifice for our convictions, where are we? Right?"

Frank nodded and said, "You're in insurance, aren't you?"

"Rupp Insurance." It was Maud Bently. She stood teetering next to Arthur. "That always makes me think of trusses, for some reason. You see, I had this doll when I was a little girl. My father was a pharmacist, right here in Fort Elbow, God rest his soul. He brought home this doll for me, all dressed up—he'd had the clothes made special—but it wasn't an ordinary doll. An adult doll, if you know what I mean. When I undressed it, it turned out to be one of those little figures truss companies gave to druggists, to advertise their wares. I mean it was wearing a truss, you know?"

124

Arthur knew. He glanced at Father Ascue. Maud saw that.

"Now, Art, stop treating me like a drunk. That's not fair."

"It never entered my mind."

Maud put a clawlike hand on Father Ascue's sleeve and said in a stage whisper, "Arthur is such a big shot since we elected him chairman of Te Deum. Underneath it all, he's really a nice guy—truss and all." She whooped, slapped Arthur on the back and teetered away.

"Sorry, Father."

"Don't be silly."

"I wish Maud wouldn't be. But she always is."

"Do you hold the policies on the parish property?"

Arthur Rupp gave him his undivided attention. "Yes, I do. What is it, a claim of some sort?"

"Oh, nothing like that. I wanted to know about liability on the playground, that sort of thing."

"Is Monsignor Entweder concerned about it?"

"This is for my own information."

Dinner was announced and Arthur said they must get together on this later. Frank was sorry he had brought up the matter. This was just not the propitious occasion he had hoped it would be.

The veiled warnings about Maud Bently were shown to be understatements once they had sat down to table. Fred was seated next to Maud and immediately she snuggled up to him, clutching his arm, wrinkling her nose, pushing her face to within inches of his.

"Take it easy, Maud," Dick Bently said.

"Take it easy, Maud," she mimicked. "It used to be Come into the garden, Maud. Now it's Take it easy." She reached for her wineglass and toppled it.

In the ensuing commotion, Maud looked pleased. The maid came in and slipped something under the cloth. Maud asked for more wine.

"I've spilled mine," she explained.

Arthur hesitated, but decided to pour.

"Did I tell you my joke about Rastus?" Maud asked.

"Oh, no!" Dick Bently groaned, smiling sickly.

"Well, there was this big buck Negro and his friend came up to him and asked whatever happened to Beulah and Rastus say Why she dead. Dead? I dint even know she was sick. She done bled to death. Izzat so? What she have? Syphilis." Silence descended over the table and Frank felt all eyes darting to him. He looked receptively at Maud and she went on. "Syphilis! Rastus, you don't bleed to death from syphilis. And Rastus say, Man, you does when you gives it to me."

Maud exploded in laughter and so did Fred and finally, if only in

125

self-defense, the rest joined in. Sheila caught Father Ascue's eye, lifted her brows, smiled an apology. Arthur Rupp glowered. Maud tipped over another glass of wine.

"That's all for you, sweetie," her husband said.

"That's all for you, sweetie," Maud echoed.

Beside her, Fred began to croon the words. For the rest of the night, every other remark was to remind Fred of a song and set him singing. Maud wanted to know if he knew "Romeo in the Clover." Fortunately he did not respond. At the moment, he was in a falsetto rendition of "The Sheik of Araby."

Later, when Maud spilled coffee on Fred's arm, it was impossible to think it accidental. The tablecloth in front of her was discolored by wine, her water had been discreetly removed and now the coffee! Fred leaped to his feet, his sleeve drenched, trying not to give vent to the rage he clearly felt. The maid led him away. The food had been largely wasted; for the most part the diners had mashed it, picked at it, rearranged it while drinking wine. Sheila Rupp seemed more bored than surprised or embarrassed by the antics. Clara's tolerant smile seemed directed at a table other than the one before her. Arthur smoldered. All the scene had lacked was for Fred, before the deluge, to intone "Te deum laudamus."

When they finally left the table and adjourned to the living room for brandy and more coffee, Frank felt less than *compos mentis* himself. Can one become drunk by osmosis?

"They were worse than usual," Sheila assured him.

"A delicious meal."

"I know. Poor Grace goes to so much trouble. She might have served hot dogs."

When Arthur Rupp suggested that they go to his den to talk about the insurance on the parish plant, Frank, reluctant now, agreed. Arthur listened to the idea for using the school and grounds during the summer vacation with neither enthusiasm nor disinterest. He took out a pencil and began to doodle on a pad.

"What I need, Arthur, is some rough idea of the cost so I can approach possible donors with it."

"Donors."

"I hope parishioners will want to come up with the amount needed."

"I see."

"It's such a good idea that I don't think I'll have much trouble."

"Has Monsignor Entweder agreed about the donors?"

"I haven't spoken with him about this yet. I want to get the facts first."

"That's not his way of doing things, donors. He's what you might call a general revenue man. No special collections, nobody's name on windows and pews and what-not as donor. Besides . . ."

Frank waited. His notion that Arthur would snap up the role of donor seemed a mad dream now.

"This whole thing just doesn't sound like the sort of thing Monsignor Entweder would go along with. Not that it isn't a good idea. It is. It is an excellent idea."

"I knew you'd think so."

"Of course I do." Arthur stood. "We must talk about it again. After you've discussed it with Monsignor Entweder. These figures should help."

Frank felt pleased when he took the piece of paper Arthur handed him. Sister Eloise would have been proud. Not that she wouldn't have been far more adroit and devious in trying to pry a donation out of Arthur here and now. There was no rush. He and Arthur could talk again after he had gone to the pastor with the idea. However absurd and embarrassing this evening had been, it seemed redeemed by the little talk with Arthur.

"Sheila likes you, Father," Clara Rupp said. "I can tell."

Frank looked at his hostess, but her expression was one of maternal concern.

"You have a fine daughter, Mrs. Rupp."

"Call me Clara. We worry about her nonetheless, Father. That's part of being a parent, I know."

"I wouldn't think she would give you cause for worry."

Sheila had seemed the one sane person here.

"She doesn't live with us, you know."

"She mentioned that."

"Did you have much of a chance to talk?"

"No, not really."

"I do wish you could talk with her sometime, really talk. Young people get so confused nowadays. I don't blame them, understand; the world has become a very confusing place. I just have a hunch that if you were to, oh, remind Sheila of things, she would listen."

It was all very enigmatic but Frank doubted that anything serious lay behind Clara Rupp's concern. After the debacle of the dinner, he could easily see why Sheila might not want to live with her parents. Not much later he was thanking the Rupps, with unction and a straight face, for a delightful evening. When he got outside, the cool night air and high sky pierced with a thousand stars seemed waiting to verify the phrase. It was indeed a delightful evening.

3 Father Ascue, at the window of his room to adjust the air-conditioner, looked out and saw Phil Bullard talking with Sister Eloise on the playground. He tossed his breviary onto his bed and went downstairs. He had been wanting to talk with Phil ever since he had spoken with Diane but whenever he remembered and called the Center Phil was out. Hilda smiled and revved her mixer when he went through the kitchen, and stepping outside, Frank was hit by the heat and the dazzling brightness of the sun. He stopped to catch his breath, shaded his eyes and saw that Phil and the nun had turned at the slam of the door. Caloric waves rising from the asphalt made them ripplingly unreal and as he went toward them he half expected that they would dissolve and disappear before he reached them.

"Here's our fund raiser now." The tip of Sister Eloise's nose was red from the sun, her eyes were hidden behind dark glasses, her smile was merry.

Phil extended his hand. "Hi, Frank. We've been speaking about Sister's idea for a summer program. It sounds great."

"It'll sound greater when the pastor approves it."

"Of course he'll approve it." Phil stopped. "I take that back. Pastors are likely to do anything, as I ought to know."

"It's only a matter of insurance," Sister Eloise said, but her manner had altered. Frank felt that he had been the bearer of bad news.

They stood talking in the sun for ten minutes and though sweat ran down Phil's forehead it did not dampen his enthusiasm. He promised a terrific bunch of kids to help out during the summer; he would be glad to help himself, just so Entweder did not learn of it. Frank could not help thinking that the pastor would never recognize Phil as a priest. He was wearing suntans and a black T-shirt; his brown canvas shoes had crepe soles and he moved about as he talked, on the balls of his feet, a boxer in training.

"Could I borrow Phil, Sister?" Frank asked when there was a lull in the exuberant planning. "There's something I have to ask him."

Phil frowned, or squinted against the sun—it was difficult to say which. He had really warmed to the subject, there in the sun. Sister Eloise said she had to get back to the convent anyway. She had been holding her veil and now draped it over her head.

"Back to my disguise as Clark Kent. Or was it Lois Lane?" Half skipping, she went across the asphalt toward the convent.

"About Diane," Frank said.

Phil did frown then, and looked over his shoulder to see if the nun might have overheard. But he was smiling when he took Frank's arm.

"Let's get out of this sun, all right?"

"We can go over to the rectory."

"I'd rather not."

They settled for the shade of the loggia but this did not get them out of the heat.

Phil said, "You saw her?"

"Yes. How have *you* been, Phil?"

"Keeping busy. Very busy. It's not as difficult as I had feared it would be. It's a lot easier than I deserve."

"It's been hard on Diane. I can see why you were worried about her. She seems lifeless, fatalistic, I don't know what. Phil, we talked of the possibility of her leaving town. Just getting away. I don't know if she will, but I hope so. I think that would be best."

Phil nodded. "That is a good idea."

"The only wrinkle is that she can't afford to."

"Afford to?"

"Money."

"Oh." Phil shook his head sympathetically but his expression was that he might have worn when hearing that some stranger was unable to take a trip.

"Could you come up with the fare if she decides to leave? I don't mean that you should give it to her directly, of course. I'll be the intermediary. She doesn't have to know where it comes from."

"You want me to pay her way out of town?" Phil was shocked.

"It's not much to ask. You're the main reason why it would be best for her to get away. I have a suspicion that she would like to leave. Can you raise the money?"

"How much?"

Why didn't he just say yes, damn it? He was annoyed that Phil should be so calculating. He had no idea of the amount; that depended on where Diane wanted to go. If she really did want to go.

"I'll tell you what, Frank. Find out how much and let me know. Of course I'll try to come up with something."

"I'll let you know," Frank said crisply.

"I do appreciate the trouble you've gone to, Frank." Phil picked a leaf from a bush beside the loggia. "It's a funny thing. Sometimes I can't believe that any of that happened. With Diane. I've really turned my back on it. That's good, isn't it?"

Frank agreed that that was good. When Phil had gone, when he was back in his room with his breviary, he repeated to himself that, yes, it was good that Phil had been able to forget Diane. If only the transition had not seemed so effortless. He recalled the vacant expression on Diane's face, her listlessness. She had obviously been more deeply affected than Phil.

Sister Eloise had called him the fund raiser and that was about how he felt: he might have to scare up the money for Diane's going, if she went, as well as for the insurance, in case Entweder should consider that to be an impediment to the summer program. Arthur Rupp had called to give him a more accurate quotation on the policy but there had been nothing like an offer of a donation from him, not even when Frank inquired again about potential donors.

"I'm afraid I can't be much help to you there, Father. Maybe Monsignor Entweder would have some ideas."

But of course he could not put it to the pastor yet. This had to be a fat accomplice. His mind turned to the affluent section of the parish and alighted almost immediately on Miss Simpson. But when he telephoned he was told she was in the hospital.

"The hospital!"

"Saint Luke's. She went in yesterday."

"Is it something serious?"

The maid was uncommunicative and repeating that he was Father Ascue did not loosen her tongue. When he had hung up, Frank went to tell Monsignor Entweder.

"Yes, I heard. The poor woman." Entweder shook his head. "A devout person, Father. We must pay her a visit as soon as possible."

Entweder's orders, if they could be called that, were usually oblique. Frank said he would go down immediately.

At the hospital, he first sought out the chaplain, Bill Keegan. Keegan was a legendary priest who had been hospital chaplain for a dozen years, never took a vacation and was said to relax by sight-reading Homer. A nun in a white habit, the old-fashioned habit, took Father Ascue to the chaplain's office and said she would fetch Father Keegan. But nearly half an hour went by before the priest appeared.

"Simpson?" Keegan's eyes seemed to dim in their pouches.

"She's a parishioner of ours. An elderly woman."

"Oh, I know who she is. She has Dr. Rather and that's something anyway. He's good."

"It's serious?"

"Terminal cancer. I thought you knew."

He wanted to say that he had had no idea that Miss Simpson was ill but of course he did, he just had not taken the signs seriously. Her trip to Rome and Fatima and Lourdes must have been a last desperate gamble, although desperate did not seem quite the word for Miss Simpson.

"Can she have visitors?"

"Who's going to stop a priest? Go see her. It'll do her a lot of good."

He had almost hoped that Keegan would tell him Miss Simpson could not see anyone, that she should be left alone. What do you say to a dying woman?

"Weren't you in Rome, Father?" Keegan asked.

Frank looked at him. Rome. That seemed a very long time ago. He nodded.

"I've always wanted to visit Rome," Keegan said wistfully. His phone rang and the expression disappeared. Frank rose to go and the chaplain lifted a hand in farewell, his attention on the phone.

In the corridor, at the desk where he was given the number of Miss Simpson's room, and in the elevator going up, Frank felt confronted by the polar facts of life: birth, death and all the ills that flesh is heir to in between. His companions in the car encouraged the thought. A young man with a dazed ecstatic look held a plant in both hands and announced that he was going to the seventh floor. "Maternity," he added and could not keep the smile of pride from his lips. A small bald man looked at him with vague, distant eyes. He carried no flowers.

When Father Ascue emerged from the car and walked down the silent corridor to Miss Simpson's room, he thought suddenly of his parents. He commemorated them each morning in Mass, but their names came forth rotelike, mere names, like those of the unknown saints of the Canon. Now in the hospital, oppressed by reminders of death, his thoughts went beyond the names to the dimming memories he could not trust, unsure whether they had been taken from life or from the surviving photographs of his parents.

Her letters came to Howard Nygaard at his office, usually special delivery, so that shortly after noon he was reading the three or four pages she had written the previous evening then carried to the downtown post office in Cleveland to ensure that her letter would be on its way to Fort Elbow while she slept her troubled sleep.

"It's here," Miss Furlong would say when she brought the letter in to him. His secretary stood before his desk, eyes shut, the letter lying in the palm of one extended hand, weighing it blind, like Justice.

"My day is complete."

It had been impossible to conceal the letters from Miss Furlong, of course: she knew that the single name and the Cleveland address were those of a client of sorts. Worse than infidelity, worse than having kept this from Char from the very beginning, as if he had known, before he knew, what this girl would come to mean to him, worse than that was the fact that he had permitted Sharon's letters to become a little joke with Miss Furlong.

"Personal," Miss Furlong had noted when the first letter came after his trip to Cleveland a year ago.

"Oh? From whom?"

Miss Furlong read the uncapitalized name. Piper.

Howard said, "Ah. The Mansfield estate, remember?"

Miss Furlong remembered. When the letters continued—and why shouldn't they? He answered every one, usually on the day he received it—he had invented a Sharon with whom to quench Miss Furlong's curiosity. A poor neurotic girl, a daughter who had never known her father and now cast the trustee of the estate into that empty role. Some truth in that, perhaps, more than he cared to admit, but it was inexcusable to cater to Miss Furlong's raised brows and dismissing smile. His ruse made the correspondence somehow a business one, no matter the "Personal" typed in red on each envelope. When he took a letter from Miss Furlong he waited for her to leave the office before opening it, his hesitation a species of apology to Sharon for letting her become an object of Miss Furlong's abstract pity.

Furtive, furtive, and that was at once the fun and anguish of it. If Sharon had wanted more than the little they had he would have stopped this months ago, before it really began, but she had no designs on him, accepted his wife as a fact of life and his children too. She seemed to have little or no curiosity about them. Once he had succumbed to the temptation to tell her that his eldest daughter was not much younger than she, but Sharon had placed her finger on his lips and shaken her head, eyes wide with that helpless wisdom she had.

When the Mansfield will had been probated, they had all assumed that Sharon Piper, not being a relative, must be an old employee or mistress Mansfield had chosen to reward from the far side of the grave.

132

Howard had flown to Cleveland and read there the report of the private investigation. The girl was twenty-seven, taught Spanish in a public high school, could not possibly have been mixed up with Mansfield. Alfred Mansfield had been eighty-three at the time of his death. The girl's mother was still alive. Howard had an idea and it was the right one. The girl was Mansfield's natural daughter. He asked her to lunch and the circuitous and compassionate way he had led up to the revelation set the tone between them.

"I don't want the money."

"That's silly. You have no choice anyway. At least we haven't. You'll get the money. Every month."

"I'll send it back."

"We'll invest it for you."

"I'll give it away."

Her eyes were moist and she was angry. He guessed that she cried easily but would not now.

"Did you ever meet him?"

"No!" Her eyes blazed and dropped.

Home had been her grandmother's house. She and her mother might have been sisters as far as the old woman was concerned. Sharon had been told her parents were divorced. In her senior year of high school she learned from her mother that there had never been a marriage. She bore her mother's maiden name as if a generation had been skipped. Her mother was drunk when she told her. She was drunk most of the time now, the grandmother having died and taken with her any discipline and restraint Sharon's mother had known.

"I hate her," Sharon said.

"Children usually disapprove of their parents."

She looked at him with genuine disgust. "I said hate and I meant it. She is weak, a parasite. She won't work, she won't live with me, to cut expenses. She insists on staying in that huge house. I suppose it reminds her of when she was a little girl surrounded by security."

"Do you support her?"

"I help. She has Social Security and something from Grandma."

"Use his money to support her."

It was a compromise she could accept. Mansfield did owe her mother something. What he owed Sharon was beyond the reach of a monthly check.

When they finished lunch they adjourned to the bar, where they spent the afternoon in its intimate half-light. It was late June. School was over. The summer stretched before Sharon. Howard got mildly drunk, drunk enough to say more than he ever would have sober, and, as the hours went by, he as much as Sharon was the topic of conversation. The fact that he was forty-five no longer seemed to matter. He had never felt forty-five, not really. When they got into the cab to go to her apartment, there was no question of why they were both so eager to be where they could be alone.

In the morning he called his motel to see if there were any messages for him. Nothing. It was difficult to believe that he could do this with impunity, that no one knew. Sharon lay beside him, watching him while he phoned. He hung up and relief gave way to the return of lust. They spent the day in bed. It was incredible. His honeymoon had not been like this. Several times he slept but when he awoke she lay sleepless beside him. Once, on her way out of the bedroom, nude, she struck a pose. He smiled and she moved about the room with supple gravity, assuming the stances of a model.

"Miss Cleveland," he said.

"No. Miss Conception."

That took the fun out of it, though he laughed. It became her name for herself with him. When with satiety guilt overcame him, she helped him wallow in it. They had dinner together, she went with him to his hotel, sat discreetly in the lobby while he checked out, then over his protests came with him to the airport.

Her letters alarmed him, excited him, confused him. And he needed them. They plotted imaginary rendezvous: they would meet in Toledo, Detroit, Chicago, somewhere. But there had been only three trips to Cleveland, the second and third of four days each. That was all. And sometimes it seemed everything. When he and Char attended those goddam meetings of Catholic married couples it was of Sharon he thought when the conversation turned, as it so often did, to the sexual "dimension" of marriage.

"You're Catholic," Sharon said, studying the medal he wore on a chain around his neck.

"By marriage."

"Don't you believe it?"

He had to think before he answered and that seemed a commentary on his faith. He said, "Yes."

"It's what I would be if I were anything."

They lay naked on her bed and spoke of religion. Before he had married Char he had called himself, vaguely, a Protestant, the generic designation permitting him, as it had his parents, to go indifferently to Lutheran, Unitarian, Quaker or Presbyterian churches on the few occasions he did go. When he joined the Catholic Church his life had been invaded by rules and rituals and priests. He would never get used to

134

priests, not even his brother-in-law. Their unnatural life filled him with distaste and awe and something like embarrassment. Sharon did not want him to speak of his family but the faith his marriage had brought him to fascinated her.

"Don't you believe it?" she had asked and he had answered Yes. And he did. If he did not would he have felt so guilty about Sharon? It had been so long since he had been to confession: he did not want to tell this to a priest. Still he went to Communion with Char since not to go would have invited questions. When they returned to their pew he knelt beside her, trying to keep his mind a blank, not wanting to think that Christ in the form of bread was dissolving within him, that sacramental presence a sentence of damnation. The first time he had received Communion in the state of mortal sin he had felt weak with fear but even that became easy to do. It was as easy as deceiving Char. Nor did he any longer feel discomfort with the children, not even with Bev, though the one thing that could summon a cold sweat was the thought of Bev discovering his infidelity. She would be wholly unforgiving, he was sure of it. He had the parallel. Bev would think of him as Sharon did poor dead Mansfield. Mercy would be out of the question. Howard was glad that God is not a woman.

"It's your baby," Yorick had said. "George's orders."

"He never mentioned it to me." The pleasant surprise of the assignment was diminished by the manner of its being given. If Yorick were to bring him news of the cardinalate it would seem a punishment.

"It's all here."

Bishop Brophy took the envelope and tossed it onto his desk. It remained there until Yorick had left the room. Inside there was a press release.

In keeping with the decision of the recent synod of American bishops, the priests of the Fort Elbow diocese were to elect members of a clerical senate. Arrangements for the election would be handled by the Most Reverend Sean Brophy, Auxiliary Bishop. Et cetera, et cetera. While he read the release, Brophy thought of Oder and others who had been pestering him about this. His answer had been a pensive look and the suggestion that the clergy proceed on their own initiative. This had been greeted with less than enthusiasm. Oder had actually had the guts to hint that Bishop Brophy himself had recently learned the penalty of incurring George's wrath. On occasion Oder could be a supercilious pain in the neck.

Bishop Brophy thought that he had borne up rather well during his three-week exile in the provinces. He had traveled all but incognito, had not opened his mouth publicly throughout his visitations and had returned to a lukewarm but not unfriendly reception from Caldron. Nor had there been much curiosity about what Brophy might have learned in his travels.

"Write it up, would you, Sean?" Caldron had said when he tried to report.

Drawing on imagination as well as memory, Brophy had composed a lengthy florid document. If Caldron had ever read it, he was managing to keep his gratitude well concealed. Brophy had steered clear of making anything like suggestions, sticking to the factual. He had taken particular pleasure in commending the work of poor Grimes. Yorick had robbed him of that small satisfaction, however, indicating that the chancellor at least had read the damned report.

"Isn't Grimes up to his ears in debt?"

"It's all in my report," Brophy said loftily.

"All what? Has he started to pay off the principal of that loan?"

Bishop Brophy had a small pestering memory of Grimes mentioning a loan.

"I thought it would have been excessive to bring back the parish ledgers, Monsignor."

"What good is a report that omits the sort of thing the bishop has to know?"

Brophy chose silence for reply. Yorick invoked Caldron as if he were making reference to the ultimate repository of standards. What a domesticated prelate the chancellor was.

The fact that Caldron had put the clerical senate matter into his hands suggested to Bishop Brophy that George now understood that initiative and loyalty are not inimical. In his own peculiar way, Caldron probably meant this as an apology for the injustice of his reaction to the statement on the seminary protest.

When Dan Donovan, the editor of the *Fort Elbow Catholic*, called to ask about the press release, Brophy invited him to drop by. He liked Donovan.

"Lydia and I wondered if you could have dinner with us, Bishop."

"Just the three of us?" It seemed a waste to devote an entire evening to just one couple.

"We wanted to see if you were free before calling others. Anyone you would particularly like there?"

"Daniel, I can hardly commandeer your guest list." Bishop Brophy settled back in his chair. This was more like it. Names slid before his mind's eye like the credits of a film. Donovan was making demurring noises in his ear. "I suppose Father Oder, Dan. What do you think?"

Dan thought Father Oder was just fine. His own suggestion, Plummet-Finch, came as a surprise to Brophy.

"Do I know him?"

"I'd like him to meet you. He teaches philosophy at the university. An Oxford man. Quite bright."

"Daniel, I am in your hands."

He had mentioned Oder only on the assumption that the senate would be discussed. Lydia Donovan, her husband said, would ensure that the bishop would be surrounded by interesting and congenial guests.

Having finished with Donovan, Bishop Brophy depressed the cradle, then released it. He began to dial. Better to speak to Oder now about the procedures for the election. A nominating committee would be the first and most important step. With a carefully prepared list of candidates, much of the mystery could be taken out of the results of the election. Bishop Brophy smiled. Grimes. He would see that Grimes made the list. Now that he himself was back in circulation, he could regard the rural pastor's plight with more objective sympathy. As a member of the senate, Grimes would have an excuse to get into Fort Elbow from time to time.

On the pad beside the phone someone had scribbled that Carl had called.

Sheila Rupp read the message with a smile and, going into the first bedroom, put her bag down and began to get out of her uniform. A tousled head emerged from under the covers.

"Who is it?"

"Sheila."

"What time is it?"

"Go back to sleep, Gladys. You have hours."

Gladys, who had not opened her eyes, collapsed sighing. With much rustling and tossing, she burrowed in, pulling the blanket over her head. And then, in a muffled voice, "Carl called."

"I know. Go to sleep."

Sheila finished undressing as quietly as she could but there was no way to make the shower soundless. There was no way to keep from humming happily either, but then Gladys must be fast asleep again. The sound of the ringing phone penetrated the racket of the shower and, dripping, her robe pulled hurriedly about her, Sheila ran barefoot down the hall to answer it.

"You're back," Carl said.

"I'm back."

"Good." He regarded each trip as death defying, seemed really surprised that flying was massively uneventful.

"I got your message."

"An hour from now all right?"

"An hour's fine."

She retraced her wet footprints to the bathroom. All the bedroom doors were closed. An hour. Three in the afternoon. She had fled to the phone without rinsing the soap from her body and it was good to get under the water again, to feel her pores open, to greet the sting.

No one understood about Carl, no one who had met him. He was quiet and seemed dull, he made no effort to impress. It was just that that had impressed her, his indifference to her reaction. He had been on a New York to Chicago flight six months ago, before Sheila had switched to transatlantic flights. It was a smooth, swift trip but he had huddled in his seat as if they were hurtling through an epic storm, had lost two engines and were on fire. Her efforts to relax him were met with moody silence but after they had landed he was the last one off and he thanked her. They walked down one of the huge ganglia of O'Hare to the main terminal, where he surprised her with an offer of a drink. She surprised herself by accepting. Her acceptance did not seem to surprise him. He asked where he should wait for her and she told him. The directions were confusing and when, half an hour later, she came into the lounge it was with the certainty that he would not be there. But he was there. And so, improbably, it had begun.

That it had continued seemed improbable to everyone but her, and to Carl, of course. From the outset there had been an easiness between them, an effortless being together that did not depend on chatter. By osmosis, in trickles and installments, they had learned of one another: there had been no biographical session when each ticked off the essential data for the other. Even her coming to know that he was divorced was not a landmark. It was not something to be curious about or brood over or lament. But it was the main reason she had not introduced him to her parents.

She had tried to tell her mother about Carl but had not got much past the point of saying that he was thirty-six. Her mother's reaction was to feign that Sheila could not possibly be serious about a man ten years older than she. It was pointless to protest, especially when Sheila herself did not know where she and Carl were headed. Not having anything definite to communicate to her mother, Sheila became secretive about Carl, or so at least it must have seemed to her parents. Did she really want things clarified? If they were, his divorce would come to the fore and though she might be able to overlook it, she knew that her parents, particularly her father, never could.

Carl showed up in a brown suede jacket and tan wash pants. Sheila was in her best cocktail dress when she opened the door. They stared at one another and Sheila laughed.

"I gather that we're not going anywhere special."

"Oh, but we are. To the cottage."

"I'll change."

"Got any coffee?"

"Look and see. I won't be a minute."

But before she could leave, he took her hand and she moved into his arms. For the first time she really felt home again. She looked up into his lean lined face, the hazel eyes, the thick hair gone mostly gray. He pressed his cheek to hers and held her more tightly. Home. She broke free and dashed for the bedroom.

When she came into the kitchen, he was seated at the table with a cup of coffee before him.

"I signed you in." He indicated the blackboard on the wall.

"Oh, nobody uses that anymore." Gladys's name was not there. There was no sure way to tell who, if anybody, was in the other bedrooms. Somehow, despite the constant traffic, there was no jam-up in the apartment.

"Who made the coffee?"

"Not I. Is it all right?"

He shrugged. "I thought we would do a little shopping, then drive to the cottage. This is no day to be in town."

It wasn't, she saw that now. When they went out to his car the air seemed filled with promise. In April they had visited the cottage but the weather had been terrible and they had spent their time in front of the fire, not venturing outside. There had still been ice on the lake and an unseasonable snow had limned the hills on the far shore.

They pushed a cart through the aisles of a supermarket, the deed inviting the fantasy that they were a permanent couple, Carl her husband, she his wife, her days of flight and rootlessness over. For three years she had wanted the feeling of belonging nowhere, of being always between flights. It was the perfect antidote to the years at home which had ended with her going off to school. But school had been a regimen of another sort, scheduled, fixed, predictable. She had put all that behind her, but Carl had made her begin to dream of fixity and a future.

How lovely it was to drive with him, to draw her legs up on the seat, lean her head on his shoulder and let the road slip beneath them. They talked little. She was almost disappointed when he turned onto the gravel road which led to the cabin. She sat up to watch it come into view. A low building Carl had designed himself, it hugged the rise of a hill and looked out over the small lake, which was surrounded on two-thirds of its shore by pasture land.

Much later, when they were on the porch, their meal done, Carl sipping a drink, the sky blurred pastels and the sun giving in its slow setting a reprieve from darkness, the peace went out of the scene.

"Your daughter?" Sheila asked.

"Yes. Catherine."

"How old is she?"

Carl sipped his drink. She was staring at him but he continued to look at the evening sky. Was he making an effort to be casual?

"Thirteen," he said. "Fourteen in September."

"You've never mentioned her before."

"No."

"Do you see her often?"

"Not really. But she's with me for a month in summer."

Which meant that Catherine would not have been with him since they had met. This revelation still seemed the admission of a major secret. Sheila felt that she should have sensed that he was a father, that there should have been some hint from him before now. This sudden, unexpected mention of a daughter loomed as a barrier between them.

"I want you to meet her, Sheila."

"When does she come?"

"She's already here. She's at my sister's now. I thought that this week . . . "

This week? She felt completely unprepared. She felt confused and angry.

"Shouldn't we be starting back?"

His face, when he turned to her, went into shadow. In April they had stayed for three days. The groceries they had bought would have permitted them to stay at least as long now. Carl finished his drink, looked out over the lake.

"Say the word when you want to go."

The first time Frank visited Miss Simpson in the hospital she looked collapsed and old, her white hair in a single braid, her eyes luminous and wide as if they already contained the secret she was going to meet.

On the cluttered table beside the bed, among glasses and pans and medicines, was her bottle of Lourdes water.

"I wouldn't have much faith if I stopped using it now, would I, Father?"

"Well, Lourdes water isn't exactly an object of faith."

She smiled confidingly. "It isn't that I have much hope of getting well."

The aged do revert to childhood as death approaches. He could imagine Miss Simpson in her teens, shy, naïve and destined to loneliness. To go single into the darkness, leaving no extension of one's self, one's flesh, was sad, but Father Ascue did not see himself huddled with Miss Simpson beneath the umbrella of that generalization. It was her he pitied, a little girl of seventy, soon to die.

It was only to make conversation and with no ulterior motive that, on his second visit, he told her of the projected summer program at Saint Waldo's.

"What a wonderful idea, Father."

"I hope Monsignor Entweder thinks so."

She asked what he meant by that and when he told her of the need to raise money for insurance she waved a fragile hand. "Money? Heavens, Father, don't worry about the money. I'll be glad to give whatever's needed."

He told her the amount and she was unfazed.

"Can I tell Monsignor Entweder of your offer?"

She said she would tell him herself if Father Ascue liked, but that would not have been good tactics. He spent half an hour with her and left elated. Downstairs he phoned Char and asked if she was busy and she told him to come right out. For crying out loud, did he expect an invitation? He took a cab to the house.

"Now don't tell me you've already had breakfast, Frank. I have a coffee cake in and we are going to eat it and no argument."

"No argument."

"That's what I said."

It was good to get out of his coat and collar and relax in the dining room, sip coffee, nibble cake and tell Charlotte all about Saint Waldo's. "Oh, I have to meet him," she cried when he told her of McTear and his tons of radio equipment in the rectory basement. On to the summer program then and to the unexpected offer from Miss Simpson. What fun it was to get outside himself and his life at Saint Waldo's and regard it as a drama.

"Who's home?" he asked at the sound of movement upstairs.

Charlotte made a face. "Bev. The poor thing. We must have woke her up."

"Is the semester over?"

"Another week and a half."

His sleepy niece appeared upon the stairs, running a brush through her hair, wearing a powder blue robe and huge furry slippers.

"Uncle Father Frank," she said sleepily. "I thought I heard your voice."

Bev brought a cup from the kitchen and poured herself some coffee. Char said, "When's your class?"

"What day is it?" Bev pulled the brush through her hair, again and again, tugging her head to one side, squinting her eyes in painful pleasure. Her mother told her what day it was.

"Ugh. I may not even go to class."

"You do need the rest. What time did you get in last night?"

"It wasn't late."

"Do you even know what time it was?"

Bev looked at her uncle with resignation. "You know, I'd join the convent if I didn't think they were all about to close down."

"Maybe if you joined they would flourish again."

"How do you like Saint Waldo's?"

He gave Bev a briefer report, not wanting to presume on her attention span, but she seemed interested enough. Charlotte, who had gone to the kitchen, discovered that this was her day to play bridge.

"Imagine. I'd forgotten all about it. I'll call and beg off."

"Not on my account," Frank asked. "I'm going. This is my day off."

"But where can you go by taxi?"

"Char, you can go just about anywhere you want by bus or taxi."

"Take our car. Someone can pick me up."

"I don't need a car."

"Of course you do. It will just be parked here doing no one any good."

It turned out to be the line of least resistance to accept the offer of the car. To refuse would have seemed an admission that he had nowhere in particular to go. He had no desire to get in touch with Wintheiser or Doyle. The thought of visiting Father Ewing occurred to him but perhaps it would be cruel to remind Ewing that his supposed replacement was busy and happy in parish life.

"You can drive me to school," Bev said.

"Good enough."

But half an hour later when he reached the campus and was approaching the Center, where Bev asked to be dropped, she said, "You know, I really do not want to go to school today."

142

"So don't."

"I should have stayed home."

"Come on along with me."

"Where?"

"I'll show you my school."

"I'm game."

He went southward on the river road for several miles and there it was, the seminary. "My alma mater," he said.

Bev shook her head sadly. "All those beautiful young men. It seems a shame."

"There aren't that many anymore. Less than a third of the number we had when I was a student. Want to look around?"

"Is it allowed?"

"Why not?"

"Would it be fair for someone as ravishing as me to show herself here? They'll take swan dives out of windows, defrocking as they fall."

He laughed. "It's not just a negation, Bev."

"It doesn't seem to bother you. Being single."

"Being a celibate," he corrected, and felt stuffy and adult.

"Do you think that will stay, priests not marrying?"

He had turned onto the seminary grounds and drove slowly under the trees. How deserted the place looked. It might have been the vacation time, but that was still a week away.

"The pope wrote a letter on the subject recently."

"He didn't send me a copy."

"You should read it. There are pros and cons, of course. But for me, it's an academic question."

"Unless you wanted to leave."

He looked at her. What a strange girl she was. She was right about one thing, certainly. Her presence would be a distraction to the seminarians.

"Why would I leave?"

"Don't you ever think of it? Oh, I don't mean leaving, exactly, but of what life would have been like if you hadn't become a priest?"

"No."

"But you must."

"Do you think married people sit around daydreaming of what it would be like to be single again?"

"Of course they do."

"Well, do you think they should?"

"You don't."

"No, and neither do you. Fantasy can take hold of us, you know that.

143

And anyway a priest has quite a long time to think about the life he's going to lead. Sometimes six years. That's plenty of time to consider what it will be like after ordination."

"But how can you really know? Phil says that that's the biggest argument against celibacy. How can a man know in his early twenties what he will be like at forty?"

"You could use the same argument against marrying when most people do, in their twenties. When is a person ready to make a promise? At forty? How does he know then what he will be like at fifty? That's a stupid argument, Bev. There isn't some stranger waiting in the future to assume our name and shuffle through the promises we dump on him. What we do now makes the person we'll be at forty."

What the hell was Phil up to, talking like that to young kids? It was the sort of argument he might formulate to justify a mess he had got himself into, diminishing responsibility by putting the blame on others. Now that he had managed to straighten himself out Phil really ought to correct the impression he had apparently made.

"Who's *that?*"

It was Eisenbarth, coming up a path which led to the river. Father Ascue stopped the car. "The rector. Come on, you can meet him."

"Lucky me."

Monsignor Eisenbarth stood like a surprised poacher, flanked by lilacs, his face as crimson as the piping on his cassock. Embarrassment gave way to surprise when his eyes moved from Father Ascue to Bev and back again.

"Good morning, Monsignor."

"Good morning, Father Ascue." Eisenbarth managed to italicize Father.

"This is my niece, Beverly Nygaard."

The monsignorial eyebrows rose, but suddenly he tossed his head as if to rid it of the madness of the times and its attendant suspicions. He bowed graciously to Bev, even extended his hand. Watching the performance, Frank was reminded of one of Eisenbarth's conferences when the rector had counseled them never to seat a woman beside them in a car. "Place her in the back seat, gentlemen. I do not care if she is your mother or even . . . " The pause was for dramatic effect, but Eisenbarth, his head thrown back, sighting down the line of his nose at the assembled seminarians, had the look of a garroted man. "Or even your grandmother," he finished in hushed tones. "Scandal. Scandal. Woe to him through whom it comes. The most innocent deed, should it have the appearance of something else, cannot, gentlemen, be undone, cannot be explained to the shocked observer." This prudent advice had been

144

annual fare and was, as a cause of hilarity among the seminarians, rivaled only by Eisenbarth's lecture on the priest as gentleman, nay, nobleman.

"Is this your first time on our campus, Miss Nygaard?"

"The very first. And what a lovely place, Monsignor. So quiet."

"Yes, it is quiet." The rector turned to Father Ascue. "You know how few students we have now."

"Under seventy, isn't it?"

"Well under. And the new class entering next fall . . . " The rector threw out his hands. "Twenty boys."

"Things can't go on like that."

"Everything happened so swiftly, Father. Everything. After the death of Pius XII . . . "

Eisenbarth shook his head, looking confused. It was difficult not to sympathize with him. For years he had ruled over a thriving institution, and now . . .

"Here's a seminarian," Frank said, and he didn't know whether he was trying to lift Eisenbarth's spirits or draw Bev's attention to what she apparently regarded as a very singular type of young man.

"So it is," the rector said. "Cole, would you come here, please?"

Monsignor Eisenbarth introduced the young man, whom Frank recognized as the seminarian who had been with Tremplin the afternoon he had received his appointment from Bishop Caldron. "The day Arthur Rupp was here," he explained to Eisenbarth.

"Ah, yes. Arthur. I want to speak to you about Arthur." He looked at the young people. "Cole, I wonder if you would show the young lady around."

"Certainly, Monsignor." To Bev he said, "The chapel is this way."

"I'm dying to see the chapel."

Cole glanced at her, smiled, and they went off.

"Arthur Rupp is quite impressed by you, Father," Eisenbarth said, taking Frank's arm. "What do you think of him?"

Frank thought of that crazy dinner party and of Rupp's dodging the matter of donations. "Apparently he's a pillar of the parish."

"Of a good deal more than the parish, Father. He is a very influential man and a very committed man. Of course you have heard of Te Deum?"

"Of course."

They walked along the path while Eisenbarth extolled the merits of Te Deum. Father Ascue listened, nodding noncommittally. He had nothing against the organization though it had always seemed rather pompous to him. Monsignor Eisenbarth descended on the nation's foreign policy with syllogistic singleness of mind. Communism is atheistic, perhaps the work of Antichrist himself. From this it followed that any adjustment with or concession to or indeed recognition of Russia took on the flavor of apostasy. It was all very bizarre. Of course, Frank reminded himself, no one else seemed to make much sense on the subject of foreign affairs either.

"Te Deum sponsors an annual citywide Communion breakfast, Father. Every July, as close to the fourth as is possible and convenient. It is quite a forum, Father."

"I should think so."

"Your name has been mentioned in discussions of this year's speakers, Father Ascue."

"Mine?"

They both came to a halt and Monsignor Eisenbarth beamed at the surprised Father Ascue.

"It has indeed. And by more than one person, I might add. Wherever did you meet Mrs. Bently?"

There was the sound of laughter. The two priests turned to see Bev coming down the path with Ben Cole.

"What got into Plummet-Finch?" Daniel asked. The evening was over and they were toting glasses and ashtrays and other debris into the kitchen.

Lydia Donovan was a one-handed helper since she still held her glass, a much fingerprinted one in which a single cube bobbed on the amber surface. She was down to straight bourbon now and no nonsense about it.

"How do you mean?"

"All that bullshit about atheism. I thought Brophy would change chairs just to get away from him."

"That's the first time I heard a bishop addressed by his Christian name."

"The advantage of the separated brethren. Or of the atheist, in Gilbert's case. Brophy *asked* him to call him Sean."

"I thought they got along all right. Not that Oder would let Harris and me divert our attention for a minute. I think he's actually jealous of Brophy. He hates being upstaged by a mere auxiliary bishop."

"Gilbert was drunk. The giveaway is when he acts sober." Daniel dragged on his cigarette. "It's that goddam British confidence that kills me. Disproofs of the existence of God! That was the endless topic. Are they possible? Are they necessary?"

146

"Are they? And which?"

"Both," he called from the living room.

Lydia brought her glass to her lips. She was leaning against the drainboard. Daniel came back, hands filled.

"Otherwise there's only agnosticism. I mean, if it is an open question, if God might exist . . . Move over, will you, honey? I'm going to drop this stuff."

Lydia moved and lost her balance and careened across the room. She put out a hand and steadied herself with the refrigerator.

"Ooops," she said.

"Let's leave the rest till morning. I'm pooped."

"It's all right with me."

She brought her drink with her and put it on the table beside the bed and began to undress in slow motion, concentrating on each item of clothing. When she was down to bra and garter belt, she sat on the edge of the bed and took another sip of her drink. Daniel in pajamas emerged from the closet and looked at her with faint distaste.

"You want your nightie?"

"Toss it to me, will you?"

Daniel reached into the closet and brought forth a flowing pink garment. He threw it and it drifted onto the bed. Lydia watched its flight in fascination. Daniel went off to the bathroom. When he came back she was in bed, propped up on her pillow, holding her drink with both hands.

"All in all, it went well, didn't it?"

Daniel yawned. "Magnificent. The dinner was delicious."

"Did they mix? The guests. Was it a good group?"

"I could have lived without Gilbert Plummet-Finch. But it was a success. Want me to turn out the light?"

"In a sec. I want to finish my drink in peace."

"If you finish it, you'll have peace all right."

"*Dona nobis pacem,*" she intoned.

They lay in silence, staring at the ceiling, their heads filled with memories of their party, feeling the combination of defeat and triumph hosts know after the guests are gone. Snatches of conversation, an ambiguous response, a gesture that might have been misunderstood. And yet Lydia was pleased. The party had had the kind of mad imbalance she strove for, the improbable juxtapositions destined for a higher unity, as Gilbert might have said, in a sniffing way, citing one of the Teutons he despised. A bishop, a liberal priest, an atheistic philosophy professor down on his luck (imagine the Fort Elbow campus snaring Gilbert Plummet-Finch, an Oxford B.A., editor of two anthologies as well as author of a much reprinted article on the practical syllogism, but also, alas, incorrigibly and blatantly homosexual), an artist, Harris, who had come as usual wrapped in a cocoon of wool, just Harris, the way she signed her paintings and wished to sign herself. And of course the Donovans, she and Daniel.

It was on the Donovans that Lydia preferred to dwell, on herself and Daniel. What were they doing in this miserable city? Daniel's *Crisis of Doubt* and her own *Married Virgins* had established them as leading Catholic intellectuals, but in this appalling place it sometimes seemed that only she and Daniel were aware of the fact. They had met in graduate school and, after Daniel flunked his candidacies, they had drifted into Catholic journalism. There had been a chancey year during which Daniel shipped story after story to the slick magazines—if any had been accepted, he would of course have insisted on a pseudonym —while at the same time doing book reviews for *Commonweal* and *America* and the *Vase of the Little Flower*. Lydia was trying to have a baby. Their bedroom had become a lab, its walls hung with elaborate charts recording her temperatures. Her menstrual cycle proved to be the eighth wonder of the world. Cycle! She suspected it of counterpoint. Dr. Barth had told her to relax and enjoy. So they had mated to music, they had mated drunk, they had fallen into casual conjugation at odd times during the day, they had whipped themselves up with the *Kamasutra*, getting as far as position fourteen, they had tried to surprise spontaneity—all to no avail. It began to dawn even on the doctors that something was wrong. There was. Daniel was sterile. Lydia's womb was tipped. It seemed ironic that two creative people could not reproduce themselves. Lydia began to make lists of geniuses who had had no children, much, she supposed, as people like Gilbert make lists of the great who have shared their inverted tendencies. After a period of melancholy, Lydia decided to master marriage on the theoretical level and thus she too drifted into journalism.

The formula for the new Catholic journalism, as she would have told no one but Daniel, was absurdly simple. One took a belief, a practice or cherished tradition and, respectively, contradicted it, recommended the opposite or suggested its dark and probably unhealthy origins. There had been a time, she understood, when, in order to become a theologian, one had to pursue a lengthy course of study in a reputable school, write a dissertation and defend it, receive a degree. Things were blessedly less complicated nowadays. After three of her articles had been published, she found herself being referred to as a lay theologian. Daniel's hold on the honorific had been secured by the publication of *Crisis of Doubt*. Perhaps it was his disappointment with their childless marriage, perhaps it was the scar left by academic failure, but Daniel managed to transpose his personal lack of confidence and his misgivings into a catchy key. Generalized, they became the undone work of theology.

Lydia's book consisted of a series of portraits, drawn from life, God knows, but each from several lives so that the women who had contributed some facets would never recognize themselves. Married virgins. Lydia was shocked to find how the nunnish ideal had invaded the wife's conception of her life style. She would not have believed that so many wives and mothers ran off to daily Mass at the crack of dawn; they belonged to Third Orders and read office every day or said fifteen decades of the rosary. It was absurd. All they lacked was a habit. Two or three particularly intense women had kept referring her to *Integrity*, a long-defunct monthly that had apparently warped their minds. One family with eight children sat silently through meals while one of their number read from an edifying book. It was all a gloss on Daniel's theme: the Catholic penchant to withdraw mistrustfully from the world into the twin evils of the ghetto and asceticism.

Her book had been well received. The only thing like a criticism had come from Camille Milhauser. "The author," she had written, "might have made it clearer that there are no longer any nuns of the kind she likens her chosen hausfraus to." *Touché*, of course, though hardly a radical criticism. The field *was* getting annoyingly cluttered with fleeing and flown nuns trying to establish their credentials as theologians. But any critical want of enthusiasm disappeared when she and Daniel published their children's version of the Dutch catechism, *Here's the Church, Here's the Steeple*. A lowland Dominican in a glen plaid suit had suggested the idea one evening over a bottle of Haig & Haig, had actually, delightful touch, secured an imprimatur for it from a missionary bishop in Lahore. He—the Dominican—was now living in San Francisco with a curious ménage.

"I wonder if God's existence *can* be disproved," Daniel said. "Logically, I mean."

"Isn't it done all the time?"

"Gilbert says not. He claims no one has ever brought it off. Till recently a disproof was regarded as making the question meaningful, so people, well, philosophers anyway, avoided the attempt."

"Does that make sense?"

"God knows."

Lydia finished her drink, put the glass on the floor beside the bed, turned off the light and snuggled up to Daniel. He lay on his back, hands behind his head, and did not respond to her overture. She put her head

149

on his shoulder and sighed. His hands came out from behind his head and he began to stroke her hair. Blood ablaze with booze, suddenly as ready as she ever was, Lydia tugged at the tie string of his pajamas and, like the nurse in the joke lifting the patient onto the bedpan, grasped him and pulled him toward her. His hands rippled over her nightgown and stopped.

"What's the matter?"

"You didn't take off your garter belt."

"Damn! Help me with it, will you?"

Daniel tugged and pulled, began to slip it over her hips. He lost his grip and it snapped like a slingshot against her flesh. She rather liked the stinging shock of it. Daniel got new purchase and began to pull again.

"Forget it," she hissed. "Forget it."

They tumbled together, their legs a cat's cradle of her garter belt, his pajama bottoms and an old copy of *Commonweal* that seemed to have been made with the bed.

When Tremplin showed up at the Center, catching him in the lounge before he could escape, Phil Bullard would not have guessed that the fuzzy spare seminary professor was the bearer of good tidings.

"We seem to be in similar boats," Tremplin said with a shy ingratiating smile.

"In what way?" He took Tremplin's arm and immediately started him on a tour. It would not help the image of the Center to have a priest like Tremplin hanging around the lounge.

"Our little demonstration."

"That was really great, Father. I've been meaning to call and tell you that. It got you into trouble?"

Tremplin sighed and rolled his eyes. Phil looked away. Tremplin had been what, four years ahead of him in the seminary, a bit of a sis, big on the liturgy. He still had those long pale hands that looked like a lotion ad in a women's magazine. Master of ceremonies in his deacon year, Tremplin had been precise, always right and a bit of a pain in the ass.

"Eisenbarth won't even speak to me. I have never gotten the complete story, Philip, but it is clear that Bishop Brophy pulled us out of the fire. And put Randolph into it, of course. I am afraid that my life has become quite uncomfortable. Except with the students," Tremplin added hastily. This addendum had only a momentary brightening effect on him. "And soon they will go off on vacation, scattered to the winds. Unless, that is, you agree to gather them, Philip."

"Me?" He had brought Tremplin to a little-used parlor, where they now sat in plastic chairs.

"Philip, they were quite sincere in their support of what you are trying to do. You must realize that you have become a hero to them." Tremplin smiled sweetly. "And not only to them. You have a constituency and with it, Philip, if you don't mind my saying so, obligations as well."

"What did you mean about gathering the seminarians?"

"Several of them have come to me and asked that I speak to you about ways they might spend their summer, relevant ways, some genuine work that would be a better preparation for the priesthood than being hidden away in the seminary for much of the year. You know how deplorably long the summer vacation can be for the seminarian."

Tremplin was serious. Phil could not remember ever having been depressed by the length of vacations. What did Tremplin have in mind anyway?

"Gosh, Jack, I don't know what I could do."

"There must be loads of things to be done here. Meeting young people, learning their problems . . ."

Oh, my God. Tremplin's eyes had drifted to the door and he looked wistfully in the direction of the lounge, where, he seemed to imagine, a thousand "problems" awaited to be dealt with. If Bishop Caldron had wanted to torpedo the Center, all he would have had to do was assign someone like Tremplin as director. Tremplin would no doubt pose in the doorway with outstretched arms. Give me your tired, your poor, your confused. The place would fold in a week.

"I have a tough time keeping myself busy around here."

Tremplin laughed, a piping ascendant laugh. Clearly he thought Phil's day was a continuum of bracing crises. And yet, despite himself, Phil began to imagine what it might be like to have a few seminarians about this summer, maybe half a dozen, hand picked. The image of himself as a model for aspiring priests, while novel, was intriguing. As a matter of fact, he would not mind testing some of his ideas about preparation for the priesthood with men still in the seminary. Suddenly he remembered Sister Eloise and Saint Waldo's.

"The guys you spoke about, Jack, are they pretty good?"

"They are among the best, the very best. You've thought of something?"

"Yes. It's not set, not definitely, but I'm working on it. I would have to reserve the right to screen the candidates, Jack. No matter how good a man may be academically, the sort of work I have in mind might not suit him."

151

"I would send them over. One by one. You could select those you want." Tremplin paused. "Be gentle with those you do not want, Philip. Let them down easily."

Phil promised to handle everything diplomatically. When he said good-bye to Tremplin—at a side door to which they came as if inadvertently and which he opened and hustled Jack through before he realized this was the end of the conversation—he remained on the walk watching Tremplin stroll out to his car. What a coup this could be. He could imagine Sister Eloise's surprise when he told her that he had secured a select group of seminarians to help in the Saint Waldo's summer program.

The park was a place of pigeons and children on swings and slides and, in the center, the destination of every path, the duck pond. It had meant so much to her as a girl that it seemed a perfect place to take Carl's daughter, Catherine, particularly after a lunch that would have been disastrous if the two of them had not pretended that the noise from the restaurant kitchen—their table was bad, an omen from the start—and the buzz of the other diners absolved them of the need to make their own conversation.

What a surprise Catherine had been. Tall, nearly as tall as Sheila, yet not much more than a child, a pretty awkward child whose sandy hair, pulled back from her forehead by a rust-colored headband, fell not quite to her shoulders.

"I haunted this place when I was a girl," Sheila said. "I just loved it. I would come here and sit by the hour, watching the ducks. Everyone feeds them so of course they are terribly spoiled. And fickle. I stopped trying to bribe them with bread and popcorn and let others make a fuss over them. I just watched. I think I felt superior to the feeders. Like the ducks do."

"It is pretty."

"Isn't it? It was even nicer then, much better kept up. See those swings?"

Catherine turned in the direction Sheila pointed but abruptly looked away. She seemed to fear that Sheila would suggest that they swing.

"I thought of them as mine. When I swung I imagined I was letting the other kids use my swings."

"Did you come here alone?"

"Yes."

Alone. It said so much and Catherine's glance, for a second, seemed to go beyond the present Sheila to the earlier self she had invoked.

Sheila had to resist telling this girl, Carl's daughter, of how desperately unhappy she had been as a child, how lonely she had been, how her imaginings in this park had been a substitute for the glorious life she was convinced all other children led. But she knew how risky it would be to follow that line; it would appear to be a bid for Catherine's sympathy and, worse, it would lead to the recognition, overt, no longer concealed, of Catherine's own loneliness.

During lunch, except for the few minutes when she had held Catherine's genuine interest with the revelation that she was an airline stewardess, she had sensed the girl's resentment. Whatever sad and inadequate life was now Catherine's had its imagined explanation in Sheila.

They had reached the duck pond and now stood by the fence that ringed it. On the surface of the pond half a dozen ducks drifted indolently. How filthy the water was. Crusts of bread and various sorts of flotsam floated there. The ducks themselves looked scruffy and unclean. The ducks of memory were impossibly white, their passage across the pond majestic, each followed by the widening perfect chevron of its wake, the water that bore them clean and clear. The neck of a nearby duck was raw, the feathers worn away. Sheila recalled her fascination and dread when she had first seen ducks mate. Knowing the cause of that raw used neck, the effect of the drake's pinning the object of his attention, Sheila wished that they had stopped at one of the benches just inside the park entrance. The disappointment of the pond and ducks, of the whole park, seemed a personal deficiency, as if she had promised much and delivered only this.

"Do you come here often now?" Catherine asked.

"No. I haven't been here for years. How changed it is."

"It's nice."

That polite reply reminded Sheila of the way children try to protect adults. Just so she might have reassured her father.

"Does my dad ever come here?"

"I don't know."

"He hates the city."

"Yes."

"So do I. That's why I like being with him in the summer. We stay at his cottage."

"Isn't it wonderful there!"

The girl's eyes went wide with surprise. When Catherine looked away, at those damned ducks, Sheila could see in the girl's effort to disguise her reaction the fact that she had been robbed of something special, something she had thought belonged only to her and her father.

"When will you be going to the cottage, Catherine?"

"Tonight, I hope."

A doomed hope, poor thing. Tonight she and Carl were going out.

"I'm sorry about these ducks. They used to be so much nicer. Everything was nicer."

"I think I should start back."

"All right."

They went back up the path again and Sheila felt utterly without resources. If only she could imagine that Catherine were a passenger in a plane, it would have been so easy to chatter with her, but each time she looked at the girl she saw Carl's daughter, the daughter she had not even known existed two days before. The worst of it was that she could see herself with Catherine's eyes, could resent herself, even hate the woman she had become. Innocently. Or had it been innocently? Was it now? Oh, God, how soiled she felt, as soiled as this park, whatever she had once been gone for good now, a scruffy duck with a raw neck. What was she but Carl's undemanding mistress? Did she seriously think she had any other future with him?

"I can catch the bus here," Catherine said when they came out of the park.

"The bus? Oh, let me call you a taxi, Catherine."

"Dad said I should take the bus home."

"It's pretty obvious he doesn't ride them often himself then. I haven't any idea what the schedule is."

"Oh, you don't have to wait. Thank you for lunch, Miss Rupp. I had a very nice time."

"Thank you, Catherine. So did I."

For a moment, with those lies over and done with, it seemed that the ice might melt, that they might come to know one another. But Catherine's eyes dropped and Sheila could not think of a thing to say. She patted Catherine's arm and, feeling dismissed, hurried away. The blatting sounds of traffic seemed an unflattering commentary on her performance.

"And how is Miss Simpson, poor woman?" Monsignor Entweder asked.

"Her spirit is good," Father Ascue said. "She has a very strong faith."

"A daily communicant for years," McTear said, uncapping a bottle of beer.

They were in the television room, supper done, McTear getting ready for his nightly session on the air. Frank decided to postpone

154

bringing up the summer program until McTear had gone. Miss Simpson's offer of the insurance money, Arthur Rupp's invitation to speak at the Communion breakfast—Te Deum or not, it was an honor and an opportunity—seemed to fit into the even flow that parish work had been thus far. He was finding his life immensely satisfying. Whatever might portend for the Church, now was now and the present was the only tense in which he could work. The night thoughts he had had after the dinner with Bob Wintheiser provided him with both stimulus and warning. Too easily he could make a worldly career of the priesthood. He knew that, not merely as a theoretical possibility now but as a warning embodied in other men. Not that he could judge them. He could not. He had no wish to. But the appearance sufficed for self-examination, whatever reality it hid. His own work seemed at once various and predictable, the surprises coming within the context of routine. Phil's confession had been a real jolt, of course, but he had found that just about any kind of problem could show up at the door when he had office hours. There had been nothing further on Diane. Perhaps he should telephone and see how she was doing. But at the moment his mind was occupied with Sister Eloise's plan for a summer program. God bless Miss Simpson. Her generosity had removed the only real impediment to the plan. He had been touched by the old woman's piety as well. Miss Simpson loved to speak of Lourdes and Fatima.

"Father," she had said once, her fingers twisted in her rosary. "What do you suppose the secret of Fatima is?"

"It's no secret, Miss Simpson."

She sat forward on her bed, excited. "Don't tell me it's been published!"

Out of the confused sequel emerged the realization that Miss Simpson's curiosity was directed at a letter that Sister Lucy, one of the three children to whom Mary had appeared at Fatima, had written to the pope. The letter was to have been opened in 1960 or after she died, whichever came first. Apparently both had come without any announcement of what the letter had contained. Frank had the vaguest memory of having heard this before.

"I have to confess that I was most uneasy throughout 1960, Father, waiting to hear what terrible revelations that letter might contain."

"There's no point in getting upset over things like that."

"Oh, I know I'm a foolish old woman. But there it is. I was consumed by curiosity." She sighed. "And now I shall die without having found out."

Frank was tempted to tell her that far greater revelations awaited her beyond the grave, but it would have been tactless to make such a remark. He did not know how much Miss Simpson had been told of the seriousness of her illness.

"I did guess, of course."

"Oh?"

"Yes." Miss Simpson made a face, that of a naughty child. "Yes, I did. Do you know what my guess was?"

How simple she was. And how good. He had heard her confession and it was as innocent as a child's. Father Keegan, when Frank had asked him, told him that Miss Simpson was even now often in severe pain and that excruciating agonies lay ahead of her.

"What was your guess?" He tried to make the question playful, but he did want to know.

"The Vatican Council," Miss Simpson whispered. "I think that Mary told those children of all this trouble and commotion in the Church— the priests, the nuns, you know. That was to be our punishment for not heeding the message of Fatima. This is worse than war, Father, it is worse than so many things one might have expected. And wouldn't it have seemed as unlikely as the prediction that Russia will be converted through devotion to the Blessed Mother? She did promise that, you remember, and who can believe it even now? So I imagined that Mary told those little children of how the pope would be vilified and that many priests and nuns would leave the Church and how confused we would all become. . . ."

Miss Simpson put her hand over her mouth to silence herself, and her eyes showed how dreadful she found what she was saying.

"Things aren't all that bad, Miss Simpson."

"Oh, but they are, Father. I've been told of a priest who says that Our Lord is not really present in the Blessed Sacrament! Can you imagine that? And there are others who say that it doesn't really matter what you believe, as if one church were just as good as another. Why, that's heresy, Father, as you know. There is heresy everywhere now. That is why I am not so very sad that I am going to die."

For a moment Frank found it difficult to dismiss this as the aimless chatter of an old and dying woman. Phil's confession came back to him and with it the thought of all the priests who had defected. If one encouraged such thoughts, it would be altogether too easy to adopt Miss Simpson's apocalyptic view of the present time. But he was saved by his knowledge of Church history. Perhaps it would have come as a surprise to Miss Simpson to learn that the Church had been in far worse condition than she imagined it to be in today. Or would she think those Renaissance popes were the spiteful fabrications of Protestants? But he

156

had no intention of arguing with Miss Simpson. Sitting beside her bed with the sounds and smells of the hospital so vivid, with the realization that in so short a time and after dreadful pain Miss Simpson would be dead, he indulged the thought that what she had said was a sort of prophetic assessment of the times.

"That's why I'm so happy to be of help on your summer program. We must keep Catholic children close to the Church, help them to know what they are. That is so important."

Frank was sure that Sister Eloise did not see her program as an invitation to a Catholic ghetto, but once more he thanked Miss Simpson.

Sister Eloise had been ecstatic when he told her he had raised the money, but he swore her to secrecy until he had spoken with Entweder, who, as luck would have it, went off the following day on retreat, inspired perhaps by Bishop Caldron's habit. Now he was back and McTear, having chugalugged his beer, bade them good night and lumbered away.

Afterward, when he reconstructed the conversation, Frank could not see what he could have said that would have altered its outcome. Certainly he had made his own enthusiasm plain enough when, having outlined Sister Eloise's plan, having mentioned that he understood the problem about the insurance and had got a quotation from Arthur Rupp, having laid the groundwork well, he produced the trump card of Miss Simpson's offer. Entweder had smiled and nodded through it all and, at the end, had seemed to share his excitement at having found the money to cover the insurance.

"You've been very enterprising, Father."

"The program is worth it, but I didn't really do anything. Miss Simpson's offer came as a surprise."

"She has always been a generous woman."

"Sister Eloise is raring to go ahead with it."

"Go ahead? Oh, I'm afraid not, Father."

"Afraid *not?*"

"Not. She must have told you that she already approached me about this. Through Sister Henry. And I said no."

"Because of the insurance."

Entweder smiled slyly. "Financial difficulties are easily grasped by nuns, Father. That was not my only reason, nor my main one."

The main reason, it emerged, was Entweder's pique at the persistent effort by a minority on the city council to halt exemptions of church property from local taxes. This was regarded as a test piece of legislation, one which, if it could be passed, would be contested and go eventu-

157

ally to the Supreme Court, where, it was hoped, the whole tradition of ecclesiastical exemptions would be stopped.

"They have no idea what a tax saving for the general public the parochial schools are, Father. Why, if all our children were released into the public school system, local taxes would soar out of sight."

"But this is a summer program, Monsignor."

"Yes, and one that would remove Catholic children from the city's obligation to provide decent recreational facilities. It would only further postpone the city council's sinful failure to do something about conditions in the upper part of this parish."

"But what about this summer and these kids?"

"My mind is made up, Father. Made up."

In the ensuing silence, the pastor became engrossed in television. Frank was seething. Finally, fearing that he would say something unsayable if he remained, he went off to his room. There he paced and reviewed the conversation, telling himself he must go back to Entweder and reopen the matter. But when the television had been turned off and he could hear the pastor preparing to retire, Frank continued to pace the floor of his room.

That night he lay awake, bereft of the contentment he had known for weeks. McTear's muffled voice lifted from the basement and from time to time there was the sound of an ancient cough from the pastor's room. After this second taste of the whimsy of his superiors, Frank found it difficult to fight off depression. He felt surrounded by apathy, by unreason, by childishness. And he did not look forward to bringing the bad news to Sister Eloise.

Part Three

7 "No!" Sister Eloise cried. "He said no?"
"I'm sorry, Sister. His mind is made up and there
doesn't seem to be any way to change it."
"But you had the money."
"Insurance isn't the problem. The reason he said no . . ."
His account of his conversation with Monsignor Entweder was deliberately factual, as if it was important to get the details right. Sister Eloise
did not need any encouragement from him in order to react passion-
ately to this shattering news. While he spoke, she opened the drawer
of her desk and dug a package of cigarettes out from under the debris.
The cigarette she took from it was crushed and bent and when she stuck
it defiantly between her lips it seemed a comic comment on her angry
expression. She did not light it and Frank did not offer to. A moment
later she took it from her mouth and pitched it into the wastebasket.
The crumpled package followed.
"I don't smoke. I confiscated those from one of my kids."
"Anyway, those are his reasons."
"Knowing doesn't help much. Reasons, no reasons—what difference
does it make?"
"It's still a good idea."
She smiled wanly. "I wonder if I'm sorrier for myself or for the kids.
Well, there goes my summer."
"How will you spend it now?"
"God only knows."
"Do you stay here in the parish convent?"
"We all go back to the provincial house, where there's absolutely
nothing to do from dawn to dark except gossip, sew and play badmin-
ton. And pray. Three months of absolutely nothing is what I face."
His own summer seemed to lie before him like an impossible flatland.
Frank went to the classroom window and looked out at the simmering
schoolyard. Heat waves rose from the asphalt and the children running

161

about down there seemed to be knee deep in mist, their shouts illusory and unreal. A few more days of school, then the playground would be closed, locked, inaccessible. Something worse than nothing faced many of those kids. He pitied them, of course, but like the nun he felt that he himself had been robbed of a season. Not that he would have taken any significant part in her summer program. It was Entweder's refusal, which the pastor regarded as an exercise in pure logic and Frank found only whimsical and cruel, that had stolen the sun from summer. The routine of parish life, until now so satisfying, seemed only routine and Entweder, his saintly if idiosyncratic pastor, a crank. But worse than his despondency was the realization that it had been effected so easily and by another's deed. He knew that, stupid as Entweder's refusal was, he should not permit it to alter his own zeal, dim his hopes, sap his energy.

"I guess I sound pretty selfish." Sister Eloise had joined him at the window.

"Wanting to do something for others rather than just while away the summer doesn't sound selfish to me."

"Nothing may have been a little strong, but nuns in quantity can be pretty boring company. And I don't like being under Mother Provincial's thumb."

"Did she know of this idea for a summer program?"

"Heavens, no. I was going to spring it on her after it was all settled. What a dreamer!"

"Do something else." But what? The range of options open to nuns was not wide. "I suppose it's too late to go away to study?"

"Wouldn't want to. That's like running away—six weeks on a shady, fun campus, playing schoolgirl again. No, thanks."

A foul ball scudded across the asphalt, pursued by a dozen small boys who had been spectators of the game. Two of them pounced on it simultaneously and then began to fight over it. The ball rolled away and was retrieved by a third boy, but the fight went on, growing vicious. Sister Eloise leaned from the window, the little fingers of each hand in her mouth. Her whistle was ear-piercing. The combatants fell apart, looked up. They saw the nun and their heads dropped. After standing there for a moment, scuffing their toes, they turned and wandered back to the game.

"I never could learn to whistle like that."

"I've been forbidden to. But sometimes it's necessary."

"How long have you been in the convent?"

"Three years."

"Where are you from?"

"Here."

162

"Fort Elbow?"

"Worse. Saint Waldo's. I went to school right here. My class picture hangs in the downstairs hall."

"Does your family still live in the parish?" He did not know her family name.

"Oh, no. My folks are in Florida now and my brother lives in the East. Providence. I'm the sole survivor."

A moment went by. "Well. I knew you'd want to know what Monsignor Entweder said."

"I wonder if I ever really expected good news."

"It was worth a try."

"Why does everything have to turn out wrong? I mean, this is supposed to be an exciting time in the Church. Everything you read, everything you hear—all over the place things are happening, new ideas, new ways of helping, change. Everywhere but here. As soon as someone has an idea in this diocese he's shot down. Look at Phil Bullard, look at the seminarians. Look at Bishop Brophy too, if the rumors are right. Not even a bishop is free. When are we going to wake up in Fort Elbow? Half the nuns in the order grumble about what's wrong with the Church, and you know what they mean: any effort to make it right. Nuns have been treated like china dolls for so long that that is what they've become. The good sisters." Sister Eloise made a face. "Well, some of us want out of that neat starched world. Good Lord, Father, I don't want to spend my life in some nunny parlor just growing old."

"Change is slow, Sister," he began, but he was stopped by her laughter.

"Slow? It doesn't exist."

"Of course it does. Your habit has changed. You've gone back to your baptismal names. . . ."

"Uh huh. Go on. What other momentous changes have there been? I'll tell you. None. The point of getting rid of those ridiculous habits was to erase a barrier between us and the people. But why do it if we don't intend to have anything to do with people after all?"

Frank looked at her, wishing he could think of something to say. He was startled by the bitterness in her voice.

"I'm sorry, Father. It's not your fault."

"Bearing with stupidity has its point too, Sister. It should make us less stupid ourselves."

"A fat lot of good that does those kids."

"I know."

"It has to change, Father. What we think we're doing. It has to change."

We have to change. I have to change. Not it. He wanted to say that aloud, to himself, to her, but it would have sounded like preaching. She already knew that anyway. He said, "It will, Sister. Don't worry."

"Me worry?" She made a funny face.

They left the classroom together and went down the stairs, where, on the main floor, Sister Gretchen, the principal, emerged from her office. She came to a halt and her long black skirt swirled and settled about her; a breeze entering by the open front door lifted her veil gently. Sister Gretchen's face, ageless in its starched frame, was smiling and serene. It seemed an odd time to realize that, aesthetically, there was a lot to be said for the order's traditional habit.

"Good afternoon, Father."

Frank greeted her and Sister Eloise, trilling some excuse, went off down the corridor.

"Monsignor Entweder tells me that you will be saying the graduation Mass for our eighth-graders."

"He hasn't told me yet. When is it?"

"Next Sunday. The nine o'clock."

"I'll be there," he said jauntily.

"It's a big day for them, Father."

"I'm sure it is."

"The sermon is aimed at the graduates, of course, and then you distribute the diplomas. Immediately after Mass, here in the school gym."

They went outside, where, on the steps, Sister Gretchen fussed on about the graduation ceremonies. She was wholly absorbed in her work, apparently without a trace of discontent. Frank could not imagine her confiding in him as Sister Eloise had. The principal had an exaggerated respect for him as a priest but, after all, he was only a man. He realized that Sister Gretchen was speaking of Sister Eloise now.

"She's still quite young, of course. And impatient. Anything you can do to encourage her, Father, would mean so much. It becomes more and more difficult for girls to grasp the true nature of the religious life. Some never do completely and many do not remain. Sister Eloise is a very generous, very dedicated young woman, but she takes things too hard."

Frank nodded and looked wise. "How will you spend the summer, Sister?"

Sister Gretchen's face became radiant. "At the provincial house! Most of the sisters will be there. After the turmoil of the school year those are such welcome months of peace. It's like a pleasantly prolonged retreat. A great opportunity for renewal, Father."

As he walked back to the rectory, Frank pondered the opposed assessments of the summer which faced the nuns. If Sister Gretchen was unduly complacent, perhaps Sister Eloise dwelt too much on causes for discontent. His thoughts returned to himself, to the house he headed for. Entweder and McTear. My God. He went in by the back door, which he shut firmly behind him. Unless the house was kept sealed, the air-conditioning was a waste. He was assailed by the aroma of cooking. Hilda, her face flushed with effort and pleasure, peeked out of her kitchen.

"Care for a piece of cake, Father? Supper's an hour away."

Frank felt his appetite respond to the invitation. Never in his life had he eaten as he had at Saint Waldo's. It was becoming difficult to fasten the waist of his trousers and throughout the day he was conscious of an uncomfortable binding at his middle. And it did not help that Hilda plied him with snacks between meals. Now, against the grain, against his stomach's gourmand leap, he said, "No, thanks, Hilda. I think I'll wait."

She withdrew, her expression mildly wounded. Frank ran up the stairs to his room. He arrived winded. If he weren't fearful of the effect on his appetite, he would quit smoking.

He read until Hilda announced supper and afterward went immediately back to his room. His isolation was intended, childishly, he knew, as punishment for Entweder. The sound of the TV came crashing down the hall. McTear was in the basement. How soporific the house seemed and, with it, the parish. It was difficult to concentrate but he finished his office and picked up a book. How little he had read since leaving Rome. His current resolution was to put himself on a definite reading schedule, to keep up on things, particularly theology. He would not succumb to the drag of mediocrity.

The phone rang and was answered downstairs by Hilda. Frank had sat forward at the sound, hoping it would be for him, a distraction, something to do that would take his mind off his discontent. Hope was draining from him when Hilda called his name.

It was Arthur Rupp. Was Father Ascue busy? Did he object to being invited out on such short notice? No? Good! The Rupps would like him to come over and Arthur would pick him up in half an hour. Frank said that he was delighted.

And, dear Lord, he was. The prospect of getting out of the rectory, even to visit with the Rupps, was incredibly pleasant. He realized that, if Arthur had not called, he would have phoned someone, Char, Father Ewing, Bob Wintheiser, anybody. In his present mood he would have welcomed an evening with Phil Bullard.

"How did you make out with Monsignor Entweder on that summer idea?" Arthur asked in the car.

"He didn't like it."

"I thought he wouldn't."

"I remember."

"Well, it was quite a bit of money."

"Money wasn't the problem. I had a donor."

"Is that so?"

Arthur dropped the topic and drove pensively. His silence caused Frank to wonder if this invitation had been tied to the hope of selling some insurance.

"You remember our daughter, Sheila, don't you, Father?" Clara Rupp asked when they were settled in the Rupp living room. Father Ascue had accepted a drink, reluctantly, remembering the unbridled revelry of his previous visit.

"Of course."

"I'm sorry about the way that dinner turned out, Father." Arthur frowned. "That Maud Bently."

"Sheila liked you," Clara said. "I could tell that right away."

Frank's smile felt idiotic. Too late he recalled Clara's saying that Sheila needed advice.

Arthur said, "She's an airline stewardess. Doesn't even live at home."

"Now, Arthur, why don't you let me tell Father about Sheila."

"I could leave the room."

"Don't be foolish."

"I mean it. You tell him. It only makes me angry. Besides, I have some things to do."

Arthur was serious. He stood and took his drink with him out of the room. Had that too been planned? Apparently not. "What a relief," Clara whispered, her eyes rolling upward. "I couldn't possibly have talked frankly to you in front of Arthur and his version would only confuse you."

Frank settled back in his chair. He was trapped and he might as well make the best of it. Besides, it was rather pleasant to be treated as the wise counselor. "How many versions are there?"

"Only one, really. Arthur pretends that he thinks Sheila is disloyal for growing up and leaving home. Of course that isn't what bothers him at all."

"What does?"

Clara brought the tip of one index finger along the back of her other hand, tracing a vein. "He thinks Sheila has lost her faith."

"Has she?"

166

"I don't know. How does one tell? When we ask her about it, she speaks in riddles."

"What kind of riddles?"

"That really isn't the right word. She talks without answering."

"What are the questions?"

"I suppose we're a little indirect too. What we want to know is: Does she go to Mass? Does she receive the sacraments?"

"Do you think she does?"

Clara shook her head slowly. "No. And that isn't the problem, not really. Perhaps it never is."

"Then what is the problem?"

Clara's sad eyes studied him for a moment. "A man. A married man. Sheila says he's divorced, but what difference does that make? I haven't been able to tell Arthur this." Clara was whispering now. "It would confirm his worst fears. Leaving home, not practicing her religion, now this. Father, would you talk to her?"

Frank waited a moment before replying and when he did he adopted a bright, brisk tone. "Clara, I'm sure that you as her mother—"

"You'd think so, wouldn't you? But I can't. I'm just no good at it. I wonder if other mothers are. I can't keep calm on the subject. The few times it has come up, well, it has been disastrous. Dear God, if Arthur ever found out, I don't know what he would do." Clara looked truly frightened. It was hard to recognize in her the bemused and maladroit hostess of his previous visit. She was a mother in pain, a wife in anguish, a confused woman. "If he found out, Father, I'm afraid that he would never want to see Sheila again. Do you know, when he objected to her having an apartment, I sided with her? She has always been so sensible."

"She seemed sensible to me."

"Oh, she is. She really is."

Frank waited for Clara to go on but she, having said the worst, seemed to think she had said it all.

"Have you met the man?"

"No! And I don't want to. Father, he is older than Sheila. There is a child, at least one, a daughter. This came as a surprise to Sheila herself. I was sure that she would come to her senses then and stop seeing him. Yet even that talk ended badly, very badly. I know she expected more from me and I had nothing to give. All I could think to say is that she must talk to a priest. I mentioned your name."

"How did she react?"

"Neither of us was very rational at the time."

"She said no."

"She said no. Of course she did. In the circumstances, it was all she could say. I know it was foolish of me to bring it up then, but she needs help. And she knows she does. She wants help. This is killing her inside, I can tell. She didn't know at first that he had been married—is married —and then to find that there was a little girl besides . . ." Clara inhaled. "Sheila met the daughter and apparently it was a very traumatic experience. For Sheila. Father, will you talk with her?"

"Of course I will, if she wants me to. But this is very delicate. I could make things worse, you know. I would be going to her knowing all kinds of things about her that she hadn't told me, private things. And I would seem to be an emissary from her parents."

"She liked you, Father. You got on. I just know she would listen to you."

It was not so much that he wanted to refuse as that he wondered what it was Clara would think he was agreeing to. She was so anxious that even the most ambiguous response from him would probably be welcome, yet he dreaded raising her hopes. If Sheila wanted to talk with him, the initiative would have to come from her. Did she intend to marry the man or what? He gathered that she was not living with him.

"Why was meeting his child so difficult?"

"I don't really know. It came as a surprise that he had a daughter, but that isn't much of an explanation, is it? Perhaps she thought he had been deliberately deceiving her?" Clara threw up her hands. "None of this is clear, I know. The point is that Sheila is desperately in need of help, religious help."

When Arthur returned from his den, he insisted that Father Ascue let him freshen his drink. "You've earned it, Father. Listening to all our troubles."

Frank made a diffident noise.

"Will you try to talk sense to our girl?"

"I'm sure that Father Ascue will do what he can, Arthur."

Later, in the car, Arthur said, "Clara worries an awful lot about Sheila. Mothers will, you know."

"I know."

"It isn't just that I want Sheila home again. I do. But mothers imagine all sorts of things." After a little silence, he said, "Sheila is a good girl, Father. She could never get into any real trouble. But it isn't wise for a girl that age to be completely on her own."

"I understand."

"I wish Sheila did."

In his room, Father Ascue unfolded the slip of paper on which Clara had written her daughter's address and phone number. He put it on his desk, wondering how in the world he was going to be able to fulfill the Rupps' request.

But it was Sheila Rupp who contacted him, several days later, by telephone.

"I don't mean to be rude, Father, but I don't want to see you. Mother told me of your conversation. I gather she extracted some sort of promise from you."

"No, not a promise."

"I don't know what she might have told you. But there's nothing for us to talk about. I don't mean to hurt your feelings. I liked you. I suppose that's why they're trying to use you."

"That isn't fair to your parents, is it?"

"Fair," she repeated softly. "No, perhaps not. Fairness has never been our long suit."

"The truth is, I didn't have any idea what I would say to you if I did call. How does one begin on this sort of thing?"

"What sort of thing?"

He laughed. "Your sinful ways, of course. Well, if you don't want to talk to me, there isn't much I can do about that."

"Father, there isn't anything to talk about. For heaven's sake."

"Good."

"I mean it."

"If only you could convince your mother of that."

"What did she tell you, anyway?"

"Would you like to get together and talk about that?"

Sheila laughed, then fell silent. Frank waited.

"Very well, Father. If you insist. When are you free? I warn you, though. You're going to be very disappointed."

"I hope so."

They set a date and he hung up. No muffled sounds rose from the playground outside his window. Despite the heat, he would have preferred to be out of the house, doing something. He had office hours this afternoon and the phone had rung but once—when Sheila called—the doorbell not at all. He should have asked her to come to the rectory now but it had seemed best to agree to a neutral place. Was Clara wrong about her daughter's involvement with a married man? He hoped she was, but why would Clara imagine such a story about Sheila? Well, he would see.

See. Learn. Find out. But what would he say to her if Clara's suspicions were grounded? Dear God, if only he could feel again the zest he had during his first weeks at Saint Waldo's. The pastor's veto of the summer program had revealed how tight, safe and comfortable the rectory routine was. Mass and census and sick calls. Business as usual. In the upper part of the parish, children for whom they were responsible ran wild and the bulk of the summer stretched before them still. They had been sacrificed to an abstract principle and one which involved the assumption that parish plants and tax-free property were the essence of the Church. The plight of those children was not imaginary, as Mrs. Purcell's visit two days before had made clear.

Frank had had office hours that day too. Hilda buzzed his room and Frank went downstairs to find a thin weeping woman waiting in one of the parlors.

"Father, he's thirteen years old," the woman wailed. "Thirteen years old!"

Was it the green youth of her son or superstition concerning the number? Little Henry had been joy-riding in stolen cars, three in all. In the third he had jumped a suburban curb and nosed into someone's family room.

"They say he'd been drinking. Henry! Father, he's only thirteen."

Frank had soothed her, he had gone downtown with her to juvenile court the following morning, he had in the process wondered if even Sister Eloise's program could have saved Henry, a pustular, sullen boy Frank half expected to whine that he was being framed.

The judge, a bald Irishman with a bulbous fuchsia nose, seemed glad to release Henry to the custody of his mother. "Understaffed," he said, almost apologetically.

"Are there many kids like him?"

"Father, it's a national phenomenon."

"I meant here in Fort Elbow."

"Too many."

"Why?"

Judge Murphy regarded him with watery eyes. "Maybe you have the answer to that, Father."

Did he mean Original Sin? That was too vague an explanation. Mrs. Purcell was waiting for him outside, to thank him. She seemed to think that Frank and the judge had exchanged some secret sign that had set her son free. Little Henry stood some distance from them, speculatively eyeing the cars at the curb.

From the courthouse Frank had gone to the hospital for a visit with Miss Simpson. As he walked, he thought of Henry and found himself resenting the boy's shifty ferret look and the mother's too effusive thanks. Why hadn't the boy's father shown up at juvenile court? Frank felt that he had been used: a priest to influence the Catholic judge and get Henry off with a reprimand. It was difficult to believe that he had done anyone a favor this morning. If he had really meant to help, he would have asked about the Purcells, about the father, and did they have other children? How was Henry spending the summer? It was too late to pursue it now. But Frank wanted to. There might be something he could do. If only Henry was not such an unlikable kid.

Miss Simpson seemed bright and on the mend. When Frank mentioned this to a nurse, he was told it was illusory. With a renewed sense of depression he returned to the rectory.

He had wanted "real priestly work" and now he feared that he had found it: sitting on dozens of sofas filling in the blanks of census cards, attending the dying or those whose release from this vale of tears was further off. Now that school was over, the parish plant wilted in the sun, entombed in silence. Except for weekends. Each Saturday morning there was a series of weddings, couple after couple plunging with vacant smiles into God knew what. On Sunday there was the chaos of the crowded Masses, the annoyance of lay lectors hamming it up while they read from Scripture or directed uncertain baritones into the mike, watched from the pews by resentful fellow parishioners. The hopes which had been invested in liturgical changes seemed to Frank inflated when he saw the thing in action. There was certainly a lot more commotion than before, but a shaggy-haired apparent addict crouching on a stool mere feet from the altar and strumming his guitar was not conducive to worship. The boy's syncopated renditions managed to throw off the crooning lector but failed to tempt the congregation into joyful song. Major Bowes would have loved it. On weekdays both Entweder and McTear said their Masses in Latin to the immense pleasure of the dozen or so faithful who paged their missals like Thomists in search of a footnote. At Frank's Mass they gripped their closed books and followed sadly the Mass in their mother tongue, all mystery and magic gone.

Sheila, when he met her at the airport restaurant on Friday, was wearing her uniform. A saucy cap dipped low on her forehead, her skirt was well short of the knee. She ordered a chocolate sundae, Frank coffee.

"Not a very good place to talk." He was reminded of the setting of his conversation with Diane.

She smiled. "I know." The whole building was aroar with echoing sounds and the restaurant was stifling hot.

"Your mother mentioned a man."

"Anyone I know?"

"That seemed to be her concern."

Sheila churned her ice cream with a spoon. "His name is Carl. I love him." Her eyes met his, deadly serious. "What's my penance?"

"Is he married?"

"No."

"Was he?"

"You're not drinking your coffee."

"I didn't really want it."

"He's divorced."

"I see."

She propped her chin in her palm. "And I can see the little wheels spinning in there." A finger indicated his forehead. "I'll bet it's chock-full of rules."

"Is his wife still alive?"

"So far as I know. Should I wish she weren't?"

"Then you don't know?"

Sheila shook her head. "Somehow we don't talk much about her."

"Just about his daughter?"

Her mouth became a line, her eyes left his.

"Hadn't he told you about his child?"

"Of course he told me. How do you think I knew?"

"What's she like?"

"I don't want to talk about her." Her voice was controlled, but angry, very angry. "Do you mind. I'm sorry I agreed to meet you."

"Carl who?"

"Oh, no."

"What does that mean?"

"Leave him alone, Father. Do you understand? You just leave him alone. Leave me alone too."

"Wait." She had pushed away her ice cream and was reaching for her bag. He put his hand on her wrist. "Please. I didn't come here to make you feel bad. Believe me. Don't go."

Her wrist relaxed and he withdrew his hand.

"I haven't much time."

"I know. Has he asked you to marry him?"

Her eyes rounded. "You've no right to ask me a question like that."

"Then don't answer it. I know I'm not doing this well. Sheila, look. Maybe it isn't impossible. Marriage. Okay, my head *is* full of rules. Most of them make sense. Some bend so far that *that* annoys people. His first marriage might not be an impediment."

"Impediment," she echoed. She was looking at him incredulously.

"Is he a Catholic?"

"No."

"A Christian?"

"I suppose so." Her answer was clipped and she stared at him as if she wondered what preposterous thing he might say next.

"If it wasn't a valid marriage, in the eyes of the Church . . ." He let his voice drift into silence.

"He hasn't asked me to marry him, Father."

"But if he does?"

She did not hesitate. "I'd marry him."

"Even if it were a sin?"

Her mouth opened, her eyes sparked with defiance, but no words emerged.

"Find out about his first marriage, Sheila. He may be perfectly free to marry you."

Her eyes lifted to the clock on the wall. "I really have to go, Father."

"Will you find out?"

She picked up her bag, slid its strap up her arm to her shoulder. That done, she sat back, studying him. Her smile was slight, almost sad. "Father, if he ever does ask me to marry him, I'll find out. Good enough?"

"Good enough."

When she had gone, he tasted his coffee, then put it down. His palate was becoming progressively more spoiled by Hilda's cuisine. Why did he feel certain that Carl's first marriage would turn out to be valid? If Sheila married him nonetheless, she would be living in sin, in the eyes of the Church. Rules. Yes, his head was full of rules. But it was not the possible cruelty of the rules that bothered him. She did not really expect Carl to ask her to marry him. Her manner had told him that. And could she trust a love that stopped short of committing itself beyond a brief arrangement? If tragedy threatened her it would not come from the Church's marriage laws.

Before leaving, he finished his coffee. It seemed a penitential act, one that in some crazy way was meant to help Sheila. The conversation had left him with the feeling that, as a priest, it was his destiny to be the bearer of bad news.

Thus, feeling inadequate and unhelpful, he moved through the week toward Sister Eloise's phone call and her surprising news. Her tone was excited, her message brief.

"I'm saved, Father! I'm going to have a good summer after all."

"Did the provincial house burn down?"

"Fat chance. No, listen. I am going to work at the Center with Phil Bullard."

"At the Center," he repeated stupidly.

"Three of us have rented an apartment nearby. Isn't that fabulous? I was certain we would be refused but Phil had Bishop Brophy talk with Mother Superior and she could hardly tell a bishop no so we're moving in tomorrow. Oh, I'm so excited."

The significance of the experiment was enormous and went far beyond the summer. Imagine, if nuns were allowed to live throughout the city, live as other people lived, out of the ghetto of the convent! It had been tried, Sister Eloise told him, it was being tried in several places, and the results were literally fantastic. Her effervescent voice sang on in Frank's ear while he looked out at the empty expanse of asphalt that might have been swarming with children.

After he had hung up, he sat listening to the sounds of tinkering lift from below. McTear now had a citizen band radio and was installing equipment in the kitchen. The idea, he was happy to explain, was that now he could be summoned instantly within a range of twenty miles. All Hilda had to do was call his car. Entweder was tolerant, Hilda vaguely excited. When the senior assistant offered to lend Frank money for a set, Frank reminded him that he did not have a car.

"You should get one," McTear advised.

"Father is right," Entweder said. "I don't drive myself but an automobile is a convenience."

Frank did not understand how priests managed to afford cars on their token salaries, let alone shortwave radios and citizen bands. Apparently it was a matter of going massively into debt and the thought of doing that disturbed him. He had never handled money in great amounts, had never incurred a debt. That whole side of life, which loomed so large for so many, was foreign to him. It was an odd thought that he had as little practical experience with money as a savage, probably less. As assistant pastor, he received seventy-five dollars a month and that was more of an allowance than a salary.

"But of course you should have a car," Charlotte exclaimed when he mentioned the conversation. "Howard and I will lend you the money if that will ease your mind. I promise that we won't foreclose and take it away."

He refused to take this as a serious offer. He wanted to think that by taking buses and cabs he was not so much leveling an indirect indictment at others as mimicking in a manner possible to him that indifference to worldly goods which his heroes, those real and fictional saints of his youthful daydreaming, had exemplified.

"I'm not sure that I want a car."

"It's not a matter of wanting, of a luxury. You have to have a car."

"I've been doing all right without one."

174

"Ha! Is that why you borrow ours?"

"I don't *borrow* yours, Char. You insist that I take it."

"Well, pardon me all to hell."

"Oh, come on. I'm grateful for the use of it. But I don't really want one of my own."

Part of his resistance was due to a recent feeling that Charlotte had too often smoothed the way for him, that, if he let her, she would increasingly give him advice and then go on to implement it. She was generous and sisterly but too insistent for comfort and he had outgrown the willingness to let her brood however benevolently over his life.

This realization of the tenacity of women had a broader base than his sister. The ruthless affection and passionate singlemindedness of women seemed all around him. Sister Eloise was not a person to be denied when she had made up her mind. Even Diane, beaten now, was in the spot she was in because of an implicit faith in the rightness of her own emotions. And Sheila. The Rupps' daughter had dismissed him as the representative of the legal, the extrinsic constraint, but he was certain that she would know a sterner taskmaster: the whiplash of her own felt certainty that whatever she wanted had to be right.

"Women are always sure of themselves," Entweder generalized when Frank had spoken to him in anonymous terms of Sheila's situation. "Sure and seldom right. On the whole, though, I have come to think that that is preferable to an unending search for the safe reasoned way."

"But a marriage is either valid or invalid."

"That's true. Does the question bother the young woman?"

"Not at all, apparently."

Monsignor Entweder sighed. "It almost never does. Man is the regretful animal, Father. A moralist in retrospect. By the time this woman comes to see that there is some wisdom in ecclesiastical marriage laws, her knowledge will be good only for remorse."

The afternoon Charlotte had urged Frank to buy a car, she asked him to stay for supper. "Howard had to go to Cleveland and Bev is caught up with a new boyfriend, plus working at the Center."

"Working?"

"Just volunteer. No salary or anything so mundane. Phil Bullard has a few nuns and seminarians helping him with a program for kids in the neighborhood and Bev is caught up in it too."

Char seemed to know little about what sort of work Bev was actually doing. Her own curiosity ran in a different direction.

"Is there any news on your nomination to the priests' senate?"

"The vote hasn't been announced yet."

"Don't be so damned blasé. Surely you want to be elected."

"No one seems to know precisely what the senate is supposed to do."

On the ballot he was listed as Francis Ascue, S.T.D. It seemed clear that his presence there was due to Bishop Brophy, but why the auxiliary thought mentioning his degree would help puzzled Frank. If he thought it was a plus he might be surprised; there was a subtle sort of resentment among the clergy directed against those who had been sent on to higher studies. In any case, Frank felt some mention should have been made of the fact that he was now the junior assistant at Saint Waldo's. Shortly after the ballots had been put into the mail, he had received a number of phone calls. Phil Bullard had professed to be delighted and said that he would push as many votes Frank's way as he could.

"We need all the young blood in there we can get, Frank. Oder is the only man over forty I'll vote for."

"Excepting yourself," Bob Wintheiser said, his tone conveying that the exception was not all that clear-cut. "I am dubious of the youngsters on the ballot. Whoever engineered it certainly had an eye for Young Turks. The definition of which is that they are chicken when it comes to principle. Of course the whole idea of a senate is utter nonsense, a sop to the democratic spirit. However valid that may be in the political realm, it has no application in the Church. But a sop makes a sap out of the one giving. How representative of sentiment among the clergy is that ballot?"

Frank did not know how to assess the ballot in those terms. So far as age went it seemed to offer a spectrum. Which made it a mystery how Phil would vote if he used forty as a cut-off age. While he was speaking with Phil, he asked how Sister Eloise was working out.

"If the two who came with her turn out to be half as good, this could be quite a summer, Frank."

To Charlotte he said, "So Bev has a new boyfriend?"

"Very new. He seems someone special. She's never talked of the others as she does of him."

"What do you think of him?"

"Me? She won't bring him near me. That's how I know it's serious."

The boy's name, it turned out, was Ben Cole.

The afternoon they took a bunch of kids to the children's zoo, Bev had volunteered to drive the VW bus Phil had borrowed from a grad stu-

176

dent and, when Ben Cole had packed the yipping, hollering bunch into the back and got in beside her, she managed to start the motor all right but the gears proved to be a mystery. There was a diagram on the dash but she could not get the stick to follow the indicated pattern.

"I thought you said you knew how to drive one of these," Ben said.

"Of course I can."

"To get it into reverse, you have to press down."

"Have *you* driven one before?"

"I've watched it done."

So they changed seats and he had trouble finding reverse too but finally he had it, they backed away, started off, and a roar of approval went up from the back seats.

"You showed me the seminary chapel," she informed Ben when Phil had introduced them at the Center.

"I remember."

"You don't look it."

"What do you mean?"

What *did* she mean? She didn't know. She reminded him that Frank Ascue was her uncle, as if by having a relative who was a priest she was less a stranger, an in-law by canon law.

"He was in my class," Phil said and Bev resented the suggestion that Uncle Frank took on importance from this association with Phil Bullard.

In the bus she said, "They're not much alike, my Uncle Frank and Phil."

"What parish is he in?"

"Saint Waldo's."

"We expected him to be appointed to the seminary faculty."

"So did we."

Ben looked at her. "Doesn't he like Saint Waldo's?"

"Uncle Frank? He loves it. No complaints at all."

"That's the way to be."

He concentrated on his driving, leaving the wild Indians in back to her. After half climbing over the seat in an effort to shut them up, Bev decided to let them raise all the hell they wanted. They didn't seem to bother Ben so what difference did it make if they whooped it up a little? The poor kids seemed to find this a real treat, a visit to the stupid zoo. At their age, they should have been there dozens of times already but, if you could believe them, none had even known there was a zoo in town. How often had Dave and Beth been there? Trying to guess, Bev felt a twinge of guilt. Would she have been this willing to take her little brother and sister to the zoo? They weren't deprived like these kids, but even so.

Once inside the zoo, Ben said, "Let them run. They can't get lost." She agreed. Their charges scattered along the walks and they strolled slowly. Ben stopped at the monkey cage and almost immediately turned away. Did he think the pink-bottomed antics of those horny little beasts would embarrass her?

"What did you mean, your uncle isn't like Phil Bullard?"

His eyes were gray and had an intriguing way of not really settling on her while they talked. She had noticed that at the seminary, when he had been asked to show her around, had thought at first it was shyness, but then realized it was because she was off limits, an instance of what he was saying no to if he became a priest. It made her feel twice as female as before, was pleasant, and she was determined that he was going to look at her, really look at her.

She said, "Phil is always bitching about celibacy. So okay, he doesn't like it. Does he have to tell *every*body? Sometimes I think he's afraid his manhood will be questioned."

"I'm sure that isn't it." My God, she had shocked him.

"What then?"

His eyes were on her, too briefly, drifted away. Honest to Pete, he made a girl feel like Miss America. She began to hum that awful tune.

"Your uncle doesn't complain about it?"

"You make *him* sound unusual."

"Well, a lot of people wonder if it will last. Celibacy. It is a rule that could be changed."

"Would you like that?"

He looked at her directly. "What do you think?"

What she thought, though this was later, was that that had been a nice note on which to get started. His awkwardness went while he talked of the separability of holy orders and celibacy and then they were distracted by the return of some of the kids and it seemed a good idea to round them up and keep an eye on them.

For a week they saw each other only during the day, at the Center, and it was easy to stay together there. Bev could almost believe that Phil Bullard conspired with them to make it easy, but of course it was silly to think that anyone noticed. There really was not much to notice, not that first week, not ever at the Center. Besides, Phil was too busy with Sister Eloise. They seemed to vie with one another to come up with new ideas for attracting more kids, doing more things, expanding the program. It was all very exciting but Bev did not kid herself about her motives. In the morning, reluctant to get out of bed, all she had to do was think of Ben and she bounded up, wide awake and eager to get to the Center. The drive-in movie was something that just grew out of their talk about the film being shown there. When Ben asked if she would like to see it, diffidently, as if he expected her to hesitate and remind him that he was a seminarian, she was already deciding what she would wear.

That night, sitting beside him in his father's car, she put her hand on his and for minutes he just left it like that until she began to feel foolish and predatory and then his hand turned under hers, his fingers grasped hers. She looked at him and saw indecision etched on his face. It filled her with tenderness and also with a slightly demonic desire to make him forget the contradiction of the situation. He turned to her and she could sense his dying resolve to take his hand away, to start the car and get the hell out of there, take her home, never see her again, and then she was in his arms and while he kissed her he groaned as if with real pain. Later that night, in bed, it occurred to her that she was the first girl he had ever kissed and she began to cry, to sob helplessly with delight and a vague shame, until she had to bury her face in her pillow so no one would hear her.

He was an hour late getting to the Center the next day and it was a very long hour for Bev. When he did arrive it was like the first day, he would not meet her eye, but then suddenly, in the hallway, when they were briefly alone, he took her hand and squeezed it painfully and when she moved against him and his arms came around her she knew that the bad time was over.

Except that it always threatened to return. Nearly every night now they went out and it was best when they had no destination, when they just drove to the beach and talked, but there remained a division in him that she just did not seem able to do anything about. She learned that it was best to steer the conversation toward the source of his uneasiness.

"Do you ever think of leaving the seminary?"

"I guess everybody does. You know."

She nodded. Everybody? To hell with everybody. She wanted to know about Ben Cole.

"Maybe it will change."

"What?"

"Celibacy."

"Maybe."

They had left the car in a parking lot and were sitting on a bench; below them the river moved darkly in the night, caught glints of light bobbing on the going water. The silence was filled with his indecision but she knew now which way the coin would fall—as long as they were together. And then he mentioned going away.

"Father Grimes? Who's he?"

"A priest I know. He was assistant at our parish when I was a kid. He has his own parish now, in a small town, and he wants me to come see him."

"For a visit?"

Ben nodded.

"How long would you stay?"

"I don't know. A couple days. It depends."

The word seemed to dangle in the dark, a hook from which her own hopes depended. Instinctively she felt that Father Grimes was the enemy, the man Ben would tell about her and in the telling she would become something else, a danger, a temptation, someone to turn his back on. When finally Ben kissed her it was she who groaned as if in pain.

Frank was familiar with her name from reading the *Fort Elbow Tribune* and he felt almost flattered when Mary Muscatelli showed up at the rectory one day. His mood altered when he realized that she had come here with a mistaken notion.

"But the pastor isn't in charge of the nuns, Miss Muscatelli. Not in that way."

"Mary."

"Mary. They have their own superior in the parish convent and of course they are all subject to the mother provincial."

"She assigns them to places?"

"That's right."

The reporter brought her cigarette to her mouth; she inhaled so deeply that her cheeks sucked in. The v of her fingers opened and closed on the cigarette and her shoulders hunched. When she spoke her words emerged like signals.

"So you wouldn't know anything about why Sister Eloise and the other two nuns have taken an apartment?"

"You could talk to them about that."

"I already have." Mary tapped her knee with her closed notebook. "I thought I might get their boss's viewpoint."

"You'll have to go to the provincial house for that. What did Sister Eloise have to say?"

The reporter looked at him for a moment, as if appraising him. Then she flicked open her notebook and began to read.

The life style of sisters had to change, the giving of one's life to Christ did not mean withdrawal to the security of the cloister. The whole point of being a nun, everyone's sister, was to be available, to be generous, to help. Changing garb might seem pretty superficial but it was in a way the key. We talk to people with our clothes, don't we? Dress is a language. Ever since I started to dress like this people aren't frightened of me anymore, they're not aloof.

Although Mary read with a droning disinterested swiftness, Frank could hear the cadences of the nun's voice in the recorded phrases.

"So I asked her if she ever got into compromising situations," Mary said.

"What did she say?"

"Sure. And didn't I?"

Mary had asked Eloise about the gold band she wore and had been told she had received it at profession. The bride of Christ. It helped a little in those compromising situations Mary had mentioned. The reporter's voice became more perfunctory and flat and finally she closed the notebook.

He said, "You weren't impressed."

"Oh, it's not that. She's sincere, that's obvious. Who knows, they may even do some good down there. But it's hardly stop-the-presses news, is it?"

"What's it like being a reporter in a town like this?"

"Don't get me wrong. It's not the town. There are all kinds of important things going on here while I'm being sent out to interview some nuns who have taken an apartment as if that were the rough equivalent of journeying into darkest Africa. It's ridiculous."

"What important things?"

She lit another cigarette and before she had waved the match out she was reminding him of the New Hampshire primary, of Johnson's decision not to run, of the Kennedy and King assassinations. Right now they were on the threshold of the national conventions and even if the Republican one would be a dud, the Chicago convention should be another story entirely.

"Father, there are people here in Fort Elbow who will be delegates to those conventions. What are they thinking? What do they intend to do? That's my idea of news, not jotting down some sweet nun's notion of what the age requires."

"So why don't you interview those people?"

"I'd love to. But I can't." She scowled. "I've become the hotshot religious reporter on the *Trib*. What a joke. With all due respect, Father, and I'm a Catholic myself, sort of, I just don't think all this hullabaloo about nuns and priests makes any sense."

"Many nuns and priests would agree with you."

"Maybe. But not all. Some of them really lap it up, believe me."

"Well, Eloise isn't one of them."

"No." Mary reached for her purse, which was on the floor beside her chair. "Why do they have to be associated with that Center?"

"Why not?"

She thought about that for a moment, then sighed. "Oh, well, I guess it's teapot enough for their tempest." She rose. "I'm sorry. I didn't mean to cry on your shoulder."

When he let her out the front door, Frank watched her walk out to her car. A Catholic, sort of. He wondered what she had meant.

No doubt Mary was right in seeing what Eloise and the other nuns were trying to do as less than sensational news, but if that was dull how much duller was his life at Saint Waldo's. It was easy for him to envy the kind of work Phil was doing at the Center, the kind of work the nuns were doing. Someday he would have to stop by for a visit.

"Is Sister Eloise in?" Frank asked when the door was opened by a pale girl with unkempt hair the color of August weeds.

"Huh?" Her nose wrinkled into a sergeant's chevrons.

"Does a woman named Eloise live here?"

"Did you say Sister?"

It occurred to him that their work here might be more effective if people did not know they were nuns. "A manner of speaking."

When Frank explained that Eloise would be living with two other women, the girl looked less stupid. Three women had taken an apartment here. Apartment seemed not quite the word for any subdivision this house might contain. It was a huge frame house whose siding was gray and weatherworn, its look as woebegone as the girl's who had opened the door. Let into the hallway, Frank searched in the dim light and found a new slip stuck into a mailbox slot.

"That's there." The girl pointed at double doors. Frank knocked on both of them. They must once have opened onto a parlor. There was no answer. He knocked again, conscious of the girl waiting behind him.

"When are they usually in?"

"Search me."

"Have you met them?"

The girl assumed an about-to-lie look, but she said, "Sure, I've met them. Who are they anyway?"

"Who did they say they were?"

"They didn't." The girl stood with her weight on one foot, her shoulders slumped in the same direction. She did not seem terribly bright.

"Well, thanks."

182

There was a pay phone hanging on the wall, surrounded by a filigree of penciled notations. He should have called before coming here; they would have had the number at the Center. When he had been unable to reach Eloise there, he had simply assumed that she would be at the apartment. But of course she could be anywhere. It had been stupid to assume that she would be sitting home in the middle of the afternoon. After all, this wasn't Saint Waldo's.

He let himself out and stood on the porch. It was a huge wooden affair which ran along the front of the house and, L-shaped, continued along one side as well. There were hooks in the ceiling and Frank could imagine a swing hanging there. Like the neighborhood itself, this house had once been elegant. Earlier occupants must once have swung on this porch, the scene before them one of affluence and ease. Both sides of the street were lined with cars, suggesting how crowded the houses were now, divided and subdivided, not really cared for, none of their occupants feeling the pride of possession or any sense of permanence.

A red Mustang stopped in the street and a girl hopped out. She called something to the driver and slammed the door. As if the slam had done it, the car shot away up the street. When she came between two parked cars, Frank saw that the girl was Eloise. His eyes went to the car disappearing up the street. Suddenly he felt trapped and out of place. He moved quickly across the porch and around the corner of the house. He could hear the sound of heels coming up the walk and then she mounted the steps and crossed the porch. The door opened and closed. When he exhaled, Frank realized that he had been holding his breath. That was as surprising as the fact that he had avoided meeting Eloise. He turned to the window beside him. The girl he had talked with in the hall looked out at him, her expression puzzled and suspicious. Feeling more ridiculous than he had in years, Frank hurried across the porch to the steps. All the way out to the street, his back tingled with the certainty that he was observed, by the girl, by Eloise, by everyone. When he reached the street he walked in the direction opposite that in which Phil Bullard had sped away in his red Mustang.

"Congratulations, Senator," McTear said. "How does it feel?"
Frank smiled. "I'm not sure. Good, I guess."
"You bet it's good. It's nice having Saint Waldo's represented in the senate. Monsignor is pleased as punch."
Frank too thought of his election in terms of Saint Waldo's, a chance of opening out from the parish, getting into other sorts of work. He had got over his melancholy, the depression that had followed on Ent-

weder's capricious reaction to the summer program. It had required some prolonged talking to himself, and prayer, but he had managed to get to work again with some semblance of zeal. Nonetheless, his first fervor was gone forever; there was no point in pretending otherwise. What had once been exhilarating was now routine. How incredibly same the days were. Entweder and McTear seemed totally content to tread the cage, to feed and sleep and do their little jobs. When he was not envying them, Frank came dangerously close to despising them. He suspected that McTear went out more often now simply to provide Hilda occasion to contact him on the citizen band. At night the senior assistant had his equipment in the basement and the lengthy conversations with far-flung hams like himself. As for himself, Frank had learned not to expect the superficial pleasure from his work that had been constant during the first weeks in the parish. There was something to be said for working against the grain of his emotions so that, if ever satisfaction returned, he would know enough not to rely on it, as though it were the motive of his work. The chance of being elected to the clerical senate had promised opportunities for something more significant than the daily round of parish work. And then Bishop Brophy had phoned to say that he had been elected.

"I want you on the Steering Committee, Father. The first session has to be carefully planned or the senate could be doomed from the start."

Frank said that he would be glad to be on it and the bishop ticked off the names of other possible members. Oder, Ewing, some others who were only names to Frank.

"Do you know a man named Grimes?"

"Jim Grimes?"

"Yes. He's been elected and I'd like him on the committee too. He's pretty far out, but I think it would do him a world of good."

Frank felt like saying that the work would be therapy for himself too but Brophy might not have understood. The first meeting of the Steering Committee would be held at the Saint Barnabas rectory.

It was not an hour after the bishop called that the phone rang again. It was Charlotte, proud and happy.

"How did you find out?"

"It's in the paper, dum-dum. Isn't it wonderful?"

Her elation fed his own and he told her of the Steering Committee. Charlotte wanted him to come out that night but he had to beg off, postponing it until the night of the meeting at the Saint Barnabas rectory. He would have to eat and run, but Char said that was better than nothing, at least they would have a few hours with her big-shot

184

brother. By the time Arthur Rupp called, Frank felt a practiced accepter of congratulations.

"I must say I'm not terribly clear on the purpose of the senate, Father."

"The general idea is to enable the clergy to advise the bishop on matters that concern them."

"Like the consultors?"

"Not quite. The senate is elected by the clergy, not appointed by the bishop."

Rupp made a humming noise. "I suppose there'll be attempts at mischief."

"What do you mean?"

"Let's just say that I'm relieved to have someone like you on the senate, Father. There are a lot of rascals wearing Roman collars nowadays. Or not wearing them. You know what I mean."

"The senate wouldn't be if the bishop didn't want it, Arthur."

"Well, I hope my fears are unfounded. You have our support. Te Deum's. I mean that."

Bob Wintheiser offered his sympathy. "I didn't vote for you, Frank. I want you to know that. You still have friends. You poor devil, what a crew to get mixed up with. Have you gone over the list?"

"I've seen it, yes."

Bob sighed significantly. "Ah, well. Perhaps it will just wither away, like the state."

"Not a very apt analogy, Bob."

"Don't be so literal. I'm surprised Bullard wasn't elected."

"It would have been more surprising if he had been. He wasn't on the ballot."

"I meant as a write-in. Anyway, lots of luck. Have you seen Gerry yet?" They still spoke of having dinner together, the three of them, but the discussion had become ritualistic.

"Not yet. Do you think he's avoiding me?"

"Why? You were only just elected senator. Anyway, I don't suppose he'll hold that against you."

Frank was glad when the conversation ended. Bob was worse than Arthur Rupp. Well, maybe not worse. Arthur seemed to think that Te Deum would be represented on the senate because Frank had been elected. At least Arthur had not asked him about Sheila, but then Clara would have told him of her call.

"Surely you don't expect me to tell you of our conversation, Clara."

"Not specifically, no. Is she all right?"

"Haven't you seen her lately?"

"You know what I mean." Clara paused. "How I wish she would settle down and get married."

"Maybe she will."

"Did she say that?" Clara's voice rose.

"I can't tell you what she said."

"She is going to, isn't she?"

"I haven't any idea and if I did, if she had told me something in confidence, well . . ."

"I understand, Father." Clara's tone seemed meant to soothe him and then Frank did get angry.

"You *don't* understand. I haven't said anything. Sheila is a good, sensible girl, as you already know. If you want to know of her plans, if you want to know whether she has any plans, all you have to do is talk with her."

"Oh, I will, Father. And thank you. Arthur and I are very grateful to you. Thank you."

And Clara hung up. Frank continued to hold the phone, staring at the mouthpiece, and when he hung up it was with a bang. He had not told Clara anything but clearly she thought he had. For several days, the memory of the conversation had made him uneasy but, since Arthur had not brought up his daughter when he called, things must be all right. Perhaps, afterward, Clara had seen how silly she had been, jumping to conclusions, and had told Arthur nothing at all.

Oder opened the door. His brows lifted in greeting and his smooth hand clasped Father Ascue's. The pastor of Saint Barnabas conferred on clerical clothing an aura of high fashion. His collar and board-stiff French cuffs, linked by facsimiles of Roman coins, were impossibly white; his black suit was tailored to perfection. A handsome face and thick gray wavy hair, worn longish but barbered and groomed, added to his undeniable presence. The only flaw was his expression, a not infrequent one on the very handsome; it seemed a reflection of the surprise and admiration he incited and acquiescence in the beholder's estimate.

"Good to have you, Father. Come in. I had *heard* that you were back from Rome." The remark seemed to suggest that Frank should have reported in long before this.

"From Rome to Saint Waldo's."

"Yes." Oder, closing the door, studied him as if to see if the remark was a comment on his assignment. "Dear Monsignor Entweder."

"Am I the first arrival?"

"The last, Father. But never mind. This way."

Unlike most rectories, that of Saint Barnabas, perhaps because it was a rather more expensive instance of the suburban homes surrounding it, had a living room; they crossed it, went down a hall and came into a study. Bishop Brophy, Father Ewing, Jim Grimes, two priests Frank knew only by sight, and a layman awaited them there. Oder presented Frank to the bishop, who transferred his drink to his left hand and shook Frank's without getting up.

"You know Father Ewing, of course." Oder's voice rippled, not quite teasingly. Father Ewing winked with both eyes and patted the cushion beside him on the black leather couch. Frank did sit there after he had said hello to the others. The layman, a shy fellow with a belligerent blush, was Donovan, editor of the *Fort Elbow Catholic*.

"How're things?" Ewing asked, taking a cigarette from a crumpled package.

Frank said things were fine. Oder, withdrawn to a sideboard on which cut-glass decanters gleamed, asked Frank what he would have and, told that he wanted nothing, drifted to the desk. They all turned to the bishop.

Bishop Brophy spoke for fifteen minutes with a spontaneity that could only have been rehearsed. He reminded them that the clerical senate was an innovation, that it was imperative that it begin smoothly. The Steering Committee was to ensure that it did and their first task was to draw up an agenda for their colleagues' consideration. There was one item, though Brophy did not suggest that it be first on the agenda, that he would like their ideas on. A countywide ecumenical conference was in the offing, indeed plans were being formulated by himself, Father Oder and representatives of other faiths. Their agreement to the idea, in advance of the convening of the whole senate, would be helpful in Bishop Caldron's deciding on the matter.

"I gather he's opposed to the idea," Father Ewing said.

"Opposed is too strong a word, Father," Brophy said, unbothered by Ewing's acid tone.

Donovan giggled. "Indifferent?"

"Incidentally," Ewing said, smothering a general laugh, "is Mr. Donovan a member of the senate?"

This question did bother Brophy. "Are you objecting to his being here?"

"Not if he's a member of the senate."

"Father, you know he isn't a member."

"Then I object to his being here, Bishop."

Donovan's face was crimson. Eyes glazed and unseeing, he directed his smile into various corners of the room, as if in search of a place to hide.

"Mr. Donovan is my guest, Father," Oder said. "I can't bring myself to think that you are asking me to expel him from my house."

"Of course not. I'm speaking of this meeting."

For some moments, the silence was absolute. Then, in a croaking voice, Donovan said, "I represent the press, Father Ewing."

"You mean what we say will be in the papers?"

"Mr. Donovan is editor of the *Fort Elbow Catholic.*" Bishop Brophy said this as if certain it would dispel Ewing's doubts.

Donovan said, "I thought the principle of press coverage of the senate ought to be established from the outset." His complexion was only pink now, his voice huskier.

"Did you?" Ewing said.

"Do we have secrets, Father?" Brophy's smile was forgiving.

"That's just the trouble. We don't. I cannot imagine a single reason why what we say here should be made public. For example, Bishop, I would hate to read in the paper any suggestion that you proposed putting the squeeze on Bishop Caldron to get his approval for participation in an ecumenical conference."

"I made no such suggestion, Father!"

"You know how newspapers are."

"I object to that," Donovan cried.

"And I object to you," Ewing said coldly. "Your right to be here is under discussion—though I don't know what there is to discuss."

Oder had stood and now came out from behind his desk. He leaned down and whispered in Donovan's ear. The editor turned crimson again, his eyes darting nervously about. When he stood he was stiff with anger.

"Very well," he said. "You are expelling the press."

Only Father Ewing laughed. "You don't look like an abstraction to me."

"I assure you, Father, I am quite concrete."

Ewing leaned toward Frank and said in a stage whisper, "Walter Concrete?"

Frank blew his nose. It seemed the only way to remain neutral. The fact that Ewing had asked him to sit beside him on the couch, the fact that when Brophy turned to Ewing he had to see him past Frank, made Frank feel that he had been placed unwillingly on the wrong side in this unexpected dispute. If Ewing had a point, so did Bishop Brophy, but in either case the points were minor, the issue unworthy of them. One thing was clear, Father Ewing had assumed the role of devil's advocate and this, however temporarily vexing for the bishop, assured Brophy the support of everyone else in the room.

"Have a cold, Frank?" Ewing asked.

Oder returned without Donovan but did not comment on what had happened. Somewhat less ebulliently, Bishop Brophy resumed the discussion. But Father Ewing was not disposed to settle for a single laurel.

"Did you say a countywide ecumenical conference, Bishop?"

"Yes, I did."

"Then why involve a senate committee in the matter?"

"What do you mean?"

"Cobb County is only one county in the diocese. The senate represents the clergy of the whole diocese. It's hardly a question for us to take up."

"Do you mind if we take it up nevertheless?" Oder asked archly. "We are all residents of Cobb County. Except Father Grimes, that is."

"Is the committee meeting over?"

Bishop Brophy looked around the room. "Perhaps Father Ewing is right. Before discussing the conference we can conclude the business of the Steering Committee. With your agreement, I shall draw up the agenda—"

"Subject to our comments?" Ewing asked.

"Of course. A preliminary draft will go out to all members of this committee for comments and approval."

Ewing rose and stretched like a well-fed tiger. "Well, I'll mosey along. Anyone else going?" He looked down at Frank, who sat immobile. Frank looked at his old mentor as if seeing him for the first time; Ewing had gone too far in playing the part of destructive crank. Bob Wintheiser would have been proud of him.

"I'll show you out, Father," Oder said.

"Very good of you. Good night, Bishop Brophy."

"Good night, Father. Thank you for coming."

"Not at all. I enjoyed it."

Brophy sighed when Father Ewing had gone. "Well, I knew I was taking a chance appointing him to this committee, but I had no idea he would be such an obstructionist."

"The bull of the Steering Committee," someone said.

"Where did you put Daniel Donovan?" Brophy asked when Oder returned.

"Upstairs. Father Swivel will be along with him in a moment."

"Good. We can't have the editor of the diocesan paper down on us. Press coverage, favorable press coverage, is of the essence."

Donovan, as it turned out, was easily placated. Oder pressed a fresh drink into his hand and Brophy apologized for Father Ewing. Jim Grimes came across the room to Frank.

"I didn't realize you were home, Frank. Did you finish up over there?"

"Yes."

Grimes crossed his arms and studied the floor. "You'll be teaching at the seminary this fall, I suppose."

"No. I'm at Saint Waldo's."

"But isn't that just for the summer?"

"No. How's your parish?"

Grimes unfolded his arms while his expression became one of serious contentment. "I love it. If you're ever out that way, Frank, I hope you'll drop in." He smiled apologetically. "It's pretty far out, of course. Stillville. I'd like you to see it though."

"Now that he's a senator, he'll be coming into Fort Elbow, won't he? You can see him here."

"He's in town now, Bev. He called this morning."

"Then why don't you talk to him here?"

"That isn't what he has in mind. He wants me to see his parish."

Ben had shown her the letter in which, while speaking jokingly of his election to the clerical senate, Father Grimes had repeated his invitation that Ben come for a visit. The letter went on and on about his stupid parish.

"You want to go," she said.

"Bev, I've known him since I was a kid. He's the one who interested me in the seminary."

"It's me, isn't it?"

"What's you?"

"The reason you want to go. Me. Us. Poor Ben is really bothered."

Of course he was. She was bothered herself. They got along so well, he wasn't like any other boy she had gone with, and yet, no matter how alone they were there was that other thing, his vocation, sitting between them, watching, condemning. Beverly was as conscious of it as he was and it was not easy to get rid of her sense of guilt. She felt that she was deliberately luring him away from the seminary and, if she succeeded, if they remained together, he would always resent what she had done. Even so, it would have been a lot easier to know what she thought of that if she could be sure that she could do it, win him over, rid them of that silent partner. Sometimes it seemed that she only

190

wanted to reach the point where she knew that she had won; then she could let him go, turning away from victory rather than defeat.

"Yes," Ben said. "I'm bothered."

They were parked in front of her house. It was late, after midnight. She put her head on his shoulder.

"I'm sorry, Ben."

"Don't be."

"Ha."

"He wants me to ride back with him."

Silence. Crickets. The sound of a late plane settling down at the airport. From several blocks away came the mounting squeal of tires but it did not end in a crash.

"Close call." Beverly shivered.

He put his arm around her. Warm. She stirred against him, getting closer. Make me chaste, Lord, but not yet. He had said that once and it seemed their motto, an admission of their impermanence. Gathered into his arms, Beverly tried not to think that he would drive off the next day with Father Grimes, go far away where he could talk about her as if she were a stranger, a danger to his vocation. She felt certain that she would never see him again, not after that. This could be their last time together. Make him remember, she urged herself. Kiss him so good he will never forget.

2   The name meant nothing to Entweder and it annoyed the old man that it did not. "You say she came here to the house?" he asked Frank. Assured that Mrs. Purcell had indeed come to the rectory for help with her son Henry, Entweder went mumbling to his office, where he searched his files of census cards. "It might be out of place," he said when no Purcell card appeared. "It might be under *B.*" But the pastor did not sound as if he believed it, though he thumbed through more cards. "We don't get them all," he conceded finally. "People come to church, maybe drop a few coins in the basket, but don't really contribute. Give them a pack of envelopes and it's another story. Then it's a matter of record and their pride is involved. But there are deadbeats, I know there are, and the census doesn't pick them up."

"I'm sure this woman doesn't have much to give, Monsignor."

"It's not the amount, Father. That isn't the point."

Entweder was a firm believer in tithing, certain that the spiritual benefits of giving a tenth of one's income to the church were incalculable. Frank had leafed through the pamphlets meant to convey this conviction to parishioners and found the arguments strange, as if avarice in the laity could be conquered by transferring it to the church. A rich parish for the poor in spirit.

There were no Purcells listed in the telephone directory either and Frank began to think that he must have the name wrong. But just as Entweder had been unable to find a name close to Purcell in the parish census files, so Frank found no plausible substitute in the directory. He put it aside as if he had failed to find hope listed there. And then he thought of the judge. He would know where the Purcells lived; it would be a matter of record.

"Purcell?" Judge Murphy repeated, beginning to shake his head. "No, I don't. Not that that means anything. When was it?"

Frank told him and, after Murphy had given the information to his secretary and sent her in search of the Purcell address, the judge began to bounce his head gently off the cushioned headrest of his chair.

"How come you're interested, Father? Is the kid in more trouble?"

"It isn't that. I keep remembering him, that's all. There must be something that can be done for boys like that."

"Like what?"

"I don't know. Something."

Murphy stopped bouncing his head. "Father, if you've got some idea that you're going to start a scout troop or baseball team and straighten out kids like"—his eye dropped to the legal pad on which he had scribbled a minute before—"like Henry Purcell, well, don't get your hopes up, let's leave it at that."

"Just leave them alone?"

"I don't mean that. Just don't hope. I've been in juvenile court longer than I like to think. After a while it gets you, the repetition, nothing new. I suppose hearing confessions must be like that. Oh, the faces change, they get younger or I get older, maybe both, but it's the same thing over and over. Theft and vandalism, theft and vandalism. And the parents. I know what they're going to say before they open their mouths. They'll promise anything to get their kids out of here. It won't happen again. But it will. Do I sound cynical?"

"I don't think they'd want you in the Elks or Kiwanis."

"Don't let me discourage you. I don't mean to. I urge you to help them."

"Am I a repetition too?"

Murphy smiled. "Not really. Haven't you heard? We have it all down to a system now. Probation officers, enlightened treatment, everybody an expert. No need for amateurs. But go ahead, start a scout troop, organize a ball team. I wish you luck."

"Where are the probation officers—here in the courthouse?"

"Right downstairs. Drop in and see them. They're full of optimism."

When the secretary brought in the Purcell address, Frank thanked the judge and left the office. He took the winding staircase to the basement.

Tony Silva, to whose cubicle Frank was led, consumed cigarettes in a way that made Frank want to quit smoking on the spot. Silva smoked each one down to the filter and lit another from the stub before putting it out in the massive tray whose ashes had a portentous look, the too soon destiny of the addict himself.

"Murphy? He always lets them off on the first offense with a warning. He refers them here only on second and later offenses."

"He's pretty pessimistic," Frank said.

"Oh, well." Silva waved his cigarette, leaving in air a tracery of uninhaled smoke. "It's best not to expect too much. I mean, we try, we really do, but the results are depressing. Once in a while . . ." His eyes drifted away like smoke, in search of an elusive cause for hope. "What was the Purcell kid up for?"

"Stealing cars."

"What else? It's not much fun being poor in a consumer society."

"He's not old enough to be thinking of cars."

"Tell it to Madison Avenue."

"Kids that age should have other interests." And then, almost to his own surprise, he began to tell Silva of the idea he and Eloise had had to use the Saint Waldo playground for a summer program. Competitive sports, dances, arts and crafts.

"What happened?"

"The pastor vetoed it."

"There you are. That's why we never expect too much."

"But surely someone must give a damn about these kids. Murphy says he handles dozens every week."

"Where does this Purcell live?" Frank read the address to him. "Baglio," Silva said. "That's his ward. He's the alderman. He is full of ideas about rehabilitating kids. Maybe you should talk to him."

"Have you tried to?"

"Why don't you see him?"

"Where would I find him?"

The address was a hardware store off Cavil Boulevard, within the confines of Saint Waldo's parish. When he entered, Frank stopped for a moment and let the scents of the store recall Dunn's Hardware, to which as a boy he had gone for jigsaw blades and model airplane kits. There was a counter in the center of the store and behind it an elderly man whose thin neck emerged from his starched open collar as if he were seeking to escape into breatheable freedom.

"Mr. Baglio?"

"No sir. What can I do for you?"

"I'd like to see Mr. Baglio."

"Personal?"

"Please."

"Joe!" the man bellowed, staring Frank straight in the eye. "Hey, Joe!"

There was an answering yell from the back room and the old man pointed at it with his thumb. Frank found Baglio taking inventory of his paint supplies.

"Father McTear, aren't you?" Baglio said.

"No, Ascue. Frank Ascue."

"I've seen you at Saint Waldo's."

Frank told Baglio that he had come from Judge Murphy and Tony Silva at the courthouse. The alderman put down his clipboard and sat on a rung of a stepladder, nodding through the explanation.

"You bet I'm concerned about those kids, Father. Do you know how many of Murphy's cases come out of this neighborhood? They're stealing me blind. It's a kind of blackmail. I turn them in and you think their parents and relatives are going to vote for Joe Baglio again? Fat chance."

"Why can't there be a summer program for them, Mr. Baglio. Something for them to do?"

"What do you mean?"

Once again, Frank described the program that had been planned at Saint Waldo's. As he spoke, he could see wariness creep into Baglio's eyes.

"Did Entweder send you up here?"

"No, of course not."

Baglio picked up his clipboard and banged it against his knee. "He's been after me for years to get a park built up here. A park! Where? I try to tell him what it would cost to reclaim that kind of property in this neighborhood. He treats it as a joke. Him. Good God, he knows the value of a dollar if anyone does. I've sent people from urban renewal out there to talk to him, to show him our plans, but until we get more federal money, there isn't anything we can do. We'd have to tax people out of business to foot the bill ourselves."

"Then a park is planned?"

"Of course it's planned. It's only a matter of time. Monsignor Entweder tells me how much money Saint Waldo's is saving the city in school expenses. Why is he telling me that? I belong to Saint Waldo's. I contribute some of the money that is saving the city those taxes. He's just got to be patient. What did he say when you told him about your summer program?"

"I think you know."

"Of course I know."

"Okay, we can't use Saint Waldo's. How about public schools? Isn't there a public school up here with a playground? Can't the kids use that?"

"You're kidding."

"Do I sound as if I'm kidding. Mr. Baglio, I've got the program all thought out. All I need is a place."

"Like a school?"

"Yes."

"Father, do me a favor. Take a walk over to Ericson School. It's two blocks away. Notice the mesh over the windows and the height of the fence around it. You open that up to the kids in this neighborhood and it wouldn't last a week. They tear hell out of it during the school year. And even with that fence and a special watch on it it's vandalized several times a year."

"But the program would have supervision."

"You?"

"I can get a dozen people."

"Not from the park board you can't. They're over their budget now."

"I don't mean the park board. I'll get volunteers."

"Volunteers?" Baglio seemed torn between interest and skepticism.

"Sure. Seminarians on vacation, nuns, college kids."

"You want to run a Catholic program at a public school?"

"It wouldn't be Catholic at all. It's a recreational program. Look, Mr. Baglio, I don't know anything about the park board or the school board or anything else. You do. You're my alderman. You're the alderman for these kids too. Why don't you look into it, see what can be done. Maybe Monsignor Entweder is right. Wherever the tax money is going, it's not into this neighborhood. Why not?"

"Okay. Okay. I'm not making any promises. I'll look into it. We'll see what can be done. Believe me, you don't want those kids off the streets any more than I do. They're stealing me blind, anything they can grab, whether they have a use for it or not. You wouldn't believe it."

Frank assured Baglio that he believed it. The alderman came with him through the store and opened the door for him. There was a sign in the door Frank had not noticed earlier. ONLY 2 STUDENTS IN STORE AT ONCE. A fragile barrier to the pilfering Baglio complained of. When he set off for the Purcell address Frank walked with some authority. He had given up too easily when Entweder vetoed the idea for the summer program. There were other ways. He would show them. Them? His pace slowed as he wondered who it was he meant to show. Entweder? Perhaps. Or maybe he wanted to show Eloise and Phil that it was possible to do something in Saint Waldo's parish.

196

The surge of bravado seeped away when he climbed the stairs to the fourth floor of the building where the Purcells lived. Narrow the stairs and steep the steps and at the top something other than paradise awaited. The railing was painted a deep chocolate and the walls a pale unhealthy green and it was possible to imagine that the mix of smells had something to do with those colors. On the fourth floor he came into a hallway where the floor was covered with a linoleum whose pattern was only vestigial after the traffic of too many feet. The door he sought revealed itself by the absence of a number, but since 1, 2, and 4 were accounted for, it had to be 3. He knocked with the sense that he was summoning squalor and grief to reveal themselves. A moment later Mrs. Purcell's face looked out at him over a guard chain, her expression annoyed, no hint of recognition in her eyes. He told her who he was.

"From Saint Waldo's," he added.

"We're not Catholic," she said and started to close the door.

"I'm not here about that. It's about Henry."

"Henry?" The door opened again, taking the slack out of the chain. "What about Henry?"

"Mrs. Purcell, I went with you downtown. Don't you remember? You came to the parish house and—"

The door slammed, a chain clanked and then it opened wide and she beckoned him in. When he had gone past her, she put her head into the hall and looked to left and right. When she had the door closed she turned to him, "You shouldn't have said that. They might have heard you. Everybody's so nosy."

"I'm sorry."

Petulance gave way to fear. "Is Henry in trouble again?"

"No, no. I don't know. I haven't seen him. I wondered how he has been. Since I saw you last."

She looked relieved but with relief came something else. She looked around, seeing the apartment with his stranger's eyes. Frank had not really noticed before but now, following her lead, he too examined the apartment. There wasn't much to see from where they stood. A living room, a square box without windows, sparsely furnished, a lone rag rug in front of the couch. Nothing matched, no piece of furniture looked chosen or cherished. On one wall was a large beautiful photograph, some northwestern scene.

"We could sit in the parlor," she said, not really suggesting it.

"All right."

In the room, he concentrated on the large photograph as the likely prize possession. There was a legend on the lower frame. Union Pacific Railroad.

"I'm out of coffee," Mrs. Purcell said, when Frank was seated on the couch.

"No, thank you. Nothing. Please."

More relief. She sat and pulled a package of cigarettes from an apron pocket. She had a match struck and applied to it before Frank could assist her.

"Why are you worried about Henry?" she asked from a cloud of exhaled smoke.

"I'm not. Not specifically. I'm worried about all the kids in the neighborhood. What do they do all day?"

"Do? What do kids ever do? Play. You know."

"Where?"

"Outside, everywhere. What difference does it make?"

For the third time that afternoon he described the program that had been planned for Saint Waldo's that summer and though this time the recital was for someone who would be a beneficiary of it he spoke with a growing sense of unreality. Mrs. Purcell listened intently as if she were waiting for him to begin saying something that might interest her. Her obtuseness prodded Frank into an ever more detailed account of the program he envisaged but while he spoke he began to wonder if any priest had ever paid a visit on his mother, spoken to her like this of an afternoon. The event would have been stored away in the priest's memory, surviving his mother, as his memory of this afternoon might still be recalled when Mrs. Purcell was dead. It was a silly thought, and depressing, as if her claim on the future was tied to his own doomed brain cells. She had greater grounds for hope than this. But thinking of his own mother brought thoughts of his father too and he said something of Mr. Purcell's possible interest in the program.

"I'm divorced." She brought out another cigarette to punctuate the remark.

"I'm sorry. I didn't know."

"Why should you? You don't know I work nights either, from six until two. A waitress. Brownell's," she added, a little flick of pride seasoning her bitterness.

He didn't pursue it. He felt too strong a desire to get out of there. If she was gone during those evening hours, who looked after Henry? One thing was clear, any program that could be arranged would have to go well into the evening hours. Kids like Henry were not loose on the streets in the daytime alone. He thanked Mrs. Purcell and she shrugged it off. Clearly she did not understand why he had come by to tell her all this. She didn't really believe him, that had to be it. At the door, she rubbed her chin with the back of her wrist and looked up at him almost slyly.

"That day at the rectory, I never said I was a Catholic."

"That's all right."

"I don't want you to think I was trying to trick you."

"I was happy to help."

Help? He felt helpless going down the narrow stairs to the street. Even if a program could be started—and suddenly that seemed an enormous *if* when he remembered his conversations with Murphy and Silva and Baglio—even if there were a program it no longer seemed a panacea for the kids of the neighborhood. But still it was something, something he could do. Already he was looking forward to approaching Phil and Eloise with the idea, enlisting their help, feeling camaraderie with people who were willing to take a chance to help those who needed it.

"Where's Catherine?" Sheila asked.

Carl's expression was uninformative. "She's gone back to her mother."

"Oh."

He had met her plane and now they were crossing the airport parking lot to his car. A jet took off, climbing overhead with a deafening roar. At the car, Carl opened the door and she slipped in; he came around, got behind the wheel, put the key in the switch, but did not start the motor.

"Catherine liked you," he said.

"Did she?"

"What is it, Sheila?"

He turned toward her but she could not face him. That would only lead to a staring match, and what was the point of that? She closed her eyes and massaged their lids with her fingertips.

"Nothing. I'm tired."

"How was the trip?"

She shrugged. "They're all alike, Carl."

But this trip had not been like the others. London. I've been to London to visit the queen. All the while thinking of Carl back here with his daughter, thinking of her parents, thinking of that ridiculous conversation with Father Ascue. But mainly thinking of Catherine. It was not resentment that she felt but fear. The girl had frightened her, had seemed herself regarding what she had become, herself a girl again,

looking without sympathy or mercy on the antics of her elders. Whatever reason Carl and his wife had had for their divorce, Sheila knew that
Catherine did not, could not, understand it, that she would never really
forgive them. Sheila had offered a different target, the alien intruder.
How easy it had been to read Catherine's judgment of her, how easy
to share it.

"I'm sorry, Sheila."

She removed her fingers and looked at him with blurring eyes.

"I should have told you about Catherine, not just sprung her on you
like that. I don't know why I didn't tell you."

"You don't owe me an explanation."

"Don't I?"

His face, if not the situation, clarified. How abject he looked, his
expression matching the sadness she felt. They were drawn toward one
another, guilt and sadness more compelling than the previous bond of
desire and love. In his arms, her breathing shallow, her heart thumping
within her, she clung to him and heard herself crying. Her cheek was
slippery with tears when he drew back.

"Let's go."

"Let's. Hurry."

Later, lying on her side, she looked at Carl's face in repose. Their eyes
met, continuing, recalling, deepening the fierce union they had known.
She had let them into the apartment, her hand trembling as she unlocked the door, had pulled him down the hall, looked into her room,
found it empty, tugged him inside and the rest had been a crazed,
passionate and almost animal coupling.

"Are we alone?"

She placed her fingers on his lips. "I don't know," she whispered.

"Shouldn't you find out?"

"What difference does it make now?"

"I don't want to compromise you."

He was serious. How curious men were. At the moment she would
run naked with him through the streets but already, for him, caution
had returned.

She said, "I love you."

"Me too."

"Narcissus."

"You know what I mean."

"Show me."

He smiled languorously, ran his hand along her hair. "You are in bed
with an aging man, Sheila."

"Ha."

She moved against him, settled into his arms, pressed her face against his chest. Mine, mine. She felt that she could devour him, perform dirty perverted acts for him. She shivered, frightened by the intensity of her desire.

"Catherine didn't like me at all," she said.

"Of course she did."

Sheila shook her head. "No. She didn't. And I don't blame her."

"She's just a little girl, Sheila."

"She will never accept me."

Silence. Her protest had gone too far, had assumed what had never been mentioned. Sheila drew her upper lip between her teeth and waited. Silence. Why didn't he say something?

When finally he did speak, he said, "Are we going to do anything tonight?"

"I don't care."

She sat on the edge of the bed. He put his hand on her back. Looking around at their scattered clothes, Sheila told herself that this was all that they would ever be, a feverish exchange of passion, no strings, their present no demand on any future. Had she ever really thought it would be different? She remembered Father Ascue talking of impediments and sin and marriage. She was as naïve as he was. She turned to Carl.

"Where were you married?"

"Good God, what a question!" Carl was propped on his elbow. She had truly startled him.

"Was it in church?"

"You don't want to talk about that."

"You don't."

"Of course I don't." He looked at her as if she had been guilty of a breach of etiquette.

"Sorry." She stood. "I'll be right back."

How ridiculous she felt crossing the room naked. She found her robe in the closet and wrapped it around her before emerging. She did not look back at Carl when she left the room.

On her way to the bathroom, she tapped on the one bedroom door that was closed. No response. She eased the door open and looked in. Helen lay asleep, on her back, mouth open. Thank God she was out like a light. Sheila wanted to creep back and tell Carl, urge him to get up and dress and wait for her in the kitchen. But she continued to the bathroom. Helen was unlikely to wake up before morning.

In the bathroom, she avoided looking at herself in the mirror. Someone had done some housecleaning for a change. No nylons hung from the shower curtain bar; the towels were clean, not damp pennants draped over the racks or scattered on the floor. Sheila turned the faucet and the doorbell rang.

She froze, feeling as she would have felt if Helen had surprised her in bed with Carl. The terrified face in the mirror was her own. But this was ridiculous. She pulled open the bathroom door and ran down the hall. "I'll get it," she called—to Carl, to Helen, to anyone.

At the front door she stopped and composed herself. Then she opened the door. Her father stood there.

"Daddy!"

"They told me your flight got in this afternoon."

"Yes. Yes, it did."

"May I come in?"

Sheila, after she had opened the door, had moved to the center of the doorway, blocking it. Her initial surprise felt frozen on her face. Her father! He looked at her with anger and alarm. She stepped to one side and he came in. Having shut the door, she turned and directed him into the living room. She could not resist one last look over his shoulder before following him. The bedroom door was closed; Carl was trapped in there.

"Sit down, Dad."

"It's time we had a serious talk." He remained standing, his hands plunged into his trouser pockets, his head to one side, but there was a strange catch in his voice, a controlled sob. "I have learned something that deeply disturbs me."

"Please sit down."

"I'll stand. Are you mixed up with a married man?"

Oh, God. Sheila slumped into a chair. This was too much. It could not be happening. Her flesh crawled at the realization that Carl was hearing this.

"Well?"

She looked at her father. How ageless he seemed despite the increasing signs of age. He was the same man who had scolded and coddled her years ago and she was his daughter, at a perpetual disadvantage.

"Please, Dad. I don't want to talk about it."

"Then it's true." He said it softly, then sat, in the center of the couch, on the edge of the cushion, his hands between his knees, his shoulders slumped. His eyes dropped to the toes of his shoes. "It's true."

"Mother told you, didn't she?"

He looked up, baffled. "Is that all that concerns you? How I found out?"

No, she didn't care about that. Her one regret was that she was causing him this sadness. She did not dislike him. She did not love him either, not in the way she supposed children love their fathers, but she did not want to cause him pain.

"Sheila, my God, I cannot believe it. I kept hoping that you would tell me it isn't true."

Why hadn't she? There are a million ways to lie. But she had been so surprised to find him at the door it had not occurred to her that safety might lie in a lie. Perhaps if Carl were not there in the bedroom, trapped, listening . . .

"Dad, it's not what you think."

"Don't, Sheila. Don't. There is no justification for . . . ." He stopped, inhaled deeply. "Tell me about it. Who is he? How serious is it?"

She found that she could tell him, could give him some version of Carl and herself, only of course it was not really Carl and herself that she described. They became stereotypes in the telling, a young unmarried stewardess and a slightly older man, divorced, who met, who began to see a lot of each other, who . . . It helped that her father would not imagine that she, his daughter, his little girl, had actually been in bed with a man, a man still married so far as Arthur Rupp was concerned. What really bothered him was the thought of an impending marriage, invalid in the eyes of the Church. Like Father Ascue, he would assume that Carl was wooing her, seeking her hand in marriage, that the only danger lay in her weakening and accepting his proposal. Sheila began to feel almost innocent.

"What about this first marriage, Sheila? Was it valid?"

She stared at him.

"Well?"

"Father Ascue told you!"

"Ascue? Told me what?"

Sheila was furious. She leaped to her feet. That snake in the grass of a priest had probably gone immediately to her parents after their talk. Wasn't that some sort of sacrilege? You were supposed to be able to talk to a priest in confidence. Of course her mother had got the story from her, in pieces, but Father Ascue had apparently tried to put it into the perspective of all those laws. Her father was on his feet too.

"Sheila, you can't take a step that you'll regret all your life."

"Let me alone, Dad. Please. I don't want to talk anymore, not now. Please let me alone. I have a headache."

"Come home with me, Sheila. There's no reason for you to live—"

"Daddy!"

She closed her eyes and gritted her teeth, controlling herself, waiting. She heard him move. His hand gripped her arm. When she opened her eyes his face was twisted with tenderness.

"Would you like your mother to come?"

"No. No, thank you. Not now."

He hesitated, then abruptly, awkwardly, put his arm about her and tugged her against him. When he released her there were tears in his eyes. He went to the door swiftly and closed it gently, noiselessly, lest even the click of the latch seem a rebuke.

The bedroom door opened and Carl appeared, fully dressed. His hand lifted, his lips moved, he seemed about to speak but no words came out. Sheila ran past him, down the hall to the bathroom. She slammed the door behind her and locked it.

"There's a Miss Rupp to see you," Hilda said, filling the doorway of the office in which Father Ascue sat.

Frank got to his feet. He had heard the doorbell ring, had listened to Hilda shuffle out of the kitchen to answer it and, trying to concentrate on his breviary, had hoped it was someone come to relieve the monotony of his afternoon.

"Come in, Sheila."

Hilda withdrew, permitting Sheila to enter, and Frank indicated a chair. When he had closed the door he turned and was surprised to find Sheila still standing.

"Do you know why I'm here, Father?"

"I'm afraid to guess. Please sit down."

"Afraid? I suppose you are." Sheila sat and stared at him. "I had no idea you would go to my parents with what we talked about."

"You were perfectly right. I didn't."

"You didn't? Then how did my father—"

"Sheila, whatever your father said, he did not learn it from me. I give you my word. I did talk to your mother. She asked if I had seen you and insisted on thinking I was answering questions she put to me. That's all that happened. I'm not blaming your father either. He's understandably concerned. I wonder if you would really like him to be less concerned."

"He came to see me. . . ." Her voice drifted off. She looked around the little room as if she were making an inventory of its contents. "Why did I come here?" She shook her head slowly in disbelief. "Do you know, I've never been inside a rectory before."

"What did your father say to you?"

She waved her hand in a dismissing gesture. "It doesn't matter."

"I don't understand."

"Does anyone? My torrid affair seems to be over. Just like that. I don't

204

want to talk about it." She shuddered, then inhaled and sat upright. "It's all over and I'm numb and I suppose I had some idea that if I came here and blamed you for talking to my father I could pretend that somehow the whole thing is your fault."

"Well, I'm glad you came, anyway."

She smiled a very small, very sad smile.

"What now, Sheila?"

"You tell me."

The remark was not flippant, it was a plea for help and one that left Frank feeling terribly inadequate. His mind churned with the dozen things a priest might say. Misfortune, reversals, disappointments—these are means God uses to show us that no matter how we try to escape Him, no matter what substitutes for Him we devise, He is the only ultimate purpose of our lives. Truths become truisms and lose their bite and yet what can we put in their place?

Sheila, as if reading his thoughts, said, "Isn't it strange that when a Catholic gets into trouble and asks what it all means the answer is always right there on the tip of the tongue, some answer learned a long time ago that has just been lying in wait for the question?" Her sad little smile reappeared. "I have been trying to feel sorry for myself, trying and succeeding. But whenever I ask myself what's the use, I keep thinking of catechism answers. 'God made me to know Him, to love Him and to serve Him in this world, and to be happy with Him forever in the next.' "

"That is the answer."

"I know. I know it, or believe it, but I don't feel it."

"Maybe even saints don't always feel it. No, not maybe. They don't. They've said as much. But feelings that don't follow understanding don't count for much. Convictions based on them can go as swiftly as the feelings."

They both fell silent, so silent that Frank could hear his watch ticking, an artful imitation of his natural pulse. Dear God, if only he could think of the right thing to say to her now.

"I've broken all the rules, Father."

Frank said nothing.

"I mean that I have sinned." She closed her eyes and said as if in a trance, "Bless me, Father, for I have sinned."

"Say it, Sheila. Say it your own way. Then, if you want, I'll give you absolution."

"What I feel is shame, not contrition."

"Do you want to make your confession?"

"Here?"

"Yes. Or we can go over to the church if you would find that easier."

"I'd rather just talk. I'm not ready for confession yet. I don't know if I ever will be."

He did not warn her of the danger of living in a state of serious sin, that that was presuming on God's mercy. Weren't those among the things she already knew?

"I want him back, Father. You think that's wrong, I know. And I know that whatever pain I feel now, having him back would only mean more pain and disappointment sooner or later. Even so, I wouldn't hesitate for a minute."

"Why?"

She stared at him. A defiant expression came and went on her face. "Because I love him."

"And he loves you?"

"Yes!" She turned in her chair and looked out the window. "Even if he didn't . . ."

"I understand."

"Do you?"

It was a fair question. Dear God, what did he understand? His vantage point provided absurdly simple, evangelically simple, remedies for most problems. Men sold their souls for the silliest things, things seldom even pleasurable when had—furtive sex, drink, money, praise. Did it really require a lot of experience to see that the meaning of life could not lie in such things, small good things which, made into idols, lost their value? The difficulty with such remedies was that those in the grip of passion or ambition could not see them.

"All I know is what you already know, Sheila. Those catechism answers. I was sent away to study in Rome but all I really learned is that wisdom is hanging onto what everybody knows already."

He looked at her, hoping that he was making sense.

She said, "I keep trying to remember the impression I had of you the first time we met, at my parents' awful party. I think it was of someone who knows what life is all about. Oh, I don't mean in a smart way. Someone who lives as he knows he should. Do priests realize how awfully attractive their life can sometimes seem to people like me?"

"People like you? Sheila, don't imagine that you are terribly different from the rest of us."

"I just meant people who are caught up in the rat race. There are times when I would love to become a hermit."

"There are no hermitages."

"But you know what I mean?"

"Sure I do. A priest like myself sometimes envies monks. I wonder whom they envy."

"The dead?"

He looked at her, startled. Was she more despondent than she seemed? It occurred to him that it was the woman who seemed to get the worst of affairs, first Diane, now Sheila. Phil, for all the anguish he had shown in this same office when he spoke of Diane, had moved with relative ease out of and beyond the involvement. Frank had not seen Diane again, but he had spoken with her on the telephone and each time her tone had reminded him of her disconsolate expression when they had had coffee together. Morality apart, women seemed to have too much psychological and emotional depth for random, soon done affairs. Frank could not help wondering what Sheila's friend was like. Had he too found it easy to drop her, go elsewhere, leave her to her own devices? But Sheila, having grazed the subject, did not really return to it. If she was not ready for confession, neither was she ready to talk of what had happened to her. For that, at least, Frank was grateful. His role was not that of confidant, but of priest. What he had to offer Sheila was no personal wisdom but the grace Christ had chosen to dispense through fumbling men. And yet, when she rose to go, he said, "Whenever you want to talk, come see me."

"Magdalenes Anonymous," she said wryly.

"Don't dramatize it, Sheila. That's worse than belittling it."

"Thank you, Father," she said, when he had opened the front door for her.

"Keep in touch, okay?"

Heat, the sound of traffic, a bright June sun. This was not the weather of despair, but of anger and violence.

"I'll send you a postcard from London."

Having closed the door, Frank felt enveloped by the welcome coolness of the air-conditioned rectory. He did not know if he had been of any help to Sheila but for the moment he was willing to settle for the thought that he had not done her any harm.

Miss Simpson lingered on, much of her time now passed in drugged slumber because of the pain. Seated beside her bed, looking at the closed lids and the round of her skull, Frank felt like a monk reminding himself of mortality. Sheila had asked that. Do monks envy the dead? It was a ghoulish thought, improperly understood, like Plato's definition of philosophy as the study of death. And who was less morbid than

Socrates awaiting execution? Alive now, soon to be dead, Miss Simpson seemed to represent one of the gates of life.

"It won't be long now, will it, Father?" she whispered to him in a wakeful moment.

"Don't dwell on it. God loves you. He waits for you." There were not many people dying of cancer to whom he would have dared to say, God loves you. No mind can encompass the thought of a just God who permits pain, but would an unjust God grant us the joys he does? He took Miss Simpson's hand in his, mortal hand in mortal hand.

Her dry lips tried to smile. "I know."

Know, not believe. Her life was summed up in the conviction that after death there awaited her an unimaginable joy. Frank prayed that he could be with Miss Simpson at the end.

"Pray for me, Miss Simpson."

She looked startled. "Oh, no, Father. You pray for me. I have led such a silly useless life."

"Let God be the judge of that. I doubt that he will agree with you."

He was less prepared to be indulgent with himself. No doubt it was true for Miss Simpson that the life she had been given, lived well, was all that God asked of her. But he was a priest, he had special obligations, and at the moment they took the form of getting that summer program for kids started at last.

Baglio led Frank to an office at the back which was separated from the storeroom by metal shelving. The alderman removed some catalogs from a chair and asked Frank to be seated.

"How are you coming with that summer program idea, Father?" Baglio sank into a chair at the desk and smiled noncommittally over Frank's head.

"Can we use the school?"

The smile gave way to a look of pain. "This is a lousy time of year, Father. Everybody's on vacation—the school board, the mayor. . . ."

"Haven't you asked?"

"I've been meaning to call you. I'm not all that clear on what you have in mind."

"But I already told you."

"The thing is, Father, the superintendent of parks thought it sounded like what they're already doing."

"They're not doing anything in this neighborhood, are they?"

"Well, there isn't a park up here."

"Just a school."

"Yes, there's a school. But that isn't in his jurisdiction."

"Look, Mr. Baglio, I don't know whose jurisdiction it's in. The fact is it's in yours. You represent these people—"

Baglio held up a seamed hand. "There are fifteen aldermen, Father. This is only my second term. Anyway, these things take time. I wish you had come to see me last winter."

"Last winter I was in Rome."

"In Rome?" Baglio brightened. "What were you doing there?"

Frank exhaled slowly. "Studying. Mr. Baglio, you want these kids off the street as much as I do. If you can't get that school opened, who can?"

"You know, it wouldn't hurt if you talked to Pollock. He's Park Board but a visit from a priest might get him off his duff."

On the way to the door, Baglio told Frank where in the courthouse he would find Mr. Pollock. When they had come out onto the sidewalk, he put his hand on Frank's arm.

"One thing, though. Try not to mention you're from Saint Waldo's." Baglio shook his head. "Entweder's name is poison downtown."

A streamer attached to the grille of Pollock's air-conditioner wavered unsteadily while the machine snarled at the humid air in the office. Pollock, his collar loosened, his sleeves rolled to the elbow, seemed caught between respect for Frank's collar and contempt for his idea.

"How many people you got to help on this, Father?"

"I can get all I need, no problem there."

"Priests?"

"Oh, no. College kids."

"Where from?"

"That isn't the problem, Mr. Pollock. I can get them."

"You understand that I couldn't promote anything religious."

"I know that."

"They'd be volunteers?"

"This isn't going to cost you a cent."

"It couldn't. I mean, my budget couldn't handle another thing. In any case, I'm going to have to have something on paper, to take to the school board. Here's what you do. You write up the sort of project you have in mind, the people you'll have running it, a few names of kids who will be involved. Get that to me and I'll see what I can do."

"You think it's possible?"

An expression of methodic doubt flickered across Pollock's face. "Possible? Sure it's possible. That's not a promise, but I'll do what I can." Pollock rose from behind his desk. "What parish are you in, Father."

"I just got back from studying abroad. In Rome."

"Going to be a teacher?"

"It's possible."

Possible. Going down the corridor from Pollock's office, Frank hoped that the superintendent of the Park Board had used the word in a more meaningful way than he had. For the first time Frank really believed that something might come of this resurrected idea for a summer program and with hope came the desire to talk it over with Phil Bullard.

When he phoned the Center neither Phil nor Sister Eloise was in; waiting for this negative news, Frank held the receiver close to his ear and listened to the sounds of activity drifting to him over the wire. The contrast with the soporific silence of the Saint Waldo rectory both angered and exhilarated him. When the girl returned to tell him that Father Bullard was out and, no, Sister Eloise was not in either, Frank left a message for Phil to call him.

"Good for you, Frank," Phil said that night when he phoned. "What changed Entweder's mind?"

"Oh, it won't be here at the parish. Actually it's not at all sure yet. I have to put it in writing in order to get the use of the public school. What I need are some volunteers to help out."

"Volunteers?"

"I remember your saying a few weeks ago that you could interest some of the kids on campus in this sort of thing."

"Oh, sure. But that *was* a few weeks ago. At the time I was turning them away here. It might not be so easy to find kids, good kids."

"I'm counting on it, Phil. I can't do this alone."

"No, of course not." Phil hummed in thought. "I know. Call Jack Tremplin. He sent over some seminarians to help out here. I know a lot more wanted to come. Give him a ring and tell him what you have in mind."

"Okay. But I can't have all seminarians. If the thing looks Catholic, well, it just won't go through."

"Once you've talked with Jack, call me back. We'll work it out, Frank. Don't worry about that."

When he had hung up, Frank had the feeling that Phil had put him off, that he was no longer as interested in the idea as he had been that day on the playground when they had talked about it with Sister Eloise. Eloise. Frank lit a cigarette and stared at his window, made a mirror by the night outside. Portrait of second assistant enjoying a cigarette. Did Phil think that Eloise would want to leave the Center and join the

210

project which had been her first idea on how to spend her summer? Of course he wouldn't ask her to stop working at the Center with Phil. She had no obligation to the old plan, even if it did involve the parish where she taught. If it went through, if Pollock got that school opened for him. His hope, when examined, seemed fragile indeed and talking with Tremplin did not help.

"Seminarians, Frank? You're kidding. This place is deserted. They've all gone home. Sitting in my room I can hear the toilets flush in the main building. Where would I find any seminarians?"

"There must be some who live in Fort Elbow."

"Most of them are working with Phil at the Center."

"Not all?"

"You wouldn't want the others."

"Why not?"

"Phil screened them, Frank. They're his rejects. Of course some are quite nice, I don't understand why Phil didn't want them. I could make a few calls."

"Would you do that, Jack? Please. This is very important."

Tremplin promised, sighing as he did so. That out of the way, Jack wanted to know when they could get together, for dinner, a show, something. Frank said that he was pretty busy now.

"Busy? Dear God, how I envy you. I spend my days reading. Think of it, Frank, you might have been assigned here. You would have vegetated, I hope you realize that. Sometimes I think of going down to the chancery and demanding to be sent to a parish. Anywhere, I don't care. I'd even take a country parish."

The thought of Jack Tremplin in a country parish remained with Frank as a comic afterimage of the conversation. Jack's complaint about days spent reading had filled him with a twinge of envy. How odd it had been to hear Jack Tremplin express envy of life at Saint Waldo. Was anyone happy where he was?

McTear had office hours and insisted that Frank take his car and that is how Hilda got in touch with him, on the citizen band, her scrambled voice bearing with it the memory of the succulent smell of her kitchen as well as the message.

The offer of the first assistant's car had decided Frank against going to Charlotte's on his afternoon off. That was becoming too much of a habit anyway. He drove south out of town on the river road, eventually pulled into a crescent-shaped parking place where there was a historical marker and a path which led down to the water.

And down he went, sliding on the loose gravel path, and found what he sought—peace, distance from city and people, the sounds all natural ones. Birds were noisy in the trees above and from time to time, out of the muddy river, a fish came up for air. It was dank and humid, the sun penetrating with difficulty and casting mottled shadows on the path where this season's leaves and last's were pasted like mementos. There were tokens of human passage too, beer cans, wrappers, cast-off contraceptives. The latter were surprising, in the age of the pill, and for a moment Frank was assailed by the image of furtive exchanges of passion here by the river, doubtless at night, the couple having left their car above and then come down here to grapple in the dark after adequate precautionary measures. He found it unnerving in the confessional to hear a girl's voice say she had sinned against purity with a boy. Some used no circumlocutions. I did it with a boy, Father. Followed by a hush. Was this where such things happened, out of doors, under the trees, perhaps on a blanket? He found it difficult to regard such thoughts with disgust. Indeed, for a moment, his breath caught and he felt at once his own aloneness and the appeal of such abandon. But then the moment passed, passed as such moments always had for him since adolescence.

His third year at Lake Glister had been the low point of his life on that score. He had dreaded the end of day, nightfall, and the trek from chapel to dorm where, after lights out, under the covers, all around him his classmates settling down to sleep, Frank had clutched his rosary and prayed that tumescence would not come. His very fear of it seemed to bring it on and with it came those dark desires, the more powerful for being vague. Lying on his back, bending his knees to keep the pressure of the blankets from his body, Frank would stare wide-eyed at the scarcely visible ceiling and try to concentrate on the mysteries of the rosary, the sorrowful mysteries, Christ tortured and crucified for our sins. Sin had become the name for what he did when he gave in, rolled on his stomach, gripped his pillow and refused to think, wanted only to feel. And, dear God, afterward the terrible letdown and remorse, actually crying, stifling his sobs, fearful that other wakeful boys would hear him and then the cold chill of wondering if they already had, if they knew what he had done. The next morning he skulked down to the crypt beneath the chapel and waited in line to go to confession, trying not to think that they were all there for the same reason. It was agony to go up to chapel afterward, to take his assigned place in the pew, once more certain that everyone knew why he was late and where he had been. But worst of all was the sweating ordeal of the confessional itself. I committed an impure act with myself, Father. And old Casey would sigh as if he recognized the voice, sigh and launch into a lengthy harangue, more lacerating because it was delivered in a gentle whisper edged with grief as if the offense had been against him and not God. The repeated resolution, the firm purpose of amendment, seemed mocked when a week or two weeks later Frank had to go down to the confessional in the crypt again. He decided that this could not go on, that he must leave. He was not worthy to consider the priesthood. There was a fierce joy to be had from considering himself the most despicable of sinners. At fifteen he had a glimmer of what despair must be. And then, almost magically, the intensity of temptation lessened; he would realize that it had been a month, two months, more. After Margaret, after Toohy, he had conquered it and it was not really until he had begun hearing confessions himself, at Saint Waldo's, that the memory of that awful period in his own life came back to him.

If such thoughts occurred to him, walking by the river, he was able to put them away like other thoughts of his boyhood. He wished his ability to identify birds went beyond robins and sparrows. Trees too were for him only oaks, elms and others. It was strange to think that the natural world was a system of classical nomenclature closed to him, but would the technical names alter his enjoyment of the greenery and bird life around him? He was content to walk and let the chirps and creaks and liquid whispers invade his mind and substitute for thinking. Finally, he turned his thoughts to what he had wanted this solitude to think about.

When Arthur Rupp had come to the rectory, Frank had hurried through a conference with a couple planning their wedding. Trying to get the conversation past ceremonial preparations to talk of the sacrament the couple would receive, he watched their faces go blank. They had no desire to hear his views on the married state. His job was to assure them that the church would be free, to give them information about flowers and seating and rehearsals. He told them that Saint Paul had spoken of marriage as a great mystery. The boy rubbed the tip of his nose with the back of his hand and the girl crossed her legs, a daring operation given the length of her skirt. In one sense at least marriage apparently held no mystery for them. There seemed little point in prolonging the session, so he let them go. He found Arthur pacing the office in which Hilda had put him.

"Father, I want you to speak to Sheila again."

"Sit down, Arthur."

"A few days ago I went to her apartment. She practically threw me out."

Arthur went into self-lacerating detail describing his visit to Sheila's apartment and his face twisted in an agony of incomprehension. Sheila had admitted to him that there was a man, that she was involved. Arthur looked at Father Ascue as if even now he hoped a denial might erase the truth and return him to the sense that all was right with the world, at least his corner of it. It would have been impossible not to feel sympathy for the man, but, listening, Frank imagined the episode from Sheila's side. No doubt that encounter with her father had brought her here to the rectory.

"Things may not be as bad as they seem, Arthur."

"What do you mean?"

"What I said. I can't say more."

"You've talked with her?"

"You know I have."

"I meant again."

"You told me yourself that she is a sensible girl, Arthur. Trust her."

Arthur glared at him. At first Frank thought that the man was angry because his loyalty to his daughter was in question, but Arthur laid a pudgy hand flat on the desk. "What is your thought on all this, Father? What did you say to her?"

"You don't expect me to answer that."

"All right, all right, you can't violate a confidence. That isn't what I meant. Generally, in cases like this, what sort of thing do you tell a girl? I don't mind telling you that I worry what priests might say these days."

Frank waited a moment, repressing his anger. "I know that you're upset—"

"Conscience. Follow your own conscience. To hell with the rules. Do what you like. Father Ascue, I don't want my daughter getting that kind of hogwash."

"Now see here—"

"No, Father, you see. I asked you, as a representative of the Roman Catholic Church, to speak to my daughter—"

Irrationally, Frank said, "Clara asked me."

"Don't quibble. I told her to. We wanted you to remind our girl of the Church's teaching, not give her some razzle-dazzle theories of your own."

And so it had begun. Frank was not so angry that he did not see that Arthur was simply redirecting his fury at a convenient target, but any sympathy the realization might have brought was pushed away by his remembering Arthur's phone call when his election to the senate had been announced. It was bad enough to be treated as if he were Te Deum's representative on the clerical senate, but to be assigned unwillingly the job of the Rupp family chaplain and then be scolded for not

214

doing it well was too much. Arthur's rerouted wrath paled beside his own and all the frustration and disappointment he had felt since Entweder's veto were dumped on Arthur Rupp.

"All right, Arthur, that's enough. I want you to shut up for a change and listen. One, I am not an errand boy for either you or your wife. Second, your daughter is a big girl now and if she has chosen to live away from her parents, that is her privilege and, believe me, her choice indicates that she is indeed a sensible girl. Who do you think you are, barging in here and talking to me this way? I suppose this is how you talk to your daughter too. No wonder she wants to keep clear of you. You might ask yourself what responsibility you bear for any trouble you take her to be in now. Maybe if you had devoted more of your energy to being a good father instead of presuming to speak for your Church and your country, she wouldn't be in trouble."

Even then he did not stop. He had gone on to speak of his own and Sheila's reaction to that ridiculous dinner party, had commented on the sterling quality of the charter membership of Te Deum, had heard himself with horror and shame but also with keen delight. Arthur sat back in his chair, his face slack, his mouth open like a fish, incredulous before this outburst. Slowly he shook his head, and when Frank had stopped, more for want of breath than of further items, said, "Well, I really touched a nerve, didn't I? Thanks, Father. You had me fooled. Now I know the kind of priest you are."

"The trouble is, Arthur, you don't know a damned thing."

Arthur rose, feigned shock in his eyes. "Swearing! A priest."

"I would advise you to leave your daughter alone."

Arthur, who had turned toward the door, wheeled. "And I advise you to keep away from her. Do you understand? I don't want you near that girl again."

"That's up to her."

They stared at one another, both trembling with rage. Groping behind him, Arthur found the handle of the door. "Forget about the Te Deum Communion breakfast, Father. Just forget all about it. We don't want anyone of your ilk speaking to us."

And then he was gone, slamming the door behind him. Frank, at the desk, stared at the accusing panels of the door and felt his anger recede and go, leaving behind numbness and self-disgust. He rose and left the office and went upstairs to his room with the feeling that he had become a stranger to himself.

That had been yesterday. All last night he had been gripped by remorse. This morning he had gone to confession to McTear, not daring to say Mass with that sin of anger on his soul. And he had rehearsed the exchange with Arthur again and again, hoping it would come to seem less awful than it was, but each time it became worse, his conduct less and less excusable. Dear God, what a stupid thing to do. He would have to ask Arthur's pardon. And he would. Soon. But that bitter pill was one he had no eagerness to swallow. Perhaps, if he thought there was any chance that Arthur might feel an impulse to apologize in turn, it would be easier, but he could imagine the triumphant reception he would get when he arrived as penitent at Arthur's door.

The only saving thing in the whole business had been McTear's almost comical advice. "Yeah, well. Try counting to ten or something. What I do when I want to blow my stack is read things backward. You know? Signs, words, anything. Next thing I know I'm all right."

Remembering McTear's advice as he walked along the river path, Frank smiled, but of course he could not smile away his appalled sense of having encountered a new and dangerous self during that crazy argument with Arthur. And a self too much like what annoyed him in Arthur. Just as Arthur refused to believe that *his* daughter could go wrong, so Frank did not want to think of his irrational behavior the previous afternoon as really his own, as showing the kind of person he was. He had never been particularly tempted to anger before, but that sort of outburst was just that—something bursting out from inside him that he had not known was there.

He did not want to brood on it; that could not help. But where was the line that separated brooding from the attempt to gain self-knowledge? If the episode told him anything it was that in a very short time, hardly more than a month, he had soured on parish work, permitted the pettiness of the pastor to sap his zeal to the point where he ranted and raved at a parishioner in genuine distress. He remembered that premonition he had had of the Church in diaspora and the thought had lost its mordant appeal. His own experience had shown him how little he could count on the present alterable organization of the Church to sustain him: pastors *were* small-minded and despotic, the daily round of the parish priest seemed to graze but not confront the deeper needs of people. If the structure was no support for his life, then, support had to come from within, but within there was the unknown darkness from which that burst of anger had come.

When he had retraced his steps, climbed the path to the parking lot and the car, Hilda contacted him on the citizen band.

"Can you hear me, Father?"

He said he could.

"Father Ascue! Can you hear me?"

He repeated that he could hear her, wondering if there was some special coded answer he should give.

"Father, press that little button when you talk. Are you doing that?"

This time he pressed the button when he spoke.

"A woman from the newspaper called, Father. I told her I would contact you right away and have you phone her but you haven't been answering."

"What did she want?"

"She wants you to phone her. Miss Mary Muscatelli. She'll be at this number for another half hour."

Frank took down the number and drove to an outdoor phone booth from which he called Miss Muscatelli.

"Where can I see you?" she demanded.

"Is it urgent?"

"I could come to the rectory now."

When he told her he was returning her call from a booth, she said she would be there in fifteen minutes and hung up. Frank replaced the phone. McTear's car was parked at the curb. Traffic snarled past. The road he was on was lined by gas stations, motels and drive-ins featuring chicken, hamburgers and hot dogs. While he waited he tried unsuccessfully to raise Hilda on the citizen band. He should have asked McTear how the damned thing worked.

It was not quite fifteen minutes later that a VW crept past him, its driver leaning across the seat to peer at him. Father Ascue waved tentatively and the little car swung in to the curb. Mary jumped out and came with a loose stride to the side of his car.

She seemed not to want to look at him. Her eyes swept over the pastel fronts of the drive-ins. "We could go in there and have a cup of coffee."

"All right."

Inside they took a table, ordered and waited as if that had been their reason for coming. Their coffee arrived in tan plastic cups.

Mary said, "You talked to Diane, right?"

Oh, my God. Frank stirred his coffee. It was not anger he felt so much as weariness. He was beginning to think that half the people he talked to wanted to know what the other half had said. Or what he had said to them. When he nodded, she said, "And offered to pay her way out of town?"

"Is this what you wanted to talk about? If it is—"

"Who asked you to do that? The bishop? The chancery?"

Frank smiled. "I doubt that the bishop or the chancellor have even heard of her."

"So it was your own idea?"

"How is Diane? You're her roommate, aren't you?"

"Yes, I am. And don't worry about Diane."

"It's pretty hard not to. She was very low when I talked to her."

"Bullard asked you to talk to her, didn't he?"

"Does it really matter? She didn't have to see me if she didn't want to. She has been through a terrible experience." He looked out the window to where traffic hurtled past. "You're a Catholic, aren't you?"

She had lighted a cigarette and, as she nodded, smoke escaped from her lips. "For whatever it means anymore. I can tell you one thing, I'm fed up to here with priests and nuns."

"Everybody's human, Mary."

She made a face and he didn't blame her. It was a stupid remark.

"Why didn't *he* leave? Bullard. He told her he was going to. He was going to quit being a priest and they would go away together and get married."

"Do you think that would have worked out?"

"No! But she would have found out what a crumb he is."

"That's a grim thought, isn't it? Being seen as we really are. We'd need God's mercifulness too if we could see ourselves that way."

"Mercy wasn't what I had in mind."

"We all need that."

A little skeptical frown appeared on her face. "I'd forgotten priests talk that way. The ones I've been meeting lately don't."

"About Diane. You don't think it would be a good idea for her to leave town?"

She didn't answer immediately. "I don't know. Maybe. I want to say no. But if she does want to go, if she needs money, I'll help her. She doesn't need money from you people."

"You're a true friend, Mary. Diane is lucky."

He had embarrassed her. She stubbed out her cigarette, tasted her coffee, frowned again. She said, "I have to go."

Outside they stood for a moment on the sidewalk. Mary watched the traffic with narrowed eyes. Suddenly she said, "You're a member of the clerical senate, aren't you?"

"Yes."

"What's this stuff about an ecumenical meeting?"

"That isn't a senate matter." He could imagine Ewing grinning.

"Whose then?"

"Try Bishop Brophy."

"I might have known. Well, so long. And thanks."

They went to their cars. Mary drove away with a roar, crouched over the wheel, shifting gears as she entered traffic, headed for downtown.

He had not heard from Tremplin. He could not reach Bullard by phone. He wanted to see Pollock at the Park Board but all he had was two typed pages of vague plans, no names, no helpers, no kids. That week Buzz, his first altar boy, was serving his Mass and one morning in the sacristy he asked the boy where he lived. The address was not in the part of the parish where the Purcells lived in their unnumbered apartment on the top floor of an odorous building. Frank wondered if any of the altar boys came from that neighborhood.

After breakfast Frank walked over to Cavil, turned left and walked in the direction of Baglio's Hardware with the improbable thought that he was on his way to recruit altar boys. Surely he would recognize some kids he had seen on the school playground, or more likely they would recognize him, and he could talk to them, try to bring the conversation around to serving Mass. Once he got to know them the next step would suggest itself. He just had to make some move or the idea for that damned program would become less and less realistic. Like setting off on a bright summer morning in search of potential altar boys.

There were no kids hanging around Baglio's when he went past; there seemed to be no kids anywhere. He walked to the corner, stood while the light changed four times and then, without a destination and with a mounting sense of the futility of this search, turned and went in the direction of the Purcell apartment. When he approached the building, his heart leaped at the sight of a kid sitting on the steps. Henry! Frank, feeling like a bad actor, strolled past the boy then stopped and turned.

"Henry?"

The boy looked up, wary, recognizing him immediately. Frank retraced his steps.

"How've you been, Henry?"

A shrug of the shoulders.

"What have you been doing?"

"Nothing." The word was a denial. Frank sat beside the boy.

"Is there any place around here for you to play?"

Frank had an absurd image of himself as Bing Crosby in *The Bells of St. Mary's*. But he did wish he were wearing something other than a suit. After all, Henry wasn't Catholic; maybe the collar made him uncomfortable. Frank heard himself telling Henry of the need for a park in this neighborhood, of all the things a guy could do if only there was a park, some sort of a recreational program. There could be baseball teams, a league even, with a trophy for the winner, and there were all sorts of things to learn. Working with a jigsaw, for example. Had Henry ever worked a jigsaw?

"Don't call me Henry."

"What do they call you?"

"Who?"

"Your friends."

"I don't have any friends."

"Aw, come on. What do they call you? Hank?"

Henry stared at him in disbelief and his upper lip curled back. He looked away then, glaring into the street. And then he spat, unsuccessfully. It dribbled onto his chin and he scooted back, away from the drip. He brought his forearm up and wiped away the spittle, looking at Frank as if he were to blame.

"Why don't you leave me alone?"

"I want to help you," Frank said, his voice plaintive but feeble too.

"Leave me alone!" Henry screamed this, getting to his feet and retreating up the steps to the entrance of the building. "Leave me alone!"

The small piercing voice lifted Frank to his feet. His body prickled with embarrassment and sudden rage. Why did the kid have to scream like that? And then, fearful that Henry would scream again, Frank started up the street. Henry was not placated by his going.

"Who the hell you think you are, anyway? Nobody wants you around here. I'm no Catholic, we never said we was. You just get the goddam hell out of here, okay?"

The strident voice pursued Frank up the street, speeding him on his way, and his ears seemed to flatten against his head as if eager to catch each enraged shout. Frank expected windows to fly up, doors to open, a hundred witnesses to watch him retreat to the corner and then, thank God, he was finally there and around it. He slowed and stopped and thought of Henry, poor little Henry who had no father and whose mother worked, who had no place to play, and he would have liked to wring the little bastard's neck.

That night Frank went down to the basement with McTear and watched him fiddle with his equipment in preparation for hours of far-flung conversation.

"What do you talk about with them?"

"Oh, this and that." McTear grinned sheepishly. "The weather comes up a lot. A guy wants to know what the temperature is here, is it raining.

I guess it's kind of stupid. We talk about the news too, of course. You'd be surprised how interested people overseas are in American politics."

Frank tried to imagine McTear explaining the preparations going on for the national conventions.

"Remember that summer program I tried to set up?"

McTear had to think a moment before he remembered.

"I've been trying to reactivate the idea."

The first assistant frowned. "I thought Monsignor gave you thumbs down on it."

"Not at the parish school." Frank told McTear of talking to Baglio and Pollock, he spoke of his visit to Judge Murphy and Silva. He could not bring himself to mention Henry Purcell.

"We do have a scout troop in the parish, you know. A guy named Reilly runs it. You ought to talk to him."

"Those kids are already taken care of."

"They're ours too, Frank."

But Frank could imagine the kids in the troop, kids who really didn't need it; their families would take them on vacations, they had plenty of other things to do. Scouting was just one more thing in a crowded life. McTear pushed away from the table on his wheeled chair and lifted his shoes to its edge.

"It's a funny thing, Frank. I mean, being where you are. Not you, anyone. I used to think of becoming a missionary when I was in the seminary. Maryknoll, something like that. There's a missionary in Central America I used to talk to. Anyway, it makes you think. Why are we here rather than somewhere else? There are all kinds of places that need priests and here we are but we're needed here, aren't we?" McTear frowned, as if in search of the thread of what he was saying. "No matter where you are that's the only place you can be. You can't be everywhere."

In a jumbled way, what McTear had not succeeded in saying made sense, Frank supposed, though he was not sure what it was. When he had gone upstairs to his room, he sat at his desk and opened a book. Read backward. Another bit of McTear's advice. And of course that was what the older priest had been giving him, advice. Do what you can do well and don't worry about all the things you're unable to do. That was sensible, of course. Almost too sensible. But then Frank thought of Henry Purcell, cursing him out at the top of his lungs. Embarrassment, anger and then a sense of futility possessed him. Bing Crosby would have known what to do.

3 "Father?"

Frank Ascue turned to face a man who had been attending his Mass every morning that week. Thin and tall, his face gaunt, he had black hair that was cut short and lay flat on his head. He smiled apologetically. Men were rare at daily Mass, young men, so Frank had noticed him. Now, on Friday after Mass, he stepped into the sacristy, where Frank was divesting.

"I'm Walter Mitchell. Here." He darted forward, took the alb Frank had just removed, opened a closet to get a hanger and draped the vestment over it. "You're new in the parish, aren't you, Father?"

"Yes, I am."

Mitchell had hung up the alb. "Mother mentioned you in a letter." He smiled as if in explanation. "I'm home on vacation."

"Your family lives in the parish?"

"Just Mother. Of course I still consider Saint Waldo's my parish."

"Home on vacation," Frank said.

"Yes." Mitchell made a little wet noise before speaking. "I am a grad student at UCLA. History. Medieval history." He smiled at Frank as if they were co-conspirators. "As you know, there is quite a little renaissance in medieval studies." He laughed at his joke. "Could I buy you breakfast, Father? I'd like to talk with you. As a priest."

"I'm expected at the rectory." Frank hesitated. "Would you care to have breakfast with me there?"

"Are you sure it isn't an imposition?"

"Not at all."

But as he took Mitchell across the loggia connecting church and house, he wondered if Hilda would mind. No rule about lay guests at meals had ever been mentioned.

"Any time, Father. Would you like something special?" Hilda rubbed her hands in expectation of a challenge.

222

"No, no. Just the usual. Not that your usual isn't special."

"Oh, get out of here, Father."

Mitchell had disappeared. Puzzled, Father Ascue went on to the dining room. Before he reached it, McTear emerged, moving swiftly.

"Good to see you again, Walter," he called behind him. "I've got to run. Big day."

McTear turned, his face a mask of relief. When he saw Frank, his eyes rolled. Before Frank could react to this, McTear was gone, thundering up the stairs to his room. Walter Mitchell awaited Frank in the dining room.

He said, "My, it is some time since I've been in this room."

"Sit down, sit down."

Hilda waddled in with fresh coffee and her smile seemed to freeze.

"Hello," she said to Walter.

"Hilda! How are you?" Mitchell, still standing by the table, made something like a bow in Hilda's direction. She ignored him.

"How do you want your eggs, Father?" Her expression was reproachful.

"Poached, I think. How about you, Mr. Mitchell?"

"Walter. Please. No eggs, Hilda. Just toast and coffee."

He meant it. He did not even butter the toast. He broke a slice into at least ten fragments and seemed to let each melt in his mouth before sipping coffee. Frank felt like Dives to Mitchell's Lazarus.

"You said you wanted to talk to me?"

"Yes." The wet noise. "About my vocation."

"You're not married?"

"Oh, no. No. You see, I've always thought—oh, for years and years—that eventually God meant me for another life."

Mitchell let that sink in. The priesthood? Well, it was not out of the question, of course.

"How old are you, Walter?"

"Thirty-three. The age of the crucifixion." Mitchell seemed to have startled himself. He actually blushed. "Just thirty-three."

"How far along in your graduate studies are you?"

"I have passed all my candidacy exams but one. That I must take over. Then there is my German. I have to work on that. It is almost impossible to qualify in German at UCLA." Walter now pronounced the initials as an acronym. "So really it is just a matter of the dissertation."

"Then you intend to get your doctorate before . . ."

"Not necessarily, Father. Not necessarily. What would you advise?" Walter sat forward as if for thirty-three years he had been moving toward this moment, his whole future, together with his immortal soul, now in Frank's hands.

"I'm scarcely in a position to advise you. I don't know you well enough."

"Just ask, Father. Anything. I mean it. Last night Mother and I sat up until nearly midnight and I told her that I have made up my mind to do *something*. I am not getting any younger, after all." He seemed to expect Frank to deny this. "Anything you must know, Father, ask."

Walter's answers to his questions, while lengthy, did not cause a clear picture of his life to emerge. Frank was curious to know what the man was still doing in graduate school at the age of thirty-three. There was a vague allusion to a teaching post, but that hint, pursued, led nowhere since, in a quince, Walter was back at UCLA. His moist manner of speech made the school sound like pastry. Frank suggested that they let Hilda clean up and adjourn to an office. The suggestion was made with some reluctance, since this was Frank's day off, but Walter sprang to his feet. Ensconced in a chair, Walter lit a cigarette, assumed an abject expression and said, "If only I had persevered in the first place."

"Then you've been in the seminary before?"

"Do you know the Capuchins, Father?"

"Of course."

"*Really* know them?" Walter did and it was a lucky thing for the Capuchins that their future did not depend on Walter's assessment of them.

"Why exactly did you leave?" Frank asked, wary now.

"Oh, we parted amicably enough. But part we did. My life, I need not say, was a shambles. It is a traumatic thing, Father, suddenly to find that one's whole life style must change. I knew some rather bitter days, I confess to that. But that is all water over the dam, isn't it? Or Walter over the dam." He laughed. "As I told Mother last night, I consider myself a blank slate."

At thirty-three? Frank was beginning to wish that he had ended this with breakfast. He planned to stop by the Student Center and see how Sister Eloise was getting on, and Beverly too. But Walter was a parishioner and, like it or not, this had to be regarded as the line of duty. Frank would have been a good deal less philosophical if he had known then that Walter would stay until noon and that there would be no saving interruptions. From time to time, Hilda's heavy tread was audible, as if she were checking to see if Walter had left, but McTear, who had office hours today, seemed to have hidden himself upstairs.

When twelve o'clock approached Frank managed to get Walter to the front door, and he had to repress the impulse to grab his arm and steer him outside. He had pieced together something of the man's history. Walter had been in nine different religious orders, usually as a seminarian but twice as a prospective lay brother. "The humblest post, Father. I would have accepted it gladly." But always, inevitably, Walter had run afoul of some inept superior. His eyes glistened as he recounted the stations on his personal Way of the Cross. "*Stabat* Walter," he cried, when he summarized his brief sojourn with the Dominicans. "Stab at Walter, Father. The old game again."

It was impossible to find out what precisely had led to Walter's amicable partings from nine sets of superiors, but on the remembered dung-heap of his reversals, Walter, Job-like, yet had it in him to hope.

"As I said to Mother last night, now is the time for me to strike again. Every day dozens of priests leave, vocations are off, seminaries are empty."

Walter did not quite say that by now standards must have fallen so low that any seminary would be glad to snap him up. Now, at the door, Frank said for at least the tenth time that, yes, if Walter needed a letter from his parish priest, he would see that he got one. He would welcome the opportunity to alert Walter's next victim. At the sound of the lunch bell, Frank pulled open the door and moved toward Walter. Walter got the hint. They parted amicably.

McTear and Entweder awaited him at table. There was a wound of a smile on the first assistant's face.

"And how is Walter?"

"Walter?" Frank pretended to think. "Walter Mitchell? Wonderful news. He thinks he has a vocation."

Even the pastor groaned. "We should have warned Father Ascue about Walter," he said to McTear.

"Was Mr. Rupp expecting you?" the woman in the outer office asked Frank. She had stood at his entrance, a stick figure in a florid dress. Her smile stretched her lips but revealed no teeth. "I'm afraid he's not back from lunch yet."

"I should have called first."

"If you care to wait, I'm sure he'll be back soon. I could call his home, Father . . ."

"Ascue. No, don't bother. It isn't important."

"Do please wait. He's usually back by now."

It seemed a personal favor to the woman to take a seat. Frank thumbed through a magazine, trying to keep his mind a blank. He did not know what he would say to Arthur and he had the bleak hope that his mere coming to Arthur's office would be understood as an apology and the ridiculous argument in the rectory forgotten. Perhaps it had been unwise to let a week go by, though it was difficult to see how any earlier effort to smooth the waters would have been easier. The receptionist, still smiling her painful smile, fussed at her desk, opening and shutting drawers, rearranging things in front of her. When she settled down to typing, Frank stopped pretending to read the magazine. The pecky cypress walls were hung with plaques. Arthur, it appeared, was a member of the Million Dollar Club, had been for years. Certificates, awards, photographs with other portly types, seemed so many emblems of affluence and success. The typing stopped.

"That's his car." The woman nodded toward the window which contained an air-conditioner. Frank had heard nothing, but a few minutes later the door opened and Arthur Rupp hurried in. At the sight of Father Ascue, he stopped.

"Good afternoon, Arthur. May I have a few moments?"

After the slightest hesitation, Arthur nodded and led him into another office. He closed the door behind them and went to his desk and sat.

"What is it, Father?"

"I want to apologize for losing my temper last week. There was no excuse for that. I hope you'll forgive me."

Arthur cleared his throat, but his voice, when he spoke, was unnatural. "No priest ever spoke to me like that in my life, Father."

"I'm sure of that."

Arthur twisted a ring on his finger. "I suppose we were both upset."

"You had far more reason to be upset than I did."

"Yes. I had counted on you, Father. With Sheila. Now . . . Well, I don't know what is going to happen."

"Pray for her, Arthur. I will too."

"Do you think it's that bad?"

Frank saw that Arthur was serious. Well, perhaps his view of prayer was not unusual.

"Nothing is that bad, Arthur. Well, I won't take any more of your time."

Frank walked to the door but, before he opened it, Arthur spoke again. "I can't change my mind about the Communion breakfast, Father. I hope you'll understand that."

"I understand, Arthur."

Although it had been easier than he had expected, Frank did not derive any particular satisfaction from having apologized to Arthur.

Which was just as well, of course. Remorse is easy, almost attractive; it was foolish to think it simply swallowed up the wrong that had occasioned it. Frank was still puzzled by the source of his outburst of anger and, riding the bus to the Student Center, he wondered what would become of Sheila Rupp. Diane, when he had last telephoned her, had spoken with a vacuous sprightliness he had found false and unconvincing, but at least she had moved beyond her despondency.

"Oh, don't worry about me, Father. I'm the belle of the ball again."

"If you should ever want to get together . . ."

"And get all serious again? What's the point of that?"

It had seemed safe to repeat his offer and again Diane had turned it aside. What did she want out of life? Surely not a parade of escorts. Nor did the work she did seem to engage her fully. A home, a husband, children—that common natural aspiration would enclose her in a sustaining network and replace what she had left behind her in Illinois, if that was indeed what she had left behind. Diane had shown no desire at all to speak of her parents. Frank wished he could do even so little for Sheila as he had done for Phil Bullard's discarded love.

"Frank!" Phil cried, when Father Ascue looked into his office. "Come on in."

"You're busy."

"Busy? Of course I'm busy. What do you think this is, a parish?"

It would have been impossible to think of the Center as Saint Waldo's. Phil took him on a tour, to classrooms where ghetto kids were being tutored by coeds, to a lounge rocking with music where an endless dance went on, to guitar classes, games, lessons in arts and crafts—the place was a hive of activity. They found Sister Eloise huddled with a mixed group in the chapel. Some of the kids were smoking, but Phil told Frank the Blessed Sacrament was not reserved there.

"We need the room. And we only let them smoke tobacco." Phil winked.

Sister Eloise acknowledged their presence with a little wave but did not break off from what Phil called her rap session.

"On what?"

"The war. What else?"

"Where's my niece?"

"I'm not sure. I think she took a bunch of kids on a picnic or something. She prefers the outdoors stuff."

Back in the office Phil sank into his chair behind the desk and emitted a whooshing sigh. "It's this way from morning to night, Frank. And I love it. Everybody loves it. The nuns, the seminarians, the college kids."

"It looks great, Phil."

Phil's expression became pensive. "And to think I was ready to chuck it all." He shook his head incredulously. "I came that close. Thank God, I snapped out of it in time."

Frank stayed for an hour and then had to force himself to go. Almost apologetically, he told Phil that it was his day off. Phil had not had a day off in weeks. Outside they stood for a moment.

"Where's your car?"

"I ride buses."

"You know, in the long run, I'll bet it's quicker. If you ever need a car, though, give me a buzz. Mine is usually parked around here somewhere."

"Tell Beverly I was here."

"I wish you could be working with us, Frank."

And that was as close as either of them came to mentioning Frank's twice-aborted hope to have a summer program at Saint Waldo's.

Mr. Cole was funny. Whenever he spoke to Beverly, he seemed to be addressing someone standing at her side—except when Ben was standing beside her. Then he had a tendency to talk to the floor or walls.

"I want you to meet my dad," Ben had said when he came for her.

"How was Stillville?"

"Boring."

"How odd. So was Fort Elbow. Sunny and boring, day after day."

"At least you had the Center to go to."

"But I didn't go there, not every day. How was whatchamacallit? Father Grimes?"

"All right."

"Have a nice talk?"

"We talked."

"Mmmm." She went on humming, undecided whether his unwillingness to tell her about it was good or bad. But now he wanted her to meet his father. Wasn't that good?

Telephoning Ben at the rectory in Stillville had seemed an inspiration until she actually placed the call and was waiting for him to come to the phone. She had shut her eyes and pressed her upper arms against her sides, holding the phone with both hands, not breathing. Would he be angry? Would he be able to talk? She feared that he might be pleased while they talked and then, afterward, wonder what the hell. But it was too late then to just hang up.

"Hi," she said when he answered, trying to keep her voice neutral, just a girl's voice.

"Bev?"

"How did you guess?"

"All the others have checked in today."

"Drop dead."

"How are you?"

"Do you miss me?"

"I've been thinking about you."

"That's nice. Had your talk?"

"You know how it is."

She frowned at the phone. "Can't tell Beverly about it now?"

"That's right."

It had gone on like that, a silly exchange, and though she could not put into words what she felt at hearing his voice and feeling that he was close again, she was glad that they were having even that stupid conversation. When it was over and she had replaced the phone, she went upstairs to her room where she sat on her bed, hugging herself and smiling like a lunatic.

Ben seemed different now, no longer mixed up and indecisive. Had he thought before that they were only a summer thing that didn't count so he could go back to the seminary? No wonder he had wanted to go to Stillville and talk with a priest he had known when he was a kid. What he had really been looking for was someone to tell him that it was all right to leave the seminary. Not that it mattered much what Father Grimes had said. Ben had already made up his mind before going there. Maybe he knew that now. The fact that it was taking him a long time, the fact that the decision was an anguishing one—well, would she really have wanted him to act differently? It could not be an easy matter to turn away from a goal he had been pursuing for so long.

"Hasn't your father ever seen a girl before?"

"Ask him."

"Who *am* I, incidentally? An old friend you met in the summer apostolate, a nun in disguise?"

"Let's play it by ear."

Mr. Cole, who was watching the second game of a twinight doubleheader, got to his feet reluctantly, nodded at her name, and slapped Ben's hand when he reached to turn down the volume of the TV. "Two strikes on the batter," he explained. "No balls."

"Who's winning?" Ben asked, as if to fill a strained silence that had not yet formed.

"Cleveland. Your father Howard Nygaard?" Mr. Cole asked the space beside her.

"Do you know him?"

"The name. You two want to watch the game?"

"We're going out," Ben said.

But they did not leave for fifteen minutes, during which Mr. Cole was obviously listening to the game, Ben spoke to her rather than to his father and she kept sneaking peeks at a photograph on a table beside the couch. She asked Ben who it was.

"My mother."

"Oh."

"She's dead."

"You told me."

Beverly picked up the picture. The woman's hair was done in an old-fashioned marcel. Bev could not discover much of her in Ben. What she saw, or thought she saw, was a vague resemblance to herself.

They went to an outdoor movie and did not turn on the sound. A silent teen-age orgy went on on the screen, and in the cars around them, while they talked.

"I had an argument with Grimes. It was pretty bad."

"He doesn't approve?" she asked vaguely.

"Maybe it's the isolation out there, I don't know. Maybe now that he's on the senate he'll find out what's going on in the world. Maybe. Do you know he actually told me he never once had a doubt about his vocation?"

"Neither has my uncle."

"He told you that?"

"Yup."

Ben shook his head. "They can't be serious."

"Maybe that's what it's like, having a vocation. Uncle Frank says it's like getting married. You just put everything else out of your head."

"He and Grimes must get along fine."

"Wouldn't he listen to you?"

"Not really. He knows it all already."

"What *did* he say?"

"He told me to forget about the seminary."

God bless you, Father Grimes! "Gee, that's too bad."

He looked at her.

"Just when I had decided to get me to a nunnery. And why not? What does life hold for me? Would you believe it, boys take me to outdoor movies just to talk my arm off? If that isn't a sign of a vocation—"

He pulled her to him, buried his face in her hair and she could smell the crisp whiteness of his shirt, actually smell it, and her arms tightened around him as if she meant to crack his ribs. How she had missed him, how she had dreamed of this reunion. Good old Grimes, whoever you are.

"Ben?"

"What?"

"Who does your shirts?"

Some minutes later, she began to wish they had gone on talking. Not that Ben tried anything. He was unbelievably chaste, but there was a new desperation in the way he crushed his mouth to hers. She drew away, turned, pulled his arm over her shoulder and then scrunched down so that his cheek was against her head. The silence deepened, seemed to become melancholy. She looked up at him. He was watching the screen mournfully. When he became aware of her eyes on him, he smiled and lowered his mouth to hers but she moved away, a finger on his chin.

"Ben?"

"What?"

"Say it."

He did not understand at first but, when he did, he looked solemn and said it very distinctly as though it were an answer to a catechism question. She lifted her face to his and clung to him, the words echoing in her ears. But her delight was not keen. It was as though she had said it to herself.

"I love you."

Howard had come downstairs because the heat in their bedroom was insufferable, though Charlotte lay in deep and open-mouthed sleep, her only concession to the heat wave an infrequent sigh whenever she tumbled over to her other side. She might have been an automated Saint Lawrence turning on the grill, basted in her own sweat, intent on getting evenly cooked. Her mouth clamped shut from time to time and she made a smacking effort to work up saliva.

Howard sat on the edge of the bed regarding his sleeping wife. Charlotte, like everybody else, he supposed, looked so vulnerable asleep. And innocent—as if by closing the lid of the mind's eye we shut out guilt and evil and have only the sinless self with which we began. Howard ran his fingers through his hair. His own inability to sleep seemed a defect. He decided to go downstairs. In the hallway, he paused outside of Dave's and then Elizabeth's room. Asleep, of course, both of them, and it was so hot, how could they stand it? He would have to have this house air-conditioned. The builder should be sued for not including it in the original plans. On the way downstairs, after he passed the landing, he kept close to the wall to avoid making the stairs creak.

He did not turn on any lights. Beverly was still out, but they had not left a light on for her. If she was going to come home at such ungodly hours, Charlotte had said, she could just find her way in the dark. No doubt Char had imagined a pitch-black house and Bev bumping around among the furniture, groping for a switch. But the house was bathed in pale light, eerily illumined. Howard went into the kitchen and opened the refrigerator; a wedge of white light, wonderfully cold, emerged. He took a bottle of beer, twisted off its cap and tasted it while still standing in front of the open refrigerator. Closing the door with his knee, he went into the living room. He was still sitting there when Bev came home.

The car pulled up to the curb, its lights went out and then the motor. There was the sound of doors slamming in the night. Footsteps and then Bev's voice, whispering. A gruffer voice whispered in reply. This went on for a minute and then was replaced by silence. Howard felt like a spy imagining what they were doing out there. Minutes went by. He wanted to clear his throat but that might sound like disapproval. Why didn't he feel disapproval? His heart was with the unknown young man out there as if they were allied as males, storming a female monolith. Strange thought. Howard felt menaced by his own weakness, not by women. Sharon. His wife. Even his daughter Beverly. What if Beverly should become the prey of some predator like himself? Even then it would be the man he pitied. The whispering began again and then, in normal tones, Bev and the boy said good night.

She came into the hall and turned on a light and Howard sat very still. To speak now would frighten the hell out of her. But she turned and saw him and said, "Oh, hi, Dad. What are you doing down here?"

"I couldn't sleep. The heat."

"It is hot." But she said it as if she had just noticed that the temperature was well over eighty and there was not the faintest hint of a breeze.

"Have a good time?"

"Uh huh." She slipped out of her shoes and came into the living room barefoot.

"Who were you out with?"

"Ben. Ben Cole."

232

"Oh."

"You don't know him."

"I didn't think so."

Bev yawned and looked at the shoes she held. "Well, good night, I guess. I'm beat."

"I'm going to finish this beer."

She leaned over and kissed his cheek. "Do you want the hall light on?"

"Why don't you turn it off?"

She did and for a minute afterward the house seemed very dark. Beverly did not avoid the creaking steps when she went up, made no effort to be quiet. It was a wonder that she did not wake the house.

His beer was warm now, its taste more perceptible. He did not particularly like beer, but he sure as hell was not going to have a drink this time of night. In too few hours he would be going to work, to work and another letter from Sharon.

He had often longed for a time of quiet when he could think through his involvement with Sharon but now that he had it he found his mind just flitting from one image to another. What he was doing was stupid, he knew that much. If he were someone else, he would find it very easy to give himself advice. They made an absurd couple, he and Sharon— because of the difference in their ages, because he had a family and a ton of responsibilities, because ninety-nine percent of the time Sharon was little more than a pen pal.

She insisted that she wanted to know everything, what he did, what he thought, felt, hoped for, hated. It was ridiculous and yet . . . Perhaps psychoanalysis was like this, a perpetually sympathetic ear, no line drawn between the trivial and important, a constant spilling of the guts. That at least was some sort of explanation: they were using one another for therapy, baring their souls without the threat of any consequences.

But was that so? Sharon said they now had all she wanted, only this, those goddam letters and, from time to time, his visits, a day or two spent almost entirely in bed. It seemed a joke his body was playing on him. Even in this heat, wishing he were upstairs in bed asleep, his body responded to memories of Sharon. Lust, disgust, a drained weariness— leaving Cleveland was a relief, both physically and emotionally. While he waited for his plane and escape, Sharon seated beside him in the terminal, he was certain that the antics they had engaged in were graven on their faces, that each wore a ravaged look which anyone could read. But Sharon at least looked only like a freshly scrubbed schoolteacher, and an extremely pretty one. It seemed impossible that her countenance bore no trace of their debauch. His own must make up for hers, two decades further up the stair of time, a portrait in the attic. Who but a wanton man could have imagined Dorian Gray?

He had returned from his last visit to Cleveland by train, wanting more time to elapse between leaving Sharon and arriving home, and Sharon had boarded the train with him. Snug in the roomette, he had held her gloved hand in his, looked at the streaked dirty window and longed to be on his way.

"It goes so quickly," she said.

"I know."

"Is it allowed to ask when you'll be coming back?"

"That's hard to say."

Squeezing her hand in ambiguous comfort, he found himself wishing that she would meet a young man, fall in love and write a farewell letter to Fort Elbow. The memory of innocence affected him strangely, made his throat tighten until he felt that he could weep for his freedom. Why didn't he make a move to regain it? He could ease off, write less, let matters simmer down, cool, stop. That way any overt stopping of it would be unnecessary.

I'm afraid to, he told himself, sitting in the darkened living room, the house seeming to pulsate with the sleep of Charlotte and his children. I'm afraid to. Having admitted the thought, he realized that he had had it all along, from the beginning. He did not believe Sharon when she said she wanted only what they had. Her ardor and tenacity, her abandon in bed, said otherwise. No woman wants nothing; her body is her barter, no matter what she says. Their meetings and, worse, his letters to her were a weapon. She saved his letters, he knew without her telling him, and his skin crawled at the prospect of eyes other than hers reading them.

No. He drove the thought from his mind. Sharon would not do that to him. Even if she were inclined to, she would know that it was a doomed game. She would gain only the destruction of his marriage, if Charlotte's religion would permit even infidelity to do that. Sharon could hardly expect both to ruin him and to have what would then be left of him.

Howard finished his beer. He should go upstairs and try to get some sleep. But he remained in his chair. Sharon would not use his letters against him, he assured himself, but at the same time he resolved to write her less, to alter the tone of his letters, make them letters anyone might read. He had all of Sharon's letters too, locked in a file in his office. He would get rid of them.

He fell asleep in his chair. He dreamed that he was on his first trip to Cleveland, when he had met Sharon, and nothing turned out as it really had. After lunch they parted, he returned to his hotel and the next day flew back to Fort Elbow and lived happily ever after. When he awoke at three he did not remember his dream but he went upstairs feeling a strange euphoria.

The world was Sheila's hiding place. When she was in Fort Elbow she spent as little time in the apartment as possible and no sooner had she returned from a trip than she made plans to go off again. For weeks she had been hurtled around the globe until she felt so weary that she could not face the thought of boarding another plane. She took a cab to her parents' house.

"Sheila," Mrs. Rupp cried when she opened the door, her eyes widening at the sight of her daughter in uniform. She took the suitcase quickly, as if fearful that Sheila would dash away. "For heaven's sake, come in out of the heat."

"Is Dad home?"

"In the middle of the afternoon?"

"I just wondered."

"I'll put this in your room. Your room," she repeated, hurrying away.

Sheila walked around the living room, trailing fingertips across a table, picking up an ashtray. She looked at herself in the mirror over the fireplace, a professional smile first, then permitted her face to sink into exhausted repose. She had her shoes off and was sitting on the couch, legs drawn up beside her, when her mother returned.

"I unpacked your bag. Half your things went into the laundry. The other half should go to the cleaner's."

"Later. I'm so tired."

"Is anything wrong?"

"Oh, no. Not that anything is right either."

"Sheila, I won't ask a thing. I am so ashamed of the way your father and I pried into your life. It was all my fault. And then your father had a dreadful argument with Father Ascue."

"Mother, please."

"All I'm saying is, blame me, don't blame your father. It was all my fault."

"I don't blame anyone." She closed her eyes and massaged them with her fingertips. She wanted to lie down and sleep for days. She felt her mother's hand on her arm.

"Come on. Upsy-daisy. You're going to take a nice warm bath and then into bed, hear? You look like death warmed over."

How nice it was to be fussed over. Sheila got to her feet and her mother scooted upstairs to draw the water. For half an hour, Sheila luxuriated in the tub, adding more hot water when it cooled, until she had it almost brim full. She could have fallen asleep then and there, relaxed and simply slipped beneath the surface to a permanent rest. She held a warm washcloth to her face and nearly swooned. Enough of that. Into bed, girl, she told herself, mimicking her mother's tone.

She could not sleep. After the bath she felt so languid, she was dead tired and under the covers, shades pulled, no distractions in the silent house. She could not sleep. The smooth bland surface of the ceiling developed, when stared at, a hundred flaws, its uniform color aping the spectrum with only light and shadow. But if she looked elsewhere her imagination formed faces from a fold in the curtain or a shadow on the wall. Shutting her eyes, she squeezed strange bursts of color from her lids. She counted to one hundred in French. Turning on her side, she hugged her pillow as if it were a lifesaver and she afloat on fathoms of water. She could not sleep. Carl. She allowed his face to form and, open-eyed, not crying but feeling that her heart would break, she reviewed in minutest detail the whole history they had shared. Mercifully she fell asleep before she came to that dreadful afternoon in the park with Catherine.

She was wakened by a tap at the door. Her mother.

"Are you hungry, Sheila? It's after eight."

"Haven't you eaten already?"

"We thought we'd wait for you."

"I'll be right down."

When she came into the living room, she had the feeling that her parents had agreed upon their strategy. Her father hugged her close. "How about a drink?"

"Okay."

"Your mother and I are having a martini."

"A martini is fine."

"Did you have a good trip?" Her father launched the question over his shoulder as he busied himself with the drinks.

"I had two whole days in Rome."

Mrs. Rupp brought her hands together. "How wonderful."

She had always been reluctant to regale her parents with accounts of her travels but now that seemed selfish. Through drinks, over dinner and still when they had returned to the living room—her mother would not hear of their doing the dishes now; she would just rinse them and leave them in the sink—Sheila listened to herself tell anecdote after anecdote, some from long-ago flights, but most from her recent parlay of trips.

"Clara," her father said. "We really should travel. It pains me to think that I have never been to Rome."

Clara Rupp said firmly that no one would ever get her onto an airplane. She gripped the arms of her chair as she said this, her body going rigid and resistant.

"Oh, Mother, don't be silly. Thousands and thousands of people fly every day of the week."

"And so do millions of birds. I won't join them, thank you."

So they had that whole discussion, the relative safety of air travel compared with any other, the whole thing leading inevitably to her father's saying that her mother ran worse risks going to the supermarket. "Remember what Fulton Sheen said, Clara. It's foolish to think that God takes care of you only on the ground."

"I don't like Fulton Sheen anymore."

"I know, I know. But he said this a long time ago."

When she returned to bed, Sheila had no difficulty falling asleep but, before sleep reclaimed her, she thought, It could always be like this, I could come home. She need not quit her job, of course, only leave the apartment with its painful associations. The girls could get someone to take her place. It was a pleasant, soporific thought, and one that she was sure would have lost its appeal by morning.

"Someone phoned," her mother said at breakfast. Her father had already gone to his office.

"Who?"

"I put the number by the phone."

Carl. Sheila crumpled her mother's note. The only safe course was never to see him again. She did not dare return his call. Thank God she was here and not at the apartment, where resistance would have been more difficult.

"Where are you going?" her mother asked later.

"Just for a walk."

"I sent some of your things to the cleaner."

"Thanks."

"Where will you walk?" Her mother seemed to fear that she was trying to escape.

"Nowhere in particular."

"Why don't you go to the park, Sheila? Remember how you used to love the duck pond? It's still there."

The Mass had been Phil's idea and it came to him, appropriately enough, during the dialogue homily at a Mass he and Father Tremplin were concelebrating in the Donovan dining room. Sister Eloise could not resist the thought that they made a strange tableau, a Last Supper by a minor Renaissance artist. But that would have been Lydia Donovan, leaning on the table, turned sideways in her chair looking soulfully at Phil, the beloved disciple, and Eloise did not find her hostess (if that was the name for her, during Mass) right for the role.

The topic during the dialogue was, inevitably, the war and the familiar judgments on it issued from them all: it was unjust, imperialistic, basically economic, an ideological imposition on a confused non-Christian Oriental people. Daniel Donovan grew visibly impatient with the litany.

"I'm tired of just *saying* these things," he grumbled. "We've all read them, heard them, said them a hundred times. *We* don't need convincing. I say that it's time we *did* something."

Lydia agreed immediately, whether out of prearrangement or because she and her husband were perfectly attuned, Eloise could not tell. Father Tremplin suggested that saying a Mass for peace was already doing something. This was greeted by an impatient murmur.

"What sort of action do you mean?" he asked Daniel.

The action Daniel had in mind had the merit of imitation; the scenario awaited them, the deed had already been done in a dozen cities. Hardy, a pink-cheeked seminarian, said excitedly that his father owned the building which housed the draft board. He could get a key.

"I think we should break in," Daniel said. "For the symbolic value."

"Key or no key, we'd still be breaking in."

"Even so."

Phil said, "They have duplicates of all the records. What's the point of destroying them?"

Daniel regarded him with exaggerated patience. "One action cannot stop the war machine. We all know that. But it is more than a gesture, far more than that."

"The symbolic value," Lydia said.

Phil's obvious reluctance encouraged her own and Eloise listened to the developing plan with dismay. It had too much the note of déjà vu and she did not like the description of it as fighting fire with fire. Making war on war was just the sort of thing they had to avoid. One thing was certain, however; they should do something. But what? And then Phil had his idea.

"If you want symbolic value, a truly peaceful action, the thing to do is to say Mass on the sidewalk outside the place in the middle of the day. Announce what you're doing and why, then do it. How can anyone object to a religious ceremony?"

The little silence that followed his remark contained an almost palpable shifting of gears and then everyone was talking at once. It was a perfect idea, making what Tremplin had called their present action a public and symbolic one as well. From across the table, Phil winked at Eloise with both eyes, as if his idea had been theirs and they had saved the group from a silly and imitation action. She smiled back at him, happy that he had reasserted his leadership and stopped the Donovans from running away with the group. Later, when they gave the sign of peace and Eloise was shaking hands with Hardy, the little seminarian seated next to her, Lydia leaned toward Phil and kissed him on the cheek. A symbolic act, no doubt.

The following day, when she and Phil set off from the Center in his car, heading for the meeting point downtown, he was obviously unenthused by what they were about to do.

"I don't really go for these group things," he said in explanation.

Of course he was a loner, but he was a leader too; he had to face up to that, and being a leader meant having followers, a group. Phil had introduced truly relevant apostolic work to Fort Elbow, alone, but the work had to involve more people and now it did. Even so, she could appreciate his dislike for group activities. She herself was not all that wild about those who awaited them on the steps of the cathedral.

It was not an impressive gathering, though Phil's arrival animated them. They got up from the steps, where they had been sitting, and Dan Donovan, puffing on a cigarette, said, "All right. Let's get moving. We want to catch the noon crowds."

It was an eight-block walk to the draft board office and they went by twos, twelve in all, some seminarians taking the lead with a hand-lettered sign. STOP THE WAR. Eloise and Phil brought up the rear and he seemed embarrassed now.

"Scared?" she asked.

He grinned. "Petrified." He shifted his Mass kit to his left hand and called ahead, "Take your partner's hand." He took hers and they swung up the street, encountering more pedestrians when they turned down Keasy. Phil and Tremplin, the seminarians too, wore Roman collars and Eloise had on her veil. Some people, curious, began to follow them.

The building was off Keasy, next to a movie theater, and the sidewalk in front of it was crowded. People stood aside for the strange procession and then they were there, forming a little semicircle around Phil. Eloise noticed the slack-jawed surprise on the faces of the people when Phil opened his Mass kit. The STOP THE WAR sign provided a backdrop for him.

"We have come here to say a Mass for peace," Phil announced, his voice clear and vibrant against the noise of the traffic and the buzz from the growing number of spectators. "Here, because this building houses a draft board, which is but one small cog in the machine of war that must be stopped before it brings ruin on the world. No more war!" He paused, then cried out again, his voice a plea, "No more war! That was the message Pope Paul brought to the United Nations and it is the basic message of Christ. Peace. No more war. Our country has become the principal threat to peace in the world and we, as citizens, as Christians, have an obligation to stop it before it is too late. The Mass we celebrate is a reenactment of Christ's sacrifice on Calvary."

"Hey, what's going on here?" A police officer pushed his way through the spectators. Phil ignored him.

"Blessed are the peacemakers. That is what Christ tells us. It is so easy to make war while telling ourselves that it is the Christian thing to do, because we are stopping atheistic communism. Did Christ make war on those who *really* threatened his life?"

The police officer took Phil's arm. "Hey, Father, what are you doing? You can't have a demonstration here, not without a permit. You're blocking the sidewalk."

"We're saying a Mass for peace, officer. That's all."

The officer was huge and had a red kindly face. "But you can't do that. Not here. Not on a public sidewalk."

"What better place to call attention to the warmongering of this country?" Donovan shouted. "This is a *public* place and we are concerned with the public business."

"We are the public," Lydia added. "Go on, Phil."

"You're a bunch of goddam pacifists," someone shouted from the enlarging crowd. "Run them in, officer."

The cop glared. "All right, cut out that kind of talk. This here's a priest."

Tremplin moved past the officer, his arms extended. "Join us in this prayer for peace, this prayer for our country. This is the way we can bring the war to a stop, by praying together."

A short, swarthy man, his face twisted with contempt, snorted at Tremplin. "You bet we can bring the war to an end. What do you think

240

we're doing over there? The way to stop a war is to win it. And that's what we're going to do!"

The police officer put his whistle to his mouth and blew a shrill blast. As if it were a signal, the little man moved forward and with him came others, a group against the group that was huddled around Phil. For the first time, Eloise felt real fear.

"Sit down," Donovan cried. "Everybody sit down."

Eloise was pulled down with the others, but Phil remained standing, guarded now by the officer. The menacing crowd, awaiting its cue from the angry little man, pressed forward, pushing the officer and Phil back. Eloise scrambled to her feet. It was stupid to sit on the walk like that; they could be trampled to death by these enraged people. She stared at them in disbelief, at the range of expressions, blank, curious, half amused, but those closest to her distorted with hate. An old woman swung her purse and caught Eloise on the cheek and the surprising pain was almost welcome. "Peace," Eloise called to the woman, trying to summon grace gathered at hundreds of Masses and pour it on that irate woman. The woman shouted an obscenity in reply.

The sound of approaching sirens seemed to relax them all; there were photographers now too, however, and when they began to take pictures, that stirred up the crowd again. The police officer was in as much danger as anyone and he kept blowing on his whistle. Other policemen arrived, thank God, moving through the crowd, dispersing it, converging on their besieged fellow. Eloise was almost surprised when she was arrested.

Lydia Donovan was already in the car they took her to. The door was slammed shut and the car began to roll, its siren first a guttural roar, then rising to a scream.

"Are you all right?" Lydia asked. Her face was pale and drawn.

"Yes. Are you?"

"My God." Lydia shivered, closing her eyes. "Did you see their faces? I think for the first time I understood why we are at war."

Eloise no longer felt fright, only a strange exhilaration. The danger had passed and been replaced by the certainty that what they had done had needed doing. If only they had not been separated like this. Somehow she had imagined them remaining together through it all. She wondered how the others were. Phil and the others.

Frank okayed and returned the proposed agenda Bishop Brophy had drawn up and, two days later, received a telephone call informing him that the first meeting of the senate would be held the following day.

"I'm sorry for such short notice, Father," Bishop Brophy said. "But I know that you'll appreciate the urgency."

"Monsignor Entweder told me that I'm always free for senate business."

"Of course." The bishop sighed. "I do wish Bullard had let us know before they acted. Oh, well. Until tomorrow, then."

Bullard? Surely the bishop wasn't serious. The demonstration in front of the draft board had been a picnic for the newspapers but it was not on the agenda of the senate meeting. Bishop Brophy must simply be assuming that it would be brought up anyway. After last night, Frank was inclined to think he was right.

Bob Wintheiser had shown up unannounced with Gerry Doyle, insisting that Frank come along with them, no excuses accepted. Frank, who had settled down for a night with Rahner, was not enthusiastic, though he was glad finally to see Gerry. Relieved too, since Gerry was thin and almost haggard, a striking contrast to Bob.

"Out where?"

"To my place," Bob burbled. "You have to meet Gilly. He is livid about Bullard and that is when he is at his mordant best. Come on, come on. Put on a collar. We shall brook no contradiction."

It was some consolation that Gerry was as bemused by Bob as he was. Frank put on a collar, grabbed his coat and felt that he was being hustled out to Wintheiser's waiting car. The three priests got into the front seat where, wedged between his friends, Frank said, "How have you been, Gerry?"

"Working my tail off, I can tell you that. Fine, though. How about you?"

"Enough, enough," Bob cried, hurtling through traffic. "No small talk. Save your energy. We have bigger game tonight."

Gilly, a short thick man with a salt-and-pepper crew cut, wearing a black cardigan and holding a tinkling drink, shook Frank's hand firmly, inspecting him as he did so.

"So this is the noblest Roman," he said, the remark addressed to Bob.

"Yet another classmate of the redoubtable Bullard. Now then, what is everyone having?"

"Bullard," Gilligan growled as his assistant busied himself preparing drinks. "When is Caldron going to give that idiot the ax? Look at that." He gestured toward the newspaper spread out on a leather footstool in front of the chair into which he now sank. Some of his drink splattered on the pages of the paper. "They've written it up as if it were the Alamo. Since when did that punk become an expert on foreign policy?"

"Your trouble, Father," Bob said smoothly, doling out drinks to Gerry and Frank, "your trouble is that you don't recognize an agrarian reformer when you see one."

Gilligan, it emerged, had been a Navy chaplain during the Korean War and he saw in Vietnam a perfect parallel to the Korean conflict. "Conflict," he snorted. "Police action. That was a war and make no mistake about it, the same war we're fighting now. The same damned war. If Korea made sense, and it did, then Vietnam makes sense. What's changed, that's what I want to know."

"Maybe Bishop Caldron is grooming Phil Bullard for the Chaplain Corps," Bob suggested sweetly.

It was Gilligan's profane opinion that Bullard would not be allowed to clean latrines in any branch of the service of the United States of America.

There was a globe in Gilligan's study, an obviously expensive one, illuminated from within as from the ultimate source of every volcano, and he made use of it in the lecture that followed, stabbing a stubby finger at Southeast Asia, drawing their attention to the great glob of China, threatening to drip southward like the paint in a familiar advertisement. Frank was aware of Bob's eyes on him, bright, encouraging, wanting to see if he was really enjoying this. Frank was not enjoying it at all. Did Bob seriously regard such harangues as an intellectual treat?

"Now you three," Gilligan said, wearying of the world. "You're classmates of Bullard. Okay. Go to him, lean on him, let him know what you think of his stunts. That's what classmates are for." He pulled at his drink. "Apparently Caldron intends to give him more rope. Well, maybe you can stop Bullard from going all the way and hanging himself. And the rest of us too. Make no mistake about that. This rubs off on every one of us."

"Tell him to forget about peace?" Gerry asked, and it was difficult to tell whether he like Bob was engaged in prodding Gilligan onward.

"Peace! Whimpering around draft boards is concern for peace? The trouble with people like Bullard is that they don't live in the real world. Say we stopped fighting. Tomorrow. Okay. We bring the troops home, every damned one of them, by tomorrow night. Would that be peace? Like hell it would. It's one big war, that's what it is. And it is going to go on and on and on."

Gilligan glared at them, his expression angry but a grim smile on his lips. The thought of an endless conflict did not bother him!

It was a triumph of sorts to get through those two hours with Gilligan without really uttering a word, though Frank had to fight the impulse to tell the pugnacious pastor that there was another side to the argument, one that could not be dismissed by emphasizing Bullard's deficiencies in geopolitics. But what would have been the point? It would have prolonged the evening and, from the moment he met Gilligan, Frank's only desire was to get out of there and home. When they did leave—as it were, dismissed from a briefing with a senior staff officer— Bob came out to the car with them, eager for their reactions to his boss, so eager that he seemed to find in their half-hearted mumbling a ringing endorsement. Gerry revved his motor and Bob sent them on their way with a mock salute, palm visible, hand trembling, British.

"Why?" Frank groaned. "How could he wish that on us?"

"You weren't impressed?" Gerry shook his head, smiling slyly. "Didn't you notice what an intellectual giant Gilly is? Why, he has the world situation in the palm of his hand."

"Are we supposed to choose between him and Phil Bullard?"

"That we don't have to do. And *benedicamus domino.*"

"You've lost weight, Gerry."

"Have I? It's been a bit of a grind."

"How is your pastor?"

"He's home again, but he hasn't much poop."

"Bob says Gilly works him pretty hard."

"No doubt. Think of the territory. Southeast Asia, China . . . Wow."

Home again, back in his room, Frank looked at the volume of Rahner he had put aside some hours before. And for what? If Bob Wintheiser ever tried another trick like that he would, friend or no friend, tell him where to go.

Now, with the possibility that more of the same awaited him at the first meeting of the clerical senate, Frank hoped that there would be a parliamentarian to keep them to the agenda. The items on it were comparatively dull, things not even Ewing could take much exception to. Well, maybe not that dull.

The fifteen members of the senate met in a classroom at the seminary and the setting seemed to carry them all back to earlier days. Monsignor Eisenbarth and Father Ewing were not affected by the room, of course; for them this was home ground. Nor was Bishop Brophy, whose seminary days had been passed in more impressive surroundings. Frank took a seat in the second row from the back. Eisenbarth and Ewing were content with the back row. Bishop Brophy called them to order.

"Monsignor Eisenbarth, would you say the prayer?"

The familiar nasal voice led them in a Hail Mary, they sat and Frank felt that he was a student again, the class about to begin.

"I am not here as one of you, of course," Bishop Brophy said with a wide smile. He stood beside the lectern, one elbow resting on it in a practiced way. "As a matter of fact, with this meeting, my own small part in the formation of the senate ends. I will not succumb to the temptation to remind you what an opportunity the senate is for the priests of this diocese nor how important such innovations are for dioceses throughout the country. You are all perfectly aware of that. I will convey to you the good wishes, and blessing, of Bishop Caldron and my own too, if I may. Now then, before I fade away, there remains one last preliminary matter, the election of your chairman. If you wish, I shall be happy to preside until I can turn the chair over to your choice for that office." Brophy's brows went up, his smile swept the room and, encountering no negatives, he said, "Very well. Nominations are open. Yes. Father Maxwell."

"I nominate Don Oder."

"Father Oder. Any others? No? Are there any other nominations? Well, well. I take it then that Father Donald Oder is unanimously elected chairman."

Brophy led the applause for Oder, then shook his hand when he came forward.

"Even before thanking you," Father Oder said, "I want to express our thanks to Bishop Brophy for all that he has done to bring this body into being. I know that no one was misled by his description of his part as small."

Bishop Brophy was sped on his way with a generous burst of applause. Oder again thanked them all for their confidence and proposed the adoption of the agenda. That done, the floor was opened for discussion of the first item, consultation on clerical appointments.

"Smooth," Ewing murmured behind Frank. "Very smooth. A well-oiled machine."

"What does this item mean?" Eisenbarth asked in a whisper. "Do they expect the bishop to *ask* a man to take a post?"

Oder was commenting on the first item in mournful tones, making veiled references to the capriciousness with which priests were sometimes assigned. Frank felt a tap on his shoulder and Ewing nodded toward Oder. "You could tell him a thing or two about that, eh?" It was a moment before Frank realized that Ewing was referring to his own appointment to Saint Waldo's. It had been weeks since he had thought of that. During the faintly anarchic discussion of the item which was destined to go on until the break for lunch, Frank found it difficult to share the discontent of the others. If he had been given his choice last May, he would have asked for an appointment to the seminary faculty. Now he doubted that he would have been happy here. Whatever his feelings about his work at Saint Waldo's, he had at least the small satisfaction of knowing that it was the bishop's will he was obeying, not his own. Most of the discussion was taken up with anecdotes of Caldron's past whimsies, though the bishop was not explicitly named. Eventually they tired of this and Oder, saying that he sensed the senate was in agreement that something must be done, asked for proposals as to the machinery of consultation. Young Maxwell was like a Trappist on holiday, eager to speak, to comment, to reply. Now he bounced up yet again to make a proposal. He suggested that the bishop simply endorse the choices of the clergy. Who knew better than the priest himself what work he could do? Ewing rose to his feet.

"I find this a very interesting proposal," he drawled. "Do I understand it correctly when I imagine myself, say, informing the bishop that I feel a calling to take over Father Oder's parish and then await endorsement of my selection?"

"An endorsement that might too readily be given," Oder said with a laugh. "No, Father. As I understand the proposal it does not envisage replacing caprice by caprice."

Ewing, less amiable, asked for a definition of caprice and into the thicket of verbal dispute the assembly all too eagerly descended. When they did break for lunch, they were where they had been an hour and a half before. Something should be done about consulting the clergy in the matter of their appointments, but they did not know what that something might be.

Jim Grimes fell in beside Frank on the walk to the refectory.

"It looks the same, doesn't it?" Grimes said, making a comprehensive gesture. "Everything so unchanged. But can you imagine it with so few students? They're below a hundred now, aren't they?"

"Well below."

Grimes shook his head. "In ten years as a priest I've managed to direct only one boy to the seminary. And recently I advised him to leave. He actually seemed to believe that the law of celibacy would not apply to him, that it has already been changed or very soon will be, I suppose in time for his own ordination. I told him he was mad. Of course he was involved with a girl."

They went up the steps and into the refectory, where they ate at the faculty table and Eisenbarth, at the center of things, looked less unhappy than he had during the morning session. Oder sat at a far end of the table, with Maxwell and the younger men. Frank and Grimes sat side by side but they were drawn into the conversation which was devoted largely to nostalgic reminiscing of seminary days, anecdote following anecdote. It grew maudlin but a palpable sense of comradeship developed at the table. Afterward, outside again, Grimes suggested a stroll and Frank went along with him. Grimes returned to the topic of the seminarian he had advised to leave.

"He was quite openly involved with a girl, Frank. In my day here, that was not only unthinkable, it would not have been tolerated for an instant. I knew a man who was expelled because of a supposed summer involvement with a girl. He claimed that he was innocent and perhaps he was but in those days even the appearance of that sort of thing was grounds for expulsion."

"The seminarians read the papers, Father. They read of all these priests marrying and what they say when they do. I suppose it does look as if celibacy is hanging by a thread."

"Perhaps. But I don't think it is the newspapers that do it. They're ruined right here. He was a good boy. I'm certain that he had a vocation and then lost it. Here. At the seminary. Think of that. He was involved in all that commotion last spring, the strike, the demonstration."

"What's his name?"

"Cole. Benedict Cole."

Frank stopped and looked at Grimes.

"Do you know him, Frank?"

"I've met him."

He was the boy Beverly was going with. Frank made the connection immediately and had the sinking feeling that he had been a witness of sorts to the steps in the boy's decision to leave the seminary. Cole had been there with Tremplin when Frank came from the chancery with news of his assignment to Saint Waldo's. Cole had been the seminarian Eisenbarth had asked to show Beverly around the campus. And Cole was one of the seminarians working at the Center with Phil Bullard where Beverly too was spending the summer.

"What kind of girl would go out with a seminarian, Frank? Can you tell me that?"

"It's hard to say," Frank mumbled.

"But then maybe he didn't tell her where he went to school."

"Maybe."

The classroom, when they returned to it at one o'clock, did not invite postprandial napping. Apparently everyone was bothered by the inconsequence of the morning session and there seemed a common resolution not to get bogged down like that again. The second item on the agenda was introduced and, inevitably as it now seemed, Father Maxwell gained the floor.

"Look, Father, what's the point of this meeting, what's the point of the senate, if we're going to waste time on the cut-and-dried? All morning we took turns saying what everybody knew before we came here. We don't have any say in where the bishop sends us and lots of men have assignments they don't like or for which they're not too well equipped. Okay. We all know that. Talking about it isn't going to change anything. Now we're going to talk about the priest and civil rights and, after that, we will all agree that we don't get paid enough. That's item three. Well, I want to talk about the priest and civil rights concretely, in terms of a practical proposal. You all know that a couple days ago a small group of people acted on their convictions. Two priests, some seminarians and a nun, plus a number of lay people, tried to stage a Mass for peace in front of the draft board downtown. Why? Because they are fed up with a crazy system that forces young men to go off to a war that hasn't a justification in the world. Okay. I move that we go on record as endorsing their action and that we ask the diocese to foot any legal bill for their defense."

Halfway through this speech, Eisenbarth was on his feet, waving his arm for recognition. Now he began to call Oder's name. The chairman's eyes did not look in his direction. When Oder pointed, it was to his assistant, Swivel, who rose to his feet.

"I second the motion. The clerical senate of this diocese has to come down on the side of peace."

"Sit down, Randy. Sit down." Ewing was tugging at the rector's sleeve. "The motion has been made and seconded. Let them speak to it."

"Are you in favor of it?"

"Let's get the lay of the land."

The lay of the land seemed to favor the motion. Five priests spoke on its behalf and, with Maxwell and Oder and Swivel, that seemed to ensure passage. Throughout the discussion, Frank was reminded of his ordeal the night before with Gilligan. The speakers took an opposite stand to Gilly's, but there was the same kind of political rhetoric, the same assumption that genuine attitudes had to be global in scope.

"Father Ascue," Oder said, when Frank raised his hand.

"This motion suggests that we declare ourselves for peace. I find that rather easy to respond to. Of course we are for peace. I doubt that anyone imagines that the priests of this diocese are warmongers who are enraged by the prospect of tranquillity." An image of Gilligan teased his mind, then faded. "Let me make a little confession. When I went through this place, they weren't offering the courses in military science, diplomacy and world politics that so many of you obviously passed with flying colors. I am going to have to restrict myself to things I know. There are two aspects of the motion I wish to comment on, the one considerably more important than the other. First, there is the matter of a law which was broken. It is not a terribly important law, but it is nevertheless a law. These people had a public assembly without a permit when there was no reason why they should not have applied for one and no reason, so far as I know, to expect that it would not be granted. That is my first point, the one of lesser importance. I suggest that we can be for peace and for demonstrations without endorsing an unnecessary breaking of the law. Is breaking a law the most effective way of arguing that a war is illegal? My second point is, as I have said, vastly more important, and it has the merit of being one that we as priests have some claim to competency on. The intention of the group in question was to say Mass on a public street under highly unfavorable conditions and with the intention to use the Holy Sacrifice of the Mass as a weapon." Frank looked around, inhaled, continued. "I don't really know what to make of this war. I *feel* it is wrong. I would dearly love to see it end. I can sympathize with, applaud, perhaps even wish to join those who oppose it. That is one sort of thing and if that is all the motion involved I wouldn't have much problem with it. But, as a priest, I do have deep misgivings about *using* the Mass in the way this group apparently intended, to taunt, to divide, to intimidate others and, far more seriously, in a way that shows fundamental disrespect for the Holy Sacrifice. If the motion should include a condemnation of the attempt to say Mass in such a fashion and in such circumstances, I would vote for it. If it does not include such a condemnation, I shall vote against it."

Frank sat down, surprised by his own performance. He had had no intention of making a speech; he had not realized until he stood up what it was about Bullard's group that dismayed him. Ewing was clapping him on the back, others began to speak without recognition and Oder was slamming the desktop with his palm, trying to restore order. Maxwell, recognized, begged them to concentrate on the simple point of his motion, peace not war, but others took up the point Frank had raised, not so much to develop it as to hem it round with hawkish embroidery. Frank had the depressing feeling that he had provided ammunition to those who would have agreed with Gilligan's harangue. But he could not regret having made the Mass the issue, however that was now turned to other ends. His intervention turned out to be a telling one. When the vote was finally taken, the motion was defeated.

"Excellent, Father," Eisenbarth whispered. "Excellent. You saved the day."

Grimes said, "Isn't it crazy? I never even thought of that, trying to say Mass on a crowded street. I was afraid we were going to be here for hours discussing foreign policy."

As Maxwell had predicted, when they turned to item three they agreed that they were not paid enough, but no one had any notion how this could be remedied, particularly now that collections, along with church attendance, were falling off. No one demurred when Oder called the meeting to a close.

"Come have a drink, Frank," Ewing said. "You deserve it."

"Thanks, Father. But not today."

"Entweder keeping you busy?"

"We take a lot of census."

"Good. Entweder's solid, always has been. You made a great speech. Eisenbarth was right. You saved the day."

Had he? Then why didn't he feel any elation? No matter how important what he had said was—and he did not doubt its importance—it seemed to have placed him on the wrong side. When Oder asked him to come along to the Saint Barnabas rectory for a drink, Frank was glad to accept.

"Just a little postmortem," Oder said. "We can learn a lot from today."

"What got into Maxwell?"

Oder shrugged and wore a sheepish look. It turned out that Maxwell too had been invited to the postmortem. Besides Frank and Oder, Swivel, Maxwell, Tremplin and Donovan settled into leather chairs in Oder's den. A cloud of gloom seemed to hang over the gathering. Maxwell glared at Frank.

"You sure as hell weren't much help."

"Gentlemen," Oder soothed. "Let us not repeat the hassle here. The fact is, Max, Frank made an important point. I agree that the underlying purpose of your motion was lost sight of. An expression of support for a group that acted on the dictates of their conscience would have been a powerful thing. However."

However, they were going to have to face the fact that the senate was not so constituted that progressive proposals were assured of automatic passage. In the future, they would have to proceed circumspectly and with better preparation. The most important proximate thing facing them did not, as it happened, concern the senate. The coming county-wide ecumenical conference was a great opportunity and they had to make the most of it.

Maxwell wanted to know if it was going to be just a rounding up of believers or what.

"I don't understand, Max," Oder said.

"My point is that we should issue wedding garments to everybody. How about the nonbelievers?"

"Harvey Gunderson!" Swivel said. Gunderson was a Fort Elbow atheist whose writings had given him a national reach.

"That's ridiculous," Donovan said. "Gunderson!"

Maxwell turned on the editor. "Don't you want atheism represented?"

"The point is, how. I would suggest Plummet-Finch."

"Plummet-Finch?"

"He's at the university, right here in town," Donovan said smugly. "A friend of mine and an excellent man."

"Let's have them both," Oder said. "Excellence *and* Harvey Gunderson."

Donovan shook his head in dismay when Oder's suggestion met with agreement.

Oder asked them all to stay for dinner, but Frank decided to leave. Oder seemed to have forgotten that Frank had come to the rectory in his car and Frank, not wanting to remind him, set off on foot.

He walked south to the freeway, turned left and set off at a leisurely pace in the direction of Saint Waldo's, three miles to the east. His original idea was to walk to where he could catch a cab, but now the prospect of the long walk home appealed to him. It was a warm evening with the sun still in the western sky behind him, no longer hot, and the sound of traffic, the noise of the city, the mechanical act of walking, brought a welcome relief from this long confusing day. He had looked forward to senate meetings, expecting something more serious than his daily round at Saint Waldo's. Today had been a great disappointment, but of course they were only beginning.

Should he have spoken up during the discussion of Maxwell's motion? The question seemed to lift from the rhythm of his walking feet. The possible sacrilegious abuse of the Mass, however important, however much it had seemed to turn the vote, was not, Frank now thought, what had been decisive for the others. There were two groups—there were always two groups—and the division was political: liberal and conservative, right and left, hawk and dove. It was foolish to think that priests had any special insight into political and military matters. What they said was only an echo of the newspapers and magazines they read, the commentators they listened to. Frank knew that he had been lucky to escape the suffocating embrace of Te Deum, though he did not like to remember what had effected his escape. Did he now want to move toward the opposition, to Oder and Bullard? Perhaps it was not fair to lump Oder with Bullard. Phil was such a strange mixture of the good and dubious whereas Oder, together with Bishop Brophy, represented a genuine effort to implement the spirit of the Vatican Council. Nonetheless, something in Frank resisted the thought of taking sides. But, if he had to, he knew that he would gravitate toward Brophy and Oder. Perhaps he had already done so, despite the unwanted praise from Ewing and Eisenbarth for what he had said at the senate meeting.

His legs were tired by the time he reached the river and after he crossed the bridge he still had some distance to go before he reached the parish house, but he persisted. When finally he was inside his own rectory, the cool air made him realize how strenuous the walk had been. He really ought to exercise more, but how? He did not want to get in with the golfing priests—nor the bowling monsignori either—and jogging bore the stamp of Arthur Rupp, who had tried to urge it on Frank.

"Father Ascue?" Hilda called from upstairs.

"Yes."

She came down sideways, slowly, her expression sadder than it would have been if she only meant to chide him for missing supper.

"I've been trying to reach you, Father."

"What is it?"

"Miss Simpson." Hilda had reached the bottom of the stairs. She turned mournful eyes on him. "Miss Simpson died this afternoon."

The body was no longer in the room when he got there. Frank stood in the doorway, looking around that empty anonymous space. The bed was newly made, not yet occupied by another patient. The top of the bedside table held only the standard impersonal items. There was no sign left of the woman who had spent the last weeks of her life here.

Father Ascue turned away and started down the hall. The emptiness of the room was almost a denial of the news that Hilda had given him twenty minutes before. Miss Simpson dead. His absence of surprise on hearing the news made it somehow more surprising and horrible. Dead.

252

"Father?"

He turned. A nun in white. Pleasant face, her expression not quite a smile. Concern. Charity.

"Are you looking for someone, Father?"

"No. No, thank you, Sister."

She went away, busy, busy, the work here real, birth and death, pain and the hope of health. How did they stand it?

There were several people waiting for the elevator and he went past them to the stairs. He had not yet prayed for Miss Simpson. May her soul and the souls of all the faithful departed through the mercy of God rest in peace. In peace. He remembered the afternoon quarrel and his mind blurred. Where was the chapel? Second floor.

From the second floor he gained entrance to a loft that overlooked the chapel. He knelt, aware of the scent of flowers. Small, ornate, dark, the chapel invited his eyes to the altar and the tabernacle there. He kept repeating the prayer for the dead. All the faithful departed. That included his parents but the thought of them as dead was a familiar one. Miss Simpson. She had told him that she was offering her pain to God in reparation for the sins of men, principally her own, of course. How profoundly simple her faith had been. The gift of suffering, a suffering so difficult to bear with dignity. In the divine economy, for all we know, Miss Simpson's sacrifice might far outweigh more dramatic deeds. That seemed a thought he had been searching for.

Below him, in the chapel, three or four patients were scattered among the pews. How ill were they? They must be on the mend if they were allowed to come to the chapel. Or was that so? Frank sat, wanting to pray, unable to pray. He would just sit there awhile. He remembered Miss Simpson on the plane from Rome and his thoughts turned to himself on that flight. How eagerly he had looked forward to getting home, not a doubt in his mind that he was destined for the seminary faculty. It was hard to believe now that he had really wanted that. What did he want? Consultation on clerical appointments? His assignment was Saint Waldo's and he had to accept that, accept it as Miss Simpson had accepted cancer, accept it and turn it into something far more than it was. He had to avoid getting drawn into the tug of war, those political groupings. Right and left. The labels did not help, were a distraction. Camps, factions, machinations, triumphs and defeats. In Rome he had imagined that there would be varying degrees of enthusiasm for what the Council had done, but was that the same thing as these opposing groups?

Miss Simpson's estimate of the turmoil had had the advantage of clarity and simplicity. Fatima, Lourdes—the Mother of God brooding sorrowfully over a world her son had died to save. Miss Simpson knew why the world, and the Church, were in a mess. War is the punishment, not the crime. May she rest in peace.

He ran into Father Keegan, the chaplain, on the main floor.

"They told you Miss Simpson died?"

"Were you with her at the time?"

Keegan shook his head. "No. But I brought her Communion this morning."

"Good."

"Have you seen her?"

Startled, Frank said, "She wasn't in her room."

"She's downstairs if you want to see her."

"Downstairs?"

"The morgue."

"Oh."

"Just take the elevator to the basement."

They parted, Keegan going in the direction of his office. Frank hurried by the elevator and out the street door into the cooling night.

Beverly had arrived at the Center at ten, coming as if to an assignation, but her day had been a slippery slide into the slough of despond. Ben did not show up. And all day, it seemed, she and Janice, Bullard's secretary, kept running into one another and exchanging the same questions.

"Have you seen Father Bullard, Bev?"

"Have you seen Ben Cole?"

They said no to one another's questions until, at one-thirty, Bev said, "Maybe we should combine searches. Want to have lunch?"

"I brought mine from home."

"Bring it along. I'll pick up something."

They ate on a campus lawn. Janice was tall and pretty and kind of dumb. Away from the Center, where she was a study in motion, she looked lost and unsure of herself.

"Do you usually have lunch at your desk?"

"Uh huh."

"Sounds awful."

"We're always so busy. You know."

254

"How long have you worked for Phil?"

"Since he came. Actually, I was there when he came, had been for a month. But, more or less, we started at the same time."

"I guess you like it."

"Oh, yes!"

Bev was distracted by a blue jay who was being chased by a band of robins. Having lunch with Janice was probably better than eating alone. Probably. But it was Janice who broke the silence.

"What do you think of Sister Eloise?"

"She's okay."

That did not seem to be the answer Janice wanted. She frowned.

"Why do you ask?"

"No reason."

Like fun. Janice seemed undecided whether to pursue this. Curious, bored, Beverly said, "Of course, I don't know her very well."

"I don't think I'd want to."

"Oh?"

"Have you ever noticed her with Father Bullard?"

"Quite a bit."

Bingo. "That's what I mean," Janice said. "She practically clings to him. Honestly, would anyone think she's a nun watching her hanging around Father that way?"

"Has he said anything?"

Janice sighed. "Men are so dumb. I don't think he even notices."

"We live in changing times, Janice. As Adam said to Eve."

Janice grew impatient. "Someone ought to say something to *her*."

Not me, Bev thought, if that's what you have in mind. She drew Janice's attention to the blue jay. The girl was pathetic. She obviously had a crush on her boss and saw Sister Eloise as competition. Weird.

When they got back to the Center, Father Bullard's car was there. Eloise was in the office with him. The sound of their laughter drifted from the open door and Janice stopped and cast a stricken look at Bev. It was too much. Bev decided to go home. If Ben Cole did show up he could just eat his heart out.

He phoned that night, late, nearly eleven o'clock. Bev was in her room, getting ready for bed.

"Where were you?" she asked. "I've had them dragging the river."

"Any luck?"

"You sound depressed."

"Hasn't he talked to you?"

"Who?"

Ben groaned. "Father Grimes really did it. He was in town for the senate meeting and told your uncle about us. So your uncle called and asked me over for a little talk."

"Uncle Frank!"

"The Reverend Francis Ascue."

"But what did he say?"

"Can't you imagine?"

No, she could not. She insisted that Ben tell her. This was beyond belief. Ben said that Uncle Frank had spent an hour scolding him, reminding him of his vocation and of the fact that he was not supposed to take out girls.

"He made me feel that I was leading you astray."

"But what did you say?"

"Say? I did a lot of listening."

"Oh, Ben, I'm so sorry."

Sorry? She was furious. All day long she had felt abandoned and now to find out that Uncle Frank was the cause. Ben Cole was none of his darned business.

"Oh, he thought it was his duty, Bev. You know."

"Didn't you tell him what Father Grimes advised?"

"What do you mean?"

"Grimes told you to forget about the seminary. Remember? He did say that, didn't he?"

"Sure he did." There was a pause, a long pause. "But if he really meant it, why did he talk to your uncle? Why did your uncle call me over there?"

So they were right back where they had been before Ben's visit to Father Grimes and she had Uncle Frank to thank for that. She felt that she would explode, but what good would that do now, on the phone, with Ben brooding again.

"You see how it is with people who never had a doubt, Ben. Don't you wish you were like that? Then you could prop up everybody else."

"You wouldn't think it was funny if you had to sit through it."

"Sit? I would have stood and saluted through the whole thing. Be grateful, Ben. Uncle Frank just has your best interests at heart. Maybe he could arrange for you to live at the seminary for the rest of the summer. Far from temptation."

"I'm surprised he didn't suggest that."

"I'll mention it to him."

"You're a big help."

"Mmmm." Humming was as sexy as she could get at a distance.

"Are you going to the Center tomorrow?"

"Are you?"

"I'll see you there. Okay?"

"Okay. Keep the faith."

Beverly hung up the phone and took a deep breath with her eyes closed. She turned and, despite the hour, screamed.

"Mother!"

Part Four

1 Arthur Rupp emerged from sleep with the sense of having been summoned. Speak, Lord. But the sound of Clara rustling beside him made it clear that she had wakened him.

"What's the matter?"

"You were snoring. Roll over."

He stifled a curse. The sleep she had shaken him from had been unaccountably peaceful. On his side, he stared at the faintly illumined window and felt absolutely awake. He could not tell from the light what time it was and the luminous dial of his watch was a blur telling him only that it was some time but not which. He eased over onto his back and looked at the ceiling. He was wide awake and already Clara's breathing indicated that she had drifted off.

Counting one's grievances is not a wise way to tempt sleep, but Arthur lay there reviewing the general decadence of the day: the waning of patriotism, the waxing of the welfare state, the crumbling condition of the Church. It was the last he fastened on, reciting to himself a familiar litany of complaints. What people refused to understand was that the Church is not a democratic institution. By its very nature it is authoritarian, its doctrines and laws products not of consensus but of someone at the top laying down the law. If a person did not choose to accept those teachings, okay; he could get out. But nowadays dissenters wanted to question and doubt and disagree and still claim to be Catholics. Even worse than such shenanigans was the incredible silence of the bishops. Why the hell didn't they crack down, break a few heads, throw the rascals out?

"Prudence," Eisenbarth answered, when confronted by this question. The rector's lips pursed, his lids dropped and he nodded as if that weasel word encompassed the wisdom of the bishops' craven failure to do one damned thing about those who were tearing the Church to pieces.

261

"Oh, come on, Monsignor," Arthur retorted. "There's another word for doing nothing. They're scared and you know it. Of what? If they're worried about losing a few priests, a few people, their current method, or lack of it, ought to be scrapped. People are confused. They can hear fifty versions a day of what the Church teaches on a given point and no one tells them what's what. And, remember, it's the rebels who end up leaving the Church. Why cater to them?"

Eisenbarth hunched his shoulders and displayed his hands like a wop selling fruit. He was as bad as a bishop. Probably still hoped to become one and did not want to antagonize his future peers.

"I thought Bishop Caldron was dead set against this ecumenical conference that's going to be held."

"Monsignor Yorick tells me that Bishop Caldron has given his permission. Reluctantly and with stipulations." A pained expression crossed Eisenbarth's face. "He has placed Bishop Brophy in charge, to ensure that the appropriate caution will be observed."

Brophy! If Caldron wanted caution exercised he should have put Monsignor Eisenbarth in charge. Well, there was no point in saying that. Eisenbarth's expression indicated that that was precisely his own thought. So Arthur had swallowed his distaste and telephoned Bishop Brophy.

"What did you have in mind, Mr. Rupp?" the bishop asked, and Arthur thought, as he had before, that Brophy could have made a fortune in insurance with that rich, confident voice.

"I understand there will be panels."

"I think you're right. Some panels are planned."

"Bishop, many of our members have a good deal of experience debating Protestants and I want you to know—"

"Debating?"

"Answering the usual smears. You know. We have a man who is particularly good on Luther." Arthur thought it was wiser to speak of himself in the third person. "Lots of juicy stuff on him that few Lutherans know."

On the other end of the line, Bishop Brophy cleared his throat several times, but each time it was a prelude to more silence. Finally he said, "Mr. Rupp, the idea isn't so much to debate our separated brethren as to remove causes of suspicion and recrimination."

"That's no way to make converts, Bishop. Take my word for it."

Brophy's laugh was a bad actor's. "I doubt that anyone will be converted as a result of this conference, Mr. Rupp. That isn't the idea at all, you see. We are going to exchange views, explore our differences, see what can be done about bringing all Christians together again."

262

"In the Roman Catholic Church?"

"That we must leave to God."

It was incredible to find a bishop in need of instruction on the Power of the Keys. Arthur gave up. His only remaining interest in that damned conference was to torpedo it. But how could he do even that when Eisenbarth—the founder of Te Deum!—was counseling prudence, caution, waiting and seeing and all the rest of it? Nor was Clara any help.

"You mustn't try to assume responsibility for everything, Arthur. There will be madness no matter what you do. Surely Te Deum is enough?"

Te Deum. Considered calmly in the dead of night, that organization seemed to its president little more than a league of heavy drinkers, people far more interested in bibulous social gatherings than in the talks and projects Te Deum sponsored. The Fourth of July Communion Breakfast, to be held on the eighth, would be a bust, there was no point in kidding himself about that. Eisenbarth would speak and his talk would no doubt be one they had all heard a dozen times before. If the man could summon half as much concern for ecclesiastical confusion as he did for secular, Te Deum might make its weight felt now when the Church needed it. It was not that the other members disagreed with him or did not share his anger, but Arthur seemed to be the only one who wanted to translate the rage into action. Oh, to hell with it.

On his side once more, he closed his eyes and tried to surprise sleep by erasing every thought from his mind. It did not work, not with a mind as active as his. Why hadn't Clara let him snore in peace? He thought of Sheila, asleep in her room down the hall, and something like content came over him.

His daughter was on vacation now and Arthur hoped that she would quit her job. Of course Clara vetoed his suggesting that to Sheila. Let her be, Arthur. Let her be. He had agreed. Thank God she was back under her own roof again. A bit mopey, maybe, not as happy as she might be, but then she had been through a rough experience.

Too late he tried to stop that line of thought. Ascue. He could not figure out that man. God knows what advice he had given Sheila and then blowing his stack like that in the rectory office. Arthur had been sure that the young priest was having a breakdown of some kind. But then he had come to apologize, and that could not have been an easy thing to do. More mystifying still, Eisenbarth had told him that Father Ascue had singlehandedly stopped the clerical senate from passing some stupid resolution in support of that demonstration in front of the draft board. You would think that a priest trained in Rome would be more predictable.

The light at the windows was brighter. Soon he would get up, don his sweat suit and go out on his morning jog. Honest to God, sometimes he wondered if it was worth it. What difference did it really make if he gained a little weight? At his age, that was the most natural thing in the world. But he knew that he would get up and go jogging. Somehow exercise and concern for the fate of the Church seemed inextricably linked, as if by giving in to obesity he would be leaving the field uncontested to all those rebels.

Beside him Clara began to snore gently. Arthur stopped his hand before it reached her shoulder. He would not shake her awake. He would just lie here and suffer, offering it up. A small cross but a real one. Gritting his teeth, pressing his eyelids closed, Arthur rode the rhythm of Clara's snoring back into dreamland.

Sheila, on these vacation mornings, went off improbably to Mass, at Saint Waldo's, feeling no affinity with the elderly women in their print dresses, hankies or mantillas on their heads, a few accompanied by their husbands, thin brittle aging men who walked several paces behind their spouses as they went up the aisle toward the front of the church. Sheila took a back pew, did not kneel, but sat in the carved curve of the seat and watched the early sunlight lay shifting cartoons of light upon the pews in front of her, the white beam, polychrome at either end, projecting downward from the stained-glass windows. It was Father Ascue's Mass that she attended.

She did not pray. Her distance from the altar might have expressed her distance from the God who was worshiped there. How could a numb heart go out to a deity defined in terms of reward and punishment, mercy and remorse, salvation? When she had thought of sin as a child, of Christ dying on the cross for sinners, it must have been someone like her present self to whom she had imagined those outstretched arms appealing. What she could not have known is that there is little resonance in the sinner to that promise of forgiveness. Only numbness, distance, an observer's curiosity.

Did Father Ascue, facing them from behind the altar, see her there? She felt the object of his gaze but was certain this was imagination. As celebrant he played a role, fulfilled a function, and must be aware of the congregation only as an actor is of his audience: a group, a collective presence. He fascinated her, nonetheless, and not in his functional role. The fact that he knew so much about her seemed to create an intimacy between them which was all the more poignant for being impersonal. Almost impersonal. She sensed that the priesthood was so ingrained in him that there was no seam between him and it and that made him different from any other man she knew. She would like to talk to him but she could not go to the rectory again nor did she want to go into the sacristy after Mass. The meeting there would necessarily be brief and inconsequential and what she wanted was to take up again the discussion of herself they had begun some weeks ago and which she had then stopped before it became too painful.

Her sense of separation from what was going on in the church increased at Communion time when the old people rose stiffly from their pews and went forward to receive. She could not do that. She was still in a state of sin, too numb to move past the sense of defeat and humiliation to some semblance of sorrow for what she had done. Only if she had been absolved from her sin could God be placed on her tongue and housed in the body she had given so hopelessly to Carl.

When she walked home she did not avoid the park as she would have liked to do. It seemed important not to allow herself to forget the pain of that afternoon with Catherine which had announced the end of her affair with Carl. Affair. She hated the word but had no decent substitute for it. The trouble with the word was really its decency, evoking afternoon teas, diplomatic troubles, the titles of mystery novels. Carl had not called her parents' home again. He must have realized that, even apart from Catherine, there was between them now that horrible afternoon when her father had appeared at the apartment and she had opened the door to him fresh from her lover's arms. If only he had come out of the bedroom the horror could have mounted and then been swept away since his appearing would have forced them into a new relationship.

Passing the park, Sheila saw the puffing figure of her father approaching on a gravel path. She waited for him, returning the wave he threw as if acknowledging expected if unwanted applause. When he arrived at where she stood, he continued to raise his knees high, jogging in place, perspiration beading his forehead. His face glowed unhealthily.

"Are you going to do that all the way home?"

"You set the pace," he gasped. "Where have you been?"

"Out for a walk."

They went up the street toward the house. Sheila was undecided whether to hurry so that her father's strenuous activity would be translated into a more forward movement or to slow down in the hope that his wind might be renewed.

"Am I going too slowly?" she asked.

"Doesn't matter," he panted. "Doesn't matter at all."

"Dad, you'll have a heart attack."

"Bah. This is the best thing in the world for a man my age."

As if to underscore his point, he began to bring his knees still higher. Sheila did hurry then, wanting to get him home as quickly as she could.

Inside, collapsed at the table, a towel wrapped around his sweating head, her father skimmed the morning paper with familiar gloom.

"Where did you walk, Sheila?" her mother asked.

Before she could frame a lie, her father groaned. "Today is that damned ecumenical conference." He slapped the paper down and gripped his glass of juice.

Sheila said, "Here in town?"

"At the Placental Hotel." Her father handed her the paper. He made a face, perhaps because of the citric tartness of the juice. "Of course that Muscatelli girl will cover it for the *Tribune*. An anti-Catholic!"

"How do you know?"

"She'd never even heard of Te Deum."

"I'm surprised you're not going, Dad."

"Ha! That sort of thing is for people like Father Ascue, not me."

"Is it open to the public?"

Her father stopped buttering toast. "Were you thinking of going down there?"

"Well, I was thinking of going downtown."

"Go to the meeting, Sheila. Listen. Take notes. I just don't trust that damned newspaper anymore."

"I didn't say I was going."

"If you do," he said, subsiding. "If you do."

After breakfast Frank went upstairs to his room and changed into street clothes but since it was still too early to set off for downtown he settled into his chair and lit a cigarette. Downstairs the phone rang. It was answered on the second ring. Not for him. He realized that it had been over a week since he had been summoned by Charlotte and he had not heard from her since. Would she forget that today was the day of the ecumenical meeting? The chance, however remote, was real and he did not want to call and risk reminding her.

She had met him prim-lipped at the door, her eyes on the departing cab. In the living room she waved him to the couch, still not looking at him.

"Kids in bed?"

"Of course. It's after nine o'clock."

"Where's Howard?"

"Cleveland."

266

"Again? Why does he go to Cleveland so often?"

"Business." Charlotte did look at him now. "Aren't you going to ask about Beverly?"

"Okay. How's Beverly?"

"She's out, no thanks to you. Frank, what on earth got into you? Do you realize that I *denied* to Bev that you could possibly have done such a thing? I could not believe it. Your own niece . . ."

"Did you know that she was going out with a seminarian?"

Char stared at him, her mouth open. "Frank, did you hear yourself when you asked that? Could you hear yourself? You sounded like—oh, I don't know what you sounded like. For heaven's sake, what's wrong with you? Beverly likes that boy. He likes her. Why did you have to try and spoil it?"

"Do you know him?"

"What do you mean, do I know him?" Char had tipped her head to one side and was trying to smile.

"Have you ever met him?"

A dozen lies flickered in her eyes. Finally, she plopped her hands in her lap. "What in the name of God has that got to do with it?"

"So you haven't met him. I'm not surprised. Doesn't that tell you something, Char? Why shouldn't Bev want you to meet a boy you say she likes so much?"

"Do you honestly think a parent meets everyone her daughter goes out with? Come on, Frank."

He wondered what Char would think of Ben Cole, if she did meet him. Frank had been almost surprised when Ben agreed to come to the rectory at Saint Waldo's, since he had made it perfectly clear why he wanted to see Ben. If the boy had decided to leave the seminary, he would most likely have refused to come. Or, having come, explained that he was no longer studying for the priesthood, thus forestalling any criticism. But Ben had not only come, he had sat there mutely while Frank reminded him that he was jeopardizing his vocation by taking out Beverly.

"By the rules of the seminary, you could be expelled. You know that."

Ben had nodded. "Yes, I know."

"It's not fair to the girl either, and I'm not saying that just because she's my niece."

Ben's expression indicated that he did not suspect Frank of having that kind of motive. He said something that suggested he had been— well, he had a lot of respect for Beverly.

"The boy is a seminarian, Char," he said to his sister.

Her laughter filled the room, caromed off the walls, rode a tinkling

267

derisive scale. Her eyes, half shut with laughing, grew moist. "Oh, Frank. A sem-i-nar-ian! You make him sound like a married man. Or a priest. A seminarian." She began to laugh again.

"It's not funny, Char."

She wiped her eyes. "Do you know something? Bev asked me once if you ever took out girls when you were in the seminary."

"What did you tell her?"

"No." She looked at him. "Isn't that true?"

"What would you have thought of me if I had?"

"Thought of you? At the time, I suppose I would have been shocked. Of *course* I would have been. Now I wonder if you wouldn't be a better priest if you had had a few girl friends."

"But would I have become a priest if I had? Char, that's my point."

"Do you know what I thought at first? When Bev told me? I thought that you were worried about her. Your niece. But that wasn't it at all, was it?"

"Not entirely, no."

"Do you know what you've made her feel like?"

"It won't hurt her a bit if she feels ashamed, Char. She ought to feel ashamed."

"Frank, have you even noticed what's going on? Every day men are leaving the priesthood. The *priesthood*, not the seminary. If this boy wants to leave, that's still okay, isn't it? I mean, you don't think it's against the law, do you?"

"I don't want Beverly to be his reason for leaving."

"My God, Frank, listen to yourself. This poor innocent boy and along comes Beverly, the femme fatale—*Beverly*, Frank!—and takes him by the nose and leads him out of the seminary. You have to be kidding. Doesn't he have a mind of his own?"

He knew that he must sound fussy and old-fashioned about this, but Charlotte should understand. If only Char had met Ben Cole, this would be easier. Frank found it difficult to sustain his position when he remembered Ben's vacillation about going back to the seminary. Asked point-blank, he had said that Father Grimes had told him he ought to forget about it.

"Well, do you intend to? If you do, of course, there's no need . . ."

"What do you think, Father?"

Shades of Walter Mitchell! No wonder Grimes had told Ben to forget about the seminary.

"I won't advise you, Ben. Don't you have a spiritual director at the seminary? Talk to him. Talk it out with someone you know. But in the meantime, you can't be dating girls. If you take Beverly out again, I'll interpret that as your decision not to go back to the seminary. You understand I'm not suggesting you stay or leave. But as long as you are a seminarian, you're going to have to act like one. Will you discuss it with someone you know?"

Ben agreed, but in a way that did not fill Frank with confidence that he really meant it. Perhaps he should have added his own advice to Grimes's: forget the seminary.

Charlotte had moved to a more general plane. "Frank, just think what is involved here. And what is involved with the priests who leave. Celibacy! Can all of them be wrong? Why not a married clergy, I'd like to know. Would it really matter? It makes me so darned mad to think that just because of two ridiculous things, celibacy and birth control, we are having all this trouble in the Church. Why can't we face up to them and get unjammed?"

It was a charmingly simple outlook: abolish celibacy, lift the ban on contraceptives, and all would be well. How saturated with sex the discussion had become in the aftermath of the Council; no matter where it began, with complaints about the Curia, the American bishops, ecumenism, talk always seemed to lead to the bedroom. All honor to sex —in marriage. But was it really the key to all problems? The trouble with a romanticized theory of sex was that it seldom seemed to match what people found in marriage. It was always elsewhere, like the sex the disgruntled celibate imagined. Celibacy and the ban on contraceptives, whatever might be urged against them, did have the undeniable merit of reminding the priest and the married Catholic that they were called to something higher than secular comfort. And then, as quickly as she had taken them to this new level, Char plunged them down again.

"Bev is out with him tonight, you know."

"With Ben Cole?"

"Yes." Her smile was tight, teasing, defiant. "Doesn't that bother you?"

"Maybe he decided not to go back to the seminary."

"Well, it's a relief not to have you launch into another tirade."

"I wasn't aware that I had."

"Frank, you talk like some old conservative pastor who doesn't know his ass from his elbow and who probably wishes the Council never took place. You sound like one of those idiots in Te Deum."

"Thanks a lot. Charlotte, if Ben has left the seminary I don't give a damn if Beverly goes out with him every night of the week."

"Well, thank you for permission. And if he hasn't?"

"I've already told you what I would think then."

"Frank, Bev and this boy could go to any number of priests, good priests, priests who are living in 1968, and get entirely different advice, even if he still is a seminarian."

"I don't doubt it."

"Who's out of step, Frank? You or everyone else?"

"I'm sorry I disappoint you."

"You do, Frank. You disappoint me very much."

Well, he had disappointed himself too. He could not make even his own sister see the point of what he was saying. Which, he thought, on his way downtown in the bus, did not exactly qualify him for an ecumenical dialogue.

The legend on the marquee of the hotel read in crooked letters: COBB COUNTY ECUMENICAL CONFERENCE. Frank paused on the sidewalk and squinted in the morning sunlight.

"Dis muzz be de place," a voice said at his side. Frank turned to face a short man whose teeth emerged from his beard like eggs in a basket. He introduced himself as Jim Salpeter. "Unitarian," Salpeter added. "Come on. Let's go in and get religion."

Inside, Salpeter led him down a hallway toward the ballroom and a Babel of excited voices. A registration table had been set up outside the ballroom doors and Frank and Salpeter got in line.

"Good God," Salpeter said. "There's Harvey Gunderson."

Salpeter indicated a thick-set man whose white hair fell over his broad forehead and accented the fiercely disapproving expression with which he regarded those around him. After they had registered, Salpeter tugged Frank toward Gunderson, who had been joined by Swivel.

"I see your pope got into the news this morning," Gunderson growled, looking from Swivel to Frank.

"Did he?" Swivel said, winking at Frank. "I missed it."

"Making a nuisance of himself again."

Swivel adopted a pained look. "I wish he'd just clip his coupons and be quiet."

"He came out for peace."

"He might advocate it in the Curia. Frank, have you met Mr. Gunderson?"

"Reverend Gunderson," Salpeter corrected and became a target for the old man's ferocious glance. Salpeter pointed at the badge pinned to Gunderson's lapel. *Hi*, it read. *I'm Rev. Gunderson.* Seeing this, Gunderson plucked it off and put it into his pocket. His eyes went around the now crowded hallway. "To think that all these men make a living from religion."

Of course much the same could be said of Gunderson himself. His Pure Reason Bookstore, together with the royalties from his own writings—Frank knew of *Fallacies of Faith* and *Godlessness Is Cleanliness* from the ad Gunderson had been running every Sunday since Frank was a boy—had apparently been the aging atheist's sole support for years.

"You call this living?" Salpeter laughed.

Frank got away from Salpeter with the sense of escaping and moved among the other clergymen, who, like himself, wore false receptive smiles. When he caught a glimpse of Oder and Bishop Brophy he went to join them.

"Aha," Brophy greeted him. "I'm glad you came, Frank. We want to put our best foot forward."

Oder looked up from a mimeographed sheet. "This morning looks pretty blah." His eyes took on a speculative look. "I hear you're in some demand as a speaker, Frank."

"Hardly."

"Oh?" Without straying, Oder's eyes seemed to exchange a look with the bishop. "Aren't you speaking at a Te Deum breakfast?"

"I'm afraid not."

Bishop Brophy leaned toward him. "But weren't you asked?"

"The invitation was withdrawn."

"By Eisenbarth?" Bishop Brophy seemed delighted.

"No. By Arthur Rupp. He decided I'm not the kind of priest he wants addressing his organization."

Oder smiled and Brophy actually chuckled. For the first time Frank felt really welcome. From inside the ballroom an amplified voice began to urge them to be seated. Brophy said he had things to do before he went in. "Come with me, will you, Don? Frank, don't go away. I want to talk with you. Perhaps we can have lunch together."

But after the morning session, which was indeed blah—a panel composed of the inevitable trio, a priest, a rabbi and a minister—Frank came out of the ballroom and was commandeered by Swivel.

"Salpeter is getting the Foyles," Swivel said, moving Frank toward the restaurant. "I've made a reservation. With this crowd it seemed a good idea. How was the morning session?"

"Who are the Foyles?"

"Dean Foyle. A peach of a pair, the Foyles. He's big on the apostolate to the homosexuals. You must have heard of him. His church is one of the few where they can have their unions solemnized. Very courageous man."

Foyle had a face of unbaked bread. Mrs. Foyle, a head taller than the dean, her purse swinging at knee level, pushed her husband before her as they came among the tables, pursued by Salpeter and Gunderson. Swivel half stood and waved a menu at them. There was no sign of Bishop Brophy or Father Oder in the restaurant. Frank felt trapped.

"This is Frank Ascue," Swivel said when the group arrived at the table. Foyle's smile made his raisin eyes momentarily invisible. He introduced his wife, Kathleen.

"Don't call me Kitty," she warned.

Only Foyle laughed. He seemed convinced that his wife was a wit. For ten minutes, while they waited for their drinks to come, he passed on quips of Mrs. Foyle's. She studied the menu and corrected him when he misquoted her. On their honeymoon she had rolled away from him murmuring, "Foiled again." She had dubbed their boat the "Ship of Foyles." When she had decided that two children were enough she suggested that they stop making Foyles of themselves. The dean went tirelessly on. When a martini was set before him, Frank picked it up as if from real need.

In the course of the meal, Gunderson tried unsuccessfully to bait the clerics but he was met with tolerant smiles until Dean Foyle grew earnest.

"The thing is," Foyle said, hunching over the table, his raisin eyes on Gunderson, "you're as much of a believer as any of us. Now don't protest. Affirm, deny, does it really make any difference? Atheism too is a kind of God relationship." He sat back, suffering Gunderson's snorting laughter. "Wait until you hear Puller this afternoon. On Christian atheism."

When they returned to the ballroom and its folding chairs, Salpeter sat beside Frank. On his other side was Mrs. Foyle. At the microphone a swarthy man named Puller was explaining the overcoming of the transcendent God. The modern mentality could not accept a God beyond time and history, Puller assured them. Demythologization was in order. The transcendent God must go. He had already died. The impossible argument went on and on. Mrs. Foyle jabbed Frank's arm with her finger and slipped a note into his hand. It was from Oder. Would Frank join him and Bishop Brophy as soon as the speaker was done? Frank had put the note into his pocket when a commotion began on the platform. Puller had stopped speaking. People were standing craning their necks. Frank rose too and saw a tall thin man pushing Puller from the speaker's lectern. There was an indignant gasp from the audience but Puller, regaining his composure, raised a tolerant hand. The man who had gained possession of the microphone raised his hand too. It gripped a Bible.

272

"We do indeed read that God died," he bellowed. "Brethren, the Son of God died for our sins."

"Oh, Jesus," Salpeter said, as they all sat down again. "Taggart."

"God Almighty fashioned this world from nothing, my friends. He sent his only son to redeem us, to buy us back from the bondage of sin."

The booming voice was filled with conviction and the embarrassment in the ballroom was palpable. Frank recognized Taggart as a man who broadcast radio sermons from an evangelical tabernacle of which he was both founder and minister. His forte lay in giving scriptural answers to the problems of the day: cigarette smoking, air pollution, Vietnam. Having gained the stunned attention of the audience, Taggart launched into a sermon that recalled the revival tents of another day. There were cries of Amen from a row of Baptists near the front.

"Aren't they going to shut him up?" Salpeter muttered.

"Listen," Gunderson said from beside Salpeter. The atheist's eyes glinted with delight. Clearly he saw in Taggart a foe worthy of his steel. "He's good."

Taggart let them have it. They were whited sepulchers, all of them, watering down the word of God. But they must not despair. Oh, no. Arms wide, his expression one of beaming expectation, he urged them to make a decision for Christ. Now. He asked them to stand up and come down the aisles and group themselves before him as a sign that they accepted Jesus Christ as their personal savior.

For a minute there was total silence. Stricken looks were exchanged. Crimson faces stared at ashen. And then there was stirring. One man got up and then another and they started down the aisle toward Taggart. The row of Baptists rose as one man. Harvey Gunderson looked around with a triumphant smile and then he too got to his feet.

"Where are you going?" Salpeter asked, aghast.

Gunderson's eyes sparked. "I'm going to debate that bastard."

More and more people rose but when they got to the aisle they started toward the exits. The group that had gathered in front of Taggart broke into a hymn and Frank heard Mrs. Foyle humming along. It seemed a good time to go find Oder and Bishop Brophy. He followed the fleeing Salpeter up the aisle.

Vents open, accelerator to the floor, the little red Mustang flew along the highway. The radio filled the car with noisy assonance, canceling the need or possibility of talk, so Eloise relaxed and let her hair whip wildly in the breeze. At the wheel, Phil now wore a serious expression, almost grim, a contrast to the playful smile he had assumed when, having started downtown to the Placental Hotel, he drew suddenly to the curb and stopped the motor.

"Let's not go," he said.

"Not go? But why?"

"I hate meetings. Particularly of the clergy."

"But this is important."

"Of course it is. But is it important that we be there?"

Eloise had frowned, tipping her head to one side, and stared at him. How boyish he was, bad-boyish. She could imagine him as one of the kids in her class, slightly devilish, the one who always got into trouble, the one she secretly preferred. This was just the sort of unexpected suggestion she should have expected Phil Bullard to make.

"What would we do?"

He shrugged and smiled a crooked smile. "Go for a drive. Just get away for a while. We'll have lunch somewhere. And talk."

With a laugh she had agreed. Why not? Suddenly she was sure that the conference would be crowded and dull, not half as interesting as everyone expected.

"So drive," she said.

Drive, have lunch, talk. Well, the talk would have to wait until lunch because the car was filled with its own roar magnified by the wind. Did his serious expression now mean that he was having second thoughts? If she could make herself heard, she might try to cheer him up. She reached over and turned off the radio. It helped, but not much. He glanced at her, a more relaxed expression on his face.

"Don't you like music?"

"That's the trouble. I do."

"I have a tin ear."

But a heart of gold. What a nice idea, really, an unscheduled day in the country.

"Where are we going?" She had almost to shout.

He slowed the car, diminishing the roar. "No place in particular. Okay?"

"Okay."

He clamped his foot down again and the car leaped forward. How she would like to drive it. Later, after they had had lunch, she would ask him if she could.

They had lunch in the Isle de France, a restaurant in a little town forty miles east of Fort Elbow.

"This place isn't bad," he said, when he had wheeled into the parking lot.

"Oh," she said sadly. "You've been here before."

"What's wrong?"

"And I had thought this was completely spontaneous."

"But it was. Deciding to come here."

"Anyway, I'm starved."

"Me too."

The suit she wore was one she had made herself: sky blue, white piping, light and nice. Phil was in clericals, because of the skipped meeting. She had not often seen him in a Roman collar and it constituted the slightest of barriers between them, diminishing the naturalness with which she met his banter and his changing moods. The flick of the hostess's eye when they entered had made Eloise conscious of what they were wearing. The woman preceded them to a table next to a false leaded window.

"Care for a drink?"

"All right. You order." She felt a little devilish herself, as if in response to the suppressed disapproval of the hostess. She could not remember when she had last had a drink. Last summer she had shared a bottle of beer with her father, but it had been a very hot day, the taking of it purely practical. Phil spoke to the waiter, who minced away. Elbows on the table, his hands in an attitude of prayer, fingertips propping his chin, he looked at her.

"Sorry we skipped the meeting?"

"What meeting?"

He laughed. "Good girl."

Girl. But of course she was a girl. For the first time, though mildly, she wondered about the wisdom of this impetuous holiday. She felt far removed from the safe contours of her life as a nun. All her theorizing about the need to get out of the ghetto of the convent into the world seemed remote and unreal. Had all that aimed at this, lunch in a town miles from where she belonged with . . .

She inhaled, expelled air, kept her laughter to a small giggle. Lunch with a priest, for heaven's sake.

"What's the matter?"

"Nothing."

"Isn't it good to get absolutely away from it all?"

"Yes!"

"I was serious when I said I dislike clerical gatherings. I don't know what it is. Perhaps it's all the collective guilt."

"What do you mean?"

"You know. What are we doing wrong? Where have we failed? Everybody knows the answers to those already. I'm fed up with talk."

"You've done more than talk."

"Have I?"

The arm of the waiter came between them, setting down their drinks. He waited for her to take hers and then together they sipped.

"Of *course* you've done more than talk."

"Even if that's true, and I'm not saying it is, there are times when I have a sense of complete futility. That's when you'd think the company of other priests would help, wouldn't you? It doesn't. If I feel low, the sight of other priests fills me almost with loathing." He leaned forward. "Eloise, think of it. I run a youth center on a secondary campus. What do I do from day to day—apart from saying Mass, of course? I talk, I counsel, I try to bring faith and life into some kind of meaningful relation."

"And you succeed."

"Do I really? The Center isn't an island, self-contained. Those kids go home, you know. They attend Mass at all sorts of different parishes. At least some of them attend Mass. How do you think what they run into there fits in with what we're trying to do at the Center?"

"Listen, if you could hear the things those kids say about you, how much you've helped them."

He seemed irked by the remark. "I mean the whole thing, Eloise. The whole thing." His eyes drifted away and a look of such frustrated longing came over his face that Eloise leaned forward, waiting to hear what he would say next. "Sometimes I think of just dropping everything. Dropping it and getting a job and doing only the most basic, fundamental sort of thing. The things without which religion has no basis. Social work, maybe. Helping people. You know."

"But you're already doing that." Did he mean leave the priesthood? He could not be serious. To cover her confusion, she returned to her drink.

"Being a priest . . ." he began. "Look, let me put it another way. Haven't you ever felt that being a nun isn't much help, that it might even be an impediment, to doing the sort of thing you became a nun to do?"

"Yes! I see what you mean."

And she did. She thought of those grandiose plans for the summer program at Saint Waldo's. She thought of the alternative of the mother house that she had escaped when she was granted permission to work at the Center. Of course she saw what he meant. All she had to do was think of all the sisters lolling through the summer months under the autocratic eye of Mother Superior and of all the sweet inane conversations. The truth was that she dreaded to think beyond the summer since, if the experiment of living in the apartment was terminated and

276

she was sent back to Saint Waldo's, well . . . It wasn't that she minded teaching kids that age, but the fact was, and this must be Phil's point, you did not have to be a nun to do that. Or was his point that you might do it better if you weren't a nun at all? And what if he was right?

This surprising question, once admitted to her mind, had a familiarity that made it stranger still. It seemed to mask a conviction she had had without knowing it. She was relieved when Phil called the waiter and ordered. Lunch was soup, a ham omelet and a small bottle of wine that made her already light head lighter as the meal went on.

When they came out of the coolness of the restaurant into the smoldering afternoon, they seemed to move with difficulty through the hot resistant air as they crossed the parking lot. The car was like an oven. Phil opened the doors wide so air could circulate before they got in. He took off his suit jacket and collar and tossed them into the back seat.

"Let me drive," she said.

"Sure."

She strapped herself into the bucket seat and started the motor. "I've only driven cars with automatic shifts before."

"The stick? That's only decoration. It's automatic."

His hand closed over hers, guiding it while the car remained motionless in the parking lot.

"See? Easy as pie."

"Easy as pie."

His hand remained on hers. She turned toward him and for a moment he just looked at her and then he leaned forward and, incredibly, pressed his lips to hers.

It had been days since Howard Nygaard had received a letter from Sharon and even so short a time seemed a liberating reprieve. Now he sat apprehensively at his desk, certain that this morning the spell would be broken. Miss Furlong came in with the mail and when the pile proved not to contain an envelope with the familiar Cleveland return address, Howard pushed away from his desk and went to the window, where he smiled benevolently out at Fort Elbow.

How cluttered with churches the city seemed. He had never noticed that before and, now that he did, it struck him strangely as appropriate. Freed from the consequences of his foolish use of freedom, he felt in the pit of his stomach the pragmatic value of virtue. An orderly life, honesty, being what one seemed—everything depended on those. More importantly, there was no peace of mind without them. It was stupidly adolescent to think that happiness is some other life than that we have chosen. The road not taken does not exist.

However belatedly, Howard felt that he had gained a profound knowledge of what life is all about. On that sunny July morning, surveying Fort Elbow as if he were being subjected to the temptations of Christ, Howard put the whole vague glittering world of otherness and elsewhere behind him. His own life, his wife and family, were all he wanted.

When he returned to his desk, prepared to work with a single-mindedness that had not been his for months, he could afford to think kindly of Sharon. He should have known better, not she. Well, he did know better now. His life, even unromanticized, was pretty good. The alternative to it, equally unromanticized, was not half as attractive.

He turned to his mail and this morning did not postpone difficult matters to some undefined later period when he could give them his full attention. He dealt with everything immediately. Miss Furlong was suitably impressed.

"These can be typed, signed and in the mail before noon," she said.

Before leaving, she hesitated, as if she were about to welcome him back. Happily, all she did was make an ambiguous gesture and leave. Welcome back. It would have been an appropriate remark. How long had it been since he had been wholly here? His phone rang and he snapped it up.

"Nygaard speaking."

There was no immediate answer. "You sound so different."

"Who is it?"

"Howard, it's *me.*"

Sharon! My God. He managed to say, "You sound different too."

"Do I?"

"Not really. It's a good connection. Did you dial direct?"

"But I'm not calling long distance. I'm here."

"In Fort Elbow?"

"Yes!"

"Well."

He tried to put surprise and the imitation of delight into the monosyllable but it came forth as a plaintive bleat.

"I wanted to surprise you."

"You've done that, all right." His laugh was choked. "How long will you be staying?"

After a pause, she said, "I don't like talking to you on the phone. Not when we're so close. Howard, this doesn't change anything. With us. My coming here."

"If only I had known . . ." What would he have done if not get out of town? "When did you get in?"

"Monday."

"Monday! What have you been doing all week?"

"Oh, I've been busy," she said coyly. "Is there any way at all that we can meet?"

"Of course we'll meet. After all, you're a client. How about lunch?"

"Lunch with my lawyer." She said it wryly.

"Where are you now?"

"Just tell me where to meet you. I'll find it."

He told her and let her hang up before he had demanded to know what the hell she was doing in Fort Elbow, what she had been doing here since Monday without his knowing. He paced his office. He went down the hall to the firm's library but young Hanson was in there so he continued on out, took the elevator downstairs, started up the street toward the Placental. Before he got to the hotel, he remembered that Charlotte would be there, at some damned meeting, and he turned into a strange bar and ordered a double bourbon.

The bartender served him discreetly and withdrew, exhibiting a professional wariness, or respect, for the morning drinker. Sharon in Fort Elbow. Good God. How ridiculous his earlier sense of liberation now seemed. He swallowed half his drink and tried to remember if anything in his last visit to Cleveland provided a clue to Sharon's incredible visit. She knew no one in Fort Elbow, only himself, he was sure of that. There seemed little point in hoping that there was an explanation of her coming here which did not involve him. But why had she waited days before calling him? The more he considered the question, the more ominous the delay appeared. He could imagine Sharon scouting his city, learning it; perhaps she had even gone by his house. Curiosity, which she had always denied having, would, once aroused, be insatiable. Eventually she would want to see Charlotte and the children. Oh, God. He finished his drink.

He would have to take a strong line with her from the outset, lest this visit become the first of many. Her coming here like this was intolerable. He would not stand for it. She had to realize that it was one thing for them to meet in Cleveland and another for her to arrive here unannounced. He burned with accusative anger. And then it dawned on him that this visit could be an excuse for breaking off with her definitively. Ah. He would be grim, he would not mask his annoyance, he would let her know immediately that she had done something irreparable. His spirits began to lift. He would turn this flattening shock to his own advantage and once again feel the peace he had known an hour earlier. He waved for the bartender.

Throughout his second drink, and he sipped this one, less agitated now, he rehearsed for the coming lunch with Sharon. Aggrieved disappointment. She should have known better than to do this. Her visit threatened his . . . No, that sounded too self-serving. Damn it, he did not need an argument. Anger was the key; he would put her on the defensive and demand an explanation of her visit.

He felt half drunk when he returned to his office, scarcely an hour before he would have to set off again for lunch. The hope of getting back onto a productive schedule had been shattered by Sharon's call and he felt nostalgic for the long-lost regime that had made work a joy.

"Where have you been?" Miss Furlong asked.

"I had an errand to run."

Her reproving look did not go away. "I didn't know where to say you were."

"Did someone call?"

"You had an appointment with Mr. Beecher at ten-thirty. I put him in the library."

"I'll see him now."

He arranged things on the surface of his desk. Beecher? He could not for the life of him remember who Beecher was. That seemed added cause for complaint against Sharon. He was lucky his partners had not noticed and remarked on his absent-mindedness.

When Beecher was shown in, Howard rounded his desk, took the man's hand and spoke toward a corner of the room so that he would not disturb his client with the smell of liquor.

"Well, well," he said heartily. "And how are you this fine day, Mr. Beecher?"

"I still can't believe she's gone," the man said mournfully.

Too late, Howard remembered the recent death of Mrs. Beecher.

Although it was noon, Beverly was still in bed when her mother telephoned.

"Are you up?"

"I had to get up to answer the phone."

"Who called?"

Good Lord. "Nobody called, Mother. Just you."

"How are the kids?"

Beverly felt a sudden surge of guilty panic. "Am I supposed to be watching them?"

"Oh, no. They're next door at the Shorters'."

"How's the meeting?"

"All right." But there was disappointment in her mother's voice. "I'd hoped to have lunch with your Uncle Frank but I seem to have missed him."

"Maybe he isn't there."

"He's here all right. I saw him."

Beverly frowned at the receiver. Her mother claimed that she had told off Uncle Frank for pestering Ben, but Beverly would have liked to hear that scolding. She would not trust herself to speak to him, not yet. He was, after all, a priest. And what a priest. Never had a doubt about his vocation. It made him sound like a machine, programmed for one thing only. Well, Ben Cole wasn't like that. Obviously. He seemed to be wavering all over the place again.

"What are you going to do?" Suddenly she was saddened by the thought of her mother all alone at lunchtime downtown.

"I thought I'd stop by your father's office and go out to lunch with him. I don't know how long it's been since we did that. Do you have anything on today?"

"Let's see. Shorts, blouse, sandals." Beverly was still in pajamas.

"Ha ha. You don't mind if I stay downtown, do you?"

"Of course not. Have a good time."

"You might keep an eye out for the kids, Bev. Mrs. Shorter will give them lunch."

"I'll keep an eye out."

Beverly hung up. She had nothing on for today. She certainly was not going to that damned Center. She was sick and tired of the place. Janice seemed symptomatic of what was wrong with it, though Beverly was sure that the girl had flipped. The other day she had confided to Beverly her fear that Father Bullard and Sister Eloise were planning to run away together.

"Cheer up," Bev had said. "Next time it might be you."

Janice had been shocked. "I don't think that is very funny."

"Actually it would probably be dull."

Of course Phil had chosen just that moment to walk in. He greeted Janice with a playful hug and the girl shook free and ran down the hall to the office, leaving Phil looking a bit shook.

"Something wrong?" he asked Beverly.

"I think she made a typographical error."

"I know I could figure that out if I had the time."

Well, she had a lot of nerve making fun of Janice. Ben had not shown up at the Center yesterday and it had not helped when he called last night to say he was going to that ecumenical meeting today.

"Do you know I forgot you had asked me to come along?"

"Would you like to?"

"I forget that too."

"It could be interesting," he said unconvincingly.

"Oh, I'll bet."

"Are you busy tonight?"

If she had had the cowardice of her convictions she would have told him to go to hell, but of course she didn't. Any enthusiasm they had now seemed to come from her. She felt that she was chasing him. Well, she *was* chasing him and any shame that involved only made her want him more. But she was not getting through to him, that much was clear. He sealed himself off from her, the part that really counted, and at the moment she could no more have asked him straight out if he was going back to the seminary than she could have asked Phil Bullard when he planned to run away with Eloise. She had recently asked Ben what he thought of Janice's suspicion.

"She's nuts."

"Granted, but do you think it could happen?"

He was silent for a moment. "I think it isn't happening."

"Frankly, Phil disappoints me. He hasn't given me so much as a tumble, if you'll forgive the expression. Not that it could lead to anything. My father. He has nothing against priests, but he wouldn't want his daughter to marry one."

Ben did not take the cue to talk about them. The coward gathered her into his arms and conversation lagged. Every girl knows that in such a situation coyness is called for, but despite herself Beverly continued to be stupidly available whenever Ben phoned, forgave him when he didn't, overlooked his not coming to the Center when he should know that she was expecting him there. Did he think she was interested in youth work, for crying out loud? She almost wished her parents would forbid her to see him, that Uncle Frank had convinced her mother that she was a wicked thing to dazzle poor Ben with her fatal charms.

It was a nice thought, her parents meeting for lunch. Her mother had said that it had been a long time since they had done that but Beverly could not remember their ever doing it. Would they be having lunch together if she had agreed to go along with her mother to that crazy ecumenical meeting? They would not. Her laziness took on the look of virtuous self-denial. Just keeping out of the way, that's me.

Beverly stood in her pajamas at the kitchen door and looked dreamily across the lawn to where David and Elizabeth were playing with the neighbor kids. Arms crossed, she enclosed her breasts in her hands. Ben's hands, last night. The memory made her dizzy. Coyness was not the only weapon that a girl had.

Chopfallen, his forehead patterned with deep-tread wrinkles, unkempt but wearing withal the authority of an Athenian in imperial Rome, Gilbert Plummet-Finch had watched the fiasco in the ballroom with amused fascination. Really, Americans were so incredibly polite at public meetings. It would have been child's play to wrest the microphone from that man Taggart and permit poor Puller to continue his nonsense. That would have been somehow infra dig, apparently, so the madman had been allowed to scuttle the meeting. Outside the ballroom, Gilbert ran into Daniel Donovan.

"My God," Donovan said, passing a hand over his pasty face on which freckles lay like fading coffee stains. "My God, Gilbert."

"I don't believe I saw you make your decision for Christ, Daniel."

Donovan groaned. "I told them they had to be careful, but they insisted on opening the doors to anyone."

"Ah, well."

"Gilbert, wait." Daniel put his hand on Gilbert's arm and, pivoting on one run-down heel, called through the milling throng. "Mary! Mary Muscatelli!"

A young woman turned, hesitated, then seemed drawn toward them by whatever force had already raised her eyebrows.

"I'm in a rush, Donovan. What is it?" She looked curiously at Gilbert.

"Gilbert, I would like you to meet Mary Muscatelli. She's with the *Tribune*. Gilbert Plummet-Finch, Mary. From the university."

Gilbert took her hand and his look of embarrassed diffidence was unfeigned. University! The Fort Elbow campus made the dreariest red-brick seem absolutely hoary with culture and tradition.

"What did you think of Taggart?" the girl asked him.

"Well, now, what *would* one think?"

"You tell me." She flipped open a notebook like a Roman waiter and Gilbert was assailed by the swift memory of a trattoria near the Pantheon where he had once lunched with an olive-skinned boy in white hip-hugging trousers and . . . With an effort he drove the lovely painful memory away. But if he was thus affected by the appearance of Miss Muscatelli's notebook, his reaction was as nothing compared with Donovan's.

"For God's sake, Mary, do me a favor. Play Taggart down. Don't emphasize it."

"Why, you old censor, you."

"Please!"

"For crying out loud, Donovan, this isn't your show. What do you care? Aren't you just covering it like the rest of us?"

"Actually, I agreed more or less to do PR for them. Play down the Taggart thing, Mary. Please."

"And what in hell would I play up?"

"This morning's symposium?"

"You've got to be kidding."

Gilbert was bored with their quarrel and not a little peeved that they did little more than nod when he said he had to toddle off.

He went down the hallway to the lobby of the hotel where his eye was caught by the entrance of a bar. Tempted, he thought of a gin and tonic, but he resisted. Arms unswinging at his sides, he walked swiftly to the exit. He hated hotels.

Hotels reminded him of that dreadful experience the previous spring when he had read a paper to the American Metaphysical Society. The bite of his argument had been borne out, Gilbert thought, by the acrimonious discussion which had followed his reading of it. American philosophers had a predilection for mere agnosticism, eschewing the stronger meat of a downright denial of a Supreme Being. Theism had few articulate adherents, of course; it was the plucky thinker indeed who felt he could steer around the accumulation of difficulties advanced against the classical proofs. Gilbert himself took the stern view that God's existence could be definitively disproved. This left him open to barrages from all quarters which, fortunately, he had met with cool cogency. When the chairman brought the chaotic session to a close, Gilbert had a deserved sense of having done a fair day's work.

A succulent dinner with two other displaced Oxonians and a rather insipid Cambridge type—were Wittgensteinians really any less obsequious asses than those Englishmen who had gone sniffing after Ouspensky?—followed by a bibulous and nostalgic bout of reminiscing had brought him to his hotel room after midnight. Alone. He was resolved to be on his good behavior during this convention, mindful of the near disaster at the APA in December. Americans could be so frightfully aggressive about their heterosexuality.

The telephone in his hotel room had begun to ring just after he had sunk into that first shallow sleep when one seems still awake. Gilbert fumbled for the phone and found it on the third ring.

"Plummet-Finch here," he said, his heart leaping involuntarily. Was it some shy admirer wanting to come up for a drink?

"Gilbert Plummet-Finch?"

284

"Yes, of course. Who's that?" Whoever it was spoke in remote sepulchral tones. Gilbert sent his hand in search of the bedside lamp. He had just turned it on when his caller spoke again.

"God."

"Oh, I say, that's not very funny. I had just fallen asleep."

There was silence on the line save for a throaty measured breathing which made Gilbert all too conscious of his mortal pulse.

"Who *is* there?"

The only reply was that ghastly breathing. The spirit blows where it list. He hung up. Not violently, as he would have liked to have done, just replacing the receiver. He picked up his pipe, lighted it, immediately put it down again. How he hated practical jokes. At school he had always been the butt of them and during a brief involvement with an analyst, when he was a tutor, the suggestion had been made that his proclivities might stem, in part, from that fact. But imagine the crudity of the caller. God on the line! Gilbert was reminded of an anecdote of Sartre's, a woman who butchered half her arrondissement and claimed, when arrested, that God had phoned up and told her to do it. Of course she was mad. Would any of his opponents that afternoon regard it as an open question whether God had telephoned Plummet-Finch?

The phone rang again, startling him. He hesitated before picking it up.

"Hello."

Again that strange and awful sound of labored breathing.

"I say, is that God there?" His mother had assured him that boys would taunt him less if he developed a sense of humor.

"Yes."

"I should have thought you'd put in a personal appearance."

The breathing became a sigh.

"You know. Drop in and say hullo."

Silence. Oh, for heaven's sake, this was ridiculous. He did slam down the phone this time and when it rang again some minutes later he refused to answer it. He got up, dressed, angry now, angry enough to go out and cruise the city and get into God knew what sort of trouble. But first he would speak to the hotel operator. He picked up the phone and heard the sound of breathing.

"God?"

"Yes."

Gilbert slammed down the phone and left his room in a rage. In the elevator, he composed himself. Doubtless his tormentors would have spies about to see how he was taking this stupid joke. He strolled across the lobby, the picture of insouciance, and went out into the night. He had one drink and then another, drinks he did not need, and then went down to the bus depot and scouted the men's room. Nothing. On a bench in the waiting room he found a copy of *Reader's Digest* and wasted an hour paging through it, amusing himself with ideas of *his* most memorable experience. A soldier went by and scowled when Gilbert looked up pathetically. Oh, to hell with this.

But he had taken the long way back to his hotel, where, once more in bed, he fell into a troubled sleep. The next day, he told the anecdote a number of times, aiming the telling at his nocturnal caller, whoever he was, hoping the man realized what a puerile joke it was. Did he seriously imagine that that sort of nonsense constituted an answer to Gilbert's paper?

Thus it was that Gilbert now left the hotel and came outside with a sense of relief. Sunlight, the noise of traffic, the press of people on the sidewalk. How delightfully banal after that idiotic meeting. He could strangle Donovan for talking him into attending it. Gilbert sighed, remembering the luncheon he had had with Daniel, Bishop Brophy and that smoothie, Father Oder. Busy, busy, busy. Well, he had agreed to take part in the silly panel they were dreaming up. "I'll call you," Father Oder had assured him. "I'll call you as soon as it firms up." Gilbert smiled. He had not told Father Oder that he did not have a telephone.

Don Oder led Frank away from the ballroom at a quickening pace though Taggart had finally surrendered the microphone and now a good portion of the participants had returned for the scheduled panel on the social responsibility of the believer. They found Bishop Brophy in a corner of the lobby, turned aloofly toward a window. When they came up to him, he seemed relieved that he had been discovered by friends.

"Was it as bad as Donovan said?" he asked when they had drawn up chairs.

"Just a little old-time religion," Oder said.

"Well, the responsibility lies with our Protestant friends. They must have invited him."

Oder suggested that Taggart's performance was all to the good, lest there be too much complacency on "how far we have come." Brophy nodded and dismissed the subject. He was looking earnestly at Frank.

"This sort of meeting has its importance, but it's more or less intramural. Now an opportunity has arisen for something with more widespread potential. Frank, you're a moral theologian."

Frank agreed that he was.

"And that's what it all comes down to now, doesn't it? A new morality. A fresh look at old problems. Have you given much thought to the Church's stand on contraception?"

"It's rather difficult not to."

Brophy sighed. "I know. Yet how many people realize there has been a radical rethinking of the matter going on in the Church? The Council should have faced up to it. Eventually that will be done, I have no doubt of it. In the meantime we seem saddled with a position that is unacceptable. Until the Church speaks out forthrightly—"

"How much time will Bantam give us?" Oder interrupted.

"An hour. You'll be chairman, Plummet-Finch will take part. We'll need another non-Catholic." Brophy put his hand on the arm of Frank's chair. "Frank, will you sit in on a televised discussion of sexual morality? I want someone with academic credentials but also someone who is abreast of the latest theological thinking."

Frank sat forward. "When will it be?"

"Then you'll do it?"

Brophy actually seemed relieved. Had he thought Frank would refuse? Throughout the day Frank had been waiting for this meeting to assume some promise of importance but the truth was that Taggart had provided the only moment of excitement in the program. No doubt there had to be a preliminary blandness to this sort of thing, a feeling-out period during which old enmities could be forgotten. Only later could there be any true working together on the part of men who had until recently been divided by centuries of misunderstanding. The television program devoted to something specific, something of undeniable importance, suggested a more immediate impact.

"Who is Plummet-Finch?"

"A philosopher. He teaches on the Fort Elbow campus, but he seems to be pretty good."

"I suppose there'll be a minister too?"

"Not necessarily. That's still open. There might be more impact in getting a secular figure. A celebrity of sorts. It's still fluid, you understand."

The idea was that the discussion would be taped at the local station, whose manager, Bantam, had assured Bishop Brophy that he would not run it at some impossible hour.

"Like after the late show," Oder said with a wry smile. Apparently Don had taped a summary comment on the Council after the last session and it had been aired at two-thirty in the morning. This experience was cited as reason for Oder's moderating the planned discussion.

Having secured Frank's agreement, Brophy looked at his watch with some surprise and got to his feet.

"Don will keep in touch with you on this, Frank. I know you'll do a fine job. I'm counting on you. People have to know where theology has gone lately."

Brophy and Oder left him there, in the lobby. Frank watched them go away among the chairs and sofas on which scattered women were now taking tea. He sat down again, not wanting to go back to the ballroom. The prospect of presenting the Church's position on sexual morality excited him, though Brophy's references to the theological avant-garde made him somewhat uneasy. Surely the bishop did not think he would endorse the more radical proposals for altering completely the traditional ban on contraceptives. Of course he could present for the record the fact that any number of reputable theologians . . .

"Father Ascue, how are you? You look so solemn."

Frank looked up to see Sheila Rupp standing in front of him, brows raised quizzically, holding her purse in both hands. He started to rise but she sat down across from him.

"Playing hooky from the meeting?"

"Were you there?"

She leaned toward him. "As a spy. For my father. I'm to report any heretical remarks by Catholic priests."

"Have you heard any?"

She sat back, laughing. "How would I know? Daddy is the guardian of orthodoxy."

"I know."

"He means well, Father."

"Of course he does."

Female voices drifted to them across the lobby, accompanied by the tinkle of cups and saucers. Sheila looked around.

"Wouldn't you love some tea?"

"I'm not much of a tea drinker."

"Oh." Sheila was disappointed.

"I'm sorry. Would you care for some?"

"And drink alone?"

"I'll have some with you."

"But you don't like it."

"Of course I do." Frank turned and caught a waiter's eye. When he had ordered and the waiter was gone, Sheila took cigarettes from her purse. Frank felt gauche, watching her light her own cigarette, but he would have felt more awkward doing it for her. It suddenly occurred

288

to him that this was not terribly wise, having tea with a girl in the lobby of the largest hotel in town, and one presently crawling with clergy. Sheila was looking at him speculatively through a cloud of exhaled smoke.

He said, "I'm surprised your father didn't attend this meeting."

"I think he wanted to, until he decided that it was a rebel uprising."

"And what will you tell him?"

"I'm not sure. What would you suggest?"

"Just tell him that the priests who came are working in the spirit of the Vatican Council."

"Do you think that would set his mind at ease?"

"Perhaps not. But it should."

"He told me it was your sort of meeting."

"Mine? What kind of priest does he think I am anyway?"

"Do you care?"

"Not really."

Their tea arrived and Sheila poured, the activity suggesting an almost domestic intimacy. Frank wondered what Arthur Rupp would make of this scene. His daughter having tea with a priest. No, not just a priest. With Father Ascue, whom he had warned never to see his daughter again. That remembered threat conferred a faint suggestion of the illicit on this happenstance meeting and Frank did not find it at all welcome. The truth was that he did care what Arthur Rupp thought of him. He had to care. A priest could not be indifferent to the impression he made; he represented so much to lay people. Frank smiled. His thoughts were echoing Eisenbarth.

"Tell me," he said, having sipped his tea. "Where have you been flying to lately?"

"I'm on vacation."

That explained her presence at his Mass these recent weekday mornings. She must be staying with her parents.

"When do you go back to work?"

"I'm trying not to think of it."

"It doesn't sound like work, but I suppose you know that. I mean, flying to Europe. Rome."

And he urged her to visit Santa Susanna the next time she was there. The American church. Paulists. Nice people. And the memories flooded back as they never had before and he told her of Rome, the endless walks and inexhaustible beauty of the city, talking on and on, as if she were the homebody and he the tireless traveler. When finally they got up to go, she offered to drive him to the rectory but he said no, he had a stop to make. He watched her leave the hotel and then turned and walked back toward the ballroom. He had seen a men's room in that direction. McTear's warning applied to tea as well as coffee.

At table that night he assured Entweder and McTear that the meeting had been a first step, not wholly successful, but at least a beginning. The pastor wanted to hear about Taggart. Apparently the evangelist's impromptu sermon had been featured in the newspaper account of the meeting.

"He feels threatened by the present mood, I suppose," Frank said. "That's understandable. Change is a painful thing."

Monsignor Entweder thought about that, then nodded. He returned to his soup and Frank, who had been about to tell the pastor of the proposed discussion on television, decided not to. At the moment Hilda's potato soup seemed a safer thing to share with Entweder.

2 Late Thursday afternoon. The next day was the First Friday of July. From outside the church came the not quite muted sounds of traffic. The setting sun illumined the curtain of his door and Frank had the sense that he and the penitents existed in shadows which neighbored a place of peace. They whispered their sins, he gave absolution and, when he slid shut the grille, he could hear them rise and go out into the light. Women and children, mainly, an occasional male adult, usually old. The kids were no problem, a rapid high-pitched whisper until the recitation was done and then the audible breathing, impatience rather than apprehension, while he urged them to do better, then said the prescribed formula which absolved their sins. He opened the grille on his left and was assailed by the smell of an inexpensive perfume. Lilac. While the woman spoke, he closed his eyes. The woman was asking him about the pill and the word, as she pronounced it, had an abbreviated vowelless sound.

"How many children do you have?"

"Four."

"How long have you been married?"

Ten years. No doubt she was in her early thirties. He could imagine the children, coming at regular intervals over the course of eight or nine years, a small house, noise, economic worries. And all those fertile years ahead of her.

"Have you tried rhythm?"

An exhalation of breath, not quite a laugh. She said that rhythm did not work. That was why she was asking about the pill. So many of her friends told her that it was all right, priests had told them so. Was it all right? Frank, his eyes open now, stared at the carved folds of the illumined curtain before him. He told the woman that she must consider her situation carefully, prayerfully. "Your conscience will give you the answer."

"But what is the Church's position?" she asked.

"I'm trying to tell you."

"You mean I can just do what I want?"

"I didn't say that. I don't know the details of your life. Only you know them. You must think of your children, your husband, of what this will mean for your marriage. Your conscience—"

"But my conscience says no. That's what I was always told before."

Frank, who had been sitting rigid in his chair, leaned toward the grille. Even if he tried he could not imagine a face for this woman. To make it easier, he pretended that she was Charlotte. "Perhaps that's the great difference in the Church today. We aren't going to receive so many ready-made answers to our questions. We're going to have to think for ourselves."

There was silence on the other side of the grille.

"Do you understand?"

The woman shuffled on her knees. "You mean that it's all right?"

"There isn't any blanket answer," Frank said, and immediately regretted the phrase. What he meant was that a simple yes was as difficult as a simple no. It depended on so many things, things only she herself could know. Was there tension between her and her husband because of the fear of another pregnancy? Would she be more devoted to her children if she had no more? Frank was terribly conscious of the fact that he was speaking in the dark to a stranger he could not see. It was impossible to think of her as Charlotte. How could she expect him to tell her what to do in so important a matter? After he stopped speaking, there was a long silence on the other side of the grille.

"Give me permission, Father."

"It's not a matter of permission."

"If you don't, I won't do it, and I should. At least I think I should. All my friends are on the pill." Her voice had become querulous, self-pitying.

"Do you think your situation justifies it?"

"I don't know, Father. I don't know. Just tell me it's all right."

And so the burden he had sought to shift to her shoulders was shifted back to his own. He could understand why she was reluctant to bear it. It was so easy to say, Follow your conscience. But what did that mean? The woman was right. It did sound like the suggestion to do what she wanted.

"It's all right."

Her intake of breath sounded like a gasp. "Thank you, Father. Thank you very much."

She was up and gone before either of them realized that he had not given her absolution for the sins she had confessed. For the next fifteen minutes, Frank half hoped that she would remember and come back. He wanted to go into her background, weigh the pros and cons, talk it over with her. He did not want to bear the weight of her decision.

That night he stopped McTear before he went down to the basement for a session with his radio. He wanted to talk with someone about the advice he had given that woman in the confessional but of course he spoke in generalities. Penitents kept telling him that other priests said it was all right to use contraceptives.

"Not me," McTear said, lighting a cigar.

"So many use them anyway."

"I know."

"What do you tell them?"

"That it's wrong." McTear released a heavy bluish cloud of smoke.

"Do you give them absolution?"

"Sure."

"But what's the point?"

McTear looked puzzled.

"If they're going to go right out and do it again . . ."

"Well, I ask them if they'll try to do the right thing."

"It seems so unrealistic to ask them not to do something they're going to do anyway."

"Oh, some of them don't. At least they don't confess it."

"What good is a rule that's always broken?"

McTear frowned at the ash of his cigar. "But that's true of everything. Frank, take anger or talking about people. They keep confessing those, we tell them to stop it, try to do better, give them absolution. Next time, the same sins over again. So what should we do? Say they're not sins? Same thing with contraception."

As usual he found McTear's simple approach disarming. There was a difference between contraception and anger or lack of charity, but at the moment Frank was not sure how to express it. He was relieved when the first assistant went on down to his radio.

The following morning, after breakfast, Frank took the census cards the pastor had set out for him and left the rectory. At Mass, when he distributed Holy Communion, he had wondered how many of those who received were using contraceptives, with a clear conscience, their doubts removed by advice like that he had given the woman the day before. The thought preyed on his mind and at the first several houses where he called, he found himself speculating about the marital lives of the women who answered his questions. Even in his preoccupation, the neighborhood seemed vaguely familiar, though he could not have taken census here before. And then he turned up the next card and understood why. A dog yipped at his heels when he went up to the door and rang the bell. Frank tried to soothe the animal and succeeded only in making it bark more loudly, making dashing passes at Frank's ankle as it did so. Behind him the door opened. It was Sheila Rupp.

"Well, for heaven's sake. Father Ascue."

Frank, aware of the dog still barking at his heels, was surprised to see Sheila. "Are your parents home?"

"No, they're not. Come on in before that darned dog bites you."

"He's all right."

"He's a menace. Daddy has called the pound any number of times but they never seem to get him."

Sheila opened the door wider and Frank went in, happy to get out of range of that dog.

"Does he belong in the neighborhood?"

"I don't know. Obviously he doesn't think you do."

Frank slipped the census cards into his pocket. "Your parents aren't home?"

"Did they know you were coming?"

"Oh, no. Nothing like that."

"Daddy's at work, of course, and this is Mother's bridge day. They actually start playing at nine in the morning. It almost sounds penitential, doesn't it?"

"If I gave that kind of penance, my confessional would be mobbed."

The remark seemed to make Sheila uneasy. She pointed to a chair and Frank sat down.

"You're still on vacation," he said.

"Yes."

"Don't you get a travel pass from the airline?"

She got a travel pass from the airline. She told him she had not the least desire to travel. All she wanted to do was sit still.

"You didn't tell me you had an argument with my father."

"I'm not very proud of that."

"What was it about?"

"It was my fault. I lost my temper. . . ." He did not want to talk about it.

"I'm not surprised. I do that all the time."

"I said some very cruel things to him. He told me no priest had ever spoken to him as I did, and I believe him. Anyway, I've apologized and I hope it's all forgotten."

"You apologized! I wasn't told that."

"There's no reason why you should have been."

"I wonder if Mother knew that you had." Sheila thought about that for a moment, then said, "Was it about me?"

"That's how it started, I guess." It did not seem to Frank that she had been the substance of the quarrel. "Your father insisted on thinking that I was giving him information about you. That I would pass on to him anything you said to me. I guess we just talked at a bad moment for both of us."

Sheila ran her finger along the edge of a cushion. She was seated on the couch and now seemed to shrink into it, out of the beam of sunlight which, till then, had lain softly on her face and hair.

"I've been attending your Mass."

"I thought I'd seen you there."

"I wondered if you would. Maybe I wanted you to think I'm a good little girl."

Frank let that go by. "How are things?"

"Things? Oh, things are fine. People aren't so good though. At first, after we talked, I went on a real work binge. No time off, Sheila the girl who could be called on anytime. It didn't help very much. Now I'm trying sitting still."

"That seems to be helping. You look different, more alive, happier."

She sat forward, moving into sunlight again. "Let's talk about you for a change, shall we? I'm tired of me. I know you went to that meeting downtown the other day. You say Mass in the morning. What else do you do? Priests have always been a mystery to me. They're so different from everybody else. How do you decide to become a priest?"

"Good Lord, that's a long story."

"Do you have a family? Where did you grow up, here in town? Tell me. You know so much about me and I don't know a thing about you."

"There really isn't much to know."

But he did respond to the invitation; he told her about Charlotte and her family; he told her about growing up too, after his parents died, and he told her about entering the seminary. Once he had begun, it seemed the most natural thing in the world to go on. It had never occurred to him that the familiar items of his personal history could be of interest to anyone, but Sheila listened with apparent delight. If nothing else, he told himself, this narrative would take her mind off her recent sad experience. When he glanced at his watch and saw that he had been in the house an hour he could not believe it. He scrambled to his feet.

"I've got to get going."

"And just when I was going to suggest coffee. Or tea. Or milk. A professional reflex."

"No. No, thanks."

She came with him to the door. The dog seemed to have disappeared. Frank went down the steps and, when Sheila called, turned.

"Say, did you want to leave a message for my parents?"

"A message?"

"Didn't you want to see them?"

Frank slapped at his pocket, then pulled out the census cards. He showed them to her. "I forgot. I'm taking census. Well, I guess we know all about your family. Good-bye."

He felt foolish at having forgotten why he had stopped by. Ah, well. If the hour had proved as diverting for her as it had for him, perhaps it had been worthwhile. Sheila was on the mend, there was no doubt of that. Her going to morning Mass was good, even if she was not receiving Communion yet. That would come, he assured himself. Just give her time.

Sheila watched Father Ascue start rapidly up the street, pursued by the little dog, who had suddenly reappeared. He stopped and held out his hand but of course the dog just snapped at him. He started off again, obviously uneasy at being barked on his way. Smiling, Sheila went into the kitchen for a cup of coffee.

It was so pleasant being in the house alone. These vacation days had been more relaxing than she would have predicted and it was tempting to think of her life just going on like this. Of course that was impossible. But she had to make up her mind about the apartment. Helen had called to say Carl was trying to reach her.

"He wants to know when you'll be back. What should I tell him? For that matter, we're curious too. *Are* you coming back?"

"I don't know."

"You're in on the rent until the first, but if you're not coming back, we should know in time. We all want to keep it a six-way split."

"I'll let you know as soon as I know."

"And what about Carl?"

She had phoned Carl from a booth, intending to tell him to stop bothering the girls at the apartment, but before she could say that, things got off the track.

"I want to see you, Sheila."

"No."

"Please, Sheila. Just that. See me."

"It would be a waste of time."

But she had allowed herself to be persuaded, sure that the time that had passed since she had last seen him would be armor enough. They met in a small bar, Carl's choice; perhaps he thought that its past associations would fan the flame again. To Sheila it now seemed only a poorly lighted place. Carl too appeared in a poor light—or newly in the bad light of the bar. He was a middle-aged man stricken by nothing more serious than the interruption of a convenient arrangement. She could not believe that so short a time before she had thought her life was bound to his. How shallow she must be to be so wholly devoid of feeling for him now. When she looked at him she saw the man who had cowered in a bedroom while she had suffered through that terrible confrontation with her father. Thank God Carl was proud. Once he had convinced himself that it was indeed over between them he did not prolong the meeting. She declined his offer of a ride, asked him to leave first. She would call a cab. Watching him go out of the bar, she had tried to feel about their affair as Father Ascue did, even as her father did, but all she could summon was wounded vanity and a sadness that she had given so much for so very little. The closest she came to sorrow was when she remembered his daughter, Catherine.

Sitting at the kitchen table, sipping coffee, Sheila wondered what Father Ascue would have said if she had told him about seeing Carl again. No doubt he would have scolded her. She almost missed the total concern he had shown her before, although at the time it had been terribly annoying. He was really very nice this morning and, in a way he never had before, he had *noticed* her. She had sensed that when she told him how she had tried to get over Carl by working hard, had watched his eyes follow her gestures, return to her face, finding there a person, not merely a poor little girl in terrible trouble.

Smiling dreamily, Sheila imagined that when she had opened the door to him he had been just himself, not the priest from Saint Waldo's. She asked him in, of course, and they talked. About what? He could have told her those things about himself and she would listen just as she had, but it would have been a prelude to something, something un-defined yet promising to be very nice and, of course, very moral. His intentions were thoroughly honorable; he was that kind of man. When finally he crossed the room to her, sat beside her, he would be awkward. He would not know what exactly to say, what exactly to do, and she would remember that she must not help him. He was shy and she liked shy men. At least she liked him. And he liked her. Anyone could see that from the way he described the sun in her hair. He took her hand. It was unbelievable how significant that could be, a man's taking a woman's hand in his. He looked into her eyes. Though he would never allude to it, he knew of her tragic affair with an older man and how much she was in need of understanding and comfort. Perhaps that was part of her attraction for him, that sadness in her past. It called forth tenderness from him but no doubt it piqued his curiosity too, her experience a complement to his shy innocence. She drew his hand toward her, clasped it in both of hers. . . .

Sheila stopped herself with a little laugh. Good Lord, she was going stir-crazy. Obviously it was time for her to get back to work, out of this house, back to the apartment, into the saddle again. When a girl sits around daydreaming about a young priest, well, really . . .

Phil Bullard told himself that this was not at all like the incident with Diane, and not only because Diane had been eager and willing whereas Eloise was shy and frightened. Virginal. Eloise had not said one word on the drive back from lunch and he sensed the turmoil going on within her, knew that silence was needed then. The kiss had surprised her. For that matter, it had surprised him too. But she had responded and no doubt it was that that had frightened her most. She had drawn back, aghast, and he did not try to hold her. This was not at all like the incident with Diane.

He had not kissed Eloise out of curiosity, out of a carefree desire to see what would happen next, where it might lead. But hadn't it been that way with Diane, an experiment? With her he had acted like a kid. Now that he thought about it, his application to be laicized seemed to have nothing in particular to do with Diane. She had been merely the occasion. It had never entered his mind that he might marry her. It was just that, having been caught in that kind of situation, he had not wanted to go on functioning as a priest. His thoughts of leaving, of putting Fort Elbow far behind him and starting over from scratch, had not included Diane, not really, although he had of course talked it all over with her. She had been an occasion, not the cause, and if Diane was now a thing of the past, that occasion gone, the underlying cause remained.

Kissing Eloise had been completely spontaneous. That was what he had told her when he drew up to the curb in front of her place, said it quietly, looking straight ahead. It was important that she know that. She must not think that he was playing adolescent games with her. He waited for her to reply, but a full minute of silence followed his remark, though she made no move to open the door and go.

"Father?"

"Phil!"

"Phil." Her voice nearly broke. "I am very sorry. It is my fault that happened."

"What do you mean, fault?"

She had closed her eyes and was biting her lip. "It won't happen again."

"Eloise, wait."

But she had the door open now and she hopped out and hurried up the walk toward the house before he could explain to her that it was just because their kiss had been spontaneous, unplanned, that there could be no question of fault.

Yesterday he had tried to reach Eloise but Sister Dolores told him Eloise was not feeling well and could not come to the phone. This morning he had overslept and when he called the house where the nuns lived some nutty woman answered and he could not make her understand what he wanted. Unable to remain at the Center, he had gone out to his car and just driven, remaining in town, driving aimlessly, filled with a happy sadness that expressed itself in desultory humming. Perhaps it was just as well that he could not reach Eloise yet. This was something they would both have to get used to. But he did want to talk about it with someone. Frank Ascue? Why not? Frank knew about Diane so there would not be the shock of disbelief. He knew these things happened. But it was important for Frank to see that this was different. This was real. Frank had as much as suggested that he get laicized because of Diane. Phil made a U-turn and began to drive in the direction of Saint Waldo's.

"No, he isn't in," the fat woman said. "Would you like to see Father McTear?"

"When do you expect him back?"

"He's here now."

"I meant Father Ascue."

"That's hard to say." The woman looked at him skeptically, as if she were wondering whether she ought to know him. "Would you like to leave a message?"

"Tell him Jack Tremplin called."

"Father Tremplin?"

"That's right."

Phil went with bouncy step back to his car. Apparently the fat woman didn't know Jack. There seemed little point in having Frank know he had stopped by. Already Phil had lost interest in discussing Eloise with him. Frank could be a pretty straight-laced guy and Phil had no desire to have his love of Eloise subjected to cold clerical analysis. What did Ascue know of love?

He headed back toward the Center now, tired of just driving around, and, while he drove, he thought of Eloise.

If he were playing games with Eloise, he would have welcomed her saying that it had all been her fault. Of course there was no fault; what had happened was spontaneous, unthinking, real. But if she insisted on feeling guilty, well, he could have built on that. Not that he would. This was not that sort of thing. He had been attracted to Eloise, he saw now, since the first time he had seen her on the playground at Saint Waldo's. What a waste for a girl that beautiful to be a nun, especially now when there was no ridiculous habit to make even the beautiful ugly.

He drew hope from the fact that Eloise had gone to the limit her order allowed in the matter of dress. The move to the apartment near the Center was a good one. Experiment indicated dissatisfaction with her life and, like so many others who had tried new ways of being a nun, she would come to see that what she really wanted was not to be a nun at all. And she liked him. He was sure of that. They had been together as much as possible since she had come to work at the Center and that was no more accidental on her part than it was on his. The kids loved her. Who wouldn't? She was bright, generous, good. . . . Phil felt his eyes blur with longing. My God, how he loved her.

A mile from the Center, he slowed to pick up a hitchhiker and was surprised when Ben Cole hopped into the car.

"I didn't recognize you," Phil said. "I'm going to the Center."

"Good enough."

"Is that where you were heading?"

"Why not?"

Funny kid. When the car was rolling, Ben began to talk of the Center and how much he was enjoying his summer there. Phil listened, thinking that he had never wasted a summer the way Ben was. At Ben's age he had worked as third cook on a diner, the Chicago to Seattle run, free and as far from seminary routine, and his father, as he could get. Phil's father had belonged to the Serra Club, a bunch of spoiled priests, themselves safely married, who encouraged young men to take up the life they had not had the guts to choose themselves. Saying that he had a vocation to the priesthood had been a sure way to win his father's complete admiration. Phil was in seventh grade when he made this announcement and his manifest destiny had been a shield behind which he could retreat whenever he got into trouble. Going to the seminary had been the line of least resistance. So had remaining there. Why hadn't he left? It was easy, maybe too easy, to say that his father was the reason, but there had been other reasons too. In Seattle he had gone to a whorehouse, a real rough place near the docks, and for a month had sweated out the fear that he had caught something from the lank-haired girl who had lain on the bed, pale as a plucked chicken,

300

watching disinterestedly as he undressed. When nothing showed up, Phil had returned with relief to the seminary. Sometimes he thought that he had gone through with it, been ordained, more out of inadvertence than decision.

"Summer's more than half over," Ben said.

"They go fast."

"They sure do."

"When do you go back?"

"I'm not sure about that."

"It's usually the middle of September, isn't it?"

"I meant I'm not sure that I'm going back."

"Oh."

"There's a girl."

"I see."

Ben was waiting for him to say more, but what? Good for you? Shame on you?

"Beverly Nygaard."

"Frank Ascue's niece?"

Ben nodded. He looked ashamed.

"Does Father Ascue know about it?"

"Father, I don't want to give up the idea of the priesthood. I would like to be a priest. But I like Beverly. I like her a lot. Why should I have to choose between them?"

"Maybe you shouldn't have to. But that's the way it is now."

He sounded like an uncle himself. And unsympathetic. The truth was that he resented Cole's telling him this, dumping his silly little troubles into the midst of his thoughts of Eloise. The suggestion that they were in the same boat, in a way, he and Cole, angered him.

Ben said, "I thought you'd understand."

"What do you mean?"

Ben was startled by the sharpness of his tone. "Do you know Father Grimes?"

"I know who he is."

"He advised me to leave the seminary."

"Well, maybe he's right. Of course, you have to make up your own mind."

"Father Ascue does know about me and Beverly. He really gave me hell."

"He could be right too."

"But which one is right? That's what I can't figure out. What would you do, Father?"

Phil looked at him, his anger fading. Cole was obviously enjoying his indecision; he seemed to consider his predicament worthy of everyone's concern, interesting, even shocking. Well, Phil knew what that was like. In Seattle, afterward, just lying there on that smelly bed, he had propped himself on his elbow and told that prostitute that he was studying to be a priest. No doubt he had hoped to shock her, to stir up in her some genuine interest. She had just looked at him.

"Yeah? Well, don't tell me. Tell it." And she had flicked him with her fingernail, painfully.

"I don't know," Phil Bullard said to Ben. "I really don't know."

Daniel Donovan put down the telephone, pushed back from his desk and—to hell with it—gave out with the old Geronimo war whoop. Thus, as a boy, he had jumped from garage roofs, swung on rope swings and charged across the playground, in the rear physically perhaps but, ah, spiritually at the head of the pack. Miss Clarity came in from the outer office and smiled apprehensively.

"Pope John is alive and well in a catacomb?"

"That was the NCR on the phone."

Miss Clarity did not cheer. "But we don't even have a cash register."

The trouble with Miss Clarity's humor was that it might very well be unintended. Cash register. The Jewish typewriter of the same youth from which the Geronimo war whoop had unexpectedly issued.

"They want to carry my story on the ecumenical conference."

"No kidding," she said. "Wow."

For Christ's sake. Daniel suspected Alice Clarity of having more contempt for Catholic journalism than it presently deserved, at least as an overall proposition. Even she should know that the *National Catholic Reporter* was about as good as you can get in the Catholic press. Apart from the old standbys like *Commonweal* and *America*, it was the one organ you could safely say had an honest-to-God national circulation, its readership the avant-garde of the Church in America, and not unread by non-Catholics either. It pained Daniel to think of the clippings, suggestions, inquiries he had sent to NCR's offices in Kansas City without getting so much as an acknowledgment of receipt. He had been positive Bullard would interest them, if only as an item in their front-page leonine growl, but no dice. The strike at the seminary had rated a few lines in that unfocused newsreel, but with no hint that its source was the *Fort Elbow Catholic*. Now, with the ecumenical conference, he had hit and hit big.

"Rewrite it for us," his caller had said. "Give it less of a local thrust. And we'll need more background." A giggle came along the line like

302

an air bubble in an artery. "You won't believe this, but some people have never heard of Fort Elbow, Ohio."

Wise apple. Did she think Kansas City was Athens? "Will do," Daniel said in efficient tones. "When do you want it?"

"Instanter. This is on spec, of course."

"Of course." Who the hell did she think she was dealing with?

Alice Clarity left his office and the sound of her typing resumed. It might have been a cash register. How did she make the bell ring so often? She must have the margins set only inches apart. He hoped that she had remembered to put a sheet of paper into the machine. Sometimes she forgot and typed half a letter before noticing. It had been a mistake to let Lydia persuade him to take Alice on. A friend of a friend, that sort of thing, and he had assumed that she would be smart and eager and grateful enough for the opportunity to overlook the lousy salary. But Alice treated the job as a quaint hobby, lived at the Y and was about as rooted in Fort Elbow as . . . As I am, Daniel thought hopefully. He had to do a bang-up job on this assignment. Who knew? Overwhelmed by his prose, the NCR might . . .

He suppressed the thought. At thirty, his life seemed, when he looked back upon it, a series of flops, one aborted career after another. Lydia was under the illusion that the two of them were in the vanguard of the Catholic intelligentsia, but their common publisher survived on atrocious inspirational novels, crap that Canon Shehan or the *Sacred Heart Messenger* would have disowned. Padded uplift novels as the foundation of empire.

Lydia. He must tell her. He picked up his phone and had to think a moment before he remembered his home number.

"Oh, Dan! How neat-o. When will it appear?"

"Next issue, I suppose." He added gruffly, "No guarantee, of course. It's on spec."

"Of course."

Two old pros running down a check list of their métier.

"I should come home to write it. I can't do anything here, anything serious."

It was understood between them that what he wrote at the office was, if not crap, not wholly serious either. Home was where serious work was done. Every night, more or less, he insisted on doing his "pages," the quota of writing on what they called his *capolavoro* and which was meant to propel them once and for all out of the midwestern morass into the eastern big time.

"What did Brophy say? And Oder?"

"I called you first."

She was moved by this order of priority, deeply; he could sense it in the tremor in her voice. He felt a tremor himself, foreseeing the grueling direction her gratitude would take that night.

"Do come home, Dan. But phone Oder and Bishop Brophy first. And Ascue too, don't you think?"

But before making any more calls, he wanted to wind down. It would not do to sound excited, particularly if the auxiliary bishop and Don Oder did not immediately grasp the importance of the NCR opportunity. Daniel went down the hall to urinate, something he always had to do when excited, but though his bladder felt uncomfortably full he stood there like a dry creek for minutes before a token stream relieved his mind and he hurried back to his desk, zipping as he went.

Once more behind his desk, he breathed deeply, wanting to squeeze the last bubbles of elation from his blood. Calm, professional, matter-of-fact, that was the ticket. Odd that Lydia had suggested he call Father Ascue too. Daniel thought about that. Lydia was a better judge of character than he was and if she saw Ascue as one of their own she was most likely right. But then Ascue had been chosen for that television program, chosen by Brophy and Oder. Yes, Ascue was definitely in and that was good. In Fort Elbow they needed every liberal they could find. Daniel pulled his phone toward him and began to dial Bishop Brophy's number.

Howard Nygaard had not taken Sharon to lunch at Brady's or Charley's or any of the usual places but to the lunchroom on the top floor of Wissel's Department Store, a place frequented by shopping matrons. From their table they had a panoramic view of Fort Elbow. Sharon stripped off her gloves, dropped them in her lap, clasped her hands together and looked out at the city as if it were Mecca and she a Moslem.

"I had no idea it was so lovely."

She gestured toward the city, enraptured, but then the glow faded from her face and she looked at him.

"I have something to tell you."

"What?"

"You're so frowny."

"I had a rough morning."

"Can we get a drink here?"

"I'm afraid not. What do you have to tell me?"

She studied her hands. "It's never the way we imagine it will be, is it? Telling someone something special?" Her eyes met his. "I've moved to Fort Elbow. No. Don't say anything yet. I want to say this right, to make things perfectly clear. This has nothing to do with us, not primarily. I was sick to death of Cleveland, of the school I taught in, but mainly of my mother. I can't bear to live near her any longer. Okay. That is why I left Cleveland. Of course I could teach anywhere, so why Fort Elbow? I wrote the school board here in May and just a week ago they told me that they had had a cancellation."

Howard picked up his water and drained the glass. He wished they had gone to one of his regular restaurants, anywhere that they could have got a drink.

"I've found a lovely apartment."

The address was in the neighborhood of the school where she would teach, nowhere near his own. She said, "Well, what do you think?"

"It's hard to believe."

"You don't like it."

It was his turn to be fascinated by the view of Fort Elbow. Sharon had a right to live wherever she liked. If she wanted to move to Fort Elbow, he could not stop her. He did not own the city. But my God, what did she mean by saying that her move here had nothing to do with them? It had everything to do with them and she damned well knew it. He could not risk losing his temper. A pleasantly quizzical expression—or so he imagined—had frozen on his face but inside he seethed. How dare she pull a trick like this?

"What does your new school look like?"

She looked at him desolately. "Do you really care?"

"Of course I care."

"This was a mistake. Oh, God, it was a mistake." Her eyes swam with tears and Howard was filled with panic. Would she make a scene here, in a lunchroom filled with housewives on a shopping spree?

"Eat your lunch, Sharon."

She looked at her food as if it had been produced by sleight of hand. A tomato stuffed with rice, mixed pepper salad, iced tea. He gave her his handkerchief but she shook her head, almost violently, and brought a napkin to her eyes.

"Please understand, Sharon. I am still trying to adjust to this."

"Adjust?" She made it sound like a dirty word.

"Yes, adjust. I wonder if you're not right. Perhaps moving here was a mistake. And for many reasons."

Such as? But she was on the defensive now and he held back. Why tell her what she already knew? He did not want to spell out the bad effects of this move on her, though they seemed obvious enough to him. His main concern was the threat it posed to him and, by God, it was a threat he would resist regardless of the consequences. His earlier concern over her mere letters seemed comic compared with her presence in Fort Elbow, phoning him no problem, coming to see him easy. But he must not panic, he must not exaggerate the spot he was in.

"Let's go someplace where we can get a drink."

Why not her apartment? Wedged side by side on the escalator, she told him how she had dreamed all morning of their going from lunch to her apartment. She had been so eager for him to see it.

"And now . . ." Her eyes filled with tears again and Howard wanted to take her arm and shake her. She could not do this to him, not in his own town.

"Of course we'll go to your apartment. I want to see it."

The apartment was a parody of femininity, chintz and lace, bric-a-brac everywhere, the three small rooms reeking of lilac. He could see what she had been doing since Monday.

"Nice."

Sharon had said nothing on the drive here and now she looked around forlornly. When her eyes finally came to rest on him, they swarmed with the plea that her move here and this apartment embodied. Despite himself, he felt his loins stir. They were safe here; no scene could ruin him. Like doomed actors they drifted toward one another and then she was in his arms, her wet cheek on his dry one, her body lifting to meet his.

"Where did you go for lunch?" Char asked that night.

"Why do you ask?"

"I stopped by your office just before noon."

"Oh, too bad. You should have phoned first."

"Aren't you even surprised?"

"That you didn't find me in?"

"No. Howard, how long has it been since we had lunch together?"

"I couldn't guess."

"Neither could I. Miss Furlong suggested that I look in Brady's but you weren't there so I had lunch alone."

"At Brady's?"

"Yes."

"I was with a client who doesn't drink. We had lunch in Wissel's lunchroom of all places."

"You *did?* That's where I was going to go when you weren't in Brady's, but I was so hungry and there was a table, so . . ."

In the bathroom he pressed a washcloth to his face. He had soaked it first in cold water and, when he wrung it out, he wished it were

Sharon's neck that he held in his hands. Today there had been no recuperative lapse of time between leaving Sharon and coming home and he had entered his house with the feel and touch of her still clinging to his body. He looked at himself in the mirror and was filled with loathing. There had to be a way out of this but, dear God, he could not imagine what it was.

Charlotte tapped on the door. "Hurry up, Howard, Frank is coming over."

Frank! It had not been too bad, talking with Frank, when Sharon was miles away, in another city. What was that line? You have committed fornication but that was in another country. Well, Cleveland anyway. But now his sin had come to town to stay and how could he spend an evening in small talk with a priest? Frank heard confessions, of course, he knew about things. Sure he did. But what would he think if he knew his brother-in-law was an adulterer. Howard repeated the word to himself, liking the sound of it. The word seemed to lend some ragged dignity to the mess he had got himself into.

When after a year as a postulant Eloise made her first simple vows, she had worn a wedding dress, a beautiful, beautiful wedding dress, the very one in which her mother had been married. With the other girls, all of them lovely that day at least, she had walked down the aisle of the mother house chapel toward Bishop Caldron enthroned before the altar. Her parents were there, her mother's eyes brimming with tears, her father grim and uncomfortable, watching their daughter dedicate her life to God. The bride of Christ. At a certain point in the ceremony they had been led away and when they returned they wore the habit of the order. A plain gold band, a wedding band, was slipped onto her finger to be a constant reminder of the solemn dedication of her life to Christ.

Eloise turned the ring slowly now, pushing it with the fleshy ball of her thumb, round and round, as if she were conjuring up the memory of that day five years before. So much had changed since then, in herself, in the life she had undertaken, in the Church. No sooner had she become a nun than the order began a series of meetings to implement the decisions of the Vatican Council. The habit Eloise had so solemnly put on at her first profession was discarded within a year and then, in graded steps, those who chose to do so began to dress exactly as they had before they entered. Only the ring remained. The novice mistress had opposed any and every change and, while under her tutelage, Eloise accepted her mentor's conservative outlook as the mind of the order. Once she was out of the novitiate, however, she had quickly joined the faction dedicated to the most sweeping changes.

Among the little group at the Saint Waldo convent, Eloise had been considered the most far out in matters of change. And now, this summer, the experiment of living outside the convent, of taking this apartment with Rita and Dolores, had put her in the very vanguard of reform. This was the context in which she had to consider the surprising relationship that had sprung up between her and Father Bullard. After the first shock, after, to be honest, some revulsion, Eloise was alternately grief-stricken at what she had allowed to happen and excited by the memory of it. But she was sincerely determined that there would be no repetition. Far more than her own fate depended on the success of the experiment the apartment represented. Dolores was of course surprised when Eloise told her she would not be going to the Center.

"But why not?"

"There are other things to be done, Dolores."

"But Eloise, that is our work." Dolores, as if sensing something, stopped. "What happened?"

"Nothing happened."

"You're afraid of something."

Afraid? That seemed a strange name for what she felt but perhaps it was the right one. She did fear that she might do something that would make a mockery and a lie of that beautiful ceremony in the mother house chapel. It frightened her that she had so easily stepped out of a character that had been five years abuilding and should be the only self she had. Kissed by a man, by a priest! When she was in high school she had let boys kiss her, after the first date, and when they did she had waited for a flood of romantic feeling to overwhelm her. It never had. She could not forget that in the daytime her dates were only the awkward boys with acne whom she had known all her life.

Dolores said, "Talking about it might help."

"Talking about what?"

"Would you like me to guess?"

"Dolores, for heaven's sake."

Dolores nodded, her look significant. Her mouth opened but immediately she clamped her hand over it. "No," she mumbled. "I can't."

"Dolores, don't be silly."

"Very well. You say it."

"I am not playing a game. I am not going to the Center. There is plenty of work to be done right here in this neighborhood."

"Father Bullard," Dolores said in a small voice.

"What?"

Dolores grew bolder. "He's the reason. Father Bullard. He is, isn't he?"

How depressing to have this turn into a convent parlor game. Discretion was not exactly Dolores's forte either. The woman simply could not keep her mouth shut.

"Dolores, you are being foolish."

But she was not to be put off by that. "And you're not. I think you've made a wise decision. Both Rita and I have wanted to say something, but neither of us could get up the nerve."

"The nerve to say what?"

"The kids at the Center say things, Eloise. We have overheard some rather nasty remarks. Of course, we knew that there was nothing . . ."

The ruptured remark became a question. Dolores was waiting to be assured that there was nothing to it. Eloise obliged and of course Dolores was not convinced. At least she did not pursue it. Now. No doubt she wanted to run off and have a good talk with Rita. Oh, dear God. At the moment all Eloise wanted was to be left alone.

But, thrown on her own resources, she seemed to have little defense against the emotions Phil had stirred up in her two days ago. When she had been in the novitiate, what she would be, what she would become, had been spoken of as the product of years of habit, of effort, and above all of prayer. Now all the layers of that constructed self had crumbled. Prayer. When she closed her eyes to pray she was met by the riot of her feelings, a montage of images: the highway moving beneath the car, the rush and roar of the wind, Phil beside her, both of them going somewhere, anywhere, away. Opening her eyes, she was grateful for the vast distraction of the sunny day.

From the window she looked out at the depressing street, at people milling about, the cars at the curb, a general air of decay and desuetude, and yet beneath it all there was the pulse of a life from which she had cut herself off when she had entered the convent. Odd that the thought of being the most troubled housewife on the block could appeal to her more than her own remote and somehow privileged life. The people here were poor. She and Rita and Dolores mimicked their poverty, but their life here was really a game, an experiment, finally an insult to the real problems their neighbors faced. It seemed a symbol of her vocation. She was a tourist in the midst of real life. She had told Dolores that there was work to be done right here in the neighborhood, but what could she give these people? She had no greater knowledge or strength than they, perhaps less. The least of these people knew more of life than she did and, standing by the window, looking wistfully out, Sister Eloise envied her neighbors.

"Good to see you back," Phil said next day, his manner neutral.

To come to the Center had seemed a declaration and Eloise was crushed that he did not respond appropriately. She was tugged away by a group of girls and they kept her busy all morning, but her mind was not in the discussion. It was unreal that they should look to her for light on anything. Not one of these girls could be as confused as she was. When noon came she avoided Dolores and Rita and went down the hall toward Phil's office. Janice came out the door.

"Is Father in?"

"No!"

The girl was looking at her with undisguised hatred. Shrinking from this incredible response, Eloise turned and ran back toward the lobby.

"Hey, what's the rush?"

Phil! She ran to him confused, and he put his hands on her arms, holding her until she had control of herself. He guided her toward the exit.

"Let's get out of here," he said.

"Yes. Oh, let's. Let's just go anywhere."

Humming, holding an unlighted cigar, Monsignor Yorick stood while Bishop Caldron read the letter from Bullard.

"Should I make an appointment for him, Bishop?"

Caldron looked up. "I don't see that he has asked for one."

"I thought you would want to see him."

"I am always available to my priests, Monsignor. When they ask to see me."

"Should I draft a reply?"

"I don't think that will be necessary. Not yet. We'll let things simmer. He may very well want to change his mind again."

The bishop smiled cherubically, a multipurpose smile, and among those purposes was the dismissal of his chancellor.

In his own office, Yorick lighted the cigar and drew on it angrily. The nerve of Bullard, writing to ask that his previous request for laicization be reactivated. Reactivated! And just like that. On again, off again, Finnegan. Did he think it was some damned vacation trip he could plan and cancel at will? Caldron should simply suspend the guy. That was the only way to handle this kind of nonsense. Of course, the chancellor had not told the bishop all he knew of the matter.

Monsignor Yorick had been unimpressed by Father Bullard's previ-

310

ous change of heart, when he had withdrawn his application to be laicized. The chancellor's contacts proved helpful, as they often had before. Tony Calcaterra was in an odd business, no doubt of that, and one that had often brought heavy-handed kidding from the chancellor. Approached on the Bullard matter, Tony, a short and hairy grade school friend of Yorick's, was coolly businesslike. He bobbed his head, made a few notes, lifting an admonishing hand when Monsignor Yorick said that discretion was of the essence. Tony promised an early report.

There was a woman, of course, a data processing operator employed by Millikens. A nice stroke of luck. The regional manager at Millikens was Cyril Horvath, whom Yorick had successfully championed in his desire to become a Knight of Saint Gregory. Bullard's letter now prompted the chancellor to get in touch with his debtor.

Horvath suggested lunch at his club and Yorick got down to business over martinis in the library. The dining room was crowded and, in any case, it would not do to spoil a good lunch with a topic of this sort.

The soul of knighted prudence, Horvath nodded sagely while Yorick spoke, his brows knitting when the chancellor told him the name of the priest.

"I knew he was a Yo-Yo, Monsignor. Remember those slanderous remarks in the paper?"

The chancellor remembered.

"Art Rupp and I agreed at the time that there was too much patience being shown that man." Horvath brought his glass to his lips but did not drink. He shook his head slowly. "A priest."

Yorick waited for Horvath to get beyond this first and understandable reaction. He did not want to waste both their times sighing over straying priests, a melancholy subject to which some laymen were inclined to devote endless lamentation.

"A weak man, yes. I want to help him by removing the source of the trouble."

"I don't understand."

"The girl, Cy. The girl."

"Ah."

"I thought that if she was transferred . . ."

"Consider it done, Monsignor. I'll make a change of scenery seem irresistible to her. I can't force her to go, you understand, but I think I can assure you that she will be out of town in short order."

"I knew I could count on you."

"I consider it a duty." Horvath gave Monsignor Yorick a significant look. A Knight of Saint Gregory.

"Of course."

With a sense of accomplishment, Yorick preceded Horvath in to lunch, his mouth watering in anticipation of the finnan haddie Horvath was describing to him.

When, that evening, Tony Calcaterra called with an invitation to bowl a couple of lines, Monsignor Yorick was happy to accept. Tony was off his game, actually rolled a gutter ball his first time up, and the victorious chancellor was expansive later over drinks. It seemed only right to confide to Tony what Horvath had agreed to do.

"What took you so long?" Tony asked. "That girl was making a habit of it."

"What do you mean?"

"Bullard wasn't the only one, you know. There was another too."

"Another priest?"

"Yeah. I was going to mention it in the report, but you had only asked about the one."

"Who is the other?"

Tony frowned in thought. "Asquith, something like that."

"Do you mean Ascue?"

"That's the name. Want another drink?"

The studios of WFEO looked like a warehouse to Frank. In one corner was a truncated kitchen, the setting of a morning show that Charlotte watched. Other props were pushed back against the walls, the sets of the local news program, the weather show, a children's hour shown on Saturday morning. A scoreboard showed the results of the previous day's major league games. More or less in the center of the room was a round table with chairs arranged around it in a semicircle. Don Oder stood near it with two men and Frank joined them. The tall man was Plummet-Finch, the philosopher, the other was a Lutheran minister named Tetzel whom Frank remembered from the ecumenical meeting. Frank said little, marveling at the calm the others showed. They were waiting for Edwin Pomodore. Oder had described him as a publisher, a native of Fort Elbow, and it was clear that Don regarded the man's agreement to participate as a coup. At a drugstore near the rectory Frank had come upon one of the magazines Pomodore published, glossy mammalian pornography of the most insipid sort.

"Of course," Oder had said when he called him. "Of course. But did you read the publisher's page?"

"I certainly didn't buy the thing."

"I see. Personally, I subscribe to *Hedone*—if only to know what my parishioners are reading. It's on every coffee table in the parish, Frank.

I don't know about his other magazines, but *Hedone* is not the usual sort of girlie book. I suspect that, in Pomodore's mind, those silly photographs are only meant to capture readers for his page."

Pomodore arrived at the studio late, sweeping toward them in a bottle-green Edwardian suit, a florid ascot, smoothing with one pale hand his long thin hair. Tweedy Plummet-Finch, who had been grumbling about the delay, emitted an angry humming noise at the sight of the publisher.

"Is this to be in color?" he wondered loudly.

Pomodore ignored the remark, if he even heard it; he was being fussed over by Oder and the director, Mouchoir. Mouchoir arranged the panelists in chairs at the table, pursing his lips angrily at Daniel Donovan, who sought to intervene. Frank and Pomodore were placed on one side of Oder, Tetzel and Plummet-Finch at the other. Donovan, who had darted behind one of the cameras, studied the arrangement with the narrowed eyes of the ideal viewer. He nodded affirmatively. Mouchoir ignored him.

"Want to warm up a bit?"

The panelists looked to Father Oder, who said he didn't think that would be necessary. "I'll say something by way of introduction, then call on each of you for a brief statement." They agreed and Mouchoir said, "Okey-doke."

He gestured to the booth, the light on one of the cameras glowed and an announcer's voice filled the studio. "The following program, a discussion of sexual morality, is brought to you as a public service by WFEO." The names of the panelists were given and the chairman introduced. Mouchoir pointed to Oder and they were on.

Oder explained the format of the discussion, then continued: "A question is sometimes raised as to the possibility of moral conviction apart from religious faith. Lest that question seem altogether too academic and abstract, I should like to point out its peculiar relevance for ecumenism today. As you all know, my own denomination, the Roman Catholic Church, has for centuries maintained that contraception is immoral. To many it must appear that this prohibition is a matter of intramural discipline, applicable to Catholics alone, along the lines of not eating meat on Friday or of attendance at Mass on Sunday. Or is a wider claim being made? Does my church hold that contraception is objectively wrong, and for anyone, whatever he may think about the matter, whatever he may do? At the moment, as it happens, we Catholics are awaiting word from our coreligionist, the bishop of Rome. The pope has appointed a commission to review Catholic doctrine on this point, thus indicating that it is open to discussion. What I suggest to the

313

panelists, in order to make our topic concrete and relevant, is that they discuss our theme with constant reference to this vexed matter. First, I shall call on a distinguished British philosopher, currently resident in Fort Elbow."

"Well." Plummet-Finch took his pipe from his mouth, put it back in, removed it once more. "I must say that our chairman's suggestion has left me aghast. If I understood him correctly, he wished to say that there are those who ask whether ethics is possible apart from religious faith. Now, I should have thought that it is their compatibility which poses difficulties. However . . ." Pipe in mouth again, Plummet-Finch began to grope for matches. Pomodore tossed a book of matches down the table. Plummet-Finch picked them up, removed his pipe from his mouth and went on. "Intellectually, sheerly as a matter of what one knows, and knows he knows, I confess that the whole topic of religion has come to grievously bore me. My surprise at the chairman's remarks increased with his suggestion that there is some problem concerning the morality of contraception. I should be inclined to say that, in the present state of affairs, it is immoral *not* to make use of contraceptive devices. We are all aware of the menacing statistics."

Plummet-Finch ticked off those statistics. The projected world population, the limits of the food supply, the psychic attrition from noise and crowding. When he was done, he sank back as if exhausted.

"Unlike the previous speaker, Professor Finch," Pomodore said when called upon, bowing at the previous speaker, who, robbed of his hyphen, scowled in reply. "Unlike the learned professor, I persist in thinking that Christianity, indeed religion generally, has content of lasting value. The task, as I see it, is to strip from it certain obscuring features so that it can be revealed for what it is, namely, the common man's notion of what life is all about. Love." Pomodore showed his teeth in a smile. "Love," he repeated. "It's that simple."

And what is love? Pomodore asked. His answer was that of the male libertarian, love is sex, basically, and sex is subjective, an experience. That copulation requires a partner, a person, and not merely complementary reproductive organs, did not seem to have occurred to Pomodore.

Plummet-Finch reached for the carafe of coffee on the table before them and, in the course of filling his cup, managed to spill a good deal on the table, distracting Oder and introducing an edge to Pomodore's voice.

"I seem to have upset Professor Finch," he said. "Or was it only his coffee cup?"

314

"Both. Really. All this *machismo* and chest-thumping is dreadfully boring. There are boys and there are girls. Surely we all knew that."

"All of us?" Pomodore asked sweetly.

Oder intervened. "I wonder if I might call on Father Ascue now."

Frank said, "The chairman's opening remarks made a good deal of sense to me and I would like to emphasize why. As I understood him, he asked whether believers of different persuasions, as well as believers and nonbelievers, can meet on common ground and find there a basis for ethical judgments. Are there ethical judgments on which all would agree? Obviously there are. It would be fairly easy for me to list a number of moral judgments on which we would all agree. The judgment, for example, that the killing of innocent persons is wrong. Of course the trouble with such agreements is that they still leave much room for discussion, not about what they say, but about their application. Would abortion be an instance of killing the innocent? In order to answer that, we would have to discuss what is meant by human life, a human person, and so on. Father Oder has made things considerably more difficult by turning our attention to an issue where agreement is not had and where it is unlikely that it will be had."

Frank went on to say that it was clear from past pronouncements of the Church that she considers contraception to be wrong in the way that killing the innocent is wrong. That is, its wrongness lies in the nature of the deed and does not follow from its being prohibited by some authority. "That is why the ban on contraception has always been intimately linked with what moralists call natural law."

Plummet-Finch, in the act of bringing a lighted match to his pipe, stopped. His swift intake of breath was the sound of shock.

"The concept of natural law is, to say the least, an exceedingly thorny one." Plummet-Finch resumed the lighting of his pipe. "The current debate on contraception within the Catholic community is in large part an attack on the concept of natural law. One thing is quite clear. If contraception is morally wrong, the reasons for its wrongness are going to have to be as clear to non-Catholics as to Catholics. Personally, I find the specific arguments advanced against contraception in the past unpersuasive and dubious. And I am one who expects that, when the pope does speak on this matter, he will present a doctrine different from that of the past."

Oder beamed. Plummet-Finch nodded through clouds of smoke. Pomodore wore a look of tardy vindication. If Donovan had been an examiner, Frank would have passed with flying colors. Tetzel, when called on, wondered about the distinction between nature and grace and pursued the thought into a theological stratosphere.

"Why are we fearful of pleasure?" Pomodore demanded, when the discussion was declared open. He looked about the empty studio as if it were jammed with masochists. "Surely the message of religion is not that pleasure is sinful. I think of God as a happy, as a playful creator, as a being who—and I suppose that even today this will shock some— a being who wants us to have fun."

"Sex as recreation," Plummet-Finch drawled. "Surely that is as banal as the Catholic position from which Father Ascue has so adroitly backed away. Where in heaven's name would the pleasure principle take us? And, really now, is any sexual experience *fun?* Oh, I suppose it is in the mindless pages of Mr. Pomodore's publications. But in real life? The profound collision of personalities involved is more often abrasive and violent. I would suggest, as a matter for discussion, that sex is aggression rather than perfumed and airbrushed fun and games."

"In *normal* cases," Pomodore emphasized, "in normal heterosexual relations . . ."

"Precisely what I have in mind," Plummet-Finch snapped.

". . . the experience of *participants* suggests quite the opposite of the professor's spectator judgment."

Oder quickly recognized Tetzel.

"I object to Mr. Pomodore's apparent suggestion that there is some connection, of a positive sort, between his publications and the Judaeo-Christian ethic. His magazines are one continuous paean to hedonism."

Pomodore smiled. "You seem to be a student of my magazines."

"No, I am not a student of your magazines. I have, however, followed newspaper accounts of your legal difficulties, largely with the pornography statutes."

"Never a conviction, sir. Not one."

"A man without convictions," Plummet-Finch murmured.

Tetzel turned to the professor. "You are an atheist, Professor?"

"Yes, I am."

"In the light of that, what in your view makes what is morally wrong to be morally wrong?"

"You mean apart from God forbidding it?"

"Yes."

"I should say a number of things. Consider our privileged example. Overpopulation brings with it consequences which range from the inconvenient to the deplorable. I would cite those consequences as a basis for saying that it is wrong, unreasonable, bad, for people to reproduce themselves heedlessly."

316

Tetzel wanted to know if an act could be bad which had no bad consequences. Since he himself was of the opinion that contraception is permitted, he suggested the example of lying.

"When it hurts no one?"

"Absolutely no one. Not even the liar himself, at least in the way you imagine, through consequences."

"Well." Plummet-Finch laughed. "In that case, it would be quite unnoticeable and I wonder if I need have any opinion about it at all."

"Father Ascue," Oder said. "I wonder if you would develop your view on a forthcoming change in the Church's stand on birth control."

"It could be said that the change has already occurred," Frank said. "The majority on the papal commission favored a change. That majority, indeed the majority of the faithful at large, could be due to the work of the Holy Spirit. Thus it becomes possible to say that the present thought of the Church—and I mean the thought of her members at large—differs from past papal statements on the matter. What the pope must do, then, if this view is accepted, is promulgate the de facto teaching of the universal Church on this matter."

Oder was delighted. "I think I would add that if that is not done, and done soon, confusion will reign. And if the old position were to be repeated, well, there would be something very like a revolution, among theologians, among pastors and, most importantly, among the laity. The Holy Spirit, speaking through the vast majority of the faithful, has been teaching a doctrine different from the papal one for years."

Plummet-Finch said, "It comes as news to me that the Church of Rome is run by referendum."

"That's too strong," Oder said. "But it can no longer be run by Olympian pronouncements from the top."

Frank wanted to add that the position he had expressed was not his own but one that had been put forward by a number of theologians. Before he could speak, however, Mouchoir indicated that only a minute remained. Oder slipped smoothly into a summary of the haphazard discussion and, when the camera lights were off, Frank had the feeling that the whole hour had been meandering and pointless. He was particularly dissatisfied with his own remarks. Things were so complicated, there was need for so many distinctions. Daniel Donovan approached the table and took Frank's hand.

"Beautiful, Father. Beautiful. You put it very well."

"It all seemed so random."

Donovan glanced at Pomodore and Plummet-Finch, who had got up

317

and were talking behind the table. "They'll attract an audience. That was the point of asking them."

"When will this be shown?"

"Not till next Sunday afternoon."

Oder joined them, putting his arm around Frank's shoulder. "Well," he said. "I think our side did very well."

3 "I thought you said that he had red hair, Bev." They were in the kitchen to get drinks and snacks before the program began on television.

"It turns in the summer. Ben would rather have beer, Mother. You and I can drink the lemonade."

"Turns?" Her mother frowned. "How much beer is there?"

"Only a few bottles."

"Then you and I'll drink lemonade. Let your father and Bill have the beer."

"Ben. Ben Cole."

"What's his family like?"

"There's just his father. Mr. Cole knows Dad, at least by name."

"Then he must be a lawyer."

Mr. Cole was not a lawyer. He was a manufacturer's representative, whatever that was. Some of Beverly's friends had suggested that her mother's erratic thinking was due to menopause, but as far as Beverly could remember her mother had always been like this.

Ben and her father were in the living room. When Ben had arrived, ten minutes ago, her mother told him warningly, "We're going to watch my brother on TV in a few minutes."

"Mother, that's why Ben's here."

"My dad is watching the ball game," Ben explained.

"Is one on?" Mr. Nygaard looked wistful.

"The Indians."

"Nationally televised?"

"He picks it up from Cleveland."

"The program starts at three," Mrs. Nygaard said. "Are you sure that's the right channel?"

"It's WFEO."

"Who wants a snack?"

So into the kitchen they had gone and now out again, bringing beer for the men, lemonade for themselves. Her father was asking Ben where he went to school.

Ben's eye caught hers. "At the moment, that's in doubt."

Smiling, Beverly served Ben first. Her father looked puzzled when she gave him his beer.

"Ben and I are working together at the Center, Dad."

"At the university?"

"Yes."

He seemed to think that located Ben in school adequately enough. She and Ben no longer talked about his plans. An unacknowledged guilt was the glue holding them together. For him, she was off limits, while she was drawn by his wavering indecisiveness. What would she think of him if he were simply another boy?

"It's on," her mother cried.

On the screen, overlaid with titles, five figures sat at a table. The announcer was speaking.

"Shhh," Mrs. Nygaard said, though the room was silent. She leaned forward in her chair while her husband slumped back in his.

"How long a program is it?" he asked.

"An hour," Ben said, his eyes on the screen.

Throughout the hour, Beverly watched Ben more than she did the program. He was as engrossed in it as her mother. Her father watched fitfully, through half-closed eyes. The poor guy, Bev thought. He looks so beat.

"Hurrah," her mother cried at some remark of Uncle Frank's. "Wasn't that good?" she asked over her shoulder.

"Great," Ben said.

"Yeah." Beverly winked at her father.

When the program was over, Mrs. Nygaard turned with a triumphant smile. "That was really great. Frank was magnificent."

"It was good," Ben agreed.

Mrs. Nygaard turned to him. "What did you think of Father Oder?"

"How do you mean?"

"I don't know." She seemed to be sizing up Ben. "Oh, I do too. He kept breaking in all the time, as if he were something more than the chairman. And he looked so smug."

"He got them through some rough spots, though."

"C'mon, Ben," Beverly said. "Show's over. Time to go sit in the yard."

When they left the living room, her mother was trying to prod some enthusiastic response to the program from her father. Uncle Frank. Uncle Frank. How could her father stand it? She and Ben collapsed on lawn chairs in the backyard.

"Whose roses?" he asked.

"Just ours. Mother bought them at the supermarket. They grow like weeds."

"Nice."

"At the moment that's in doubt."

"What?"

"Where you go to school."

"Oh. He really put me on the spot. What was I supposed to say?"

"You tell me."

He did not want to talk about it. From several yards away, the sounds of a badminton game drifted to them.

"Maybe you should go talk to Father Grimes again."

"Or your uncle."

"There's always me. In a pinch." She pinched him.

"I did talk with Phil Bullard, Bev."

"Who hasn't?"

"About that."

"You did! What did he say?"

Ben looked angry. "Nothing. He was as bad as Grimes. And no more help than your uncle. He seemed to resent my asking him about it."

What did he want, a declaration of independence drawn up by a certified expert? Uncle Frank had told him only what he had just said on TV. Make up your own mind. "Maybe Phil is too wrapped up in his own troubles."

"Eloise?"

"You've noticed."

Ben pulled a blade of grass from the lawn and consulted it as if for the mystery of being. "I don't think he's long for the cloth."

"Nor she for the veil. Not that that will involve a big costume change for either of them."

"It's pretty damned depressing to hear kids making cracks about those two at the Center all day. I mean, there is still such a thing as scandal, isn't there? If he's going to leave, why the hell doesn't he just do it?"

Beverly took the blade of grass from his hand. "Amen," she said.

Lydia Donovan got up and turned off the television set. Daniel lolled in his chair, pleased with the program, which he had watched with a proprietary air.

"A real bombshell, wasn't it?" he asked his guests.

Phil Bullard's brows settled at unequal heights. "Frank Ascue as radical—I can't believe it. What did you think, Eloise?"

"About Father Ascue? He's changed."

"How do you mean?" Donovan asked.

Phil said, "I always thought of him as cautious."

"One thing is safe to predict," Daniel said. "He is going to get one helluva lot of attention because of this. National attention. My story on the ecumenical meeting should appear in next week's issue of NCR. This will make a better story."

Lydia wished he had let her mention the NCR piece. That would have been less look-at-me-ish. "Coffee anyone?" she asked.

No one wanted coffee and Eloise, bless her, repeated her offer to help with the dishes.

"Are you sure you don't mind?"

Eloise was sure and Lydia led her into the kitchen. It was time to get down to the real purpose of inviting these two. Daniel had been getting crank calls at the office for over a week, some half-hysterical girl demanding that the *Fort Elbow Catholic* do something about the so-called nun who was seducing Father Bullard at the Student Center.

"Maybe there's something in it, Dan," Lydia had said.

"Seduce is a transitive verb, my love. Philip Bullard is not some green curate susceptible to the wiles of a designing female. There have been rumors, however."

A little phoning around had convinced Lydia that there was something definitely afoot between Bullard and Eloise. Hence the invitation. The couple had to be shown that there were some lay people who sympathized with them and who would stand by them if they contemplated a serious step.

In the kitchen, herself washing, Eloise wiping, Lydia said, "Phil would have been a natural for that panel himself."

"I know. But the Center is everything to him. His whole life is there."

"You two are the most dedicated people I know."

Eloise blushed prettily. "Certainly Phil is."

"He thinks a lot of you too, that's obvious."

Eloise looked at her with alarm but Lydia soothed her with an understanding smile.

"I've heard, oh, I don't know how many discussions, but when you see the cruelty of celibacy in the concrete, well, it's enough to break your heart."

Silence.

"Lydia?"

"Yes."

For a moment Eloise just stared at her, clearly torn between the appeals of prudence and revelation.

"Go ahead, Eloise. Saying it is the first step."

"I have no one to talk to. No one."

"You can talk to me."

Lydia dried her hands. To hell with the dishes. She poured them each a cup of coffee and, seated at the kitchen table, Eloise talked her heart out. She was just a poor confused kid, Lydia decided, and head over heels in love. That meant a rough road ahead, for her and Phil. It meant leaving behind the work they both loved, leaving town too. They could not stay in Fort Elbow.

"When?" Lydia asked.

"We don't know. We just don't know. Oh, dear God, it is so good to be able to talk to someone about it. We have only each other and it has to be secretive. We have to pretend. It's awful. Honestly, there have been times when we thought of simply running away."

"That's understandable."

"But we want to do it right. Phil has to be laicized and I should be released from my vows."

"Have you both made applications for that?"

"Phil has."

Lydia lifted her cup and stared at its contents. "That could take years, Eloise."

"Years!"

Lydia nodded. "The real tragedy is that the swiftest way is to go ahead and marry. And then . . ."

"But that would be . . ." Her voice dropped away. Sinful? Surely she didn't expect Lydia to believe that all they had been doing up to now was holding hands.

"That's the tragedy. Bishops are actually forcing priests to commit sin. After the fact, laicization is just routine. How many priests have been laicized *before* they left?"

"I don't know."

Neither did Lydia, but the question had rhetorical force. "My advice would be to go ahead. If there is any fault, it's the bishop's, not yours."

She is pretty, Lydia thought. In a girlish, athletic way. How old is she? At the moment Eloise seemed a pathetic child.

"I still can't believe that this is happening."

Lydia patted her hand. "It's called love."

When they returned to the living room, they found Daniel in one of his more pontifical moods, lecturing Phil on the weaknesses of the Church in Fort Elbow.

"Can I get an interview with Caldron? Can I, for God's sake, even get in to see Yorick? That withered bitch of a woman at the chancery doesn't even know who I am."

"It could be worse," Phil said. "You might get in."

Dan laughed his piping laugh. He really cannot hold liquor, Lydia thought. Particularly when he starts this early in the day.

"I don't know what I'd do for information if it weren't for Brophy."

"Brophy's all right."

"Brophy's great! It will be a sad day for this diocese when he goes. I don't know why he hasn't gone already."

"He was only consecrated three years ago."

"Seniority, seniority," Daniel snarled. "But Brophy is a real leader. He could be a national leader."

Daniel had dreamed for so long of making a national impact himself that he had become obsessed with the idea, particularly since the phone call from NCR. He tipped his glass and some of his drink escaped the corner of his mouth and ran down his chin. He wiped at it with the back of his hand.

"I've got to get out of this burg," he said.

Bullard glanced at his watch and then at Eloise. "I think we should get going."

Thank you, thank you, good-bye, good-bye, but Daniel delayed them in the hall, getting back onto the subject of Bishop Caldron and Monsignor Yorick. Finally he subsided and Eloise and Phil skipped out to his car. Watching them, Lydia could not help wondering where they were off to now. She followed Daniel back into the living room.

"Daniel, it's true!"

"Of course it's true," he groused, his thoughts still on his ecclesiastical adversaries.

"I mean about them."

Daniel looked at her vacantly.

"Eloise and Phil Bullard. They want to get married."

"Well, I'll be damned."

"Maybe Father Ascue would like a TV dinner," Monsignor Entweder said when Hilda asked for menu suggestions. McTear guffawed, then grew serious.

"Television," he said with disgust. "Remember how great radio used to be? Now it's nothing but music, commercials, junk. It's a real shame."

"Are you criticizing Father Ascue's performance?" the pastor asked McTear, smiling roguishly.

"I didn't get a chance to see him. It was nine in the evening in Vienna." McTear always spoke with an Austrian duke on Sundays.

"How about pork roast?" Frank said to Hilda. There was no point in responding to Entweder's clumsy teasing about the televised panel.

"Is that okay with everybody?" Hilda asked.

It was okay with everybody. The pastor gathered up his napkin and, looking like an apprentice parachute packer, began to fold it.

"I'll take office hours this morning," he said. "To release the young for wider fields of endeavor."

"This is my day off," McTear reminded him.

"So it is." Entweder stood, the process affecting only his legs; his torso remained stooped and he looked at Frank over the rims of his glasses. "Did you get the message that Father Ewing telephoned?"

"Yes, I did."

"He seemed very anxious to speak with you."

The call had come when Frank was out and he simply was not up to returning it after his lunch with Bob Wintheiser.

"I won't be put off, Frank," Bob had said. "Of course you can get away for lunch. I'm coming and we're going."

Not to have gone after that would have seemed cowardice. Frank might be bored by Bob but he would not be intimidated.

"A drive-in?" Bob yelped, after asking Frank where he would like to go. He put his car in gear and it leaped away from the curb. "I might have known. You've gone completely mad."

"I'm almost completely broke."

"I suppose you just turn over your salary to SNCC or some other worthwhile charity. I'll pay for your lunch, Frank."

Bob did not even wait for their drinks to come before he began to discuss the panel.

"I watched it with Gilly, Frank. Can you imagine the humiliation? He kept saying: 'But he sat right here. He seemed solid as a rock.' Over and over. What was I supposed to say? Now he's convinced our whole class is corrupt. Even I may be suspect."

"He didn't like it?"

Bob dropped his frenetic manner. "What in God's name got into you, Frank? Do you realize the harm you've done?"

"To whom?"

The drinks came and Bob took his from the waiter's hand. He looked at Frank as he drank. "I could say *you*, Frank. It was like cutting your throat in public. Has the chancery said anything yet?"

"Yet?"

"Do you imagine you won't get called on the carpet? Of course you will. You're no Bullard, Frank. People may take you seriously. Do you think anyone listening to you won't think contraception is perfectly okay?"

"That isn't what I said."

"Oh, but you did. All they have to do is make up their own minds. Now what do you think that sounds like? It sounds as if the thing itself is neither right nor wrong, only neutral. All one needs is the proper attitude. Well, the proper attitude is very easily had."

"Bob, you know that when people talk of birth control they can mean any number of things."

"Right now it means only one thing. The pill."

"*The* pill?"

"What do you mean?"

"Bob, several very traditional moral theologians have suggested that some of the contraceptive pills are actually devices to aid nature, that they don't interfere with a natural process so much as assist it, and, consequently, don't fall under the principle according to which artificial means have been condemned. These are very traditional moralists, Bob. Not wild-eyed fanatics."

"And you accept their argument?"

"It is at least plausible. One thing is for certain—the matter is extremely complicated. In such circumstances, each confessor and each penitent has to make his own decision."

"That isn't what the pope said, Frank."

"Why do you suppose there's a papal commission to study the ban on contraception?"

"Pope John did that."

"And Pope Paul retained and enlarged the commission. What do you think all those people are doing?"

"Whatever they're doing, nothing has changed."

It was that kind of lunch. When Frank got back to Saint Waldo's, he was not sure what he had ordered or if he had eaten it. During the conversation he had stopped being angry with Bob and started feeling sorry for him. Bob could not deal with the most obvious difficulties with his position, but he was adamant. Frank sensed that his old friend would feel that the world was crumbling if he had to give up his inflexible view. There must be many priests like Bob. What they clung to was not a well thought out position but a familiar unexamined framework. That was why they reacted as to a personal attack when contraception was discussed in new ways.

There had been other reactions to the panel, favorable ones. Daniel

Donovan was ecstatic about the appearance in NCR of his account of the ecumenical conference.

"This thing is snowballing," he assured Frank. "I think you'd better ready yourself for national exposure, Father."

"Me? But there are dozens of people who would say what I said."

"Maybe. But you're young, you have a degree in theology, you've been blackballed in your own diocese—"

"Blackballed!"

"A man trained to teach theology made assistant pastor in a backward parish? What would you call it? Phil Bullard drew my attention to it, but of course it's obvious."

"The only thing that is obvious is that I'm at Saint Waldo's."

"Another thing," Donovan said, ignoring the disclaimer.

"What?"

"Hartshorne Prince. He's a native of Fort Elbow, you know. I phoned him yesterday and he is definitely interested. I sent him my articles airmail special delivery this morning. A network man is going to look at the taped discussion. You may be seeing yourself on the national news in a day or two, Father."

If he had ever dreamed of such a possibility, Frank would have hoped to react with aplomb, but he was filled with excitement. For an hour after his conversation with Donovan, he was literally dazed, as if some fraction of a minute on a network newscast was equivalent to the Beatific Vision. It was all he could do to keep away from the phone. He wanted to call Charlotte and tell her this. He lay on his bed, his mind reeling with the notion that millions of viewers from one end of the country to the other would hear his name, listen to him speak. He would be a spokesman for the Church in America! That night he watched Prince as if they were old colleagues, heard disappointment escape him like a gasp when the half hour was over and there had been no mention of the great debate in Fort Elbow, Ohio. A strange depression, then a resurgence of hope. There was always tomorrow.

He awoke during the night, roused by McTear's ascent from the basement or his own mad dreams, and lay thinking of the exhilaration and the euphoria that had coursed through him, that coursed through him still. The possibility of being the object of national attention had so captured his imagination that, he realized with terror, he would do almost anything to get it. Was this what had gripped Phil Bullard, if only on a smaller scale? That lofty addendum seemed a symptom of his state. He forced himself to repress his excitement, tried to clear his head and regain perspective. Could he remember anyone other than politicians who had figured in Prince's newscasts during the previous week? He could not. How evanescent such fame, or notoriety, was. It frightened him to see how the mere possibility of it affected him and he began to hope that Prince, just because he was a native of Fort Elbow, would be disinclined to take seriously anything that happened here.

After Mass the following morning, his hopes leaped up once more and the day seemed aimed at Prince's program. And Frank did appear. The clip figured in a Princely essay on the current turmoil in the Catholic Church, its proximate background in the Vatican Council, its present manifestations, its likely direction. Frank's face looked out at America for perhaps ten seconds but, gripping the arms of his chair as if gravity were insufficient to keep him in it, he followed his own words with complete absorption. Until he went to bed that night, an interval filled by congratulatory calls, he walked as unweighted men would tread the moon.

"We made it," Donovan said in choked tones.

"I saw it."

"Congratulations."

"The same to you." Donovan had drawn fleeting mention as the bright and innovative editor of the diocesan newspaper in Fort Elbow.

Bishop Brophy, Oder, Tremplin, Bullard and, of course, Charlotte phoned. And Father Ewing, who said he would like to have a chat, soon. Frank went out for cigarettes, half expecting to be mobbed when he entered the drugstore, but of course no one gave the slightest indication of having seen him on national television.

Two days later, Father Ewing was pacing the seminary road when Frank drove up in McTear's car. He closed his book but retained a preoccupied air when Frank, having parked the car, walked toward him.

"I'm reminded of a few months ago when you came here from the chancery."

"It seems longer ago than that."

"Doesn't it? Care to go in or would you like to stroll?"

"I could use some exercise."

They walked to the gate and back again and then along the peripheral path which marked the limits of the seminary grounds. Memories of hundreds of such walks came back to Frank, evening walks after supper, enjoying a cigarette, exchanging the endless intramural gossip that occupied so much of seminary life: of classes and exams, of the faculty, of books being read.

"I've been following your career," Ewing said sardonically.

"At Saint Waldo's?"

"Ha." Ewing scuffed along with downcast eyes, then stopped abruptly. "Frank, you're all wet on this birth control thing. There isn't going to be any change in the Church's teaching. If I were a betting man, I would bet anything on that."

"I might take the bet."

"Might? You sounded surer on television."

Frank hesitated. He did not want to ask the older man what kind of contact with lay people he had recently, what sense he had of their impatience. A rule that no one obeys is a very dangerous sort of rule; widespread ignoring of it was a species of refutation. That could lead to the ignoring of more fundamental teachings as well.

"Let me ask you this, Father. Would you want to defend the traditional position, natural law, all of it? Even those on the papal commission who favor the traditional teaching admit that they cannot defend it."

"Of course they can defend it," Ewing said. "So can you."

"No, Father, I can't. I mean it."

"What is the purpose of marriage?"

"There are several."

"All right. But what is the main one?"

It was a reminder of exams. Frank knew the answers that Father Ewing wanted. The chief end of marriage is the having, nurture and education of children. The end of marriage is the *bonum prolis,* the good of the child. It would have been easy to tick off those answers; the difficulty lay in handling the objections to them. Even the rhythm method was a recognition that not every act of intercourse had to aim at a possible pregnancy.

"How does nature provide for the good of the child, Father? After a woman gives birth, she isn't immediately capable of having another child. There is a cycle of fertile and infertile periods. Why? Say it is because, if a woman were constantly fertile, she could not humanly care for the children she has. Now, if a pill simply ensures infertility, it is aiding and perfecting a natural provision for the good of the child."

Ewing shook his head. "That isn't what these pills do. Some are abortive. Others sterilize."

"Granted there are pills and pills. But even if there is none now which would act in a way I described, no doubt one could be devised. If it were, do you think it would be morally wrong to use it?"

"Yes. It would still be an artificial means."

"So is bottle feeding."

"You know that doesn't apply."

"Father, what of the majority report of the papal commission?"

"What report?"

"It's been published. Someone leaked it to the press. They favor a change, Father, and the majority is sizable."

"Who published it?"

"The NCR."

Ewing's jaw dropped. "And you accept it as authentic?"

"I don't think anyone has questioned its authenticity."

"Well, I do. I question anything that appears in that rag. I can't stand to read it anymore. In any case, the commission is not the pope."

"But the pope wouldn't ignore the advice of a commission he himself appointed."

"If they advise artificial means, of course he'll ignore them."

"I hate to think what would happen if he did."

"What do you mean?"

"People wouldn't accept it. Bishops, theologians, lay people."

Ewing smiled grimly. "Henry the Eighth."

"It's not the same thing."

"The principle is. The Church would lose a whole country rather than give up a principle."

It was useless, Frank decided. He hated to argue with Father Ewing. The only effect of their talk was to convince Frank that what he had said on that panel was reasonable. Ewing was too ready to hurl anathemas, to stigmatize his adversaries as heretics, to do just about anything but address the issue. Surely the pope would not behave like that. The very fact that he was taking so much time on the matter was proof that he did not find it simple. Even if the pope were to do what Ewing hoped, it would be too late. His very conscientiousness in weighing the matter so long had created a vacuum into which theologians and confessors had entered, anticipating his decision, presuming that he would alter the Church's position. Given this, it was conceivable that the pope would end by saying nothing, simply let things go on as they were going. Better that than to react as Father Ewing would, attempting to saddle people with a teaching no one seemed able to defend.

"Frank, if you can't accept the Church's teaching, if you don't understand it, the least you can do is to remain silent. Caldron won't tolerate a public attack."

It was a low blow to invoke the specter of disciplinary action by the bishop. Frank had not heard from the chancery. He had never seriously thought he would. Until now. Reacquainted with Ewing's intransigence and suspecting that he might very well represent the official view of the diocese, Frank could imagine himself receiving some kind of admonition. A remark of Bishop Brophy's, gnomic enough, now seemed a veiled promise of support if Yorick or Caldron raised a fuss. He began to feel what Donovan had called him, blackballed, silenced, conspired against.

The door of the main building opened and Father Sweeney appeared, old, bent, squinting against the sun.

"You young men should be out golfing on a day like this."

Sweeney came down the steps and joined them and they talked of the weather, of the unusual temperateness of late July, not too hot, not too cold.

"Except at night," Father Sweeney said. "It cools down wonderfully at night and I find I can sleep right through without getting all knotted up."

"Well, Frank," Father Ewing said. "I'll let you go."

"Off to the golf course, Father?" Sweeney asked Ewing.

"I might get in nine holes at that." Ewing spoke like a drunk suggesting that he would have just one. Everyone knew that his summer was spent tramping an endless fairway.

Frank remained with Father Sweeney after Ewing had gone inside. The ancient spiritual director of the seminary, his cassock shiny and so old it seemed faintly green in the sunlight, looked at Frank with clear alert eyes.

"You seem troubled, Father."

"Not really. Father Ewing and I were having a very difficult discussion."

"He is quite upset by the line you've been taking."

"I know."

"Is everything else all right?"

"Yes, Father. Thank you."

"Why don't we get in out of the sun? Or are you in a rush to be off?"

The prospect of a chat with Father Sweeney was suddenly attractive. It had always been a pleasure to drop by the old priest's rooms as a seminarian. Sweeney had been Frank's confessor and spiritual adviser, unfailingly sympathetic; the fifty years in his post had not dulled his interest or compassion, though the difficulties of young men studying for the priesthood must have come to seem highly predictable to him.

"I have been reading the most extraordinary book," Father Sweeney said when they were comfortably settled on wicker rockers on the porch of the main building. "An account of some recent apparitions of the Blessed Virgin in Spain. Garabandal. I'm probably mispronouncing the name. Reminiscent of both Fatima and Lourdes, particularly of

331

Fatima. I've been amusing myself with the thought of visiting there, though from all accounts the village is all but inaccessible."

Father Sweeney had always had a keen interest in Lourdes and Fatima, alluding to them often in his conferences to the seminarians.

"Wasn't it remarkable that the pope flew to Fatima?"

Frank had forgotten about that. How quickly we have become used to the pope flying about the world. Not that that had been the first papal recognition of the appearances of the Blessed Virgin to some Portuguese peasant children in 1917. Father Sweeney would have been a young man at the time those strange events, witnessed by thousands, skeptics and otherwise, had occurred.

"Was there anything about them in the papers at the time?"

"Oh, I'm sure there was. Somewhere on the back page. I don't remember reading anything about it then, though. For that matter, have we read of these Garabandal happenings?"

"I haven't."

"It's no wonder. We are so benumbed by sensational events we wouldn't give it a thought anyway."

"One of our parishioners who died recently was extremely interested in Fatima."

"Of course, of course."

"She was very curious about the secret revelations."

"Ah, well. Did she know that they had been published? In Germany, I believe."

"I'm sure she didn't. What was the secret?"

Frank had spoken in a light, almost bantering tone and Father Sweeney frowned out at the lawn.

"It is very interesting, Father. And not a little frightening. It concerns the second half of the twentieth century. Now. The Blessed Mother told those children that in the second half of the century there would be grievous dissension within the Church. Bishop would attack bishop and cardinal cardinal. There would be attacks on the pope himself. Unless . . . "

The message of Fatima was penance, prayer, devotion to Mary, the sacraments. If men did not turn from vice and pursue virtue, great evils would befall the world. Frank had read the earlier almost apocalyptic messages, those which had predicted a second world war and the atomic bomb. He supposed that he accepted them, though of course he need not. It was difficult not to feel a chill of apprehension while reading such things, difficult not to become curious for more clues as to what the future would bring. But that was a curiosity best kept in check; when it got out of hand, a certain fatalism ensued or one lost sight of

332

the major means of salvation: the Mass, the sacraments, prayer. Frank had known seminarians, and others, who had been carried away by their interest in private revelations. There had always been a flourishing sub rosa industry providing mimeographed accounts of strange happenings in South Dakota, a stigmatic in Chicago, unlikely events in unlikely places.

When Frank rose to go, Father Sweeney walked with him to McTear's car. As they approached it, the squawk of the citizen band became audible. Father Sweeney looked on in amazement while Frank answered. Hilda told him that Lydia Donovan was trying to reach him.

"Did she say what she wanted?"

"No. But it sounded important."

Frank signed off and Father Sweeney shook his head.

"Ingenious."

On the way back to Saint Waldo's, Frank thought of the parallel between leaking the majority report of the papal commission to the press and the unsanctioned printing of the secret of Fatima. Similar and yet so different. Father Sweeney's credulity bothered Frank, and he was bothered by being bothered. Certainly Sweeney had always been a level-headed spiritual adviser. How to express it? Well, he thought, imagine going on television and speaking matter-of-factly of what the Blessed Virgin Mary had said to some illiterate children in Portugal and Spain. Imagine doing that while flanked by Pomodore and Plummet-Finch. Everyone would think him mad. But were the Incarnation, the Resurrection, Christ's miracles, less incredible? Those basic mysteries of faith become so familiar we no longer sense how extraordinary it is to accept them.

A traffic snarl distracted him and, when he was out of it, he remembered Mrs. Donovan. What could she have been calling about?

Eloise stood at the window of the motel unit looking out at the blue-green surface of the pool. It all seemed make-believe. The sculpted concrete basin, that unreal water, a tiled apron on which, in chairs, a few people sat. Bodies. Some kids in the water, their heads like bobbing apples, their voices muted and distant, like some party of her childhood. Games. Happy laughter. The novitiate too. She pressed her eyes shut. Phil was off somewhere, getting ice, getting liquor. They did not need ice, she did not want a drink. The room was very cool, almost cold. She shivered and opened her eyes.

The lifeguard was a girl. She sat apart from the bathers, her long slim body baked brown from a summer beside that pool. Her hair was pinned up in back, she wore giant sunglasses which emphasized the delicacy of her profile. Beside her chair there was a cloth bag with a braided handle and a design stitched on it, giving the effect of a sampler. She was knitting, the mechanical task permitting her to keep an eye on those kids in the pool.

Eloise turned and looked at the room: plastic, veneer, dresser, chairs, lamps. A television set. It all looked unused and new. This motel, near the Interstate, had not existed last summer, the land on which it stood had recently been only a field, some portion of a farm. What had it been used for before it became a farm? A hundred years ago, a thousand years ago? She thought, with a sense of the elusiveness of reality, that this bit of space had always been here, its contours changing, under water, under ice, emerging into air and put to any number of uses, but mainly just a scene which altered without reference to human beings. And now this cube of a room with its standardized furniture, a resting place for travelers. Or for illicit lovers. The beds. Two huge beds. She turned back to the window.

Like that girl knitting out there, her concern for others had been generic, almost impersonal, everyone, no one in particular. Those in trouble, those who needed her. All that was going to change. Her love would be concentrated now on Phil, primarily on him; only the surplus would be available for others. Just as that girl would eventually marry and forget the summer hours by the pool, on guard, fulfilling a function.

The door opened and Phil came in, holding a plastic bucket high. His look was triumphant, his smile untroubled. She ran to him and he took her in his arms and she was conscious of his male smell, of the strong arms holding her against him. Bodies. She had forgotten that people are bodies, bone, flesh, sinews, heat and smell, and this choking desire that filled her with sadness and joy made her want to sob helplessly. Phil loosened his embrace and stepped back.

"Now for a drink."

She nodded, her smile forced. No matter where she turned, she saw him. The dresser was at least six feet wide and there was a mirror equally large on the wall behind it. A reflected Phil freed plastic glasses from their wrappers, dumped ice cubes into them, picked up the bottle he had brought. When he handed her a glass, she put it immediately to her lips, pretending she wanted it, that the smell and taste of liquor did not evoke the faintest promise of nausea.

She had not been surprised when he had brought her here, though he had said nothing of where they were going. He did not seem to feel as awkward and frightened as she did, thank God. God. She did not want to think of God. She did not want to think at all. Phil went to the window and drew the drapes and that was better. He came back and sat on the bed, patting a spot beside him. There was no doubt in the world why they were here, but for a moment she wanted to play dumb, to pretend surprise. But the moment for protest had long since passed. If she had been going to say anything, she should have spoken when he pulled in at the motel, when he told her to wait while he went in and got a room, when he returned and drove to the door of their unit. She had put herself entirely into his hands. Whatever they were doing was his decision. She had abdicated when she left the apartment and fled to the Center and Phil. She went and sat beside him on the bed. When she felt his arm about her, she went stiff. He tugged her toward him and she relented, almost collapsed against him, seeking some place to lay her head. He brought his glass to his mouth and she heard him swallow.

"I love you," he whispered.

She nodded. Love. That was the explanation.

"You're my wife."

That husky remark seemed to sanction what they were doing. Phil went on talking, the sound of his voice soothing; she did not really listen to what he said. He would leave and she would leave, they would leave together and then—but the sequel promised only happiness. He put his glass down on the table beside the bed, stretching to do so, and she clung to him and then his arms were tightly around her and she closed her eyes and lifted her face. With his lips on hers, in a darkness produced by her closed lids, she felt his hands upon her create a shocked tremor. Oh God, God. She pressed her mouth painfully against his, wanting him, hating this, allowing him to ease her back upon the bed, desire rising in her, trying not to think of her body, of her underwear, of the faint sound of kids playing in the pool outside the window.

FORT ELBOW, OHIO, July 25—Rev. Philip Bullard, a Roman Catholic priest of the Fort Elbow diocese, was married today to Sister Eloise Leger in the chapel of the Catholic Student Center here, where Father Bullard is the director. The ceremony was performed by Father John Tremplin, a member of the faculty of the Fort Elbow Seminary, and was attended by close friends and followers of the couple.

Father Bullard's controversial direction of the Catholic Student Center has attracted local attention. His marriage today raises serious questions about his ability to remain in his post. In reply to questions put to him after the brief ceremony, Father Bullard indicated that he had not been dispensed by his superiors from his vow of celibacy. Asked if his marriage could be regarded as an act of defiance, he said, "I find that a strange question. I married Eloise because I love her. If our marriage has significance beyond that, and I suppose it does, whatever we might wish, perhaps it will stand as a symbolic and prophetic deed. I certainly would not mind if other priests, caught in the anguishing web of the celibate life by a youthful promise made on the basis of inadequate knowledge, took courage from our action. Dissent from the rule of celibacy is widespread today, both here and abroad," Father Bullard said. "The bishops can ignore this only at the risk of courting real disaster."

While the bridegroom spoke, his new wife stood at his side, pretty and serene, nodding agreement with what he said. Asked about their future plans, neither was able to give a definite answer.

Father Bullard said, "Of course I—my wife and I—would like to continue our work here at the Center, but that does not seem likely. At any rate, this is the kind of work we want to do, dealing with young people and their problems, bringing to them the message of charity and justice in more relevant forms."

Sister Eloise, a parochial school teacher in this city, came to work at the Center this summer. With two other nuns of her order, she has been living in an apartment in an impoverished neighborhood nearby. Their residence had been described as an experiment in a new mode of life for nuns.

The new Mrs. Bullard wore a powder blue suit. A yellow rose was pinned next to the simple gold cross which, she said, indicated that she is a nun. When asked if she had received permission to marry, she looked to her husband, who said no.

Inquiries at the chancery of the Fort Elbow diocese drew only a No Comment from the Right Reverend Rabanus Yorick. Father Ewing, professor of moral theology at the seminary, and a colleague of Father Tremplin, said that, if the marriage had taken place as reported, Father Bullard is automatically excommunicated from the Roman Catholic Church. An excommunicated Catholic cannot participate in the sacraments of the Church. In Father Bullard's case, Father Ewing went on, there would be suspension of faculties as well. This means that Father Bullard can no longer say Mass or perform other priestly functions. Father Ewing declined to comment on what action might be taken against Father Tremplin.

Father Tremplin said, "I considered it my obligation, under both canon and civil law, to perform this marriage ceremony. Has love no rights?"

Monsignor Yorick's office seemed less of a haven now. He could imagine hordes of screwballs marshaling in the hall, preparing to crash in upon him with questions and demands. "What in the name of God is happening in the Catholic Church?" The chancellor's much-thumbed copy of that blast by the *National Review* no longer delivered up the consolation it once had done; now the titular question seemed a threat.

Miss Muscatelli's account of the Bullard wedding looked up at him from the open newspaper on his desk. While he read the story, one of Yorick's hands had drifted to the phone; he felt an impulse to call out the troops, sound the alarm, press the panic button. But of course Bishop Caldron would already have seen the story. It was Tremplin's appeal to canon law that infuriated the chancellor. One stole home

336

from second base and appealed to the umpire for support. Well, Tremplin would catch hell and no mistake. He would be out on his ear. He would howl, of course, and the newspapers and television would pay more attention to his yelping than to the fact that he had, by his action, suspended himself. Why couldn't there be at least one newspaper that presented this kind of crazy news for what it was?

The *Fort Elbow Catholic?* Look at the way Donovan had featured that ridiculous ecumenical conference. Rumors had come to Yorick that Donovan considered himself to be working under the heavy hand of censorship. My God! The paper pretty effectively concealed the fact that George Caldron was the ordinary of the diocese. Its pages were crammed with Brophy and Bullard. And Ascue.

Ascue. Monsignor Yorick had been flabbergasted by Tony Calcaterra's linking of Ascue and the little data processor at Millikens. Horvath had got her out of town, thank God. The chancellor wanted to doubt Tony's story about Ascue. The son of a gun had not been all that accurate on Bullard. Why hadn't his report mentioned the nun? Still, Tony had been half right on Bullard and it was difficult to discount entirely what he had said about Ascue. What were things coming to when you could not even trust a man trained in Rome? Ewing had really been shaken by his protégé's flirting with heresy.

"I want you to know that I'll stay on here indefinitely," Ewing had said to the chancellor.

"Good," Yorick said but immediately he bristled. Ewing would damned well stay where Caldron put him.

"I don't want Frank Ascue replacing me," Ewing said sadly. "And that is something I would not have believed a few months ago."

The trouble was that Ewing could not last forever. Eventually he would have to be replaced. And so would Tremplin, immediately. Yorick rubbed his face with both hands like a Neapolitan. Maybe it was a good thing enrollment at the seminary was down so low. They could get by with a reduced faculty by doubling loads. That would raise a few howls but it would not be the first time seminary professors had felt oppressed by the chancery.

There was another source of the chancellor's despondency, one that he was reluctant to admit even to himself; he feared that Caldron would react as he had too often of late. Patience, procrastination, no lowering of the boom. Yorick dreaded the possibility of a bland statement, post facto laicization and bye-bye Bullard.

He was startled by the buzz of the intercom and Caldron's request that he come in. How had George got into his office without being seen?

337

Yorick's sense that life in the chancery had changed profoundly increased. He did not even know when the boss was in.

Bishop Caldron sat frowning at his desk, his pudgy hands folded before him.

"Philip Bullard appears to have lost patience with us, Monsignor. When did he make his second request for laicization?"

"Two weeks ago. Tomorrow."

"He can scarcely complain of the law's delay, can he?"

"His first request came in last May."

"Last May," the bishop mused. "Two months ago. How swift the course of true love is."

"The bride is a nun."

"Even so," Caldron said enigmatically. "Had we heard from her?"

"No."

"I'd like you to contact her superiors to see if they are as surprised by this as we are. I will see Father Tremplin at once."

"Good," Yorick cried, and the bishop's brows raised. "Do you want to issue a statement on the marriage?"

"Yes."

Action at last. Yorick returned to his office with a bouncing step. Tremplin first. His dialing finger gouged the eyeless holes, digit to digit. Tremplin's voice quivered over the wire.

"Today?"

"In the bishop's exact words, at once. I trust you can make it, Father."

"Well, if this is a summons . . . "

"That is exactly what it is."

Yorick banged down the phone with satisfaction. This is what they should have done from the beginning, when Bullard began to act up. A few heads on the block might have saved the neighborhood. You have to let people know who is boss. Caldron's motto, *Illum oportet crescere,* had never struck Yorick as apt, particularly since it evoked the *me autem minui* of the text from which it was taken. That God's increase might be man's decrease was a nice thought, unless that man was a bishop. On those not infrequent occasions when he had permitted his thoughts to pursue the daydreams of ambition and had imagined his own coat of arms, Yorick favored such possibilities as *Quaerens quem devorat.* He had mentioned this once, on a fourth Scotch at a priests' retreat and with no reference to himself, and been reminded that Saint Peter had been speaking of the devil. "Which is what a bishop should be ready to give his clergy," Yorick replied, unglad for the taunting. Now, finally, Caldron had his back up and Yorick did not envy young Tremplin the session that awaited him. He could not resist the hope that

Tremplin would attempt to debate with the bishop. George Caldron did few things better than lead an upstart adversary to the precipice. Remember that his going easy on Brophy had led to those sweet weeks of exile in June.

Brophy. Yorick picked up his phone. The call to the mother superior could wait.

The surprise of Bullard's marriage had rekindled in Bishop Brophy the desire to escape from Fort Elbow before the place went up in smoke. This was certain to bring a crackdown and Sean Brophy had no wish to be George Caldron's agent in any effort to whip his clergy into line. It seemed a good time to consult his eastern mentors and get the lay of the land. Decisions on two dioceses, good ones, and a third not unthinkable were still pending and he wanted to know where he stood.

The news was not encouraging. The gist of the message was that he was being insufficiently wise as a serpent and not quite as simple as a dove. Brophy listened with a renewed distaste for vatic pronouncements further obscured by Scriptural double-talk.

"Your statement on the seminary strike hurt you, Sean," the archbishop said. "It hurt you in New York and, worse, it hurt you in Washington. You have acquired the label of the fiery young liberal of the American hierarchy."

The pleasure of knowing that he was discussed in the East was of course diminished by the apparent drift of the discussion. Not that Sean Brophy did not accept the label mentioned.

"What did *you* think of my statement?"

"It is not my reaction we are talking about." A promise of sharpness came into the cultivated voice. "In any case, the Delegate is aware of my interest in you."

"Have the appointments been made?"

"I am afraid so."

Brophy sighed. The American hierarchy was not unlike the railroad, for which his father had worked. One grew old as a fireman, waiting for some decrepit engineer to retire or die. Bishops were no more likely to retire from their sees than engineers from their cabs and they had the same perverse longevity.

"It's been nearly three years," Brophy said, trying to keep his voice level. "Three years in Fort Elbow, Ohio."

"Indeed." The archbishop had not been in favor of Sean's accepting the appointment as Caldron's auxiliary, but Brophy had not dared pass up the chance, fearful another might not come. His background had not bred into him any confident sense of droit du seigneur.

"I know. You told me so."

"I believe I did point out possible pitfalls. But come now, cheer up. Perhaps there is some way you can balance the impression you've made."

Touch all the bases? Mend a few fences? Of course he could do that. But was that really the answer? The rasping voice of the cardinal, the next man he called, said definitely not.

"You go on being Sean Brophy, do you hear? No trimming of sail now. One, it won't work and, two, there is such a thing as the vanguard. Don't shun the label they've stuck on you. Earn it. Be what you are, and what they know you are, and they won't be able to hold you back. They accept me now, if only as a crank, but at your age I couldn't have been the auxiliary in Podunk. These are different times. Go with the spirit of the Council, Sean. Speak out. Bother them good. The rest will take care of itself."

"Eventually?"

"Maybe sooner than you think."

Bishop Brophy grasped that promissory straw, went with the cardinal and against the archbishop, telephoned Don Oder.

"Thank God we had the sense to keep Bullard off the senate. And the ecumenical conference." The pastor of Saint Barnabas sighed in troubled relief.

"I wish he had been on both," Brophy said.

"You're not serious."

"Oh, but I am. In any case, it's too late now. Don, did you have any idea what Bullard was up to?"

"I hardly knew the man."

"We should have known, Don. We have to know everything that affects moving this diocese in the direction set by the Council. We goofed on Bullard. I just hope that he gets his bride out of town fast. The issue now is John Tremplin."

"Tremplin!"

"I suppose you hardly know him either."

"Sean, Tremplin is in deep and deserved trouble. You know that. Canon law—"

"His status in canon law is one thing. There are other considerations. We cannot let George Caldron crucify Father Tremplin."

"He's bound to suspend him."

"Is he? To which canon do you refer?"

"You know that he'll be suspended."

Brophy let his annoyance pass. A leader had to shore up his troops when the going got rough. Saint Crispin, pray for us.

"Don, it is precisely that legalistic image we have to shed. What after all did Tremplin do? Look at it through the eyes of your average American, Catholic or not. A young couple wanted to marry. Tremplin is deputized by both civil and Church law to perform marriages. If he refused them, if everyone in his position refused them, what is that couple supposed to do? Live in sin?"

"They are anyway. The marriage ceremony didn't prevent that. And now Tremplin's in the same boat."

"And out of Peter's bark?"

"What are you getting at, Sean?"

"A meeting of the senate."

"Oh, no!"

"Oh, yes. Look, I am not asking that you say what Tremplin did is kosher. Not at all. You can emphasize that he acted contrary to the letter of the law. Do emphasize that. But at the same time, point to the positive side of what he did. His compassion, his disponibility, his courage."

"Do you know Tremplin, Sean?"

"I've met him, of course."

"He's no tiger, believe me."

"All the more reason for him to know that a substantial number of his fellow priests are in sympathy—partial sympathy—with what he did."

"How do you figure in all this?" Oder asked after a pause.

"I am with you all the way. You'll see."

But first Oder had to be made to see the desirability of the course being urged upon him. Patient suasion over forty-five minutes instilled the beginnings of passion in the prudent pastor of Saint Barnabas.

"It's time we stood up and were counted, Don."

"Just to be knocked down and counted out?"

"One or two might run that risk, yes. But all of us?" Brophy let that sink in. It was the main point, really. George Caldron would be left with no alternative to tempering justice with mercy. He would not want to face, or even seem to face, a general revolt by his clergy.

The conversation with Oder, added to his eastern calls, seemed a full day's work. But Brophy had no opportunity to rest on his laurels. His phone began to ring as soon as he hung it up. It was Monsignor Yorick.

"You on a party line or something? I've been trying to reach you all morning."

"We must install a hot line."

"What do you make of Bullard?"

"Is George upset?"

"Now what do you think? Bullard had made a request to be laicized but apparently he couldn't wait. A couple lousy months and he couldn't wait."

Brophy smiled. Yorick was beyond belief. The two laicizations that had gone by the book in Fort Elbow had taken three years apiece.

"What is George's reaction to John Tremplin?"

"He's in with the bishop now. Why don't you come over? We should put up a united front. The publicity on this thing hasn't even begun."

"Has George asked for me?"

"Do you need a special invitation?"

"Now, Monsignor. I do have a crowded schedule."

"Yeah. Well, maybe George will send for you anyway." Yorick paused and Brophy could imagine him stroking his hair. "Tremplin. Did I ever tell you of the conversation I had with that guy a couple years ago?"

"I believe you did."

"So I really can't say I'm surprised."

"I suppose not."

"What gets into these guys, Sean? Can you tell me that?"

"I wish I could. I wish I had the time."

"They're nuts. It's the only explanation. Sometimes I think we ought to have them all psychoanalyzed before they're ordained."

Brophy, who had once commended the growing practice of providing psychological counseling in seminaries and been answered by Yorick's highly imaginative and unflattering thumbnail sketch of Freud, smiled joylessly.

"You may be right, Monsignor. You may be right."

Frank Ascue stood with Sheila Rupp looking out at the asphalt playground where so short a time ago Eloise had been skipping rope with the kids, her veil dancing with the effort. It was easy to think that if the summer program here had been approved by Entweder, the nun would never have come to know Phil Bullard, at least so well. If only she had spent her summer at the mother house with the other nuns. If, if, if . . . Given Phil's previous involvement with Diane, Frank wondered how solid the marriage would be. Poor Eloise. Would she eventually look back with regret to the day that she had met Phil Bullard on this playground?

"She lived right over there, didn't she?" Sheila asked.

"Who?"

"The nun who married the priest."

"Yes, she did."

"I hope they'll be happy."

And that, Frank thought afterward, was at least a different reaction. Others had expressed rage or shock, triumph or amusement; the simple human hope that Eloise and Phil would be happy was refreshing. Among the clergy, the fact of the marriage had disappeared behind abstract discussions of celibacy, authority, obedience. John Tremplin's suspension had been all but eclipsed by the generalized debate.

Bishop Caldron's statement had been crisp and correct. There was no justification for what Tremplin had done and he must have known what fate awaited him. He might have longed for that fate; Tremplin had a compulsion to be a victim. His remark, quoted in the newspaper, repeated when he was suspended, seemed somehow pathetic and self-referring. Has love no rights?

When Oder called to tell him of the senate meeting, he asked Frank if he was free for lunch. Frank said he was.

"Just you and I and Bishop Brophy."

They had lunch in the hotel where the ecumenical meeting had been held and, alluding to that, Brophy said, "Let's hope this lunch will preface another triumph. You did a splendid job on TV, Frank. It is more important than ever now that the voices of reason and moderation be heard."

There are those, Brophy went on, patiently if sadly, and they are undoubtedly sincere and zealous men, who persist in retaining a notion of the Church which has been superseded by Vatican II. These good men regard the current ferment with suspicion. He smiled. "They literally think that the Church is coming apart at the seams." Well, they are right. It is. The old Church is crumbling. But of course the seamless garment of the essential Church survives. Dialogue, questioning, searching, yes, even doubt, characterize our times. Disputed questions cannot be settled by appeal to a book of outdated rules. We must be innovative, compassionate, sensitive to the Spirit. To make a long story short, we have to prevent the Tremplin case from turning into a scandal that would irreparably damage the Church in Fort Elbow.

"It seems to have died down," Frank said.

"If only that were true."

"Does he intend to appeal?"

Brophy and Oder exchanged a glance. "We need your help, Frank," the bishop said.

At the moment, the bishop said, Tremplin was crushed, near the breaking point. "Apparently he is fearful that if he leaves his room he will return to find his things moved out of it. So he has holed up at the seminary." Bishop Brophy sipped his daiquiri. "Father Swivel has been with him, trying to keep him calm. Unfortunately, he does not seem to be the man for the job. For one thing, he doesn't really like Tremplin. Never has, it seems. Well, we have enough trouble without adding a personality conflict. Tremplin must be made to see that he has sympathy and support, that there is still hope."

Frank said, "Maybe he should move out of the seminary."

"Oh, no," Oder said. "Then he would seem to be acquiescing. Legally he is in the wrong, there's no doubt of that. The need is to push the whole affair beyond legalism so that his deed can be seen in a new light. Tremplin made the point himself. Has love no rights?"

"A higher tribunal," Brophy said, turning his glass slowly. "What do you think, Frank?"

"You want me to talk to Tremplin?"

Brophy put down his drink. "Take him under your wing, Frank. Bolster his spirits. Let him know that in the coming meeting of the senate his case will be considered. Sympathetically. In a new light. You're the only one who can do it, Frank."

Frank looked at the two men hunched toward him. He wanted to object that he did not know Tremplin well, that he did not like what he did know. If Swivel had a personality conflict, so did he. He recalled Tremplin telling him of saying Mass in the trunk room, his paranoid remarks about Eisenbarth. "Why me?"

"Tremplin has asked for you," Oder said.

"*We* need you, Frank."

How could he refuse? Jack Tremplin faded into the background. The important thing was that the auxiliary bishop of the diocese and the president of the clerical senate were asking his help, telling him he was indispensable.

"All right. I'll talk to Jack."

He returned to the rectory as to a provincial outpost, come from the very font of power and influence. McTear was in the kitchen, tinkering with Hilda's end of the citizen band. Entweder was in his study, napping in a leather chair. The house seemed dead, a joke. In front of Entweder was the map of the parish on which the pattern of census calls was recorded. Frank tiptoed by the pastor and rearranged the flagged pins haphazardly.

That night Frank was wakened from a restless sleep by the ringing of his telephone. A sick parishioner, fearful of his approaching end? He groped for and found the phone.

"Father Frank Ascue?"

"Yes. Who is it?"

"Bishop Brophy suggested I call you. Your degree is in theology, right?"

"Moral. Why?"

"Great. What we're doing is rounding up theologians to sign a statement on the new encyclical. We want to grab the ball and run with it before the bishops say anything."

"Encyclical? What encyclical?"

There was a gasp on the line. "Haven't you heard?"

"No. What happened?"

"Pope Paul has just issued an encyclical reaffirming the traditional ban against birth control."

Part Five

1 Frank Ascue's image of his personal past was a line whose calibrations represented the months and years of his life and which he could trace backward to six, five, four, to the vague point where his memories stopped. For historical time he had the image of the globe itself which, spun counterclockwise in the mind, revealed the centuries, each arriving over the horizon unaltered, the constant in the constant change of the earth on which those dramas had been played. Rewinding history to the time of empire, Frank reversed the direction of memory, turned the globe slowly, watched the christening of the West, the fusion of religious, cultural and political streams which had made Europe and later her colonies what they distinctively were. The relics of that past were scattered in the present century, in monuments and mottoes, in our language if not in our hearts. Like the altar Paul found in Athens, they spoke of an unknown God, a forgotten God. The West had long since been unchristened.

Frank knew he shared a cultural ambience with unbelievers, knew that he as well as they read with distaste of faith healers or those visionaries who gather on hillsides awaiting the end which does not come. For most of his contemporaries, the believer, the priest, is not different from the evangelistic quack with secret information about the end of the world. The Incarnation, the Passion, the Resurrection, heavenly bliss are no longer part of the common cultural lore. Frank recognized his own divided mind, a mind only half baptized; like anyone else he found the objects of religious faith antagonistic, strange, out of step with the times.

This sense of a division within him increased in the wake of the issuance by Pope Paul VI of his encyclical letter *Humanae Vitae*. With half his mind, Frank regarded that distant hollow-eyed figure enunciating his unexpected and discordant edicts as he might have the Dalai Lama. A citizen of what has been called a contraceptive culture, he heard the head of his Church, the bishop of Rome, the successor of Saint

Peter, the vicar of Christ on earth, declare that contraception is in and of itself immoral. He heard and inevitably reacted, at least in part, much as did his non-Catholic and unbelieving contemporaries—with shock, outrage and disbelief. And of course this was news, big news, and the startled Catholic would read the story, hear it discussed on television, realizing as he did that to his fellow citizens he was now emphatically in the same class as stage-struck wonder-workers and those small sad crowds huddled on a morning hillside expecting the world's last day.

The morning after he had received the surprising telephone call from Washington, Frank Ascue returned from saying Mass to find both Monsignor Entweder and McTear still in the dining room. The pastor hummed and rattled the newspaper and McTear smiled strangely at Frank and then looked away.

"Oh, good morning, Father," Entweder said, as if he had not noticed Frank come in. "I was absorbed in the paper."

The pastor disappeared from view, holding the paper wide before him so that the story on the encyclical was facing Frank. McTear cleared his throat but said nothing. This tableau was disturbed by Hilda's entrance with Frank's eggs. She stopped to stare at Entweder.

"Are you still here, Monsignor? Didn't you get enough to eat?"

But it was McTear who rose, mumbling like a naughty schoolboy, and left the room.

"Just dawdling over the paper, Hilda," Entweder said. "The pope has issued an encyclical."

Hilda, having put Frank's plate in front of him, held the edges of her apron as if about to curtsy. She looked at the pastor with a puzzled expression.

"It's been on the radio. Is it important?"

"Oh, indeed it is. A most significant document." Entweder lowered the paper and looked ingenuously at Frank. "Had you heard of it, Father?"

"Yes." Frank buttered toast with a smile that began and ended on his lips. "Early this morning. I had a phone call."

"From Rome, Father?"

Frank did not take his eyes from the surface of his toast. "From Washington."

"D.C.?"

"D.C."

"Well, well."

Entweder dove behind the paper again. Hilda shrugged and left the room. Frank felt like an ass for mentioning last night's phone call. Had he expected Entweder to be impressed? Had he wanted to impress him? Frank found himself thinking that that call in the night had allied him with others and that he did not stand alone against his timid pastor's triumphant delight in the encyclical. Entweder was muttering unintelligibly, apparently reading. After a minute, he folded the paper, pushed it toward Frank and began to towel himself with his napkin.

"I am interested in your reaction to the news, Father, but I have to get to work."

Frank left the paper where Entweder had put it, dying to snatch it up and read, unwilling to give the pastor the satisfaction of seeing his reaction to the newspaper account. Entweder, standing now, blessed himself and lapsed into a lengthy and silent grace after meal. Finished, humming almost gaily, he left the room. Frank reached for the paper, read the headline, then put it down again. He would finish breakfast first, squelch his curiosity. But it would have been hard to say whether the greater penance lay in reading the paper or postponing it.

When he had hung up his phone earlier that morning, Frank switched on his light and saw that it was after two o'clock. He could not remember if there was a time difference between Fort Elbow and Washington, but it was late enough in any case. He lit a cigarette, propped up his pillow, did not lean back against it. He was stunned by the news of the encyclical. Had the pope made no distinction at all between means of contraception, between kinds of pill? His caller's voice had trembled with a passion Frank found it easier to share than he would have to name. Anger? Rebellion? A sense of having the ground cut from under him? That he certainly felt. What could the bishops do now but go along with the pope? Frank wondered if he should have let his name be added to the dissenting statement which had been read hurriedly to him over the phone. He remembered nothing of what it had said. It was then that Frank picked up his phone and dialed Bishop Brophy. It was answered on the third ring.

"This is Frank Ascue, Bishop. Excuse me for calling so late. I just heard about the new encyclical."

"Ah, then they did contact you?"

"Just a few minutes ago."

Brophy sighed into the phone. "The fat is in the fire now, Frank. To tell you the truth, I was afraid this was going to happen. Did you sign that statement?"

"I said they could use my name."

"Good. It should appear in the same issues that carry news of the encyclical itself. That should blunt the blow a bit"

"How will the bishops react?"

"That depends on reactions like this dissenting statement, Frank. Even so, it is going to be extremely sticky."

"I should have signed the statement, shouldn't I? I mean, that won't be misunderstood?"

"Of course you should have signed it. Frank, is there any way we can avoid being misunderstood nowadays? You know I'm not one of those who divides the Church into heroes and villains. There are honest differences on how to move the Church into the twentieth century. I know that. I respect that. But this encyclical is a backward step and it is up to us to try to diminish the damage it will do. That will entail being misunderstood, of course. It's a small price to pay, Frank."

The call finished, cigarette and lamp out, Frank felt cheered by the conversation. A bishop had approved what he had done. Others too had expressed their discontent with the encyclical. But it was not easy to fall asleep again. It began to bother Frank that he had reacted before reading the encyclical. He did not even know the name of the document. Lying in the dark, pursued by such thoughts, he remembered Rome. Against his closed eyelids he could see the traffic on the Corso and the policeman on his pedestal in front of the monument in the Piazza Venézia. In memory Frank drifted down Vittorio Emanuele, across the bridge and up the Via della Conciliazione, past the Columbus Hotel, to the Vatican, to that immense pile that seemed to diminish in size the longer he had been in Rome. Rome. He could see the shuttered rise of umber walls, feel the stifling air, hear the constant plash of water that seemed to confer coolness even on marble it did not wet. That Rome was a tourist's delight and, like so many meccas of the camera-bearing wanderer, an anachronism, an overblown past decaying in the soot and sun of the present. There are no underground parking lots in Rome to relieve the gutted streets because everywhere beneath the feet, awaiting careful pick and shovel, are all those layers of the past, a national treasure, buried, precious. Frank's thoughts returned to the Vatican, to the Bernini columns which reached out crablike to embrace him, to pull him into the enclave where lived the vicar of Christ whose unread letter on contraception Francis Ascue, priest, had declared unacceptable to him.

At breakfast, as earlier saying Mass, Frank could not take comfort from the thought that Bishop Brophy had applauded his dissent, that there were many theologians around the country whose names would be listed with his own beneath that statement. The pope's official and considered word on any subject was something a Catholic heard with respect, pondered, accepted almost instinctively. But Frank's instinctive reaction had been no and what he had said no to was not yet clear to him. All he knew was what he had been told, that the pope had reaffirmed the traditional ban on any form of contraceptive.

Frank had honestly thought that there would be either no word at all from the pope or a cautious acceptance of the pill, of some sort of pill. He had not taken the position he had on the panel in a spirit of rebellion; he knew that what he had said had already been said by any number of theologians before him, not least by the experts who served on the papal commission. Of course an encyclical was not an infallible document, but would lay people understand that when they heard theologians dissenting from it and urging them to follow their own consciences?

His uneasiness diminished somewhat when he finally gave in and picked up the newspaper again. The dissent from the encyclical appeared to be international and Frank's own action was lost in a number. Eighty-six people had signed the theologians' dissent. One shy and indiscernible digit in a large and growing number, he was crazy to worry about the consequences for himself of what he had done. What was important was quantity, the number of those who questioned the pope's judgment; that must certainly weigh heavily and, if the newspaper was right, those objecting to it would constitute a majority of those saying anything at all.

"Well, Father," Entweder called from his study when Frank went down the hall. "What do you think?"

The pastor was seated at his desk, boxes of collection envelopes piled before him. The taking of the census kept turning up people who were not supplied with envelopes and the pastor immediately mailed them a box, inscribing the address with a huge orange fountain pen.

"Every contribution helps," Frank said.

"Indeed it does." Entweder blew on his handiwork to dry the ink. "Have you read the paper?"

"Yes."

Entweder picked up another box, consulted a list at his elbow, began to write. "Rome has spoken," he said solemnly.

"Discussion seems to be continuing, Monsignor."

"That's as it should be, I suppose. Among theologians. But on the pastoral level, we must not confuse the faithful. Not in the confessional, not from the pulpit. We shall say what the pope has said and that is all."

"Very well." Frank certainly did not intend to debate the pope in the pulpit of Saint Waldo's.

The temptation to argue was strong, but Frank went on to his room. Entweder's soft-spoken ultimatum did not anger him. *Roma locuta est, causa finita est.* Rome has spoken and that is the end of it. Not Entweder, but the teaching authority of the Church had spoken. How inviting it was to let that settle the matter, to accept the judgment, pass it on and stifle his own doubts and downgrade the real and imagined difficulties people had always had with the Church's stand on this subject. Conform, assent, accept. Frank found himself sinking into the comfort these thoughts brought when he remembered his promise to pay a visit on John Tremplin. Who would have thought that that distasteful task would present itself as a welcome distraction from the news of the day?

Napoleon on Saint Helena, Mussolini on his mountaintop, John Tremplin in his room on the first floor of a residence hall at the Fort Elbow Seminary. The exalted parallels were entertained by Tremplin himself, political precedents deliberately chosen, though earlier religious martyrs might also, if remembered, provide him consolation. Boethius imprisoned at Pavia, Aquinas in the family castle . . .

He had not shaved for days. His eyes were sunken and inflamed, he was constipated from the weird diet his self-imposed incarceration entailed. Swivel had brought him sacks of hamburgers, pizza, fried chicken once, and the remains of these far from festive repasts littered the room. He had not let the nun come in to clean, not since the first day when he had noticed the reproachful look in her eye. He had closed the door on her, feeling like an alcoholic surprised by a representative of the great sober world outside. He wished that he did drink, but even the Mass wine made him half ill.

Mass. He could not say Mass. He was a eunuch and for what kingdom's sake? It was all so unfair. Has love no rights? He had read and reread the newspaper account of Phil's wedding and his own quoted remark had acquired the status of a motto. They said they were behind him now —at least Swivel said they said that—but his fellow priests were out *there*, free, still able to function as priests, while he was here alone, holding the fort against the threat of eviction. What did their support mean, aside from wishing that supercilious bore Swivel on him, Swivel who brought him cooling food from half a dozen of the cheapest drive-ins? The food did not matter; he really did not care about food. God knew he did not miss the refectory fare. A wave of nostalgia washed over him when he remembered the hunger strike last spring. What a triumph even this might be if only the boys were here, his boys. Tremplin was just a tiny bit disappointed that the seminarians had not converged on campus, drawn from their far-flung vacation locales, to protest the injustice being done him by the institutional Church. It piqued him too that his deed had been all but buried in the report of Bullard's wedding.

Some hero Phil Bullard had turned out to be, skipping town with his bride and not so much as a fare thee well to the friend who had risked so much on his behalf. Tremplin could have become quite indignant over this ingratitude if he had not himself volunteered to perform the wedding ceremony. Indeed, he had had to persuade Phil to let him. He had heard the rumors about Phil and the nun, of course. What else could he do but drop in on Phil?

"This is another opportunity, Philip. You must act and you must act publicly."

"What the hell are you talking about, Jack?"

How to put it, that was the problem. I know about your affair? Nothing so direct would do. But indirection had its pitfalls.

"One hears rumors."

"Rumors take at least two, Jack."

"So do many things."

Phil had glowered at him, heaven knew why; he stood and seemed about to succumb to his rather boorish habit of hustling his friends out of the Center.

"Isn't her name Eloise?" Aha. That had done it. Phil's frown deepened and then was gone.

"Yes, her name is Eloise." Phil sat down once more.

"I assume it's serious."

Phil mastered a threatened repetition of that unattractive frown. "What do you want me to say?"

"I'll marry you, Phil!"

Dancing brows and a flop of the wrist—how Jack hated it when people acted like that. Couldn't Phil be serious?

"Have the wedding right here. In the Center chapel. Nothing furtive. Do it publicly. I'll say the nuptial Mass, Phil. We'll pull all the stops."

Phil's indecision lasted only a moment. He sat forward and his expression was all the agreement Jack had needed. Phil did grow impatient during the little homily Tremplin felt constrained to deliver; Phil seemed to think his deed required no rationale. But he had to be made to see that the rule of celibacy constituted moral duress; they had all agreed to it only because it was a condition of ordination. Since there is no essential connection between a celibate life and holy orders, the institutional Church's rule of celibacy was blackmail pure and simple.

"There is a vast recent literature on the subject, Phil."

"I've heard."

Of course one of Phil's charms was the fact that he was not an intellectual; he never had been. All Tremplin's memories of Phil in the seminary were in athletic settings: Phil, flushed and sweaty, making a perfect pivot on the basketball court; Phil on ice, posed for a face-off in hockey; Phil at first base, opening and closing that butterfly of a mitt. Brawn, just brawn. Yet of late Phil had exhibited the courage of action as none of the self-styled intellectuals had. So it mattered little that Phil Bullard had not thought through at an abstract level what he was doing and why. Indeed, theory seemed stale, flat and unprofitable to Jack Tremplin himself. *Le coeur a ses raisons.* Has love no rights?

In the prison of his room, John Tremplin longed to discuss the theory that theory is useless, and with someone with at least half a mind. They had sent him Swivel! Swivel, who camped in front of the television, watching ball games and uttering grunts of delight or dismay. How could Donald Oder stand having that ass in the same house with him? Tremplin had thrown Swivel out. He jerked the plug of the television from the wall, silencing the infernal din, and screamed at Swivel to leave his room. Swivel had scampered off, of course. Well, the next move was up to *them.* If there really was all this vaunted support for him, they could just send Frank Ascue here. He would accept Frank's word.

It had been such a disappointment when Frank had not been assigned to the seminary faculty. If only he had been, everything might have been so different. Ewing had refused to show his own disappointment, of course; he would not deign to receive condolences, but it had been obvious that he had been crushed by Caldron's failure to replace him with Frank. For three whole years the man had babbled on about his days here being numbered, and the prospect had, Tremplin supposed, made him less difficult to live with, though it was not easy to imagine a more abrasive colleague than even a hopeful Ewing had been.

No doubt he and Eisenbarth were busy conspiring against him now. Tremplin's eyes darted to the door, seeking reassurance from the chain in its socket. Oh, wouldn't they just love to toss him out of here? Tremplin was gripped by a sudden chill. Where would he go? He had pestered Phil on that point, asking what he intended to do when he left. He needed these walls around him; he needed to know that, if he cared to look outside, he would see the familiar campus of the seminary. This place had been his home for nine years; six as a seminarian and, after an interval in graduate school, three as a professor. No student could match his contempt for the place or top him in finding fault with it, but now, to his own mystification, he discovered that the only identity he possessed was bound up with the Fort Elbow Seminary.

He wished that he had even a slight desire to imitate Phil, but the thought of courting a woman, nun or not, made him want to gag. He was burden enough to himself. His only hope would have been to find someone utterly self-reliant, someone like Mother, a person on whom he could depend for strength and who would know without being asked what step he should take next. But Mother had actually married again and was living in bovine content in Sarasota, snug with her retired druggist. How he needed someone. And they sent him Swivel. Frank Ascue would be another story, but it had been over twenty-four hours since he had pitched Swivel out and there had been no word from anyone. Of course he refused to answer his phone. Tremplin wiped his eyes, hard, and eventually his tear ducts responded. He looked around his room with blurring eyes. Napoleon on Saint Helena, Mussolini on his mountaintop . . .

On the front porch of the main building of the Fort Elbow Seminary, Father Ewing and Father Sweeney continued to rock when the car came in the road.

"Who is that?" Father Sweeney asked.

"I don't know." Father Ewing stopped his rocker and leaned forward. Frank Ascue? Yes, it was. He got up and started across the porch. "I'll go see."

Frank was out of the car and, seeing Father Ewing, stopped. Doesn't look too happy to see me, Father Ewing thought, unable not to smile.

"Well?" he said.

Frank looked puzzled, or tried to.

Oh, to hell with it. Be magnanimous in victory. "What do you think of the new encyclical, Frank?"

"It surprised me."

"Did it really?"

"I wasn't the only one."

Father Ewing's feelings of exultation evaporated. He growled and shook his head. "I hope you're not thinking of taking exception to the pope. All this garbage about it not being binding. We can't be Catholics and wonder whether or not we'll listen to the pope, Frank. Isn't that right?"

"Well, when he speaks *ex cathedra* . . ."

"Whenever he speaks. You've read *Gaudium in terra.*" Wasn't that

357

the title of the conciliar document he had in mind? No matter. Frank must know that a Catholic cannot ignore the ordinary magisterium.

"The debate is going to continue," Frank said. His eyes went beyond Father Ewing as if he were searching the seminary campus for a lost docility. "Whether or not that's wise."

"There have always been gripers and complainers."

"Maybe you're right."

"Of course I'm right."

"How is Jack Tremplin?"

Ewing groaned. "Do you plan to visit him?"

"I hear he's taking it pretty hard."

Ewing twirled a finger around his ear. "He's out of his head. He hasn't been outside his room for a week. If he doesn't snap out of it soon, he'll be carted off to the funny farm. I think he's drinking."

"Tremplin?"

"Well, he isn't eating anything."

"What does he say?"

"Say! He won't come to the door or answer his phone. Even if he did, he probably wants to talk to me about as much as I want to talk to him."

"The poor devil."

"He deserves what he got, Frank. I don't bear him any ill will, but he's been asking for it for a long time."

Frank stood with crossed arms, his feet apart. "He certainly can't just stay in his room like that."

"I know. I suppose he wonders what difference it makes. I mean, the bishop can't simply reinstate Tremplin, even if he would admit that he did something wrong. The funny thing is, he won't admit that. At least he hasn't yet." Ewing made a face but then, quite suddenly, his expression changed. "Say, what is Oder calling a senate meeting for?"

"I think he wants us to discuss the impact of Bullard's wedding, Tremplin's suspension, all of it."

"My God, are you serious?"

"The encyclical has overshadowed it for the moment, of course, but the reaction is still there. Some people hope the bishop won't go as hard on Tremplin as he might."

"Frank, Frank," Ewing moaned, grasping the other priest's arm. "Don't get mixed up with the kooks. Please. Tremplin won't even help himself. He did something seriously wrong; there is absolutely no doubt about that. He is finished here at the seminary, finished in the active ministry, at least for a long time. You should pray that he'll see the harm he's done if you really want to help him."

"I do pray for him, Father."

358

Let it go at that, for God's sake. At least for now. He drew back and studied Frank. "Are you getting any exercise?"

"Not much. Of course I walk a lot."

"So did the Volga boatmen. Look, how about some golf?"

"I haven't golfed in years."

"No wonder your mind's decaying. Let's go out. Nine holes, eighteen, whatever you say."

"I don't know."

But Ewing detected a wistful note and he pursued it until its pitch was pure and ungrudging. When they parted, he felt slightly better about Frank. Tomorrow, on the golf course, fresh air, open sky, with a five handicapper's chance to play tutor, he would get through to Frank, he was sure of it. The boy had drifted in with the worst bunch in the diocese. Well, there is nothing like golf to restore a sense of proportion.

Golf. Everyone kidded him about it, but the truth was that lately even a leisurely nine holes left him exhausted. The thought that he was doomed to remain at the seminary, perhaps to the end of his days, did not help, of course. He felt doubly betrayed: by Caldron or, more accurately, Yorick, and now by Frank. He did not want to be replaced by Frank Ascue, not now.

When he had closed the door of his room behind him, Father Ewing stood for a moment, breathing as deeply as he could. The slight exertion of the stairs had left him breathless and, if he inhaled deeply, he almost blacked out. A constellation of spots formed before his eyes and danced away like flying saucers when he tried to concentrate on them, to make them real specks rather than projections from his brain. His familiar comfortable room attracted and repelled him. This and the adjoining bedroom had been home for decades. He looked at his cluttered desk, at the books jammed into the shelves which covered two walls. How he had read when he was in his prime, and not narrowly either; he had ranged far beyond his field, into history and biography, even into fiction, seeking the living context of moral issues so that he could avoid hackneyed examples in class. Frank Ascue had spent hours here and his youthful eagerness had caused a recurrence of energy in a jaded professor.

Father Ewing crossed the room slowly and sat in an easy chair by the open window where the breeze that rippled the curtain played across his brow. He was perspiring like someone who had just finished thirty-six holes. He leaned over to loosen his shoes and for a crazy moment wondered if he could straighten up again. He did and sat back in the chair, eyes half closed, looking at his shelves of books. So many memories. He was tired, very tired. If only Frank had proved more solid and

Caldron and Yorick less capricious, this could have been a wonderful summer. He would have been packing those books, preparing to move. Move. Now the thought of a new job and different responsibilities was unattractive. Just think of the energy that would require. I am old, he thought. I have grown old without noticing it.

Visiting Tremplin was a decent thing to do. An act of charity. Best to think of it that way. Visit the sick, comfort the sorrowful. The corporal works of mercy. Yes. Frank was a good boy. Whatever Oder was up to, Frank would interpret it as mercy to a wayward colleague. Nothing wrong in that, nothing in the world. Frank was basically solid. He would get through it all somehow. Crazy days. Hard on us all. Sweeney had said that Frank had a deep devotion to Mary. Such a man never went wrong. Should say fifteen decades a day himself instead of five. Said them too quickly anyway. Distracted. Grumbling, always grumbling. Old. Concentration, composition of place, a good prayer life. How easy it was to forget the basics: prayer, sacrifice, obedience.

Father Ewing reached for his cigarettes. The package exerted its weight in his hand, oddly heavy. He shook it and several cigarettes fell to the floor. He would pick them up later. He put a cigarette in his mouth, flicked his lighter, inhaled. Pain in his chest. Should quit. He smiled. That velleity had sprung to his mind so often over the years, but he had never stopped, not even for Lent. He looked at his hand as if it were a foreign object. He could not feel the cigarette between his fingers. He moved his hand and there seemed a delay between the sending of the signal and the slow movement of his fingers. The cigarette slipped from them and, startled, he leaped to his feet. Pain swept over him. Something seemed to be jerking him higher and higher, as if he might rise to the ceiling. His right hand shot out and he watched it, dazed, and then he fell. The floor rose to meet him, slowly, dreamily, but before he struck it there was a blaze of light behind his eyes, the end of time.

Sprawled ignominiously on the carpet, the body that was no longer Father Hubert Ewing was destined to lie there twenty-four hours before it was discovered.

Frank had been rapping on Tremplin's door at half-minute intervals for at least three minutes, observed suspiciously by a nun who did the cleaning, before there was any response. The nun had come around a corner of the hall, disappeared immediately, walking backward, then come out again to stare at him. There was the rattling of a chain on the other side of the door.

"Who's there?"

"Frank Ascue."

The door opened a crack, as much as the guard chain permitted, and Tremplin, looking ungodly and sick and demented, blinked out at him. The room behind him was dark and Jack seemed to find the dim light of the hallway blinding.

"Thank God you've come," he cried.

The nun had inched closer to get a glimpse of the recluse. Tremplin's tear-filled eyes opened, he saw the nun and looked accusingly at Frank.

"What is she doing here!"

"Take it easy. Let us alone, Sister."

"I'd like to clean that room."

"No!" Tremplin said.

"You don't have to let her in, Jack. Sister!"

"It hasn't been cleaned for days."

"*Sister!*"

The nun gave Tremplin another look, getting it right, then hurried off to the convent with her tale.

"Did she go?"

"She's gone. Open the door."

Tremplin was trying unsuccessfully to look down the hallway. "Is anyone else out there?"

"Jack, open that door or I'm leaving."

The door slammed, a chain clanked and the door reopened, wide. It did not frame the figure of John Tremplin. Bedsprings jangled and Frank went in, groping for the light switch. The place smelled ripe. Windows shut, drapes drawn; it must have been ninety in there. He found the switch and flooded the room with light. His eyes moved around the room and to the bed. Tremplin, a sheet pulled to his slightly bearded chin, peered at him with tragic woebegone eyes.

"See what they have done to me?"

"Come off it, Jack. No one did this to you." Holding his breath, Frank went to a window, pulled aside the drapes and raised the sash. Air rushed in, seeming almost cool, incredibly fresh.

"Look at it, Frank. My cage. Let others know what you have found."

"Who, the Bollandists?" Frank shook his head. "I'm sorry I sent that nun away. This place needs a shovel."

"This is what happens when you stop caring." Tremplin looked around his room with awe. "I understand the poor now, Frank, those who live in slums. Squalor can be willed, you know. It is an objective correlative, the outward expression of inner desolation."

"What's wrong with your phone?"

"I disconnected it."

The cord had been pulled from the wall. The television was not plugged in. Tremplin's typewriter was. A sheet of onionskin paper was in the roller with several lines typed on it. Frank bent over to read and Tremplin bounded from the bed, dashed to the typewriter and ripped the page from it. His lavender boxer shorts were covered with bugs.

"What are those?" Frank asked, backing away.

Tremplin looked at his shorts, then clicked his teeth. "It's a pattern, Frank. For heaven's sake, I'm not lousy."

"Get dressed."

"Why should I?"

"Get dressed!"

Tremplin tilted his chin in defiance but wilted under Frank's gaze. His shoulders slumped and he went to a chair and extracted a pair of trousers from a pile. While he was stepping into them, he began to cry.

"I only wish George Caldron could see what he has done to me."

"You ought to be ashamed to let anyone see you like this." Frank put a cigarette in his mouth. "I wonder if it's safe to strike a match in here."

"Oh, ha ha."

Tremplin went to a corner of the room and removed a cover from a birdcage. The canary inside began to bleat. Frank struck the match.

"Have you been feeding that bird?"

"Of course."

"Go shave."

Tremplin's hand went to his chin and stroked the stubble there. "No. I have always wanted to grow a beard. I was afraid to be mistaken for a missionary, but there's no danger of that now."

"Get in there and shave."

Tremplin obeyed meekly. He was obviously eager to have someone tell him what to do. Why couldn't he take orders from Bishop Caldron? While Tremplin shaved, Frank tried to put some order in the room. He retrieved the onionskin sheet from the basket where Tremplin had put it.

"August 5," it read. "The fourth day within the octave of my unjust suspension by Bishop George Caldron, may his tribe decrease. Once on television I saw a woman interviewed who had spent years in a communist prison and she told of the devices she had used to retain her sanity. Do not underestimate the resourcefulness of the human mind, George Caldron. I shall not crack!"

Within the octave. Had Tremplin put a time limit on his self-imprisonment? Frank doubted that Jack knew what day it was.

When he had finished shaving, Tremplin came out of the bathroom and put on a cassock. He looked pale and haggard still, but almost human. Seated in a chair, he ran a finger along the edge of his Roman collar and once more his eyes filled with tears.

"Remember the first weeks in the seminary, Frank? Remember what a delight it was finally to be wearing a cassock and collar?"

"I remember." Dressing the part had seemed to make one a priest already. That had passed quickly, of course, and one became conscious of the years of study still ahead.

"They have taken all that away from me."

"I thought you'd given up wearing clerical clothes."

"You know what I mean. My memories." Tremplin looked sadly about him. "Has love no rights?"

"Why did you do it, Jack?"

"Do what?"

"Marry them. If I know Phil Bullard, he would have been perfectly happy with a justice of the peace."

"Oh, yes. *He* would have. But I was not acting for them alone, Frank. Don't you see, it was a protest. We are hemmed in and stifled by all these impossibly picayune rules. They were a couple in love who wished to solemnize their union before God and man. They were in *love*, Frank. We must not forget that. Love sanctifies—"

"Is patient, is kind, is not puffed up. . . ."

"Very well." Tremplin clamped his mouth shut and adopted a hurt expression. "Why have you come to me?"

"Didn't Swivel tell you?"

"Swivel!"

"He said that he told you and you wouldn't believe him."

"You tell me."

Frank told him of the coming senate meeting. There would be a qualified expression of sympathy and support for Jack, a request to the bishop that he review the case with an eye to the possible extenuating circumstances of Jack's deed. While he spoke, Frank wished that Oder and Brophy could see the man they regarded as a victim of an impersonal and legalistic institutional Church.

Howard Nygaard, when it became clear to him that the fear he had felt when Sharon told him of her move to Fort Elbow was baseless, was tempted to take a different view of his involvement with her. The arrangement was a sophisticated one, was it not? Worldly and debonair, he was awaited across town by an extremely pretty young lady who never tired of lavishing her affection upon him. He did not pay her rent;

363

she was self-supporting; there were no ties that bound him to her save those arising from his excess of animal spirits. Sharon was simply a little secret that need never come to the surface. He could grow old like this, with a wife and mistress too, but if, in the normal course of events, Sharon drifted away from him, he would make no attempt to hold her. He could imagine their good-bye. Mature, understanding, his eyes would crinkle with melancholy understanding which somehow would be exactly the appropriate attitude for the scene. Farewell, farewell.

But of course that was not at all the way things were. Together with his fear of being found out had gone his anger too and in their place, stronger than before, was a feeling of possessive tenderness toward Sharon. Her availability, as if she had no other purpose in life, affected him deeply and such guilt as he had stemmed from the fact that he was a taker, a user, one who was never inconvenienced by this affair even when it had changed locale and thereby become both more frequent and preoccupying. It was Charlotte who irked him now, not Sharon.

How in the name of God was he supposed to respond to his wife's excitement about something the pope had written on contraception? Charlotte seemed undecided whether it was the end of the world or the beginning. In either case, it struck Howard as being massively unimportant. While Charlotte jabbered on about marital relations, a nodding Howard found his thoughts traveling back to Sharon, to her apartment and the peace it seemed increasingly to represent.

"There will be a revolution, Howard. There really will."

An overthrow of the pope? Howard was not at all clear as to whether the pope could be deposed, voted out of office, replaced. That is what a revolution suggested to him, but Charlotte had lesser things in mind.

"CFM has to come out against the encyclical, Howard. We will just say flat out, No, thanks. We don't agree with the pope and we are the ones affected by this silly encyclical and we are perfectly capable of making up our own minds."

Howard did not follow Charlotte's speech closely but his bodily presence was all the audience she needed. She strode around the bedroom, her robe floating behind her, and Howard compared the familiar contours of her body with the lither ones of Sharon's. Charlotte had a good figure, he could not deny that. And she was pretty; she had a mature handsomeness which was in its way more attractive than unformed prettiness. Why Sharon? She could not be explained simply by a desire for novelty. That could have been satisfied in any number of less involving ways. No, Charlotte had a fatal flaw: her goddam mouth and all this crap about the Church, the pope, CFM, on and on endlessly until he wanted to pick up his pillow and throw it at her. He should be grateful that she had so much to distract her. Would any other wife have been so incurious about her husband that she would not have guessed he had another woman? He could not imagine deceiving Sharon as easily as he did Charlotte.

Even after the light was out, Charlotte continued to lecture in the dark, her voice addressing the ceiling, not modulating at all when he simulated sleep and a slight snore. When she did subside, she continued to mutter, winning argument after argument with some imaginary opponent. The pope? Most likely. Welcome to my bedroom, Your Holiness. Excuse the mess. The lady? My wife, your enemy, the savior of the spouses of the world. She is sailing into menopause, shaking her fist at those who would question her right to use contraceptives, should she ever feel inclined to mate, should her depleted husband be up to the task. Charlotte was asleep. Minutes before, her muted grumbling had been audible but now she was asleep. As he did so often, Howard slid from bed and went downstairs.

There in the unlighted living room where he had once pondered a dilemma of which Sharon was the unwanted horn, he pondered it anew and his discontent was aimed at the ceiling, at the bedroom above and his angry revolutionary wife. These solitary meditations in the living room late at night had the added bonus of a conversation with Beverly when she came in.

"Have a good time?" he asked this night as he had so often before. The question was really only a way of letting her know that he was sitting there in the dark.

"No."

"No?" Her not following their little script almost annoyed him. His question usually drew some noncommittal noise or a yawning yes. Beverly came in and sat across the room from him, a huddled silhouette, his daughter.

"Who were you out with?"

"Ben. Ben Cole. You probably don't remember him."

"Of course I remember him. Where did you go?"

"Nowhere. Just around. You know."

You know. How could he know? He summoned memories of this Ben, but he had only met him once, one Sunday, the day Frank had been on television. Funny kid.

Beverly made a strange noise and he realized that she was crying. My God, what was wrong? His little girl, crying. Howard got up, crossed the room put his hand out, groping for her shoulder and finding the top of her head. He left his hand there, feeling like a blind Old Testament character blessing the wrong child. Beverly began to sob aloud and he moved his hand to her shoulder. How frail she seemed, how young. He heard her purse open and the rustle of a tissue.

"Tell me about it," he said, praying that she would not. Charlotte, not he, should be soothing Beverly.

"There's nothing to tell."

He sat beside her on the couch. "There must be something."

She leaned her head against him, snuffled, said nothing. Get control of yourself, Howard prayed. Go upstairs to bed. A good night's sleep, tomorrow a new day. He was conscious of the fact that his arm was rigid where Bev's forehead leaned against it.

"Why don't you run up and go to sleep?"

In trying to nod, she rubbed her head against his arm. He wanted to hold her and console her, but that would have seemed too hypocritical. Oh, God, why was everything so complicated? Beverly pushed away and he knew that she was looking at him.

"How come you're always down here, Daddy?"

Daddy. How young that made her sound, as young as Dave and Beth. The thought of young lives dependent on him made Howard frightened and sad. He wanted to be only himself, himself and Sharon, yet he was tied to his children by bonds that could not be seen and that very fact exerted an irresistible tug at his heart.

"I couldn't sleep."

"Do you ever sleep? Dad, you can't work all day and sit up all night. You'll collapse."

"I was just about to go up."

She changed her position on the cushion beside him. "Do you wait up until I get in? Is that it?"

"Of course not."

"I'll bet!" She said it tenderly. She wanted to think that and he realized that he wanted her to. He patted her cheek and she leaned forward and kissed him.

"All right. Your vigil's over. I'm home and you can go to bed." She stood and tried to tug him to his feet.

"Go ahead, Bev. I'll be along in a minute."

It was a pleasant thought, himself as concerned parent, unable to sleep until his daughter was safely home. He listened to Beverly go upstairs. Why had she cried when she came in? Some misunderstanding with the boy? Or was it something more serious? No, it couldn't be. Not Beverly. She was still just a kid, really.

When some minutes later he did go up and passed her door, Beverly called out in a soft voice, "Good night, Daddy."

"Good night," he whispered. "Good night."

366

Beverly heard the creak of the bed when her father lay down. The thought of him waiting up for her to come in brought tears to her eyes again. What a fool she had been to cry like that downstairs. What would he think? It would be so nice if she could talk to him, really talk to him, tell him about it, but of course she could not. There wasn't anyone she could tell—least of all Ben.

She lay on her back, the covers pulled beneath her chin, and stared at the ceiling. Wavering chips danced overhead, reflections of some light passed on by half a dozen surfaces. When she was a kid and had the front bedroom, she had loved to lie awake and watch the way passing cars made the windows move swiftly around the room, bending at corners and at the meeting of wall and ceiling. She had imagined that evil men had flung her bound on a busy road and that the traffic was hurtling harmlessly past, her life charmed, a triumph of the good. And, hearing her parents talking downstairs, she would think, They do not know the danger I am in; they go on talking while at any moment I may be crushed to death. Her vulnerability and their ignorance of it brought on the sweetest tears of self-pity. And so she lay now, weeping in her bed at night, her parents peacefully asleep, and the danger was no longer imaginary.

Tonight she had tried to tell Ben. She had tried to maneuver the conversation to a point where it would be natural to say it, but he was so incredibly dense. And chaste. If the conversation even came close to that, his only thought was to repeat their resolution that it must not happen again. It was important to him to believe that it had been a mistake, unintended by either of them, a moment of weakness. She could scream when he started that damned preaching and of course she wondered if his resolution stemmed from the fact that it had been, after all, pretty darned disappointing. The first time—and it had been that for both of them—was supposed to be awkward and clumsy; he should know that as well as she. Well, it had been, but it was more than a disappointment. It had been ridiculous.

They had often gone down along the river path before, kidding about what the other couples were up to down there—at least she had kidded. Maybe all around them on their blankets other couples were talking of the rest, insisting on their difference from everyone else. They sat and talked, lapsed into silence, began to kiss, to make love. Up to a point. Where that point was had kept shifting until a month ago she had sensed that it was not there anymore, not for him, not for her, and dear God all those slushy verbs were right, she wanted to surrender herself

367

to him, give him her all without restraint and it would be so beautiful. Beautiful, beautiful. She kept repeating that to herself throughout, trying not to notice his ineptitude, since that was his charm, he was so innocent, and did it really matter that it never did become beautiful? It was all over before it began and then, God, God, Ben was crying, sobbing his heart out, and she had been frightened, at first because someone might hear him and then because his tears became an insult. They must have sat there for an hour afterward, saying nothing. She had to take his hand and she looked at him staring out at the water as if everything good and beautiful in the world had just sunk without a trace. On the way back up the path to his father's car, on the drive home, she sat beside him feeling that she had raped and ruined him. What a mistake it had been to let him act like that. She realized that as soon as she had gone inside and lay, like this, in bed, thinking over the evening. She should have been filled with wistful happiness, a melancholy pleasure in the knowledge that she had turned that big corner and shown him how much she loved him. But he had robbed her of that and she felt then as she had ever since: guilty, a destroyer, the cause of it all. And like a damned fool she had let him refer to it with solemn obliqueness the next day as what they must never do again.

Had she gone along with him out of some wily certainty that, with the passing of time, in the natural course of events, it would happen again, no matter what resolutions they made, and that the next time he would react differently? Perhaps. Perhaps she had promised herself that next time she just would not let him treat her like that afterward. He had to see the significance it had for them. She had convinced herself that it was really good that it hit him so hard, because then when it happened again he would realize how much in love they must be. But the only repetition there had been was his preaching about it and she could see that he was actually preening himself on the fact that, having fallen once, he had recovered his strength. So she made a little resolution of her own. She had had all she could take of Benedict Cole. He was as bad as all those other creeps she had gone out with, utterly self-centered. How had she ever thought that he was different? She had waited for the right moment to give him the big bad news—she was as much of a dramatist as he was. And now she had missed.

She had really missed. It was not a delay, a fluke, anything like that. That one awful time and it must have happened and she had to tell Ben and she simply could not. Beverly gripped the covers, her eyes pressed shut, and shook her head up and down, her chin bouncing off the sheet held taut between her fists. She would tell Ben tomorrow when they went swimming and if he tried to get out of it by bawling or giving her a sermon, well, she did not know what she would do.

Side by side, their bodies oiled, the sand beneath and above a hot relentless sun and all around them others seeking in this purgative place the anticipatory pleasure of having been there, Ben and Beverly looked at the troughed, glittering water where swimmers bobbed like buoys between the shore and the raft on which stick figures stood hugging themselves and shivering improbably in the record heat. Beverly was propped on her unbent arms, palms pressed behind her against the bean-bag feel of the blanket, her legs stretched equally unbent before her, the heel of one foot in the cradling toes of the other. Sweat ran down her forehead, down her nose, under the bridge of her sunglasses, which slipped until they could slip no lower on the fleshy part of her nose. She felt hot and sticky and thoroughly bored. They had not talked. She had not talked. She could not imagine how they could have a serious talk here or anywhere.

"Let's go in."

"Better wait, Bev. It hasn't been fifteen minutes since we had those hot dogs."

Careful, careful. She stood and dropped her sunglasses onto the blanket. Shading his eyes, Ben looked up at her. She was wearing her new suit, which scarcely covered her, but he looked determinedly into her eyes as if gaining merit in the process.

"Come on," she urged.

His nose wrinkled and he shook his head. "Wait a while, Bev."

She turned from him and started toward the water, gyrating her hips in an exaggerated way. But she reached the water without his coming to join her. She just kept on walking into the water until it was knee deep and then dove.

She swam laterally to the shore, wanting to get away from the laughing sputtering crowd of bathers. Turning on her back, floating, her chin pointing to the sky, sustained and enveloped by water, she sought in the blue above her some hint of a way out of her worrisome plight. Caught. Like other girls, she had assumed a mocking grin at the possibility, as if life and love and going with boys was a lottery and she unquestionably one of the winners who would never find herself on the porch of the casino fingering the little silver-plated revolver. Caught. It was so ridiculously melodramatic. Why couldn't she just tell Ben that she had missed her period, just that, and let him take it from there? Well, for one thing, she was afraid that he would not know what she meant and she would have to explain all that to him. But even if he understood, even if, to take the happiest result, he rose to the occasion, took her in his arms and without saying it made it clear that he would do the decent thing, even given that, was that what she wanted? The whole arch of the sky above invited her No. No, because she too would feel caught and with him it would not simply be that marriage would snare him sooner than he had thought; he would see this as the reason why he was not going back to the seminary and she would always be the scapegoat for the future regret he seemed to spend most of present getting ready to feel.

A wave slapped at her face, water got into her ears, but then the lake calmed and she continued to float. Contained by water, she thought of the watery world which would form within her and there too a little creature would be afloat. The process begun would go heedlessly on until that tiny swimmer was ready to be washed ashore. Unless . . . She did not pursue the thought but interrogated the sky. It was blank and vast, indifferent; no answer reached her. She rolled over, surprised to see how far she had floated. She began to swim slowly back.

When she got to the blanket, Ben looked as if he had not moved a muscle in her absence.

"How was it?" he asked.

For answer, she stood over him and shook what water still clung to her onto him. He grabbed her wrist and tugged her down. She landed in his lap, looked into his eyes and breathed heavily. "Take me."

The slightest of frowns but then, in a bantering tone, "Where?"

"Home."

"You're kidding."

But she was not. She freed herself and began gathering up things, stuffing them into her beach bag.

"Let's go."

"But I've only been in once."

"You had your chance."

She turned away before she could see if he took that for a double-meaning remark. He got up, shook the blanket, to the annoyance of their neighbors, folded it, followed her across that festive Sahara to the parking lot. The silence on the drive home was welcome. There, she patted his hand, got out of the car and skipped to the door, her terry-cloth robe flying.

No one was home. She called through the downstairs and then went upstairs. No one. She showered and while she did so twice turned off the water to listen but what in the roar of the water had sounded like the downstairs door or voices was not. The dress she put on was dressy; no reason for that, she just felt like it. The emptiness of the house began to bother her. Silly. In this house no one told anyone else their plans for the day; they just came and went. Her father would be at work and God only knew where her mother was. She must have taken Dave and Beth along or stashed them with a neighbor. Even so, Beverly felt deserted. The closing of the Student Center after Phil Bullard married Eloise had deprived Bev of a usual destination. She had no place to go, no one to talk to. The house seemed to imprison her.

Downstairs, she looked into the living room and she remembered her father sitting there in the dark when she came in from dates. But the room did not seem the same in daytime. How awful to think she kept him up, sleepless until she got home. Every night and for so long, sitting in the dark, sipping beer, smoking, waiting. How easy it was to talk to him, knowing that he had for her an unquestioning love. He would know what to do. She took her purse and ran to the door. She would go see him at his office.

At that hour downtown-bound buses were all but empty and the trip was swift, a minimum of stops. When she got off, Beverly had to stop and think how best to reach the building where her father's office was. Somehow that seemed symptomatic of her indifference to him, and she was filled with a desire to make it up to him. And wasn't seeking his help now the best way she could show her love and her dependence on him?

In the lobby of the building, scanning the directory on the wall, she felt like a little girl come to see her daddy. She had called him Daddy the other night, the word just slipping out of her helpless terror. Well, she was helpless and alone now, more so than she had been when she was a little girl. The feeling persisted when she went up in the elevator, and no wonder. She *had* been a little girl the last time she had been to his office.

She entered timidly and waited until the receptionist finished on the phone.

"Mr. Nygaard? Did you have an appointment?"

"I'm his daughter."

The woman's face lit up with phony delight and she looked at Beverly with real curiosity. Just as suddenly the light went out and she became sad.

"But your father has already gone home."

"Oh." Her disappointment seemed to have no bottom. She stood there looking at the woman as if she had just denied some self-evident truth. All the awkwardness she had felt a moment ago would have been swept away by the sight of her father, but now it had increased.

"He left early," the receptionist said. "I'm so sorry."

"He went home?"

The woman nodded, sympathetic. Home. Beverly escaped before the receptionist could call in her father's secretary to see Mr. Nygaard's lovely daughter. She decided against the elevator and walked down six flights of granite steps, the stairwell deserted in the busy building, down to the street floor and outside where she wandered vaguely back toward the bus stop. No place to go. But this was downtown. There were hundreds of things to do downtown. Like? She had too little money in her purse to want to shop and a movie at that time of day was insane. Home. She did not want to go home. Home was where men told their receptionists they were going when they wanted to get out of the office early. Her father could be somewhere near, in one of these bars. Of course she could not go looking for him, the desolate daughter of the town drunk.

If her father really had gone home, he would be there by now. She began to hurry toward the bus stop. The bus she boarded was jammed and the return trip took almost twice as long. Beverly burst into the house, calling out as she had earlier. No one answered. She went upstairs, she went out into the backyard, she ended up in the living room, seated in her father's favorite chair, staring at nothing. Alone.

Bending over the ball on the practice green at the Belvedere Country Club, Frank felt the awkwardness of one who has been too long away from the game though his body tried to recall the proper stoop and arrangement of feet. His hands opened and closed on the grip of his club. The putter, bronze head, wooden shaft, was a relic, a gift from his Uncle Harry, his first club.

The practice green was bordered by a low hedge and overshadowed by great cottonwoods whose soft seeds drifted onto the bent grass, providing easy excuses for missed putts. Frank had the green to himself, and no wonder. The dark clouds were ominously low in the sky and a chill wind rustled the leaves. Rain was inevitable, he had known that when he left the rectory, but he had been unable to reach Ewing and suspected that nothing less than a typhoon would deter him. Ewing had not been at the club when Frank arrived, brought by a McTear shocked at the thought of someone arriving at the clubhouse in a cab, so Frank had gone out to the practice green, slipped into his golf shoes and settled down with his putter. This practice seemed more and more all the golf he was likely to get today.

At the sound of a horn Frank turned, but he did not recognize

Ewing's car in the parking lot beyond the hedge. Before he could putt again the horn sounded once more. A hand emerged from a window and waved at him. That was all he could see, the hand: the windshield was opaque with reflections. Frank waved tentatively and Sheila Rupp's head emerged, adding a smile to her wave. When he returned to his ball, Frank was conscious of her there and it did not help his reading of the green. A minute before he had felt the pastoral isolation of the course, not knowing whether he welcomed or resented the memories it brought back. Sheila brought back both the present and the wider world whose fairways were untracked and no pars posted. The first drops of rain began to fall.

The branches of the cottonwoods swayed wildly in the wind now. A wall of rain moved up the ninth fairway and players on foot and in electric carts dashed for cover. Again the horn sounded in the parking lot. Scooping up his ball, Frank ran to the hedge, cleared it, and raced toward Sheila's car with the rain pelting on his back. He pulled open the door, clambered inside and shut the door after him in one not altogether graceful movement. Rain thundered on the roof of the car and, settling into the leather seat, aware of the wet smell of his clothes, Frank wiped at his face. Sheila was looking at him with an amused expression.

"I couldn't believe it was you," she said.

"Golfing? It's practically a clerical sport."

"I meant the clothes."

His suntans and knit shirt were not up to the sartorial standards of the Belvedere, but of course she must mean that this was the first time she had seen him in anything but clerical clothes.

"What brings you out here?"

Sheila wore a pretty florid dress, shades of yellow and brown, and white heels. Her hair, which fell to her shoulders, seemed affected nicely by the rain, ends separating and curling, creating an indistinct nimbus.

"I dropped Mother off for a bridge luncheon and then was distracted by this strange man on the putting green."

"Some day."

"I'm afraid you're out of luck. This rain is going to last."

"I haven't golfed in years."

It was a simple fact, but it came forth sadly, as if his profoundest hopes were being drenched by the rain. They sat and listened to the sound of it on the roof; the windshield was a molten blur of running water and the side windows had begun to steam up. Frank took a package of cigarettes from his shirt pocket, discarded several soggy candidates and offered Sheila a dry one. Having lit hers, and one of his own, he rolled down the window an inch and tossed the match out. Through the stitching rain, he could see the blurred bulk of the clubhouse. Was Ewing there? If he was, he would be dry, and there was a bar. Seeing the building from the car, cut off from it by the rain, Frank saw it as he had years ago, as someplace he did not belong, off bounds.

"Were you going to golf alone?"

"No. I'm waiting for someone." He turned toward her. "Another priest."

"I was never much of a golfer."

"But you have played?"

"Oh, yes."

"Here?"

She nodded. "My parents don't really approve of the sort of people who belong here, yet their membership is important. Business, I guess."

"I used to caddy here."

"You did!"

He smiled as if it were a little joke. "Yes."

She wanted to know all about that, when it had been, what summers, and then she wondered if she could possibly have seen him in that improbable role. He had already wondered that. He rubbed at the window and, peering out, felt that if the rain should let up he might see his younger self out there, walking down the hill toward the caddy shack. From the practice green he had seen the caddy shack where a dozen years ago he had whiled away the boring hours between rounds. He had only glanced at it, then turned away, as if in denial. Why had he found it so humiliating to be a caddy? He had liked being out in the open, had always loved this course. As the memory of his parents faded, receding into a mythical past, it had been easy for him to believe that their early death had deprived him of a more satisfactory youth. And it had been boring sitting around that shack, waiting to go out, his name on the list the caddy master kept, disponible. Yet going out was often worse. Usually the foursomes were talkative and the caddies ignored but from time to time he was addressed as himself and there would be the mounting uneasiness as the disinterested questions continued. When the dreaded one was asked ("Where do you go to school?), he would say that he went to LaSalle, the Christian Brothers school. He had learned not to tell the truth, to say that he was a student for the priesthood and went to school at Lake Glister. When he had answered truthfully, he had been pursued by questions throughout the round. "Don't you like girls? How can you tell at your age that you want a life like that?" On and on, with Frank becoming more and more embarrassed. If he lied to avoid that, he told himself that it was not his own embarrassment he wanted to avoid, but the faintly mocking remarks about the priesthood. Now, sitting in Sheila's car in the parking lot, with the rain noisy on the roof, he felt the return of that old sense of inferiority, of not belonging, and the fact that he was dressed as he was altered his relation to Sheila.

"How are things?" he asked, groping for his lost status.

"Things? Oh, all right, I guess." She dragged on her cigarette, then let the smoke escape without inhaling it. Had she accepted the cigarette only out of politeness? "Have you ever quit smoking? I have. The worse part of it is that you begin to imagine an endless stretch of days without cigarettes. One at a time, the days are easy enough, but the thought of that blah future makes it hard." She smiled, but not very joyfully. "That's pretty much how things are."

"Just take it one day at a time then."

"Right. This is my first cigarette in months."

"If I had known, I wouldn't have tempted you."

She looked at him. "How about you?"

"Me?"

"How are things with you?"

The ready answer did not form itself upon his lips. Looking at her, thinking of how much he knew about her, of the things they had talked about together, he found that he wanted to say it. "Not so good."

"Oh?"

"It's a long story."

"So? Here we are, stranded. We might be on an island."

Hadn't he read somewhere that strangers caught like this often tell one another all about themselves, finding in the impersonal intimacy a powerful attraction? A person could say aloud and with impunity what he would normally say only to himself. Eventually the air raid stopped, or rescuers came, the strangers parted and never saw each other again. Of course that did not quite apply to Sheila and himself, but the racket of the rain seemed a convincing backdrop: the roar of the surf, the sound of falling bombs. She knew Monsignor Entweder ("Know him? He baptized me."), she knew his good qualities, so she could understand that his criticism was not total, but even so, the pastor's squelching of the summer program had been hard to take. Very hard to take. Sheila nodded. She understood. "What about caddying?" she asked. "Couldn't some of them do that?" "Caddies are a thing of the past, Sheila. Automation. Carts." "I hadn't thought of that." The human beast of burden replaced by the electric carts which zipped over the greensward with cardiac cases, near traffic jams on the fairways; it was really a shame.

Humbling as being a caddy had been, the money was welcome. And on Monday mornings they had been granted the use of the course; that was when Frank had learned to golf, striding the Belvedere course at the crack of dawn, mimicking the members. When the sun rose into the sky and the dew lifted (he had a vivid memory of the track a ball made on a dewy green, throwing up water like a car tire in the rain), the sound of women on the first tee would drift over the course. Monday was ladies' day as well as caddy day. But Sheila did understand what a shame it had been that the Saint Waldo summer program had not gone forward. She understood too when he spoke of the panel, of the encyclical, of Bullard and Tremplin and Ewing too. Frank wiped at the window again. On the parking lot, puddles had formed in every depression and their surfaces were stippled with bombarding rain.

"Isn't Bullard the man who married the nun?"

"Yes."

"Did you know him well?"

"We were classmates."

She considered that for a moment. "How do priests react to another priest's marrying?"

"In all kinds of ways. Mainly negative."

"I suppose."

He tried to explain it to her, the solidarity that grew through the seminary years, the way it was. As he talked, hands on his knees, khaki pants, this setting with its unsettling memories, the priesthood seemed again something in his future, not yet his, and he felt as he had trying to explain his vocation to those mocking members so many summers ago, thus conferring on Sheila the status of the remote and privileged on whose pleasure he had waited in the shade of the caddy shack's overhang. The smell of rain, of leather and, faintly, of her perfume. His voice sounded defensive and, annoyed, he became critical of Phil Bullard.

"So you don't blame her?"

"Eloise?"

"Usually the woman gets the blame."

"I'm not blaming anyone," he said.

Sheila put her head on the seat back and Frank let the subject drop. Listening to the rain, forgetting his grievances, he let his mind go blank. It was peaceful sitting there, enclosed by the rain, everything else shut out. An interlude. Soon the rain would stop and he would get out, their being here like this forgotten. How could he be blamed for taking shelter from the rain? Blamed? He glanced at Sheila. At least she had not acted as though their sitting here like this meant anything. She had closed her eyes. Her profile seemed very distinct against the background of the steamed window. The round of her chin, her full mouth, the lower lip puffed out as if in thought, delicate nostrils and closed lids, their lashes miniature fans. How various and complicated the human face is when looked at closely; its parts cease to be parts and assert themselves against their sum. Sheila was pretty, he knew, but it was a puzzle where exactly the prettiness was, since it seemed neither the parts taken alone nor all together. Frank turned away, bothered by a memory of Kreuger, a caddy like himself, a grinning, likable, dirty-minded kid, full of apocryphal stories of being importuned by the women he caddied for, his rounds, if you believed him, full of phony searches for lost balls in wooded roughs and out-of-the-way dales. Kreuger claimed to have bedded the daughter of a member whose house was on the road which ran parallel to the seventh fairway. His story had taken on credibility when he had been observed scaling the fence, approaching the house, knocking on the door one afternoon when her parents were at the clubhouse. Kreuger's smirk after that had become intolerable, his bragging masterpieces of innuendo. What had happened to Kreuger? What had happened to them all? Could any of them have had a more improbable future in store than his own, a priest? It was strange to be reminded of the time before his final commitment had been made, when ordination had been years ahead. What else might he have become? Would he have prospered and joined the Belvedere? A good job, on the way up, membership good for business. He had been driven to the club by his wife and, caught by the rain, they were sitting in the parking lot waiting for it to let up. She was expected for bridge, he hoped to get in at least nine holes. At home there would be a child or two.

When he turned to Sheila he found her staring at him. Her eyes, their whites moist, bordered by folded flesh, were accented by the dull light they caught.

"Do you think of them as traitors?"

He did not understand.

"That priest and nun who married."

"Yes. Yes, I guess so."

She closed her eyes. "This is nice."

"Yes."

Shivering, she folded her arms and hugged herself. Her eyes remained shut, but her chin lifted slightly. He could see the vertical lines in her lips. He felt like Kreuger. A lucky break, stranded in the rain with a member's daughter, the rest obvious. He could hear Sheila breathing now. Her eyes opened, their look defenseless, vulnerable.

He said, "The rain's letting up."

"It's pouring."

"I'd better check to see if my partner is waiting in the clubhouse."

"You're frightened."

The pupils of her eyes seemed many colors; in the inner corner a little bud of flesh glistened. Lashes, brows. The eye a metaphor of the body.

"I'd better go."

"Stay."

Her expression was solemn. What did she want? A kiss from a priest in a parked car? He felt an almost physical pressure on his shoulders, pressing him toward her, but he knew he would not do anything, if only because he feared making a fool of himself. He found the door handle and pushed the door open.

"You'll get drenched," she said, her tone mocking. (Don't you like girls? How can you tell you want a life like that?) The rain was falling on the arm which held the door open and on the leg he had put outside.

"I'll be all right," he said and got out. He shut the door and walked across the parking lot, walked right through the puddles with raindrops falling on his head and working right through to his scalp. He had come to the end of the parking lot when he remembered his putter. He turned and looked back at the car. It might have been unoccupied. He went slowly back to it. When he opened the door, Sheila was sitting forward, her hands on the wheel, her head on her hands. She looked up, startled.

"I forgot my putter."

"Oh, for God's sake."

He took the club and, before he closed the door, stooped and put his head inside. "Sheila, I'm sorry. I . . ."

"Why don't you go catch pneumonia or something?"

He closed the door again. It had been silly to allude to it. To what? Nothing had happened. He did not want to go to the clubhouse. He had left his bag propped against a tree beside the practice green. His shoes sounded mushy when he went for it. Slinging the bag over his shoulder, he looked down the hill toward the caddy shack. In a moment he was running toward its promised shelter.

The shack was locked, unused. Benches along its walls, under the deep overhang. Frank sat down next to a water fountain, rusty tap, stained porcelain basin. No handle. Had Sheila wanted to see if he was like the man she had been involved with? Like Bullard? Running his hand along the bench on which he sat, he felt the carved initials of an earlier time. Lead us not into temptation. Trying not to listen to Kreuger and his dirty talk. He would not even have known what to do with Sheila, how to hold her, how to kiss her. He had never kissed a girl. That thought settled sodden in his mind as he stared out over the impossible green of the fairway; the rain continued to fall, fell like inexhaustible *lacrimae rerum*. If he had had any sense at all, he would have asked Sheila for a ride back to the rectory.

2 The funeral Mass for Father Ewing was said in the seminary chapel and everyone present sensed that he was witnessing the end of an era. Out of deference to the often expressed views of the deceased on the new liturgy and, in a way, perforce, since the seminary master of ceremonies, John Tremplin, was now *hors de combat,* Bishop George Caldron offered a solemn requiem Mass in Latin. The clergy assembled in the choir stalls which filled the nave of the chapel leaned into the Gregorian chant, their voices quivering with nostalgia for the dear gone days when they had stood in these very stalls as students. The collective tremolo had an added fittingness as a mark of sorrow for the loss of one of their number. Seated in the sanctuary on the diminutive throne on the Epistle side, Sean Brophy looked across at George Caldron, more definitively enthroned on the Gospel side, at Father Foster placing with practiced hands the miter on his bishop, and it would have been difficult to say whether the auxiliary bishop was concealing his amusement at the medieval display or was slightly envious of Caldron's having elected to say the Mass himself. Brophy was attended by Father Oder since his chaplain, young Garish, was away on an extended retreat.

One whitecap in the sea of surplices in the choir stalls, Frank Ascue felt a deep sense of fellowship with the other priests. Across the aisle, toward the front of the chapel, Monsignor Eisenbarth occupied the rector's place and ranged beside him was the depleted corps of the seminary faculty. Father Ewing seemed conspicuously absent from that stall and Frank's eyes drifted to the draped catafalque in the center aisle. It took an act of faith to think of Father Ewing as lying there. How many of these men had known him as teacher? Frank wondered, and Ewing's reply, "Too many," came immediately to mind and elicited a little smile. This chapel, these stalls, seemed some sort of parable; each year they filled anew with possible replacements for the present clergy, generation following generation. But of course many had sat and knelt and stood in this choir who had not continued to ordination, changing their minds and leaving before the decisive step of major orders. When one was a seminarian it was possible to think that these years of study were a survival course, that only a few would make it to the priesthood and a seemingly permanent status. But Phil Bullard too had put in six years in these stalls, had been ordained a priest and now was gone. He represented a new category of alumnus, one that had been unimaginable only a few years ago. Would Phil ever recall his days in the seminary and feel the sweet nostalgia Frank did now that was a function of the music, of this gathering of priests, of the special camaraderie of the clergy? Better that he did not.

Monsignor Eisenbarth preached a moving tribute to his departed colleague, the tone for it set in the precision with which he moved from his place to the center of the sanctuary, bowed to the bishops in turn, and then, facing the clergy, concealing his hands in the sleeves of his surplice, consulted the rose window in the organ loft for half a minute before beginning to speak. He stressed Hubert Ewing's loyalty to the promises he had made to God as a young man and his obedience to the will of the bishop. "It can happen, as perhaps some here know, that the assignment given us does not match our own estimate of our talents. How easy it would be to brood on the difference between duty and inclination, to become sullen and sour and grudging in the performance of our daily tasks. Those of us who knew him well were aware of Father Ewing's zealous hope that one day he would be transferred from the important but seemingly remote work of teaching to a pastoral post where the theory might become practice, his practice, and not merely that of his former students. That hope was never realized. What I wish to stress today is not the existence of that hope of Hubert Ewing's but his mode of conduct as a professor, as a priest, despite that hope. He did his work. He gave what was asked of him. Daily he lived the vocation to which he had been called and he was faithful to the promises he had made. He did his work. He was faithful. May each of us today, in paying respect to Father Ewing's memory and in commending his soul to God, ask for the grace to imitate these salient features of his life."

Eisenbarth's peroration was spoiled by the opening of the chapel doors. Heads turned from the front of the chapel to the back, where, in the open door, silhouetted against the outside light, John Tremplin stood. Tremplin came inside, allowing the doors to close, and started up the aisle between the facing banks of choir stalls, his heels clicking defiantly, calling attention to his shoes, apparently of green suede. The startled eyes lifted from shoes to flared trousers and then to the rib-hugging cut of the jacket of the yellow suit he wore. A pink shirt, a psychedelic tie and, emerging from this sartorial surprise, the wagging head of John Tremplin, his face dominated by a manic self-satisfied smile. Tremplin made a smart right-angle turn and took a place in a pew whose surpliced occupants rolled back like a commanded wave. And then, from the altar, Bishop Caldron's thin voice intoned the Credo and the chapel filled with relieved and fervent song.

Someone tugged Frank's sleeve and when he turned, an elderly priest pointed to the back of the choir stall. Frank went up to the back pew and looked down at the agonized face of Father Oder.

"Frank, get him out of here."

There could not be a doubt in the world who was meant. "How?"

"I don't know. But get him out."

Frank nodded. The imperative was categorical. He went down the steps to the aisle and, as if under cover of the singing, went back to John Tremplin and grasped his arm. Jack looked at him haughtily but gave no resistance when Frank led him into the aisle and then toward the door, increasing the pace so that by the time they reached the door he was propelling Jack. Once outside, he gave Tremplin a push that sent him careening off balance through some intricate footwork that saved him from falling on his face.

"Hypocrites," Tremplin shouted, when he had established himself flatfooted and was facing Frank. "Hypocrites!"

"What in the name of God do you think you're doing?" Frank went to Tremplin and again gripped his arm. "We are burying a man, don't you realize that?"

"As one who has already undergone the process, let me assure you—"

Frank shook him into silence. "You're crazy."

"Perhaps." Tremplin freed himself, smoothed his sleeve, seemed pleasantly distracted by his attire. He looked at Frank. "Either crazy or finally in possession of clarity. I have, as you might say, lost my faith."

"You've lost your mind."

"None of it makes sense, Frank. None of it. That dawned on me in a blaze of light. I have been hoodwinking myself for years. So have you. So have they." Tremplin gestured toward the chapel.

"When did you decide to leave your room?"

"That is what I am explaining. I began to think, really think, about what was grieving me. Frank, have you any idea what our life looks like when inspected from a rational point of view?"

"Jack, I am going back to chapel. Are you through making an ass of yourself?"

"Oh, quite through. I have written a long letter to George."

382

"Will you stay out of chapel?"

"With pleasure." Tremplin's chin dropped and his look softened. "This is good-bye, Frank." Jack seemed intent on investing the moment with some mad solemnity. Frank, whose hands were clenched in fists, would have liked to hit Jack, really clout him, and the desire exhilarated him more than it shamed him.

"No hard feelings?"

Tremplin extended his hand. Frank looked at it, saw a network of lines, the bitten nails, and all he could think was that that was the consecrated hand of a priest. As were his own. He unclenched his fists. The pathos of the figure before him, his recent mournful thoughts about the man whose body lay in chapel, made it less difficult to take Tremplin's hand and shake it. An absurd adieu. Jack turned and, arrayed in that incredible costume, minced away along a seminary walk, heading into the waiting world.

Frank returned unseeing to his place in chapel, to the remainder of the Mass. Afterward they all filed out after the coffin. The seminary road was lined with cars, one of them McTear's, in which Frank would drive Entweder to the cemetery. On the walk outside the chapel he stood, looking for the little pastor, and was aware of grateful glances from the passing priests. Monsignor Yorick strode toward him.

"Good work, Frank. What in hell did he think he was doing?"

"Saying good-bye."

The chancellor frowned. "You're kidding."

"That's what he said."

Yorick said something profane and they were joined by Bishop Brophy, whose presence caused others, among them Oder, to gather around. The consensus was that Frank had done a noble thing in hustling Tremplin out of the chapel.

"Well, Frank," Swivel said expansively. "It looks as though this place is going to be home for you, doesn't it?"

There was a murmur that might have been approval but what Frank noticed was Yorick's frowning dissent.

When he arrived at his office in the morning, Howard Nygaard wished only to get safely behind his desk, to have a cup of Miss Furlong's coffee placed before him and to be assured of at least half an hour of solitude during which he went through the psychological exercises which enabled him to face another day. After an all but sleepless night, the coffee was a necessity to slam his nerves back into some semblance of alertness. The solitude of his office, the one place his guilt did not seem to occupy, enabled him to lift his thoughts above the dilemma represented by Sharon on the one hand and his family on the other, above and onto the neutral plateau where it was possible to get some work done and thus justify his taking his percentage of the firm's income. Thank God their clientele had stirred up nothing but routine problems for years and his tasks, like those of the other senior partners, were almost mechanical. But this morning his progress toward his office had been arrested by the receptionist adding to her Good morning a startling piece of information. Howard came to a halt as if wires had been pulled from above.

"My daughter? Here?"

"Uh huh." Mrs. Hinkly's fifty years were supposedly disguised by the angoralike wig which sat on her head like a helmet. "Didn't she mention it? I told her that you'd gone home early."

"What time was she here?"

Mrs. Hinkly's smile contracted on her prominent teeth and her eyes darted beyond Howard. He turned to see that Miss Furlong was there.

"Did you see my daughter here the other day?"

"Your daughter?"

"I told you about it," Mrs. Hinkly whined. The receptionist, who had clearly considered herself the carrier of bright news, was puzzled by this strange turn of events.

"It doesn't matter," Howard said, and plunged into his office. He could sense that behind his back the two females were exchanging startled glances, nor did he blame them.

He sat at his desk, dropping his attaché case on the floor beside his chair. Miss Furlong came in with a cup of coffee, placed it on the desk and fussed a bit, obviously waiting. Howard said nothing and in a moment she left him alone. Sipping coffee with narrowed eyes and raised brows, he felt that Beverly was standing before him. What did she want? What expression would be on her imagined face? The memory of her crying the other night when she came in from her date took on an ominous meaning. He had assumed that she was weeping over her own troubles, troubles that could not possibly be serious, but now he could not avoid the thought that he had occasioned her tears. Why hadn't she mentioned her visit to the office? Howard went back over the time since Mrs. Hinkly said Beverly had dropped in here. He had gone from the office to Sharon's and from there home. Beverly had said nothing at the dinner table and it seemed to him now that he had been struck by her preoccupied air. My God, she knew! Somehow she had found out about Sharon. What had she intended to say when she came here? What would she say when finally she confronted him with her knowledge of his infidelity?

Sweat began to form on his forehead, aided by the heat of the coffee, but it was the sweat of fear. Beverly could never understand, never. He could not expect that she would. The possibility that his own daughter might accuse him was a far more frightening prospect than anything Charlotte might say if she should find out about Sharon. Any marriage contains enough grievances on both sides to provide some semblance of an excuse for straying, but Beverly would be the envoy of innocence, unable to see how her father could do such a thing, certainly unable to forgive it. What in the name of God could he say to her that would not make matters infinitely worse? He could not expect to reach her with a bill of particulars against her mother; any such attempt would increase his own guilt immeasurably. If he should hear his own case from Beverly's viewpoint he would not hesitate to bring in a verdict of guilty.

It helped to have put the worst possible interpretation on Beverly's visit first. There were other possibilities, of course, and Howard tried to confer on them such probability as he could muster. And, after all, it was possible that her visit had no significance at all. She might simply have been downtown and looked in at his office and, not finding him in, forgotten all about it. Of course. He smiled. He returned to his now cooler coffee, seeking in the familiar taste the reassurance that this was a morning like any other. But even this more appealing view of Beverly's visit had its unsettling side. First Charlotte and now Beverly had come here to find him gone, and on both occasions Sharon had been the reason for his absence. Char was no more likely to come here than Beverly but the fact that they both had, and recently, suggested that a pattern of the unlikely might eventually lead to the discovery that he spent several hours nearly every day with a young woman at her apartment.

For an hour his mind veered from one interpretation of Beverly's visit to the other and the more he thought of it, the less consolation he could find in either. For there was an appeal that he could not deny in the possibility that he was discovered, that his duplicity could cease. What a relief that would be. But how in the crunch would he resolve his dilemma? Would he abandon Sharon for his family or vice versa, presuming that both options were open to him? The chance that he was not yet discovered seemed only a temporary comfort, since it seemed to him now inevitable that eventually he would be. He picked up his phone, intending to call Sharon, and surprised himself by dialing home. He was almost startled by the sound of Charlotte's voice.

"Oh, Howard, I'm so glad you called. I forgot to mention it this morning. CFM is tonight."

"Tonight?"

"Now don't say you can't make it. You haven't been to a meeting for months and you know it's awkward for me to go without you. After all, the whole point is that we meet as couples."

"I suppose. What are you doing?"

"Doing?"

"I wondered if you'd like to come downtown. For lunch."

"Just you and me?"

"I've felt badly since that day you missed me here."

"Howard, what a nice thought."

"We can meet here."

"But I can't! The meeting is at the Hogans' tonight and I told Sally I'd come help her get ready. Now don't say there isn't anything to get ready; I know there isn't. But Sally is the sort of person who has a breakdown at the thought of that many people in her home at one time. And I want things to run smoothly for this meeting. We have to decide what we are going to do as a group about this encyclical."

"Well, some other time then. All right?"

"You will come to the meeting, won't you?"

He said he would. The call seemed to earn him balancing points on some score card that was being kept somewhere—in heaven, he supposed—and he found that he was able to get to work. But at the edge of his mind throughout the day was the talk he must have with Sharon when he stopped to see her on his way home.

"I really hate my mother," Sharon said almost musingly. They lay on her bed. The shades were pulled but the late afternoon sun was bright upon them, illuminating the billowy white curtains. Howard felt that he was supine in a model bedroom in *House Beautiful,* but the thought was not critical. He now found Sharon's apartment attractive and tasteful.

"Hate your father," he advised.

"How can I? I never knew him. I know my mother."

"It isn't her fault that you never knew your father."

"Don't think it bothers me not to have known him."

"Doesn't it?"

She stirred beside him and he could feel her eyes on him, but he stared at the ceiling where amorphous patterns formed and dissolved.

"Oh, I guess it does. But I doubt that my mother would have been very different if they had married and all the rest. She is a thoroughly

386

repulsive person." Sharon tossed away from him and banged her head into a pillow. "Sometimes I wish I were dead."

"You don't mean that."

"I wonder. Not being in the same city as her doesn't help as much as I had hoped it would. Just knowing that she exists . . ."

From outside came the sound of afternoon traffic. His shock was not profound. But her malice was contagious and, closing his eyes, he imagined that that was how Beverly would speak of him if she knew of this apartment, if she could see him now. That his daughter might wish him dead did not, as he had expected, fill him with self-pity, providing a means of transferring his guilt to someone else, since after all he did not wish anyone dead. Or did he? He lay there and thought of himself as dead and it seemed almost a solution. All those he was now wronging in different ways would unite to mourn him, think only good thoughts of him, forgive or forget his mistakes. He had a vision of Charlotte and the children, and Sharon too, all of them in black, kneeling in a front pew while he lay in a box in the middle aisle, the object of everyone's sorrow and tears.

"Oh, Howard, I'm such a horrid person." Sharon rolled toward him, crushed against him, struggled to get her arms about him, until almost reluctantly abandoning the delightful image of his own funeral he gathered her in and held her close and thought how much she needed him, how much she depended on him.

Sharon had not told her mother that she had moved to Fort Elbow. She had simply disappeared from Cleveland without a trace. Why didn't the old woman sound the alarm, report Sharon as missing, hire private detectives? Did he see in that a way of escape? Sharon dragged kicking and screaming back to Cleveland and the mother she hated, Howard left as if abandoned, with only his family exerting a claim upon him. It was because Sharon was here almost incognito, without roots, that her dependence on him was total. He found it hard to realize now that, in the beginning, he had resented that. He was her only contact with the world beyond this apartment. Whatever responsibilities his family imposed upon him seemed to pale before the claim of this girl, who clung to him there on the bed, pressing her youthful body to his aging one, seeking to draw from him the patrimony that life and chance and human weakness had robbed her of.

Monsignor Randolph Eisenbarth's necrology, when he permitted himself to dwell on it—and in the days following Father Ewing's funeral he found it difficult not to—was depressingly long and forever growing longer. His parents, two older brothers, one niece, assorted more distant relatives, and also, and this is where the list lengthened, fellow clerics. Revered older priests, his models of long ago, had gone on into the next life one by one; they had been joined by members of his own generation until it was possible to believe that all around him his cohorts were being mercilessly cut down. I alone have escaped to tell you. Monsignor Eisenbarth had been affected all out of proportion to his relations to the man alive by the sudden death of Father Ewing.

Hubert's age somehow did not diminish the shock. For all his disgruntled ways, Ewing had been one of the most vivacious members of the faculty—think of all that golfing—and only a few years the rector's senior. The manner of his going induced long thoughts, of course. How horrible to have the body found like that. Father Sweeney had stopped by for a chat and, worried when his knock went unanswered, let himself in and found Hubert sprawled upon the floor. The future contained his own inevitable end, of course, but Monsignor Eisenbarth did not like the thought that his mortal remains might one day, and soon perhaps, be found lying on his floor.

His eyes dropped to the carpet of his office, a thin and faded carpet that had come with the room. It would afford no cushion to his fall. Father Sweeney's discovery of Ewing's body might have been more grisly than it was. Ewing had been smoking, predictably, and the cigarette he had been holding when the attack claimed him had smoldered on the rug, burning a sizable hole but then mercifully going out. How easily Father Ewing's clothing might have been set afire. The rector shivered. Fire, air, earth and water—any of the elements might be the instrument of death and he found none acceptable. If only he could be assured of slipping gently away while sleeping, to be found in bed, decently covered, the thought of dying would be easier to contemplate.

He must not brood. When he was younger, he had thought death would lose its strangeness, perhaps even its fearsomeness, with age, but the fact was that now when he found it impossible to ignore that millions had died before reaching his age, life's attractions increased enormously. It was difficult not to think of all he had yet to do. Such eminence as he had reached fell so far short of what he had aspired to that his life had a decidedly unfinished look to it. Unfortunately that was no assurance that he still had years to live. Ewing too had hoped for more than he had. What a depressing thought that his own ambitions, like Hubert Ewing's, would more than likely be frustrated.

The morbidity of these thoughts was reduced by asking himself what he could do now, in his present position, that he was not already doing. Ewing had urged vigorous action during the hunger strike and the picketing last spring and he had sat here, counseling patience, trying without success to convince his colleague of its wisdom. He knew that Ewing had considered him a coward. For that matter, Arthur Rupp had lost faith in the moral courage of the founder of Te Deum. They are right, Monsignor Eisenbarth thought gloomily. I have become an artless dodger. Where is the moral indignation, the lust for combat, that I used to have?

He sent his fingers rummaging across his desk and turned up Oder's letter announcing a meeting of the clerical senate. It was as usual an enigmatic letter. Recent unspecified events were to make up the agenda. Monsignor Eisenbarth was certain that others, perhaps most others, in any case the clique that had formed around Brophy and Oder, knew perfectly well the purpose of the senate meeting. He was excluded from the councils of power. For one who had always been close to the center of things, with two doctorates, a monsignor in his early thirties, the youngest man ever appointed rector of the seminary, as close to George Caldron as it was possible for any mortal to be, this was a bitter realization, and all the more bitter because of what it indicated. The bishop of the diocese was no longer the exclusive source of power. The senate was an innovation which was all the more threatening because of George Caldron's visible aging. Eisenbarth had felt ineffectual, even humiliated, at the first meeting of the senate, unable even to be recognized by the chair. The one group whose attention he could claim was Te Deum, and even they were disenchanted by him because of his timidity. Yes, timidity. It did no good to call it prudence. Ewing, it turned out, was right. He should have dealt severely with John Tremplin. Imagine the man creating a scene like that at a funeral, and in full view of the bishop!

His eyes dropped to Oder's letter, which he read again with renewed annoyance. He should demand to know what precisely this meeting was to be about.

When he reached Father Oder on the telephone, however, Monsignor Eisenbarth was the victim of his own courtly manner. For a full five minutes he exchanged pleasantries with the chairman of the senate and then tentatively approached the purpose of this call.

"I have been looking over your letter, Donald. The letter in which you call another meeting of the senate."

Oder sighed. "I'm afraid that this is a more demanding job than I had imagined."

"Organizational work has a way of tyrannizing over one," Eisenbarth agreed. "That was the reason I felt I must put down the reins of Te Deum."

"I haven't heard much of it since you did," Oder said kindly.

"Oh, it is thriving, Donald. It really is."

This reassurance met with silence and Eisenbarth decided to strike into the deep.

"What is on the agenda for the meeting?"

"Did you want to suggest an item, Monsignor?"

"Yes," Eisenbarth said, surprising himself. "Yes, I would. It has struck me that the senate might sponsor a discussion of the new encyclical. A thorough discussion. Perhaps we could invite some outside speakers."

"You mean an open meeting?"

"Of course. This need not be restricted to members of the senate. Any priest might come. We could provide a thorough airing of the matter, pros and cons, but conducted on a respectable level, a theological level."

"Actually I had been thinking of canceling the meeting."

"It might be a good idea to postpone it. Next week is much too soon for a carefully planned meeting. We would not want to sponsor anything hurried or incompetent. The Holy Father needs and deserves all the support we can give him in these hectic days."

"Well, Monsignor, your idea is certainly worth considering. For a future date. I think I can say that next week's meeting will not be held."

"What was to have been the purpose of it?"

There was a pause and then, in a strange shift of topic, Donald asked, "What has happened to John Tremplin, do you know?"

"I am told that he has taken up residence in a downtown hotel." The rector sighed. He did not add that he had been told that John Tremplin intended to have the bill he was running up sent to the chancery for payment, allegedly as a claim against underpayment for services rendered in the past.

Before hanging up, Oder said, rather condescendingly, that he would give serious thought to the rector's suggestion of a senate-sponsored discussion of the encyclical. Monsignor Eisenbarth felt that he had been dismissed as a crank.

Then, as he did increasingly now, he replayed the conversation in his mind, amending it so that his part became the principal one. But Oder's somewhat peremptory tone haunted him. Too late it occurred to him that he might have told Donald that it was somewhat presumptuous to call meetings at the seminary without prior consultation and approval of its rector. His own unpremeditated suggestion of a meeting devoted to a serious discussion of the encyclical seemed the real heart of the conversation, not least because it was something he could pursue without any encouragement from Oder. Why, he might just go ahead with

390

it and force Oder to go along; the calling and content of meetings were not the exclusive prerogative of the chairman. It might be well, as a general principle, to establish that fact early in the history of the senate. Monsignor Eisenbarth smiled at the prospect of diverting the clerical senate, a dangerous experiment in democracy, to the ends of the hierarchy. It could be said without uncharitableness that Donald Oder was altogether too much influenced by the anarchic currents within the Church; he was certainly not the man to stage the sort of discussion of the encyclical that Monsignor Eisenbarth had in mind.

Te Deum. The organization he had founded had been a force for good over the years but, alas, Donald Oder was right: of late it had not been making itself felt. Oh, Monsignor Eisenbarth was willing to share the blame for that, it was not Arthur Rupp's fault alone. Arthur had a combative spirit but it was increasingly clear he needed more direction than he had been receiving from Te Deum's founder. Remembering the zeal which had led to the forming of the organization, back in those terrible days when the communist menace was being mocked by the liberal press and treated as if it were a drunken dream of Senator McCarthy, Monsignor Eisenbarth dismissed the idea of trying to battle Donald Oder for supremacy in the senate. He already had an organization. And he had a cause. Te Deum must come massively to the support of the Holy Father.

Stirred by his own thoughts, the rector got up and went to his window. On the porch outside, Father Sweeney was pacing slowly, reciting his rosary. How unperturbed, and edifyingly so, the old man was by the current turmoil in the Church. Only this morning, Eisenbarth had found himself stating his own fears to the ancient spiritual director.

"Father Sweeney, would you have believed ten years ago a prediction that such things would be going on in the Church?" The occasion for this remark had been an item in the paper about a monsignor who was giving up that title because, he said, to retain it might suggest a loyalty to the pope he no longer felt he could promise since the issuance of *Humanae Vitae*. A few days before, the rector of a seminary for retarded vocations had suggested that the pope stood convicted of heresy because he was in disagreement with the majority of Catholics on birth control. "I simply cannot believe that this is happening," Eisenbarth had said plaintively.

"But it was all predicted," Sweeney said with a bittersweet smile. "At Fatima."

"It's the fifteenth century all over again," Eisenbarth said, ignoring Father Sweeney's familiar trump.

"Things will get worse, Randy. Much worse."

Monsignor Eisenbarth wished that Father Sweeney would show less relish for these dire predictions. Perhaps relish was the wrong word. Yet how placid the old man looked now, telling his beads while all the media crackled with news of dissension, revolt and schism. It was difficult not to envy Father Sweeney his conviction that unspectacular prayer and penance, not debate, were what the times required.

But each has his gift from the Lord, and Monsignor Eisenbarth's had always been debate and controversy. He went back to his desk and telephone. He had other calls to make.

"Poor Randolph," Bishop Brophy said, his eyes on the point where the thick base of his glass met the rounded arm of the leather chair in which he sat. Both he and Frank Ascue had been the silent addressees of Oder's end of the telephone conversation with Eisenbarth: words for the rector, grimaces of commentary for his guests. "I feel sympathy for men of his generation. It's not simply that they were unprepared for *aggiornamento;* they all have this very different picture of the priesthood. I've sometimes thought that it isn't the going of the Latin that bothers them so much as the realization that their knowledge of Italian is no longer an asset. They thought of themselves as in the foreign service, the Vatican diplomatic corps. They've all been on overseas assignment—at home. They are a lost generation."

Oder made a face. "Eisenbarth is years younger than Pope John was when he was elected."

"Are you suggesting that there are better things in store for Randolph? A cisalpine ultramontane pontiff from Fort Elbow, Ohio?"

Frank Ascue smiled but Oder was as usual impatient with any levity not his own. Or had he turned the edge of the remark against his vulnerable self? The pastor of Saint Barnabas was in as definitive a cul-de-sac as the rector of the seminary. Frank had known reversals, he certainly could not have been pleased about being sent to Saint Waldo's, but he was still young, while Don had probably reached his personal summit and that was, in its way, odd. Donald Oder was a brilliant man and had always been regarded as such locally. Naturally George had not taken advantage of this. Don's knack for investments had provided him with a comfortable financial cushion; he had a vast and perused library and was indeed one of the best-read priests Bishop Brophy knew. The bishop's eyes moved over the shelves in Oder's study with the approval of one who no longer has time to read himself, really read that is, the kind of in-depth pursuit of a subject one liked to hope would someday be possible. Yet to what purpose Oder's erudition? The parishioners who liked his professorial sermons were vastly outnumbered by those who found them tedious. Had Donald ever dreamed of teaching? Too bad if he had. Unlike Frank, he had no advanced degree.

"He suggested that the senate sponsor a discussion of the encyclical," Don said. "Outside speakers. A real do."

"I can imagine the speakers he has in mind," Bishop Brophy said.

Frank put out his cigarette. "It would be easy to get a good discussion going on the encyclical. Maybe we should."

"A discussion? Speeches?" Oder looked at Frank with disappointment. "Whatever for? Aren't you sick to death of lectures and talks? I am. I suspect everyone is."

"But things are so confused just now. There hasn't been any official diocesan statement on the encyclical, yet people read the papers. They know what's going on everyplace else."

"Of course they read the papers, but how many do you think would come out to hear a discussion?"

Frank sat back. "Maybe we should get something into the local paper then."

"Not the *Fort Elbow Catholic?*" Don teased.

Bishop Brophy said, "What do you mean, Frank?"

"I don't know. But I do know that there should be some guidance on the matter in the diocese. At Saint Waldo's we mentioned that the encyclical had come out and that was about it. Monsignor Entweder didn't want any questioning of it. That's all right, maybe, in the pulpit, but people know it is being questioned. By theologians, bishops, cardinals."

"What about it, Don?" Brophy asked. "You did that series on the Council for the *Tribune,* didn't you? Couldn't you put together something on the encyclical?"

Oder raised a staying hand. "Not me. Please. I am no theologian." He looked at Frank. "You're the man for it, Frank. If you think it would do any good."

"Coming from me, I know it would do no good. Something like that should carry weight. It should come from someone in authority. Like you, Bishop Brophy. If you would . . ."

"I? But, Frank, I am no theologian either. Of course I've been keeping up on the current discussion, as much as my schedule allows, but I could scarcely contribute to it."

"Let Frank write it for you," Don said. "That's the solution. He can sketch out the theology of it, you can revise it as you like and it could appear in the *Tribune* under your name."

"I'd have to think about that."

"Sean, Frank is right. For a week now we have all been waiting for some American bishop to step forward and speak in his own name. There is a vacuum waiting to be filled. This is a great opportunity."

Smiling pensively, Bishop Brophy settled back, thus encouraging Don and Frank to continue their blandishments. The suggestion grew more attractive as he thought of it. A dramatic and personal statement, Sean Brophy addressing the nation. The National Bishops Conference, through its spokesman, had been reacting to comments on the encyclical like a dazed boxer. Behind the scenes, Bishop Brophy knew, any number of bishops were in sympathy with the dissenting theologians, but no one had stepped out from the official solidarity to voice anything like a criticism of *Humanae Vitae*. Several courageous bishops on the Continent had been heard, single voices like that of the Archbishop of Munich, a collective voice from the Netherlands. Even the Canadian bishops had shown more spunk than their counterparts on this side of the border. Clearly there was a role here in search of an episcopal player.

"All right," he said. "Work something up for me, Frank. Something good, something solid, but remember the audience."

Past the point of decision, Bishop Brophy felt gripped by the same certainty he had known when he issued his statement on the picketing seminarians. But this time he would not get into a position where George might try a punitive reprisal.

"The time is ripe," he said.

Ripeness is all. There is a tide in the affairs of men. Bishop Brophy's mind crackled like Bartlett's *Familiar Quotations* as he warmed to the idea. Good Lord, this could be the really big one. He rose to his feet.

Oder said, "God knows Fort Elbow can use an authoritative voice to rally around."

Brophy gave him a small smile. Fort Elbow! The impact he dreamed of went far beyond Fort Elbow. But if Frank and Oder showed themselves deficient in imagination, could he plead innocent to the same charge? Like everyone else, he had been biding his time, awaiting some signal from above, acting like a follower rather than a leader. The whole point of the present crisis in the Church was that they must all get over that structured view of things: the employers and the employed, the engineers and the firemen. The times were such that priests could take the play away from bishops and an auxiliary in Ohio could steal a march on the National Bishops Conference by going over the heads of his peers to the people of God themselves.

"Where's Garish?" Brophy asked.

Frank said, "He told me he would be in church."

"I'll have Swivel fetch him," Oder said.

"Come on, Frank. I'll drop you at Saint Waldo's."

As they walked out to the car, it seemed providential to Bishop Brophy that he had suggested earlier, when he and Don had been chatting and Tremplin's antics at Ewing's funeral came up, that they give Frank Ascue a call. Frank had performed excellently that day. For that matter he had done extremely well on the television panel. Frank was a good man, a very good man, and he would be playing from strength in drafting this statement. After all, Frank was a theologian. An S.T.D. who was second assistant at Saint Waldo's. Bishop Brophy shook his head. Well, something could be done about that now. With both Tremplin and Ewing missing from the faculty, the seminary would be in a severely weakened condition and who could George turn to if not to Frank Ascue?

"How are things going at Saint Waldo's?" Brophy asked when they got to the car.

"I'm kept pretty busy," Frank said, and then added, "I like it."

But of course Bishop Brophy could not really believe that.

Monsignor Eisenbarth's visit to his office was like an absolution for not having jogged the last few days. What a tonic to hear the old crusader's tone in the monsignor's voice once more, a glint in his gray eyes and the nervous movement of his hand through the high-rise of his still thick hair. Eisenbarth was clearly girded for battle and Arthur Rupp felt like a fleet summoned from mothballs, a rifle cleaned of its preserving grease, a grenade whose pin had finally been pulled.

"Excuse my bursting in like this, Arthur, but we are not granted the luxury of leisurely preparation. Can you mobilize the membership? A good turnout is of the essence."

"We've all been waiting for something like this," Arthur said with unconcealed excitement. "Don't worry about the turnout."

"We can't afford another Fourth of July," Monsignor Eisenbarth said pointedly.

Arthur resented that. Was Eisenbarth suggesting that Te Deum had fallen into incapable hands since he had stepped aside? Or, sinking thought, when he spoke of speakers did he have himself in mind? No, no, he had said outside speakers. As for the crack about the Fourth, well, they could not afford the luxury of recrimination either.

"We will steal their thunder, Monsignor."

"We need the laity with us. We shall have the bulk of the clergy, of course. I have already spoken with Monsignor Yorick. I wanted to clear this with the chancery from the outset and the chancellor said that it was the best news he'd had since the encyclical itself."

Arthur resented this order of priorities. Sometimes he wondered if Eisenbarth took Te Deum as seriously as he claimed to do. He certainly took it for granted.

"The fact that Father Oder knows our plans—and I take full responsibility for that—introduces an unsavory factor." Eisenbarth's eyes narrowed with the shrewdness of one who knows the ways of the world. "It would be naïve not to expect that the other camp will eventually see the importance of this meeting. I predict that they will in their turn seek a spokesman who will seem to speak with authority. Our own choice must be governed by that possibility."

"We could organize a claque," Arthur said. "Drown him out."

"No, no, no. Hooligan tactics are out, Arthur. We are speaking of Te Deum. Our choice of a speaker must already make the basic point. We want someone of unarguable eminence and authority, someone beside whom their own spokesman must appear a marginal figure."

Arthur ceded grudgingly to Monsignor Eisenbarth's gentleman's code, though he could not share his confidence in the power of presence and argument. Eisenbarth would not step into the gutter and he could not abide the thought that the organization he had founded might lust to do so. Arthur rather liked the thought of turning the meeting into a donnybrook. Eisenbarth's revelation that the opposition was already alerted to their plans suggested to Arthur that the meeting could be torpedoed. After all, Oder was the chairman of the senate and behind him lurked the gray eminence of Bishop Brophy. Into a stacked clerical deck Te Deum would bring the wild card of the laity. For days dissenters to the encyclical had been invoking the authority of the voiceless lay majority. Well, by God, Te Deum would show them that lay people were foursquare behind the pope, as every Catholic ought to be, and if some priests were not, then they ran the risk of getting their noggins rapped.

"I wonder if we shouldn't bring Cyril Horvath into this," Eisenbarth said. "The three of us could get together for luncheon."

"Horvath?" Arthur said testily.

"Why ever not? He's a prominent layman. Arthur, he is a Knight of Saint Gregory."

Arthur looked accusingly at his preceptor. Of course Horvath had been knighted by the pope. *His* friends had some notion of noblesse oblige, or was it largess?

"Oh, I don't care," Arthur said petulantly. "Should I phone Sir Cyril now?"

But, lucky, lucky, Horvath's secretary said that he was out of town. Considerably relieved, Arthur assured Monsignor Eisenbarth that he would contact Horvath at the earliest opportunity.

"The main thing, Arthur—and this is totally in your hands—the main thing is the speaker. We need a star!"

Arthur was so anxious to speak to Clara of this wonderful turn of events that when Eisenbarth got up to go he did too. He put Eisenbarth in his car, waved him off and, when he was gone, dashed to his own car. The Rupp Insurance Agency would have to sail on without its captain for a time.

"Oh, Arthur," Clara cried with delight. She held her hands in front of her, clenched into fists, making her rings pop out. "Finally!"

"I am calling a meeting of the executive committee for tonight. Here." He took Clara's hands, knobby with rings, palms dry but warm. "I have to invite an outside speaker. A real headliner."

"Who?"

"Buckley. Bozell. Someone of that caliber."

"Oh, Arthur. Arthur."

She flung her arms about him and squeezed. It was an emotional moment. They clung together, faith justified, hope fulfilled, love remaining and intensified.

"Is there any coffee?"

"I'll put on a fresh pot."

In his den, Arthur positioned himself at his desk, cleared his throat, rehearsed with moving lips, picked up the phone and asked for the long distance operator.

Clara tiptoed in while he was on the phone, put an empty cup before him and mouthed the message that the coffee would be ready soon. Arthur nodded, his attention on the instrument at his ear. It was good to have Clara's respect again. His drooping spirits, a consequence of Sheila's return to work as well as to her own apartment, but also of the publicized reaction to the encyclical, had led to his failure to jog. Clara had said nothing but her disapproval was palpable.

Arthur had no luck with his call to New York. His ear filled with the chatter of a series of operators while the Fort Elbow girl was shunted from number to number. Clara came in with the coffeepot and filled his cup.

"Would you like me to try that number, sir?" the operator asked when yet another string of digits had come her way from New York.

"Of course."

He might have admired the technological marvel which permitted him to chase his prey about a city hundreds of miles distant, but his mood was more that of Captain Ludd. Where the hell was the man? Probably whizzing about Manhattan on his motor scooter, if you could believe the dust jacket of his most recent book. Reluctantly, Arthur drew a line through the top name on his list and instructed the operator to go in search of Number Two.

Success was not to be his until he came to his seventh name, a name added while listening to the lengthy regrets of Number Four. Arthur had gone down his list with the sense that something very important between Clara and himself depended on his emerging from the den victorious. When he had his man, he put down the phone and went into the living room like a blacksmith taking a breather from the forge. Clara looked up expectantly, a little apprehensively too. He had been over an hour on the phone.

"Thaddeus Chorzempowski," Arthur announced.

"*Prince* Thaddeus?" Clara squealed.

"He was honored to be asked and delighted to accept."

Clara broke down; ecstatic tears filled her eyes. Needlessly, Arthur ticked off his headliner's qualifications.

"And a *prince* besides," Clara burbled joyfully. "An authentic Polish prince." She took Arthur's hands and might have led him in a polka had he not restrained her. A prince indeed. A Polish prince. He grinned malevolently. Take that, Horvath, you Hungarian knight. But underneath his own delight in having secured so eminent a speaker, Arthur felt a current of peasant sullenness pass through him.

The little Franciscan took half a minute to get settled in the pulpit before he said a word and there was restless movement rather than anticipation in the pews. At the front of the church, on either side, two mounted fans reminded Howard of the cowling on the old Stinson. Did they still make Stinsons? As a boy in Minneapolis, he had loved to hang around Wold-Chamberlain field, where in the prewar days, before commercial aviation had been a big thing, a boy could wander into the control tower to kibitz or prowl through the hangars among the private planes. There had been a blue Stinson into whose leather seat he had loved to settle and pretend by the hour that he was aloft. Make-believe remembered, the trigger those fans, while the little Franciscan told them all about himself, where he had been, what he had done, and parish bulletins moved monotonously before bored faces, supplementing the inadequate fans. Howard would have given much to be only another bored parishioner, essentially innocent, looking forward to Sunday dinner and hours in front of the television.

Only cowardice explained his being there, in church, at Mass, his family beside him in the pew. But if his presence was pharisaical, hypocritical, within he prayed the prayer of the sinner. Lord, have mercy. Lord, have mercy. And what if mercy came? It would do him no good. He was caught in a situation of his own devising and there was no way out that did not entail pain, for others, for himself. For Charlotte. The way out was out of his marriage, away from his family, to Sharon. He wished that his pulse did not quicken at the prospect of a life with her.

Sharon, when he arrived at her apartment yesterday, peeked around the door, her hair in curlers, face scrubbed and youthful. She might have been a child but for the wise look in her eyes.

"I didn't expect you." She opened the door, keeping out of sight: vanity, prudence, what? The door shut behind him and he stood for a moment with closed eyes. The little apartment was steamy, filled with the aromas of soap and shampoo. When he turned, he saw her bare feet showing forlornly from under her robe. He held her close, caught up once more in the passion that was the only explanation of them. Her throat tasted soapy to his lips. They moved toward the bedroom, marionettes in a farce, clinging to one another.

Afterward, Sharon beside him, her head on his shoulder, those damned curlers painful against his cheek, he listened to the early evening traffic beyond her chintz curtains.

"A penny."

"Hmmm?"

"What are you thinking about?"

"Cleveland."

She snuggled closer, as if Cleveland were a code word which explained it all.

"Have you let your mother know where you are yet?"

She stiffened. "No."

"You really ought to, Sharon. She must have reported you missing."

"You're kidding. That would involve making up her mind to do something. She is completely incapable of that."

It had been a mistake, getting her started on her mother. The by now familiar catalog of complaint went on and on. Howard had a very vivid image of Sharon's mother, though he had never met her, a central figure in the scenarios of helplessness and ineptitude that Sharon sketched.

"If she had had the least bit of guts, she would have gone after him. My father." She spat out the word. "She let him go on living his comfortable life while she endured the shame of raising me. He lived only a few miles away and she never bothered him, never demanded that he help.

Why should he have been allowed to go on as if nothing had happened while she turned into a drunk and moped about, convinced that she had thrown away her life once and for all."

"You should have told her that."

"I did!" Sharon slid away and looked at him with angry eyes.

In the pulpit, the little Franciscan was droning on about his experiences in the missions of Central America. "We had a jeep there, an army surplus jeep, and let me tell you . . ."

Howard looked down the pew at his family. Charlotte's eyes were shut, Beverly sat stoically, her mind obviously miles away, David was making an airplane of the parish bulletin. Beth slept, her head resting on her mother's arm. He had meant to plead illness when Charlotte wakened him for Mass, but he had got up with the solemn feeling that this was one more thing that he was doing for the last time.

Howard closed his eyes and recent conversations with Charlotte and with Sharon echoed in his head.

"When do you start teaching?"

"Not for weeks. Why?"

"I haven't taken a vacation yet."

"Do you have to?"

"I don't want to."

"Maybe you should, Howard. You look tired. You *are* tired. When you fall asleep here I hate to have to wake you up."

"I could take my vacation here."

"Mmmm."

"No, wait. Maybe I'm serious. At the office I could be on vacation and at home I'm still working."

"And at night?"

"Night?"

"You'd still go home, Howard."

"Not necessarily. Look, what I'll do is take a trip to Cleveland. We could have *days*. What's the matter?"

"Nothing."

"Tell me. I thought it was a pretty good idea."

"Oh, it's a great idea."

"Sharon, I didn't mean to hurt your feelings. Don't *cry.*"

"I'm not crying."

"Well, your eyes are. What is it anyway?"

"Your family."

"My family!"

"Howard, I keep thinking of them. I don't want to, I just do, and I feel like—oh, you know what I feel like. I should have stayed in Cleveland."

"Don't say that."

"You were angry when I moved here and you were right. You should have stayed angry. You should have just turned me around and sent me back to Cleveland where I belong. It was different there. Then you didn't have all these obligations—"

"Sharon, stop. I love you."

"You love me. And you love your family. No, I want you to. I'm not that kind of bitch. I want you and it hurts to know that I'm pulling you one way and they're pulling you the other. I did not want to do this to you."

"Have I complained?"

"Howard, you can't want this. Just this."

"It won't always be like this."

"What do you mean?"

"I'm giving it thought. I'll think of something, Sharon. It'll work out. I promise you."

"I'll go back to Cleveland."

"No!"

"Char, I can't carry on a conversation through a closed door."

"Then open the door."

"I am sitting on the toilet, all right?"

"So what? Howard, open up."

"Can't you please let me do this by myself?"

"Are you sick?"

"No, I am not sick."

"You've been in there for hours."

"I just this moment sat down."

"Can you hear me?"

"I can hear you."

"Then listen. This meeting—it's an open meeting, not just Te Deum, the public can come, and we're going, CFM."

"What meeting are you talking about?"

"It's to be a discussion of the encyclical."

"Are they still talking about that?"

"Still? You're kidding. It hasn't even begun, believe me. This is a revolution. Where have you been?"

"Char, wait a minute."

"Did you hear me?"

"I heard you. I'm going to flush the toilet. I'll be right out."

"Howard, no! I won't have that on my conscience."

"Will you listen to me, Sharon? Just listen. I've already made up my mind. That isn't the issue. It's all settled."

"Did you talk to her?"

"I am going to talk to her."

"But you haven't yet?"

"Sharon, she is not an easy woman to have a conversation with. I can't explain. But I will talk to her and there is nothing to discuss. I have already decided."

"But your children, your little children . . ."

"I know. I *know.* I've thought of all that. Do you think I like that part?"

"You can't do it, Howard."

"I've already done it. We make decisions in little bits and pieces, not even knowing that's what we're doing. Until it's too late and then—"

"It's not too late, Howard."

"I didn't mean it that way."

"I don't want this, Howard. Don't think that you are doing this for me. I never asked this, I never expected it. I won't be responsible for those little children."

"Stop talking about my children!"

"Did I bring this up?"

"You're goddam right you brought it up. You moved here, didn't you? You left Cleveland and came here and just called me up after the fact, surprise, surprise. What in hell did you think you were doing?"

"I was changing jobs."

"Don't make me laugh. You could have had a million jobs in a million different places."

"So I'm to blame?"

"Yes, you are."

"Thank you very much."

"Well, thank you too. What is this, accusing me of deserting my children? They're not going on welfare, you know. I'll provide for them."

"I don't want it. I don't want it. Stop talking like this."

"Sharon, come here. Look, I can't go on like this. I can't do this to you. No one is to blame, Sharon. These things happen all the time."

"Don't. Please don't. We're not statistics."

402

"No one's statistics. You know what I mean."

"I know that I want you to forget this crazy idea. You are not going to leave your family. What's wrong with the way things are?"

"It's tearing me to pieces, that's what's wrong."

"I'll leave. I'll go back to Cleveland."

"No!"

"Howard, what do you think?"

"It sounds okay."

"Okay? Is that all you can say? Howard, it's fantastic, that's what it is. We're going to bring baby buggies, placards, everything. We're not going to let them forget for a minute what it's really all about."

"Char, let's talk."

"Talk? We are talking."

"No. You're talking. Let's us talk. About us. I don't give a good goddam about that meeting, all right? I don't care about the encyclical or the baby buggies or any of it. I'm tired. I want to talk."

"Well, pardon me all to hell. I'm sorry I've been boring you."

"How are the kids?"

"What do you mean, how are the kids? Go upstairs and look if you want to know how the kids are. They're in bed. I put them to bed before I started boring you."

"Where's Beverly?"

"Out."

"She's always out."

"So what? You're always in Cleveland."

"I haven't been to Cleveland for a long time."

"Why not? Maybe it would do you good. Maybe then you wouldn't be bored with me so easily."

"I'm bored with that meeting."

"Well, I'm not!"

"I know."

"What's that supposed to mean?"

"I don't know. You tell me."

"Tell you what? Is this what you meant by talking?"

"No, this isn't what I meant."

"You're tired. You're always yawning, do you know that? Since we're criticizing, I can tell you that. You're always yawning and you look exhausted. Bev says you sit up half the night. Are you worried about her?"

"No, I'm not worried about her."

"She thinks you are."

"Well, she's wrong."

"Maybe you should be, Howard. Do you know that I had a long argument with Frank because of the boy she's going with? I told you but I suppose that bored you too and you didn't listen. Frank talked to the boy and I talked to Frank—"

"I don't want to talk about Frank!"

"Howard, what in God's name is the matter?"

"Nothing's the matter."

"Then stop shouting at me."

"I'm tired."

"If you're tired go to bed and get some sleep. You're all on edge. Now you've got me on edge. Go upstairs, Howard. Take an aspirin, get a good night's sleep."

It was when they all heaved to their feet to recite the creed that Howard saw the way out of the crazy dilemma he was in. He turned the idea over for the rest of the Mass; it still seemed good when they had returned to the house. Early in the afternoon he drove downtown to his office, put a sheet of anonymous paper into Miss Furlong's typewriter, and pecked out a note to Sharon's mother. Your daughter is in Fort Elbow. He typed out the address. Sealing the envelope, putting a stamp on it, taking it downstairs and outside and then into a mailbox and it was done. What was done? Oh, dear God, help me out of this. I cannot help myself. Help me out of this and I will be so good. I'll spend more time with the kids. I won't mind Charlotte's endless chatter. I'll be everything you want me to be.

For a week Frank had been at work on the statement for Bishop Brophy and it was like returning to school after a long summer vacation. It recalled the feeling of purpose and excitement with which he had written the first draft of his dissertation. His room was a chaos of open books, journals, newspaper clippings, and seated at his typewriter, trying to bring together into a cohesive whole the bits and fragments he had culled from a variety of sources, he no longer felt himself to be an insignificant curate in a backward parish. Father Ewing had left his personal library to Frank and many of the books scattered around the room had been brought back from a foray to Ewing's shelves at the seminary. Through his reading Frank was in contact with minds that challenged his own as well as one another. And, of course, it was difficult not to think how important a role what he was writing was destined to play in Fort Elbow. As he typed, Frank was trying to find Bishop Brophy's voice, a voice that would speak with authority and yet convey the perplexity and division which existed among the best theological minds in the world. If the experts were not unanimous, it was dishonest to suggest to the average Catholic that everything was clear and settled.

Both the pastor and McTear were curious about this new activity, the sound of typing, the scholarly disarray of the room, when they stopped by to investigate. Frank answered their questions with sibylline indirection and sent them away more curious than they had come. That added to the fun of it, of course. On secret assignment. An anonymous power behind Bishop Brophy. The closest he had come to divulging what he was up to was with Char when she was complaining about the confusion reigning in the diocese over the encyclical.

"Frank, why doesn't somebody *say* something? Why don't you?"

"Be patient."

"Patient? My God. Even Father Oder has been utterly spineless on this. Not one single mention of the encyclical since it came out. And now Te Deum is preparing a rally of true believers. There has to be something to balance that."

"There will be."

"What?"

"I can't tell you."

Fortunately Howard got them off the subject. If he had not, Frank was certain he would have told them, after swearing them to secrecy, of course, but he knew what that would have been worth.

It was Donovan who told him that Manspricht Deutsch would be in Cleveland.

"When?"

"Day after tomorrow. To give a talk on the encyclical. I wish to God we could bring him here. To counter Prince Thaddeus."

"Where is he staying?"

"Do you know him?"

"I heard him once. In Rome."

Frank had a vivid memory of the German theologian who had looked so youthful he might have been a fellow student rather than a transalpine professor of theology. Deutsch was actually in his mid-thirties, a canon lawyer by training, who had been catapulted into fame by his book on the Church and poverty or, more accurately, by an American lecture tour arranged by a handful who had read a translation of the book printed by an obscure press in Pocatello. Deutsch had been invited to speak at a seminary in Ferrous, Pennsylvania, and the result had been sensational. His mild-mannered denunciation of the wealth of the Church and of the baronial lives led by the hierarchy, his aspersions on the Vatican investment portfolio, had electrified an audience which, as chance would have it, included a stringer for *Time*. Invitations poured in and Manspricht, in the hands of a good lecture agent now, had crisscrossed the country, speaking for mounting fees and leaving in his wake thousands of devoted fans. In the few years since, he had come to America twice a year, written fifteen books, bought a villa on the Costa Brava and become a symbol of intelligent low-key dissent in the Church.

Donovan had no idea where Deutsch would be staying in Cleveland but that posed no great problem. Frank could call the chancery and get the information he needed. He had already decided that this was an opportunity not to be missed. An exchange with Deutsch before he put the statement for Bishop Brophy into final shape was an undreamed of stroke of luck. Somewhat to his surprise, Donovan indicated that he knew of the statement Frank was preparing.

"I think he wants me to look it over," the editor said. "From a journalistic point of view."

"That might be a good idea. It's not an easy subject."

"I'll see what I can do," Donovan said, a trifle smugly, Frank thought.

Four days later Frank approached the desk of a Cleveland hotel, asked to see Father Deutsch and, after a moment, was told he might go up, Deutsch was expecting him.

From the time Deutsch opened the door of his suite Frank felt perfectly at ease. In shirt sleeves, his wavy blond hair slightly rumpled, his blue eyes crinkling in welcome, Manspricht Deutsch certainly seemed to carry his reputation lightly. He had a bottle of Scotch, he ordered ice, he sat Frank down and assured him the visit was not an imposition, the talk he would give that night was one he had already given a dozen times before on this tour.

"Fort Elbow," Deutsch mused. "Have I ever spoken there?"

Frank told Deutsch that he had heard him speak in Rome.

"During the Council?" Deutsch leaned toward him, searching Frank's face with a pleased smile.

"Oh, no. Just two years ago."

"Two years ago." Deutsch frowned, consulting his memory.

"At Sacrae Legis."

"You lived there!"

"Yes."

406

There was a moment of silence and then Deutsch said, "My own degree is from Heidelberg."

"I know."

"There are some good men in Rome."

The ice came then and, after he had poured drinks for both of them, Deutsch sat down again. "Well, Father, what has the reaction been to the encyclical in your diocese?"

"Actually there hasn't been a good deal."

"Who is your bishop?"

"George Caldron."

Deutsch licked his lips, as if he were trying the name along with his drink. He shook his head. "Young, old, what?"

"Old. Quite old. In his mid-seventies. We have an auxiliary too. Bishop Brophy. He wants to issue a statement on the encyclical. I'm helping him with it. That's why I wanted to have this talk with you."

"Ah." Deutsch sat back, closed his eyes, nodded slowly. When he looked at Frank his expression was serious. "It is imperative that the bishops resist the encyclical. Unfortunately, the American bishops have not been noted for their independence. I find that difficult to understand. This vigorous young country, so free, so expansive. Yet, the bishops . . ." Deutsch shook his head sadly. "They are seldom intellectuals, though, am I right?"

"Most of them are, well, good businessmen."

"Perhaps they will take heart from the Dutch and German bishops. The war is not lost, Father. Perhaps not even the battle. Voices are being raised all over the world, courageous voices." Deutsch smiled, showing short even teeth, a Teddy Roosevelt smile.

"Certainly the argument of the encyclical is difficult." Frank spoke with the conviction of one who had been poring over the text for a week.

"Argument? It simply repeats the traditional confusion. Muddling around a bit in biology and sociology, true, but basically the same misconception."

"I've never understood the traditional position," Frank confessed. "I learned to repeat it, of course, as well as answers to the usual objections, but . . ."

"Even if the argument were valid it wouldn't matter," Deutsch said, his lips wet from an interrupted dip into his drink.

"I don't understand. If it were valid, well, then—it would be valid," Frank ended lamely.

"Father, I will give you a précis of my talk for this evening." Deutsch settled back, running the tip of his finger around the edge of his glass, closing his eyes for a moment's thought. "Imagine that the traditional argument against contraception is valid. Concede that it is, that all objections can be met. Say that the natural law position is as airtight as the pope could wish. Now, even granted that, it would remain utterly irrelevant. Can you see why?"

Feeling like the foil in a Platonic dialogue, Frank said no.

"It is simple. If the encyclical expresses what is the right thing to do, or not to do, it is perfectly clear that we cannot rely on people to do the right thing and thus hold off the population explosion and the crush of war and famine it will bring. Do you see? It is ethics that is irrelevant. The only way to stop this mad growth of population ethically, if the pope is right—and he could be, it is not impossible—would be for the vast majority of people to become saints. That is, of course, an absurd expectation. People are not saints. This is the real argument against the encyclical, the reduction of it to absurdity. It demands the impossible. And it misunderstands where the weight of moral authority must fall. When you read the encyclical, you could imagine that the problem is that too many people are using contraceptives. But this simply is not so. Far too few are, even in the West, where of course the rabble do not employ them. The elite are weeding themselves out of the population. Without contraception, without a way of limiting population which does not depend on self-restraint, we are doomed."

"Do *you* think the encyclical is right, ethically?"

"I am saying that that makes no difference."

"Because we are doomed if the future depends on people acting well?"

"Exactly!" No matter how wide Deutsch's smile became, all the teeth it revealed were the same size. "Aristotle said it, Father. Most men are bad. In previous times, even the cumulative effect of evil did not threaten the race as a whole. Now it does. Oh, it would be nice to leave everything to individuals and live with the result. But that is a luxury we cannot afford. Men have lost the right to decide for themselves how many children they will have or even if they will have any at all."

"But why not simply say that using contraceptives is the ethical thing to do?"

"I will tell you something, Father. To say that is only to make a virtue of necessity. I suspect that it would be as difficult to show that contraception is moral as it has proved to be to show that it is immoral. The fact remains that that is not the question. The question is survival. Now there are those who wish to construct an argument from that. If survival, then contraception." Deutsch laughed dismissingly. "The end justifies the means. The argument already repudiates ethics. Let us be honest. We do not really care, we cannot afford to care, whether or not contraception is moral. Morality takes us back to those good old days when individuals could decide these matters for themselves. You recognize the slogan? Decide for yourselves? What it means now is that the individual can no longer decide for himself. So much for all this emphasis on personal conscience. Depend upon it, Father, states will soon remove even the semblance of individual choice in these matters, in the name of individual privacy, of course. Contraceptive agents will be put in our water supplies. One will need a license to have a child. The matter has moved beyond the quaint individualistic ethics of yesterday. Survival is too important a matter—politically, if you will—to be left to the individual conscience. This is the real problematic and it is time that we recognized it and stopped all this archaic moralizing."

"You have a very grim view, Father."

Deutsch beamed. "I know. I know. But you see how dreadfully out of tune with the real issue *Humanae Vitae* is. It astonishes me that theologians, dissenting theologians, accept the obsolete framework of the document and attempt to meet it on those grounds. Honesty, Father. Honesty. That is what the times require. In a day when one man's private decision could seal the fate of us all, we cannot permit such private decisions. I speak of the bomb. Everyone sees the point there. We do not want the fingers of moralizers anywhere near those terrible buttons. Sex is a button every bit as destructive."

Frank felt that he was being addressed from the far side of the looking glass, though Deutsch's wide-eyed placid manner was disarming. The man had a Nietzschean vision, beyond good and evil. If survival depended on man's being honest, would honesty become obsolete too? This conversation was not turning out to be as helpful to him as he had hoped.

"The real madness, Father," Deutsch said, pouring them each another drink, "the true and certifiable madness is to make the survival of the race depend on the expectation that weak men will do heroic, ascetic deeds."

On his third drink, riding the rising tides of alcoholic confusion, Frank tried to convince Deutsch that any race that survived on his terms would not be the human race.

"It never was! Not in the Greek sense. The rational animal." Deutsch chortled. "What have I been saying? Once it may have been true that man's irrationality could not destroy the species and we could afford the luxury of our stupidity. Now we see the real dimensions of our situation. Every ethics was addressed to a few. We have evolved beyond ethics."

"Perhaps the encyclical addresses a few too. An elite."

409

"Of course it does. An irrational elite."

And that, Frank thought later, waiting in the Cleveland airport for his flight to Fort Elbow, is the other side of the intellectual life. For a week he had been delighting in the intricate play of the mind on the vexed issue of sexual morality, enjoying the sinuous course of the arguments. But thought had a way of escaping into an unreal stratosphere where any sense the words expressing it might have could not be translated into ordinary significance. Whatever the value of Deutsch's thoughts, and Frank had found them increasingly unreal as the conversation progressed, it surely was not as a possible component of the statement he was preparing for Bishop Brophy. Not that he considered the afternoon or the trip wasted. Now whatever he wrote would seem sanely conservative when compared with the far-out speculations of Manspricht Deutsch.

While he waited for Frank Ascue and Daniel Donovan to complete their tasks, Bishop Brophy rather enjoyed the thought that two versions of the statement he would make were in preparation. Had not FDR too played members of his staff against one another, rubbing them together like flint and steel so that the resultant spark was unequivocally his own? Daniel Donovan was petulant, his style the whimper of a beleaguered but articulate man, but what he wrote was strong, full of echoes of the better minds he read. Frank Ascue would provide an orthodox vocabulary, a sense of the context of the problem, of its historical and theoretical presuppositions and, Brophy had no doubt, a solid brief for the cause he intended to espouse. Donovan's reward would be the satisfaction of knowing that for once in his life at least he had got the toe of his loafer into the corridors of ecclesiastical power. Frank Ascue? The bishop smiled. *Quid pro quo.* An appointment to the seminary faculty, the delayed dessert for the time he had served in Rome. It was to the end of ensuring that reward for Frank that Bishop Brophy now ascended the steps of the chancery, elbows angled back, chest out, chin up, his knees moving like the pistons of a very well-oiled machine indeed.

"Good afternoon, Agnes."

The old girl lifted her bottom from her chair, bent forward, her air generally deferential.

"Good afternoon, Bishop Brophy."

Agnes, Agnes, *qui tollit peccata mundi.* Brophy waved a kind of blessing at Caldron's cousin and continued down the hall to Yorick's door. No "Come in" answered his knock. Yorick preferred to greet a caller on the threshold, blocking the way should it be someone he did not wish to see—and that was nearly everyone.

"Oh, it's you."

"As if anyone not expected would get this far."

Yorick went back around his desk and picked up his cigar. Its wet, ragged end held his attention, as if it were some metaphor of the times. "You going to that Te Deum shindig next week?"

"I haven't been asked, Monsignor."

"Would you like me to arrange it?"

"I wish you wouldn't."

"That could be a great opportunity for you, Sean. To put the encyclical into perspective. Know what I mean?"

"I think I do."

Yorick put the mutilated cigar between his lips and brought a lighted match to it. "Quite a parlay. You and the prince." Yorick expelled a cloud of acrid smoke. "He speaks for the intellectuals, you let them know what the hierarchy thinks. That meeting might end up doing a lot of good around here."

Brophy should not really have been surprised at the chancellor's assessment of the prince. He would not of course tell Yorick his own view of that Polish charlatan. There is a time for war and a time for peace. Chorzempowski had been on the fringes of the Beck government which had helped Adolf carve up Czechoslovakia after Munich. When Hitler had turned on Poland, the prince and others like him had come yelping westward warning of the rise of a new barbarism. After the war, the prince's target had become Yalta and, more generally, godless communism. Chorzempowski was professionally an obscurantist and anti-intellectual, lending credence to the rumor that his doctoral dissertation had been turned down by his professor at Cracow.

"Prince Thaddeus," Yorick said. "I've met him, you know."

"In Fort Elbow?"

"No. In Rome. During the Council."

The puffing on that foul cigar became decidedly smug. Yorick had a way of referring to his attendance at the Council which seemed aimed at reminding Brophy that he had not been there. That he had not been was one of the great regrets of Bishop Brophy's life. But the last session was over before he was made bishop and, while it was going on, he had been anchored to a desk in Washington, following the debates in *The New Yorker* and *New Republic*, dying to be there. He had made an effort to go as a correspondent, but his offer had not been taken seriously by the two secular reviews he approached—they preferred disgruntled ex-seminarians, not a cleric obviously on his way up. In desperation, Brophy had made an inquiry at several Catholic monthlies, a secret that would go to the grave with him, not least because they too had turned him down. But, my God, what if they had taken him up on his offer?

"He lives in Rome, doesn't he?"

"A good part of the year. But he is an American citizen now, you know."

Bishop Brophy knew. Not a year ago he had helped dissuade some young Turks who were seriously considering initiating deportation proceedings against Chorzempowski because he had not dropped his title. Brophy agreed with cooler heads who thought the man got altogether too much attention the way it was. Besides, he never referred to himself as Prince, leaving that to his sycophantic admirers.

"It could be a real opportunity for you," Yorick said.

"How so?"

"He'll draw a crowd."

Into the silence thus created, the chancellor pumped more cigar smoke, further clogging the room. Against his grain, Brophy went directly to the point of his visit. "That was a nice touch, Ewing's will."

"The money to the caddy master or the wad to the missions?"

"I was thinking of his personal library."

"Oh, yeah."

"Frank Ascue will make good use of those books."

"Let me tell you something, Sean. *Entre nous.*" The chancellor hunched forward as if suiting deed to words. "Enter noose," he repeated. "I'll bet Ewing would have changed his will on that score. Do you know he told me he was willing to stay on at the seminary indefinitely, just to keep Ascue off the faculty?"

"Indefinitely turned out to be a short time, didn't it?"

A look of fugitive sadness flickered across Yorick's face. "Yeah."

"Ewing. Tremplin. The seminary faculty has been decimated."

"Did I tell you about Tremplin?"

Brophy looked at the chancellor. Surely not the old story about Tremplin on the Council?

"Know a guy named Plummet-Finch?" Yorick asked. "Teaches philosophy or something at the Fort Elbow campus?"

Brophy frowned, discouraging this kind of gossip. He had already heard the sordid rumors.

"I always knew Tremplin was a nut," Yorick said. "Saying Mass in the trunk room, running down the pope, inciting the seminarians to riot."

"Picket."

412

"What's the difference?"

For half a minute they both seemed to be remembering that Bishop Brophy had more or less championed Tremplin on the picketing occasion. The auxiliary bishop wished that he could get some kind of control over this ridiculous conversation.

"As far as I'm concerned," Yorick said, "I think that Father Ewing's dying wish should be respected."

"His dying wish?"

"That Ascue be kept off the seminary faculty."

If muscle control were merit, Bishop Brophy's smile would have assured his eternal salvation. "Spite won't replace Tremplin and Ewing, Monsignor."

"Spite!"

"Can we afford not to make use of a man trained like Frank Ascue?"

"How well do you know him, Sean?"

"Frank? I think I know him rather well."

Yorick shook his head. "That television panel. Signing that statement. The guy's a heretic."

"Oh, come on, Rabanus."

"There's more, Sean. I can't say what, but there's more. These guys. You think you know them, but . . ." Yorick sucked on his cigar and yelped. His angry drag of what remained of the cigar had brought its blazing coal into contact with his fingers.

"Hurt?" Brophy asked, almost hopefully.

Yorick, sucking his fingers, moaned.

Brophy got to his feet. What a waste of time this visit had been. He had certainly not advanced Frank Ascue's cause this afternoon.

Mrs. Ryan's face was tragic when she intercepted him before he could go upstairs to his room.

"Is something wrong, Mrs. Ryan?"

"I pray to God there isn't, Bishop."

"Well, what is it?"

"A telegram came for you."

Aha. He thanked the housekeeper, soothing her superstitious soul, and mounted slowly to the first landing and then, out of sight, bounded the rest of the way. The yellow envelope was propped on his desk. He ripped it open. Long. Very long. His eyes dropped to the sender's name and he felt like kneeling to read the message. But he read it standing. He read it again while pacing the room, his face suffused with a smile. He sat at his desk and read the telegram again. Only then did he pick up the telephone and send his reply. Not bothering about wordage, but crisply anyway, so as not to make his profound gratitude cloyingly obvious, he wired the Secretary of the National Bishops Conference that he would be delighted to serve on the committee and would come to New York this weekend for the scheduled meeting.

Like the trip to Cleveland to see Manspricht Deutsch, his regular parish duties seemed to Frank a remote source for what he was trying to put into Bishop Brophy's statement. Taking census in a section of the parish near the rectory with its huge old houses, a few occupied by retired couples still clinging to the home in which they had raised their families, some become rooming houses, others now owned by young people with large families who preferred a well-built house in the city to the homogeneity and obsolescence of the suburbs, he often found the talk coming around to *Humanae Vitae*. Mrs. Fellows was perhaps not typical though she had been a memorable housewife.

"Hi, Father," she said, holding open the porch door. "Come right on in."

A little boy held onto her denim skirt with one hand and had the other jammed into his mouth. When Frank came onto the porch a little girl skipped out from the living room, where a television set was aroar.

"Okay if we sit out here?" Mrs. Fellows said, scooping toys from a sling chair. "We don't get the sun here until afternoon. Susan, close the door or turn down that darned TV."

Ignoring her mother, Susan stared at the visitor. Mrs. Fellows, having cleared the chair, waved Frank to it and there was a bad moment when, expecting to encounter the chair, he just kept descending. Bottom met bottom eventually but his knees were chin high and Frank felt both helpless and foolish. Two more children, both girls, came onto the porch. Their mother put a hand successively on each child's head and spoke a name as if she were then and there conferring it.

"Not that you'll remember them. Say hello to Father, kids."

A mumbled chorus. Frank felt challenged but decided against repeating the names. His posture in the chair had robbed him of all dignity; even his smile felt clownish and apologetic.

"I just made Kool-Aid for the kids, Father, if you'd like a glass. It's not half bad. Or I'm getting used to it. I don't have anything else made. If you'd like coffee . . ."

"Kool-Aid sounds good." His words had the makings of a jingle. All but one child disappeared with Mrs. Fellows. Inside, the volume of the television went down and then a moment later went up again. The little girl stared at Frank.

"What grade are you in?" He put his hands on his knees with a

414

reminder of the sensation he had felt as a kid getting ready to mount his stilts. The child did not answer. How old would she be? He guessed seven. He stared out at the street for a time but when he turned back to her the girl still looked at him.

"Do you go to school?"

The girl nodded.

"At Saint Waldo's?"

"No!"

This was shouted from inside by Mrs. Fellows. The television had been quieted again. She came out onto the porch and handed Frank an orange plastic cup in which an ice cube bobbed on an emerald surface.

"They go to public school. Those that go."

"How many do you have?"

"Six."

"Really?"

"I know, I know. And I can remember when we used to be congratulated for it. The reason they go to public school—"

Frank stopped her. "You don't have to explain." The parish school was crowded as it was; besides there was the expense, however nominal.

"You mean apologize. Believe me, I'm not. Parochial schools aren't what they were when I was a kid. Then they were better than the public schools, really better, academically, besides having religious instruction."

Frank nodded as if he too saw the better ship of the past sinking in the west. "There were more nuns then, Mrs. Fellows. Well-trained nuns."

"How do you like the Kool-Aid?"

He sipped it, wearing a judicious expression. It was grainy and very sweet. "Not bad."

"The kids love it." Suddenly she sat forward, her eyes sparkling. "Say, what's the story on the nun who ran away with the priest?" She made it sound like a nursery rhyme. "I mean, she taught right here in our parish school and there hasn't been a single mention of it in the pulpit or parish bulletin. How come? It seems odd to have to read that kind of news in the *Fort Elbow Tribune*. Of course everybody's talking about it, particularly those with kids in the school."

"What could we say?"

"That it was wrong!"

"Surely you wouldn't want them condemned from the pulpit."

Mrs. Fellows hunched her shoulders, as if to become a more substantial interlocutor. "Not them maybe, but surely what they did should be condemned. It was wrong, wasn't it?"

"Well, yes. The way they did it. Of course, there's nothing wrong with marriage. . . ."

Mrs. Fellows laughed. Round merry face, reddish hair cut short, she seemed amiably belligerent, as if she had been dying to plunk a priest down in this sling chair, put a glass of Kool-Aid in his hand and have a good talk. Frank wished that he felt more mobile; it was going to be a major operation getting to his feet again.

"Who said there was? There's nothing wrong with being a nun either, is there? My sister-in-law is a nun and she's nuttier than a fruit cake. The fact that we have six kids really embarrasses her. Last time she was here she left a pamphlet on family planning. I'm serious. Isn't that a switch? We really did used to be praised for having a large family—and that was when we only had four kids. Now we're practically scolded. Sister Maureen—that's her name now; it used to be Sister Mary Purgata—talks about nothing but the population explosion. South America. Japan. India. Does she expect us to give some of the kids back? Know what she reminds me of?"

Frank shook his head.

"Of when I was a kid and wouldn't eat something, say cauliflower, something icky, and my mother would say, think of all the starving Chinese. How my eating cauliflower was supposed to help them, I don't know. I mean, it was already cooked. Do you think a man and wife ought to sit down with the population statistics before they go to bed?"

"Well, it is a serious problem."

"In this country?"

"It will be."

"Have you ever driven around this country? We're campers, so we've seen a lot of it. Do you know that most of Pennsylvania is empty countryside, woods, hills? And that's the east. People talk as if we were shoulder to shoulder. Where? In Manhattan?"

Frank sipped his Kool-Aid. He was reminded of southern Germany, whose woodlands and wilds had come as such a surprise to him. Mrs. Fellows's smile had become skeptical.

"I saw you on TV, when you knocked the encyclical."

"That panel was taped before the encyclical appeared."

"Well, you knocked the pope anyway. What do you think of the hullabaloo now?"

"About the encyclical?"

She nodded, pulling a crushed package of Pall Malls from a pocket of

416

her skirt. The cigarette she extracted from it was bent and broken. She kept the longest part and lit it.

"All these priests having the time of their lives criticizing the pope. I can't believe it. What really kills me is this talk about limiting the size of your family as if that took courage. You know, virtue. Nine times out of ten, it's pure selfishness. The day couples with one or two kids start sending checks to the starving Armenians I'll believe they're thinking of someone beside themselves."

"I suppose just about anything can be done for the wrong reason."

"But can the wrong thing be done for the right reason?"

Frank shrugged. Theological distinctions lay upon his tongue, along with the Kool-Aid, but he doubted that Mrs. Fellows would appreciate a little lecture on subjective and objective guilt.

"Do you know I got a call this morning from some birdbrained woman who wanted me to go over to the seminary next Monday and picket some meeting because there would be speakers there who agree with the pope? And this is a CFM group!"

"From where?" There were no CFM groups in Saint Waldo's. Monsignor Entweder thought that the parish had enough organizations already with the ushers' group, the Ladies' Benevolent Society, the PTA and the Men's Club.

"I don't know. Saint Barnaby's? Something like that. I told her I'd be more likely to picket the pickets. If I had the time, which I don't. The reason we live in this dump is to be as far as possible from people like that, suburbanites. They want to live like a TV commercial and call it being a good Catholic."

"What sort of work does your husband do?"

"He's an engineer. Electrical."

"You have a nice family."

She looked thoughtful. "It's scary having kids today, Father. No one can frighten me with stories of too little room, not enough superhighways, not even with the claim that there won't be enough food. It's the whole tone of life I worry about. You know? I mean, is this or is this not a vale of tears?"

Once more Frank stopped himself from qualifying her remarks. He adopted a pensive look instead.

"Sometimes we talk about going to Australia. Or Alaska. Do you know you can still homestead in Alaska? I want my kids to know what life is really all about. I mean, it's a test, isn't it?"

"I suppose that is a tempting thought, to get away." Frank had been shuffling through his census cards; now he dealt the Fellows card onto his knee and clicked his ballpoint pen. Mrs. Fellows took the card and pen and filled in the card herself. Frank refused the offer of more Kool-Aid but accepted her help in getting out of the chair.

"Three cheers for the pope," Mrs. Fellows called after him when he was going out to the street. Frank turned, smiling, and split his fingers in the peace sign. Somehow he was sure that Mrs. Fellows would interpret it as Churchillian confidence in victory.

Mrs. Fellows's remark about the CFM group that was contemplating picketing the Te Deum meeting at which Prince Thaddeus would speak preyed on his mind throughout the morning. He had little doubt that it had been Charlotte who had called Mrs. Fellows. That afternoon he borrowed McTear's car and drove out to his sister's, not calling first, wanting to give the impression that he was just dropping by, so that the subject of picketing could come up naturally and casually and he could try to convince her that it was a foolish idea.

The Nygaard lawn did not compare favorably with the green barbered expanses which flanked it. Unmown, dry, shot through with some flowering weed, the grass gave the impression of an abandoned Eden. The shrubbery was limp and dull, rusting unwatered in the August sun. Walking up the driveway from the car, Frank looked into the open garage at a chaos of toys, bicycles, wagons, one flat football, out of season, out of air. What a lot of garden equipment was there, rakes, hoes, spades, a mower, a fertilizer cart, all looking as abandoned as the yard. A trike with a missing wheel blocked the walk to the front door and, stepping over it, Frank found this desuetude a commentary on Charlotte's family and her busybody interest in Te Deum. He glared at the weeds in the lawn. The family that sprays together stays together. When he pressed the bell no sound came, though only the screen door was closed. Out of order? My God. He knocked on the aluminum frame, then turned away, to protect his eyes from the bright sunlight on the silvery screen.

"Uncle Frank?" The bodiless voice was Beverly's.

"Is your mother home?"

Her answer was the sound of the door unlocking. It opened and his niece, barefoot, in shorts and halter, her hair damp with perspiration, peered reproachfully at him. Ben Cole. He had not spoken with Beverly since the day he summoned Ben to the Saint Waldo rectory. "Come in out of the sun."

And into further chaos. Had the house always looked so uncared for? Yesterday's newspaper lay on the couch and on the floor was a large

418

greasy bowl in whose depths some unpopped kernels lay. Old maids. Beverly's eyes followed his about the room. Was she, too, surprised at this mess?

"Let's sit out back. I just came in to get something to drink."

In the kitchen, he ignored the dishes in the sink and the remnants of lunch upon the table. The wall calendar still stood at July. He nodded when Beverly asked if he would like iced tea. What was he doing here? Even if Charlotte had been home, the visit was ridiculous. His hand closed around the glass Beverly gave him; it was still warm, the temperature of its contents not yet having penetrated the container. The lower screen of the back door bulged outward and when Beverly held it open for him, with her knee, the bulge seemed explained. He had imagined the younger kids ramming their heads into it. A comic strip of long ago teased his memory. Rodney the Rock.

They sat in the shade of the house on lawn chairs whose aluminum arms were cool. Frank chose that moment to remember that he should be working on that statement for Bishop Brophy. He seized on the thought as if it were his excuse to go.

"I can't stay long. Where's your mother?"

Beverly shrugged. She sipped her tea, her eyes on the end of the yard where a swing set rusted in the sun. One plastic seat hung from a single chain, looking condemned and executed; the other had been raised to within two feet of the crossbar. The slide looked warped and unsafe. A single cheery note was provided by the pink hollyhocks along the fence but Frank suspected that they antedated the coming of the builders and this house.

"I just dropped by."

"It's been a while."

"Yes."

"How's Saint Waldo's?"

Her eyes grazed him, went to the next yard, returned in a lazy disinterested arc to the swing set.

"I never had a chance to talk with you about that boy. Ben Cole. Your mother said . . ." He stopped. It was dishonest to pretend that he had come to speak to Beverly about that. The fact was that he had been relieved when that nutty conversation with Charlotte turned out to be the end of her interest in the matter. Beverly was looking at him strangely.

"Maybe you were right about him after all."

"Oh? In what way?"

"Telling him to go back. To the seminary."

"That isn't what I told him."

"It's what he heard. What he wanted to hear. You were right about me too. I *was* trying to lure him away. It seemed something I owed my sex, the women of the world." Beverly laughed dryly. "Show him what he was missing."

"Then it's all past tense?"

"I'm just tense in the present now."

"I got the idea that he intended to leave the seminary. The point was, he had to make up his mind, one way or the other." Frank rubbed at his forehead. Sweaty. The glass of iced tea was sweating in his other hand. He did not want to talk about Ben Cole.

He said, "You ought to be at the beach on a day like this."

"The little kids are. With the neighbors."

"Why didn't you go along?"

"Have you been to the beach lately?"

Her tone dispelled his image of unpopulated expanses of sand, cool inviting water; he imagined the bathers shoulder to shoulder under the sweltering sun, the sand pocked with washed-out castles, footprints, the debris of snacks. Better the backyard and a glass of iced tea than that.

Beverly said, "He can't make up his mind and I've made up mine not to help him do it."

She was back to Ben Cole. "That's sensible. I guess that's all I was trying to say to your mother."

Beverly seemed no more impressed with the importance of what he said than he himself was. A dating seminarian seemed wholly innocent in the face of the general erosion. Frank stared at the ragged lawn, thinking of Phil and Diane, of Sheila and that nameless man, of all the voices of penitents who had been filling his ears with a multitude of woes. And he thought of Howard, almost with sympathy. This house, this neighborhood. And Charlotte. If his sister seemed part of the nature of things to him, she was, after all, someone Howard had chosen and it had to be difficult to come home to that constant inane chatter, far more difficult for Howard than it was for Beverly. This was temporary for her. She must already see the end of her stay in this house. Her life was about to begin. But for Howard, this would be all he could expect to have. It was a depressing thought and not to be dismissed as due to the persistence of adolescent fantasies. Howard would not have to be in pursuit of some impossibly romantic alternative to want something better than this. The very disloyalty of the thought gave it authority.

"She didn't really mind. Mother. Your talking with Ben. Why should she?"

"But you did?"

"At the time." Beverly's profile was not a clear blend of Charlotte's and Howard's. There was a Nordic pensiveness in the brow, the eyes, the bridge of her nose. Charlotte's chin, though subtly different; more molded, perhaps from less exercise. "Maybe you did me a favor." Beverly smiled but it did not brighten the tone of her voice.

"You think he'll go back to the seminary?"

"I don't know. I don't care either." The extra sentence lay falsely between them. Beverly sat up in her chair, crossed her legs, and the toes of her suspended foot looked bunched and vulnerable. Her partially visible sole was very smooth, and dirty. "Maybe I'll go away."

"Away?"

"To school. You know. Why should I attend the Fort Elbow campus?"

"You mean Columbus?"

"Why should I even stay in Ohio? There are a million colleges."

"Anything more specific?"

Beverly seemed surprised. Those million colleges had apparently seemed a single destination. "Maybe California. Someplace in California."

Frank had no idea how easy or difficult it was to change schools, but surely this was rather late in the summer to be thinking of that. Perhaps Beverly was just permitting herself some vagrant thoughts as protection against this dull and stifling August day. His reaction to the yard and house returned and he sympathized with her desire for flight. California. Australia. Elsewhere issued its constant invitation. He set his glass beside his chair; it tipped over and what was left of the ice cubes slid onto the grass. They both watched them settle on the blades, geometrical solids destined to be drawn sunward.

Beverly walked out to the car with him, padding barefoot down the driveway, a glass of iced tea in her hand. When he got behind the wheel, she brought a forearm to her head, to wipe away perspiration, to shade her eyes, in a gesture of farewell. He took it for the last and waved to her. When he drove away he found that he was glad that Charlotte had not been there. She and Mrs. Fellows were at opposite ends of a teeter-totter and he was in search of its fulcrum, some balanced view between the extremes. The thought of the research awaiting him in his room was welcome. The real world is a messy place. Look at Beverly. The poor kid, wanting to get away, anywhere, someplace else. Like Mrs. Fellows and her dreams of Australia and Alaska. What they wanted was peace, happiness, but the geography of happiness is not terrestrial. He smiled. His thoughts went to such phrases nowadays. He would have to finish up that darned statement and get it to Bishop Brophy. Speaking *ex cathedra* could get a little tiresome.

For Daniel Donovan the prospect of Bishop Brophy's statement on the encyclical was the one bright spot on the local horizon since *Humanae Vitae* had appeared. Father Ascue, when Daniel phoned him, said that, yes, he had finally shaped the thing up.

"Could I drop by for it, Father? Maybe we could look it over together."

After a slight hesitation, Ascue said, "I thought I'd give it to Bishop Brophy first."

"He's out of town."

Daniel had been surprised himself to learn this at the cathedral rectory and it had not been easy to persuade the housekeeper to check out Brophy's room for some indication of where he had gone. The telegram had been on the bishop's desk. Surprise had given way to dismay. Would Brophy be able to resist the corrupting influence of the higher councils of power? Daniel was intent on saving Brophy from any weakness along those lines. He assured Father Ascue that Bishop Brophy was indeed out of town. He added that he himself would be right over.

Out of town. The phrase recalled Kansas City and Daniel felt a dryness in his throat. He had not been wholly honest with Lydia in telling her of that disastrous trip. It was difficult to say whether things had gone badly because he had drunk too much or if he had drunk too much because he had sensed how badly things were going. They had treated him like a fool and his notion that they were considering him for the staff of NCR had turned into a hideous joke. No one seemed to remember having asked him down for an interview. Looking over their letter later he had admitted to himself that its message was ambiguous. Yet, beforehand, both he and Lydia had taken it for a feeler. In the dismal aftermath of the trip the letter's remark that Daniel was the kind of editor needed today and the hope that they might soon discuss with him matters of common concern did not read like a demand that he catch the first plane to Kansas City to discuss contract terms. Only one person there had connected him with anything other than the *Fort Elbow Catholic* and she was an angular girl with a withered arm who wanted to know if he was related to Lydia Donovan, the author of *Married Virgins.*

"Only by marriage," Daniel had tartly replied.

He took the bus back to Fort Elbow once he knew they would not pay his expenses. Rolling through the Midwest he wished that he could rid himself of his absurd ambitions. Farmhouses far back from the road, guarded by stands of trees, the little towns whose walks men strolled in complacent anonymity, the stops where they had coffee and breezy waitresses chatted with the driver. Daniel noticed all this and felt welling up within him a fierce desire to be like the rest of men. A small life, a happy one, some simple job that did not promise to change the world. And, at night, coming home to Lydia, who would have spent the day playing bridge, puttering in the garden, baking. That vision of the good life had made him want to cry out with longing in the swaying bus. He just had to get away from Fort Elbow and his dreams of importance and influence. And then Brophy's request that he back up Ascue on the projected statement, keep it intelligible and direct, had brought him back to the real world.

Of course Daniel did not intend to wait for Father Ascue, simply to edit the statement the priest would write. As soon as he had hung up the phone after speaking with Brophy, he had called to Alice Clarity, asking her to bring him everything they had on *Humanae Vitae*.

"On what?" When Alice wrinkled her nose like that, her front teeth gave her a rabbity look.

"The encyclical," Daniel explained.

"Oh, yeah."

She left his office sinuously, reminding Daniel what lust was like. That was as far as it went. He had far more important things to do than indulge in raunchy reveries about Alice Clarity. She brought in folders of press clippings and Daniel flipped open the top one and immediately went to work. He sorted and pasted and typed for hours, exhilarated by the way the thing seemed to assume its own shape. The result would be at once a pastiche of clippings and an original statement, one that would put Brophy in the vanguard of dissent, yet sustained by authoritative cohorts. The auxiliary bishop would be the mouthpiece of the Holy Ghost as well as of the diligent ghost hacking away in the editor's office of the *Fort Elbow Catholic*. It conferred a sense of power to cast himself in the role of one addressing the Catholics of the nation. Through Brophy he would exhort the other bishops to stand up and be counted. The day was past when the Vatican could drop a bombshell like that encyclical and expect everyone to knuckle under. Collegiality was the clue. The American bishops had been wary of the idea of collegiality before the Council and had taken little advantage of it since. It was a crime that bishops from the very cradle of democracy should be so goddam eager to kowtow to the Curia. American theologians, thank God, were more adventurous and independent. Through this statement their dissent would issue from the mouth of at least one bishop. Once Brophy spoke out, other bishops would join him. You had to give him credit for seeing this opportunity. In a leadership vacuum, someone had to step forward. And Donovan began to fear that some other ambitious young bishop would see and seize the chance before Sean Brophy had fired a shot.

Ascue's reaction when he told him Deutsch would be in Cleveland encouraged Daniel. Perhaps Ascue would come up with some things he could fold into his statement. It went without saying that his, not Ascue's, would be the basis for their united efforts.

The Saint Waldo rectory, which Daniel had never seen before, was quite a little surprise. Leave it to the clergy to set themselves up royally. It was the nicest house for blocks around and was surmounted by an enormous antenna. Daniel became aware of an eye upon him. The door had opened a crack and what seemed to be a woman looked out at him suspiciously. Her eyes dropped to the briefcase in his hand.

"No salesmen," she said, closing the door.

"Wait!" Daniel yelped. "I'm here to see Father Ascue."

"Are you selling anything?" The door did not quite open again.

"Tell Father Ascue that Daniel Donovan is here." Daniel turned his back on the woman and glared out at the street. He was startled to hear the door shut behind him. Furious, he wheeled and lunged at the doorbell and kept his finger on it until the door opened.

"Hello, Daniel," Father Ascue said, looking at the finger still pressing the bell.

"Who *is* that woman?"

"Come in."

Daniel went in. From the end of the hall a huge woman looked at him with suspicion before disappearing.

"She hates salesmen," Father Ascue explained. "She once bought a set of encyclopedias."

"I'm surprised she knew what they were."

"That's part of her complaint. This way."

After some preliminary sparring in the office Ascue led them to, after in as offhand a way as he could manage Daniel had mentioned that he too had roughed out a statement, they agreed to exchange what they had done and then talk over uniting them. Daniel took Ascue's to a window. The statement was what he had expected, what Brophy must have feared: a term paper for a class in theology. He did admire the fairness with which Ascue weighed the pros and cons, followed both sides into their common and conflicting assumptions; moreover, the treatise ended with a sane statement on the encyclical. It was not an infallible document. On the other hand it was the thought-out opinion of the Holy Father, whom no Catholic would wish to ignore. And of course he quoted the Council on the ordinary magisterium. Daniel

424

could imagine what Brophy would make of this too-balanced and there-fore wishy-washy statement.

How cool and quiet the rectory was; it might have been a hemisphere removed from the hot, muggy street outside. From the window where he stood, Daniel looked out at a lawn that was concealed from the street by a brick wall which encircled the yard and met the loggia joining church and house. How well they live, Daniel thought. And then: Wait until the revolution.

This bastion of middle-class comfort was one of the targets of the present mood, Daniel assured himself. The rectory must have cost at least a hundred thousand and most likely it had been built at a time when parishioners who could afford houses were making payments on ten to fifteen thousand dollar places.

Behind him he could hear Ascue turning over pages. He hoped, not too strongly, that the priest would not have the usual critic's vanity. He turned to see that Ascue had finished and was restacking the pages, making a neat pile on the desk. He did not look up. Daniel did not like that tapping finger.

"That's just a draft, Father."

Ascue lit a cigarette, as if to gain time. "It's pretty strong, isn't it?"

"Of course it is." Temper, temper. Daniel sat down. God, how he hated amateur criticism. "Bishop Brophy *wants* a strong statement."

"But maybe a more balanced one, don't you think? After all, he's a bishop himself. I'm sure he doesn't want to suggest that he's the only non-idiot in the hierarchy."

This was going to be hairy, Daniel could see that, but he could not risk the satisfaction of telling Ascue to stick it up his ass. He needed at least his apparent collaboration. Daniel stooped over, fumbled in his briefcase and brought out a notebook. He opened it, placed it on his knee and punched the button on his ballpoint.

"What are your suggestions, Father?"

Some hours later, back at his desk, Daniel looked with disgust at the notes he had forced himself to take while Ascue went on and on. Dear God, what a crucifying session that had been. Ascue, it was all too clear, was only a fair-weather liberal. If he had his way, Brophy's statement would become a paean to the pope, a rallying cry to back the bishops in the difficult decision they must make. The bishops! Authority. Ascue agreed that the whole point now was that individuals had to decide for themselves. So why refer to the bishops as if they could decide for others? Daniel sighed. It was going to be quite a trick to feed some of

425

Ascue's language, from the notes, from the draft the priest had prepared, into the final statement, but it could be done. It had to be done.

Daniel went back to work in the awareness that, in a few days, Prince Thaddeus Chorzempowski would invade Fort Elbow. The man was an ultramontane of the worst kind who had transferred to the pope as temporal liege lord all those powerful sentiments his displaced title stirred up in his exiled breast. Daniel could imagine the charge of lese majesty being leveled against anyone who wished to discuss the encyclical seriously, the likening of sincere questioners to a motley mob of revolutionaries. The prince no doubt represented a very special point of view but the damnable fact was that he would be here in person while Bishop Brophy was away in the East subject to God knows what blandishments. Daniel pushed away the clutter on his desk, his notes, his previous version, Ascue's draft, and turned to his typewriter. Come, Holy Ghost, he prayed. He had to get this thing done and delivered to Mary Muscatelli at the *Tribune* while there was still time.

After Daniel Donovan's visit Frank was assailed by memories of the anarchic statement the editor had seemed seriously to think that Bishop Brophy would be delighted to issue in his own name. It was clear that *Humanae Vitae* represented only a symptom to Donovan and that, in discussing it, insofar as he had, he was after a far larger target, the Church itself, the hierarchy, the notion of authority. Frank had begun by imitating a conservative reaction to the incredible piece Donovan had put together and ended by finding the borrowed sentiments almost his own. Of course the whole meeting had been a waste of time. Bishop Brophy would need only a glance at what Donovan had written and into the wastebasket it would go. His more careful statement would be more to the bishop's liking. After all, Brophy intended to interpret an encyclical for the faithful, not announce his withdrawal from the Church.

On Saturday night he did not go immediately downstairs when Hilda rang the bell for dinner but even so he was the first one into the dining room.

"Darn that television," Hilda said. "Sometimes I think he expects me to serve his meals up there."

Frank had been aware of the pastor's color set, in the way that neighbors of airports are aware of jets: hearing, he had not heard. He glanced at his watch.

"The news."

McTear came in, stood by the table, got his bearings, sat down. Frank suspected that the first assistant was not sure what meal he was being summoned to until he saw the table.

"Where's Monsignor?"

The clump of feet upon the stairs answered McTear's question. When Entweder came in, he directed a wondering smile at Frank and then at the soup tureen that Hilda set before him. He did not begin grace.

"I never would have believed it," he said.

"It's minestrone," Hilda said.

"Bishop Brophy was just on the news. Prince's program. From New York. He made a marvelous statement."

McTear, eying the soup hungrily, said, "What about?"

"The encyclical. *Humanae Vitae.* Bishop Brophy urged every Catholic to accept humbly the guidance of the Holy Father, Christ's vicar on earth. He said that if the pope was wrong, and he didn't for a minute believe it, he would rather be wrong with the pope than right with a small group of radicals who seemed more interested in publicity than the good of the faithful."

McTear was still waiting for the punch line. Frank stared at the pastor, trying unsuccessfully to believe that this was a little joke. He thought of the hours he had spent writing that damned statement. He thought of Daniel Donovan. "Poor Donovan," he said aloud, but the editor seemed no more of a fool than he did himself.

The pastor and McTear looked at him, puzzled. When no explanation was forthcoming, Monsignor Entweder bowed his head over the steaming soup and said grace before meals. In English.

3 Frank told himself that he should feel relief. Back in his room, which Hilda on his instructions had left all but untouched during his struggle to prepare that statement for Bishop Brophy, Frank looked around as if at a deserted battlefield. Relief. He could forget the tortured effort to follow the advocates and the enemies of the Church's traditional stand on birth control. Did the arguments really matter? He went to a window, closed a book lying open on his air-conditioner and looked out at the parish plant, rosy in the evening sun, heading into night and the promise of a drop in temperature. What good would his statement have done, really? It was difficult to believe that all those words, sentences, paragraphs, a beginning, middle and less than conclusive ending, would have reached one single human heart. Had he himself ever acted on the basis of such a presentation as that? The whole effort seemed futile, an exercise conducted above the heads of men, a game for experts whose antics did not interest any audience. So he was well out of it. He should feel relief.

But what he felt was betrayal. It was difficult not to think that Bishop Brophy had less interest in what he said than in its usefulness for himself. How else interpret his 180-degree shift on the question of the encyclical? Publicity was what Brophy had wanted and now he had it on a national scale. Frank could imagine him gloating in New York. And why New York? Donovan had said that Brophy was out of town but had not seemed to know where. Frank reached for his phone, hesitated, then drew it toward him. He dialed the Donovan number and, with the phone held away from his ear, listened to it ring and ring. Poor Donovan. If he felt betrayed how must Daniel feel?

Books on the floor, books on the bed, the top of his desk a mess from which his typewriter rose, the instrument of his folly. He recalled the sense of importance with which he had tapped out the final draft of his statement. He got up, shuffled through the papers, arranging the carbon of what he had written. When it was stacked, the pages in order, he tore it neatly in two and dropped it into the wastebasket.

As if activated by his unsuccessful effort to reach Daniel Donovan, his phone began to ring. Charlotte.

"Well," she said. "Brophy really lost his nerve, didn't he?"

"If you want to call it that."

"There's nothing else to call it. He really let us down. Do you realize what this will do to people? If *he* is going to defend the encyclical, where are we? Not that I'm really surprised."

"Oh?"

"Frank, he's out of touch with people. I wonder if there is any bishop who isn't. Brophy seemed an exception, that's true, but obviously he wasn't. When the chips are down, they all stick together."

"I guess you're right."

"What is he doing in New York?"

"I don't know."

Charlotte sighed. "What kills me is that Te Deum meets day after tomorrow and they are going to have the time of their lives. They will make it clear that Brophy capitulated."

"Charlotte, it's only a meeting."

"They have Prince Thaddeus speaking."

"Would you go to hear him?"

"You're kidding."

It was only after he had hung up that Frank remembered what Mrs. Fellows had told him. He did not call Charlotte back. For one thing, the thought of her picketing the Te Deum meeting did not seem important. For another his phone began to ring again.

Bob Wintheiser hoped that Frank was edified by what Bishop Brophy had said about the encyclical. Frank said that edification might not be just the right word.

"All right. How about admiration? Don't you think he knew that a lot of scrambled people expected him to waffle on the issue, even come out against the pope? In a way, they have been his constituency. The kooks. Up to now, that is. It took courage for him to say what he did, considering."

"Considering?"

"Considering his past performance."

"You may be right."

The next caller was Arthur Rupp, chortling with delight. In his elation he was more than willing to let bygones be bygones. This was a time for unity and celebration.

"Father, you're welcome to attend the Te Deum meeting at which Prince Thaddeus will speak. It's not often that you get to hear someone of that caliber."

Frank agreed that that was true.

"It will be a great day for Fort Elbow."

"Have you thought of asking Bishop Brophy, Arthur?"

"As a matter of fact, I have. Can't reach him. Still out of town, I gather. Monsignor Yorick has agreed to come."

"Where is the meeting being held?"

"At the seminary. There'll be loads of room. I wonder if you could announce it from the pulpit on Sunday?"

"You'd have to speak to Monsignor Entweder about that."

Entweder's phone was ringing when Frank came out of his room. He went downstairs and outside, going halfway across the loggia, where he sat on the ledge and lit a cigarette. The night was warm. Saturday night. He looked at his watch. In fifteen minutes he had to be in his confessional. He pushed away from the ledge and dragged on his cigarette. He dreaded the thought of all those mournful voices in the dark, whispering through the grille. Dear God, may there be no confused people asking about birth control. What could he tell them? Perhaps he should refer them to Bishop Brophy's statement. At least the words Brophy had spoken in New York had the merit of being his own. Frank put out his cigarette, hopped over the ledge and set out across the playground, walking briskly.

Low clouds hung over the school and in the distance there were flashes of lightning. He remembered how the rain moved up the fairway when he had been putting on the practice green. From the street in front of the church came the sounds of automobile horns. Sheila in the parking lot. He felt a single drop of rain. Sitting beside her, there had been minutes of peace before things had gone wrong, before he had remembered that he was a caddy and she a member's daughter, before . . . Before what? Had he escaped from temptation, dashing into the rain, or only from his boyish hopes, borrowed hopes at that? It was ridiculous to think that Sheila found him attractive, that she had been consciously leading him on while they sat there in the rain. And yet, when he had gone back for his putter, she was embracing the steering wheel and had snapped at him like a woman scorned. More raindrops fell, a hot wet smell began to lift from the asphalt. Frank sprinted for the church, entering by the sacristy. His breath came short. He knelt on a prie-dieu from which he could see the tabernacle in the sanctuary. In the church there were the nervous coughs of early penitents. Outside the rain was really coming down now. *Rorate coeli desuper.* Advent. But this was Pentecost, the time after, months and months of it, on and on until the end of the world and Advent again. The tabernacle, bronze, was enclosed by a silken tent. Behind the locked door, in golden cups, hundreds of white disks were God become the food of man, that miracle the result of words he spoke at Mass. It seemed a strange and unlikely thing, nothing anyone could possibly believe on a rainy Saturday night, betrayed by an auxiliary bishop, obliged to sit until nine o'clock in a confessional where by the wave of his hands and speaking other words he would wash away sins. The coughing in the church became a summons. Without having prayed, Frank rose, crossed the sanctuary and hurried with downcast eyes to his confessional. He did not want to see and recognize any of those waiting to confess their sins.

Donald Oder phoned at ten o'clock, wondering where Frank had been.

"Hearing confessions."

"Till this hour?"

After he had finished, Frank had come out of his confessional to find McTear waiting for him. They went outside and stood on the front steps of the church. The street had a washed look. The rain had stopped, but traffic moved wetly past them.

"The pastor really liked what Brophy said." McTear spoke to the passing cars. The semaphore at the corner was repeated indistinctly in the wet surface of the street.

"Yes."

"He's never really liked Brophy, you know."

"Why not?"

McTear thought about it. "I'm not sure."

Hilda had a snack waiting for them when they returned to the rectory and they stood around in the kitchen, sipping coffee, eating Boston cream pie, saying that the rain certainly hadn't cooled things off much. When McTear said it was time to get down to his radio, Frank hated to see him go. On the way up to his room he could hear the phone ringing. "Hearing confessions," he told Oder. "Have you been trying to reach me?"

"I suppose you heard Sean Brophy on the news tonight."

"I heard about it."

"Well?"

"What is he doing in New York?"

"Aha. You see the connection. He has been asked to serve on a bishops' committee to prepare a statement on *Humanae Vitae*. Obviously he couldn't wait to go on record himself."

"That's his privilege, I guess."

"Privilege? Oh, hardly that. His obligation. We must all get behind the Holy Father in this trying hour." Oder did not seem to be taking pleasure from his mimicry. In normal tones, he said, "Of course this puts Sean in a rather embarrassing position."

"How do you mean?"

"Well now, he can't very well have it both ways, can he? *Viva il papa* in New York and then the statement you and Donovan prepared for him here."

"Obviously he won't be using that now."

There was silence on the line.

Frank said, "I doubt that he even saw it."

"But that can hardly be. It's in tomorrow morning's paper."

"I'm sure you're wrong, Father."

"Frank, I have an early copy before me now. I went out to buy one as soon as Daniel Donovan told me it would appear. It makes for an odd front page, Frank. The New York statement in one column. Your extended statement beginning in another. And, between the two, the beaming face of our own Sean Brophy."

Some minutes later, Frank was hurrying up Cavil Boulevard to the drugstore. He brought the *Fort Elbow Tribune* back to his room and read it. What Oder had said was true. Frank called Daniel again and again but each time all he got for his pains was a ringing that stopped only when he put down his phone.

The seminary on Long Island occupied an erstwhile estate bequeathed to the Church by a "good Catholic layman" some fifty years before, a gift motivated by piety and, perhaps, the slightest twinge of guilt at how his wealth had been gained. The seminary buildings overlooked the Sound and had the artful expensiveness that Bishop Brophy associated with the Church he loved and served. The chapel in which he had just said Mass that Sunday morning, concelebrating with the other members of the hastily named and convened committee of the National Bishops Conference, alone had cost a million and a half, and that in days when a dollar was a dollar. The guest suites were a marvel and so too had been the dinner which Brophy was now walking off, following a path which gave a commanding view of the water and led toward the donor's mansion, which now functioned as a sort of local Castel Gandolpho. Brophy's colleagues had repaired to their rooms for a nap or a belated tussle with the newspapers, but the auxiliary bishop of Fort Elbow, Ohio, chose to savor these surroundings and daydream of a personal future lived in a similar setting. In imaginings lost, he invested himself with the pallium and gratefully accepted the red hat from the next and progressive pope. ("We wish to thank you," the white-clad figure murmured, surprisingly in an American accent, "for your initiative during the reign of Our esteemed predecessor of blessed memory." Whereat the pontiff winked.) Thanks to the preeminence of his imagined future see, Sean Cardinal Brophy would be the confidant of presidents, a member of innumerable commissions, honored guest of the powerful, the no longer missing link between the City of God and the City of Man.

This pleasant reverie was interrupted by the sound of someone calling his name. Brophy turned to see the young cleric the chairman of the committee had brought along as recording secretary. Brophy could not help comparing the young man with Garish. If his own master of ceremonies had the look of one who, in the world, might have hoped to rise to an International Harvester franchise, young Father Healey was the clerical counterpart of the suave young man from Chase Manhattan, instilling confidence with his computerized precision.

"Sorry to bother you, Bishop Brophy, but the call seemed urgent."

"Thank you." They started back toward the seminary and Brophy was pleased anew by the fact that Healey did not patronize him by treating him like the provincial prelate Fort Elbow might suggest he was.

"The cardinal was quite insistent."

The cardinal? Well, well. No wonder Healey was diffident. "Where did he call from?"

"He said you'd know the number to call."

It got better all the time. Hamming a bit, Brophy paused to look out over the Sound. On the horizon, a boat with a wind-bellied spinnaker striped like an Arab's tent inched along. Healey, taking his cue, stopped too. The young priest clearly liked this unhurried response to so eminent a summons.

Back in the building, he thanked Healey once more and assured him that there was nothing he needed at the moment. In his room, he settled into an easy chair and reached indolently for the telephone.

"What in God's name are you up to?" his patron demanded when he came on the line, the question prefaced by no amenities. "Of all the idiotic statements I have ever seen, yours is surely the worst. I simply cannot believe you would write such tripe."

Bishop Brophy rolled to the edge of his chair, gasping for breath. "Statement? What statement?"

"Don't tell me you have lapses of memory too?"

Brophy closed his eyes and worked his jaw muscles. Against his closed

433

lids he saw the image of an admiring Father Healey. He opened his eyes. "Your Eminence, I don't know what statement you are referring to. Surely you can't mean my remarks on television last night?"

"Of course I don't. Wait, let me read it to you. That may refresh your memory."

"I'd appreciate that, Your Eminence."

Listening to the prose read with consummate sarcasm by the man who was his ticket out of oblivion, Bishop Brophy felt his scalp lift as if for the taking. The visions he had indulged in during his postprandial stroll seemed a mad commentary on this moment: the pallium, the red hat, the confidant of presidents. My God. If the cardinal could believe he was responsible for what he was reading, Sean Brophy would be lucky to get Wyoming.

"I didn't write that," he interrupted. "Where did you get that?"

"In this morning's edition of the *Fort Elbow Tribune*. Someone was kind enough to send me a copy by special messenger. I had an idea it might be you."

Bishop Brophy blew a blast of angry air into the phone. Ascue and Donovan? It had to be. "Your Eminence, there has been a terrible, a ludicrous mistake. You must believe that this is the first time I have so much as heard what you have been reading. I have a suspicion what must have happened. I asked a young theologian, Father Ascue, and Daniel Donovan, the editor of the diocesan paper, to work up some background material for a statement on the encyclical. Neither showed me what he had written. I have the dreadful certainty that it is their work you are reading."

"The byline is the Most Reverend Sean Brophy."

"That is a libel."

"You never laid eyes on it?"

"Never."

"All right." The cardinal breathed heavily and Brophy was reminded of the sobriquet the man's rugged appearance had earned him with his smoother critics: the primate of America. "I don't know what you're going to do, Sean, but you had better do it fast. This could ruin you. And I mean ruin you."

"Did you hear my statement on television?" Brophy asked plaintively.

"That's in this paper too. Side by side with the other."

"My God."

"Take care of it, Sean. Fast."

"I will, Your Eminence, I will."

He sat quivering with rage after he had put down the phone. Not

434

since that absurd session with George Caldron last May had anyone dared speak to him in such tones. Ascue and Donovan! Those damnable fools. Were they completely mad? How bitter it was to recall that he had counted on Frank to balance Donovan. And to think of the two of them getting together, concocting that ridiculous article and sending it to the *Tribune* under his name! But he had to control himself. He removed his cassock and collar, rolled up his shirt sleeves, prepared to stay the hurricane. The cardinal had counseled him to take the radical route before but obviously he too had come to see the risk in that. Brophy began to wonder about his earlier assumption that he owed the cardinal his appointment to this committee. Although he had phoned him here, he had made no mention of what his presumed protégé was up to in New York. The archbishop? Good Lord. What would *he* think of that article if it had affected the cardinal like this? That some enemy had sent copies to all his friends seemed too obvious a truth to question. This is the turning point, Brophy thought solemnly. The way he acted now would determine whether or not he had the stuff of which real churchmen are made. He smiled a joyless smile and reached for the telephone. First things first.

"Operator, I want to make a long distance call to Fort Elbow, Ohio. Fort Elbow," he repeated, then had to spell it for her and suffer her giggle when he had. "Father Francis Ascue. Saint Waldo's rectory. I don't have the exact address."

"Is he listed?"

"Saint Waldo's will be."

"But not Francis Ascue?"

"No."

Not yet. Frank would not be listed yet. But he would be. Oh, would he be listed.

Frank had awakened at six, reached for the phone and dialed Donovan's number. He knew it by heart, having dialed it until two in the morning without success. The ringing in his ear might have been coming from the opposite side of the earth, some unpopulated place. Where in hell had Donovan disappeared to? Of course he must be at home, simply ignoring the phone, fearful Bishop Brophy would call. Frank would have liked to dress and go out to Donovan's house but this was Sunday and he had two Masses to say, the nine and ten-thirty. Groaning, he rolled over but sleep would not come.

Ten minutes later he got up and walked to his desk. He took the paper back to his bed. It was true. The article, Donovan's article, was there on the front page, attributed to Bishop Brophy. It read worse than it had the night before, even worse than when Donovan had brought it here to the rectory. Daniel must have lost his mind. What he had done was not simply stupid, it was illegal, printing something of his own as if it had been written by another and without that other's consent. But how could the *Tribune* run both stories on the same page, an account of the televised remark and Donovan's crazy article? The first account had been written by Mary Muscatelli. Frank looked up her number in the book and called her. After half a dozen rings a sleepy voice answered.

"Miss Muscatelli?"

"Who's that?"

"Frank Ascue. Father Ascue."

"Oh, yes. What time is it?"

Frank glanced at his watch, decided not to say. "Early. Look, I'm wondering about this morning's paper. The stories on Bishop Brophy."

"I'll bet you are."

"Did Donovan give you that article you've attributed to Bishop Brophy?"

"Why?"

"He wrote it, Mary. I doubt that Bishop Brophy ever saw it."

"That isn't what Donovan said. He said you two—"

"He said what?"

The sound of a match striking came over the wire, then the rustle of exhalation. Frank expected smoke to emerge from the receiver. "Donovan explained everything, Father. To me and to the editor. You had prepared this statement for the bishop, to counter the Te Deum meeting tomorrow. Brophy had been called out of town but he wanted that article in the Sunday paper."

"Didn't you call Bishop Brophy?"

"No. Why should we?"

"Because of what he said on television. *You* wrote that up. Surely you noticed the contradiction."

"Father, let me tell you something. Nothing anybody has said on that encyclical since it came out makes any sense to me. Sure I noticed the contradiction. It wasn't the first time."

"Bishop Brophy is almost certain to sue."

"Who, me? He'll have to sue Daniel Donovan. He told us what he told us. Me, the editor, others. Why are you so concerned? Even if you helped write the thing—"

"I had nothing to do with it."

"Maybe you better sue Donovan too."

"Maybe." What a ridiculous conversation.

"Is it really six-fifteen!"

"I'm sorry. I had to find out—"

The line had gone dead.

Among the announcements he read at both his Masses was one which said that Te Deum would sponsor on the morrow a public meeting at which Prince Thaddeus Chorzempowski would speak on the recent encyclical issued by Paul VI. As soon as he had finished the ten-thirty Mass, Frank set out in McTear's car for Donovan's.

He pressed the bell, he knocked sharply on the door, he rang the bell once more. It was in order; he could hear it ringing inside. And then came sounds of movement. A moment later, the ravaged face of Lydia Donovan looked out at him.

"Father Ascue," she said, apparently without surprise.

"I would like to speak to Daniel."

"He isn't here." She worked her lips, as if to moisten her mouth. An aroma of liquor spiked the freshness of the August air.

Frank opened the door and stepped inside. "Is he at Mass?"

"No."

Frank felt like throwing up windows in a Johannine gesture, to let in a little fresh air. The living room was a mess; the ashtrays were filled with scarcely smoked filter tips, papers were scattered over the floor, among them the *Fort Elbow Catholic*. A blanket lay contorted on the couch. A pillow too. He looked at Lydia. The rumpled Mrs. Donovan had obviously spent the night on the couch, fully dressed.

Scratching her head and yawning, Lydia walked in stocking feet across her husband's publication and collapsed on the couch. She waved vaguely at a chair.

He remained standing. "Where is Daniel?"

"I don't know." Her voice was bewildered.

Patience, patience. She was like one of those confused children who stumbled in from their naps when he visited parishioners in the afternoon.

"When did Daniel leave this morning?"

"He wasn't here all night. He didn't come back."

Frank sat down. He felt oddly deserted because Donovan was not here. "He was gone all night?"

"Yes. We were watching the news. . . ." Her eyes went to the television set as if she were trying to reconstruct the scene. Frank looked too and was surprised to see an inaudible Taggart haranguing them. He got up and turned off the set.

"Bishop Brophy came on. And we had just been celebrating his finishing the article for Bishop Brophy. He ranted and raved. I tried to calm him, to get him to eat. I'd made such a nice supper. Crab, wine . . ." Her mind went in pursuit of last night's menu.

"And watching the news?" Frank said helpfully.

"Daniel never misses Hartshorne Prince. Not since he mentioned Daniel that time." Lydia seemed touched by her husband's loyalty.

The conversation proceeded like a crossword puzzle and Frank filled in the squares on the cue of her disconnected remarks. Daniel had reacted to Brophy's statement in New York with disbelief, then with fury. He would not let Bishop Brophy back out of the statement Daniel had prepared.

"Had Brophy ever seen it?"

Lydia ignored him. Daniel had determined to release the statement to the newspapers. Lydia tried to convince him it was too late, but he was adamant. He had fled the house armed with a crab fork. And with a copy of the statement he had written for Bishop Brophy. Frank shook his head.

"Bishop Brophy will kill him. Have you seen today's paper?"

Lydia looked at the floor but only the *Fort Elbow Catholic* and yesterday's *Tribune* were scattered there. Suddenly she froze, head cocked. Her face took on a stupefied expression. Then Frank heard it too. A groan. They were both on their feet in the same instant. Frank followed Lydia into the bedroom. Daniel was spread-eagled on the bed, his loosened tie draped over his chest like the bend sinister. He groaned again. Lydia sat on the edge of the bed and began to shake him.

"Alice," he moaned.

"Daniel, you're not at the office. You're home." She made a face at Father Ascue, who stared with disgust at the undone editor.

"Is there coffee, Lydia?"

"I don't think it will do any good."

"Why don't you make some anyway?"

She seized upon the suggestion. Something to do. When she had left the room, Frank grabbed Daniel's ankle and pulled him off the bed. An instinctive genuflection saved Daniel from crashing ignominiously to the floor. Elbows on the bed, he looked at Frank with flaming eyes.

"What the hell's going on?"

"Good morning, Daniel."

"Yeah." Daniel's eyes went out of focus and again he groaned.

Frank left the room, joining Lydia in the kitchen, not caring to witness Daniel's efforts to regain his balance on the whirling planet. Daniel stumbled noisily after him, stood in the doorway, looked abjectly at his wife.

438

"What time did you get in?" Lydia spoke with an insouciance Frank found manic.

Daniel looked at the spot on his wrist where his watch should be and shook his head. "I don't know." He tried to focus on Frank. "I took care of old Brophy, Father. I really fixed him."

"Is that what you call it?"

"That article? The one we wrote? I gave it—"

"The one *we* wrote? Don't be ridiculous. That was yours alone, Daniel. You're going to tell Bishop Brophy that. I had nothing to do with it, with writing it, with giving it to the newspaper."

"But we talked," Daniel said, confused.

The phone rang and Lydia answered it, a wall phone hanging right there in the kitchen. Her eyes widened with fright and she brought her finger to her lips.

"Daniel? I'm afraid not, Bishop Brophy. Can I take a message?"

Lydia frowned and nodded. "All right. Yes. Yes, Bishop Brophy. Tonight."

She put the phone back on the hook very deliberately. "He's coming back tonight. He wants to see you."

One could see what Daniel would look like as an old man, if he survived. His mouth was slack, the skin around his eyes gray, his hair matted. "Oh, my God," he groaned.

"Daniel, you're going to have to tell Bishop Brophy I had nothing to do with it."

"Oh, Father, please shut up." Lydia glared at him. "Can't you see he's sick? Leave him alone. Just leave him alone. Bursting in here, thinking only of yourself—"

"Lydia," Daniel groaned.

Frank thought Daniel was interceding for him—God knew he needed help; Lydia's impatience, her accusation, made him feel like a fool—but Donovan lurched to his feet, sweat popping from his forehead. Lydia took his elbow and guided him out of the room. Frank waited a moment but the sounds of retching sent him to the front door and outside. How crazy to worry about himself. Brophy would see in a minute he had had nothing to do with the article in the paper. Poor Donovan. His troubles had only begun.

After Sunday dinner Father Oder left Swivel with "Friar Tuck," the Franciscan who helped out weekends, and became incommunicado in his den, his mood fluctuating between anger at Bishop Brophy for his turnabout on the encyclical and a pleasure of which he was not wholly proud when he studied the beautiful contradiction in which Sean had been caught on the front page of the Sunday *Tribune*. Of course it might have been only a local contradiction if Father Oder had not sent copies of the newspaper to Brophy's powerful friends. Why had he done this? Once Frank Ascue had removed all doubt that the bishop had not even seen the article Donovan had published under Brophy's name, the contradiction was only apparent. And Donald Oder wished that it were not so. What particularly irked him was the realization that Brophy had been using him, yes, and the senate too, for his own purposes and, when those purposes did not require it, simply went on his way, without even informing his putative ally. Nor was Oder much mollified when Bishop Brophy telephoned.

"I'm trying to reach Frank Ascue," the bishop said without preliminary.

"Have you tried his number?"

"Of course I've tried his number," Brophy snapped.

"Well, he's not here."

"Don, I'm in New York."

"You are! I hadn't heard." Fingers crossed, a mental reservation—he had not heard it from Brophy.

"It's a long story."

"Yes?"

Brophy made the long story exceedingly short. How he would have loved to gloat over that appointment, Oder thought. A summons to New York, one of a select few . . . On any ordinary occasion, Brophy could have filled an afternoon with it but of course, as the bishop's tone made clear, this was not an ordinary occasion.

"Incidentally," Oder said, when the bishop paused for breath, "I enjoyed your article in the *Tribune.*"

Brophy's sputtered retort was music to Oder's ear. He settled back in his chair, prepared to enjoy this.

"It isn't your article? I don't understand. The style . . ."

"Don, I never saw the damned thing. I still haven't seen it. All I know are the portions which were read to me on the phone."

"Someone called?"

"It's a long story."

"Another one? I've been wanting to talk with you but of course I had no idea how to contact you."

"Everything happened very quickly."

"I can see that. No wonder Daniel just presumed on your consent to publish your article."

440

"*My* article!" Brophy went into a rage. "I've told you, Don, it isn't mine. Donovan and Frank Ascue are responsible for it."

"Frank?"

Brophy sighed in confirmation. "I thought he would tone it down. Dear Lord! How could they do this to me?"

"I'm sure they were only trying to help you."

"Help me? I'd like to wring their necks. They are going to have to issue a statement, explaining what happened. They have to make it clear that I never laid eyes on a thing they wrote. That's why I'm flying back tonight."

"That ought to clear everything up," Oder said cheerily.

"It better. Don, get hold of Frank. I want him to meet my plane. I talked with Lydia and she claims she doesn't know where Daniel is. Protecting him, of course. Will you do that?"

"Of course. Of course. How is the committee work going?"

That was like asking Adam about Eden after the fall. Poor Sean. Again Oder assured Brophy that he would have Frank meet his plane.

"And Mary Muscatelli. Have her there too. I want her to take down the statement on the spot."

Later, eating crackers and cheese and sipping beer, Oder reflected that Brophy's connections were indeed formidable and, if his past performance was indicative, he would very likely squirm out of this difficulty. It might even turn into a *felix culpa*. Food for thought there for the pastor of Saint Barnabas. He hoped he had not gone too far, teasing Brophy on the phone. Unpredictable as he was, Bishop Brophy was a powerful friend to have.

It was nearly ten o'clock that night when the front doorbell rang. Oder remained seated in his den, but he laid the book he had been reading against his stomach and waited. On the second sounding of the bell there was movement overhead and then the housekeeper started reluctantly down. Before answering the door, she looked into the den accusingly.

"Someone's at the front door, Father."

"Would you see who it is, Ruth?"

"Now that I'm down here."

"I'd rather not see anyone."

But he came to the door of the den and peeked down the hallway when she opened the front door. From out of the night the drunken voice of Daniel Donovan demanded to see the pastor. Ruth glanced down the hall and Father Oder shook his head violently but, alas, with the housekeeper thus distracted, Daniel pushed into the house, spied the pastor and came lurching toward him.

"I've got to talk to you."

"Of course, Daniel. Of course. Knock and it shall be opened."

Oder cast a despairing look at Ruth and received in return an unsympathetic scowl; she slammed the door and went back upstairs to her Sunday movie on television. Meanwhile Daniel had gone into the den, where Father Oder found him in a state of semicollapse in a leather chair.

"I want to go to confession, Father."

"In your condition? Better wait, Daniel."

"Okay. Let me have a drink then."

"Do you think that would be wise?"

"No. Let me have one."

Oder nodded to the sideboard and Daniel got up and went to it. Once there he stood, his back to Oder, his shoulders slumped. There was the sound of sobs. Daniel was not being coherent; all Oder could make out was clarity and adultery. Well, he couldn't have it both ways. He went to Daniel, patted him on the back and mixed a drink for him. Grasping the glass, Daniel turned to Oder. "Thanks."

"That's all right, Daniel. Sit down."

"He's coming in tonight. I'm supposed to see him, meet his plane. Lydia doesn't want me to."

"Bishop Brophy?"

"I'm in real trouble. Even Ascue has turned against me."

"In what way?"

"He says he had nothing to do with it, that he didn't write a thing."

"And he did?"

"We talked it over, he made suggestions. I have the notes."

"Well, then."

"But who'll believe me? I'm through, Father. Finished. And in Fort Elbow!" Daniel peered at Oder, certain he would understand that this was nadir indeed. "I thought I was doing him a favor. That remark he made in New York. You know that isn't what he thinks. It can't be what he thinks. He thinks what I wrote. What Frank Ascue and I wrote. It's a great statement." Suddenly remembering, Daniel fished in his pocket and brought forth a crumpled telegram. "Read that."

"From Bishop Brophy?"

"No. Read it."

The NCR had wired to ask that a copy of the Brophy article be sent them pronto. Oder looked into Daniel's proud haunted eyes.

"Have you sent it?"

"You're kidding."

"It's already in the public domain, Daniel. No doubt Bishop Brophy's desire to disassociate himself from it increases its interest."

"It's a good article. A damned good article. It deserves national attention."

"There you are then."

Was it pointless whimsy thus to encourage Daniel and further Brophy's embarrassment? But it did not seem right that Brophy should get out of this so easily. After all, he had commissioned Daniel and Frank Ascue to write a statement for him, and certainly not of the tenor of his remarks on television last night. He ought to be made to sweat a little anyway. For much the same reason Oder counseled Daniel to meet the bishop's plane. Bring the principals together, that was the ticket. Oder was almost tempted to go to the airport himself.

Only every other light was on in the airport terminal and the place had the forlorn look public buildings have when deserted. The clean-up crew had its work cut out for it. The seats in the waiting room were covered with debris; ashtrays, heaped with candy wrappers and ice cream sticks, gave off the acrid smell that ashtrays have in the dead of night. The coffee room was closed, the ticket counters were closed, the cigarette counter was closed. One couple sat in the waiting room, yawning and bored. From behind the metal door of the baggage room voices were audible.

Frank continued walking through the building and came out on the field side. Before him the runways sparkled like a fallen Christmas tree in the night. The sky was overcast and the spot from the tower, when it flicked past, illumined the clouds and brought them close. It was difficult to believe that another flight was expected. Who had answered when he had telephoned half an hour ago, to verify that the plane from Cleveland was due at eleven forty-five? Frank turned and looked at the terminal building. High above him the glass panes of the tower shone brightly and there were other lighted windows below them. Frank went back inside.

He was not really surprised that Daniel was not here. He hoped that he would not come. He wanted to speak to Bishop Brophy first and alone, make certain that he understood that this stupid trick had been Daniel's, not his. As he had earlier, he felt uneasy about wanting to put the finger on Daniel but the fault was his, no matter what he said; the article Daniel had given the newspaper without Brophy's permission was vintage Donovan prose. The couple still sat on the bench, staring

443

at him. They might have been waiting for a disaster. And then through the revolving doors came Mary Muscatelli. The hand that held her purse strap splayed in greeting.

"You here to meet Bishop Brophy's plane?" she asked.

"That's right. Look, about this morning . . ."

She shrugged it off. "Thank God you're here. Father Oder called to tell me Brophy was coming in but I don't quite trust that man."

Mary looked around the terminal waiting room, nose wrinkled. "Ye gods, what a place." She glanced at her watch. "Let's wait outside, all right? We've got time."

They stood on the sidewalk, staring across the parking lot toward the road from town. A car was coming in from the highway. They watched it sweep around the curve and head for the stand in front of the entrance. Even before it stopped, they could hear a loud argumentative voice. The back door of the cab opened and Daniel Donovan shot out, continuing to move at roughly the same speed as the braking taxi. He went away up the curved sidewalk, ranting unintelligibly. The driver hopped out and went in pursuit of his fare. He caught Daniel by the arm, turned him around and marched him back to the entrance of the terminal.

"Drunk," the driver explained to Mary, who had gone over to him.

"Hello, Donovan," she said.

"You know him?" The driver was relieved. "He had to come to the airport. If it wasn't a priest who put him in the cab . . ."

"They stick together," Mary said significantly.

The driver looked with startled eyes at Daniel, glanced at Frank's collar. Mary nodded in confirmation. "Monsignor Borgia," she said.

"Take me to the airport," Daniel demanded.

"Pay the taxi, Daniel. This is the airport."

Frank could believe that Daniel was half acting the role of drunk. Would his eyes fail to focus so comically without help? Could the derangement of his clothing be totally artless? The staggering seemed completely theatrical. Daniel was searching his pockets for money while Mary and the driver watched. Finally success. Daniel pressed a wadded bill into the driver's hand.

"Thanks." The man glanced at Frank. "Thanks, Father," he said to Donovan.

"Bless you, my son."

Daniel started toward the building and Mary took his arm and steered him around the revolving doors. Frank followed, watching them skate ahead of him across the expanse of the waiting room. Mary put Daniel on a couch.

444

"There's a coffee machine," she said to Frank. "I'll get a cup."

When Mary returned with the coffee, she held it clawlike, but still her fingers were regularly bathed with it. Her face was distorted with pain. "It's hot as lava." She gave the cup to Daniel, who held it with both hands, unbothered by its temperature.

"It's hot," Mary warned him.

"I'm drunk."

"You're drunk. Drink that coffee and then you'd better go home."

"Brophy. I have to meet Bishop Brophy."

Mary lifted her brows at Frank. To Daniel she said, "Does Lydia know you're here?"

Daniel began to cry. "I'm a sonofabitch. What time is it? I lost my watch."

The plane was due in twenty minutes. Mary whispered to Frank, "I'm going to call his wife. He shouldn't be running around loose."

"Good idea."

"Daniel, do you have a dime?"

He plunged his hand into his pocket, brought it out and coins fell everywhere. Mary and Frank chased them down, stamping on cartwheeling quarters and pennies, then picking them up. No dimes. Frank found a dime in his own pocket and gave it to Mary. "You'd better hurry."

"Gotta talk to Bishop Brophy," Daniel told his coffee. "Gotta explain."

"I'll talk to him, Daniel. There's no need for you to be here."

"Lydia didn't want me to come."

"She was right. Mary is calling her. You can go home. I'll talk to Bishop Brophy."

"We saved him," Daniel said with feeling. "From himself. Our article saved his soul."

"Your article, Daniel."

"Right! NCR wants it."

Frank looked toward the phone booths, wishing Mary would hurry. That quickly Daniel fell asleep, sitting upright, half a cup of coffee in his hands, his head tipped to two o'clock. Frank took the cup and set it on the floor. When he tapped Daniel's shoulder the editor slumped sideways in slow motion and assumed a position more attuned to sleep. Frank lifted his feet onto the couch. Daniel bent his knees, got into the fetal position, gave forth a sighing sob and began to snore.

What a picture he made, disheveled, disgraceful, drunk. The poor guy. Frank told himself he must convince Brophy to go easy on Daniel. Donovan meant well, so did his wife, so did all kinds of other lay people who were trying to find their place in the new Church. Mistakes? Of course they made mistakes. Who didn't? Frank had no doubt whatsoever that Daniel really thought he had done Bishop Brophy a favor by publishing that absurd article on the encyclical, that he truly regarded the action as one which would save Brophy from himself. Mary came back, shaking her head.

"What did she say?"

"She's coming for him."

"No point in waking him until she gets here."

"No." Mary looked at the sleeping Daniel, then at Frank. "Lydia's a bit out of it herself."

"How so?"

"She seemed to think I'd been with Daniel for days. Wanted to know what I'd been doing with him."

Some once popular tune whose melody he could not quite remember and whose words came to him only in snatches had invaded Bishop Brophy's head when he boarded the plane at LaGuardia. *Fly the ocean in a silver plane.* Trying to drive it away only brought it buzzing back like an angry fly. *See the jungle when it's wet with rain.* The wretched song recalled the lassitude of adolescence, induced thoughts of chucking it all, putting in for the missions like Cardinal Leger. He saw himself in a simple white soutane, striding a jungle path, surrounded by smiling hordes of pink-gummed savages whose immortal souls he had just saved by means of an intense homily in their own snarled dialect. *Just remember till you're home again . . .* In Cleveland, forced to wait an hour and a half for the flight to Fort Elbow, he had half expected to be led out to a Ford trimotor for the final leg of his journey. *You belong to me.*

Jo Stafford or Margaret Whiting, one of them, but what year did the song date from? He had never succumbed to the temptation to order those albums, songs of the thirties, of the forties, of the fifties. He doubted that they would ever put one together for the sixties. Who would want it? Nostalgia was an inappropriate emotion for a man on the way up; it was the future he longed for, but he was Irish enough to want to slobber over the past, to rue and lament and see life as tragedy. Tonight, approaching Fort Elbow in a plane carrying only four other passengers, having against his usual practice avoided companionship, Bishop Brophy sat in somber solitude and let the fought-against emotion do its stuff.

A fair tenor when he did not force his voice into a lower, more authoritative register, he might have made it in show business. He had

446

the professional's need for an audience together with his mild contempt for those he played to. A crooner perhaps, but no, he could not have settled for anything so vacuous. In his present menaced situation, the thought of a helpmate was teasingly attractive and for the first time Sean Brophy really felt what must be driving so many men toward laicization. What sort of wife would he have had, he wondered. Trying to imagine her, he found that she was as vague as the song. He could not even summon a clear image of Jo or Maggie. How he wished he could forget that song. Concentrate. Think.

But his thoughts turned to Caldron and Yorick and what now seemed the suddenly swollen ranks of his adversaries. The cardinal would throw him to the wolves in a minute, he had no illusions on that score. And he had detected in Don Oder's voice the cautious distancing with which another's potential fall is met. Oh, he could be swiftly isolated, there was no doubt of that, and, irony, irony, just when out of the blue he had been picked for that committee. Which had, after all, been the archbishop's doing.

"I know you'll give it all you have," the archbishop had said when Bishop Brophy got through to him.

"As it happens, I'm flying back to Fort Elbow tonight. But I'll be back late Monday."

"Do you think it wise to leave, Sean?"

"I wish I could avoid it. Someone has done something truly incredible." Brophy manufactured a laugh *ex nihilo* and went on as if with a droll story. "The most absurd attack on the encyclical, the hierarcy, the pope."

"But surely Bishop Caldron can handle that?"

"Ah, but there is more," Brophy said with forced brightness. "This diatribe was printed under my name."

"*Your* name!"

"A friend phoned and read portions of it to me. Of course I had never laid eyes on it. The ones responsible are proving impossible to reach by telephone so I really must run out there and straighten this out before it turns into something serious."

"What an extraordinary thing to have happen."

Brophy sighed. "I know."

It helped a little to make his apparent doom the topic of light conversation, to treat it as something that might have happened to anyone. But to think of anyone else in his predicament was to think of someone with an impossible task on his hands. Any denial would only increase suspicion. Which was precisely why the denial must come from others.

As the plane began to descend on Fort Elbow, Bishop Brophy

gripped the arms of his seat and felt set upon by enemies unworthy of him. Daniel Donovan, of all people. And Frank Ascue. Frank had seemed so sane, so reliable, an outstanding young man. How could he have permitted this to happen? Would the two of them be waiting when the plane landed? Of course they would be. They had to be. But against the grain of his optimism Bishop Brophy could imagine not finding them at the airport. Well, he would rout them out, track them down, do what he had come home to do. Home. Fort Elbow. Oh, God.

He was the first one off the plane and moving purposively across the ramp when he noticed the Muscatelli girl waiting at the gate. Good, good. The press was here. And then he noticed Frank Ascue and felt a surge of anger. Better concentrate on Mary Muscatelli, ignore Frank for a moment, let him feel the chill.

"Well, well. Miss Muscatelli." He turned to look at the other passengers straggling from the plane. "Don't tell me there was a celebrity aboard and I didn't notice."

"Just you, Bishop."

"Ha ha." He took her arm and went on into the terminal. Frank came along. Out of the corner of his eye, Brophy had seen Ascue's look of eager apology turn to anxiety. Good. Let him sweat. To Mary he said, "How could you possibly have known I'd be on that plane?"

"Is it true that you had nothing to do with the article in this morning's *Tribune* that was attributed to you?"

"Quite true. There has been an incredible mix-up and I flew back here to look into it."

"Donovan is here," Ascue said behind him. "Over here."

"The work of the committee is going nicely," Brophy said to Mary. "Quite confidentially—"

"How could Donovan make such a goof?"

"Have you asked him?"

"It's been difficult to talk to him."

"I know. I know."

Ascue had gone ahead and they followed him among the chairs and couches. He came to a stop. Donovan lay there, asleep on a couch. It was all Bishop Brophy could do not to spring at the sleeping figure. Ascue shook Donovan's shoulders. Daniel moaned. Ascue shook harder. Daniel rolled onto the floor, easily, with scarcely a thump, and lay a boneless heap at their feet.

"He's drunk," Mary explained.

"I can see that," the bishop said. "Let's get him off the floor."

Brophy stooped, caught Daniel under an arm, and strained. How could so small a man weigh so much? Frank Ascue took the other arm.

448

They did it in stages. First, a seated position on the floor, then tugging him onto the couch, finally pulling him to his feet. A cherubic smile came over Daniel's face while this was going on. Now his eyes opened.

"Bishop Brophy," he cried.

"Hello, Daniel."

Donovan lurched forward, put out his arm and leaned against Brophy. "About that article, Bishop Brophy."

"Yes, Daniel. I've come back to hear all about it."

"Good. Did you read it? It's great. NCR—"

"I had nothing to do with it," Frank Ascue said, addressing no one in particular, speaking for the record.

"Oh?" Brophy said.

"You did too," Daniel said. "We talked. We collaborated. I took notes."

"That article is yours alone, Daniel."

"Daniel! Daniel!"

Lydia Donovan came running toward them, her hair a mess, feet in slippers, tugging a raincoat about her. Her eyes blazed when she looked at Brophy.

"What are you doing to Daniel?"

"Take it easy," Mary said. "Daniel's all right."

"You stay out of this," Lydia snapped.

She reached out, to free her husband from the need of Brophy's support, and her raincoat opened with the effort. She stepped back and the nightgown she must have tucked up loosened and fell to her ankles. They all stood there watching its descent as if it were a curtain falling on an incredible scene.

Mary Muscatelli got the Donovans out of there. Bishop Brophy sat down and for the first time looked Frank Ascue in the eye.

"Well, Frank. This is a pretty kettle of fish."

"Yes." Frank did not sit down. Ignoring him had not had the desired effect. Frank was distant but composed and Brophy did not like the expression on the young priest's face.

"How could you do this to me, Frank?"

"Do what, Bishop?"

"Print that godawful article as if it were mine. I won't have it, Frank. When Mary comes back here I want you to give her a statement, tell her what happened—"

"And what do you think happened?"

"What do I think happened?" Brophy rose slowly to his feet. "I'll tell you what happened. I asked you to prepare a statement for me, a sensible statement, a theologian's statement. I asked Donovan to help you. Naturally I expected to receive what you two did, revise and rewrite. I did not authorize you to send it to the newspapers. *That* is what happened. I've been made to look a fool, speaking out of both sides of my mouth. Well, by God, you are going to straighten things out. Do you understand? You are going to make a statement to the newspaper and you are going to make it perfectly clear that I had nothing whatsoever to do with that stupid article or with its publication. Ah, Mary."

Mary Muscatelli came up to them, brows raised at the tone of Brophy's voice.

"Did I miss something?"

Brophy summoned a mirthless chuckle as if from the depths of memory. "Not at all. Father Ascue has something to say to you. Now then, I'll leave you here. I must get to bed. I'm flying back to New York tomorrow."

He did not say good-bye to Frank. Imagine asking him that. And what do you think happened? Did he think this was some kind of game? Did he imagine that he could print any kind of drivel under a bishop's name and get away with it? In the cab, on the way to the cathedral rectory, Brophy scrunched in the corner, glaring out at Fort Elbow. He had been the victim of fools, however briefly. Well, now it would be straightened out. Despite the hour he would call the editor of the *Tribune* and insist that Frank Ascue's explanation appear on the front page, as prominent as the hoax itself had been. Vindication. Brophy tried to take pleasure from it and couldn't. Ascue. What had got into him? At least Donovan had the excuse of being drunk. Brophy shook his head, trying to clear it. *Fly the ocean in a silver plane.* The thought of the next day's return flight to New York was not welcome. *See the jungle when it's wet with rain.* But all he could see was Fort Elbow, dry and deserted in the middle of the night.

Frank watched Bishop Brophy swing through the revolving doors and outside. He was stunned. Brophy had not asked him what happened; he had told him. Frank wondered if he had even read the article which had brought him flying back from the East. Perhaps, as with the encyclical, Brophy had not had to read it in order to know that he did not like it. But actually scolding him like that, in this public if deserted place, telling him what he must do. Frank felt memories of the boyish vulgarity of the caddy shack flood his mind and it was all he could do not to make an obscene gesture after the departing bishop. When Mary Muscatelli spoke he turned to her, startled, as if she could guess what he was thinking.

450

"Want to sit down, Father?"

"No. No, I'd rather stand."

"Suit yourself. Well, what's it going to be? Can you give me something printable on that article of Brophy's Donovan turned over to us?"

"It wasn't his."

"So he said. Who wrote it?"

Looking at her, Frank could imagine what Brophy had assumed he would have to tell Mary, that he and Donovan had fobbed something of their own off on the bishop, printed it as his without his permission. For a moment the reporter held the fascination the executioner must hold for the condemned, the end, a way out of it all, total destruction. How incredibly welcome that seemed. He could tell Mary what Brophy imagined had happened and thus wash his hands of the whole mess, cleanse himself of what propelled the bishop now, the lust for exoneration. I did it. *Mea culpa.* It's all my fault. But of course the moment passed.

"It's a long story, Mary. Maybe we should sit down."

When they were seated side by side and Mary had her notebook open, Frank felt again the flicker of a desire to take equal blame with Donovan. He looked across the room at the couch where the forlorn editor had lain, drunk and asleep. But a lie would be of no lasting help to Donovan. Only the full truth might diminish his plight. So he began by telling Mary that he had suggested to Bishop Brophy that a statement on the encyclical would be very useful since there had been no local discussion of it. Brophy had agreed and had asked Frank to prepare a rough draft of such a statement. Apparently he had made the same request of Daniel Donovan. At a certain point in their separate labors, they had conferred, exchanged manuscripts, commented on what the other had done. Daniel had taken on the task of collating the two pieces. And then, with Brophy called suddenly out of town and the Te Deum meeting imminent, Daniel had decided to release the statement to the press, to balance what he feared the speaker engaged by Te Deum would say.

"And Bishop Brophy never saw it or gave his permission for its release?"

"No."

"Did you see it first?"

"The version that appeared in the paper? No."

"How much of it was yours?"

Frank thought of Daniel, pathetically assuring Brophy that the article was good; he thought of the bishop so eager to turn the fire on somebody else, anybody else. "The article you printed was Daniel's."

451

"His alone?"

Why didn't she look at him? He felt that he was giving damning evidence at a trial. "Yes."

She did look at him now. "And you disagree with it, like Brophy?"

"That doesn't matter."

"Father, look. Obviously you didn't have anything to do with the piece we printed. I don't have to use this background material you gave me. Why should you be mixed up in it at all?"

"Because I am."

"Bishop Brophy? But obviously he doesn't know what really happened. He wouldn't expect you—"

"I wish you'd give the full story."

"How long have you been a masochist? I'll read it back to you."

While she did, Frank followed her voice as if from a distance. The story did exonerate him, making him as innocent as Brophy. Somehow he would have preferred guilt. Poor Daniel.

"Okey-doke," Mary said, flipping her notebook shut. "Daniel will be lucky if the *Tribune* doesn't sue him."

"I doubt that it would be worth their while."

"Money? This is worse. It's the principle of the thing."

"I'm glad it's over with."

Mary slapped her knee with her notebook. "Do you know, I'm almost sorry Brophy is getting off so easily. He doesn't make a very plausible victim."

"He was this time. He never saw that article."

"And now he's off the hook." Mary's voice was sad.

"Whatever happened to that roommate of yours?"

Mary's expression did not change; it just froze. "She left town. Like Bullard. I wonder why."

"What do you mean?"

"I don't know."

The door through which the passengers had entered opened and the crew of the plane came in, talking happily together, the pilot, copilot, two stewardesses. Frank recognized Sheila Rupp at the same moment she did him. Sheila looked as if she would have liked to stop, to go back out the door, but her companions bore her on, straight toward Frank and Mary Muscatelli. Sheila looked at Mary, at Frank, at Mary again. Frank got clumsily to his feet. The two men, noticing his collar, nodded, then they too darted a glance at Mary, who had remained seated. Sheila had put on a professional smile and would have just swept by if Frank had not spoken.

"Hello, Sheila."

"Father Ascue, what a surprise." She kept her eyes fixed on him as if she must force herself not to look at Mary. Why did he feel that she wanted him to say something, anything, that would explain why he was sitting here after midnight in the airport terminal with a girl? Perhaps because he was trying desperately to think of something that would take that shocked expression from her eyes. But nothing occurred to him and after an awkward moment Sheila went on with her companions. Frank slumped back onto the couch.

"Good grief, Father. Have I compromised you?"

"Don't be silly."

"Thanks a lot."

"That isn't what I meant."

"I know, I know. Don't get shaken up over that too."

"Shaken up?"

She seemed to reconsider. "Your statement. Remember?"

But of course that wasn't what she had meant. She shoved her notebook into her purse, tossed her head, said she had to get going. Did he have a car? He had to admit that he did not. How bitter to remember that he had imagined whisking off in a cab with Bishop Brophy, or perhaps in the bishop's own car, come to pick him up, jabbering away in the back seat, explaining to Brophy what an incredible thing Donovan had done.

"Come on, I'll give you a lift. Saint Waldo's, isn't it?"

"That must be out of your way."

"Father, at this time of night, nothing is out of my way. I'm going to have to get downtown and type this up before I'm through so what's the difference? Come on."

Seated beside her in her Volkswagen, his knees seemingly under his chin, he felt much as he had in Mrs. Fellows's sling chair. Mary drove with abandon and Frank kept both hands on the dashboard grip during the wild ride to the rectory. The little car made such a racket, Frank was sure it would wake the house when she stopped at the curb and gave several jolts of gas to the motor.

"Thanks very much." He opened the door. "I'm sorry to have made work for you."

"Weep not for me," Mary said, winking. "If you have second thoughts, you can call me during the next hour or so and I'll keep that background out of print." She slapped her purse, which contained the notebook and his statement.

"You already have my second thoughts."

Then what were those that came to him in his room? He did not regret having done exactly what Brophy had ordered him to do. Doing

453

it had seemed almost as sweet as revenge. Eventually, Brophy would learn the truth and then . . . Then what? Did he imagine a remorseful Brophy coming to him, abjectly begging his pardon? The attempted laugh became a cough. His throat felt sore. He put out his cigarette, one he did not remember having lit. What a stupid habit. Forget about Brophy. And remember Sheila, her shocked expression, the accusing look she had tried not to give him, the way her whole manner had cried out for an explanation he had been unable to give. *I scandalized her, Frank* realized, *I really did.* And he could imagine Sheila comparing that scene in the airport terminal with another one, in a parked car at the golf course, in the rain. He did not want her to think that he and Mary . . . The only way he could stop this train of thought was by saying his rosary, letting the beads slip through his fingers, the Glorious Mysteries, the Resurrection, the Ascension, the Descent of the Holy Ghost . . . During the third decade, trying to meditate on the Holy Ghost descending upon the Apostles, Frank descended into a restless sleep.

With something of the vanity of an author Frank read several times what he had dictated to Mary Muscatelli the night before. It was on the front page of the paper, enclosed in a box under a caption which ran: HOAX EXPLAINED. His words had a distant impersonal look; he admired their crispness, brevity and flow. Almost, he could abstract himself from what he had made public. A shriven sinner now, his burden lay there on that impermanent page, off his shoulders, exorcised. Though neither the words nor the action had been his, Frank felt the reader would see him as guilty as Donovan. What he was ridding himself of was the responsibility for suggesting to Brophy that he make such a statement on the encyclical, as well as his timidity in not telling Donovan point-blank what he had thought of the earlier version the little editor had brought to the rectory. Remembering a seething Daniel taking notes while he commented on his supposed collaborator's prose, he could believe Daniel felt that he had come far more than halfway to incorporate another viewpoint into the final version.

Frank folded the newspaper carefully and left it in the center of the dining room table. He was alone. Had Entweder and McTear read his explanation? No doubt, no doubt. Ah, well. It was too bad they had not dallied over breakfast to discuss with him the depths to which he had fallen. The pastor might have drawn from his vast fund of experience to produce a few well-chosen words of advice. And McTear would no doubt have had some rule of thumb to follow in future cases of a similar kind. Count to ten, read backward, foul your typewriter ribbon, speak no evil. Sheila.

When he parked in front of the Rupps' he could see up the driveway to the gaping garage, door up, car gone, empty. Of course they would already have left for the seminary and the Te Deum meeting. At the front door, Frank pressed the doorbell and waited, standing sideways, looking up the street as if with curiosity. When the door opened, he would turn, surprised, as if it were he who was being called on without notice. But the door did not open. He rang again, resumed his waiting stance, pursing his lips and emitting a little tuneless half-whistle as he stood there. Should he ring a third time? Why not? If she had not gone with her parents, she would most likely still be in bed. She had got home quite late the night before. It would take her time to get presentable, come downstairs, open the door. He imagined the itinerary she would take. The side of him which was nearest the door tingled in expectation. On the way here he had rehearsed what he would say, the explanation he would give her to erase the possibility of scandal, but now he was beyond the need of that. It was odd to be so concerned with saving his good name when he had probably opened himself to the scorn of the entire city with that too fulsome statement on Brophy's article. The third ring brought no one to the door. Frank walked slowly out to McTear's car, still hoping that behind him the door would open and Sheila call out to him. This did not happen. Behind the wheel again, he sat and wondered what he would do. Had she after all gone with her parents to the Te Deum meeting? Unlikely as that seemed, it was a possibility. He started the motor and slipped the gear to Drive.

He parked on the far side of the seminary campus and came across the lawn, approaching the classroom building from behind. Some twenty-five yards from the building, he left the walk to cut across the grass. When a little sports car came suddenly around the class building Frank, without thinking, stepped behind a tree. He stood there, feeling absurd. Why this stealth? He realized that he felt like a pariah, that it was not going to be easy to show himself here, particularly here, with this sort of people. He peered around the tree, his fingers light on the gnarled bark of the old oak, and saw two men get out of the parked car. He recognized Plummet-Finch first, then John Tremplin. Mary Muscatelli rounded the building and came toward them.

"Hello, hello, hello," she said. "What brings you two here?"

Plummet-Finch just stared at her, frozen in the act of shutting the car door, brows raised. He turned to Tremplin as if demanding an explanation of this predatory female's presence. Tremplin, in pale blue shirt, black tie, white seersucker jacket, made a sound suggestive of postnasal drip.

"This is Miss Mus-ca-tel-li, Gilbert."

The remotest hint of recognition established itself in Plummet-Finch's face.

"The reporter," Tremplin said.

The film leaped to life. Plummet-Finch slammed the car door and took Mary's hand. "Of course." Now he looked around, nostrils flared, enthralled. "Such a lovely place."

"Just out sightseeing?" Mary asked.

Tremplin had been rendered philosophical by his surroundings. "Nine years. I lived here nine years."

"I'm amazed you left," Plummet-Finch said.

"And now you're back," Mary offered.

"Yes." Tremplin threw back his shoulders. "Are they here?"

"They?"

"Te Deum. Caldron's claque. You know who I mean."

"John," Plummet-Finch urged. "You simply must show me around."

"Now?"

"Now!"

Mary stepped back, as if fearful Gilbert would stamp his foot. "What *are* you doing here?"

From the inside pocket of his seersucker jacket Tremplin produced a sheaf of paper. He made a little defiant gesture with it.

"You'll see."

When the voices had died away Frank stepped out of hiding. He walked to the back door of the class building from which, between lectures, they had emerged for a cigarette in the winters of his youth. Dry yellowing butts trampled into the ground made a mosaic that might have dated from his own time here. Frank stared at the trod-upon cigarette ends and at a crumpled Camel package whose cellophane wrapper was beaded with condensation. No message for him there. He opened the door and looked inside at the narrow staircase, rubber treads gritty with dirt, rising between tongue-and-groove walls, to the first floor, from which came a roar of voices. Frank closed the door. He decided to go to the main building first.

He closed the screen door behind him. The hall before him was empty but he could hear people talking around the corner where the rector's office was. Eisenbarth was saying, "His Highness is in my room, glancing over his talk." The rector's tone was one of scarcely suppressed delight. Clearly today was a major event.

Frank went toward the stairs which led to the second floor, turned and looked toward the rector's office. A dozen people were in the hall, the men paunchy and florid, the women elaborately coiffed and clad. In their midst, shepherd to the flock, stood an ecstatic Eisenbarth. Arthur Rupp was at his right hand, Clara next to Arthur. No sign of Sheila. It was Eisenbarth who saw Frank first. He stopped speaking and the others too looked at Frank, blank-faced, and then, when the whispering began, with a shock of recognition. Ten seconds, twenty seconds, Frank looked back at them. He could not possibly go up to Clara and ask where Sheila was. It occurred to him that she might be in the classroom building and he could have kicked himself for coming here. Then, at the sound of a door opening, the group turned away from him as if on cue. A shaft of sunlight emerged from the opened door of the rector's office and fell upon the polished linoleum of the hallway. Riding the beam, descending as if from high, Prince Thaddeus Chorzempowski appeared. He stopped, wreathed in light, "morning's minion, kingdom of daylight's dauphin," and extended his arms in greeting. The elite of Te Deum were drawn toward him even as he advanced upon them, tall, aristocratic. His brightest smile and warmest handclasp was reserved for Arthur Rupp. He bowed from the waist to an embarrassed but delighted Clara. He thanked her for her hospitality the previous evening. Frank, wanting to get out of the way of the coming exodus, scooted up the stairs.

In need of a destination, he went to Father Ewing's room, shutting the door behind him, collapsing into his old teacher's easy chair. These books now belonged to him. Frank let his eyes drift over the shelves and felt no lilt of possessiveness. Ewing had bought a surprising amount of history and biography. The fiction was mainly Russian. Bequeathing his books to Frank was a deed Father Ewing must have done before their falling out, no doubt when he still thought of Frank as his successor here, the professor of moral theology, carrying on the great tradition. How I disappointed him, Frank thought. And then: How I disappointed myself. But how? His life since he had returned from Rome seemed a downhill slide when he looked back upon it. This morning he would have liked to think of himself as a victim of the stupidity of others but of course that was hardly the whole story. He had been naïve and ineffective, that most menacing of men, a well-intentioned one. Again his eyes drifted along the shelves of books. He was supposed to be educated. He had an advanced degree. Yet he knew nothing, nothing that mattered. His hands lay on the arms of Ewing's chair, a priest's hands. He turned them over, then put them palms down again. How quiet the building was. They had all gone to the classroom building, the prince, Eisenbarth, the Rupps. Frank got to his feet. Perhaps he could look in on the meeting without being seen. He could find out if Sheila was there.

He went back the way he had come and entered the classroom building by the back door. The hallway, flanked by classrooms, was packed with people. The prince might just have arrived. He stood inside the front entrance, surrounded by his escort, talking with Bishop Brophy, who, taller than the prince, dominated the scene. It would not be easy to find Sheila in this crowd, if she was here. Finding her seemed now to give point to his day, although Frank was no longer sure what they had to talk about. He pressed into the crowd, grateful for the anonymity it afforded, and suddenly found himself next to Father Grimes. Frank said hello, almost into Grimes's ear. The priest turned and his smile faded like a speeded film. He said something but in the noise Frank could not make it out.

"Quite a turnout," Frank said.

Grimes looked around as if he would want a head count before agreeing with Frank.

"How is your protégé?" Frank asked.

"Who?"

"Ben Cole."

"I don't know."

"I had a talk with him."

"Did you?"

"Yes."

Grimes turned, concentrating on Brophy and the prince, and Frank felt dismissed. If he had needed an indication, he now knew what the reaction to his explanation of Brophy's statement was.

Led by Brophy and the prince, the crowd began to surge up the stairs to the *aula maxima*, where the prince would speak. Frank moved off to the side, not wanting to be borne along with the crowd. Mary Muscatelli came sidling along the wall with Daniel Donovan in tow.

"What are you doing here?" she asked.

"I'm not sure," Frank said, smiling.

"Then you're in the wrong bunch. All these people are sure as sin. Any reactions on your confession?"

"Not really."

"Be patient. There's a law against suicide, you know. Hara-kiri, performed with pen or sword."

Daniel Donovan, wedged against the wall next to Mary, looked reproachfully at Frank.

"Thanks a lot, Father Ascue," he said sullenly. "Thanks a lot."

"You didn't like my explanation?"

458

"You're kidding."

"Did he leave anything out?"

Frank wondered if Donovan had expected not to be mentioned at all in the account of how that article had found its way into print. "Perhaps we should have collaborated on that too," he said coolly. "Didn't you find it accurate?"

"Okay, okay," Daniel said. "Sure, that's what happened. But you might have said a few things in favor of the statement. Just because Brophy chickened out you don't have to. Remember, Father, *we* were right."

"I'll try not to forget."

"Tremplin is here," Mary told him.

"I know."

"Don't you find that surprising?"

"Nothing he does could surprise me."

"He brought a friend." Mary batted her eyelashes and smiled primly.

"Let's go upstairs," Daniel suggested. "We wouldn't want to miss this."

"Coming up?" Mary asked Frank.

"In a minute. You go ahead."

"They're picketing out front. Did you notice?"

"No. Who is it?"

But Donovan began to push her gently toward the stairs and Frank stepped back to let them through. To get further out of the crush, he went into a classroom.

"Frank!" John Tremplin sat at the desk in front of the room, papers spread before him, pen in hand. Plummet-Finch was at the side of the room, seated on a windowsill, looking bored.

"Frank, wait," Tremplin cried when Frank started to back out of the room. Frank had not been quick enough. Jack had let his hair grow and it hung unimpressively over his ears. His eyes were bright with excitement. "I want you to see this."

"What is it?"

"A proposal. I was going to hold it for the next senate meeting but I think it will get more publicity here today."

What it was, Tremplin explained, his hand on Frank's shoulder, forcing him toward the desk, was a demand for sympathy and support for the League of Estranged Priests, which he, Tremplin, was organizing.

"I've written to Phil Bullard, Frank. There must be hundreds of us. Your separated brethren."

"And cistern," Plummet-Finch drawled.

Jack ignored his friend. "Talk about an underground church, Frank.

459

We make up a counterchurch. They can't ignore us. They need us, you know they do."

"But I thought you lost your faith."

Jack stared at him. "What's that got to do with it?"

"I'll read it," Frank promised, reaching for the pages Jack held.

"But I'm not quite finished."

"Later, then."

"Will you be upstairs?"

"That's where I'm going."

And it was. The hallway was now deserted and so were the stairs, though the upstairs hallway was now jammed as the lower had been minutes before. Clara Rupp seemed to have been cast adrift by Arthur and now stood smiling vacantly in a relatively uncrowded corner. Frank pushed his way through to her.

"Hello, Father Ascue," she said, smile dimming, then firming into place. "I'm surprised to see you here."

"Arthur invited me."

"He did?"

"Of course that was several days ago."

She put her hand on his arm. "I'm sorry, Father."

Frank was not certain of the source of her sympathy, only that it was genuine. "Thank you."

"You were very brave to take everything back like that, Father. I for one am proud of you."

There seemed no point in correcting this interpretation of what he had done. "Is Sheila here?"

"Sheila? Heavens, no."

"I'd hoped to see her."

"Oh, Father, I wish you would." She looked over his shoulder, then drew him closer. In the aula, Bishop Brophy had begun to speak, presenting Prince Thaddeus to his Fort Elbow audience. "I really should get inside but I mustn't lose this opportunity. Father, you were good for Sheila, you really were. For a time she was almost her old self; she came home—"

"She's not living there now?"

Clara's eyes widened and she shook her head. "She's gone back to her apartment."

"I see."

"Will you talk to her again, Father? You have carte blanche. I won't say a word to Arthur, we won't interfere. Just talk to her."

Frank agreed. He could have hugged Clara for giving him a reason to visit Sheila, a priestly reason. He could, on the margin of talking to her about herself, explain his presence at the airport last night. Mary a reporter, the statement in the morning paper, simple as pie. Clara told him the address of Sheila's apartment, thanked him with moist eyes, and suggested that they go inside. In the doorway of the aula they met an exiting Bishop Brophy.

"Frank, I want to talk to you." To Clara he said, "I'm going to have to rush off, much to my chagrin. Better hurry and get a seat."

When Clara had gone on, Brophy suggested that they go downstairs, out of range of the prince's voice. Brophy bounced down, on top of the world, Frank following more slowly.

"I've got to catch a plane," Brophy said, looking at his watch. He faced Frank now, a serious but benign expression on his face. "Thank you for clarifying matters, Frank. I really appreciate it."

Frank nodded.

"And I want to apologize for last night. I'm afraid I was rather sharp with you." Brophy ran the tips of three fingers across his forehead, removing metaphorical perspiration. "Things are so hectic just now. I shouldn't have lost my temper with you. All right?"

"All right."

They shook hands.

"It was nothing personal," Bishop Brophy said. "You understand that?"

Hate the sin and not the sinner? Brophy in his magnanimity was harder to take than he had been last night.

"Good-bye, Frank," Brophy said with a wave, and sailed out the front door. Squeals and shouts greeted his appearance.

In a moment he was back, throwing to the floor a wet object that had adorned his shoulder. He stared at it with disgust. His angry eyes lifted to Frank.

"There's a bunch of crazy women out there! They *pelted* me, with God knows what." His eyes were dragged unwillingly to the thing on the floor. A wet stain was forming around it. Frank noticed a splotch on the bishop's back as well.

"Frank, I have to get out of here. I have a plane to catch."

"Go out the back way."

"Where is it?"

Frank showed him. With escape assured, Brophy considered the condition of his clothes. From the aula upstairs came a storm of applause. Brophy slipped out of his jacket, studied the wet spot and, looking first at Frank, brought it to his nose and sniffed. Upstairs the voice of the prince resumed speaking.

"Seems to be only water," Brophy said.

"It'll dry in a minute then."

"That's a sacrilege," Brophy growled, putting his coat back on. "Canon what is it? Assaulting a cleric."

"They wouldn't know."

Brophy seemed to want to argue the point but again he glanced at his watch and thought better of it. "I really must run, Frank. Thanks again." He darted to the stairway which would take him safely out of the building. "For everything," he called over his shoulder, and then was gone.

Frank went out the front door and, as he had feared, saw Charlotte there, surrounded by other women. She stayed the pitching arm of a comrade who was about to festoon Frank with a sopping disposable diaper. "A friend. A friend. Hold your fire."

"What in God's name are you doing?" Frank demanded when he was face to face with his sister.

"Just a little Catholic Action."

"Charlotte, you insulted a bishop."

"Oh, Frank, for heaven's sake."

"That is serious, Char. I mean it."

"Frank, *he* insulted *us.*" Her eyes lit up. "He insulted you too. Denying what you had written, urging us all to fall into line, reproduce like crazy—"

"Charlotte, take these women and get out of here. Go home where you belong. Take care of your family. You've become a meddlesome shrew. No one appointed you to look after the Church."

"Who appointed Te Deum, Frank? Why should they have a meeting here?" Her voice broke. She had been visibly stung by his remarks.

"Go home, Charlotte," he said more calmly. "Please."

She stepped back, smiling bitterly, or trying to. "Have you sold out too, Frank? Like Brophy?"

"*Bishop* Brophy," he corrected.

"Brophy, Brophy, Brophy," she taunted, and just like that they both shed ten or fifteen years. Frank wondered if she would stick out her tongue at him.

"Charlotte, take these women and get out of here."

"You've sold out," she announced. She turned to the others. "He's no friend of ours. Let him have it."

"Char, for the love of God."

But her command was heeded. Incredibly, he found himself the target of flying diapers. He stepped backward, dodging, trying to get out of range and then, feeling like an ass, took off up the sidewalk at a half run. He was heading for the administration building, going in the opposite direction from where he had parked McTear's car. It seemed the part of prudence to take a long circuitous route, trying to shake as he went the lingering indignity of his departure. Dear God, what had happened to Charlotte? She seemed to have gone over the edge. But it was not only his sister he felt he was escaping when he was in the car and driving away from the seminary.

Sheila's smile of welcome was not for him. She stood in the open doorway staring at him and if her smile did not go away it altered in quality.

"How did you know where to find me? Or are you taking census again?"

"You're not living in Saint Waldo's parish here. Your mother gave me the address."

"I see."

He had left his collar in the car, along with his suit jacket, and was wearing only his Selma shirt, open at the neck. Would she ask him in?

"I ran into her," Frank said vaguely.

"And she asked you to save my soul again? Come in, come in." Sheila stepped to one side and made a little mock curtsy when Frank entered.

In the living room they stood, facing one another. She said, "Well?"

He sat down, unasked. "I've had a bad day. Did you read the paper this morning? No? Well, why should you? Would there be any news if no one read the paper? I had a quarrel with my sister."

Sheila sat down across from him, her sardonic expression gone. "Was she the girl I saw you with last night?"

"No. That was a reporter, from the *Tribune*. I was giving her a story for the morning paper. I don't suppose you read the Sunday paper either?"

"What's been going on?"

He told her, in detail, in a rush of words that surprised him, and even while he talked his anger with Charlotte increased; he should be telling her this, appealing to his sister for sympathy or whatever it was he wanted, and here he was spilling his guts to a girl he hardly knew and who could not really care about all this ridiculous stuff. But he blathered on, even telling her of Plummet-Finch and Tremplin and of Jack's League of Estranged Priests.

"Do you ever hear from that other one, your classmate, the priest who married the nun?"

"Phil Bullard? No."

"Did they just disappear?"

"I guess so."

Disappear. She made that sound bad but no doubt that was just what Phil and Eloise had wanted to do, get away forever from those who had known them before, be just themselves. Why not?

"Well, you have been having a bad time."

He shook his head. "I don't know why I told you all this."

"You had to tell someone."

"Yes."

Did she remember the afternoon they had sat in the rain in the parking lot of the country club? He wished he could think of a way to bring that up, to tell her he was sorry. Frank tried to remember the occasion as like this one, the two of them talking—and what was wrong with that?—and then he had leaped from the car and spoiled it, had come back and made it worse by saying he was sorry. But sorry for what? Because she had talked to him and he to her?

"I went to your parents' house this morning. When you weren't there I went to the seminary. That's why I was there."

"To find me?"

"Yes."

"You just asked Mother where I lived?"

"No. She told me."

"Why?"

He hesitated, he did not want to lie. "She said I was good for you."

Sheila smiled wistfully. "You were. For a time."

"Just for a time?"

She looked around the room. It might have been any room. Belonging to so many, it belonged to no one. Whatever character it had it owed to its owner, not its occupants.

"I moved back here."

"Why not?"

"I could say for convenience. Daddy is not the easiest person to live with."

"No."

"I'll make some coffee. Or would you rather have tea?"

"Either one. It doesn't matter."

"Come on. You can help me."

Down the hall to the kitchen, where she busied herself at the stove. Frank stood at the window and looked away across the rooftops, a gloomy view of tar-patched roofs, forlorn chimneys and, only blocks away, the downtown area. Had she meant convenient to the airport? They sat at the kitchen table, waiting for the coffee to boil. The place mat in front of Frank was plastic, patterned, and in its grooves were

464

crystals of salt or sugar. The bulletin board on the wall reminded him of Charlotte's. Charlotte. Across from him, Sheila, elbows propped on the table, chin in her hands, looked at him.

"You really needed to talk, didn't you?"

He laughed. "I guess so."

"Don't stop."

"I didn't leave much out."

"It's good for you to feel that, the need for someone. You'll understand people better."

"I wonder if people are meant to be understood?"

"You know what I mean."

"I know what you mean."

How omniscient he must have sounded when they had first talked. She had said then that she could see the little wheels spinning in his head, all those rules, all those answers. Now his head simply spun. He wouldn't be much good to anyone now but he hadn't been much good in the past either.

The coffee boiled and in a minute she poured it. She glanced at the clock as she did so.

"Do you work today?" he asked.

"Nooo."

"I'll go after I drink this coffee."

"For heaven's sake, don't hurry."

But he did hurry. Already he was beginning to feel uneasy when he thought of how he had burst in on her and just started to babble. A momentary weakness? But he had been looking for her all day. He had done what he had come to do. The coffee was very hot, but he kept sipping at his, not wanting to leave it. She had gone to the bother of making it. He finished half the cup, then said he had to go. She got up immediately. Frank felt foolish. Had she been waiting for him to say that ever since he came in? They were going down the hallway to the front door when the bell rang.

Sheila stopped and looked at him, clearly rattled. Frank did not know what to say. Why should his presence here embarrass Sheila? He could not make out what thoughts were flitting behind her eyes. Finally, with a gesture of resignation, she went to the door and opened it.

The man standing there was the ruddy middle-aged type often seen in cigarette commercials. He leaned forward to kiss Sheila, saw Frank, noticed Sheila's stiffening, and used the motion to come inside. Without looking at either of them, Sheila said, "Carl, this is Father Ascue. Father, Carl."

They shook hands. Frank said, "I was just leaving."

"Father Ascue," Carl repeated. The name seemed familiar to him. The newspaper? A better explanation came after Frank had gone past Carl and turned to say good-bye. The man stood next to Sheila now, his arm about her waist. Sheila smiled vaguely, her eyes not settling on anything until finally they met Frank's and he understood.

"Well, good-bye," he said.

"Good-bye, Father."

"Glad to have met you," Carl called, and the door closed.

So Sheila had come full circle, back to her unmarriageable friend. Months ago, weeks ago, Frank would have felt sadness. He turned and started down the stairs, his head filled with the lamentation he had poured out to Sheila, of sitting in a car in the rain, of Daniel Donovan and Bishop Brophy and Charlotte and every other damned thing, and what he felt was jealousy.

Part Six

1 The funeral that morning was conducted according to the new liturgy and Frank missed the Dies Irae and the haunting solemn Kyrie of the old Requiem Mass. Their measured monophonic grief would have been a more appropriate farewell to the small white coffin in the middle aisle. The altar boys did not know what they were supposed to do and they followed Frank about like lost sheep, their eyes wide with dread at the sound of weeping in the front pews. One church, one altar, the identical scene for baptisms, weddings, funerals. There would never be a wedding for the boy they were burying today. It had been so short a time since he had been brought here as an infant to have water poured over his head, salt placed on his tongue and a candle lighted to symbolize the beginning of a life that would never end. His earthly flame had been extinguished all too soon. Frank wondered what comfort his parents derived from thoughts of that other life. He nodded and one of the boys lifted the censer with a clank of chains. Frank sprinkled incense onto the smoldering square of charcoal and, in thin bluish lines, the sweet smoke began to lift. Signaling God, he felt that he had forgotten the code. The body in the coffin seemed an unreadable clue.

Frank rode to the cemetery with Jacoby the funeral director, in the front seat of the hearse. How elegant a last ride we get. The hearse, like the first car behind them which carried the parents and a brother and sister, was a Cadillac. Gray upholstery, the metal stippled where it showed, a sense of quantities of unused power as they made their solemn way through the streets of every day. Jacoby, gloveless now, lit a cigarette and sighed. If that was an overture, Frank chose not to respond. One functionary to another, their business unshared grief? Jacoby was in his forties, prosperous and pink and mournfully efficient. He hummed now as he drove. Perhaps undertakers come to regard mortality as a flaw in others, one they themselves had escaped. In his right hand Frank held a ritual book, a folded stole and a little silver tube with a pocket clip. McTear's, it contained holy water for the final sprinkling of the casket before it was lowered into the ground.

There was a canopy over the open grave and rumpled sheets of unconvincing artificial grass concealed the mounds of earth. They came across real grass with the coffin to do the final obsequies. The pallbearers slid their burden onto the rollers over the open hole. A cry escaped the mother when she saw where they had brought her child. While he read from the book, sprinkled holy water, read some more, Frank felt that his words were escaping into an indifferent air filled with the sound of birds, distant traffic and, high above, leaving in its wake puffed widening parallels, a passing plane. And then it was over. Frank went to the mother but had no answer to the massive question which swam in her tear-filled eyes. He touched her arm. She turned away. Hands were shaken. One left an envelope in his. Frank stuffed it quickly into his pocket. To return it might have seemed an insult. His stipend. His fee. The laborer worthy of his hire. Jacoby waited to take him back to Saint Waldo's. In the hearse, he offered Frank a cigarette.

"You haven't quit," Frank said. He felt that he should say something.

"Bad for business, you mean?"

"Is it?"

"How many deaths from lung cancer would you say we've handled?"

"I wouldn't know."

"None!"

"Really?"

Jacoby nodded in delight. "Not a single one. Not that that proves anything."

"No."

"As for business, you and I aren't likely to run out of clients, are we, Father?"

Professional camaraderie out in the open now and why not? Frank said, "The poor little kid."

Jacoby looked at him, then understood. "He wasn't an easy job. You led the rosary at the wake last night, didn't you?"

"Yes."

"What did you think?"

"Think?"

"The boy. He looked all right? He was a real mess when we got him. A fall like that is sometimes worse than an auto accident. The parents thought he looked good."

Jacoby's work was ghoulish, his technical pride pathetic. Did executioners too delight in a job well done? But that was not fair to Jacoby.

He had not created the age, invented his trade or fashioned the ideal of a lifelike corpse.

"It was no place for kids to be playing."

"I know. I know. But what can you do? The owner had it posted. She's safe. Not that some lawyer won't try to talk the parents into a suit." Jacoby shook his head, frowning sternly. There seemed to be a pecking order among the carnivores.

"There should be a playground in that neighborhood."

"Where would you put one?"

"They could tear down the kind of building he was playing in."

"They represent taxable property, Father. No city council is going to take that property off the rolls unless some federal program makes it up to them."

"I thought the place was condemned."

"It's a first-class building site."

Frank had no reply to that. Jacoby concentrated on his driving. Back in the land of the living, Frank was conscious of the grotesqueness of the vehicle in which he rode.

"Here we are," Jacoby said, when he pulled up in front of the rectory. "See you, Father."

Monsignor Entweder, wearing black trousers, house slippers, a short-sleeved shirt and a straw hat with a wide and wavering brim, was puttering in a flower bed by the house. He turned at the sound of the car door. Frank started up the walk, then went across the lawn to Entweder.

"Lovely day, Father. Was that young Jacoby?"

"Yes, it was."

"I've been meaning to talk to him. About the parish calendars. Did he say anything about them?"

"No."

Entweder shook his head. "He's ducking me. His father always provided parish calendars. God knows we've been good to them. Besides, it is excellent advertising. Their name on every kitchen wall in the parish."

"He didn't mention them."

"I'm not surprised."

Entweder returned to his flowers. How thin the old man's shoulders were. Frank decided not to say anything which would place another burden on them. He had expected the pastor to say something, anything. Inside he went upstairs to his room, closed the door and stood at the window, looking out at the ebony expanse of the playground.

Where the asphalt had cracked, weeds had pushed through and were now going brown in the August sunlight. At the far end of the playground he could see a gate, closed, locked. Did Entweder see any connection between this morning's funeral and his veto of the summer recreation program? Was there a connection? The boy had been a pupil in the parish school. He might have been playing here rather than in that condemned building. He might have been. So many things might have been. He thought of Eloise and wondered if she would still be Sister Eloise instead of Mrs. Bullard if she had been able to spend her summer out there with the kids. The question was less important than another. How many kids had suffered in less noticeable ways than death from the pastor's pigheaded refusal? Meanwhile the empty playground baked in the sun and Monsignor Entweder puttered in a flower bed.

Shortly before noon Bishop Brophy phoned and asked Frank to come see him the following day.

The address indicated that the office was in a sleazy part of town, but when Beverly called the number listed, the phone just rang and rang, unanswered. It did not seem possible that there would be no one there to answer the phone, so there must be some sordid emergency. But calling the number at ten-minute intervals without response convinced her that that was not the explanation. Finally she called the doctor's residence and a Negro voice, the maid, answered.

"When is the doctor in his office?"

"Which office?"

Beverly looked at the open page of the telephone directory and for the first time saw that there were several office addresses by the doctor's name. She read off the sleazy address.

"The doctor is there from six until seven."

"I'd like to make an appointment."

"Oh, you don't have to make an appointment."

"Just go?"

"That's right."

Beverly thanked her, hung up, left the phone booth. The name she had decided to give when she made the appointment seemed like extra money in her purse, a treasure yet to be spent. Surely it was an odd procedure, simply to show up at a doctor's office without an appointment? But the very oddity seemed a recommendation. She was looking for a doctor unlike the ones with whom she had had to do throughout her life, someone as shady as the neighborhood he practiced in, taking on its moral coloration and flexible approach to the code that governed the rest of the city. The doctor's residence had been a very good address, but of course he could afford to live well, raking in money as he must from the miseries of the poor. This thought had an elusive logic that Beverly in her distraught state found convincing.

The booth she had called from was in the bus depot and, leaving it, she walked over the stained tile floor of the waiting room, among the clusters of plastic chairs on which travelers waited in rumpled resignation to be summoned to departure gates. How crowded the place was. So many young people, unkempt, mobile, what goods they carried crammed into canvas bags which served as pillows while they waited. Beverly envied their going, wished that she too could take a bus out of her identity into a welcoming strangeness which would not accuse. Naïve and innocent as these young people looked, she knew they were wise enough not to have been caught as she was. Would they have the information she needed? Ohio did not have the permissive laws which would have made her plight a minor one, quickly and antiseptically remedied, her benefactor calling "Next!" as she left without her burden. Elsewhere, that is how it could be. New York? Or even better, London. To Europe via Icelandic Airways, she knew the legend: the bus-fare flight to the Old World which, knowing all, forgave all.

At the far side of the waiting room was a cafeteria. Beverly went through the line and took her cup of coffee to a table where she could look out at the street. A bad part of town. Derelicts, furtive passers-by, the suggestion of sin. The coffee was awful. She added sugar, which made it worse. But it was only her ticket to occupy this table and wait. It was two in the afternoon. The doctor's office hours began at six. What on earth would she do until she could go there and for the first time tell another human being the trouble she was in? For the moment at least she would sit at this table in the bus depot cafeteria, pretend to drink coffee and seek in the street those whose troubles were worse than her own. Oh, all ye that pass by the way. Stations on Friday during Lent when she was a kid, the church odd at night, lights on, the stained-glass windows reduced to ashy grayness, the leaded joining of the chunks of glass suggesting a photographic negative, and down the center aisle, following the cross, the priest came, stopping and facing the stations in turn. Jesus falls for the first time. Her throat tightened in sorrowful identification. Beverly falls for the first time. But once was enough in her case. My God! A fallen woman, done in by a vacationing seminarian. Her smile was small and bitter; the lump in her throat increased in size. It wasn't fair. Veronica wipes the face of Jesus. And Mary Magdalene washed and anointed his feet. The solace of faith lay in those images, learned in the past when she was a child before this crazy present when

473

her mother pelted a bishop with sopping disposable diapers and came home crying hysterically about some argument she had had in public with Uncle Frank.

What had that been about? Beverly put her elbows on the cafeteria table, hunched forward on her chair, stared unseeing at the window and tried to lose herself in an anguish not her own. Her mother had really flipped. She had crossed some line that up till now had made her fussing over the parish and her CFM group and her brother the priest a harmless quirk. Some silly meeting at the seminary about that encyclical and her mother had mobilized her troops; the phrase was hers and apparently she meant it seriously. She was making war on the hierarchy for reasons not too clear, but whatever they were she had thought Uncle Frank shared them. And he hadn't. But pitching diapers at a bishop! Why?

"Frank scolded me, Howard," her mother cried. "In public. In front of my friends. I couldn't believe it. And then we just let him have it."

"You what?"

Her mother's eyes were wide and wild, searching for understanding, but her father's expression seemed fearful of her reply. At least the little kids were in bed.

"We let him have it. We threw diapers at him. Wet diapers," she added, as if in extenuation.

"You threw dirty diapers at Frank in public? What in the hell for?"

"Not dirty diapers. Wet ones."

Her father had looked to Beverly for help, but what could she say? Not that she would have had a chance to get a word in even if she had wanted to. Her mother began to babble about the need to protest that encycylical and about the symbolic value of wet diapers. Beverly had given up trying to understand and she saw that her father had too. What was clear was that her mother was nearly hysterical. She leaped to her feet and announced that she was going to telephone Frank. That is when her father took over. He persuaded her to take some tablets and go to bed. In the morning, things would look different. Beverly listened to him cajole her mother up the stairs. The muffled monologue went on for a time in her parents' room but eventually there was silence and then the sound of her father's feet upon the stairs. He came into the kitchen, went to a cupboard and poured himself a drink. No ice. No mix. A good-sized drink. He joined Beverly at the table. For a long time he said nothing. Finally, his drink half finished, he shook his head.

"It's got worse since Frank came home. This religious thing."

"I know."

"Why?"

474

The question was serious. Her father was looking at her expectantly, as if she had the clue to her mother's behavior and could give it to him. This reminded her that he had not always been a Catholic and, even though he had been one longer than she had, she had been one from birth and thus might have some secret he could not expect to have. Of course she didn't.

"Dad, everyone's gone crazy lately. Priests, nuns . . ."

"Okay, okay. But it's their business. It's not your mother's. It must be because of Frank. Your mother is so identified with him she seems to think she's half a priest herself. And now, arguing with him in public . . ."

"They'll make up."

"That's an odd way to put it."

"You know what I mean."

He seemed to decide he did. He picked up his drink, shifted to sit sideways in his chair and, not looking at her, said, "I've been meaning to ask you. Why did you come to the office a couple weeks ago?"

"I wondered if they had told you."

"Did you want it kept secret?"

"I just dropped in, that's all."

"You haven't been there for years."

"I know."

They sat as if they had hit upon the reason for her going to his office that day. Remembering why she had gone, Beverly stared at her father's hand which enclosed his glass. After her mother's outburst, the two of them sitting in the quiet house, it would have been far easier to talk to him than it could possibly have been at his office that terrible afternoon. Easier, but still utterly impossible. Dad, I think I'm pregnant. Even forming the sentence in her head brought a clamminess to her whole body. The ceiling light seemed suddenly harsh, far too bright; she felt faint. She could not clobber him with her troubles. His face was drawn, the lines from his nose to the corners of his mouth deep, giving his mouth, even in repose, a kind of vulnerable smile. She could never tell him. She could never tell her mother. She knew for certain then that she would have to take care of things all by herself, and soon.

But she had let the days slip by until finally she had gone downtown to the bus depot to look up doctors in the phone book. Ben had called in the meanwhile and asked to see her. Why? He had been at the seminary for the big meeting and was sure she would want to hear all about it. His voice, while controlled, seemed to carry the same mad note her mother's shriller one had carried the night before. Beverly said that she had a headache. Ben did not seem terribly disappointed. The morning after the seminary meeting, her mother had slept until after ten o'clock. Whatever sedative her father had given her the night before had knocked the props from under her. She came downstairs groggy and yawning and did not mention the scene of the previous night. Hunched over a bowl of cereal, she asked where the kids were. Beverly said that they were outside.

"Did you feed them?"

"They had breakfast."

They had had breakfast before Beverly herself came down, the messy evidence all over the breakfast nook: soggy flakes afloat on milk in bowls, puddles of juice on the table, crusts of toast. From the back door Beverly had watched them climb like monkeys on that darned swing set. She cleaned up, had a cup of coffee and a slice of toast, opened the paper and did not read the write-up of the talk some prince had given at the seminary the day before. She did the dishes, vacuumed, dusted, busy, busy. Back to the kitchen and more coffee and then her mother came down.

"What are you going to do today, Bev?"

"I don't know."

"They ought to open up that Center again."

"Uh huh."

"It's a crime, just stopping the things you kids were doing down there."

Beverly escaped to her room before her mother got going on that. Her voice had taken on the whining tone which was a sure sign that she was onto another conspiracy of the bishop or someone.

Up the street from the bus depot was a theater and Beverly bought a ticket, not really noticing what was playing. Inside, she paid for a box of rubbery popcorn and took it into the dark, which smelled strongly of disinfectant. She settled down with her popcorn but soon, mouth open, not chewing, just stared at the screen where, incredibly, a man and woman, nude, were making love in bed The film was grainy and from time to time a webby blemish appeared in a corner of the screen, a dusty smudge in the projector, perhaps, while the woman moaned, her face sweaty, her lips moving all over the mouth of the man who pressed her down. Beverly became very conscious of the pores in that photographed flesh, of the obscenity of doing what they were doing in front of a camera, the deed real or mimicked, it didn't matter. She felt disgust and pity and then stopped thinking of a camera and crew a few feet from that bed, recording this prolonged and noisy lovemaking, saw magnified before her, bright in the dark, a summing up of all that was pathetic and attractive and sad and beautiful in being human. No satin sheets, no overwhelming scent of perfume, no violins: just two naked people, perspiring and moaning and wanting of what they were doing something far more than it could possibly provide.

She sat through it all. When it was over she remained, while people moved swiftly up the aisle anxious to get out of there. The movie began again. A dirty movie, that's all that it was. Her shock gone now, Beverly watched almost clinically. Why did people want to see such things? What was *she* doing here? Someone was trying to get by. A man. She half stood and he brushed against her, took a very long time about squeezing past her into the row of seats. Beverly wanted to scream. As soon as the way was clear, she stepped into the aisle and fled up it to the exit. Outside it seemed so bright. She had sunglasses in her purse and she put them on and began to walk in the direction of the doctor's office. It was nearly five-thirty.

She had to cross a bridge which spanned some railroad tracks. How almost rural the scene below her was, the steep banks rich with late summer weeds, a wavering line of greenery between the two sets of tracks, some especially sturdy growth, of no botanical interest, which survived the grazing passage of trains, day after day. The sun was hot. The traffic over the bridge was heavy. The end of the day. Exhaust from the cars swirled at her, noxious, visible, and she felt nauseated. It might have been connected with her condition and she began to walk faster, wanted to run, felt that she could burst in on that strange doctor and just blurt out to him what the matter was.

She went past the place without realizing that she had and then retraced her steps. It was an old house, in good repair, painted white, the windows covered with screens which reflected the sun painfully. Beverly went up the short walk and mounted the steps. Through the aluminum screen door she saw a plaque affixed to the inner door. DOC-TOR RANDALL. 11–12. 6–7. She opened both doors and went inside to find herself in a hallway. Directly ahead of her a closed door said PRI-VATE. To her left another closed door. WALK IN. She walked into a crowded room. Along the walls of what had once been a living room and in the dining room beyond were chairs, chairs and people sitting in them, people wearing the patient vulnerable resentful expression people wear in doctors' waiting rooms. Beverly felt very conspicuous, the object of every eye, when she crossed the room and looked into the dining room. There were at least two dozen people waiting, adults, very old, mothers with children. No nurse. No receptionist. A fat woman holding a sleeping baby looked receptive.

"What do I do?" Beverly asked.

"You want to see the doctor?"

"Yes."

The woman smiled. "You wait."

"Isn't there a nurse?"

The woman shook her head.

Beverly sat beside her. The others had returned to their magazines. On the floor sat a little boy, moving a plastic car back and forth, completely engrossed in his monotonous play. Beverly picked up a magazine.

If the doctor saw patients only for an hour, he could not possibly handle all these people. There was a radio on a little shelf on the opposite wall. It was playing. Another sign. DON'T CHANGE DIAL. It wasn't even six o'clock. Was the doctor here yet? Someone must have turned on that radio. Someone must have unlocked the door so that these people could come in. But fifteen minutes went by before a door opened in the other room. A little man in a tan cloth coat looked at those waiting in both rooms and then, nodding to an old man, tall, extremely thin, who sat nearest the door, went back inside. The old man followed, the door shut. There was a palpable rise of spirits among those still waiting.

It was going on seven o'clock before Beverly, changing chairs like everybody else each time a patient was summoned by the doctor, made it into the dining room. There were six people ahead of her. She despaired of getting in and yet she could not bring herself to get up and go. If she did get to see the doctor, she would be the last. A pimply boy had come in after she did, taken one look at the number of people ahead of him, made a face and left. Beverly knew that they would be wondering at home where on earth she was. She had told her mother that she was going downtown to shop. If she had had any idea she would be this late, she would have fashioned a more appropriate lie. She would say that she had gone to a movie, had lost all sense of time. That was easy. What was hard lay just ahead, talking with the doctor. If she got in to see him.

When he came out for the next patient, he looked wearily at those remaining. Beverly both feared and hoped that he would ask them to come back the next day. But he said nothing, only nodded at the nearest patient and disappeared again into his office. Was he the kind of doctor she sought? Beverly could not tell. He was old, nearly sixty, she guessed. He did not have the scrubbed neat look she associated with doctors. His cloth coat was unpressed and not particularly clean. She decided that his eyes were shifty, not quite honest.

"You're the last," he told her, unnecessarily, when her turn finally came. It was eight o'clock.

"I know."

"I'll turn off the radio. Go on in."

His office was very small. An old desk, cluttered, a chair beside it. On the other side, against the wall, there was an examination table. One door seemed to lead to the back of the house; the other must be the closed one she had seen when she came in. She was standing when the doctor came in and he pointed to the chair beside his desk. She sat with relief, trying to keep her eyes away from the examination table. Seated himself, he pushed at the desk and rolled slightly away from her.

"And what's the trouble?"

He was obviously tired but his voice had been kind. He no longer seemed dishonest or shifty. Beverly had no uncles other than Frank but, if she had, they would be like this man. Kind, wanting to help her. When she tried to answer his question, she couldn't and then the tears came. The doctor said nothing. He just sat there, watching her, waiting for her to stop. She managed to clamp her mouth shut and began to breathe through her nose, trying to control herself.

"All right now?" he asked.

She nodded.

"How long has it been?"

"How long?"

"You've missed a period, haven't you?"

"Twice!"

He nodded, not at all surprised, and that helped. Of course. He faced this all the time.

He said, "So there isn't much doubt, is there?"

"I guess not."

"Are you married?"

His hands on the arms of his chair looked bony, short. He was rocking slightly.

"No."

He hummed, turned toward the desk, said nothing.

"I don't want to have a baby."

"You can always put it up for adoption."

"No!"

His forehead wrinkled and he pursed his lips. He got to his feet and she was certain he would tell her to leave. He motioned toward the table. He pulled a screen from the wall, unfolding it as he did. She heard water running when she went behind the screen. She did as she was told, she endured the examination with eyes pressed shut, feeling like an object, a thing, worse than the woman in the bed in that awful film, but she felt a tremendous relief too. She had told someone and now efficient and specified things were being done. And then they were back in their chairs by the desk.

"You shouldn't have any trouble bearing a child."

"I don't want it."

"That is, if you are definitely pregnant."

She did not seize that straw of hope just as she had refused to take pride in his verdict that she could bear children easily. "I'm pregnant," she told him.

"How have you been feeling? Any trouble in the morning?"

She closed her eyes. "No."

"It's much too early for that, of course."

"Doctor, I cannot have a baby. I don't want to have it."

"What's your name?"

"Lillian. Lillian Marvin." She had had to think of the name she had invented for the occasion and when she said it it was obviously a lie.

"Why did you come to me?"

"You're a doctor."

"There are many doctors."

"I had to choose one. I chose you."

"Why?"

"I just picked your name out of the book."

"I see. Do you live in Fort Elbow?"

"Yes." As soon as she said it she wished that she had said no.

"Young lady, if you came here expecting to make arrangements for an abortion, you're wasting your time and mine. Abortions are illegal in this state. Even if they were not, I would never accommodate you."

"Then tell me where I can go. There must be someone. . . ."

He scowled. "You could try Colorado, of course. There are other places."

"I mean here."

"Even if I knew of someone, I could not tell you. That would make me an accessory." He stopped himself. "Do you live at home?"

"No."

"But you have parents?"

Looking at the floor, she nodded.

"It is my experience that girls underestimate their parents' ability to cope with this sort of thing. You have had to accept it. They can accept it too."

Beverly shook her head. This had all been a terrible mistake. She stood, wanting only to get away. Her shame was less for her condition than for having expected this man to perform an abortion. She turned toward the door.

480

"That will be ten dollars."

He had pulled his chair up to the desk and was rearranging things on it.

"Ten dollars?"

His brows lifted. "Yes. For an office call."

She did not have to look in her purse to know that she did not have ten dollars. It had not even occurred to her that she would have to pay him. Visits to the doctor had never entailed the exchange of money. Bills came to the house. . . .

"Can you send me a bill?"

He looked at her for a moment, then took a pen from his jacket pocket. "What is the address?"

In her relief she gave him the correct address.

"What was the name again? Your real name, please."

"Beverly Nygaard."

That freed her. She opened the door and got out of there. Now she would have to watch for the mailman and intercept that bill. It seemed to give her a purpose in life. But, when she was on the bus, she realized that her afternoon had been a waste of time. She was exactly where she had been before going to see that doctor. She laid her cheek on the window and watched the houses slip by, numb, tired, too sorry for herself even to want to cry.

The door of Bishop Caldron's office closed, there was the sound of confused footwork in the hallway and Agnes stood in the chancellor's doorway, tears streaming from her eyes. She tried to speak but in the process lost control of her jaw. It trembled, her hand came forward in a beseeching gesture, and then she was sobbing aloud. Monsignor Yorick, rendered mute by this spectacle, rose from his chair. When Agnes put both hands to her face and fled down the hallway, the chancellor went to his door and watched the wailing woman round the corner into her own office. He turned and looked at the intercom on his desk, certain that soon it would summon him into Caldron. The die was cast. The news was out. The final death of hope was so painful that he did not even resent the boss's order of priorities. At the moment, it seemed somehow fitting that he should inform his ancient cousin before he told the chancellor of the diocese.

What sun there was this gloomy day struggled through the blinds and lay like an unsuccessful alloy on the chancellor's bowling trophies. *Sic transit gloria mundi.* His office took on an unfamiliar look and, in the grip of emotion, he could see it as he had the first day he had entered it as its rightful occupant, successor to Jimmy Stark, who had gone on to a job in Washington and from there to a southern see and an early death in an automobile accident. Stark's office, he had thought of it when he took over and now, when his tenure here was drawing to its close, it seemed his predecessor's place again. What imprint had he made on it, after all? The trophies would go with him and a few open windows would cleanse the air of cigar smoke. The transience of things seemed suddenly as visible as the meager sun upon the enduring brass of his bowling trophies. And then, like a last trump, the intercom crackled and Caldron's thin voice invaded the chancellor's reverie.

"Would you step in here, Monsignor?"

"Poor Agnes," Bishop Caldron said, shaking his head, causing his chin to sway over his pectoral cross.

"She was crying."

"I know. I know. Weep not for me but for your job." Caldron looked up. "I refer to Agnes. Sit down, Rabanus. Please."

"Did you fire her?"

"Oh, no. Not directly." The bishop began to run the dull edge of a letter opener over the pink puff of his thumb. "You are an excellent chancellor, Rabanus."

"Thank you, Bishop."

"It is a thankless job. I have often wondered how you have managed to endure it for so long."

"Oh, I think of being in a parish, from time to time."

"Do you? Any particular one?"

"It was only daydreaming."

The bishop turned in his chair and looked toward the window. "I am getting on, Monsignor. In a few weeks I will be seventy-five years old." In profile the bishop looked an ageless elf. Snow-white hair, pink chubby cheeks, his eyes, veiled in thought now, but alert and bright. "I have submitted my resignation."

Bishop Caldron was rocking slowly in his chair, causing the slightest squeak which, to Monsignor Yorick's painfully sensitive ear, took on a melody at once gay and taunting. Why did he suspect that Caldron knew that the announcement came as no surprise to his chancellor?

"Resignation!"

"Yes. I have given it much thought. I have prayed over it. I came to see that it would be selfish of me to retain my position while my powers diminish. My natural powers. As soon as a man in a diocese this small needs an auxiliary, well, his days are numbered." The bishop swung back to face Yorick. "I would like to reward you for your faithful service,

Monsignor. A parting gesture. Now, what parishes have you thought of in those daydreams of yours?"

"There aren't many open at the moment, Bishop."

"Let's not worry about that. Just tell me where you would like to go and we'll see if we can't arrange something."

"I hate to be the cause of a man's being moved from a good place."

"What is your idea of a good place?"

"This is very difficult." If he really had carte blanche, he would name the best there was, but it would not do to appear greedy and callous at the outset of negotiations. That the conversation had turned to his own future made the boss's confirmation that he was quitting less hard to take.

"Saint Barnabas?" the bishop said.

"Don Oder's place? But he built it from scratch." Yorick could not keep the gurgle of excitement from his voice. Saint Barnabas was loaded, a real plum. And what would Don Oder do if told to pack up and leave?

"And he has done a good job?"

"An excellent job."

"Would you be interested in Saint Barnabas, if it were open?"

"That's not very likely, is it?"

"As it happens, it is very likely."

"Well, in that case . . ."

That settled, his future assured beyond his wildest hopes, Monsignor Yorick relaxed in his chair. The occasion called for a summing up. He and Caldron had come a long way together. It was a sweet sad thought that now, when his lengthy stay in the chancery was coming to its end, he and the boss might have the kind of talk he had so long hinted to others was their daily fare. And then peace like a bubble burst, leaving a soapy punished taste.

"Any idea who will succeed you, Bishop?"

"Can there be any doubt?"

"Brophy?" the chancellor croaked.

"It would have been cruel for me not to propose him, though of course there was no obligation." Caldron smiled. "I daresay he thought he would have to go to some out-of-the-way place in the event of my resignation." The smile faded. "Or death."

"Then he's accepted?"

"Accepted?"

"Bishop Brophy."

"Do you mean, has he been informed?"

"Yes."

Caldron's smile returned. "Not officially."

Hope like a whipped but loyal dog stirred in Yorick's heart. "I'll prepare a press release on this, Bishop."

"I've already done that, Monsignor." Caldron plucked a piece of paper from a basket on his desk and handed it to the chancellor. "As you will see, my plan is to retire to the mother house of the nuns. The older ones at least seem glad to have me there. I will end my days as a chaplain to nuns."

"There are worse things, Bishop."

About to go, Yorick felt retained by the bishop's thoughtful expression. "Nuns. The choice of the mother house for a place of retirement dates me, I suppose. Rabanus, as a young man I thought of nuns as the conscience of priests. They had such a wily innocence in the way they stormed heaven, an unworldliness that often went hand in hand with financial wizardry. The handmaids of the Lord. Those the phrase still fits are as old as I. I confess that the young ones frighten me. Change. Change. How threatening it seems when one is old. I feel a terrible longing for things as they were when I was a young priest. Ah, well. I shall meditate on Augustine, dying in Hippo, reciting the penitential psalms while the barbarians descended upon his city. But I am becoming morbid. You can release that announcement at once."

"Crass as it seems, Bishop, the first question will be about your successor."

"That news will come."

"I'll tell them that."

"No need to make an announcement about Saint Barnabas either, Monsignor. Not yet."

"Of course not."

Back in his own office, Monsignor Yorick sat at his desk and pondered the significance of his own good fortune. Saint Barnabas! New church, new school, debt free, the parishioners loaded, and that rectory! There had to be a catch. What would happen to Oder? Brophy and Oder. My God. It was all too clear. Oder would be Brophy's right-hand man, perhaps the new chancellor or vicar general. It was not necessary to be as old as Caldron to find change unwelcome. Would Oder resent the fact that he was taking over the parish Don had seen develop from a twinkle in his eye to one of the most attractive in Fort Elbow? Or would he adopt a protective attitude toward his successor, retain a faintly proprietary air toward the parish he had built? More likely the second and that had its disadvantages too. Yorick did not want Don Oder breathing down his neck for the rest of his life. The truth was that, in his daydreams, it was not a city parish he had thought of, but rather a good place in the sticks, near a lake, with the promise of fishing and, in the fall, hunting. Not too much work and a leisure that would not plague his conscience since there was really not all that much to do. Mass in the morning, a few calls, the rest of the day his own. He knew how those birds lived. No assistant either. At Saint Barnabas he would need at least one. Swivel there now. Well, not for long. He would not keep that clown around. He wanted some level-headed youngster who knew how to take orders. Maybe Garish. Sean would be glad to be rid of him. Oh, it had to be Saint Barnabas. He would die of boredom in the country, where it was necessary to drive miles to shoot the bull with another priest. Besides, he wanted to be nearby and watch how Brophy would do as Number One.

If he accepted. Monsignor Yorick was well aware of Brophy's powerful connections in the hierarchy. Indeed, he had often been mystified by Sean's coming to Fort Elbow in the first place. The man had the outsider's inability to see what a great little diocese it was. Yorick was sure that, if something better—better in Brophy's estimation—presented itself, he would not take Fort Elbow. Would he even appreciate what a fine gesture Caldron was making, considering the ups and downs of the auxiliary's career since coming here? Monsignor Yorick had not yet notified the newspaper when the call from Eisenbarth came.

"I must have an appointment with the bishop, Rabanus. When could I get in?"

"Is it important?"

"Have I ever bothered the bishop with something unimportant?"

"I wasn't suggesting that, Randy. But things are pretty hectic around here just now."

"They are here too, Monsignor. Do you realize that in a few weeks the fall semester begins?"

"I hadn't thought of it," the chancellor said dryly.

"How can we open with two less faculty than we had last spring? The bishop will simply have to let me have at least one more man. Even then, each of us will have to carry a heavier load."

The chancellor snorted. As far as he was concerned, seminary professors got away with murder. A couple classes a day and they moaned about a heavy load. If they ever decided to earn their keep, they could handle the curriculum with fewer men than Eisenbarth had left. Ewing and Tremplin had accounted for only four courses between them.

"How about Father Sweeney? He's always telling me how much he misses the classroom."

"His duties as spiritual director are more than a man his age should be asked to shoulder," Eisenbarth said stiffly. "Rabanus, I must insist on an appointment with the bishop to discuss this."

"Did you have someone particular in mind for the faculty?"

"Yes."

"Is it a secret?"

"No, it is not a secret." Eisenbarth was growing impatient. "Francis Ascue is the only man with a degree in theology not already on the faculty. I shall ask the bishop to appoint him here. As you may know, the bishop told me that eventually Father Ascue would replace Father Ewing. We both thought that would be some time in the future, of course."

"Let me read you something, Randy."

Yorick picked up the release that Caldron had typed out. Reading it over the phone to Eisenbarth was like playing a practical joke on the rector. There was gasping on the line. The rector was as surprised as Yorick himself would have been if he had not found a draft of Caldron's letter of resignation in the bishop's wastebasket a week ago.

"Dear God in heaven," Monsignor Eisenbarth cried.

"You see what I mean when I say things are pretty hectic around here."

"Who is taking over?"

"It looks like Brophy."

"Oh, no!"

"Cheer up, Randy. He'll put us on the map. Just think what a vigorous young man could do with a moribund diocese like this."

"Please don't joke about it. Oh, my God. He did not have the right of succession. I never dreamed . . ."

"Maybe you should speak to Brophy about your faculty, Randy."

Eisenbarth mumbled something, a soul in purgatory, and the chancellor put down the phone. His own wounds healed with the realization that others were far more vulnerable than he to what lay ahead for Fort Elbow. Poor Randy. He was probably kicking himself now for not having got a parish before the roof fell in. What could he expect to get from Brophy?

And then it occurred to Monsignor Yorick that Eisenbarth would most certainly get Frank Ascue for his faculty if he asked Brophy for him. The chancellor's brow knit. That was something that must not happen. Frank Ascue was not the kind of man to be involved in the training of future priests. The next thing you knew, he would pull a Bullard or a Tremplin and if there was one thing Fort Elbow did not need it was another demoralizing event of that kind. Brophy could not know what Ascue was really like and, Yorick decided, it was his duty

486

to tell him. Like Caldron, the chancellor decided, he too would make a parting gesture.

When he was asked to dinner at the bishop's residence, Sean Brophy knew that something out of the ordinary was up. He could count the times he had been invited by Caldron and none of those occasions had been merely social. There was no point in dwelling on that humiliating breakfast last spring when Caldron had sent him into weeks of exile. Bearing grudges was the mark of a small man, not consonant with charity, and was unprofitable besides. Even so, it was with some apprehension that he presented himself for dinner, nor was he particularly relaxed by Caldron's affability throughout the meal. The older man's charm had prefaced the falling of the ax before. But afterward, withdrawn to the study and brandy and cigars, Bishop Brophy found his superior's compliments easeful.

"I won't say that I expected less of you, Sean, but I was delighted at the way you reacted to the encyclical. Your handling of the Donovan contretemps was sure and decisive."

"We're going to have to find a replacement for Donovan, George."

"Has he been fired?"

"Not yet."

Caldron smiled. "Do you have someone in mind?"

"There is a very good young woman at the *Tribune*. Mary Muscatelli. She might take it."

"Offer it to her."

"If you'd like."

"It's your wanting it that counts, Sean. You see, at the moment it is my own replacement I am thinking of."

"Yours!"

"That's right. Sean, I am resigning. That is definite. I have proposed you for Fort Elbow. Of course my recommendation will be accepted. I want you to succeed me."

Puffing on his cigar, Caldron sent up little circles of contentment and his eyes had the glow of a parent's watching a child with its Christmas gifts. Sean Brophy, on his part, was having the sensation he imagined a girl must have when she is proposed to by the wrong man. His position was delicate. He could not deny Caldron the pleasure he took from offering his auxiliary Fort Elbow on a platter, but by the same token he could not say anything that would be construed as acceptance. Of course it was not George Caldron he would have to refuse, however much it was his offer that would be rejected.

487

"But what will you do, George?"

"Retire. To the mother house. I shall pray and read and pray some more. Perhaps I have earned the right to prepare for death at my leisure."

"You've earned a good deal more than that. The mother house, though? The nuns would keep you busy."

"As chaplain? That's fine with me."

"Couldn't you stay right here?"

Caldron shook his head. "No. No. That is very generous of you, but I intend to bow out definitively. You would not want an old man looking over your shoulder, Sean. Certainly you have had enough of that in the last few years."

"It has been a pleasure working for you, George."

Caldron brushed that aside. "Fort Elbow is in very good shape, Sean. Financially, spiritually. In general terms, you already know that. You will be pleasantly surprised when you see the details. I flatter myself that I shall be turning this diocese over to you in far better condition than I received it."

So saying, Caldron drifted into a reminiscing mood and Bishop Brophy was glad to encourage him. Caldron's predecessor had been dead three months before George arrived on the scene and his welcome had not been warm. "They had gotten on so well without a bishop, they seemed to think they could continue that way. And of course they regarded me as a mere whelp. I was forty-nine years old."

Brophy got through the evening without making any overt response to Caldron's offer of Fort Elbow and, on his way back to the cathedral rectory, he congratulated himself on his diplomatic skill. Oh, he realized that George had not for a moment doubted that his auxiliary, however tacitly, had fallen in with the plan of succession. His inevitable disappointment could only be cushioned by an alternative appointment for Sean Brophy, one that Caldron could not blame him for preferring to Fort Elbow, Ohio. Brophy looked at his watch. Too late to get on the phone now. First thing in the morning, then. The time had come for his mentors to pay off on their promissory notes.

"Take it!" the cardinal bellowed the following morning.

"Take it?"

"Certainly. One, there's nothing better open. Two, you hurt yourself badly with that stupid article. Three—"

"But that article wasn't mine!"

"I know that. You know that. But how can you explain the fact that the damned fools who wrote it felt they could put your name to it?"

"Who would expect an explanation of that?"

The cardinal mentioned another eminent name.

"But that's not fair. Would it help if I talked to him?"

"Help you? No. I would advise you to give that gentleman a very wide berth."

"I always have."

"And vice versa."

"What was three?"

"Three?"

"You were about to give me a third reason."

"All right. Three. Fort Elbow is a damned good place."

The archbishop was no comfort either.

"That is very generous of Bishop Caldron."

"I suppose it is."

"You would be surprised at the animosity that often springs up between a bishop and his auxiliary. There have been some classic cases. Not that I ever thought of George Caldron as a petty man."

"We've gotten along," Brophy said miserably.

"Forgive and forget," the archbishop said cheerily. "It's the only way."

"Yes. I forgot Wyoming myself."

"Fort Elbow is every bit as good, Sean. You are very fortunate."

"I seem to remember you warning me against coming here."

"Did I? But then that was prior to all your difficulties."

"Difficulties?"

"Now let's not rake all *that* up."

"Forgive and forget?"

"Precisely."

Brophy left his room and went out to his car. When he was getting into it, young Garish dashed into the garage.

"Mrs. Ryan told me you'd come out here, Bishop. Don't you want me to drive?"

"That's all right, Father. I'll drive myself."

"But I'm not doing anything."

"Take the day off."

Garish puzzled over this suggestion as if the bishop had just offered him the kingdom of the earth from the pinnacle of the temple. Obviously he must refuse. It occurred to Brophy that he would soon be able to reassign Garish and the thought softened his heart.

"Come on, Father. You drive."

From the back seat, Bishop Brophy looked out at Fort Elbow. Square One had turned out to be the entire game. The certitude that he was meant for greater things would die hard. He looked out at the city with altered eyes, seeing it not as a temporary stage but as the definitive setting of his labors.

"Where do you want to go, Bishop?"

"Just around. Drive around, Father."

"Anywhere?"

"Well, stay in town."

No, Garish was not too bright. Bishop Brophy thought of Jim Grimes. Grimes would appreciate a better parish and Stillville might not overtax Garish. Suddenly the thought of all those priests and parishes and the power he would have to shuffle them around when he took over Fort Elbow cheered him up. The city assumed a new importance under his benevolent eye. It was a great little town when you got to know it. On the go, lots of hustle, nice people. Your midwesterner was a lot more attractive than anything you were likely to find on either coast, even the eastern. Regret tried to reassert itself with that reference to the East, but Bishop Brophy suppressed it. Why, just think what a man with ideas could do for this diocese when even George Caldron had put it into such fine shape.

"Let's swing out to Saint Barnabas," he said to Father Garish. "And take the freeway."

"Congratulations," Don Oder said, his tone toying with irony, wariness and deference too. "This is a lucky day for Fort Elbow."

"And for Sean Brophy, Don. Let's be clear about that. I am delighted by all this."

"Of course."

"Don, how tied down to Saint Barnabas are you? Emotionally, I mean."

"Why do you ask?"

Don had been visibly shaken by the question. Recalling his friend's bantering manner during his recent troubles, Brophy was tempted to play on Oder's apprehension. But this was no time for games. Forgive and forget.

"What would you think of being rector of the cathedral. *And* vicar general?"

"I'd like it," Don said unhesitatingly.

"Good."

The first experience of distributing his new largesse put Bishop Brophy in an expansive mood and, in the congenial company of his old friend and future right-hand man, he settled down to a detailed discussion of what the new administration of the diocese would do. He stayed for lunch. It was two o'clock before he remembered Garish. Don sent his housekeeper to fetch and feed the young priest in the kitchen. She had found him in church. On the way back to the cathedral, Bishop Brophy apologized to Garish for having forgotten him, but the young priest insisted he had not felt neglected.

"This isn't much of a job for you, is it, Father?"

"It's all right."

"Wouldn't you rather be *doing* something, though? You weren't ordained to be a chauffeur."

"I don't mind."

But there was a wistful expression on Father Garish's face.

During the next few days, Bishop Brophy spent much of his time considering the changes he would introduce when he took over. The delightful thing about reassignments was that the diocese seemed made up of a vast clockwork where moving one cog moved all the others. When George told him he had promised Yorick Saint Barnabas, Brophy agreed, of course, even though it entailed rethinking the shuffling he had had in mind.

"Congratulations," Yorick said that night, appearing at Brophy's door. "George told me this afternoon."

"Only this afternoon? I thought you knew all along."

"Not officially," Yorick said grumpily.

"And let me congratulate you on Saint Barnabas, Monsignor."

"Thanks."

"I knew you wouldn't want to stay on at the chancery."

"No. Sean, there's something you should know. Eisenbarth wants another man for the seminary faculty. To make up for Ewing and Tremplin. I suppose he'll be talking to you about that."

"I can see his point."

"He wants Ascue."

Brophy's expression grew thoughtful. "Yes. Of course he would. Frank has a degree—"

"I wouldn't put Ascue out there."

"Oh?"

"Is it all right if I shut the door?"

"Of course. Come in. Sit down, Rabanus."

Yorick closed the door almost stealthily and, when he sat, scowled more fiercely than usual.

"I've always hated gossip, Sean. And tattletales. But this is serious.

Look, you know Ascue. He signed that stupid dissent to the encyclical. He was on that panel. He helped Donovan with that article."

"Yes, I know all that."

"There's more."

"More?"

Bishop Brophy listened with growing distaste as Yorick went on. Where did Rabanus pick up this kind of gossip?

"That doesn't sound like Frank Ascue to me, Monsignor. Does it to you?"

"Do you mean do I want to believe it? No. But it's true. There's no doubt of that."

"And when was this?"

"Early in the summer."

"How do you know of it?"

Yorick became uncomfortable and his scowl darkened. "A detective."

"A detective! My God, you're not serious. You hired a detective to follow Frank Ascue?"

"No, no, no. I asked him to check out Bullard."

"But what for? Monsignor, I can't believe this. Good Lord, if this got out, the chancery hiring detectives to spy on the clergy, can you imagine what the reaction would be?"

"Who said anything about hiring him? This guy was a friend of mine. He did it as a favor."

A favor! Bishop Brophy stared at Monsignor Yorick. Thank God the man was getting out of the chancery. He was beyond belief. A detective!

"Sean, whatever you think of the method, facts are facts. Ascue was mixed up with some girl. The same girl Bullard was."

"The nun?"

Yorick smiled sourly. "This was before the nun."

"I'm sure there's some explanation."

"So am I," Yorick said meaningfully. "I felt that I had to tell you this."

"Frankly, I wish you hadn't."

Yorick seemed briefly to share that wish. He began to tell Brophy of his boyhood friend who had become a detective. Nice guy. It is a much misunderstood profession. Bishop Brophy wondered if Yorick was recommending the man's services. It was a relief to get Yorick out of his room, something he managed to do by shifting the topic back to Saint Barnabas and then, before Yorick could wax eloquent on what a fine parish he was getting, excusing himself.

"I am beginning to see what a job I'm taking on, Rabanus."

"You'll do all right, Sean."

"Thank you."

"About Ascue. I felt I had an obligation. Morally. Okay?"

"I know how hard it must have been to say."

But the damnable fact was that, once a doubt like that got lodged in the mind, it was difficult to expel. Frank Ascue? Impossible. But so many impossible things turned out to be all too possible. Frank was a natural for the seminary faculty. By all rights, he should have been assigned there last spring. Well, that is where he would be assigned. There had to be a way to give Frank the chance to deny what Yorick had accused him of. There had to be a way of making sure that Frank Ascue was unlikely to go over the hill.

Sharon had said that her mother was incapable of action and, as the days passed, Howard came to believe her. Perhaps it was a mistake to think that she would feel as strongly about her daughter as Sharon did about her. Meanwhile the game he played was that of trying to convince Sharon that they would go away together, start life over in a new town.

"Howard, don't be silly. What would you do?"

"What do millions of people do? I'd get a job."

"Doing what?"

"Anything."

"You're a lawyer."

"Not much of a one, Sharon. It's not something I need. There must be thousands of mindless jobs, jobs that pay pretty well. It would be nice to have a job I didn't have to take seriously. Just put in my time and take my money. The law, any profession, tries to claim you heart and soul. I'd be free of that."

"Sure you would. You could pump gas."

"Or sell shoes," he said, only half jokingly. "Have you ever thought how free a shoe salesman is? Eight hours and that's it. He doesn't take home the memory of hard-to-fit feet. Just puts in his time."

"Oh, Howard, be serious."

"I could be a waiter. Or a salesman. And there's always insurance. I know men who have become wealthy selling insurance."

"Social Security."

"Social Security?"

"Your number. You have to give your number to get any sort of job. You'd be traced in a week."

"You haven't been."

"Nobody's looking for me."

That seemed too true and his suggestion that he and Sharon start life anew together became less a fantasy. Perhaps he would have to do that anyway, in the end. He began to practice gaining emotional distance from Charlotte and the children. Beverly did not present the problem he would have thought. When he came home at night now she would be in the backyard, sitting in a lawn chair, listlessly staring into space. Summer. Dog days. Vacation. In a few weeks school would begin again and she would come alive. No need to worry about Beverly in any case. The little kids existed in a world of noise which need not be permitted to rise more than belt high. He patted their heads, a stranger's benevolence, made no effort to decode their excited confidences, mixed a drink and drifted with the paper into the living room. All news is bad news. The world in chaos. He felt more at home in it than in his own house. Meals were hectic: the television aroar in the next room, Charlotte darting back and forth to the kitchen, Dave and Beth, blank-faced, their ears straining to follow the inanities on the invisible screen. Beverly sullen. Every unhappy family is unhappy in its own way.

"I phoned Uncle Frank to see if he's heard anything about when the Center might open again." Charlotte, returning from the kitchen, talking as she came, sat and drew her wrist across her perspiring forehead. "This heat."

Beverly said nothing. Her eyes lifted to look at her mother, then dropped to her plate.

"Not a word, not a hint. Even Frank seemed unconcerned."

"How is Frank?" Howard asked, to distract Charlotte from Beverly's silence.

Frank? Frank was fine. Of course Saint Waldo's rectory was air-conditioned. Couldn't they buy an air-conditioner or two, at least for the upstairs? It was impossible to sleep in this weather. But Charlotte herself slept like a top. The CFM would hold no meeting until there was a break in this heat wave. Of course that was dangerous, upsetting the rhythm of routine; people would get used to having Wednesday nights to themselves.

The little kids escaped. Howard did too. While Beverly helped her mother carry dishes into the kitchen, he went out to the backyard and sat in a lawn chair. He could hear Charlotte talking in the kitchen. Ten minutes later he came inside and announced that he was going to a driving range to hit a bucket of balls.

Next day, having lunch with Sharon downtown, tempting fate and why not, he saw her again as he had that first time in Cleveland, as he had when she came to Fort Elbow, and what he saw was a young girl, someone not much older than Beverly, no one he could possibly be having an affair with. Did she find him strange in this strange setting? They had lunch at Brady's. Howard felt that he was at table with his daughter. They had nothing to say to one another. Thank God, it was a noisy place, surrounding them with an impersonal bonhomie. They parted outside on the street, stiffly, formally. Howard returned to his desk confused. Which was the interlude, Sharon or the past twenty years? Once life had been an immense lobby lined with doors. He had entered one and gone down a corridor which grew progressively narrower. The walls converged, so did the floor and ceiling. The hand in his was Charlotte's. Had he waited too long before turning to go back?

That night Charlotte told him that they had been invited to the Risks for bridge.

"No. I'm not up to it."

"Up to bridge? It's a game, Howard."

"I'm exhausted."

"We can come home early."

"Did you already accept?"

"Why would I refuse?"

"Call and tell them we can't make it."

"I will not. Howard, it has been weeks, months really, since we've done anything."

"You and I will go out. I don't want to play bridge with the Risks."

"Out where?"

"To dinner. To a movie. I don't know. Out."

Charlotte was delighted and he found her reaction pathetic. How long had it been since they had been anywhere but those goddam CFM meetings?

They went to a restaurant north of town, on a bluff overlooking the river, their table enabling them to see the lights of Fort Elbow twice —winking in the distance and again in the water. In the glow of the table candle, Charlotte's face assumed attractive shadows.

"Was it bridge or the Risks?" she asked, running a finger up and down the stem of her glass.

"Both."

"What do you have against the Risks?"

"All those meetings. Charlotte, I can't stand those goddam meetings. Or those people."

A neutral setting, pleasant surroundings, it seemed the place to bare his soul dispassionately. Charlotte did not leap to the defense of the CFM group and, if her eyes dropped to her drink, the lift of her brows

495

seemed receptive. He could believe that he would now tell her everything and it would be calmly over.

"Church, priests, popes, all that crap, Charlotte. I'm fed up to here with it. If I never hear another word about religion it will be too soon."

"I know. I know."

"Think of those meetings, Char. People sitting around talking about what? Marriage, contraception, on and on." She nodded and he felt anger rise in him. "I mean you too. I don't know you at those meetings. Ever since Frank came home, you've been worse. I can't stand it anymore."

"I'm sorry."

"I am through with it all. I mean it. I've gone to my last meeting."

But she only nodded contritely. She looked out over the river, sipped her drink, put it down. "All right."

"What do you mean, all right?"

"I agree with you."

"I can't believe it."

"Neither can I." Her tone encompassed a wider incredulity; she continued to look at the river. After a minute, in a strange voice, she said, "Howard, I'm worried about Beverly."

"Beverly!"

"Yes." Charlotte opened her purse. "Have you ever heard of a Dr. Randall?"

"No."

"Neither had I. Look at this." She handed him an envelope.

"What is it?"

"Look."

A bill. An office call. Beverly Nygaard. Howard looked at Charlotte. "What's wrong with her?"

"I don't know."

"Didn't you ask her?"

"Howard, I'm afraid to. Why didn't she mention this?"

"Well, it's hardly a secret. She had the bill sent to the house."

"But Dr. Harrington is our doctor."

"Maybe she doesn't like him. I don't."

"Howard, I'm frightened."

"Oh, for God's sake."

"What can I say to her?"

"That's pretty obvious. Ask her why she went to see this guy." He glanced at the bill. "Randall." He stuffed it back into the envelope and handed it to Charlotte.

"Would you ask her?"

"I think you should, Charlotte."

He wanted to tell her of the nights he had talked to Beverly when she came in from dates, of the night that she had cried; he wanted to tell Charlotte that it was her job to provide a sympathetic ear for their daughter. He himself was too preoccupied. With Sharon. My God, how could he get back to his discontents now? If he had been able to continue he would have reached the point where he could tell Charlotte that it was impossible for them to go on together. But Beverly's visit to that doctor had deprived him of his role as judge, a phony one in any case. He was the accused. He heard Charlotte agree to speak to Beverly. On that note they ordered a meal which they ate in silence, taking turns being captivated by the lovely view of the river and of Fort Elbow in the distance.

At home he said that he was going to have a nightcap. Charlotte, yawning, shoes in her hand, stopped on the stairs. Whatever it was she had wanted to say, she did not say it. She made her flatfooted way upstairs and Howard went on to the kitchen.

The clink of ice in his glass was like a leper's bell when he took his drink into the living room, where he sat in the dark and felt defined by the solid geometry of his house, this cube of a room, those upstairs, containing his wife and children. Beverly. Crying that night on the couch. So quiet and withdrawn lately. Why? He smiled in the dark and it was as unreal as smoking in the dark. Nothing was wrong with Beverly. A speck in her eye while shopping, perhaps, and she had been unable to get rid of it, so into a doctor's office for first aid and the thief sent a bill for ten dollars. That or something equally innocuous. It was foolish to imagine it was something serious. Charlotte would talk to her and the mystery would dissolve.

But Charlotte was reluctant to speak to Beverly. Two days went by. His whispered insistence received her complete agreement. Then why the hell didn't she go upstairs right now and ask? Would he want to? They had been through all that. This was her job, a mother's job. All right, then let me do it my way. When? Tomorrow.

The following day Sharon phoned to ask if he was stopping by later.

"I won't be able to. Something has come up."

"A client?"

"No."

"At home?"

"I'm sure it's nothing."

For no reason, they talked on for ten minutes. About what? He asked her when school began. He asked if the heat bothered her. Would she like an air-conditioner? With windows open she got a nice breeze; she

497

didn't mind the heat. Two strangers talking, or two very old friends for whom everything important was understood and conversation could meaningfully consist of trivia.

"I'll try to come tomorrow."

"Don't think you have to."

He laughed. There was silence. He said, "I want to."

That night Charlotte promised once more to ask Beverly tomorrow. Without fail. And this time she did. When she phoned him at the office the next day, her voice was husky and she spoke so rapidly and in a whisper that it was a minute before he understood what she was saying.

"I'll come right home."

"No. Don't. There could be a mistake. That man took no tests. I've made an appointment with Dr. Harrington. He'll take her right away. We'll be leaving in a minute. Howard, my God."

"How is Beverly?"

"All right."

"Is she there?"

"Yes."

"Let me talk to her."

"I mean she's upstairs. Howard, if it's true—"

"Charlotte, you're right. Take her to Harrington. Let's find out first whether . . ." He could not say it. He felt a thousand ears cocked to catch the humiliating news. Nygaard's daughter knocked up. He bristled at the prospect of smirks and derision, more wounding because they would never be openly expressed.

"If it is true, something will have to be done immediately." Charlotte's voice dropped. "She's coming down. Good-bye."

He cradled the phone. A baby. A grandchild. But pride did not prove a worthy opponent of shame. It was easier to think of Beverly as a child than as having one. Beverly crying in the darkened living room. The boy, of course, what was his name? Why not marriage? There need not be any fuss at all.

He pushed away from his desk. It was impossible to go on as if Charlotte had not phoned. Unwanted babies turned his thoughts to Sharon. She did not answer her phone but he decided to go to her apartment anyway.

Before going upstairs, he rang the bell, but no Sharon awaited him in her doorway when he reached the landing. He knocked on her door. No answer. Coming unannounced like this, he felt like a burglar letting himself into the apartment, but he could not wait in the hall and he did not want to go away and then return. Where else did he have to go?

Prim and neat, so unlike his home, the apartment had an almost unoccupied look. Sharon had rented it furnished. Howard took off his suit jacket and sat on the couch. Slipping out of his shoes, he lifted his legs onto the couch. Sun on the curtains, a feminine aura clinging to the room, peace. He closed his eyes, determined not to think. Why had he come here? His family, his life, was falling prematurely apart, not waiting for his going. His going. Fantasy. Fantasy. Beverly's trouble seemed a message he must bring to Sharon. His daughter, an unwanted pregnancy, Sharon: they seemed terms in search of a syllogism. Thank God, he had arrived here before Sharon. Think. What would he tell her? But it was far easier not to think. He lay on the couch for an hour, not wholly awake but not sleeping either, the sounds from the street outside reaching him through many muting filters. His mind was a plateau, no peaks or valleys. His effort to disengage from his family had been doubly frustrated. Charlotte had disarmed him by agreeing that she had become a religious fanatic and now Beverly. He felt caught more securely than ever in the past he had longed to escape. A life of his own, that was all he had wanted. And Sharon.

He opened his eyes and looked at his watch. Late. He got up and stood indecisively by the couch. He felt very sleepy now. He put on his shoes. How quiet the apartment was. He wandered toward the bedroom, stood in its doorway, and noticed that there were no slip covers on the pillows, that the bed looked flat beneath the spread. The closet door was closed, so were the dresser drawers. Nothing on top of the dresser. He crossed the room and eased the top drawer of the dresser open, slowly, watching himself in the mirror as he did so. The drawer was empty. All the drawers were empty. He opened the closet and saw only a row of hangers on the crossbar. He reached out, touched one, and set off a sympathetic jangle in the other narrow triangles. Gone. Sharon was gone.

He found the note in the kitchen, pinned to the table with the saltcellar. "H. Mother found me. I'm going. I don't know where. This is best. Forgive me." She had signed it with her lips, a pink print, serrated, open-mouthed. He took the note with him when he left.

In his car, he sat behind the wheel, gripping it, not wanting to start the motor yet. I am free. He took the note from his pocket, read it again. Had she imagined him pressing his lips to the parting imprint of hers? He crumpled the note and dropped it out the wing window onto the street. Staring straight ahead at the hood ornament, he watched it blur and waver. Tears. Happy? Sad? Just tears. He had to get home. Home to his wife and daughter and—dear God, he had no doubt of it now—to trouble. Real trouble.

The news of Bishop Caldron's resignation and Brophy's succession seemed only another irony to Frank and he preferred not to dwell on it. The change did not really matter. Bob Wintheiser took the news as if it were the first reversal in his otherwise sunny existence.

"My God, Frank, can you imagine what lies ahead? Ecumenical razzle-dazzle, televised press conferences, taking both sides on every issue. I predict a binge of relevance. The man is an intellectual disaster."

"I seem to remember you telling me he was brave."

"Well, yes. A single lapse into virtue. Frank, he's a clod."

"How many quiz kids in the hierarchy do you know?"

"I don't mind his being dumb, but being too dumb to know you're dumb is something else. And Don Oder as right-hand man! It's enough to send a man to the Trappists."

"Did I ever tell you of the Trappist abbot I met in Paris?"

"What about him?"

"He wore a hearing aid."

"You're kidding."

"Cross my heart. No more silence in the monasteries, and they have newspapers, magazines—"

Bob raised a horrified hand to stop him. "How about the Carthusians?"

"They seem to be holding their own."

"Thank God for that. Gilly talks seriously of going back into the chaplain corps."

"Isn't he too old?"

"He's in the reserve. And the pay is fantastic. Did you know he's a colonel?"

Who but Gilligan would see the army as a redoubt of peace and tranquillity?

"Brophy may not make any difference at all, Bob."

"I wish I could believe that."

"What can he really do?"

"Do? Frank, he has us all in the palm of his hand. Where he says we go, we go."

"Okay. But so what? One parish or another, one assignment or another, what difference does it make?"

"It makes a hell of a lot of difference to me, I can tell you that. But it's the whole tone of the diocese. Look at the way he vacillated on birth control. Well, the next thing will be abortion. Then euthanasia. Look at England. How do you think Brophy will handle those things? I'll tell you

500

how. He'll lick his finger, raise it high and see which way the wind is blowing."

Frank laughed at the image of Brophy signaling a fair catch.

"And don't kid yourself that Brophy won't have trouble raising money. The big donors just don't care for that kind of man, and why should they? Any minute he's likely to play radical and suggest they got their money by theft. You can't expect them to underwrite that sort of garbage."

"You don't know him very well, Bob."

"I don't want to know him. I don't want him to know me. The less I have to do with him, the better. And yet we could be stuck with him for life. Our only hope is that he will be promoted out of here. In the meantime, we'll pay the price of his trying to make that happen. He wants to be known from coast to coast. Only when he makes his mark as the fair-haired boy will we get rid of him, for what comfort that is."

They might have been young executives pondering the significance for them of a change in the head office. Frank doubted that Bob's fears were well founded, or at least well phrased. He felt that he knew Brophy now, too well. The man's opportunism could easily lead to conformity, joining the club, business as usual. His choice of Oder was no real indication of the direction he would take. Bob might worry about the inroads liberalism had made at the chancery, but Frank had seen that the so-called liberals, like their opposites, were governed by the ideal of success, of making it. They too would manage to make a farce of the Church. At a time of the ascendancy of the business ideal, dioceses had become model corporations, conservative, careful, wealthy. In the present mood, Brophy might succumb to the canons of advertising, public relations, some version of the cult of youth, but the motive would be the same: riding the current rising wave in the U.S.A.

"Keep the faith," he advised Bob.

"What else is there?"

Hope? Charity? "You may be right."

"Incidentally, Frank, if you have some spare cash, there's a good local stock you might be interested in. Fort Elbow Screw. They've just gone public and have a great future. The shares will never be lower."

"I'll keep it in mind," Frank said with a straight face. "Where did you hear about it?"

"From Swivel. It's a matter of the children of darkness being wiser than the children of light, Frank. He heard it from Oder. Whatever you think of the guy, he's got a Midas touch in the market."

"I can believe it."

"How about dinner tonight?"

"I can't. I'm sorry. I'd have to rush it. I'm going to my sister's."

"I suppose I really should stay home and commiserate with Gilly."

Bob stood, pulling in his stomach as he did. He wore a Selma shirt, oxford gray slacks and loafers whose soft leather had the many wrinkles of comfort. Now in late August his face looked less pasty. Frank walked out to the car with him. Standing beside it, the reflected sun igniting its metal, Frank felt an impulse to tell Bob about the funeral several days ago, about the thwarted summer program, everything. He wanted to ask Bob if this was the life he had dreamed of as a seminarian. Of course he said nothing, fearing it would lead to a repetition of the conversation they had already had. For Bob what was wrong with the world was symbolized by the change of regimes at the chancery.

Howard came for him and on the way to the house discussed the weather with the thoroughness of a meteorologist. Frank agreed that it was nice to have the heat wave over, the nights cooler and the prospect of autumn ahead. When they arrived, Charlotte was waiting for them. The door opened as they came from the car to the house. Charlotte took Frank's hand, unusual enough in itself, and held it until he was inside. Her smile did not match the wary confusion in her eyes.

"What would everyone like to drink?" Howard asked even before they were seated. Charlotte turned to Frank, focusing the question on him.

"Anything," he said.

Howard had martinis mixed and why didn't they drink those? He was hardly out of the room before he was returning with the drinks. He said cheerily, "Just like last May, isn't it, Frank? When you first got home?"

Last May seemed as distant as childhood. Then his life had been on an upward curve; he was the returned expatriate, armed with a degree, on the threshold—or so he had thought—of appointment to the seminary faculty, before him a pleasant and somewhat prestigious life with Charlotte bursting with pride in him.

Charlotte said, "Frank, we need your advice."

As if on cue, Howard sank into his chair, all ebullience gone. Charlotte, at the opposite end of the couch from Frank, met his eyes for a moment, glanced at Howard, then stared at her drink as though she wondered where it had come from.

"It's about Beverly."

"Beverly?"

What a relief. Charlotte might never before have seen a human being laugh, the way she looked at him, and then she began to talk, in a rush, piling words on top of words. Howard gasped when she said it and Frank too received the incredible message as a physical blow. He did not know what to say.

"She is nineteen years old," Charlotte went on. "She cannot have a baby. It would ruin her life. Thank God we found out while things are still in their very early stages."

"Where is she?"

Two sets of eyes lifted to the ceiling. "She'll come down later. Of course she wants to talk to you too."

"When did she tell you?" It seemed the safest thing to concentrate on facts. Still stunned, Frank felt that the tortoise which supports the column on which the earth rests had been revealed to be a figment of the imagination. The myth of the solid givenness of Charlotte's life and family was completely exorcised now.

"We found out a few days ago. I took her to the doctor. Tests were given. There's no doubt about it. It's true."

"Who?" The way he said the world would have been an elocutionist's delight: no candle could have survived his saying it. "The boy."

"Does it matter, Frank?"

"Doesn't it? What does *he* say?"

"He hasn't been told."

"I see." See! What did he see? There had to be a way out of this.

"Beverly refuses." Charlotte looked prim. "It's who you think, Frank. I'm sure of it."

"If there were any chance of marriage," Howard said plaintively, "everything would be different. We could help them out, get them started. That's no problem."

Frank's heart lifted. "Did you tell her that?"

"She absolutely refuses to admit that the boy is responsible," Char said.

"Why does that surprise you?" Howard asked. "She doesn't want to marry yet. She is sure the boy doesn't either."

Charlotte's lips smiled. "He wants to be a priest. All right. That's his business. This is Beverly's." Charlotte settled rigidly into the corner of the couch. "What do you think we should do, Frank?"

Do? Wasn't it obvious that Beverly had to be rescued from all this? She was too young to have this happen to her. Feeling slightly fraudulent, Frank directed the question back to Charlotte. He did not believe they had no plans, that they had not already decided. And, though Charlotte put it tentatively, her reply made it clear what the solution was. She could take Beverly to London, where such things were handled routinely and safely. No one need know. The whole thing could be swiftly over and then forgotten. Beverly would have a chance to go on as before. Howard and Charlotte both watched him now, tensed for his reaction, expecting a resounding No. And that No formed in his mind, he could hear it, but its sound arrived down some minor avenue, it bore an alien accent; it was not at all what he felt. That No was the response of a moral theologian and he was involved here as uncle and brother. The pregnancy had to be stopped. My God, they were talking of Beverly. She mustn't be hidden away somewhere until she had the baby, living months of shame only to have the child taken from her before she even saw it. He could imagine that plaguing her for the rest of her life. Somewhere a child of hers being raised by strangers. She might pass it on the street and not know it. It wasn't fair to chain her to her mistake. Charlotte and Howard did not need to be told that. They were expecting another reaction from him. But what would the voice which was not his go on to say if he let it come in from the wings of his mind? Its message could not have the simple clarity of the course Charlotte proposed to take and which Frank in his guts approved. This was no time for debate and argument. Besides, abortion, like every other issue in moral theology, was impossibly murky and controversial. When does human life begin? No one knew, not really. In the earliest stages of pregnancy, the fetus could be regarded—was regarded by many—as no more autonomous than a cyst, an appendix, its fate decidable by the woman who housed it. The sanctity of human life? Yes, but whose? A possible one or Beverly's? This could alter and ruin Beverly psychologically. What had to be done was clear without argument. He did not want to see his niece discussed like some damned case.

"Let me talk to Beverly," he said.

Howard stirred. "I'll ask her to come down."

"No. I'll go up."

Upstairs, he could hear a radio going on the other side of the closed door of Beverly's bedroom, the volume low but not low enough to diminish the jangling primitive beat, the shrill animal joy. Frank knocked softly and waited. When the door opened, Beverly stood there, face scrubbed, eyes dry, her expression vacant. Frank went in and sat on the bed, hands flat beside him. He could feel the little tufts on the bedspread. The room was done in shades of blue and was somewhere between a boudoir and a college dorm. A stuffed animal was propped on the pillow, a pennant hung on the wall. Notre Dame. Beverly sat in the chair at her diminutive desk. The radio continued to spill forth that damnably thumping music; somehow it seemed an appropriate accompaniment.

"They told you," Beverly said.

"Yes."

She lifted her chin, but the little act of defiance did not stop her blush. Frank turned away, not wanting her to think she must look at him.

"Ben Cole?" Howard's suggestion. Marriage. The idea seemed a way to shut up that dispassionate apodictic voice in his head.

"This has nothing to do with him, Uncle Frank."

"That's not very likely, is it?"

"You know what I mean."

"I know what you mean," he said, surprising himself. But this *was* none of the boy's business. Frank remembered talking with Ben in an office at the Saint Waldo rectory. He had not liked him. He could not imagine Beverly being tied to him for life. This concerned only them, the family. Ben must not learn of it.

Beverly was breathing rapidly now and he prayed that she would not cry. His prayer was not answered. She did not try to disguise her tears. Frank felt his heart contract. The poor kid. His niece. And yet, except for the tears, she seemed the same Beverly. Was it really possible that she would have a baby unless something were done to stop it? She was so young. But he thought of those items which appeared from time to time in the newspaper: an eleven-year-old girl in India had had a baby, a ten-year-old in Tanzania; sometimes there was a photograph, a solemn dusky face whose expression tried to accommodate both motherhood and childhood. One felt pity but revulsion too. In America, nineteen was almost as freakish an age as ten or eleven elsewhere. Beverly must not become a side-show attraction.

"Uncle Frank, I'm so ashamed."

The remark brought him to his feet, seemed to save him from himself. Beverly had addressed him as a priest, pleading for help.

"I'll give you absolution, Bev. All right?"

She was startled at first, but then she nodded. "Yes. Please."

Saying the words, making the sign of the cross over her, his sense of treason left him. This was how he should act in this situation: bringing forgiveness, making things as if they had not been, pity, pardon.

"Let's go downstairs now."

"You go ahead, Uncle Frank. I'll be down in a minute."

Down to the living room then, where Charlotte and Howard might have been sitting in silence since he had left them. They waited for him to speak.

"She'll be down."

"Did she say anything about the boy?" Howard asked hopefully.

"Forget him," Frank said sharply. "She doesn't want him to know."

"Couldn't you talk to him, Frank?"

"No, Howard. Beverly would have to agree and she never would. Even if the boy knew and wanted to marry her, well, what chance does that kind of marriage have? Nearly none. You know the statistics." Frank was irked with Howard for making him say this.

"Some seminarian," Charlotte said in a small voice.

"Yes."

When Beverly came down, she and Charlotte began to talk of the trip to London, and it seemed a conversation resumed. Was it Beverly who had suggested that Uncle Frank be consulted? Frail and frightened, she sat now between her parents on the couch, a problem enclosed in protective parentheses.

Frank felt an overwhelming desire to leave. He did not want to stay and hear them discuss what they were going to do, their voices relieved, speaking with a kind of determined heartiness. He did not want to know the details. He said that he had to get back to Saint Waldo's. Beverly had regained some semblance of her usual jauntiness when she said good-bye.

"I'm such a dum-dum, Uncle Frank."

"It runs in the family."

"When did this ever happen to you?"

Frank held Beverly a moment, soft hair against his cheek, his flesh and blood. Charlotte came out on the step with him and while Howard went on to the car she stood there under the front light. Gray streaks in her hair, the lines in her face deep.

"It's the only way, Frank."

"Yes."

"Simple and quick." There was a catch in her voice. Did she still expect him to forbid the trip?

"When will you go?"

"The day after tomorrow."

Howard was waiting. Frank got into the car and, as Howard backed down the driveway, he looked at Charlotte still standing under the light, her face in shadow. If she was relieved that he had not made a fuss, if she would certainly have contested the expected line had he been able to bring himself to voice it, she was nevertheless deeply disappointed in him.

"God, what a mess," Howard said.

"It's not an easy decision."

They drove in silence to the rectory but when Howard pulled over to the curb he shut off the motor.

"That boy, Frank. The seminarian. I'd like to kick his ass sky-high.

What kind of kid is that? A seminarian, he wants to be a priest, and he's out doing it all summer."

"Let's hope he never becomes a priest."

"By the time he gets there, they'll be letting them marry, won't they? Maybe that's a good idea."

They sat as if examining the goodness of that idea from every angle. Again Frank felt the need to escape. He was privy to too many secrets, implicated in too many decisions. He told Howard he had to get to bed.

"Sure. I'm sorry. And, Frank? Thanks a lot. For being there tonight."

The remark had an unfinished sound, as if Howard too were disappointed in an adversary who had given up without firing a shot. In the moment before Frank opened the door, the silence seemed to await his opening volley, however belated, but he got out of the car, said good night and went up the walk toward the rectory door. Behind him the car started up and Frank turned as if to catch a glimpse of the seat he had vacated and, with it, his duty as a priest.

In his room, Frank did not turn on the light, did not undress, but sank into his easy chair and lit a cigarette. However difficult it would have been to say what was expected of him, it should have been easier than remaining silent and thus endorsing the decision they had made about Beverly. They had wanted him to disagree, he was sure of that now, just as he was sure that they would have ignored what he said. Exhaled smoke billowed in the lesser dark admitted by the window. The breath of life, visible as a carrier of noxious fumes. He felt physically weak. They had expected better of him—or worse; some argument or reminder, the lifted staying palm of the moral policeman. And they were right to expect that. Why had he remained silent?

He sat in the dark, a meeting point of coordinates of space, one single human being whose function as a priest demanded that he occupy as well a vantage point above it all and be the dispassionate assessor of the deeds of men. Dear God, he did not want to be a judge, a spectator, the bureau of standards of the acts of mankind. Was it distaste for that burden, more than the itch of the flesh, which accounted for men leaving the priesthood? It *was* an attractive thought to sink into the mass of men, to become only oneself with no claim to authority, groping in the dark like everybody else. Once men had entered religion in quest of obscurity, wanting to leave behind the whole worldly system of rank and prestige, to become the least of men, individuality deemphasized by the tonsure and uniform habit, a member of a community, lost in a sea of sameness, at least to the outward eye. Were anonymity, the rejection of the claim to special status, a liberating leveling which made life possible, now sought in the world?

He lay his arms flat on the arms of his chair, drew his feet toward him and, sitting erect, might have been awaiting the throwing of the switch or the dropping of the cyanide capsule. We are all on death row. What had brought him defenseless to this chair late on a Thursday night, weak-limbed, guilty for not having spoken the words which had been prepared for priests to utter? Surely his list of grievances was not a cosmic indictment which somehow excused him. A clutch of shallow churchmen, betrayals, ambition. And one frightened girl in suburbia who would have a baby unless a healing technology saved her from the consequences of her folly. Beverly's face formed in his mind and he refused to see it as tragic. She was in no real danger; remedies for her difficulty were all around her. Charlotte would take her across half the world if necessary, and could—the flight to London was scarcely more than another household expense.

Frank remembered the shacks on the outskirts of Rome, built by hopeful newcomers from southern Italy; he remembered a place near the Via Nomentana where on the edge of the city a luxury apartment building had gone up and, in a ravine behind it, in its very shadow, grimy families had gathered and built shelters with materials stolen from the construction site. They worked at night; in the morning another shack was there and occupied and no one had the heart to drive them out. So it had remained, that juxtaposition of squalor and luxury; the occupants of the apartments must look down on those huts and shelters and see there a colony from the great mass of mankind. Did they wonder why they were inside and the others outside? Thrift, hard work, self-improvement? No doubt, no doubt. But the base on which such virtues rested had itself been given and was no achievement. Those who dwelt in the shacks in the ravine had been deprived of even the opportunity of thrift, of work that paid well, of a self to improve. Beverly and Howard and Sheila and Bullard and Eloise and Miss Simpson—and of course himself—were all residents of the apartment building, their troubles real enough, perhaps, but, regarded from those shacks outside, their very troubles must appear delights.

Beggars on the streets of Rome, Gypsies, women seated on the sidewalk, a baby at the breast or held up as an exhibit of need while the pedestrians, Frank among them, flowed past, unheeding. Gypsies of course were professional beggars, consummate actors, thieves, wanderers. Of course. That was the interpretation which soothed the passer-by, gaining strength from the curse the Gypsies were apt to throw after him. Frank had been shocked by the Gypsies and the squatters, but he had become used to both. Had he ever thought of them when, in the lecture hall, discussions of morality went on? He must have, he was sure he had. And how had he put the two together? Did one choose to be a Gypsy? No more than a child chose to be born into one of those drafty shacks on the edge of Rome, a reminder in the Eternal City of the precarious claim we have on time. What must such a child think of the stream of traffic, of the horizon thick with buildings so unlike the shack in which it lived? Did it see another race which led a dreamlike existence, demigods? But there was a more anguishing contrast. While those squatters lived in the poverty of Christ himself, across town—had they even heard of him?—the vicar of Christ lived in Renaissance splendor, surrounded by pomp and incalculable treasure. Of course some popes have been ascetics, but isn't asceticism practiced in a palace an affectation, a mockery of the unchosen poverty of the bulk of men?

Frank slipped out of his shoes and kicked them into the dark. The rug was abrasive beneath his stocking feet. In the window, the air-conditioner purred; he had not turned it off when Howard came for him. Who was he to decry the comfort of the pope? Would life make more sense if men were equally uncomfortable? He shook another cigarette from his pack and lit it. The match flared, burned, suffocated when he blew upon it. A standard image of the brevity of life. What the hell was he sitting here for, encouraging this jumble of thoughts? He had disappointed himself tonight. All right. No. Disappointment was too mild a word. He had failed in his obligations; he had encouraged a course of action he should have condemned. He had in effect approved of abortion. But would he really feel better now if he had laid down the law as presumably Bob Wintheiser would have? He pictured Bob dispassionately bringing the cookie cutter of doctrine down on the individual dough of Beverly Nygaard and it was easy to feel distaste. And what would Bob have made of his performance? His indictment would not be private. Bob would speak for the Church. Frank could imagine Bob explaining how wrong he had been not to stop Charlotte and Howard, to dissuade Beverly, and how could he answer him?

His room seemed less dark now but it was still dark enough to conceal what he was looking for, what he seemed to have lost, what Bob still had. Forget about Bob. It was his own jumbled, confused thoughts he had to think. The less than grand inquisitor was within himself, and so was the object of his scorn. He settled back in his chair and tried to relax. The unexamined life is not worth living. But what if it is the only kind that can be lived? Could any human life bear up under examination? Single lives added up to the bloody violent flux of history, the disease, poverty, cruelty and injustice, the unhappiness embedded in even enviable lives, suburban lives, those whose wants were largely artificially induced. All right, but they too were stumbling toward the grave, trying not to pose that sweeping adolescent question: What does it all mean? Providence. God responsible for every least detail of creation. *The Holy Ghost over the bent world broods with warm breast and with ah! bright wings.* But if God's love explains everything, it must be equally present in childhood innocence, natural beauty, unquestioned moments of happiness *and* in cancer, poverty, war, famine, flood—in the whole catalog of goods and evils—and how can the flaws in the plan be ascribed to someone else if the plan in its totality is his? Frank knew the answers. Dear God, they formed in his mind along with the questions, words, words. Man is the creature God permits to fashion himself, freely, responsibly, as the bearer of the consequences of his deeds. If men had been created good, incapable of evil, they would not be men, their goodness would be no accomplishment deserving of reward. God was determined that men be free. But the consequences of one man's abuse of freedom were not restricted to himself; they were too often heaped on innocent heads as well. How does the theory account for those miserable kids in the shacks on the edge of Rome? Heaven. They can attain heaven, the utopia beyond time. But would that make the cruelties and injustices, the ache in the belly, the shivering in the morning when the tramontana blew through the shack, as if they had not been? Why did future bliss have to be erected on such a sordid base?

Frank got up and began to undress. In pajamas, he turned back the covers of his bed, but did not lie down. Why should he stir up all these crazy questions? Why not? Was he afraid of them? Of course he was afraid. It is a dangerous thing to inspect the foundations of one's life. When he was a kid and first realized the significance of the earth's being a globe, knew that beneath the solid earth there was, if he probed deep enough, only more air as thin as that above him, he had wanted to fall to the ground and hang on to something. If he was afraid now to see that faith's interpretation of life is an even thinner air, he was more afraid of avoiding the questions.

The blurred semilight of the window brought a memory of his parents. He heard his breath catch and was filled with the stunned confused pain he had felt when he was first told that he would never see them again, that they were dead. Of course no one had used so stark a term, but somehow he had been told. How old had he been? Nine, almost ten. He thought of that little orphaned boy with an almost impersonal tenderness. He must have awakened one night shortly after it happened and stared at the window of his room. His father had been forty-one when he died, his mother still in her thirties. They had been taken unconscious and fatally injured from the scene of the accident to die in a hospital in Wisconsin among strangers. Death by accident. Had he thought that it was accidental that people died? Of course he had. So did everyone else. Who could bear to think of that inevitable destiny when to think of it forced the judgment that life is absurd. If death is the end, life makes no sense, none at all, and death *is* the end. By the billions, men have been born, they scrambled for food and shelter and pleasure, they died. What did it matter if that sentence was laden with dozens of subordinate clauses? A man was born into luxury, was coddled, fondled, raised lovingly, was fed, clothed, housed luxuriously, led a pleasant life into an uncomplicated old age and expired without great pain. The modifications could not obscure the simple truth that one was born, lived and died. Could reflection on the process deliver up a meaning? Why had one been born? His coming into being had been as statistically unlikely as the child's forming now in Beverly's womb. Why that particular conjunction of seed and egg? To call it random, a matter of chance, while true enough, ran the risk of seeming an explanation. After such a beginning, how could the sequel be rational or make sense? Any account of human life had to begin with the recognition of its radical gratuitousness and absurdity and to call it absurd meant only that the demand that every single human life make sense could not be met. It certainly was not met by saying that on the average or for the most part or eventually some few men or generations of men would be happy. The demand was that every solitary human life make sense and whether it was the demand that was absurd or the fact that it could not be met, absurdity was the result. All men are mortal. Roses are red. Sentences equally easy to say, but the first, when one sits sleepless in his room at night, conscious of having betrayed his vocation, led to a search for the support of the vocation which could give the indictment meaning, embodied an image of an earth swarming with men at different points on the arc from birth to death, all heading into the dark. And the inexhaustibility of the supply, the permanence of the species, could not soften the fact that each individual must die and cease to be. Such is human life seen by the unofficial eye and it was to that he brought the notion of a life beyond and of a providence operative now and in every least detail. But providence did not make the absurdity disappear, it did not meet the demand that every single human life be seen to make sense. The answer was too broad; by encompassing everything it fit nothing in particular; it explained both good and bad, hunger and cruelty, cancer and the happy cries of kids at play. As a reason, providence included unreason.

511

What did he want? What did he expect? He would have liked his faith to be only a description of the facts, but surely he could not claim to be surprised to see that belief in providence went against the grain of the evidence. Faith was believing that what does not make sense makes sense. The crucifixion of the understanding, the denial that man is the measure of what is rational. That is what he had not been able to say to Beverly and Charlotte and Howard tonight. Do the irrational thing, accept the absurdity, bear the child and either keep it or put it up for adoption and by so doing lay it open to a whole set of consequences for which it would not be responsible. Visit your sins upon your children. Forget that the chances of that fetus having formed in the first place were next to nil, that miscarriages happen all the time, that too many children are being born already. Do the mad thing and know that it is mad. Of course if he had put it that way he would have had to tell them that what they planned to do was equally mad. There was no assurance that the plane to London would not crash, that Beverly would not contract some disease in the process of getting rid of the baby, that she would not be plagued for the rest of her life by what she had done. None at all. If one was going to look the absurdity of life in the eye, it was necessary to be consistent. The devil's advocate had to admit that it was not faith alone which came into question when one looked unblinkingly at the facts. Every interpretation met an identical fate. Progress, a utopia within time, a classless society where injustice no longer existed? Even if the goal were feasible—and who could look about him and think it was—it could not justify the uncounted generations which had not shared in it, those billions of lives which had been anything but utopian. They had to be regarded as logical premises lodged in the historical sweep toward heaven on earth, grist for the mill, teleology without a planner. The thing was rife with contradictions. But any heaven, in this world or beyond it, seemed to devalue the individual, and what good was an account of human life which did not apply to every single man? A theory which did not involve a heaven of one sort or another was only an armed truce with absurdity, an acceptance of the fact that not every man counts and, if only some, why not us? But the happiness of an elite is lived under the storm cloud of mortality.

Frank lit the wrong end of a cigarette and the filter burned brightly, giving off an acrid smell. To bed, to bed; he should get some sleep. What good did it do him to score off the opposite of faith? So's your old man. A creaking sound. Entweder turning over in bed, an old man's sigh as he slipped once more into sleep. What dreams awaited him there? Frank thought of himself grown old in the priesthood, looking back upon his life. He would have moved among men with a communicable disease, urging them to ask after the meaning of life so that he might tell them what it is. But he would also have to tell them that the answer did not fit the facts in a neat and satisfying way, that the trick is to believe that it does, though in a fashion we cannot understand, not yet. Later, after this life, we will see that it all made sense. Well, it is an odd kind of reasonableness which has a past tense but no present. Does it all make sense right now? To say Yes is to accept an answer one did not and could not grasp. It was cold comfort to know that any other pact with life went equally beyond the facts. The poor devils who believe that all we need is more information, more education, more under-standing, and evil and injustice will vanish from the earth have to ignore the fact that after centuries of enlightenment, with universal education a fixed tradition, this is the bloodiest era in history. They have to cope with the fact that more blood has been spilled in the name of progress and freedom and humanity and the future than in all the religious wars. Frank had been to Dachau. He had entered the village on the back of Tony's motorcycle and their way had been blocked by a herd of cows being prodded through town. After that sleepy pastoral interlude, the camp. The imagination cannot encompass what hap-pened there, cannot encompass the slaughter of millions in Russia and China and Indonesia, the holocausts of Dresden and Hiroshima. And it had been the beneficiaries of the enlightenment who perpetrated those crimes, not the undeveloped nations. Yet the simple faith in science and education flourished. Every evil called for study, more information, a report, the facts. As if facts had healing power. It was absurdity com-pounded.

And religious faith looks just as foolish. The pox is on every house that claims to hold the answer. If the myth of progress is absurdity com-pounded, so is faith, so is belief in God. Not belief in general, but the belief that by invoking God life made sense in detail, that it made sense that Beverly was pregnant, that her parents should turn to him for a clear and intelligible answer in their distress. And that would go on and on—people turning to him. He was a priest. That was his function, to bring God to men, to interpret his ways which are so manifestly not our ways. The prospect filled him with weariness, with distaste. It would not be so bad if he could just say Mass, dispense the sacraments, speak in vague terms of this vale of tears. And that is what it is, a ravine where most are weeping much of the time and where for the rest sorrow lies around any corner. Dear God, he felt like scuttling out of the sight of others with his faith, hugging it to him, a sickness, not letting it be known that he had it lest he be asked what in this mad circus another human being ought to do. But if he was not willing to stand convicted

513

of belief in God, to bear public testimony to it, to be a folly and a scandal, he could not be a priest. He had not been a priest tonight and his betrayal of his vocation had been more subtle than Bullard's or Tremplin's or Entweder's. He had refused to be a sign of contradiction. He had been afraid to admit that all the answers came out of thin air, a chilling tramontana, the winds of doctrine asserting that the irrational makes sense.

Frank sat on in his chair wondering if he could present this bleak picture of faith to others, wondering if he would be able to live with it himself. Had he ever before fully realized that beneath the Church, beneath the priesthood, beneath the familiar routine of his day, underlying all the ready answers and moral judgments, was the thinnest of air and that faith is the assertion that instead of thin air there is the firmest of foundations, that the apparent nothing is something? Now when more and more people surmised that what the Church taught was not what any reasonable man might think upon reflection, it would be increasingly necessary to admit the thin air on which it all was built—and then deny that it is thin air. Who would rush to adopt that version of faith? Would he?

What do you ask of the Church of God? Faith. How do you know it is the Church of God? Faith. What enables you to see beneath the flawed surface and the long history of quarrels and abuses, of making do or riding high, a divine institution? Faith. The single answer to every question, even to those which had not yet been asked, a remarkable thing is faith. Frank sat very still, holding his breath, and his ear reached beyond the night sounds of the rectory to pick up the noise of traffic, doubtless from Cavil Boulevard, blocks away. Even at this hour, people were spinning through the dark, pursuing a light they cast before them. So let your light shine before men, including yourselves. Frank got up and went to his window, which looked out over the playground. A corner of the church was visible, the sacristy, the hulk of the school and, beyond, empty for the summer, the convent. How deserted it all looked. What moon there was filtered through clouds and the asphalt expanse was not a solid color, shades and shadows, vague elongated images projected by a feeble hidden source of light.

His mind seemed at once as clean and clear as the playground below his window and a mad jumble of odds and ends. Phrases, definitions, half-remembered disputes contended for recognition, but what emerged from the chaos was the thought that he was twenty-eight years old and that for half his life he had been either preparing for ordination or been a priest. Twenty-eight. He felt both young and old. He wanted to sink back on the realization that for thousands of years the faith had

514

been there, that all those centuries of belief provided some kind of support for himself. He wished now that he had not encouraged these night thoughts. He could imagine, he could feel in his bones, what it would be like not to believe. It would be so easy to draw back and view what had gripped him all his life as crazy, as too primitive or too sophisticated, in either case more than a man could bear. Any sense that he had had of the permanence of things was gone. Too many things had happened. Frank turned from the window and, at the sight of his bed, longed to fall into it and into sleep, but the doors he had opened would not shut at his command. A man who is prevented from sleep soon begins to hallucinate, to go mad, to lose contact with the fragile self which depends on regular doses of unconsciousness. What would the world seem like to him if he went without sleep for three days or four? How silly convictions are if we can be separated from them so easily, no need for torture or argument, just a bare room and a burning bulb and a little jolt whenever we begin to nod. And the mind, the mind, our claim to distinction, source of our pride, house of our beliefs and hopes, would scramble far worse than in a nightmare.

Across the shadowy asphalt of his mind a surprising sentence approached. I do not believe in God. Only a sentence, the shape of a thought, his assent not given, but his imagination swarmed to the task and again he felt what it would be like if that thought became his own. Men who left the priesthood wanted more than, in the quaint phrase, to be reduced to the lay estate; they wanted out of it all, out of faith, out of the stark demand for God that still remained when the bitching was over and they realized that their target was not celibacy or the stupidity of bishops or the irrelevance of the Church. Between himself and unbelief was only the ghostly barrier of his will, an inner switch unthrown. It all came down to himself. Alone. The accuser was the accused. If the denial of faith would come so easily, was not the fault in himself? Was he not culpable in the same way as a man who suddenly realized that he no longer loved his wife? However sudden the realization, it sprang from a long series of small acts of withdrawal no one of which had seemed important at the time, but their cumulative effect is felt in the moment of realization. If a few hours of introspection brought him to a point where the denial of faith meant only the dropping of a single barrier, well, that was a judgment on his life.

Frank imagined himself down there on the playground, looking up at this window. What would he think if he should see the second assistant pastor of Saint Waldo's standing there in imminent danger of losing his faith? A moment later he was slipping his trousers over his pajamas; he pulled on a sweater and, in slippers, opened the door of his room.

He went to the stairs and started down them slowly, cautiously, though he really did not care if he was heard leaving the house. He let himself out the back door and, when he had eased the screen door shut behind him, stared out over the playground. Then, as if he were keeping a promise to himself, he walked out some twenty yards and turned to look up at his room. The oblong of the air-conditioner in the lower window and, above, a pane made into a mirror by the moonlight straining through the cloud cover. So much for the thought that he could have been the object of a judging eye.

He started across the playground, moving deliberately, hands clasped behind him, the way he had strolled the peripheral path as a seminarian, and now his judging self was in the window of his room, looking at him down here, walking away into the dark. Twenty-eight years old. A priest. His eyes darted toward the church. A priest. Once in Arles, with Tony, drinking at an outside table under the giant sycamores, he had listened to his friend explain why he had not remained an Anglican and could never have taken orders in the church of his birth. "It isn't simply that the cleric is either a mad eccentric or an out and out socialist, Frank, though of course that was part of it. Capital punishment, antivivisection, marches on Trafalgar Square with Bertie Russell in the lead. I much prefer the quirky vicar with his butterfly collection or devotion to irregular Greek verbs. A priest offers sacrifice, he dispenses the sacraments. Everything else is no more peculiar to the priesthood than the Ten Commandments."

He had agreed with Tony, more or less. Mass and the sacraments. The poor have the gospel preached to them. But there were other things; the blind see and the lame walk. Frank had never been confused about the function of the priest. Was he confused tonight? He did not think so. That was not the problem. But he could imagine Tony's distaste for the turmoil he was in. Very bad form. Tony, Bob Wintheiser too—he knew how ridiculous he would seem to them.

The bicycle racks behind the school threw a distorted barred shadow onto the asphalt. Frank looked up at the windows of Eloise's classroom. The two of them standing there, full of plans, full of hope. Only a few months ago. Sad. Silly and sad. They had dreamed of making this asphalt desert bloom all summer with the shouts of kids at play. What if Entweder had agreed, what if the summer program had gone into effect? Would he be preening himself now on his effectiveness in his first assignment? And Eloise? He remembered how she had leaned from the window, fingers in the corners of her mouth, and whistled at those fighting kids. He could hear that whistle now, troubling the air, stopping the fight or, more likely, only postponing it. When he reached

516

the far end of the playground he stopped. There was a gate but it was locked, a chain looped through and fastened with a padlock. The metal was cool as night on his fingers.

The day was overcast and the narrow chancery building looked mottled gray, its granite steps unwashed and steep, when Frank went up them the following morning. Hollow-eyed, still feeling the effects of too many cigarettes the night before, he did not look forward to his appointment with Bishop Brophy. Inside, he looked into the office where Agnes had sat, but it was empty. Caldron's photograph still hung on the wall. My last duchess. A door closed. Footsteps in the hall. Frank came out of the office to see a smiling Father Grimes coming toward him.

"Father Ascue! How are you?"

"Is Bishop Brophy in?"

"Yes, he is." Grimes seemed to be bubbling inside. He said in a stage whisper, "He's given me a new parish."

There was no need to ask if it was better than the old one. Frank congratulated him. Brophy had not waited long before beginning to distribute his largesse.

"Frank, about Ben Cole. I saw him last night. He told me of the talk you had with him. I think it did him a world of good."

"Oh?"

Grimes beamed. "He's going back to the seminary."

"Is he?"

"To tell you the truth, I'm really not surprised. I must have sounded pretty negative when we talked about him before, but there is a lot of solidity in that boy. I always thought so. That's why I tried to interest him in the priesthood in the first place."

"I guess I don't know him very well."

"He had a bad summer. That can't be denied. But maybe it's all to the good. Get it out of his system. Better now than later, certainly."

"Yes."

"Ben's coming back to Stillville with me. When I invited him last night I had no idea I would be transferred. Well, now he can help me pack."

"I better get in to the bishop."

"Lots of luck, Frank."

Behind the desk where George Caldron had sat for so many years was Bishop Brophy, affable, very much in charge, loving it.

"Sit down, Frank. Sit down. Things are still in a state of transition here. I hope you'll excuse that. But some matters won't wait until we're ready for them. How is everything at Saint Waldo's?"

"All right."

"Do you like it there?" Bishop Brophy settled back, smiling.

"I've nothing to compare it with. It's my first assignment."

"That's true."

"Except for Rome."

"Ah, Rome. Frank, I don't have to tell you that your degree represents a considerable investment on the part of the diocese." Brophy sat forward and put his elbows on the desk. His smile was replaced by an almost theatrical expression of concern. "Are you happy, Frank?"

"At Saint Waldo's?"

"In general. As a priest."

Frank showed his palms, hoping that would suffice. How would Brophy react if he should reveal his thoughts of the previous night? The chancery, Grimes, Brophy—in the light of day, it was possible to think of it all as a well-oiled machine, its place in the cosmos clear, the role of priest no more puzzling than that of physician, lawyer, soldier.

"You have no"—Brophy made a wavering motion with his hand—"no doubts, anything like that?"

"Why do you ask?" Had his harrowing night left readable traces in his eyes, his tone of voice?

Brophy sat back once more. "Frank, these are difficult times. I don't have to tell you that. Fort Elbow has been rather fortunate when you stop to think of it. Only a handful of men have left the priesthood. Maybe we've passed the peak on that; I don't know. I hope and pray we have. Of course two of our departures were rather noisy. Bullard. Tremplin. For a seminary professor to leave has got to have a demoralizing effect on his students."

"At least it happened during vacation."

"Tremplin? Yes. I can't have a repetition of that."

"That's not very likely."

No, Brophy agreed, it wasn't. A bishop could not base his judgments on rumors. There were always rumors about the clergy. People took a perverse pleasure in the discovery that priests are human, capable of making mistakes. They exaggerated when mistakes were made, as if a priest's lapse called the standard into question. Rumors meant little. In the last analysis, it was a matter of trust.

"Rumors?"

Brophy turned away, as if searching the Fort Elbow skyline for something as evanescent as rumors. Frank would understand that everything finally came to this desk, facts, estimates of how jobs were being done, important things, trivial things. And rumors too, of course.

"About me, Bishop?"

Brophy's brows lifted. "Would that be possible?"

Frank felt a superstitious shiver pass over him. Brophy, his spiritual superior now, was tuned into his soul; somehow he knew how Frank had reacted at Charlotte's, he knew of the thoughts that had kept him awake last night. Nonsense, of course, but what if he did know? Frank said, "Anything is possible."

"Yes."

A silence formed between them. It was clear that Brophy had heard something about him, but what? He did not want Brophy to ask him again if he was content and happy as a priest. Whatever he had been called on the carpet for would soon be on that desk to which everything finally came. Brophy cleared his throat but it was a moment before he spoke.

"Frank, the school year starts in two weeks. As you know, there are two vacancies on the seminary faculty. You are the only possible replacement." Brophy's smile was firmly back in place now, as if the act of speaking had pushed away whatever doubts he had been entertaining. "I am assigning you to the seminary faculty as Father Ewing's successor."

"The seminary," Frank said.

"I'm sorry you couldn't have had more forewarning, Frank. By all rights, you should have been assigned there when you returned from Rome. Well, no need to go into that. You are the only moral theologian I have."

Moral theologian? My God. "How soon must I decide?"

"Decide?" Brophy's features tended toward the pug but now his face took on a bony look.

"I have to think, Bishop. I can't say right now."

"Frank, the school year is nearly upon us. Monsignor Eisenbarth is understandably worried about staffing his courses."

"The weekend, Bishop. Let me have the weekend."

Brophy was visibly displeased. Frank had robbed the occasion of its joy. Whatever rumors Brophy had been referring to earlier had been set aside to offer Frank the position for which he had been trained, the position he must have wanted. The bishop had not been expecting a request to think it over.

"The weekend," he repeated. "I don't understand, Frank. Is there some reason . . ."

"I have to get away. I need time to think about it."

"It *is* a serious step," Brophy said dubiously. Then his eyes took on a glint of comprehension. "You mean a sort of retreat?"

"Yes."

"Excellent idea, Frank. Take the weekend. Go away. If you stay at Saint Waldo's, you won't have a minute to yourself before Monday. I have to have your acceptance on Monday, Frank."

"I'll know by Monday."

"Good. Good."

Brophy was obviously making the best of a situation he did not like at all. He stood and came around the desk to walk Frank to the door. "I remember the retreat I made before my consecration," he said, seeking an analogue of Frank's weekend. Of course no one refused to become a bishop. How could Frank refuse the obvious assignment for him? But when he had opened the door, Brophy said, "There'll be lots of reassigning in the coming months, Frank. I couldn't promise that you would stay at Saint Waldo's even if..." But of course that alternative was impossible. He clapped Frank on the shoulder. "Till Monday, then."

"Thank you, Bishop."

He could feel Brophy's eyes on his back when he went down the hall. How could the bishop's doubts fail to return now? Doubts. Rumors. What kind of rumors? It did not matter. They could not be worse than the truth. Yet even as he walked away from the office, he felt an impulse to turn and go back, to tell Brophy that of course he would join the seminary faculty. Of course, of course. He had been an arrow aimed at that target for years. Last May he would have accepted the assignment without hesitation, with delight, with the certainty that he was going where he belonged. To teach moral theology. Ewing's rooms could be his, Ewing's lecture hall as well as the books he had bequeathed to Frank. Moral theology. He kept on walking down the hall away from the bishop.

When he came outside, the sun had broken through the clouds and, gilded by its beams, Father Oder was bouncing up the steps.

"Aha. Frank. Have you talked with Brophy?"

"Yes."

"Well?"

A twinkle in Oder's eye, the insider's smug omniscience; he had known all along.

"We talked," Frank said.

Oder's face darkened in sunlight. "You already said that."

Frank smiled at the erstwhile pastor of Saint Barnabas. "He gave me the weekend off," he said brightly, and started down to the street.

2 The Franciscan Retreat House, ten miles outside Fort Elbow, was a building of blood red brick which stood on an irregular rectangle of dry grass surrounded by woods. McTear drove up a gravel drive lined with whitewashed rocks and came to a stop at the entrance of the building. Frank reached over the seat to get his bag.

"Want me to come get you on Monday?" McTear asked.

"I can't ask you to do that."

"You didn't ask. I offered."

"Thanks, Father. But I'll try to get a ride. Maybe someone from here will be going to town."

McTear shrugged. "Either way. Have a good time."

A good time. Somehow the words were appropriate coming from McTear. Frank thanked him again and got out of the car. McTear was already busy with his citizen band radio when Frank closed the door. It seemed ungrateful to suspect that one reason the first assistant had offered to drive him here was to test the range of that radio. Before the bell was answered, McTear was on his way, tires crunching on the gravel as he circled down to the county road which would take him back to town.

The walls of the guest room to which the porter led him were chalk white. The tile floor of the corridor they came along had been recently polished and Frank's soles stuck to the waxy surface. The porter, in his habit, a white knotted cincture twirling in his hand, shuffled along in sandals, making a little whistling sound. He had introduced himself as Father Leo and was delighted to learn Frank's name.

"Francis?"

"That's right, Father."

The porter seemed to think the name explained Frank's presence here. When he opened the door of the room they were greeted by a hot musty smell. Father Leo crossed to a window and opened it.

"The other has no screen, Father. If you do open it, make sure you close it at night. At least while you have lights on. Bugs."

The porter checked the washbowl. Clean towels, a wrapped cake of soap. He turned on the water, then turned it off. Everything in order.

"Just a private retreat, Father?"

"That's right."

"Most of our men help out in parishes on weekends."

"In Fort Elbow?"

"Some."

"Do you?"

The thought seemed to alarm him. "Oh, no. I stay here."

Too old? The man in charge? Whatever the reason, Father Leo seemed to consider weekend work out of the question for him. He closed the door softly behind him when he went out.

A bed whose spread was as white as the walls, beside it an oak table on which a plastic ashtray sat. One straight-back chair and a desk. No reading lamp. In the ceiling fixture one bare blub. Above the bed a crucifix, a plaster corpus affixed to a wooden cross, the body painted, a wound in the side, nailed limbs, blood upon the brow from the crown of thorns. An almost smile on the lips of the dying God. Frank had never felt comfortable with Franciscans and that crucifix seemed an explanation. He put his bag on the bed and pulled the chair to the open window. Sitting, he looked out at the trees and saw only the forest of his own confusion.

The past three months had been a declension arrived now at the accusative case. He had been doing the work of a priest, had seen from a new vantage point the Church in his native land, got some glimpse of what his life might be. It was not at all what he had expected, yet he was not sure where the strangeness lay. Had he wanted to take part in the work of an esteemed and efficient organization, his faith as American as apple pie? That morning at Mass, after the consecration, holding the host, Frank had stared at it and felt his faith waver, felt again that there was nothing but air beneath him. Did he really believe that that disk was God as a result of words he had spoken? He had driven the thought away. I believe. Help thou my unbelief.

He got up and went to the bed, where he undid the clasps of his bag. He changed into old clothes, khaki pants, sneakers, a knit shirt, then transferred the contents of his pockets. He left the building by the door he had entered, going swiftly past the porter's office, then went around back where he found a path which led into the woods. The blacktop gave way to dirt, the edges of the path became less distinct, eventually it reached a lake. For a stretch, the path led past stations of the cross.

522

Frank glanced at the pictures, faded from their exposure to the seasons. There was the sound of voices ahead, of splashing; he came upon a beach. The path rose away from it. Frank stopped to look down at the bathers, three heads bobbing in the spangled water. He supposed they were Franciscans, fellow priests enjoying an afternoon swim. Their voices echoed off the water, sounding young. Tomorrow they would go off to their weekend assignments. The lake and the path reminded Frank of the minor seminary.

So long ago. Himself an undoubting boy who wanted to be a priest. Walking slowly now, conscious of the smell of vegetation, fern, sumac, other nameless species, the growth and decay of nature, he tried to remember what his thoughts had been when he first began to study for the priesthood. Was it strange to demand of the boy he had been convincing reasons for what he had become as a man? What had the Church seemed to him then? It would certainly never have entered his mind that priests and bishops might wonder what it was all about. The Church is the Church, what it had always been, carrying on Christ's mission. But now he had heard its theologians, become one himself; he had seen its pastors and chancellors and bishops in action. Professionals, men doing a job, their function performed out of habit and routine. Wouldn't it be more difficult for them to stop than to continue? In that, surely, they did not differ from the rest of men. Could he himself continue? Bullard. Tremplin. He did not want to think of them; his doubts bore no resemblance to theirs. Phil had been a thwarted Don Juan and Jack—well, Jack was Jack. He did not want to think of others.

Dear God, how easy it was to think of himself as a victim. The victim of Caldron, of Brophy, of Donovan, of Charlotte, of Arthur Rupp. And of Sheila too? How, remembering Sheila, could he think of himself as different from Phil Bullard? If their weaknesses, his and Sheila's, had happened to coincide, what might not have happened? After he had left Don Oder on the chancery steps this morning it had occurred to him for the first time that Brophy's odd questions and reference to rumors might have been prompted by his visit to Sheila's apartment. But how could he possibly know of that? Frank recalled the lofty contempt with which he had thought of Phil Bullard's affair. If he himself had done nothing, he scarcely deserved credit for it. Sins of omission. Beverly. My God. With an effort, Frank directed his thoughts to Entweder, as if in search of where things had begun to go wrong. Entweder was not malicious; it would have been far easier if he were. The pastor thought of himself as a principled man. His refusal to okay the summer program had been based on principle, on a crazy principle. But what of his own concern for that program? The plan had seemed utterly simple and sane. Parish kids had no place to play during the summer. The school playground was there. The conclusion followed as night the day. He could imagine Bob Wintheiser saying that what he had wanted to do was social work, not the work of a priest. But it was not fair to demand that what he did must differ. The difference lay in his doing anything at all. Of course a philanthropist might perform the acts of a Christian, feed the hungry, clothe the naked, comfort the sick and dying. Miss Simpson. If his soul did not feel like a shriveled fist within him he would pray for her. It would be more fitting if she should pray for him. Would she pray that he be once again the young priest on the plane from Rome, eager to go to work?

He turned to go back, unwilling to make the full circuit of the lake, unsure that the path would take him around it. If only he could leave on this path the self he had become, a disillusioned priest seeking in a weekend of solitude the desire to go on, to advance to the point where the choice Bishop Brophy had given him would make some sort of sense.

The dining room had plain wooden tables, only one in use. Frank joined the others, all of them Franciscans, all wearing their robes. He still wore the clothes he had put on for his walk. Father Leo introduced him to the others and the response was amiable enough, though Frank sensed the usual distance of religious from the mere diocesan priest. They asked where he was stationed and if he was a native of Fort Elbow. They asked how long he would be staying in the House. Did he know Saint Barnabas parish? The last questioner was fat and melancholy. Perhaps forty. Once in the missions.

"I help out there weekends," he said. His name was Bonaventure.

"Did you know that Father Oder has been transferred?"

"No!"

That quickly Frank was back in the world of clerical gossip. What kind of a bishop did he think Brophy would make? Would there be a big shake-up? When the meal was over, Father Bonaventure asked Frank along to the rec room.

"Care for a drink, Father?"

"Do you have beer?"

"Anything you want."

That did not seem exaggerated. There was a refrigerator in one corner of the room and shelves covered with an impressive array of bottles. From the refrigerator Bonaventure got beer for Frank and ice for his own glass. That he poured half full of gin, sprinkled some tonic after it, and led Frank to chairs along the wall from which they could follow a billiard game while they talked.

524

"Ever been to Central America, Father?"

"No, I haven't."

"Great place. Really great. I spent ten years down there. In our missions."

Bonaventure obviously wanted to talk about it and Frank listened, the anecdotes punctuated by the click of balls as two friars played a silent and very serious game of billiards. Father Leo, carrying a bottle of 7-Up, came and sat next to Frank. In the far corner of the room, the rest of the House ringed a television set. It might have been the recreation room of the seminary—except for the drinks, of course. Throughout the evening there was the sound of shuffling sandals as the men went to the bar to replenish their drinks.

Bonaventure leaned toward Frank, glancing at Leo. "This place." He made a face. "I'd give anything to be back in the missions."

"Any chance of that?" Frank asked.

Bonaventure shrugged, then frowned. "Some of our young men oppose the whole notion of missions. They seem to think it's some kind of imperialism." He shook his head. "Strange people coming into the order nowadays. Isn't that right, Leo?"

The porter grinned. "Saint Francis was strange."

"Sure he was. But *holy* strange."

"Aren't vocations down?" Frank asked.

Bonaventure bent over and moved his palm parallel to the floor. "Way down. And lots of men leaving too, of course."

At ten o'clock, Bonaventure stood. "I better hit the sack. I'm off to Fort Elbow in the morning. A wedding. You get the short end of the stick doing weekend work, I can tell you that."

"I think I'll go up too."

"Care for a nightcap?"

"No, thanks."

Leo came along and in the hallway said to Frank, "What time would you like to say Mass, Father?"

"Does it matter?"

"Not at all. Come, I'll show you where the chapel is."

Inside the chapel, Leo knelt and Frank did too, conscious of the other priest beside him. Minutes went by. When Frank looked at Leo, the older priest's eyes were shut, his face expressionless. It would not have been easy to guess Leo's age. He could have been as old as Entweder. How long did he intend to remain? Frank had assumed that Leo had knelt for a little perfunctory prayer, a visit, but the porter was clearly more absorbed here than he had been in the rec room sipping 7-Up. Frank slipped from the pew and went up to his room.

He did not turn on the light. He wanted both windows open. He moved the chair to the window without a screen, opened it wide and sat looking out at the night. At first it was very quiet and then, like the music of the spheres, the pulsating sound of crickets became audible. He looked up at the sky, cloudless, a darkness which gradually revealed its lights. How immense, cold and remote it was, the dots of light random. Who knew how many galaxies swirled away out there, pushing toward the unimaginable limits of space? Frank, looking at the night sky, felt on the threshold of some important thought, but he began to yawn as if not even the cool summer evening air contained enough oxygen to keep him conscious. He resisted the impulse to go to bed. He had come here to think things through. But the yawning continued, deepened, making his eyes water. When he did get up to cross the room he wondered if he would make it. He lay on the bed fully clothed. A little nap and then he could take up his meditative vigil. Before he drifted off he thought of Father Leo, kneeling in chapel, his face in prayer one of impossible contentment. A little edifying act for the benefit of the visitor? But Frank drifted into sleep as if on the strength of Father Leo's prayer.

The next morning when Frank went down to the chapel all the altars were in use, Franciscans in fiddle-back chasubles saying half a dozen unsynchronized Masses. Father Leo had just begun and Frank decided to serve his Mass rather than say his own. Ritual, familiar words, all the gestures prescribed, the commemoration of Christ's last meal with his friends before he died. Do this in memory of me. All over the world the command was being kept, day after day, and had been over the centuries. Leo said Mass briskly but with the same complete concentration that had struck Frank the night before. At Communion time he received from Leo's hand the twice-hidden God.

Breakfast was informal and Frank had his alone at a table out of the traffic. The Franciscans seemed in a hurry, their weekend assignments beckoning. Afterward Frank went up to his room and lay upon the bed. He intended only to close his eyes but it was eleven o'clock when he awoke. Into his old clothes and downstairs, he wanted to walk that path again. When he passed the porter's office, Leo called to him.

"I wondered where you were."

"I fell asleep," Frank said sheepishly.

"Good. You looked tired when you came. Where are you going?"

"I thought I'd take a walk."

"Let me show you around."

Frank wanted to say no. He had come here to be alone, to think. But the porter was already guiding him out the door. They started down the path, walking slowly, and when they came to the beach, empty now, it looked inviting in the sun.

"You should go swimming while you're here."

"I didn't know you had a lake. I didn't bring a suit."

"I'll find one for you."

"Maybe later."

Leo was wearing his habit and the brown robe recalled Bonaventure's lamentation of the night before. The Franciscans were falling apart. Not only the diocesan priesthood, but the orders too were crumbling. Assisi, Siena, Padua—all those Franciscan cities. Would Francis recognize as his brothers the men in the rec room last night, playing billiards, drinking too much, inert before a television set? The mendicant orders had originally been a judgment on a Church grown fat and decadent. Now they were part of what was wrong. Frank thought of yesterday's swimmers, their carefree voices lifting to the path. A day at the beach, later an evening in the rec room. Poverty, chastity and obedience.

"How long have you been stationed here?" he asked Leo.

"Nearly eleven years." He had had to think, his lips moving as he counted silently.

"What did you do before?"

Leo smiled. "I was a teacher in our seminary."

"What subject?"

"Philosophy."

Leo was a Scotist and they talked a bit about that, not much—Frank had never read Scotus—nor did he defend himself against Leo's assumption that he was a Thomist. From teaching philosophy to this. But why? Of course he could not ask. He did ask Leo how long he had been a priest.

"Forty-two years." He had not needed to count this time.

"You've seen a lot of changes." When Leo smiled, as if at a remark on the weather, Frank said, "In the Church. In your order."

"Oh, yes."

"We can't go on this way."

Leo looked up the path, seemed about to reassure Frank that their walk could continue, then understood. "How do you mean?"

"The Church is crumbling, Father. Oh, maybe not the essential Church, but the one we have always known. It's going. Well, let it go."

Once begun, Frank went on, as if a prophetic vision were forming for him on the path, among the trees, and all he need do was read it off. The Church was not worth keeping in its present form. Nor were the Brophys the answer. If anything, they would magnify the problem and

527

hasten the diaspora. Let the mortgages be foreclosed, the portfolios sold off, the luxury be shed. It would happen in any case. It ought to happen. What had to be stopped were efforts to preserve the Church as it is, whether these were conservative or the more insidious Brophy kind. Relevance, updating, the caricature of *aggiornamento:* a better packaging job. The prospect of this gloomy future exhilarated Frank and his step was light as he swung along the path, Father Leo at his side. When he stopped speaking, it seemed only an interlude, as if further insight into the future would shortly be granted him.

Leo said, "You've obviously given it a lot of thought."

"It would be hard not to think of it."

"I suppose." They had reached the far side of the lake. The old priest cocked his head. Through the trees came the sound of cows lowing. "Come on," Leo said, leaving the path. They went only a short distance before coming upon a pasture. There, on a patch of grass half in sunlight, half out, they sat.

Frank lit a cigarette, awaiting Leo's comments on what he had said, but the old priest seemed content to gaze at the half-dozen cows, black and white, angular bones under slack skin, a picture of tranquillity.

"You don't agree with me, Father?"

Leo tugged at the grass, pulled up several blades, put one in his mouth. "I don't disagree either," he said, not quite smiling.

Suddenly the little Franciscan's untroubled look seemed the expression of a simpleton. How ridiculous it had been, in chapel, to imagine that this man was, well, holy, a kind of saint. Apparently he had been too inept even for the faculty of a Franciscan seminary and had been put out to pasture here, at the Retreat House. Well, he belonged here, munching on grass, like the cows.

"How long have you been ordained, Father?" Leo asked.

"Three years."

He nodded and Frank turned away. Now it would come, the avuncular reassurance. He was young, Leo was old, with time he would understand. Frank now wished that, if he had had to unburden himself here, he had talked to Bonaventure, who at least had some sense of what was going on in the world.

Leo said, "It's a difficult life."

"Yes."

But Leo did not go on. When Frank turned back to him, the old man was looking vaguely at the horizon.

"Where did you teach?" Frank asked.

"In Washington."

"And then they sent you here?"

"Yes."

"Why?"

Leo did not seem to understand the question. "Why?"

"But you must have gotten a higher degree in order to teach. Why would they send you here?" He hesitated, then added, "As porter."

"But why not?"

"I was sent away to study."

"Where?"

"Rome."

Leo brightened. "That is where I studied too. Are you teaching now?"

"I've been doing parish work."

"Ah."

"The bishop wants me to join the seminary faculty now."

"You'll enjoy teaching."

"Did you?"

"Oh, yes."

"We don't have many seminarians now. Less than a hundred."

"We are being punished," Leo said softly.

"Punished?"

"Yes. You and I. Priests, the laity. God is punishing us, Father. We have much to answer for."

"That's what I was saying before."

"I see." The old man nodded with sudden approval. "It is not easy for a man to recognize his faults."

Frank flipped away his cigarette and, watching it send up a column of smoke, told himself that he should quit. Leo got to his feet with surprising agility and Frank got up too. They went back through the woods to the path. They spoke little on the way back. Once they stopped and Leo pointed toward the sky where a hawk was being harassed by two blackbirds. Frank lit another cigarette before recalling his desire to quit. Maybe after he finished this package. Sacrifice. He remembered now what it had been like when he was a kid, what had made him want to be a priest in the first place. How easily he had dreamed of the life before him, longed for it, wanting its denials which were meant to remove the barriers to love. Love. He had dreamed of a willed inner desolation into which God might enter, a chosen emptiness only God could fill. But he had wanted to be flattened on his own terms, he had wanted to write the script himself. Now, brought low, all he could think to do was to level an indictment at others. The promised sacrifice was his and where was the throb of love?

Beside him, Leo hummed in a tuneless way, vaguely reminiscent of a Gregorian chant. Did the old priest miss it? Who didn't? A difficult life he had called the priesthood, and it was. It would always be difficult. Leo no longer seemed a simpleton. What was he? Perhaps just a priest trying to pursue the ideal in this crummy assignment, porter in a not very thriving Retreat House whose personnel were so unbusy they went off to weekend work.

"Would you like a bathing suit, Father?" They had reached the beach.

Frank suddenly felt uncomfortable as the object of the old priest's concern, wondering what tasks Leo had postponed to come on this walk with him, but at the same time he could imagine Francis offering him a bathing suit; for that matter, he could imagine Christ himself offering it. No solution to global ills, just a bathing suit.

"I think I would," Frank said.

"Good." And Leo smiled as if Frank had just made his day for him.

Back at the House, Frank took the bathing suit Leo had scouted up for him to his room. He sat at the desk. There was stationery in the drawer. He placed a sheet before him and sat there, pen in hand. During retreats as a seminarian he had always kept a notebook. Outlines of conferences, written meditations. There was so much he would have liked to write, a jumble of thoughts pressed on his mind, but he could not get a handle on them, did not know where to begin. He looked at the garish crucifix, suppressed the aesthetic reaction. Calvary had been ugly too. He heard himself humming, like Leo, a scrap of chant from Tenebrae as it had still been celebrated when he was a boy at Lake Glister, the *Christus factus est,* each syllable seeking its neum on that restricted ladder of sound while the heart supplied the complement to thought. Love nailed by hate, for me, for everyone. His eyes dropped. The blank page did not invite his thoughts. He remembered the sheet of paper in Tremplin's typewriter and put away his pen. It seemed wiser to go swimming.

He went swimming Sunday too, in the afternoon, after a lunch of cold cuts, potato salad and iced tea, he and Leo and the brother who ran the kitchen sharing a table. Leo was delighted when Frank said that he was going to the beach. It is not easy for a man to recognize his faults. I not they. The best of a bad job. And, for now, a solitary swim.

When he returned to the House, Father Bonaventure came up the gravel road in a jeep, tooting the horn and waving when he recognized Frank.

"Yorick," he cried, hopping from the jeep into the cloud of dust his braking of it had raised. "Do you know Monsignor Yorick?"

"The new pastor of Saint Barnabas?"

"Geez. You might have warned me. What a guy. Come on, I'll buy you a beer."

Frank hesitated, then agreed. When in Rome. In the rec room, rummaging in the refrigerator, Bonaventure said over his shoulder, "Yorick said you teach at the seminary." He turned, two sweating bottles of beer in his hands. "Is that right?"

Frank remembered the flight from Rome, sitting between Kieffer and Miss Simpson, a brand-new theologian returning to his diocese, eager to get to work. Only a few months ago but, dear God, what months they had been. He tried to alter his feeling with a smile. A moral theologian, but penitent, not judge. A difficult life. I not they.

"Yes," he said, accepting the beer from Bonaventure. "I start this fall."